WHO WE ARE, WHO WE HAVE BEEN, WHO WE WILL BE . . .

On a lifeless planet strange markings appear in the sand, threatening the sanity of the man who has come to explore them.

An actress plays roles in real-life dramas through a time channel that is about to shut down.

A creation myth, featuring two artificial intelligences, is passed down for future generations.

An angel appears before Cotton Mather, the apparition of a researcher in search of her own faith.

The nonhumanoid body of the Anomalous Man is protected by millennia-old glacial ice—while the figure's dreams run rampant over the scientists who approach him.

In an alternate future Jack Kennedy, hero of the communist revolution in America, poses a threat to President Lee Harvey Oswald.

Plus 22 other extraordinary stories of cosmic questions, great frontiers, and all the fascinating possibilities of

FULL SPECTRUM 5

FULL SPECTRUM 5

EDITED BY
Jennifer Hershey
Tom Dupree
Janna Silverstein

BANTAM BOOKS
New York Toronto London Sydney Auckland

This edition contains the complete text
of the original trade edition.
NOT ONE WORD HAS BEEN OMITTED.

FULL SPECTRUM 5

A Bantam Spectra Book

PUBLISHING HISTORY
Bantam trade paperback edition published August 1995
Bantam paperback edition / September 1996

ISBN 0-553-57522-8

Published simultaneously in the United States and Canada

Bantam Books are published by Bantam Books, a division of Bantam
Doubleday Dell Publishing Group, Inc. Its trademark, consisting of the
words "Bantam Books" and the portrayal of a rooster, is Registered in
U.S. Patent and Trademark Office and in other countries. Marca
Registrada. Bantam Books, 1540 Broadway, New York, New York 10036.

PRINTED IN THE UNITED STATES OF AMERICA

OPM   0   9   8   7   6   5   4   3   2   1

The Editors would like to
dedicate this anthology
to Lou Aronica

CONTENTS

FULL
SPECTRUM
5

SIMPLY INDISPENSABLE

Michael Bishop

N
o one should have to deal simultaneously with a spite wall, a boomeranging lover, and the coming of the su-'lakle.

No one.

Between Beirut and Damur, I own a faux-adobe towerhouse on the Mediterranean. Its picture window takes in my shelf gardens, a switchbacking mosaic walk, the crude but clean hovels below my cliff-chiseled estate, a strip of tawny beach, dozens of jumbled floating docks, and the green and creamy cloissoné waters of the Med itself. Every time I behold it, this panorama storms me like a SWAT team: it completely takes me over. If I were deprived of it, I would . . . well, who knows?

Thing is, Bashir Shouman wished to deprive me of it. A month back, he'd bought a wedge of cliff below the limestone wall at the bottom of my property. He paid eight homesteader families in the scrap-and-cardboard hovels there a total of three million Lebanese pounds to abandon their shambly homes.

Not, mind you, because he wished to build his own magnificent dwelling on this stony ledge, but because the purchase enabled him to nettle me. To stab me in the heart. You see, he'd hired a crew of fellaheen—Arab coolies—to raise a cheap ugly wall between my tower and the sea.

"Why?" asked Lena Faye, in response to my grousing.

"To block my view," I said. "To stand atop it and thumb his ouzo-ruddied nose at me."

Lena Faye Leatherboat had concorded in from Tulsa to share the view with me. No. I lie. Actually, she'd come to talk me into returning home from Lebanon to take up my old anchor post with Okla*Globe. And, as I soon found, to recharge an affair that had gone lapsed-cola flat months before Levant Limitless Broadcasting, Entertainment-and-News (LLBEAN to our wiseass competitors) spirited me off to Beirut.

"No," said the leanly fey Ms. Leatherboat. "I meant, why does this Showman fella—?"

"*Shou*man, not *Show*man. For pity's sake, don't call him Showman. He'd *love* that."

"Why does he want to block your view, George?"

"Out of spite, what else? Vicious, unappeasable spite. It's a spite wall."

Tenderly, Lena Faye traced the shell of my ear with a fingertip. "What *occasioned* his spite?"

"It's a Semito-Phoenician thing. Drop a toad on one of these guys, he comes after you harder than a hockey goalie."

"What did you *do* to him?"

"Bashir Shouman hosts a products-demonstration thing called *Getting the Goods* on ShariVid opposite my own *Forum/Againstum* on Levant."

"Title's familiar, but I've never scanned it."

"My first week here, the head of the European Mercantile Authority, Tito Malcangio, was a guest. In passing, I told Malcangio that Shouman played with high-tech toys for a living. I swore *Forum/Againstum* would knock him off his mechanical camel—an expensive Iraqi amusement product I once saw him demonstrate—in less than six months. Malcangio hoo-hawed. Said Shouman besmirched the reps of all true sales and marketing pros."

"You insulted him."

"I made an observation. And a prediction. *Malcangio* insulted him."

"Then Malcangio should get the spite wall."

"He lives in Milan. Shouman's a Beiruti. Unfortunately, these days, I also qualify."

"My poor Cherokee."

On my nomaditronic bed in my library-cum-relaxall, Lena Faye and I stared at my cactus gardens and the boat lights bobbing on the horizon. Shouman's spite wall already partially blocked our view of the favela sprawling downslope. That wasn't so bad, but in another few days his coolies would have raised the wall high enough to revoke my vantage on the eastern Med.

Then I'd have no view, only a window on the stuccoed and whited backside of a barrier whose sole purpose was to humiliate and vex me. It had no other use. Maybe I could post adverts on it or beam one of those premixed copulatory laser shows against it. No, nix that. The imam on Damur Ridge, if I showed such smut, would have his followers convert me into a choirless castrato. Nix everything but my mounting frustration and rage.

"Don't you have any recourse?" Lena Faye said. "I mean, of the legal sort."

"Over here, no. This isn't the fragmenting U.S. Over here, folks can do with their land just what they like—dogs, fellaheen, and furriners be damned."

"I can't believe that. Surely there's a law."

"I've asked the president of Levant Limitless—"

"LLBEAN?"

"Listen. I've asked her to pull strings. To offer *baksheesh*. To threaten. But Shouman's pit-bull intractable."

"And his wall keeps going up."

"If I lose my view, Lena, I'll—" I stuck, sighed, resumed: "With all I've got to do, with six hours of holotaping hanging over me, this view's indispensable to my mental health."

"Come back to Tulsa. You're indispensable to me, George. As I've found to my pain in your absence." When Lena Faye kissed me, I gunned the bed a dizzy one-eighty away from the window.

Facing away from the sea, gazing upon the loveliest Leatherboat ever to emerge from Enid, I felt a rush of calming metabolic chemicals.

"*Maleesh.* 'Never mind.' Nothing's indispensable. The world keeps turning."

Lena Faye had her head thrown back, her long neck agleam. She started. Something in the window had her attention. She fought to sit up. "Turn the bed back around! *Now!*"

I pivoted the bed, elevated its headrest, revved it toward the window. Shouman's unfinished spite wall had no power to deny us a view of the plasmic lightshow writhing like a lost aurora borealis in the midnight skies over Lebanon. This kinetic event—whatever it was—flowed lavender, lime, orange, indigo, even a profoundly eerie red. It *rained* light. This rain flashed from the tin-roofed huts, flare-illuminated the beach, painted and repainted the bobbing docks. It turned the sea into a crumpled foil mirror that caught, and muted, and softly echoed back, the multicolored cries of this inexplicable happening.

Lena Faye clutched me. Unashamedly, I clutched her too. The terrible lightshow continued to blaze and flicker. Then, without any incremental slackening, it ceased. The night sky over Lebanon was nothing but night sky again, an inverted bowl of moonlight and palsied stars.

"Lord, Mr. Gist, what a hello! Do you stage the same airborne gala for all your old flames?"

I hugged Lena Faye tighter.

Serious now, she said, "What *was* it, really? A new Israeli weapon? An electrical storm?"

"Lena Faye, I have no idea. I doubt it's the former. That would jeopardize the peace. An electrical storm? Who knows? Not me. I'm no meteorologist."

Before I could react, Lena Faye had pivoted the bed and dialed up Levant's round-the-clock news coverage on my vidverge wall. We watched three or four replays of the event, as taped from the roof of our studio in the Sabra Intercontinental Hotel.

Rafika Ali Sadr, the midnight anchor, noted in five or six different ways that so far no one had a convincing theory for the untoward lightshow, which, just moments ago, thousands of people in Beirut and environs had witnessed "live and in shivering color." Then she began airing all the conflicting "expert" feedback, and I retrieved my multiflicker in order to mute the idiotic row among the talking heads.

"Hey, Mr. Gist! I was watching that! Don't you want to find out why the sky started sizzling?"

"We'll know by morning. Why tune in the guesses of a thousand and one egotistical crackpots, whether Arab, American, or Trobriand Islander."

"But—"

" 'Spontaneous ozone-layer decay.' 'Chain-reaction molecular combustion.' 'Projected hologrammatic illusion.' Do you really think any of those blind stabs on target?"

She didn't, or said she didn't to placate me. Whereupon we consummated our reunion. Thirty minutes later, Lena Faye was fast asleep, seemingly blissfully so.

Careful not to wake her, I eased out of bed and strolled to my picture window. Bashir Shouman's spite wall loomed in the darkness downslope, an architectural obscenity, the three-dimensional Muslim equivalent of a Bronx cheer. It loomed far more forcefully in my awareness than did the weird event that had interrupted Lena Faye's and my conversation. Damn Shouman. Damn him to the gaudiest hell ever imagined by a vindictive iman.

Without my view, I'd . . .

Unbidden, my vidverge wall snapped on. Faintly, it lit 1) my library, 2) Lena Faye's lovely slumbering form, and 3) my stunned nakedness before the picture window.

In virtually thoughtless self-defense, I tinted the window with a thumb touch and telegoosed the bed into another room. That left me buff upright in front of my screen as it cycled through hundreds of fi-opt channels. I tried to kill it with my multiflicker, but it refused to slide back into blank and docile wallness. In fact, I felt that it *needed* an observer; that it *wanted* that observer to be me.

I, I mean: Cherokee George Gist of the popular gabfeed *Forum/Againstum.*

The channels on my vidverge wall stopped flipping—as abruptly, by the way, as had the spooky-ass lightshow. A figure emerged from the digital fi-opt signals coursing through my scrambler, a ghost of many thin and motile colors. Green predominated, the green of a diluted kiwi-fruit drink.

The head of this wraith—humanoid after the fashion of a splayed bullfrog—reminded me, with its capelike fins and the fins' hypnotic hula-ing, of a manta ray. From the hidden neck down, though, the wraith's watery greenness hinted at a narrow "chest," pipe-cleaner "arms," and static-riven "legs" that may, or may not, have ended in a pair of nebulous "feet."

The image was a cartoon, a whimsical computer-generated assemblage of migrating pixels. Whimsical and scary at once, for the creature's "eyes"—I grokked, taking hasty inventory— looked just like those of Pope Jomo I, who, along with three other religious bigwigs and a virrogate for a lottery-chosen viewer, would appear on this coming week's cablecasts of *Forum/Againstum.*

Like Pope Jomo's, the things's eyes gleamed big, brown, and wise. They didn't belong in a manta-ray-shaped head, granted, but today's vidverging hackers can do almost anything with sendable images. Given my screen's refusal to obey my off button and the weirdness of the figure astutter on the wall, those pious eyes held and calmed me.

"George Gist?" My unit speakers lapped me with a "voice" like seven cellos twanging in concert.

"Guilty." I walked to my rotary chiffonier and dialed out a robe, which I cinched about myself. The robe fell only to midthigh, but better a quarter clad than jaybird nude before the pontiff's unmistakable gaze—the peepers, so to speak, of the Holy See. I faced my image-bearing wall.

"We are the su'lakle," the creature shimmering there said in its echoey cello tones.

" 'We'? You look like an it. But who knows how many of you pesky cablejackers have conjured this lie?"

" 'Lie'? *We don't lie. But, we confess, su'lakle is a syllabic rendering of the* [garbled] *physical sequence by which we denominate ourselves."*

"What?"

"Sorry to confuse. We are a kind of plasma-energy entity of no small venerableness."

" 'We'? You keep saying 'we.' Please name the buttinsky electronic felons in cahoots with you."

" 'I'—the 'I' you now see—am a concentrated distillate of the cosmic intelligence that has just come to Earth. If you prefer the singular, I will gladly use it."

"Good. On *Forum/Againstum* I talk to jackasses in herds. Here at home, it'd be a huge relief to entertain crackpots like you—if I really must—one at a time."

" *'Crackpots'?"* the thing on my wall said in its multiple-cello voice, sounding offended. *"A disparaging term, correct?"*

"It's late, Mr. Ukulele. What the hell do you want?"

"To appear on Forum/Againstum."

"You and ten million other humans starved for a nanosecond of celebrity."

"I am neither a . . . a ukulele nor a human being. I am the deliberately sublimated essence—the spokesentity—of an antique sentient species here self-styled the su'lakle. Don't be obtuse, Mr. Gist."

"I'd be obtuse if I bought this. A dupe conspiring in my own unprincipled scamming."

"Hardly. You see, Mr. Gist, you're—"

"Look, you've hacked your way into my relaxall in the dumbass guise of Manta Man, or the Stingray Kid, and I'm supposed to *reward* you with a stool next to the simseats of my guests this week?"

"Roger-yes. Pope Jomo, Imam Bahadori, the Dalai Lama, and evangelist Jennie Pilgrim. I'd like to palaver—rap—with them. In order to reach as many of your kind as possible."

"Roger-yes," I mocked. "Do you have any idea how long it took me to arrange this historic tetracast?"

"*Mr. Gist, you—*"

"Listen, vidiot, why not hack your way onto *Forum/Againstum* the same way you've raped the privacy of my home?"

"*I am no hacker, Mr. Gist. Nor a pixel-built virrogate. I observe, therefore I am.*"

"In Marx's immortal words, horsefeathers!"

"*And therefore you are too—along with your planet, solar system, galaxy, and surrounding galactic clusters.*"

"The coaxial cops will have you traced and busted by morning! And our scientists—real ones, not cranks—will know by then what caused tonight's honky-tonk glowstorm!"

"*I doubt both such outcomes.*"

"I have a warm female companion in the next room. I'm going in to her now, Mr. Ukulele. Shut my wall unit off when you're through playing around with it."

I moved to rejoin Lena Faye. The ray-headed thing on my screen began to quake more violently than ever. Its erratic motion halted me. As I watched, it *stepped* from the flat cage of the vidverge wall into my house. There, facing me like a burglar, the su'lakle floated in three dimensions, like a person-shaped pocket of neon mist. Less than an arm's length away, it radiated neither heat nor coolth, but a dry, spreading tingle. The hairs on my knuckles stood up. My nape hairs swayed. A fine electrostatic disturbance helixed through my bowels.

"*What crackerjack systems-crasher could do this—drift in air before you as an independent being?*"

"You're a hologram."

"*I am? Projected from where, by whom, and through what mechanism?*"

Like the su'lakle, I was trembling—but for different reasons. "Who knows? By Bashir Shouman. By means of a secretly deployed nanoholocaster."

"*A hologram is often a kind of telepresence, Mr. Gist. I, though, inhabit this space with you, even as the filtered-to-essentials spokesentity of my larger Self.*"

Truth? Gobbledegook? I had no idea.

"Touch me, Mr. Gist."

I hesitated, then reached out and pinched the su'lakle's eel-ish arm just below its, uh, "elbow." The plasmic "skin" between my thumb and forefinger had a filmy elastic moistness; it followed my tug, more like a biddable mist than a pinch of rubber, and then seeped rather than snapped back into place. I couldn't imagine a virrogate able to interface to that peculiar degree with consensus reality. Maybe the creature wasn't lying.

"Give me a spot on Forum/Againstum *with Pope Jomo and the other sacred worthies."*

"But . . . but what'll I call you?"

Su'lakle, I argued, wouldn't do—not, at least, until Levant's subscribers understood the being's origins and nature. Even then, they'd probably regard it as just another electronic wave-function virrogate.

After all, in the recent past, randomly selected subscribers had come on *F/A* as my "Faces from the Rubble" interviewees in the identity-concealing teleguises of Socrates, Cleopatra, Torquemada, Queen Elizabeth I, Pocahontas, Sir Isaac Newton, Sojourner Truth, Teddy Roosevelt, Amelia Earhart, Mahatma Gandhi, Brigitte Bardot, Gamal Abdal Nasser, Buddy Holly, the Pink Panther, Stephen Hawking, Stephen King, Jessica Rabbit, Tina Turner, and Salman Rushdie (a virrogate sent packing in midbroadcast to avert a global epidemic of Islamic riots). The su'lakle's current look, to put it frankly, had less authenticity than had J. Rabbit's.

"Call me Joe," it said.

"Joe?"

"Yes. Joe Way. A participant without a sacerdotal honorific perhaps requires two names."

Bewildered, I agreed. The su'lakle stepped back into the two-dimensional realm of my vidverge unit, then disappeared by obligingly shutting the unit off.

I summoned my nomaditronic bed back from exile and lay down beside Lena Faye. No one, I mused, should have to deal at the same time with a spite wall, an ex-fiancée, and the un-announced arrival of a star-struck plasma being.

I got up to find Lena Faye sitting in front of my vidverge at a table set with bagels, strawberry jelly, cream cheese, and a pot of Earl Grey. I joined her.

"Hey, slugabed," she said. "Despite your certainty to the

contrary, the world still lacks a decent explanation for last night's pyrotechnics."

"Nobody's suggested fireworks?"

"Of course. Along with dozens of other screwy guesses. But those *weren't* fireworks. The only fireworks I have any empirical knowledge of, George, took place"—nodding—"in that bumper-car bed of yours."

I spread some jam on a bagel and took a bite. I poured myself a cup of tea, which Lena Faye had brewed to a satisfying strength and temperature.

"If you won't come back to Okla*Globe," she said, "I could come here. I'd bet LLBEAN, ShariVid, or AvivTel could use another savvy p.r. flack, wouldn't you?"

"Say LLBEAN instead of Levant to management, they'll boot you out faster'n a CableCom inspector."

"Have talent, will travel."

"Lena Faye, I just can't think about that now. I tape the biggest shows of my career this afternoon."

"Congrats." She deformed a bagel with her canines, the jam on her mouth as red as something more dire.

"Besides, you're supposed to get me back with obscene amounts of cash, corporate flattery, and—"

"Good lovin'."

"Which you've just offered to bring *here*. Meanwhile, Okla*Globe can go jump. If this is savvy recruitment work, Lena Faye, nobody here in Beirut will recognize it."

We ate for a time in silence. Nadia Suleiman, Levant's morning anchor, efficiently ticked off all the theories so far proposed for the peculiar aerial phenomenon that'd signaled "Joe Way"'s arrival on the stage of Earthbound history. None of the theories mentioned the su'lakle, of course, or came anywhere near the bizarre truth of the matter.

It did amuse me, though, to hear Nadia report that a spokesperson for the New Millenarian Ecumenical Council convening this week in Beirut claimed that the lightshow marked God's joyous personal blessing on the momentous proceedings of the NMEC.

"Ha ha," I said mirthlessly.

"At least that has a certain befitting poetry to it. You just grump and cynicize."

"Because *I* know what really happened."

"Do tell."

To Lena Faye's incredulity, consternation, and mounting

alarm, I did just that. She believed me. I warmed to the telling because she so obviously did believe, and tried to comfort me, and in fact eased me through the rest of the day to the taping that would secure *Forum/Againstum*'s status as the premier gabfeed on any of the global vidgrids.

Pope Jomo, Imam Bahadori, the Dalai Lama, and Jennie Pilgrim, spiritual leader of the World Evangelical Union (WEN), had all come to Beirut for the New Millenarian Ecumenical Council (NMEC). Other attendees included an assortment of hatted rabbis, skinny Hindu mucky-mucks, the prophet of the Baha'is, voodoo *houngans*, the head of the Eastern Orthodox Church, Wiccan hierarchs, saronged Theravada and Mahayana priests and bodhisattvas, African tribal shamans, and maybe a dozen sachems from mainline, borderline, and off-the-wall Protestant Christian denominations.

I'd tried to round up a representative sampling of spiritual leaders for this week's episodes of *Forum/Againstum*, but the Pope and Imam Bahadori had threatened to withdraw if I made them share Levant's studio—even as holojections—with more than two other council attendees. In return for this concession, they'd offered me six hours of their precious time, all of which I hoped to tape on a single afternoon for a full week's worth of programs. No one else in the infogabshow biz had ever managed such a coup.

If not for Bashir Shouman's spite wall, my internal struggle over Lena Faye, and the anomalous shuffling of "Joe Way" into my overloaded *F/A* deck, I'd've thought myself the luckiest chap in town, if not the whole rosy world.

Levant's studio well in the Sabra Intercontinental Hotel was wrapped by a field shield. Behind the shield, as audience, sat five tiers of educated foreigners and Beiruti locals.

Envision, then, six vivid figures on the set, four of them holojections in simseats, one an eccentric emerald virrogate (who'd materialized in the well as a substantive presence an hour before the coming of the others), and me, Cherokee George Gist, in a Danish chair of shiny aluminum tubes and interwoven flaxen straps.

Imam Bahadori, Pope Jomo, and the Dalai Lama sat across from Jennie Pilgrim, me, and our flickering pseudo-virrogate, Joe Way. A dozen autocams gyro-gimbaled around us at different heights and angles, all under the control of Khalil Khalaf, *F/A*'s Maronite Catholic director.

"Good evening, ladies, gentlemen, and brighter-than-average children," I began the taping. "This evening we commence a series of shows on which I plan to browbeat our distinguished guests about their respective spiritual positions and the fading hope for harmony among religio-ethnic factions and their increasingly rigid doctrinal positions."

With courteous fervor, my handpicked audience applauded. Via satellite and fi-opt cables, millions more would thrill, later, to this same lead-in. I then introduced the Pope, the Imam, the Dalai Lama (who, even as a holofeed, didn't look much like either the dead artist Salvadore or a Peruvian camel), and the large but attractive Jennie Pilgrim.

"And I'm Joe Way," said the su'lakle in its many-celloed voice. "From deepest outer space."

"DOS, eh?" said the Dalai Lama's holojection from his suite in the fully renovated Hotel St. Georges. "Is DOS a freshly protected cyber territory?"

"Mr. Joseph Way comes to us tonight," I said hurriedly, "as the proxy virrogate of our far-flung viewers, to represent them in a telegab of great historic importance."

"Joe. Joe Way. Not Joseph."

"Johweh?" said Pope Jomo in his Kikuyu-flavored English. "I hear echoes of both my name and that of the tetragrammatic Hebrew deity."

"Pardon me, Your Popeness," Joe Way said as quickly as a cello section may do, "but, in your view, what comprises the most basic heartfelt desire of any sentient entity?"

I tried to retake control: "If you'll wait a—"

"Salvation and eternal life in God's very presence," said Pope Jomo readily enough.

"Amen to that," said Jennie Pilgrim. The two beamed at each other. (Given their status as holos, beamed is something more than a metaphor.)

"Nirvana," said the Dalai Lama. "Preferably after a good leg of lamb and a glass of fine wine."

"A passionate blessèd martyrdom," said Imam Bahadori, "followed by heavenly immortality."

"Does anyone in the studio of a more secular persuasion have a differing opinion?" asked Joe Way, the wings of his manta-ray head rippling subtly.

Beyond the field shield, several members of my audience boldly spoke up:

"Earthly immortality!"

"More money than King Croesus and Austin-Antilles Corporation combined!"

"Eternal youth!"

"An unending orgasm of painful cosmic sweetness!"

"Power!" cried one pale, marmoset-eyed young man. "Power, power, and *more* power!"

Lifting my hands, I stood up and shouted: "QUIET!"

My studio audience quieted.

"Better! Much better! *Forum/Againstum* isn't five minutes old, people, and you've let this green virrogate usurp both my role as host and the religio-philosophical agenda embodied, at least potentially, in the presence of these estimable spiritual leaders! Let's get back on track! Okay?"

"Actually," said Jennie Pilgrim with a melancholy sigh, "the 'most basic heartfelt desires' shouted out here testify to a real eschatological ignorance and a nasty decline in age-old Judeo-Christian values."

"I concur," said Imam Bahadori, visibly gloating.

"*Actually*," Joe Way put in, "*although wrong, these desires do have their honesty to commend them.*"

Annoyed, I turned on the su'lakle. " 'Wrong'? Isn't one's basic heartfelt desire a matter of private choice? How, then, can you label any single such opinion *wrong?*"

"Mr. Way is correct," Pope Jomo said. "The basic heartfelt desires spoken out here are bankrupt illusions. None bestows true happiness because all are—"

"Happiness!" shouted a member of the studio crowd: a late response to Joe Way's question.

"There is only one route to genuine happiness," the Pope said. "Namely, the Way, the Truth, and the Life."

"*Wrong again*," said the su'lakle. "*One's most basic heartfelt desire is the* route *to happiness, but that route is 'the Way, the Truth, and the Life,' or 'martyrdom for Allah,' or 'out-of-body perfection' only to those who have given up on that longing which has dwelt hidden within them since the first conscious moment of their being.*"

Khalil Khalaf gave our global audience a skillful close-up of Pope Jomo's handsome ebony face, wreathed in a smile. "As I still say, that longing, whatever it is, is an illusion. One must sacrifice it to that which has lasting, and obtainable, spiritual validity."

I couldn't help myself. Looking directly at Joe Way, I said, "But what *is* that longing?"

"*Indispensability.*"

Everyone—guest, studio-audience member, or tape-delayed Levant Limitless Broadcasting subscriber—gaped at Joe Way. In his guise as a pseudo-virrogate (if the oxymoronic irony of that term doesn't render it totally meaningless), Joe Way pulsed like a living mist, kaleidoscopically kinking inside the illusory integument affording him his green-glowing creaturely outline.

The Dalai Lama, a bald, brown, spexware-bearing man in his late twenties or early thirties, recovered first. "Nonsense, Mr. Way. I know many persons with the soulfulness to wish for nothing more—in worldly terms—than to live forever in that perfect instant just before sunrise. Or to make some small but lasting private contribution to our species."

"And if you want *secular* basic heartfelt desires," the Right Reverend Ms. Pilgrim said, "I've known two or three half-decent but unsaved gentlemen who longed for nothing but a lake, a johnboat, a cane pole, and lots of time to fish. For them downhome bubbas, indispensability didn't enter the picture atall."

"*These desires came upon them,*" Joe Way said, "*after the world had disillusioned or corrupted them.*"

"After reality'd set in," Jennie Pilgrim countered. "And they realized how hard this world works to thump the backsides of malingering spiritual babes."

"Amen," said Imam Bahadori, surprising both her and me.

These guests could've conducted *Forum/Againstum* without benefit of host or studio audience. Exasperated, I tried to wrench my program back from the su'lakle: "Tell me, Imam, what issues do you plan to raise at the general session of the NMEC this Friday?"

"*It nonetheless remains the case that all human beings—indeed, all conscious entities universewide—long at bottom not for power or immortality or spiritual riches, but for that attribute, alone among attributes, that confers them all; namely, indispensability, the only quality that assures the being possessing it that if aught evil befalls it, including its own extinction, the universe and all its many components, sentient or otherwise, will perish in train. Face it. All human grief stems from the hurtful knowledge that the universe has so little care for one's own existence that the end of that existence will affect neither the operation nor the integrity of the universe a sparrow's fart. Selah."*

"How about that, Pope Jomo?" I said. "Do you—?"

"With due respect, I must point out that your flamboyant virrogate's opinion is nonsense," said the Pope.

"*Allah akbar,*" said Imam Bahadori. "The only indispensable Being is God Himself. Does Mr. Way intend to imply that we should all strive to become as God?"

"I have no problem with that ambition," said the Dalai Lama.

"Well, *I* have beaucoups with it," the Right Reverend Ms. Pilgrim retorted. "Smacking, as it does, of self-idolatrous pride."

"Each person here wishes at heart, or once upon a time wished, that he or she were indispensable to the health of this physical reality," said Joe Way unequivocally.

Jennie Pilgrim said, "Gist, you've unleashed an infantile ijit on us. A mewling babe."

"Alexander the Great died. Caesar died. So did Mohammed, Queen Elizabeth, Shakespeare, Newton, and Sadat. Even Einstein died. Ditto the Marx Brothers, Jack Benny, Buckminster Fuller, Clark Kent, Dick Clark, Imelda Marcos, and Norodom Sihanouk. The world continued without them. Secretly, we long for such a profound in-knitting with the world that, should we grow sick, or falter, or even lapse and die, the world that these famous ones left without even rippling its basic contours would, as a direct consequence, founder in shock and fall to irreclaimable nothingness."

The Rev. Ms. Pilgrim wrinkled her brow at the Dalai Lama. "This is a guy thing, right?"

His Tibetan Holiness shrugged.

"I didn't expect to encounter such denial among you," Joe Way said, splotchily pulsating emerald, lime, and radioactive chartreuse. *"Perhaps it's a function of the trained-up religious frames of mind pheromonically drawn to the NMEC."*

At that, several members of my studio audience began to whistle, boo, and/or stamp their feet.

The Pope raised one long, eggplant-purple hand. "Hush."

Everyone hushed.

The hand stayed up, in calming benediction. "It seems to me that this one anonymous viewer"—the Pope gestured at Joe Way—"has stolen a disproportionate amount of our time with pathological musings of a private and, I trust, treatable nature. Now, however, I would—"

"*I know whereof I speak. Because the august telepresences here this evening refuse to acknowledge their most basic inborn longing does not mean that I have misnamed it.*"

"Look," said Jennie Pilgrim, "who are you, anyhow?"

Oh, God, I thought. Don't answer that.

"*How do you know?*" Imam Bahadori asked the su'lakle before it could ID itself.

"*Because I am in fact a being possessing the attribute for which all of you long. Indispensability. Instant by instant, I help sustain the fabric of reality.*"

Imam Bahadori raised an eyebrow. "You are God?" His lip curled in contempt. Then he began to snicker. But, thank God, he demanded neither Joe Way's immediate exile nor a sacrilege-avenging global manhunt and a beheading.

For, of course, only Lena Faye and I, of all those in the studio, understood that the su'lakle existed as the fabricated material essence of his kind rather than as the virrogate of a geographically distant human viewer.

The Dalai Lama leaned toward Joe Way. "I beg you, sir, to repeat your last assertion."

"*I am indispensable.*"

"Really?"

"*Simply indispensable. I help sustain the world. My end would speed that of this expansion-contraction phase of this particular universe at its every spatial-temporal extension.*"

"I think we'd better break for a message from Glom-Omni Foods and Printed Circuits," I said.

Khalil Khalaf, bless him, took that desparate cue and cut away to a spectacular canned pitch for hydrosnap peaches and high-torque magnelev motors.

I looked up and saw Lena Faye sitting among some Beirutis on our studio's highest tier.

She smiled. In Cherokee hand language, she signed, Don't get rattled. You're doing fine.

The six-hour taping floundered on. Joe Way dominated the first hour, which aired later that same evening, but had only a couple more bombshells to drop, petards he lobbed during the taping's third and sixth hours.

"*Reincarnation within this expansion-contraction phase of*

this particular universe does not occur," he informed the Dalai Lama in the third hour. "*You hope for it in vain.*"

By this time, the other guests had begun to humor him as if he were an unhinged brother or an incontinent pet cat.

"I don't hope to return to the world of *maya* as either a housefly or a bodhisattva," the Dalai Lama said. "I hope to escape the cycle of death-and-rebirth entirely."

"*You hope for that in vain as well.*"

Jennie Pilgrim shot the Pope a conspiratorial look. "Do you mean to say there's no such thing as an eternal afterlife?"

"*Depends on what you mean by eternal.*"

"Pardon?"

"*We su'lakle have gone through this six or seven times before, Reverend Ms. Pilgrim. Souls caught in each cycle's afterlife get funneled into the primordial singularity from which the next cosmos bursts forth. They emerge as unconscious matter. The intervals are so long, though, that most gladly, or perhaps indifferently, relinquish awareness out of boredom. Moreover, the crowding during the epoch of ultimate collapse is terrible. Who wouldn't want to pull a terminal phase-shift back into affectless nonbeing?*"

For a moment, no one—I chief among the speechless—could think of anything to say to this. Then a professor from the American University in our audience said, "The souls of sentient creatures don't migrate into a region of sempiternal superspace?"

"*No way to get to it,*" Joe Way said shortly.

The rest of that hour, my other guests discussed the links, conspicuous or subtle, among their belief systems. Joe Way stayed silent. In fact, I had the nagging suspicion that he had gently withdrawn his essence from the pseudo-virrogate on the stool to my right.

Toward the end of the sixth hour, despite two weeks of heavy preparation and a slew of off-camera cue cards, I'd just about run out of questions. I realized *Forum/Againstum* was in deep trouble when Imam Bahadori produced some laminated photos of his kids and I took a genuine interest.

Jennie Pilgrim, by choice a single woman, jumped to the show's rescue. She leaned around me and said, "Mr. Way, I've been meaning to ask, How is it, exactly, that you think you're 'simply indispensable' to the universe."

The su'lakle had gone pretty pale over the past two and a half hours. His swirly-curly innards looked more like watered limeade than melting emeralds; the fins on his manta-ray head drooped like windsocks on a still desert night.

"Mr. Way!" Jennie Pilgrim insisted. *"Mr. Way!"*

At last the su'lakle appeared inhabited again. *"Forgive me. My 'mind' wandered."*

Ms. Pilgrim restated her question.

Joe Way's answer took several minutes. Anyone interested in its details need only consult—quickly—any video of my final *Forum/Againstum* broadcast. Basically (Joe Way told us), he, or his virtually immortal kind, had the ability to perform recurrent key observations at the quantum level that *"support the structure of the physical universe by actualizing a sequence of key observables in such a way that the fundamental physical laws that govern the cosmos cohere."*

Pope Jomo winced. "Oh, Mr. Way, you make my head ache. Of what 'kind' are you, if not the human kind?"

"A su'lakle." And steeling myself for the inevitable hostile reaction: "An alien energy being."

"From DOS," said the Dalai Lama evenly. "Deepest, Outer, Space." This idea passed unchallenged, as if everyone in my studio, future-shock junkies, had already suspected as much.

A woman in a silk sari stood up. "Are you saying you can select among the many potentialities of microscopic particles? Can, in fact, direct the observer-induced 'collapse of the wave function' that obtains in quantum mechanics?"

"Yes, I am," said Joe Way, audibly relieved.

"But no one can dictate the value—the position, or energy state, or momentum—that the specific measurement of a particle actualizes," said the woman, sitting back down. "No one."

Replied Joe Way, *"No one human. So far as I know, we su-'lakle alone, at least for now, have that talent. We not only understand the structuring subatomic codes, we can twiggle them."*

(*Twiggle?*)

"How?" Lena Faye called out from her lofty perch.

"The su'lakle—I am One—intrinsically possess a quality of intensified self-reference or-observation enabling us to alter our own consciousness. We thus influence 'reality' through externally directed observations of several specific sorts."

"This must be very hard work," said the Dalai Lama.

"No lie. Often, though, we can peer through the maya *of this spacetime realm to the suprareality of the overcosmos."*

"Again, a claim to Godhood!" said Imam Bahadori angrily.

Jennie Pilgrim said, "Mr. Gist, you've let a funny-farm hacker loose on yall's premises."

"*On the other hand, collapsing this realm into 'reality' from its various superpositions, eon after eon, eventually acquires a debilitating tediousness. Even if the actualizers—we su'lakle, along with a few other observing species across the cosmos— initially accepted that responsibility out of equal measures of self-challenge and love.*"

And those were Joe Way's last words during the sixth hour of our taping, an hour that wouldn't get fi-opted until this coming Saturday evening.

Khalil Khalaf signaled *Cut!* from his director's booth. I'd successfully shepherded my human guests, and the wild card of an incognito interstellar visitor, through a grueling marathon taping session.

So, of course, I began contemplating the best spot in my towerhouse for another Peabody or Emmy.

Unceremoniously, Pope Jomo I, Imam Bahadori, the Dalai Lama, and Jennie Pilgrim vanished. Who could blame them? They'd given me over six solid—i.e., unbroken, substantive— hours of interview time; they deserved medals.

Only Joe Way remained on the well's floor with me, because, of course, he was a plasmic distillate of the su'lakle rather than a holojection.

As my studio audience filed out, Lena Faye picked her way down the stairstep seats to join us. We hugged each other. Khalil Khalaf eyed her from his booth. He knew for whom she worked and had no doubt why she'd come.

"Mr. Way, I have a question," Lena Faye said.

"*Please.*" (Permission to ask it.)

"Why did you bring Earth's religious leaders—all of us—the message of your local 'indispensability'?"

"*Why?*" The cello voices sounded confused.

"Yes, why? I mean, what did you, or *do* you, want us to do in response to that message?"

A damned good question. I should have asked it myself. And I *would* have, I think, if I hadn't striven so hard to make it appear that the su'lakle was "really" a virrogate of one of my randomly selected viewers.

Joe Way shifted before us. The manta-ray wings of his "head" flapped a kind of querulous veronica.

"Do you want us to do you homage?" Lena Faye asked. "You know, *worship* you?"

The gaseous emeralds swirling inside the su'lakle throbbed brighter, as if she'd blown on a green fire. "*Absolutely not,*" Joe Way said.

"What, then?"

"*In time,*" he said, "*I hope to persuade you—your species, I mean—to supplant us, the su'lakle, in the indispensability business hereabouts. Voluntarily.*"

With that, he convoluted once, slowly, and funneled upward in a keening rush that hurled him out of the studio, as if he'd popped into another continuum through the tip of that notional funnel.

Three evenings later, after the first four episodes of my NMEC tapings had appeared, Lena Faye and I had dinner together on the sidewalk outside the Green Line Café. To stymie both gawkers and would-be autograph seekers, we sat near a trellis bearing oligs (hybrid olive-figs) and thoroughly enjoyed each other's company.

I seemed to be falling in love with Lena Faye again. Why she wanted *me*, though, I had real trouble figuring. For some months before leaving Tulsa, I'd treated her as a mere human accessory. And even since her arrival in Lebanon, our mutual sacktime notwithstanding, I'd generally shown more interest in F/A's global ratings and the likelihood of more infogab awards than in shoving our relationship into something moderately akin to permanence.

Now, though, I was beginning to perceive that Lena Faye had always seen in me the inhering eidolon of my better self. She had always believed in and struggled to free it, when a woman of less patience, and a less atoning vision, would have written me off as Superjerk. Now, I theorized, her fastidious observations of the microscopic virtues in me were actualizing them—collapsing them into being—in the day-to-day realm of human interactions. Maybe.

Anyway, I was thinking seriously of abandoning Beirut and of marrying Lena Faye Leatherboat.

Suddenly, a gang of youthful Shi'ites came marching toward the café jogging placards up and down; they wore stained white sandwich-board pullovers bearing upon them militant slogans in Arabic script: *Only ALLAH Is Called For. The Green Thing Is a Devil. Satan Lies in Many Colors.* One pistoning sign held a startling message in English:

> *"George Gist, atheist!*
> *We have no need*
> *Of his gabfeed greed*
> *Or Godless creed!*
> *Bleed him from his crown,*
> *Run him out of town,*
> *Uproot him like the weed!"*

"Uh-oh."

Lena Faye took my hand. "Sort of catchy."

"They're looking to catch me, that's how catchy it is. I wish you wouldn't trivialize this."

"Tighten your sphincter, George. Let them go."

It was good advice. The protest, obviously provoked by the week's first *Forum/Againstum*, had a noise-making rather than a vengeance-taking agenda, even if one of its signs read like a death warrant. It seemed highly likely that Imam Reza Bahadori himself had sent these young zealots out. In any case, they marched loudly but harmlessly by.

"I'm no atheist," I said.

"No?"

"I believe—" I thought a moment. "I believe in the Great Spirit." Another thinking spell: "Or *a* great spirit."

"*The* or *a*? Which is it? Investing in lower-case stocks doesn't require much capital."

"Small investment, small risk of woe."

"Small hope of a bracing return." Lena Faye nodded after the noisy Shi'ites. "Those guys have no doubt you're *the* weed in their spiritual garden."

"Me? I'm a high-profile media spear-carrier."

"Meaning you think the demon-weed they should *really* take out after is poor old Joe Way."

"I don't think they should take out after anybody. I think they should give it a rest."

"Some people have strong opinions, Mr. Gist. Some people *commit*."

"Some people scare the holy sand out of me."

"Not me, I hope." Then: "I believe in love."

"Great song title. It's been used, but so what?"

We left the Green Line Café and wandered along the Rue de Damas to a bistro called Hobeika's Den occupying most of the bottom floor of a bank building gutted in the anarchistic and self-cannibalizing 1980s. No signs of rubble, pockmarks, or

over-ups today: Hobeika's Den looked spanking-new, a high-
ech watering hole with vidverge mirrors, game screens, a vo-
uptuous animatronic belly dancer, and a carpark band with
vired flutes, guitars, and percussion sets.

As soon as Lena Faye and I got inside, we could tell that
he Tarabulus Music Militia's lead singer, a young Druze in a
psychedelically embroidered kaffiyeh, was singing, in kind of
pastard cockney, a hard-rock curse called, if the recurrence of
pne phrase means anything, "Simply Indispenserble":

> "S really arfly risible,
> A daftness indivisible,
> To so much pride surscepterble,
> E thinks e's [bump! bump!] 'simply indispenserble'!

> "E'll avtah take some sass fum us
> To be so bogon blasphemous,
> Cause it's crudely indefenserble
> To claim e's [bump! bump!] 'simply indispenserble'!"

The crowd in Hobeika's Den, or a major part of it, was *dancing*
to TMM's syncopated heavy-pedal scorn. Someone had even
programmed the belly dancer to punctuate the *bump! bump!*s
with staccato hip swings—unless, of course, its microcircuitry
simply triggered automatic kinetic feedback to whatever music
it "heard."

"Cripes," I murmured.

"Don't be profane."

I lifted an eyebrow. Then I took Lena Faye's hand and led
her to the cappuccino-and-cordial bar. I'd just drawn a stool
out for her when a bearish man in a lapel-less silver-lamé jacket
and a gold-foil keffiyeh grabbed the stool and shoved it toward
the dance floor. Lena Faye's eyes widened. Otherwise, she
showed no sign of alarm.

> "S awtuhgedder winceable,
> At on barmy princerple,
> Lahk e's ploom invincerble,
> E sez e's [bump! bump!] 'simply indispenserble'!"

"Gist, you camel-dung pig-dog dormouse! You dare to show
up in public?! To push your shameless mug into a place where

living flesh-and-blooders can do you the infinite justice of spit
ting in your eye?! *Phfffthhhhhht!*"

With the back of my hand, I wiped a bleb of saliva from m
cheek. (Ha ha, you missed.) Then: "Lena Faye Leatherboat
allow me to introduce you to the mild-mannered Bashir Shou
man. Mr. Shouman, Ms. Leatherboat."

"An honor," Shouman said, kissing Lena Faye's wrist befor
turning back to me. "Have a care, you pig-dog! You sully he
name merely by appearing in her company! Your depravity, lik
your cableglom, has no discoverable limit!"

> "Allah is de Prince-uv-All,
> But Joe Way's blubber-dense, yer-all,
> Is skin so fiercely flenserble
> To swear e's [bump! bump!] 'simply indispenserble'!"

"See?! See what your mendacious gabfeed has wrought? Now
I know why you call it *Forum* plus *Againstum*! You stand
against all decency! You lie to up-puff yourself!"

"Translation: Levant's ratings have annihilated ShariVid's i
our contending time slots," I told Lena Faye.

"Say on, say on!" Shouman raged.

"Mr. Shouman doesn't like adjusting to this hurtful fact. We
even plastered him *tonight*, with Joe Way sitting there abou
as talkative as Tar Baby."

"I could ask the Ayatollah Sadr to do string figures on my
program! Or hire Kuwait's soccer team to kick around a ball ir
ClingFlex thongs! My ratings would also soar! But never do I
pander! Never do I *manufacture* attractions!"

"I *manufactured* the Pope?"

"Not him! Not Imam Bahadori! Not the Dalai Lama! No
that veil-free Pilgrim woman! Not them, but the unscrupulou
fraud of your so-called DOS 'energy being'!"

> "E sneers at pious protocols
> N kicks at commonsense, yer-all!
> Is power's awl ostenserble,
> But, yah, e's [bump! bump!] 'simply indispenserble'!
> No way, Joe Way, no waaaay!"

"Joe Way is for real," I said.

"He's a see-throughable holojection which some deluded
people"—nodding at the Tarabulus Music Militia—"lack the

commonsense to see through. They suppose your meretricious Gumby-ghost is lying, never considering that the lie springs instead from you, you pig-dog!"

"It doesn't," Lena Faye said quietly. "I know Joe Way to be exactly what he has claimed."

This assertion, from this source, gave Shouman pause. How could Lena Faye speak false? He sidestepped his doubt:

"You corrupt even the most innocent, you garbage thrower; and chaos descends!"

"Unlike your spite wall, which keeps going up."

"And will do so until it has left your towerhouse as blind as its dungball-eating occupant! You deserve to see no farther than a man in a windowless box!"

"Like Wigner's friend," I said.

But Bashir Shouman didn't hear me. He had elbowed his way outside onto the Rue de Damas. Meanwhile, it had taken nearly the last of my psychic energy to keep from trying to choke the vituperative crap out of him.

"You did good," Lena Faye told me.

The MMT combo had finally brought "Simply Indispenser-ble" to a crescendoing end. Now the boys were crooning, "Bright are zuh stars zud shine, / Dark izzuh sky. / I know ziss luv ufmine / Will nevuh die."

Pretty. Truly pretty. I was astonished.

At my place south of Beirut, Shouman's hired hands worked more furiously on his spite wall, as if he'd offered them bonuses to speed up its construction. Before Lena Faye's and my eyes, it was turning into something less like a wall than a prodigious monument to malice. People in shacks farther down the hill tottered upslope just to watch the ugly barrier grow in width and height.

"The bastard," I said.

"At least he's putting people to work," Lena Faye said.

"I need a bazooka. I know where to get one, too. There's still a dilapidated arms depot at the old Burj Al Barajinah ref-ugee camp, and it'd be—"

"Stop talking rot."

"Yessum."

"If you do stay here in your adobe tower, simply turn the wall's stucco backside into a laser-mural canvas. You could switch the mural out every month or week or day, depending on your attention span."

"Ha ha. I'd already thought of something like that."

Lena Faye had only four more days of her working vacation for Okla*Globe in Lebanon. On Monday morning, I'd escort her to the airport either to see her off or to accompany her back to the states. Okla*Globe's final salary package was definitely attractive, and for additional inducement there was Lena Faye herself. . . .

Meanwhile, my vidverge wall showed that, although hostile local reaction to Joe Way's *Forum/Againstum* gigs had developed slowly, it had now begun to heat up. This anger had its roots not only in various Islamic groups (the Sunnites, the Shi-'ites, and the Druze), but also in the Christian community (Maronite Catholic, Greek Orthodox, Greek Catholic, etc.). Ten thousand Jews also live in Beirut nowadays, and their religious leaders were attacking me and Levant both for putting Joe Way on the show and for excluding a qualified representative of their own faith from the cablecast.

"*Two* Christians this come-lately Cherokee *goy* has on his gabshow," Rabbi Moshe Hillel Silver told Nadia Suleiman in a spot between reports of Shi'ite street protests and of a Maronite picket line outside the Sabra Hotel. "Not a single Jew. You call that balance?"

"He's right," Lena Faye said.

"I know. Tell that to Pope Jomo and Imam Bahadori."

"My, how you can crab-sidle, injun."

The protests against Joe Way and the outrageous su'lakle message of their indispensability to this region of the cosmos—and against my gabfeed for providing them a forum—were now receiving at least as much cable coverage as the proceedings of the New Millenarian Ecumenical Council.

The NMEC, however, appeared to be in as much disarray as Beirut's streets, parks, and beaches. Officials from the Big Three monotheistic religions suffered excruciating trials of conscience accommodating to the session-opening prayer rituals of Wiccans, animists, goddess worshipers, voodooists, and idol devotees. And vice versa. Nor did these partisan brouhahas prevent internal bickering among all the denominations, cults, cabals, and sects within either the major or the minor spiritual alignments. A spokesperson for Pope Jomo I announced that His Holiness would depart Beirut a full two days before the closing ceremonies.

"Why?" our reporter Mitri Ahad asked this flunky.

"Unfinished business at the Vatican." The spokesperson did a rude preemptive heel-pivot.

Then my vidverge screen disclosed that a large party of Druze protesters had joined the Maronite sign-wielders on the sidewalk below Levant's studios in the Sabra. Despite their common purpose—namely, reviling me, my employer, and F/A—the two groups clashed with one another about tactics, sidewalk territory, and even the su'lakle's degree of insidiousness as an extraterrestrial Satan. Police moved in, but placard poles, with much accompanying cursing and shoving, began to jab about like pikestaffs.

"Do you think Nadia's safe up there?" Lena Faye asked.

I was about to say, "I think so," when the picture on my wall crumpled in zigzag bands and scrambled away to static. Before I could use my multiflicker to repair the picture, the static resolved itself into the manta-ray-headed phosphor-dot image of Joe Way. This image stayed two-dimensional only long enough for him to acquire focus and to step out of the vidverge as his old viridescent self. This time, though, he had to *duck* to get fully out, and when he straightened again, he resembled a hammerhead shark upright on its tail, or maybe the freakshow version of the not-so-little brother of the Melancholy Green Giant.

"Joe," I said fatuously. "What's up?"

"*Ignorant members of your species don't believe I'm what I say I am, or else they assume I've somehow insulted—blasphemed against—their frail sectarian notions of the godhead. They think I've arrogated to myself the creative energies and the abiding omnipotence of God by using your infogabshow to declare the fact of my indispensability.*"

"Unfortunately," I said, "that's true."

Joe Way flickered from one side of my relaxall to the other like a pacing would-be suicide. "*How can I ask your species to take over the observational task of local universe-sustenance if I'm not believed? Even if I were to give you a simplified subatomic transition kit, full instructions, and intensive techno-spiritual aid, your species' disbelief—your intolerant wrathfulness—would probably sabotage the takeover, and with it, inevitably, much of the enveloping cosmos.*"

Lena Faye said, "Even if every human being alive believed you, I'm not sure we'd rush to accept the responsibility you're trying to stick us with, Joe."

"*Nonsense. It's a great honor.*"

"We probably couldn't do it," I said.

Joe kept up his spectral golemesque pacing. *"That's true. But mostly because your kind fatuously assumes indispensability equates with divinity."*

"It doesn't?"

"Of course not. The su'lakle—finite entities at least passably comparable to your own species—operate on a divine mandate, a ukase from God Wholeself."

"What's God like?" Lena Faye said.

"You'll never really know until you take this job."

"So God exists?" I said.

Joe Way stopped pacing, and with Pope Jomo's all-too-human eyes—a su'lakle affectation of cagy ulteriority—fixed me with a condemning/forgiving glare. Believe me, to escape it, I'd've gladly kevorked.

"Mr. Gist, you're descended from a man named Sequoyah, who taught his people how to 'write.' True?"

"Yessir."

"This Sequoyah, alias George Gist, once said, 'We have full confidence they will receive you with all friendship.' "

"Maybe. I never heard that before."

"My final F/A segment airs tomorrow night, ne pas?"

I nodded.

"Tape a segment to append to the cablecast. Announce that to demonstrate the earnestness of su'lakle intent, along with my capacity to do whatever I say, I will put on a 'pyrotechnic spectacle' not long after your announcement."

"When exactly? And where?"

"Midnight. Across an unmissable arc of sky over Al Biqa Valley, directly east of Beirut."

"But why?" Lena Faye said. "What's the point?"

"To make a point. Human beings like shows. Next week, I will appear on Forum/Againstum again to explain simplistically how humanity may acquire indispensability."

"But I've already booked next Monday's guests."

"Pshaw," said Joe Way. *"After Saturday night's spectacle, Levant's subscribers will clamor for my return."*

When he was gone, back through my looking-glass vidverge unit, Lena Faye said, "*Quel* ego. Kinda like one of my beloved Superjerk's greatest hits."

We flew from Damur Ridge to the Sabra Hotel in one of Levant's helis and set down on the aviary landing pad. The disorder in the streets had come under an uneasy modicum of police control, but I was happy we didn't have to try to enter the Sabra from the ground.

In Levant's studios, I taped the add-on that Joe Way had asked for and turned around to find both Lena Faye and myself facing a uniformed officer of the United Nations Near Eastern Security Service (UNNESS), which President Balthazar Hariri regularly dismisses as UNNESSesary.

"Mr. Gist," the officer said, "I'm Colonel Patrick Rulon. I'd like to see all the tapes of *Forum/Againstum* on which the virrogate Joe Way actually speaks."

"Why?"

"Purposes of evaluation and security. Are there forms I need to fill out?"

"No, you can see 'em. Did you hear me tape that business about Saturday night's lightshow in Al Biqa?"

"I did."

Nothing else, not even a smile, just "I did." So I took Rulon to a corked booth where he could review the first and third hours of this week's cablecasts and then preview the one scheduled for tomorrow night. I gave him a multiflicker so he could fast-forward through Joe's silences or back up and replay his odd pronouncements about "the heart's most basic longing" or su'lakle indispensability.

When he emerged from the booth, in which he'd spent less than an hour, Rulon handed me the tapes. "Interesting."

"What did you think of them?"

"I just told you."

"How do they bear on Near Eastern Security?"

"That stuff has *global* implications, Mr. Gist. Keep it under your hat."

"The last episode you watched cablecasts tomorrow. Then there's that Al Biqa thing."

"Yes, I know. Night." The colonel beat a tight-lipped, tightassed retreat.

Lena Faye: "What was that all about?"

"Pissing on bushes," I said. "Territory."

The following afternoon, even before the last of the NMEC programs was to appear, Lena Faye and I took my Levant heli out to Al Biqa and landed on a hilltop from which we'd have a good view of Joe Way's promised midnight spectacular.

The stretch of irrigated valley to our east lay below us like a beautiful gridded quilt of lavenders, salmons, and jades. The most unusual feature in the landscape, though, wasn't the crops (leafy tobacco here, tangled grape arbors there, apricot and cherry trees on islandlike ridges), but the spaced-out wind turbines—tri-petaled pinwheels set atop spindly latticework derricks—generating power not only for the hamlets of Al Biqa but also for Sidon, Tyre, Byblos, and parts of Beirut. The blades on those turbines pleasantly hypnotized us as we picnicked on cheese and bread, polished off a couple of bottles of wine, and waited for The Show.

Meanwhile, about a mile away, a convoy of military trucks crawled up a hill into a concealing stand of fruit trees. (It may have joined others already positioned there.) Also, once Joe Way's last episode of *Forum/Againstum* had concluded, groups of sightseers in buses and touring cars began to filter into the area, via the main highway from Beirut and dozens of rutted *muhafazah* roads. We saw these last arrivals by their headlamps and taillights, not by the shapes and colors of the vehicles, which, in the gathering dark, registered primarily as amorphous creeping shadows, small smudges on the vaster, darker smudge of the valley floor.

"What time is it?" Lena Faye said.

Before I could check my digital, the sky flashed once: a great, silver-veined lilac throb.

This lilac throb, occupying more aerial territory than a hundred overlapping full moons, faded slowly away, but the sky kept glowing, as if God had turned on a monstrous scallop-shell night-light behind the star-dusted scrim of space. Someone sitting on our picnic blanket murmured, "Wow." It could have been either, or both, of us.

I don't have the heart to describe in its entirety what the su'lakle showed us over Al Biqa. Imagine the biggest and most complex Fourth of July celebration you've ever seen, heard of, or read about. Then cube it. At least.

Even that doesn't quite convey what we witnessed, though, because the bursting rockets, drifting fireballs, parachuting teardrops, and migrating color streams continuously deformed into sky-borne images: fields of lion-maned flowers, roaring Niagaras, breaking *tsunamis* of Oriental-carpet figures, flaming baobab trees, translucent calving icebergs, oddball animals at play or at rest, faces human or disturbingly alien, spiraling keyholes to other continua. Et cetera.

"You know what's weird, George? What has my gut strings twanging really strangely?"

"What?" I was propped on my elbows, my head thrown back, my mouth stupidly agape.

"I've got a hunch they're dumbing this hurly-burly down."

I glanced over at Lena Faye.

"You know," she said, "for us. Condescending. Dumbing it down for our sakes. It could be ten times as spectacular if we had the brains, or the sensory apparatus, to take in their very best. Maybe a thousand times. You know?"

I didn't want to think about that. Usually, I hated fireworks; they boomed and hissed, scintillated and glowered, and all you could do was watch big-eyed and of course moan in orgiastic approval with the rubes around you. This thing the su'lakle had set shifting kaleidoscopically across the sky, though—it was different. I had the feeling that they were not so much patronizing us poor *Homo sapiens* as subtly trying to reorganize our brains through our eyes, to carve fresh pathways through our gray matter by preprogrammed visual stimuli, to refold our convolutions in evolutionary ways we wouldn't fully twig to until they'd left.

Joe Way's manta-ray-shaped head took shape in the fading remnants of their final image, an energy-storm parody of *The Creation* from Michelangelo's Sistine Chapel work. That was what *I* saw. Lena Faye read into it the spare and moving cover illo on Art Spiegelman's *Maus*. (Who knows what everybody else on hand beheld or thought they did?) She and I agreed, though, that emerging from this last image was Joe Way. The head, with its weirdly compassionate eyes, floated over Al Biqa, appearing to sustain its hover by means of its fins' endless rippling. This head occupied as much sky as the first lavender throb had done.

"*In order to acquire indispensability,*" Joe Way began in a thundering overture, "*you must—*"

From the ridge a mile away, the UNNESS vehicles parked amid the fruit trees began firing a concentrated barrage of scathing laser energy at the su'lakle. Vehicles hidden in other parts of the valley joined this attack. The rays—dozens upon dozens of them—launched upward in furious, vindictive assault. Bombs detonated in Joe Way's cheeks and boccal region. The energy comprising and tethering together the features of the entity's startled face began to dissipate. One of its rippling wings detached and floated off toward Tripoli, pulling into tat-

ters as it drifted. The other, hit several times in a row, vented
an emerald glow of gigantic phosphenes and evaporated.
Shortly thereafter, Joe Way closed his Pope Jomo eyes, and the
midnight sky—the *old* midnight sky—reasserted itself, sealing
Lena Faye and me, Al Biqa, Lebanon, and maybe even the
world itself into the benumbing boxes of our workaday lives.

I scrambled up and shook my fist at the UNNESS encamp-
ment a mile away. "You idiots! You blooming xenophobic idiots! You may've just ruined everything!"

"They couldn't hurt the su'lakle, could they?" Lena Faye
said. "Beings who sustain the cosmos."

"Look!" I told her. "Just look! Where is he? Where are they?
What's happened?"

The valley filled with the honking of all the touring cars and
buses whose drivers and passengers had come out to witness
the midnight show. Honking, cursing, keening. An obstreper-
ous mix-and-match symphony of outrage and disappointment.

My God, I thought, the whole planet sounds sick, grievously
wounded. Sick unto death.

I guess it takes a while for a system as far-reaching and complex as the universe to unravel. Despite the chaos, anger, and
traffic tie-ups in Al Biqa after UNNESS's ostensible preemptive
strike on the su'lakle, most sightseers managed to get safely
back to their homes. Lena Faye and I, of course, simply lifted
off from that hilltop and whirlybirded homeward.

On our way, seeing the flairs and bonfires illuminating a
multivehicle collision, we took the time to land, investigate,
and help two badly injured people—a woman in her fifties and
an unrelated child of five or six—aboard our Levant heli for
transport to a medical facility. Indeed, I flew them to the
Danny Thomas Memorial Hospital in Beirut, refueled on its
roof pad, and undertook three more such missions—Lena insisted on coming along on all of them—before returning to my
towerhouse on Damur Ridge. We arrived home just before
dawn. There, we turned on my vidverge unit for reports of the
aftermath of the fatuous UNNESS assault on the su'lakle.

Instead, we got Joe Way in his viridescent manta-ray-headed
guise. This time, though, he refused to step away from the
screen into the authentic three-dimensionality of my relaxall.
He peered out at us like an alien prophet.

"Joe!" Lena Faye cried. "I thought they'd destroyed you!
Your species, I mean!"

"Fat chance," he replied. *"They disrupted the surface of a hologrammatic display projected from the interstices of this spatial-temporal continuum. Nothing more. That ill-advised action, however, has determined me—us, if you like—to abandon the task of observation to you without delay or instruction. I return to offer my apologies, for I know you two human beings, at least, as entities somewhat better than even you yourselves suppose and so not necessarily deserving of this kind of abrupt rejection. As for your species as a whole . . ."*

"You're leaving?" I said. "You're simply going to pull out? What will happen to us? Joe, we don't know diddly about universe-sustenance!"

"We haven't succeeded all that spectacularly in holding our own planet together," Lena Faye added.

"Shit will happen," Joe Way said. *"Some of it will result from active manipulation of macrocosmic, as opposed to quantum, forces, and much of it will mystify and frighten you. This manipulation will be punitive. But the worst may stem from the psychic impact of our withdrawal on adjacent observer species, many of whom will follow our lead in abandoning the sustenance game. That's all I care to impart. Goodbye."*

"Wait!" Lena Faye and I both called out.

But Joe Way faded away, and my vidverge unit commenced to operate exactly like a vidverge unit.

Since then, despite repeated U.N. pronouncements about the legitimacy—yea, the *urgency*—of its laser disruption of the unpredictable alien energy beings who'd appeared on *Forum/Againstum* as "Joe Way," the cable-watching public has reacted with either withering scorn or outright indifference. Maybe the latter response is the more common. After all, most folks assume the entire Joe Way phenomenon just another example of TV hype, from the distillate's "scripted" remarks on my show to UNNESS's self-authorized and, yes, highly colorful "ambush" in the valley.

Firm believers in Joe Way, however, want an investigation into the incident. They also demand the literal head of the chief administrator of UNNESS and a concentrated international effort to retrieve and reassemble the insulted alien(s). They have no faith in the U.N.'s promises that the untoward events of the last few hours—occurrences that seem to require the suspension of immemorial "natural laws"—will cease as soon as the jet stream gets back to normal, or martens reinfest the cedars of Qurnat as-Sawda', or the planets of our solar system realign.

"Right," I say. "Or Siddhartha Gautama reappears wearing an NBA warm-up jacket, some Bombay Gear tennis shoes, and a pair of virching goggles."

We sit in my relaxall either monitoring the vidverge unit or looking downslope at Bashir Shouman's spite wall, which his busy-busy fellaheen workers completed yesterday while Lena Faye and I were picnicking in Al Biqa. It effectively blocks our view of the beach, the docks, the sea. Shouman's hired hands left themselves some stuccoing to do on its uphill face, but why should I care whether something so evil in intent and true to its function looks finished? My consolation, now that Lena Faye and I appear to be trapped here, resides in the certain knowledge that the wall will prove useful to Shouman for only a short while longer.

Sadly, with no one to make the key quantum observations that undergird the structure of the universe, the universe will cease to cohere. The center won't hold; things will fall apart. The problem appears as grave to us as was the ruination of the ozone layer to our grandparents.

Okay, *graver.*

"About five minutes ago," Lena Faye says, "I realized that reality truly is breaking down."

"How?"

"Your bathroom scales. They weighed me seventeen pounds lighter than yesterday. Impossible, of course. On the other hand, George, I *feel* lighter—you know, semiafloat even when my feet're touching the floor."

"I know." I *do*: Sometimes, walking, I curl my toes to get better purchase, to keep from drifting away.

The vidverge unit gives us a window on the anomalous events now occurring in the outside world. (The available vid-grids keep changing, though. Levant holds steady, but CNN, ShariVid, ABC Overseas, and Okla*Globe have fi-opted out, leaving behind either static, noisy Milton Berle kinescopes, or geometric test patterns framing the profiles of Amerindians like Pontiac, Tecumseh, and Geronimo.) The first anomaly that Nadia Suleiman reported today was the disappearance at the end of its runway of any flight attempting to leave Beirut International. The big jets would lift off, squeeze into a shimmering slit in the air, and vanish like a magician's pigeons. At least three jets got airborne—and vaporized or interdimensionally transported—before airport bigwigs noted that such wholesale fishiness was bad for passenger morale, ordered an investigation, and closed the facility down.

Other strange things have occurred. Without any warning, the bank building housing the Green Line Café reverted to its rubble-filled condition of over thirty years ago. No one was hurt but the drum-set operator of the Tarabulus Music Militia, who had stretched out under a table after last night's final session. A Syrian soldier vacationing on the Ramlet el Baida beach spontaneously grew a tail (apparently, a spider monkey's) and began collecting money in a stolen fez. The Ferris wheel on this same beach started releasing its cars at the top of its arc, until not a single gondola remained, and people citywide could see the released cars drifting upward and southward like giant bubbles. The streetlamps on the Avenue Charles Helou grew palm bark, heavy green fronds, and coconuts that looked exactly like bowling balls. The horses running in the eighth race at the revitalized Hippodrome crossed the finish line in a neck-and-neck tie without even a nose's difference among them. Elsewhere, the Canadian army invaded Alaska, the Eiffel Tower lifted off with a hundred-some tourists aboard, the Taj Mahal turned into a tangy-smelling construct of melting tangerine Jell-O, and at least a million two-foot-long lobsters with WIN WITH TIM buttons taped to their carapaces swarmed ashore on the southernmost tip of the Malayasian peninsula. An oil firm struck a creme-de-menthe deposit in Tierra del Fuego. Denver, Colorado, collapsed into an immense sump of some kind, and all over the world statues of sundry eminent persons began coming to life, no matter how long their commemorated subjects may've been dead.

At long last, here on Damur Ridge, night has fallen. For a while, I doubted that it would. I figured snow might fall, or pfennigs from heaven, or the self-pared toenails of feathered protodinosaurs. Lena Faye and I look out the picture window of my towerhouse. Kon Ichikawa's 1958 film *Enjo* flickers on the backside of Shouman's spite wall, subtitleless. I have no idea how it's being projected there, from where, or why. The acting has an earnest panache.

Above the pain and melodrama of *Enjo*, the sky is visible. Shouman's spite wall has not risen high enough to blot it from our view. I think of TMM in the Green Line Café doing "And I Love Her" after pounding out "Simply Indispenserble." And I pull Lena Faye to me as snugly as I can. She rests her head on my shoulder. Friendly stars blaze in their familiar places, but the full moon shines down—pale, knobby, and large—like a face on Mount Rushmore.

"It's bad, isn't it?" Lena Faye means the cosmos, or this goosy portion of it, without the su'lakle.

"Yeah. I'm afraid so."

"I can't fly home, but if you'd like to be alone, I can get myself a room in a hotel—the Sabra, maybe."

I look Lena Faye straight in the eyes, replay the TMM cover beginning "Bright are zuh stars zud shine," and shake my head.

"Uh-uh," I tell her. "Tonight, Ms. Leatherboat, I couldn't possibly do without you."

Once again, we look outward and up. The spite of our kind rebounds on us immediately, for overhead, without any fuss, the stars—all of them—have begun to go out.

[For Michael Morrison, for advice and forbearance]

THE INSIPID PROFESSION OF JONATHAN HORNEBOM

(Hommage à Heinlein)

Jonathan Lethem

1.

It was nearly dark. Jonathan Hornebom rushed along the sidewalk of Fourth Street, toward Barrow, terrified. He had to get home and see if the awful thing had recurred. He jostled a pair of tie-loosened businessmen as they strolled away from the subway, and nearly knocked into a teenager who was attempting to climb the curb with a skateboard. "Watch it, dude—"

"Sorry," muttered Hornebom as the teenager clacked away.

At Barrow Street he fumbled open his ironwork gate and went into the entrance under the stoop, to his studio. He pushed past the old canvases, those that had already received the damaging marks and those that had escaped, to the easel on the back wall, where his newest work sat covered. He pulled the sheet aside and then recoiled in horror.

The child in the foreground was just as he'd painted it. Eyes wide and shimmering, brimming with tears. The background, a field of flowers, was intact. But the sky—across his soft blue and white sky was another of the horrendous shapes, a terrifying black cyclone of bones and tendons. A bird-beast, with shining black eyes that mocked those of the child.

The shapes were, as always, painted into his work flawlessly, as if by his own hand. Indeed, he had to suspect his own hand, for want of other suspects.

But the additions were unimaginably gruesome, visions he could barely stomach, let alone originate.

The changes in the paintings forced him to confront the gaps in memory that made a patchwork of his days. He'd tried to ignore the inconsistencies. What was the importance of a lost hour, now and again? Amnesia he could live with. But if he was capable of committing these unspeakable desecrations of his work, what else might he be doing during the missing hours?

Or could there actually be a hidden tormentor, some mastermind capable of timing his attacks on the paintings to coincide with Hornebom's blackouts?

Enough! He had to know.

2.

Harriet was about to close up the office and go upstairs to her apartment when the phone rang. She thought about letting the machine pick it up anyway, and then she thought about her bank balance and reached for the receiver.

"I—is this Harriet M. Welch, the investigator?" The voice had a slight German accent.

"Right," she said.

"My name is Jonathan Hornebom. I'd like to talk to you, if I could."

"Talk."

"I—I'd rather—"

"You mean in person."

"Could I? Your office address is quite near."

"I'll be here for another half an hour," she said, putting her feet back up on the desk. She opened her drawer and took out the catalog that had come that day from Wily E.'s Surveillance Supplies and a half tomato sandwich left over from her lunch.

When Hornebom pressed the doorbell she buzzed him in without looking up, but when he entered the room she pushed the catalog into the trash basket along with the sandwich wrapping. The products were crap. She smiled up at Hornebom and said: "Mind if I smoke?"

"No, no," he said, and shook his head.

She lit a cigarette. "Sit down." She watched him put himself in the seat across her desk. He was younger than she'd guessed, but seeing his primness and reserve she understood her mistake. He was dressed like a character actor, in a gray suit, cravat, white gloves and a bowler. His hair was white but it still covered his head, and his pinched, severe features were overwhelmed by his eyes. They were deep-set, ringed, and huge. An eagle's eyes, if he'd met her gaze. Instead they darted away.

"What can I do for you, Mr. Hornebom?"

"I—I can't explain. I'm afraid it may be the stupidest thing you've ever heard—"

"That's a contest you can't hope to win. What's the problem? A woman? A business arrangement that's soured?"

"I have blackouts," Hornebom managed.

Harriet frowned. "You drink?"

"Never."

"I'm not a doctor."

"I'm not looking for one, not yet at least. I need to know what goes on during my—missing time. Because something's happened to my work."

"Your work?"

"I'm a painter. And someone, or something, is changing my work while I'm . . . out."

"Changing how?" Harriet stubbed out her cigarette, not sure whether she was intrigued or annoyed.

"Adding to my paintings—terrible things."

"Okay, wait a minute. You make a living from painting?" Her skepticism showed in her voice. He didn't look the type.

"Well, yes."

"So you're good. Or famous, anyway. Because you have to be, to make a living from art, right?"

"I . . . have a reputation."

She worked the story out of him. He lived alone, in his own brownstone, his studio in the basement apartment. (She upped her fee mentally.) The gaps in his memory were not in themselves disruptive. He'd find himself in the park, or in front of his television, or seated in a restaurant, with no memory of how he'd gotten there. But never anywhere unexpected, or unlikely.

Then, two weeks ago, he'd returned to his studio to find the first of the alterations. Nightmarish beaked and taloned things looming in his skies. Defacements, but expert ones. Either some ingenious tormentor with more knowledge of Hornebom's comings and goings than he himself possessed was destroying his work or, more horrifying to contemplate, he was destroying it himself.

"I want to be followed," Hornebom concluded. "I want you to track me like a suspect in a crime. Find out what I do, where I go. I'll pay for a full report. And if it's not me committing the artistic atrocities—"

"Would you want them arrested?"

He shuddered. "Report to me first, please. Let me decide."

"Does anyone else have a key to the studio?"

Hornebom shook his head. "My housekeeper has the upstairs key. But there's no interior stair. It was designed as a separate apartment. I have the only key."

"I'll need a copy," Harriet said. She was captivated now by the problem, the logistics. The possibility that Hornebom was merely insane she shunted to a rear part of her brain; she wanted a puzzle to solve, a locked-room mystery, and she wanted more of the checks that Hornebom now wrote out so readily with his trembling, gloved hands, one for her first day of work, and one as a standing retainer. She wanted a series of them, to pad the lining of her hemorrhaging bank account.

Assuming the first one didn't bounce, that was. He was as seedy as he was dandified, and from what Harriet had seen of the young, MTV-fresh SoHo art scene, Hornebom couldn't cut it in that crowd.

He agreed to bring her a copy of the key in the morning, and to slide it under her door if she was not in. What she didn't say was that she meant to be on his tail by then.

The guy was nervous enough as it was.

3.

He started with coffee and pastry at an Italian bakery on Sixth Avenue, then walked uptown until he found a locksmith's. She followed him back to her office, where he rang, waited, and finally slipped the copied key under her door.

Then back to Barrow Street. He went downstairs, into the studio, and she set up with a newspaper on a stoop across the street. It was a nice enough day to be paid to kill time on the prettiest street in Manhattan.

When he emerged again, an hour later, she ducked down behind her paper. He swiveled on his heel and strode up the street, at twice his previous speed. She gave him half a block and started after, quelling a pang of curiosity about the studio itself. She still didn't have a key in hand, and anyway, he looked like a man on a mission.

Her heart was pounding. The old game, still magic. Just give me someone to follow, she thought, and I'm a kid again.

On Seventh he hailed a cab. She jumped into the street and grabbed the next one, commanding the driver to follow. He raised his eyebrows but didn't say anything. Hornebom's cab shot uptown, jerking through traffic, catching stretches of timed lights, then squeaking to a stop every block for six or seven red lights in a row, and Harriet's followed. Several times they swam together in block-long seas of identical yellow cabs, and Harriet had to help the driver stick to Hornebom's. They crossed town at Fifty-third Street and finally pulled to the curb in front of the Museum of Modern Art. Hornebom paid his driver and sped into the lobby of the building, and Harriet had to surrender a twenty in her haste to follow. Six-dollar tip, but she'd charge it all to Hornebom.

She pushed through the crowds milling in the outer lobby just in time to catch sight of him paying for his ticket and passing on into the museum. Fair enough; painter wants to look at paintings. Was he in his blackout phase? She couldn't know. She got in line for a ticket and watched him heading up a packed escalator.

She handed over her ticket and hurried through the turnstile, but the escalator was too crowded for her to do anything but stand still and wait her turn, and when she got to the top he was nowhere to be seen. She ducked into the permanent collection, a labyrinth of gigantic paintings that seemed to Harriet mostly flat fields of bright color, and scouted the rooms, searching for a glimpse of his white hair. He was not there.

She took the escalator up another floor. The exhibition was labeled "Anxious Furniture: Surrealist and Dada Objects and Sculpture 1916–1948," and it seemed to be what had drawn the crowds. Perhaps it had drawn Hornebom. She jostled her way into the first of the rooms. The admirers of the vast paintings downstairs had had to stand in the middle of the rooms to take in their full scope, but the displays here were in glass cases and were mostly quite small, so the crowds bunched tight around them. Harriet found it completely annoying. She wanted to poke the groups apart to see if Hornebom was hiding in among them. Instead she bumped her way around from behind, trying to ignore the inanely reverent comments. She didn't know anything about anxious furniture, but she had the distinct feeling she was in a room full of jokes being taken seriously.

She was ready to declare him lost and go back to explore his studio when suddenly there he was, standing still in a stream of moving bodies, in front of one of the glass cases. She let a few people pass and then found a place in the group around him, a few heads back. Standing up on her toes, she looked over his shoulder.

There were three objects in the case. On the left a teacup, saucer and spoon, all normally proportioned, but covered completely in fur. On the right a metronome topped with an eye, or a photograph of an eye, and otherwise unaltered. In the middle was an object that seemed a combination printing press and toy cannon: two-foot-high wheels with a complex assembly of rollers and handles suspended between them, and a gun barrel pointing out at the viewer.

Hornebom stood alone, seemingly frozen there, while groups filled in around him, and trickled away to be replaced again, and again. Harriet began to think he was in blackout mode now, whether or not he had been on his way up here. But no, Harriet suddenly noticed, Hornebom *wasn't* alone. Another man stood as an island in the stream of oglers. He was young, a few years younger than Harriet, with a little beard that did more to reveal his age than to hide it. He had set up a little to one side of the case, and was staring intently at the exhibit.

Harriet watched as the younger man became aware of Hornebom, who was planted so conspicuously in front of the case. She melted back farther into the crowd, to watch without the risk of being noticed herself. The younger man squinted at Hornebom as though recognizing him, then, looking back at the case, took out a small spiral-bound notebook and began jotting notes with a pencil.

Harriet reflexively patted at the notebook she kept in the kangaroo pocket of her sweatshirt.

The younger man went on writing, staring at the objects in the case, and occasionally glancing up at Hornebom. Hornebom remained seemingly oblivious, his gaze fixed on the middle object in the case.

Suddenly self-conscious of her participation in their odd threesome, she shuffled along to the next case, and followed the flow around the adjacent room, glancing back every few minutes to confirm Hornebom's presence. Finally she allowed herself to risk losing him, and finished the loop of the exhibition, which deposited her back at the entrance.

She peered in: they were both still there. She started in again, and nonchalantly scooted up behind the young man with the beard. In his notebook was a sketch of the cannon/printing press. He looked up suddenly, and around; she turned her head the other way and walked quickly off.

As for Hornebom, an hour had passed since she'd followed him into the museum, and still he stood entranced.

She went downstairs and, keeping her eye on the flow through the exit gates, leafed through the exhibition catalog on the gift counter. She found photographs of all three of the objects in the case. The teacup was labeled "Breakfast in Fur," by Meret Oppenheim. The metronome was "Object of Destruction," by Man Ray. And the device in the middle—the one the man with the beard had been sketching—was "Bird Camera," by Max Ernst.

Harriet was hungry, and tired of the museum. She went and found the sandwich counter in the courtyard, turning her back, for the moment, on the exit. If Hornebom escaped she'd go back downtown and check his house, and if he wasn't home she could inspect the studio. A good plan: she treated herself to roast beef and a large Coke, on the client.

By the time she was done the crowd had thinned. She went upstairs. At first she thought they were both gone, then she spotted the bearded man, sitting on a bench across the room from the glass case.

He looked up, and for the second time she had to turn quickly to keep from meeting his eyes. Sloppy, she chided herself. She scooted into the next room, then turned and looked back. He was gone from the bench. Well, never mind. It was Hornebom she should be troubling with. Where was he?

"Hello."

She turned around to find the young man with the beard standing before her, smiling.

"Hello," she said.

"Are you with the security staff?" he asked, still smiling pleasantly.

"What?"

"Here at the museum."

"No, no. Excuse me." She craned her neck around, worrying that Hornebom was in the room.

"Because you seem to be watching me or following me or something."

"Not you. Forget it."

"The old guy, then. The one staring at the Ernst thing."

"Quiet," she commanded. They were attracting attention.

"He left, if that's what you're worried about. So, if you weren't following me, would you have coffee with me?"

"Shhh. I—I just had a Coke. Where did he go? No, don't talk. Let's go downstairs."

They made their way to the garden. Harriet led him to a table in the farthest corner, and sat so that she commanded a view of the entire yard behind him.

"You don't work for the museum either," she suggested.

"Nope. I'm Rich, uh, Richard DeBronk. I'm a student. A graduate student, I mean. At Hunter."

Professional loafer, Harriet supplied to herself. It fit his bumbling manner, and her suspicions of him eased. "Well, I'm Harriet Welch," she said. "What do you know about the man you saw today, Mr. DeBronk?"

"What do I know about—Well, what do *you* know, I mean, why should I tell you? If you're not working for the museum, what are you doing asking me questions?"

"You asked me out, Richard. This is a *date*. This is my feeble conversational tack. Have you ever seen that man before?"

DeBronk assumed a thoughtful pose. "I don't think so." He squinted at Harriet. "But he did look kind of familiar. Are you some kind of cop?"

"Have you seen him in the exhibit upstairs before?"

"Are you suggesting that I have nothing better to do than stand around in museums all day?" He tried on an indignant expression, then discarded it with a shrug. "You *do* work for MOMA, don't you? You saw me here before."

"You're making spontaneous confessions, Mr. DeBronk." She wanted to strangle him. "I don't care if you live in the museum. Can you help me by answering my question straight, or am I wasting my time?"

"Who is he? I *swear* I know his face."

"His name is Jonathan Hornebom. He's—"

"That's *Hornebom*? You mean Hornebom the crying-clown painter?"

"He's a painter, yes—"

DeBronk literally slapped his knee as he laughed. "I don't believe it."

"What's so funny?" She felt a protectiveness, of her case, of her client.

"You know those wide-eyed dogs and mimes and little ragamuffin kids, you *must* know them. He's just, like, the worst painter in the history of the twentieth century. I can't believe that's really him. I thought he was dead."

"Well, I guess not. Assuming we're talking about the same man."

"There couldn't be two. God." He shook his head.

"I guess I'm not too familiar with contemporary art," Harriet said.

"This would be more like familiar with contemporary dentist's offices," said DeBronk. "I can't believe a guy like that would show his face around here. Or want to. I mean, what do you think he was *seeing* up there?"

"I'd like very much to know."

"So what's the deal, why are you following him?"

"I'm not really at liberty to discuss it. And I should go. Here's my card. Please get in touch if you think of anything useful." She stood up.

"Is this your home phone? Can I see you again?"

"Leave a message."

"What are you doing tonight?"

4.

She saw him through his window, upstairs, from her place on the stoop across the street. The studio key was in her pocket now, but she didn't quite dare to investigate it with him upstairs and awake. Maybe after he was asleep.

She went to Seventh Avenue for cigarettes, then paced his block, smoking, for nearly an hour. Nothing. She spotted him behind the curtains a few times, passing between rooms, sitting reading in a chair. *You are boring, sir,* she reported to him in her head. *That'll be five thousand dollars. Or maybe you'd like to leave me your house in your will.*

On her fourth cigarette the sun finished setting. She was just about to head back to her apartment when Hornebom appeared at the top of his stoop, locking his door and tightening his scarf around his neck. She hurried around the corner, and watched as he headed for Seventh. In the dark she was more confident following close at his heels, and she tailed him to Waverly Place, where he went into the Coach House restaurant.

Here it was: her chance at his studio. She clutched the key in her pocket and half-ran back to Barrow.

She felt her excitement rise as she finally crossed the street and went through his gate. As a child her delight had been entering houses surreptitiously. Housesitting or babysitting, she'd always made copies of the neighbors' keys, and returned uninvited later to drink in the feel of their lives, the traces that lay everywhere.

She'd learned about adult life that way. Except the adult life she'd made for herself was nothing like that, contained none of those vulnerabilities. What she hadn't told the graduate student at the museum was that the office number *was* her home number; she skimped on bills by not keeping a phone upstairs. Her little apartment was nearly bare, would tell an intruder nothing.

She'd made her childhood spying her work, and she'd made her work her life.

She unlocked the basement door and slipped inside, into near-total darkness. Street light trickled in through the half-windows, and it occurred to Harriet suddenly that Hornebom had made an odd choice putting the studio in the basement: no natural light. If he owned the entire brownstone, why not the top floor? She remembered the graduate student laughing in the garden of the museum.

She groped along the wall for the light switch, and when she found it, flicked it on.

There stood Hornebom, wearing a madly smeared smock that reached to the floor, and holding a dripping brush. He whipped around, exposed in the light, and she saw, in place of his head, the head of a monstrous bird, black eyes shining, beak narrowly open to reveal a pointed pink tongue nestled there, and curling at the sight of her. Then it was gone, her vision, and instead the human Hornebom bore down on her. He scumbled with his brush on the palette in his left hand, then raised it to her. "Do you need repainting, my dear?"

Her hand instinctively flicked the switch back down, as though the light had called him into being. He couldn't have been painting in the dark, went her wild thoughts, so he hadn't been there at all.

Her legs, finding this logic not quite satisfactory, carried her stumbling backwards, and out. She turned and ran through the gate, and across the street.

A woman was walking a small dog, and woman and dog looked up at Harriet as she fled the house. The street was quiet, and astonishingly normal. Harriet looked back; the basement was dark, of course, and there was no way of knowing if someone was inside.

Harriet stopped and looked back. The dogwalker passed, nobody came out of the basement studio.

Face burning with confusion and anger, Harriet half-walked, half-ran back to the Coach House. There was Hornebom at a table in the back, sipping fussily from a glass of wine, looking near the end of his meal. She turned away an urge to burst in and demand an explanation, instead ducked her head from the restaurant window and hurried home, suddenly terrified, and chilled to her heart by the night wind.

As she let herself into her building she heard the phone ringing behind her office door. She went into her office, and listened as her answering machine picked up the call.

"Hi, it's Richard DeBronk . . . we talked today, and I was just wondering, even though I don't really have any useful information for you, I mean about the crying-clown man, whether you might want to have a drink with me or something later tonight, or if tonight's not good—"

She grabbed the phone and switched off the machine. "Hi. Where do you want to meet?"

"Oh, hello. You're there. I, uh, I guess I didn't think of a place. I wasn't actually expecting—"

"White Horse Tavern. It's on Hudson and Eleventh."

"Wow, great, I guess you probably need some time—"

"I'll be there in ten minutes. Where are you coming from?"

"Chelsea, no problem, I'll be there soon. Uh, great."

Harriet was cold and afraid, the universe having opened up a gap she couldn't begin to account for. Her fear made her jump at an invitation she would otherwise ignore. Within half an hour she had herself shrouded in the almost medieval coziness and gloom of the White Horse, bolstered from within by Irish coffee, and enveloped in the loopy, discursive talk that was looking to be Richard DeBronk's trademark.

5.

"—original dissertation topic was the Freudian content of Max Ernst's work, the interrelations between some of his imagery and specific case studies in Freud, right? Good solid research topic, you know? I mean, the Surrealists all worked with dream imagery, automatic writing, they all loved pseudoscientific techniques—so it's not a revolutionary thesis, but I'm *explicating* the details, nailing it down, right? Art history departments are built on this kind of stuff, there's thesis work like this piled up to the ceiling; they give you your assistant professorship and then burn the dissertation to keep warm.

"So I was just digging around, verifying dates of paintings and collages so nobody could screw me up questioning the lines of influence and stuff—with historical assertions, it's like proving plagiarism in court, you have to demonstrate *access*. The connections can't just seem fertile from our vantage point, it has to have been at least *possible* that it would occur to the people involved. Okay, so I was working on sources for Ernst's collage novels—you've seen Max Ernst's collage novels, right?"

"Uh, no."

"Oh, God, you've got to, they're great. *The Hundred Headless Woman*, and *Une Semaine de Bonte*, which translates to something like 'One Week of Kindness.' They're these pictorial novels made up of collages—well, at least everybody *thinks* they're collages, but I'll get to that. Anyway, they're all these really striking images of people with rooster heads, lion heads, Easter Island–statue heads, and they're all in these domestic melodrama situations, performing these bizarre acts on each other. It's this vision of the world as a surreal nightmare, an endless series of revelations of the monstrous things just under the surface. So you can see why it relates so well to Freud—it's like Ernst is exposing the 'unconscious' reality."

"I follow."

"Well, okay, so it's widely asserted that Ernst's source material for these pictures, these *hundreds* of collages, was woodcut illustrations from Victorian pulp magazines and children's books, right? Because they *look* like those kind of illustrations, everybody just made this assumption. Only a handful of the Ernst originals even exist—what everybody's working from are the published books. Well, I went back to the originals, I dug them out of some private collections, and I discovered something very weird: they're original engravings."

"Maybe you've lost me."

"They're not cut up and pasted together. You can't find any seams. What's passing for original collages are single, engraved images. If some kind of combining of elements ever occurred, it was at some earlier stage, and then Ernst, for no apparent reason, painstakingly reproduced his collages as original engravings. And nobody has any of the earlier versions, the actual collages. But anyway, that's not even the weirdest thing."

"Okay, I'm baited. What's the weirdest thing?"

"The presumed sources don't exist. The images originate with Ernst. No illustrations anywhere correspond to any part of any collage. I've wasted six months searching every possible archive, and I'm sure now. *The 'collages' have no sources.*"

DeBronk couldn't mask the triumph on his face, didn't even really try.

"This is a big deal," Harriet suggested tentatively.

"This is a *huge* deal. This is my career being made. Because discoveries like this aren't just lying around everywhere."

"So—the object in the case, at the museum—?"

"Well, now I'm trying to track down the real process, the methods Ernst used to create these images that he pretended were collages. He didn't own engraving tools of that type during the years the collage novels appeared. I've opened up huge mysteries about his process, his motives, and I want to try to solve some of that myself, present a finished package when I drop this bombshell, you know?

"Just before the collage novels appeared, Ernst created the object in the case, the 'Bird Camera.' There are numerous sketches for it in his notebooks—unlike a lot of the famous Surrealist objects, it wasn't just tossed off. It's a very complicated design. The plans for it have been generally regarded as a sort of elaborate hoax, a pretense that it had some function. That kind of coy crypto-science is very typical of the Surrealists. So everyone's just always assumed that it was a nonfunctional object, a pretend machine. But after Ernst created 'Bird Camera' he didn't sell it, wouldn't let it out of his studio. He even took it with him when he traveled, and it's a pretty bulky object."

"You think—"

"I'm sure of it. It's an image-fabrication machine, some weird unique design that Ernst came up with. The collages began appearing right after the 'Bird Camera' was finished."

"Can you prove it?"

"The museum won't let me near it. It's on loan from a museum in France—Ernst had to leave it behind when he fled the war. It'll be in New York for two more weeks, then back to Paris. You know, it's insured for millions of bucks, it's fragile as hell—all that stuff is, because the Surrealists weren't really sculptors, they just threw their things together. And I'm just a nobody graduate student. If I tell them why I want to see it I blow my scoop."

"Wow."

"Yeah, wow. You want another drink?"

He went to the bar and brought back two more Irish coffees. "Decaf, don't worry. So—now you."

"What?"

"Your turn. You have to tell me what you were doing there, at the museum. Your card says 'Investigator,' but I don't even know what that means."

Harriet was brought unexpectedly back to Hornebom. She wondered if Richard DeBronk could see her stiffen.

"I'm a researcher," she said. "Like you. Sometimes it involves . . . footwork. Hornebom led me to the museum. I still don't know what he was doing there, but I'll find out."

DeBronk made a face. "C'mon. Context, context. Why are you following the crying-clown man?"

Harriet sighed, and some of the tightness in her chest eased. "He hired me. It's an . . . unusual case. He's been suffering blackouts. And somebody's changing his paintings."

"That can only be a good thing," said DeBronk, grinning.

"Well, he doesn't think so. He hired me to investigate . . ."

"And?"

"I don't know. I went to his studio tonight, while he wasn't there. And . . . something was wrong."

"His studio? You have the key to his studio?"

She nodded.

He put his hand on her arm. "Take me there—"

"No!"

He put his hands together, pleadingly. "I promise not to tell anyone. But it's irresistible, it's too funny. I have to see it. Please."

"No. Stop. I don't want to talk about this anymore. I shouldn't—it's a breach that I told you anything."

"Sorry."

She shivered. Too much alcohol, too much caffeine. Too many questions. "Listen. Thanks for calling. It was interesting hearing your story. I've got to get to bed."

6.

Harriet switched on the television to drown out her thoughts as she fell asleep. She caught the end of the opening credits of the Midnight Movie—"Directed by Alfred Hitchcock"—as she climbed into bed. Perfect. She built a fort of pillows and blankets around her and settled in to watch.

It wasn't one she'd seen. A classic Hitchcock icy blonde and a hunkish hero were flirting in a pet shop. An amiable enough opening, but Harriet knew Hitchcock. Sure enough, the situation quickly darkened—a possessive mother had her claws in the hero. A pair of lovebirds were purchased at the pet shop by the blonde, intended as a gift for the hunk, but undeliverable—a symbol of something, Harriet was sure.

Then real trouble began. The lovebirds began to swell and deform, bursting the bounds of the wire cage, until they were the shape and size of men, cloaked in feathery three-piece suits. They shook themselves loose of the shards of cage like chicks freeing themselves of eggshells, cocked their heads briefly at one another and then climbed through the frame of Harriet's television set, and into her bedroom.

"Mademoiselle Welch," said the slimmer of the two birds. "We must speak with you."

"Interloper, meddler, hypocrite," said the stout one.

Harriet tried to rise from her bed, and found that somehow she couldn't. Tried to speak, and found herself voiceless.

"Breton is rather upset. He feels you are interfering with the development of a most promising pupil," said the slim one.

"Hornebom must be left alone," said the stout one. "You are not to investigate the case of Hornebom. To continue is punishable by excommunication from all you hold most dear."

"My name is Eluard," said the slimmer bird. "Don't let Breton upset you, he's merely saying how important it is—"

"We'll have you thrown to the sparrows!" Breton squawked.

It's the good bird/bad bird routine, Harriet thought.

"It is crucial, in selecting an investigation," said Eluard, "that you not inadvertently disrupt another, perhaps more crucial investigation already underway. We trust your error was in the nature of an oversight—"

"The sparrows that rend and devour!"

"To investigate birds you must become a bird," said Eluard.

"Creatures that live to shred hope!"

"Sleep now, Mademoiselle," said Eluard, nudging Breton back toward the television. "You've been warned."

7.

Harriet woke up angry. Hornebom was playing with her, and she resented it. Her idiotic dream was galling confirmation of her own susceptibility to his trick, his stunt, whatever it was he'd pulled off in the studio. In the bright light of morning it was clear to her that it had been nothing more than a clever special effect. The question was, What was the odd little man up to? What motive did he have for involving her in his games?

She'd find out, that was for sure.

She dressed and went out, grabbed coffee and a donut on Greenwich Avenue, and got to Barrow just in time to see Hornebom hurrying down the stoop, his collar up around his neck, his gaze darting nervously up and down the street yet seeming not to take her in.

She hesitated as he scurried up the street toward Seventh. Her urge to confront him vied with her curiosity, and lost; she trailed a safe distance behind.

Half an hour later she followed him into the "Anxious Furniture" exhibition and watched as he planted himself in front of "Bird Camera."

After fifteen or twenty minutes she approached him, partly just out of boredom with the alternative.

"Mr. Hornebom," she said, stepping up behind him, "we need to talk."

He turned and stared at her with a look of horror, and then darted away.

"Wait a minute—" she said, and took off after him, ignoring the stares she drew.

Hornebom made straight for the nearest guard, a stout black man stuffed like a sleeping bag into his gray polyester uniform. "Help me, please. This woman has been following me."

"Hmmm?" The guard roused slowly to Hornebom's frantic request. "She botherin' you?"

"I want you to arrest her," Hornebom said as Harriet arrived.

"Her? I ain't no cop," said the guard.

"What is this, Hornebom?" said Harriet. "Don't pretend—"

"Please, sir, help." Hornebom cowered from Harriet. "She won't leave me alone."

They were beginning to draw attention away from the nearest object, sugar cubes trapped in a wicker cage.

"This is ridiculous," said Harriet. "He *hired* me—"

"I've never seen her before," said Hornebom. "But, as you see, she's quite insistent. Please—"

Another guard, a middle-aged woman, stepped through the circle forming around them. "Let's get her out of here," she said. Harriet became suddenly conscious of the fact that Hornebom, in his suit and gloves and carefully combed white hair, looked every bit the helpless Uptown victim, while she, in her torn sweatshirt and gray Adidas, probably appeared thuggish.

The black guard put his hand on her arm.

"We can hold her for the police if you want," he said to Hornebom. "But you gonna have to stick around to make a statement. The museum don't have no charges to press, we'd just kick her out."

"I'll press charges myself," said Harriet. "I've got Hornebom's personal check in my desk. I'm *working* for him."

"Keep it down," said the first guard. "This a museum. You can argue it out when the cops get here."

"Okay, people," said the female guard. "Back to the show." The two of them steered Harriet back through the crowd, toward the lobby. Hornebom scurried after. They pushed through a door marked "Personnel" to a tiny room where a third guard, an overweight man with a pink, bloated nose, sat at a desk with coffee and newspaper.

"We gotta sit on these two," said the first guard, jerking a thumb at Hornebom. "He wants to press charges." He pushed Harriet toward a chair against the wall.

"What a day," groaned the guard with the pink nose.

The female guard pushed the door closed, but just as quickly it pushed back open, and Richard DeBronk popped in. "Excuse me," he said.

"Personnel only," said the guard with the pink nose.

"Richard—" started Harriet.

"I think I can clear this up for you if you'll give me a minute," said Richard, grabbing the hand of the guard at the desk and shaking it vigorously. "Doctor DeBronk. I'm in charge of the outpatient clinic at St. Belfort's."

"Should I get a cop now?" said the female guard.

"There's no need for a cop," said DeBronk. "This is a mis-understanding between two patients, two very *unstable* patients. I assigned Harriet and Jonathan a museum trip today, and it's one hundred percent *my* fault if they created some kind of problem."

Harriet groaned. She could tolerate DeBronk rescuing her—barely—but this performance was getting a little campy.

Hornebom began to turn red. "I see no reason why—this preposterous—"

DeBronk put a warning finger in the air. "Now, Jonathan. Why don't you run along, and we'll see you back at the residence. You shouldn't let Harriet provoke you so easily. Here—this nice lady will help you find your way downstairs." He stage-winked at the female guard, and nodded broadly at Hornebom, who could only bluster incoherently.

The pink-nosed guard opened the drawer of the desk and took out a bottle of Pepto-Bismol and poured from it into his coffee.

"There you go, that's good," said DeBronk, nudging the female guard and Hornebom back through the door.

"What about her?" said the first guard, looking at Harriet. Harriet stuck her tongue out at him.

"She can be a little tricky," said DeBronk. "I probably ought to re-hypnotize her—"

"Jesus Keeerist," said the guard with the pink nose.

"Okay, never mind. Here, do you need me to sign something?"

"We gotta 'incident' form—"

"Let me save you the paperwork. Harriet, you sit still. Let me fill that out for you, sir. My apologies for all this trouble."

He went to the desk and took the form away from the guard. "This pen doesn't work—" He dug in the drawer, knocked the newspaper from the desktop, and mixed a sequence of profuse apologies to the guards with stern admonitions to Harriet not to move a muscle—"remember what happened the day you got loose at the zoo . . ." The guards rolled their eyes. Finally he signed the bottom of the form with a flourish—"R. De-Bronk, Ph.D.—that's 'Piled Higher and Deeper,' hah hah"—came out from behind the desk, and took Harriet's arm.

And out they went. Harriet tugged free as they left the museum and rushed to the street corner, looking for Hornebom.

The river of cabs attested to his likely easy escape. DeBronk caught up with her a minute later.

"I'm going to kill him," she said. "First I'm going to make him tell me what the hell he's up to, and then I'm going to kill him. Did you see—"

DeBronk nodded. "I'd just gotten there when you went up to him," he said. "I caught the whole thing."

They walked back to the portico of the museum.

"He's trying to make me a pawn in some game he's running," she said. "But he picked wrong. I'm going to nail him."

DeBronk nodded. "If there's anything to nail. He seems kind of out of it to me."

"An act. Trust me."

He smiled. "I do, actually."

"What's that supposed to mean—Hey, speaking of *acts*. What *was* all that crap?"

"Ulterior motives."

"You're quite the little bullshit artist, Doctor DeBronk."

"Thank you."

"Don't take it as a compliment until you stop bullshitting, please. What ulterior motives? Are you flirting with me?"

"Well," he said, grinning lasciviously, "there *is* a palmed set of museum keys in my pocket." He jingled his loot. "But that doesn't mean I'm not glad to see you."

8.

"—you have to help me, Harriet, I can't do it alone—"

She and DeBronk were in her office talking, over sandwiches and coffee, when the door buzzer sounded.

"Yes?" she said into the intercom.

"Miss Welch? It's Jonathan Hornebom. May I speak with you?"

She looked at DeBronk, who shrugged. "Just a minute," she said, and clicked the intercom off.

"You can't be here," she said. "After what happened, it can't turn out that I know you. It guts my case against him if he recognizes you from the museum, and thinks we're collaborating."

"So hide me."

"Hide you. Is this what it's always like to hang out with you, DeBronk?"

"Hey, you're the one with the comic-book career."

"Shut up and get in the closet."

She buzzed Hornebom in and slid the sandwiches into her desk drawer. He opened the door to her office and she said, "Sit down."

He sat, meekly. "It's probably too soon, I realize. But I couldn't help wondering if you had—some sort of update. Any information at all, regarding the past two days."

"I might."

"Oh, good. I've been—there's been more changes. In the paintings."

"I'm sure."

"Well—oh, dear. Do I need to bring our account up to date?" He pulled out his checkbook and pen.

"That's not exactly the problem, Mr. Hornebom. Before you fill that out I need to ask you a couple of questions."

"Of course."

"I'm not necessarily in a position to protect you if what I uncover is evidence of criminal activity on your part, or even criminal *intent*. Do you understand that?"

"Oh, God, what have I done?"

"Just answer my question, please."

"I understand." He sank his head into his gloved hands.

"Okay. The second thing is that I'm no more interested in playing victim than I am accomplice or accessory. In the latter regard I *might* find a way to turn a blind eye to things—but if you fuck with *me* I'll take you down, and fast. Got that?"

The sudden rough language was a calculated effect, and Harriet saw it work. Hornebom gaped at her, slack-jawed.

"Please tell me what I've done," he finally managed.

"Please finish answering my questions. What were you doing at the museum today?"

"The museum? I've no idea—I've no memory of today. That's the problem, you must believe me. Please!"

Harriet made a face, stalling. Finally she said, "Go ahead and write me a check—make it for two more days."

"Yes, of course." He scribbled it out, staining his glove with ink, and tore it from the book. As he handed it to her he spoke in a near-whisper. "Will you tell me, please, what you know of my activities—"

"You've been visiting the museum. And something's definitely wrong with your studio. That's my report for today. Go home, Mr. Hornebom. I'll call you when my work is complete."

"Please—"

"I don't want to interfere until the pattern has become clear," she said, and as she said it Eluard's warning from her dream echoed in her head: *important not to disrupt another, more important investigation*—

Hornebom nodded in a deflated way, and went to the door. When he was gone, DeBronk came out of the closet and sat in the seat across the desk from Harriet.

"He doesn't remember," he said.

"Or it's a superb act."

"Maybe you'd better fill me in on this now."

She did, from the beginning, without skipping anything but the idiotic dream.

"Well," he said when she'd finished. "It's obvious what you need."

"What?"

"Same thing I need—a partner. If he's playing some game, he's counting on your being alone. If there's two of us, one following him, the other staking out the studio—"

"Whoa. Slow down."

9.

Harriet didn't finish losing the argument until they were outside the darkened rear entrance to the museum. She gave up when he began fumbling at the door with the stolen keys. She pushed his hand away and whispered: "Wait!"

"I told you, I'm going in with or without you."

"Whatever. But you can't just break in like that. Jeez. Here, you need this."

He stared at the device she pulled out of her bag. "What's that?"

"Well, the main security system's probably motion detectors. On all the floors and maybe in the displays, too. This thing averages out the kind of motion disturbances that trigger alarms. Like a steadicam. So it'll cloak us from that kind of system."

"Wow."

"Of course, if they've got something else we're dead meat."

"Oh."

They crept inside. No alarms sounded.

The halls were half-lit, eerily so. Empty, the lobby was oppressively huge, and crossing it Harriet felt exposed, like a cat in a cathedral. They stopped at the frozen escalator and listened; surely there were overnight guards. Just as surely, in Harriet's experience, those guards were sequestered in some room like the one she'd been taken to earlier that day, and surrounded with some combination of booze, cigarettes, radio, cards, or pornographic magazines, if not all of the above.

Hearing nothing, they tiptoed up the inert steps, two floors, to "Anxious Furniture." In the gloom of the emptied museum, Harriet was suddenly aware of the strange, vibratory power of the pieces in the exhibition. Ogled by throngs, the objects had been reduced to monkeys in cages. Now they were somehow predatory, feeding on the darkness and silence and leaking it back out in purified form.

DeBronk unlocked the case containing his and Hornebom's mysterious favorite. He plucked "Bird Camera" off its perch and eased it through the narrow opening in the back of the case, then wrapped it up in his coat, making a bulky, obvious bundle.

Richard looked at the empty spot in the case, between the metronome and the teacup, guiltily. Then, suddenly inspired, he handed "Bird Camera" to Harriet. He snuck out into the hall, and came back with a small red fire extinguisher.

"Cigarette," he whispered. She gave him one. He stuck it into the nozzle at the top of the fire extinguisher, to which it imparted a jaunty continental air, and put the new object in the case in place of the missing Ernst.

On the second floor they froze, hearing noises from the lobby. Someone on patrol. They waited until the sounds trickled away, then slipped back through the lobby and out, unharassed, booty intact.

They ferried it in a cab back to her office. DeBronk unwrapped it on her desk and then sank into her chair, holloweyed.

"What?" said Harriet.

"We stole it. I can't believe it."

"Yeah, we stole it."

"One of the major pieces in Ernst's career. This is like the most fatal thing I could possibly do in my profession. I can't believe it's sitting here. We took it out of the museum."

"What, are you going to fall apart on me now? You had to, you *said* you had to. Christ."

"It's just—"

"Here." She opened her bottom drawer and handed him a bottle of whiskey.

"Wow," he said dreamily.

"What now?"

"You really keep whiskey in your desk. Like a private eye." She rolled her eyes.

He shook his head. "You're just so cool." He took a slug from the bottle. "Okay. Paper, paper, I need paper." She opened the upper drawer and pulled out a few sheets of her stationery. "Scissors. Need to cut it down a little—" She supplied scissors. He took another bolt from the whiskey bottle, and set to slimming the paper. He checked it against the width of "Bird Camera," then cut off another sliver.

"Okay, here goes," he said, manipulating the knobs tucked under the cannon end of the sculpture.

"You know how it works?" Harriet was the nervous one now. What if they destroyed it?

"I memorized the notebook pages where he designed this thing," said DeBronk. "They were all I had—until now." His tongue stuck out of one side of his mouth as he eased the fitted paper into the maw of the press, then flicked the knob underneath the right-hand wheel.

There was a flash at the mouth of the cannon, as though it had fired. A click, a grinding of gears, and the paper was drawn into the heart of the machine.

A pause, then the paper rolled smoothly out the other end, like Polaroid film. DeBronk hurried around the desk and caught it as it fell loose.

The engraving was in the style of a nineteenth-century woodcut illustration, but it showed the corner of Harriet's office. Harriet was just at the edge of the frame, her shoulder at the bottom of the left corner, the side of her head and ear visible along the left edge.

Hovering in the space of the room, and filling the center of the engraving, were the two birds from Harriet's dream, Breton and Eluard. Eluard was smoking a pipe, and Breton was holding a bright, metallic-looking sphere which intersected the lobe of Harriet's ear like a hoop earring.

"It's incredible!" said DeBronk. "It's an original Ernst! An original *posthumous* Ernst!"

Harriet stared. "It's a photograph," she said. "That's me."

"Not a photograph, exactly. A Max-o-graph, for Max Ernst. He's like another Leonardo. God, this is so great."

Harriet couldn't find voice to express her apprehension about what the "Maxograph" revealed.

DeBronk began excitedly cutting more paper to size and loading it into the tray at the back of the device. "Do one of me." He aimed the cannon at himself. "Push the button."

She turned the knob, and "Bird Camera" snapped another shot. DeBronk with the head of a crocodile, wearing a top hat, and holding a figurine of a naked Aphrodite.

In the air over his head flew a small black sparrow.

"It's like a Surrealist party toy," said DeBronk. "The conceit is that it uncovers psychical reality, takes a picture of the subconscious world. He must have programmed the etching blades with thousands of images. And it combines them to match what the cannon lens is aimed at. It's brilliant."

"Let's—let's take a Maxograph of someone else."

"Okay. Outside." He scooped up "Bird Camera" and they went out onto the street. Holding it at chest level, he aimed it at a young couple walking on the other side of the street.

A giant rooster walking an ape on a leash, in a hail of disembodied breasts. The buildings behind showed a variety of nightmarish dramas half-hidden behind the window curtains.

"Wow, he's even got it programmed so Loplop is in each picture," said DeBronk.

"What's Loplop?"

"Not what, who. Loplop was a bird character, sort of Ernst's imaginary alter ego. He put Loplop in a lot of the collages."

Not all of those birds are named Loplop, Harriet wanted to say, but the words didn't come out.

"Harriet, I'm going to be famous. It's okay that we broke in, nobody will care."

"I'm happy for you."

"What—what's the matter?"

"Nothing. Nothing, just I need a favor, okay? No questions."

"Sure."

"We have to take a picture, a Maxograph, of Hornebom. Right away."

He smiled and shrugged. "Sure, sounds hilarious. Let's go."

She bit her lip. They walked to Barrow Street. Hornebom's studio lights were on. Harriet stopped DeBronk at the stoop across the street. "His house first."

"The famous Hornebom residence, exposed by the all-seeing Bird Camera," he announced, and turned the knob. Flash.

Water poured out of the windows of the upper floors, to

meet the flames licking out of the windows of the basement studio, producing clouds of steam that drifted off and mingled with the clouds of the night sky. The moon, above, was being mothered like an egg by an enormous vulture.

Harriet shuddered, then caught herself. She had to know. "I want—I want to catch him painting," she said. "With that thing."

"You can include the Maxograph with your report, as evidence," DeBronk suggested merrily. They slipped across the street and through his gate, and went to the ground-level window of the basement studio. Harriet peered over the top. There he was, back turned, shoulders draped in the spattered smock. She pointed. DeBronk aimed "Bird Camera."

Something, some noise or disturbance in the air, alerted him. As the cannon flashed, he turned and saw them. "Run!" Harriet whispered, and, in the grip of some unnatural fear, turned and fled herself.

DeBronk caught up with her as she unlocked the door to her office. "Look," he said, holding out the Maxograph.

It was Hornebom with the maniacal bird's head she'd hallucinated the night before.

The painting he was working on was of Harriet herself, her huge eyes flooding with tears.

Before she could utter a word, the phone in her office rang. Suddenly sure it was Hornebom, she pulled the door shut again, not even wanting to hear him record a message, not even wanting to enter a room he'd so recently inhabited.

"Upstairs," she said, half gasping.

DeBronk followed her into her apartment, and while she was carefully locking the door he put "Bird Camera" on her counter and spread the nightmarish Maxographs out on her kitchen table.

"No," she said when she turned and saw them. She scooped them up and put them in a drawer with a pile of folded tablecloths.

"What's the matter?"

"Nothing. I just don't want to look at them—at night."

"You're acting strange."

"Yes, I know." She launched herself toward him, to shut him up, and for other reasons. Kill two birds, she caught herself thinking.

The kiss started badly, their teeth clacking together, but lasted long enough that they put the mistakes behind them.

"Wow," he said.

"You should get rid of that stupid little beard," she said. "It makes you look like a boy with a beard."

"But if I shave it off, then I'll just look like a boy."

"No, if you shave it off you'll look like a young, um, guy."

"Fellow, you mean."

"Young man. Young guy, dude, something. Not a boy with a beard."

They kissed some more.

"I thought you were going to complain about the scratchiness," he said.

"No, I like that. But it looks stupid."

They went into her room and lay on the bed together. Suddenly he sat up. "Just one more Maxograph," he said. "I have to do the television—"

Harriet sighed.

"Please." He kissed her, then pulled away and got "Bird Camera" out of the kitchen. "Something Ernst couldn't have imagined, something that didn't exist—" He switched her television on. *Star Trek*.

"That should do it," she said.

He got back on the bed beside her and aimed the cannon eye. Flash.

Kirk and Spock in each other's arms, Bones glowering in the background. The tricorder in Spock's hand had been changed into a small gray dove, which he held to the captain's breast.

"Spock, Kirk, I never knew," said DeBronk.

"Seems like a hint," said Harriet. "You know, 'Birds do it, bees do it, even Kirk and Spock do it'—mmphh."

He kissed her, putting "Bird Camera" and the new Maxograph on her bedside table.

Then, for a long while, only the sound of their breathing and the babble of the television.

"I wonder," he whispered. "If someone took a Maxograph of us now . . ." Their clothes were all on the floor.

"Probably you'd turn out to be Hornebom," she said. "So let's skip it—ooh . . ."

Finally they were still as well as quiet. They lay together on the pillows as the television blared: "Now, for the first time offered to the general public, never before available, a unique six-CD package: Goof Hits of the Fifties, Sixties, Seventies, Eighties, and Nineties! That's right, all these hits—" As the voice listed songs, a snippet of each played underneath.

"—'Flying Purple People Eater,' 'The Streak,' 'Convoy,' 'Rainy Day Women #12 and 35,' 'Surfin' Bird'—"

At that moment a flock of birds rushed through the television screen and into the room. They landed on the floor and grew into a scowling, feather-suited jury, Eluard and Breton at the fore.

"Doesn't she know about the Bird?" said one. "I thought by now everyone had been informed regarding the Bird."

"She should know about the Bird," said Eluard. "We told her that Bird was the Word."

"Yes, in the Beginning was the Bird," said another.

"We must exact our punishment," said Breton.

"Dada ooh mow mow," said a bird in the rear.

Harriet found again that she couldn't move or speak. She and DeBronk were trapped, naked and immobile in the bed.

"Perhaps we should make our objections more clear," said Eluard.

"Perhaps we should rend flesh from bone," said Breton.

"Please, Aragon, will you silence Breton. Tzara, where is Tzara? Ah, Tristan, please, if you will, elucidate for this Adam and Eve the gravity and direness of the situation."

A bird with spectacles stepped up to the bed. "You must understand that we are only the Sons of the Bird. The True Bird is everywhere, and he is far more powerful, more dangerous than we handful of Sons. For so many years the Bird Who Is Everywhere ruled unopposed, and his was a cruel reign, spasmodic in its violence, brutal in its indifference.

"Then we Sons were born, out of the ashes of the cruelest, bloodiest birth spasms the Bird had ever known. There had been Sons before, but scattered, isolated, helpless to sound the alarm. We were the first Sons to band as we did, though indeed we too were helpless in the face of the Ravages of the Bird, the Ravages that were to come.

"Among us Sons was one known as Loplop, Bird Superior. He, more than any other, could glimpse the Bird Who Is Everywhere. His unerring finger found the Bird out, warned of its claws."

"Loplop must live again!" said Breton.

"You must resist interfering any further," concluded Tzara somberly.

"How can they be trusted? You see they have His camera. How will Hornebom find it here?"

"It is true," said the one called Aragon. "It is not enough now that they desist. Damage is done."

"Take her hostage!"

"But this could be called advantageous," said Eluard. "Bunglers they may be, but they freed His instrument from its tomb, they returned it to use—which Hornebom himself could not do."

"It must be delivered," said Aragon. "Take the man, leave her with the camera. When it is delivered, she shall have him back. When we have our Loplop, Eve shall have her Adam."

"Revenge, excommunication!" shrieked Breton.

"No," said Tzara. "It is enough that we take him. Away, now."

The birds rose, flapping, into the air of Harriet's bedroom, and as they swirled through the air in a vortex toward the television, DeBronk rose up from the bed and shrank, until he circled away with them into the drain of the screen.

The cyclone of birds left not a single feather. Harriet fell asleep.

10.

Harriet didn't want to think about what had gone so wrong that DeBronk left without "Bird Camera" or, from the look of things, most of his clothes. The utter jerk. She stumbled out of her bedroom and into the kitchen.

She opened the tablecloth drawer and stared at the stack of Maxographs. In the light of day the images were unconvincing, and she couldn't imagine what had scared her so much the night before. They were clever, the device that had produced them was clever, certainly, but it was clever nonsense, and she was tired of it. Art. She was swearing off art now, generally. And swearing off clever, nonsensical art historians in particular.

She made coffee and considered her situation. The sculpture in her bedroom was stolen property, important stolen property. She would have to get it back. And her client was bullshit. She needed to drop him. She suddenly wondered if Richard De-Bronk was Hornebom's colleague. It would explain a lot. DeBronk had suggested that it would take two to *uncover* Hornebom's hijinks, but wasn't it equally true that it would take two to *produce* them?

The only thing that kept her from returning the uncashed

check in her wallet was ... well, the uncashed check in her wallet. Her account cried for it. She'd contracted to trail him for a third day and deliver a report, and if she did so she could rightfully keep the money.

One more day of surveillance wouldn't hurt. It might even clear up a few things.

For Harriet, shadowing was therapeutic. It placed her in her deepest, truest self, her pleasure in stealth, her core of ancient curiosities.

She picked up Hornebom at his door and followed him to a café for coffee and newspaper. She found her own copy of the paper while he was engrossed in his: no mention of the missing "Bird Camera."

He caught a cab, heading uptown, and she did the same, thinking: *Rerun.* Sure enough, Hornebom's cab pulled up at the museum. Harriet told her cabbie to stop.

Suddenly it hit her: *If they were working together, Hornebom wouldn't bother to come back up here. "Bird Camera" isn't here.*

A chink opened in her skepticism, and through it she glimpsed a horror-film sequence of images from the night before.

"Uh, Sixty-eighth Street and Lexington," she told the cabbie.

"What?"

"I changed my mind."

The cabbie shrugged, turned the wheel, and honked his way back into the flow of traffic.

She paid her fare and ran into the bustling lobby of the main building at Hunter College, working her way through mobs of students to the information desk.

"Graduate offices for the art history department," she said. "409."

She went upstairs in the elevator, and in room 409 found the secretary for the department.

"I'm looking for a Richard DeBronk," she said.

"You'll have to wait in line."

"What do you mean?"

"Well, dear, he wouldn't ordinarily be around *here.* He's writing his dissertation—doesn't require that he appear at the department much. But he *is* teaching an undergraduate class across the street, and they've called twice this morning looking for him."

"He didn't show up?"

"If he did, they didn't let me know about it. Last I knew, the class was waiting for him."

"What's the room number?"

Harriet went downstairs and out, and into the annex across the street. She found his classroom just as the last of the students were giving up waiting.

"DeBronk didn't show up?" she asked.

"Nope."

"He's a flaky type, right? Does this often?"

"What are you, from the administration? He's never missed a class before."

Harriet's heart sank. DeBronk was a real person, with real responsibilities and connections in the world. Not just some capricious con man.

Where was he?

She went outside and caught a cab home. At her office door she paused, then looked inside quickly to see if there were any phone messages. No. She rushed up to her bedroom, switched on the television, and began flipping channels.

On channel nine a *Partridge Family* rerun was just starting. The opening credit sequence, a series of animated partridges hatching from eggs. But instead of the Partridge Family, the newborn birds turned into the cabal from Harriet's dream: Eluard, Breton, Tzara, Aragon, and several others. They smiled and waved as one by one they were introduced.

At the end of the sequence came the one continuing character who wasn't a Partridge, who wasn't hatched: the talented family's beleaguered, whining manager, played in today's episode by Richard DeBronk.

To add to the manager's usual humiliations at the hands of the Partridge children, DeBronk was naked. As the show opened, the monstrous birdmen were at their instruments, bobbing together as they played, Breton singing lead, a scabrous "Surfin' Bird" in a thick French accent.

DeBronk scurried around the perimeter, wringing his hands, his penis flapping, insisting hopelessly that they practice some other song.

Horrified, Harriet snapped the television off. She sat stunned for a minute, as the impossible truth sank in. Then she grabbed "Bird Camera," stuffed it into a shopping bag in the kitchen, and ran downstairs, and out.

At Barrow Street Hornebom was already back in his studio, wearing his spattered smock. She crossed the street and knocked on the window. He went on painting, his back to her. She let herself in with the key.

As she stepped into the studio there was a rush from the canvases lining the walls, and she was surrounded by a posse of sad-eyed children, looming, top-heavy homeless-person clowns, and puppy watchdogs with enormous, weepy eyes. They massed all around her, hemming her in, backing her toward the door. The puppies growled gently, the children murmured to themselves—"Is the nice lady a bird too?" "Where's my daddy?" "I just want to play house, but there's nothing but bullies on my block"—and the clowns chanted in singsong voices—"Gotta cheer *up* the birds, *they're* not nasty birds they're just *grumpy*, can't let 'em getcha down, uh, yeah, but who's the *lady* with the package? Don't want no birds in *here*, gotta make Mr. Hornebom happy, he's the *boss*, oh ho—"

Their gabbling rising to a roar, the clowns and puppies and children floated up to loom over Harriet, threatening to smother her with their marshmallow-soft bodies. She struck out at one and it burst like a balloon, spattering gobs of oil paint all over her arm.

"Hornebom!" Harriet shouted over the din. He went on frantically painting, tossing off new children and puppies and clowns who instantly rose from the canvas to join the barrage. "Hornebom! I have your report!"

"I don't need a report," he said without turning. "My situation is all too clear."

"What situation?" She swatted the forms away from her mouth and eyes.

"I went to the museum." He turned and looked at her accusingly. "Someone had stolen the bird detector I'd been coveting. The shock of it opened my eyes."

"I've got it for you, right here—"

"No, no my dear, I can see the birds all by myself now, I don't need it. I've been thrown back on my own resources, I understand now. The birds are everywhere. It's just me and my children, that's all I can count on." He smiled maliciously. "For instance, you my dear, I see that you are a bird, like all the others. How frightening that a few short days ago I was so blind as to walk into your nest and ask you for help. As though you could help me!"

He dashed off a pair of enormous, weepy disembodied eyes, which were so impatient to join the throng that they floated off the canvas by themselves, before their maker could surround them with a clown.

Harriet pushed the forms away from her, but as they met the resistance of others pressing behind them they began to melt together, like soap bubbles, and form the beginnings of one huge clown, whose oil-paint hide was much thicker than that of his miniature brethren. "You're as much a bird as me," said Harriet. She began backing toward the door, overwhelmed, and wary of the gigantic clown in the making.

"It's no good trying to fool me now!" screamed Hornebom. The children and puppies and clowns began flowing directly off his brush and pouring toward her. "I see the birds, I see you! They're everywhere! It's only me, I'm all alone, only me and my children to save me! I see the birds!"

"There's one bird you haven't spotted," said Harriet. She elbowed the puppies away from the shopping bag and drew out "Bird Camera." One sheet of her stationery, cut to size by DeBronk, was left in the tray. She jostled the clowns between her and Hornebom, trying to clear an unobstructed view. The giant clown lay sprawled at her feet, embryonic, yet already struggling to its feet.

Flash!

The collage that emerged showed Hornebom with a beak. Good enough. Harriet charged into the mass of clowns and children and puppies and held the paper out to Hornebom. "Take it! Look!" Her body dripped with oil paint. The giant clown seized her legs.

Hornebom snatched the paper away from her.

He dropped his brush. The clowns and puppies and children all held where they stood, yipping and sniffling and chortling in melancholy voices.

Hornebom seemed to fade, his certainty gone. The paper he held grew larger, extended easel-legs to the floor, wooden ruler-arms outward, and a long easel-neck upward. The neck was topped with a small, round bird's head, with a comb like a rooster's.

"Finally," said the easel-bird. It shook itself with a clatter, then stepped over and kicked the giant clown away from Harriet's legs. "How do you do. My name is Loplop."

"Harriet Welch," said Harriet.

"Very good choice, mademoiselle, to turn the camera on my poor son. Thank you." The voice that issued from the little red bird's head atop the easel-body was soft and mannered, with a slight German accent.

Hornebom stood looking dumbfounded.

"Yes, Jonathan, you are my son. I am your father, though you never knew me. This is a wrong that must be righted. A bird that must be captured on canvas, so to speak."

"My father died in Germany," said Hornebom softly.

"No, your adoptive father died there. Your true father, Max Ernst, left your mother never knowing she was pregnant with you. He—I—moved often and quickly in that regard. Regrettable, perhaps. Max lived many years in France and America never knowing he had this son. But I, Loplop, came to know of your existence, your emigration to America, your . . . ah, career."

"Ernst or Loplop—which are you?" asked Harriet.

"Ah. Ernst was Loplop. His secret identity, his bird self, both horrible and wise. But when Ernst died I, Loplop, lived on."

"Why didn't you come forward sooner?"

"This is a rare freedom I enjoy now. When it is over I shall go back to the margins, trapped in museum depictions, flourishing occasionally in the seams between things, like the other Sons, but unable to speak aloud. I did what I could, I tried to direct his hand—"

"The altered paintings," said Harriet.

"Yes. I added a glimpse of the Bird to his soporific canvases."

"But the Birds," whispered Hornebom. "The terrible Birds."

"Yes, we are all terrible Birds," said Loplop. "I was the Bird when I treated your mother so badly, during that terrible time when all of Germany seemed endlessly Birds. But I painted what I saw. You have spent your life running from the Bird, and so the Bird is never named, never mastered."

Loplop turned to Harriet. "My son had a powerful Surrealist magic in him. Despite his never knowing his heritage, it knew itself in him. But he put it to very poor use. Jonathan is a reverse Icarus. His father equipped him with wings, but rather than fly too near the sun, he never left the ground." He scowled at the puppies and clowns and children, who were now beginning to scurry and melt back into the canvases that lined the walls of the studio.

Loplop took "Bird Camera" out of Harriet's hands. "My little toy. Jonathan won't need it now—you must return it to its place in the museum." He stilted over and put it into the shopping bag, then looked at a watch on his wooden wrist.

"Hurry home now, you have to free your friend from the television. *Sesame Street* will be over in a few minutes."

"What about The Sons of the Bird?" asked Harriet.

"I'll see to that. Breton is a scoutmaster at heart, always checking and revoking memberships, slapping wrists and handing out medals. You mustn't take it too seriously."

He looked back at Hornebom, who stood hapless in the midst of his canvases, his eyes nearly as large as those he ceaselessly depicted.

"Please leave us," said Loplop. "I have many apologies to make, as a father." He paused, scowling. "And my son has equally many to make, as a painter."

11.

Their house is not exactly in the city, but the city can be seen from the nearby promenade. It's a part of Brooklyn Heights where it is possible to live in brownstones very much as lovely as Hornebom's, without living anywhere near Hornebom himself. Her success as an expert in museum and auction security, due in large part to her celebrated rescue of Max Ernst's "Bird Camera," permits her to run the agency at a remove. He still teaches, but not because he has to.

There is not a single television in the entire house.

EVITA, AMONG THE WILD BEASTS

S. A. Stolnack

She clearly didn't belong in the gallery. She stood apart from our little group, fingering the thick, glossy brochure the museum gives to all who want one, avoiding eye contact with the others, and ignoring the paintings on the walls. A few of the other women whispered among themselves and gave her odd, catty looks; but aside from the fact that her face reminded me of a woman I once met inside Manet's *A Bar at the Folies-Bergère*, she meant nothing to me. She could have been the most famous (or infamous) personality in Buenos Aires and I would have been blissfully ignorant. You see, *I* am a Dilettante. I have no interest in current affairs.

Because of her association with the Manet, though, this woman did interest me—if at first only slightly. Seeing her recalled the week of subjective time I had spent wandering the gaslit world of the *Folies-Bergère*. That had been my first long-term trip inside the Simulacrum; and her face brought on a faint nostalgia, as a whiff of a woman's perfume along the Boulevard might bring a tiny, jeweled tear to one's eye, for reasons long lost to memory and buried deep within the darkest recesses of one's unconscious.

I went up to her. She stood uncertainly before Sisley's *June Morning*, her eyes directed toward the painting, though her thoughts were clearly elsewhere. I could feel the disapproval of

the rest of the group like a weight on the back of my neck.
Prudes, I thought. *Stuck-up Bourgeoisie.*

"Charming, don't you think? It's one of my favorites."

She looked up at me, clearly startled that anyone would
speak to her.

I went on offhandedly. "There is a certain nonchalance in
Sisley's work, almost a floweriness, that I find appealing. Almost rustic in his simplicity. Though refined rather than primitive. Don't you agree?"

There was the faint look of the trapped animal in her eyes
as she smiled timidly.

"I don't know much about paintings."

Her accent was startling. It reeked of the Barrios, of poverty.
I almost recoiled in shock, but caught myself. Though something in my face gave my thoughts away; because her dark eyes
hardened, and whatever good will that had existed in that
timid smile was gone.

"Forgive me if I seemed shocked," I said softly. "It's just
that your voice—you sound very much like my poor dead sister." A lie, of course. I never had a sister—only brothers. Nor
would she speak like a ragpicker if I did.

Her eyes softened, though a certain wariness never left them.
"I'm sorry—"

I closed my eyes and made a negating motion with my hand.
"You couldn't have known."

The guide came in and introduced herself then, and while
she explained the workings of the Simulacrum and the sensory
creche to the uninitiated—a lecture I've heard a hundred times
or more—I contemplated the woman beside me.

She was perhaps twenty years old. Her lips were slightly too
thick and her nose a bit too big, but taken as a whole she was
not unattractive. She seemed nervous by nature: like a bird
always poised for flight. She listened to the guide's lecture with
a wide-eyed intensity that I found endearing, as if her life depended on her complete understanding of artificial realities,
sensory fields, holistic paradigms, and the like. *Poor fool*, I
thought. It makes no difference *how* the Simulacrum works, or
what jargon one uses to describe its workings; all that matters
is the quality of the experience. This is the Dilettante's creed.

When we moved as a group into the staging room, I offered
her my hand and helped her into her creche, and then took
the one beside hers. She was clearly uncomfortable with my
attention and at a loss as to how to discourage it. I decided to

bide my time, play the helpful, vulnerable friend. It would make an interesting game. I could not help but think of Faust's seduction of Gretchen; though in reality I've always modeled myself more as a Mephisto than a Faust.

Our first work was Monet's *Two Haystacks*. As we lay like corpses in our creches, the guide went through her standard monologue about Monet's series of fifteen paintings of the haystacks, and the different effects that time of day and weather had on each one. Then the mist cleared and the painting became reality around us; the vague farm buildings in the distance took form and color yet never lost their vagueness; and we stood inside the soft magical reds and blues of Monet's quiet world.

We walked in a field beneath a pastel-yellow sky. The light was diffuse; there was no sun. The sound of our footsteps on the hay stubble was joined by the distant whisper of scythes, but we saw no one save our little group, there was no movement but our own, there was not even a breeze to stir the few stalks of hay that had escaped the mowing.

The woman walked beside me. She had been transformed into a slender, pale-haired peasant woman, while I was bearded, tall and dark, with a thick chest and strong, blunt hands. The coarse fabric of my shirt and trousers was pleasantly rough against my skin.

"It's so beautiful," the woman whispered. Her eyes shone, and she looked around as if not quite believing what she saw.

"Oh yes, quite," I said. In fact, Monet rather bored me. True, he was interesting visually—his mastery of light and color could sop up all the attention the eye could bring to him, at least in his mature works—and the technicians had done a competent job incorporating the rest of the senses into the world. But I had outgrown Monet long ago. He had come to be so—so *respectable*. Like an old, familiar, slightly eccentric yet harmless uncle. And Impressionist landscapes, I'm afraid, are rather dull. I understood why the tours often began in a peaceful pastoral scene: it gave the uninitiated a chance to make a gradual transition to the more challenging works that lay ahead. Who, for instance, would want his first journey into the worlds of art to be an encounter with the aggressive and ignorant Vlaminck? But after a while, Monet and the pastoralists became tedious.

I bent and picked up a starry pink-headed wildflower that had twined itself around a stalk of cut hay.

Access, data, I subvocalized. *What is this flower?*

Centuarium Martinum, the Simulacrum responded. *Common name, Daniel's century. Member of the Gentian family. Members of the family are smooth-foliaged herbs with opposite, non-petioled, simple, entire leaves on a four- or five-toothed calyx and—*

Terminate.

I held out the flower to the woman.

"It's called Daniel's century," I said. "A member of the Gentian family."

She looked at the flower dubiously. But there was a tiny gleam of pleasure in her eyes.

"Go ahead, take it."

She reached out and took the flower, carefully avoiding all contact with my fingers. I could see a faint blush of color spread across her face.

As I watched her, a very strange feeling came over me. There was more wonder in watching her blush than I'd experienced in more than a year's subjective time inside the Simulacrum. I felt a warm glow inside me, and a strange happiness—perhaps I was blushing also. What a beautiful, shy creature she was! Yes, I thought, with only a trace of guilt; I *must* seduce her.

We walked on. The guide's voice was a faint monotone inside my head. I could have turned her off, but since I knew the woman beside me would be listening and hanging on every word, I decided to keep her on in order to score a few easy points.

Once, during a lull in the guide's rather flat narrative, I turned to the woman and said:

"Monet once said that his subject was not the thing in the view, but rather the experience of viewing—the continually unfolding process of perception. To him, that process was the painting's *raison d'être.* I find that quite profound, don't you? What mattered to him was the experience, and nothing more."

I was quiet after that. Let her ponder what I'd said: perhaps I could plant a seed that would grow into a desire for her own act of genuine "experience."

The woman glanced over at me with a serious, thoughtful expression.

"Words are easy for you, aren't they."

I looked down, feigning embarrassment. "I've always been rather good with facts. But with emotions, the words are not easy." I glanced over at her. She was looking off into the distance, and I'm not sure she even heard me.

As we walked past the haystacks and toward the distant farmhouse, I heard someone call my name.

"Martin."

To our left there was an ancient hedgerow that bordered the field. The guide stood alone in its burnt-umber shadow. I excused myself and walked across the field to her.

The guide's name was Teresa. She and I had crossed paths for years, though we didn't know each other well. It was said that she had been a Dilettante once, until she'd used up her inheritance and had been forced into the odious position of having to work for a living. Our circles of acquaintances overlapped but rarely brought us together.

"Where's the rest of your flock?"

"I sent them up ahead," she said. She nodded toward the woman with whom I'd been walking.

"Watch out for that one, darling."

"What do you mean?" I asked innocently.

She smiled. "The woman is a saint. A genuine religious phenomenon. She could be a danger to an innocent fool like you."

"Her, a danger? To *me*? You're joking."

"Why don't you meet me tonight at my apartment? Just before sunset." She leaned closer. "I'll show you something."

I glanced at her body, then looked into her eyes. Yes, the invitation was there. Because she was a guide she didn't change her appearance in the Simulacrum as the rest of us did—she was our one anchor in the shifting realities through which we traveled. I hadn't noticed before, but there was a certain animal attractiveness to her that pleased me.

"Will you show me something about your saint also?"

She smiled again. "Of course, darling."

"I'll be there. Now, if you will excuse me."

"Until tonight," she said. "Just before sunset."

I walked back across the hay stubble toward my "saint," who had almost reached the old thatched-roof farmhouse by the time I rejoined her. To think of her as some kind of "religious phenomenon" was amusing—and I must say rather intriguing. Teresa's warning, instead of convincing me to stay away from the woman, had the exact opposite effect. I thought it all nonsense, of course. But what would it be like, I wondered, to seduce a saint? Would there be thunderbolts? Fire and brimstone? Voices of angels?

Our next painting was one of Cézanne's 1906 *Mont Sainte-Victoires*. We entered the frame on a hilltop overlooking a valley jumbled with houses and patches of forest. Blocky green clouds scudded across a hazy purplish sky. The pungent smell of pine resin was thick in the air. The mountain sat like a king in the distance, but it never took shape as a whole: a line here or a slope there would become distinguishable, then would shift and fade back into vagueness as another section came into focus. Such was Cézanne.

I looked over at the woman beside me. This time she had dark eyes and touseled chestnut-brown curls. There was a thoughtful, faintly tragic expression on her face that, with the eyes and hair, made her look like Manet's famous portrait of Berthe Morisot, *sans* hat.

"Forgive me for not introducing myself sooner," I said as we lingered on the hill. The rest of the group had started down into the valley. I watched them step carefully among the flattened, misshapen blocks of color. "Martin Fierro Gutierrez Clemente y Salvador, at your service." If she recognized my family name as one of the ruling Hundred, she didn't show it. It didn't matter. I had disowned everything but my inheritance long ago. I held out my hand.

"Christina Maria Calderon," she said. She gave me a sidelong glance as if to see if I recognized *her* name. *Child*, I thought. *Saint or no saint, Dilettantes have no interest in the poor's little dramas.*

We shook hands. I felt an electric thrill pass between us as we touched. She—Christina—released my hand as quickly as she could without seeming rude. We began our descent into the valley.

"How did she die?" Christina asked quietly, a few moments later.

I frowned. "I beg your pardon?"

"Your sister."

"Ah." I kept my eyes on the path as we made our way down toward the houses clustered in the center of the valley. Grass, rock, shadow; light, color and texture.

"It was an accident. My sister loved to fly," I said, improvising as I walked. What kind of sister would this woman like me to have?

"Each day, she flew her glider from the cliffs outside the city—some days she would be up for hours, riding the currents of air above the *Río*, or soaring far to the south above the

Pampas." I wiped my eyes and stole a glance at the woman. She was like a little bird transfixed.

"She must have loved the freedom," she whispered.

"She was only twenty years old. She'd never had a boy-friend—she was too shy." I was beginning to warm to the fiction. "One day something happened. A part of her glider failed as she was taking off from the cliff. A wing collapsed. I—I was standing at the edge when it happened."

"My God—" She turned chalky white.

"Yes." I wiped my eyes again. "I was the first one to her body at the foot of the cliffs."

Christina's eyes were shining with terror and pity. "I'm so sorry."

I turned away so she wouldn't see the grin that was splitting my face.

We toured two more paintings—the Sisley we had seen in the gallery, and Gauguin's *Haymaking in Brittany*—before we finally came to one that really interested me. It was Matisse's *The Red Studio*.

Red. Red beyond belief. Vibrant, alive, almost pulsing. Red walls, floor, ceiling; red table, dresser, chairs. A box of artist's crayons lay on the table by my left hand as I entered the frame. There was a goblet, a house plant, a few busts. Paintings of nudes on the walls. Canvases leaned against the wall in a corner. The red grandfather clock struck twelve. There was a simultaneous intensity and serenity to the room that defied all my attempts to comprehend it.

The tiny studio was crowded with the guide and the rest of us, about a dozen in all. But I shut them out—shut out even Christina for a while, and simply experienced the extraordinary red room. I offered myself up to the color, surrendered to my senses. My body began to vibrate in harmony with that vivid red. I became a single enormous sensory organ, a raw nerve dedicated to the perception of red. I grew, expanded, became a universe of red; and I shuddered with such profound pleasure that for a moment I lost consciousness.

How can "reality" ever approach this level of intensity? What hold can a world of poverty, ugliness and brutality have upon one who has known such transcendent pleasure? My brothers, with their notions of duty, patriotism, honor and the like cannot begin to fathom my world. They are all bound by their greed and their desires to build more monuments to themselves, to perpetuate the family name and the family legacy. In their striving they experience *nothing*. They are no better than the lowest *pobrecito*. But I am beyond pitying them: I have seen past their limited horizons and values and I will not look back. Let them follow me, along the Dilettante's path, if they are brave enough.

I looked around and saw Christina watching me thoughtfully. I smiled and gave her a bold look. She met my eyes for a moment, then looked away as the color rose to her cheeks.

The guide gathered us up a short time later, and I took the opportunity in the confusion to speak to Christina.

"If you ever feel like a personal tour," I said, "I would be happy to offer my services. I have friends in the museum who can arrange to have the gallery opened after hours."

She looked down at her shoes and said nothing.

Later, when we came out of the Simulacrum, I handed her out of her creche. That familiar electricity was still present—perhaps even more so in the flesh.

"May I see you home?"

She looked startled at the thought. "That would be impossible. I—I'm meeting someone."

"Will we meet again?"

She looked down. "I don't think so."

"That is too bad," I said, feigning sadness. "I think my sister would have liked you." I offered my hand. "Goodbye, then. It has been a pleasure talking to you."

We shook hands, and she made a hasty exit.

I followed her outside, and from the top of the granite steps watched her, on foot and alone, turn the corner at the far end of the block.

I followed her, of course. I wanted to find out where my little bird lived. She may have thought that I was out of her life forever; but I had other plans.

She led me into successively poorer and poorer sections of the city. At each turning the streets became more filthy, crowded, and dangerous. More and more buildings were gutted and vacant, more dark, staring *pobrecitos* lounged upon the stairways or in the trash-filled lots. It was like a descent into hell.

And on every other street corner were the General's soldiers, with their armored vehicles, tear gas canisters, automatic weapons and riot visors. They oozed malice and power the way the *pobrecitos* oozed hate and poverty, and I walked a fine edge between the two, knowing that if I slipped too far from that edge on either side I would fall away from light and life and would never be seen again.

Finally she turned and went up the stairs into a squat, ugly brown building. I followed her in—the door had been torn off its hinges and lay on its side in the dim entry. There was a shrine or altar of some sort, with fresh lilies laid before it, in the gloom beneath the stairs. The sound of her footsteps echoed in the stairwell; I listened to her ascend three flights. Then there was silence for a few seconds. I heard a key turn in a lock. A door opened, then closed again. The *snick* of the lock was loud in the silent stairwell.

I climbed the stairs quietly and stopped on the third-floor landing. The hall was dark and empty. The small window at the far end let in a little gray light.

Then I heard Christina's voice, followed by the voice of a man. Was my little saint married? An unfamiliar woman said something, and then the man began to shout. Of course. The mother and father. Of course she would still be living at home.

I could make out little of what the man was shouting, in his thick accent of the gutter. Something about disgrace, spoiled opportunities, the family; he was working himself into a frenzy. Christina shouted back, only once. The mother was shouting too; I could not tell whether she was on the side of Christina or the father.

A door to one of the apartments on the floor above me opened. I ran down the stairs as quietly and as quickly as I could, and left the building.

That night, I arrived at Teresa's apartment a half hour before sunset. She met me at the door in a diaphanous blue gown that left little to the imagination, and made it clear what her intentions were for the evening.

We went out onto her balcony. The weather was warm, the sky cloudless; now and then a faint suggestion of the sea wafted toward us on a warm breeze from the *Río de la Plata* somewhere not far to the east. Her apartment was fifty stories up, and overlooked the main east-west boulevard of the city. The sun was slanting toward the western horizon below the level of the buildings, but shone through the gap that the boulevard made between the skyscrapers like some rare celestial alignment. The faces of the buildings along the boulevard glowed a languid, luminous rose in the horizontal rays of declining light.

Teresa stood close beside me. With her so near, the events

of the day and my little games with the timid Christina seemed far away indeed. I turned to her, and was just about to suggest that we go inside and share a glass of ambrosia when a faint sound drifted up from a long distance off.

I strained to listen, and soon heard it again. It was the sound of voices raised in song. I leaned out over the rail of the balcony and looked into the canyon between the buildings. We were very high above the boulevard—high enough that the idea of falling and eventually striking the ground seemed only a theoretical possibility: something the mind can ponder but the body cannot grasp. My belly clenches at fifty feet, but fifty stories is beyond my body's understanding.

There was something far to the west, a smudge of darkness on the street, sprinkled with intermittent flashes of reflected sunlight. The singing grew louder as the dark smudge approached along the boulevard. There were colorful pennants, like little red, yellow, blue and green clouds, floating along above the darker mass. I looked at Teresa.

"Is this what you wanted to show me?"

She handed me a pair of zoom lenses. "Pay attention to the head of the procession."

I took the lenses and focused them on the darkness below me. The Brazilian optics collected and processed the fading light remarkably well: the figures jumped into focus with such intensity that I almost sprang backward into Teresa's arms.

A sea of faces. Unwashed, swaying, many of the men sweating and shirtless. Some musicians. Women dancing. The deep sound of their singing boomed through the canyon between the skyscrapers and grew louder by the minute. Here and there throughout the procession were platforms carried on the shoulders of the men, and on the platforms were effigies of a woman in white.

I swung the lenses back and forth, looking for the first platform. I pulled the zoom back, saw something shining among all those dark faces and bodies. The lenses refocused themselves and I uttered a grunt of surprise.

She was dressed in purest white. My little bird. She was like a beacon shining in the middle of a sea of darkness. She sat upon a throne of burnished gold, carried at the head of the vast procession. Behind her swarmed thousands upon thousands of fervent, singing *pobrecitos*.

"What's this?" I whispered, awestruck by the vastness of that sea of poverty—and that Christina should be there at its head.

"The Procession of the Shirtless Ones, darling." *La Procesion de los Descamisados.* "Your friend on the throne is Santa Evita, and beside her is The General."

Yes, I realized, refocusing the lenses; there was a young man in a general's uniform on the platform too, on a throne beside Christina's. He was too young to be a real general.

I tore my attention from the street long enough to give Teresa a sharp glance. "Who is this Santa Evita? Why is Christina down there—and what general does the man represent? There have been so many."

Teresa smiled and looked at me through lidded eyes, like a *jaguar* of the northern forests sizing up its prey. "You really don't know, do you? But then you *are* a Dilettante, aren't you, darling. Politics and history bore you, don't they." She ran a finger along my arm. "I was a Dilettante once too, you know. I understand you. Paintings and poetry are all that excite you . . . and—something else?"

I looked away, feigning indifference. "I really do wish you would stop babbling and tell me what is going on."

"Poor innocent," she murmured. There was something vaguely hostile in her tone that I did not understand. Perhaps she was jealous, because I was still a Dilettante and she was not. She stroked my cheek, and let her hand slide down to my chest. "Come inside, and Teresa will help you forget about your little saint."

I allowed her to lead me inside, still dazed by the vision of the shining figure at the head of that enormous mob. Teresa's body was thick, languid, like a well-fed animal's. Yet she was easily aroused and quite explicit in her desires. The sound of the procession rolled over us, thousands upon thousands of voices, and I could feel the building sway as their song resounded through the canyon between the skyscrapers.

I was twelve years old when I saw poverty for the first time. I remember my father taking me and two of my older brothers out of the family compound at Las Cruces, and driving out into the town. We drove for a long time. The wide, tree-lined boulevards with their grassy dividing strips became narrower and narrower, the walls around the houses grew lower and lower, until they became simple chain-mesh fences with a spiral of razor wire at the top. Then even the fences disappeared. The houses grew smaller. The streets became dirtier. Graffiti ran like a multicolored fungus over every solid surface. And then the buildings sprang up much bigger than before—but they were dark, ugly, with gaping holes where windows should have been.

I remember the people staring at us as we drove by in our big black Mercedes with its escort in front and back; I remember the crumpled faces of the poor, how they stared with such a burning in their eyes that it terrified me. How could such poverty, hatred and ugliness exist? To the surprise of everyone in the car—including me—I began to sob uncontrollably.

On the street, an old man with rotten teeth picked up a rock and threw it at the car. His face was twisted into a horrible expression of raw hatred. I was so terrified, I wet my pants. My brothers, who were both older, made faces of disgust. My father ignored me. I think he was ashamed for me.

Finally my father had them stop the car in the most devastated area we had yet seen. There was a muddy field with dilapidated shacks and lean-tos squatting haphazardly in the mess. I remember clearly a sagging blue plastic sheet draped like an enormous tablecloth over one wooden box. Other shacks were made of cardboard or corrugated metal. Naked children ran among puddles where human shit floated in a sheen of oily water.

There were bulldozers and tanks lined up along one side of the field. My father gave a signal. As we watched from the car, the bulldozers advanced slowly. They knocked the crude buildings to the ground, crushed the wood and plastic and metal into the mud. The inhabitants of that hell ran for their lives, and when they were safely out of the way they just stood and watched. Almost all of the poor standing on the edge of that muddy field were women or children. I remember vaguely wondering where all the fathers were.

My father said to us in a distant, almost nonchalant tone, "If you remember only one thing in your life, remember this: All that separates you from them is money, backed by power. And if you ever forget it, they'll either tear you to pieces, or you'll end up right there with them in the shit and the mud."

I think it was my father's attempt to instill in us a work ethic; but all it did for me was teach me to be afraid of the poor, to hate power, and to loathe ugliness.

When I returned home from Teresa's apartment after our night together, I queried the System about Santa Evita and the *Procesion de los Descamisados*. Teresa had told me more as the night went on, but only enough to whet my curiosity. She had been more interested in reliving, through me, her own life as a Dilettante than in furnishing me any real facts.

The System had an astonishing amount of information on file—I learned, to my surprise, that this Santa Evita was an actual historical figure.

She had been beloved by the poor, and had died young. Eventually the Old Catholic Church had canonized her. When the Government finally outlawed the Church, they kept Santa Evita to placate the poor, and over the years the Procession had evolved into something the Church Fathers would have recognized, but with a far more ghastly end than they could ever have envisioned.

Every five years, a young woman is picked to represent the saint. It is a great honor: her family is given gifts of money and food, and treated like celebrities. They need never worry about going hungry after that—the Shirtless Ones see to it that they are well provided for. And for one entire month every five years, each night at sunset the Procession winds through the streets of the city.

The System archives had some excellent video records of Processions going back thirty years. I watched, transfixed by the video terminal's snakelike gaze, as the images played out before me: the half-naked men working themselves into a frenzy, the musicians, the women dancing in the streets. An unbroken line of tanks and armored cars flanked the route through the city, but there was never any trouble between the *Descamisados* and the military—on this night at least, the poor were satisfied with venting their passions through the Procession rather than through violence. Always the same song reverberated in the valley between the skyscrapers: I could never make out the words, but the melody, at once both mournful and ecstatic, haunted me. And always there was the image of the shining woman in white at the head of the sea of poor.

On the last night of the month, the Procession meanders like a lazy river through the streets of Buenos Aires. The *pobrecitos* sing and dance, and light torches. Everyone is happy, exhausted. Many collapse along the way as the night progresses. Finally, the Procession ends near dawn at the cliffs that overlook the *Río*. And when dawn first touches the highest skyscraper in Buenos Aires, they tie Evita and the General to their golden thrones, set the platform alight with their torches, and send it tumbling over the cliff and onto the rocks below.

• • •

Two days later, Christina was back at the gallery. I was surprised to see her; to be honest, I'd given up on her, after seeing the video archives. She would be dead at the end of the month. But there she stood, like a gift from the gods thrown at my feet. Clearly it was my destiny to seduce her.

"It gives me great joy to see you again," I murmured, taking her hand.

"I—thank you," she said. She stared intently into my face for a moment, then averted her eyes. I think she was as surprised to see me at the gallery as I was to see her. They were touring through the Fauvists as part of the day's program, and I have always had a fondness for that short-lived movement's brashness and intensity. Matisse was a Fauvist at one period in his career.

I handed her into her creche. We toured a Delacroix, the obligatory Monet, a Degas, a Renoir. I never left her side; and as the day progressed she became more spontaneous, less conscious of herself and of me. I was enchanted. In each painting she had a different face and figure; but her shy, musical laugh and the gleam of pleasure in her eyes, once she grew more comfortable with my presence, were constant elements of her nature.

We frolicked in Sisley's summer *Landscape*; we sat quietly transfixed in Degas's *Dancing Class* as the dance master put his flock of little ballerinas through their exercises; we adventured in tall sealskin boots and thick fur coats through Derain's *Snowscape at Chatou*. In another Derain, *The Turning Road*, we picnicked in the blue shade—the blue of an old blue bottle—beneath a tall vermilion tree. Below us, men and women moved slowly along the road and across a bridge that curved to the left above a river. Teresa winked at me and took the rest of the group on ahead.

There was a certain quality of a Gauguin paradise in this Derain—but the colors were intensified, heightened beyond anything Gauguin would have done. This, of course, was one reason of many why Derain was a Fauvist and Gauguin was not.

" 'Christina, *chez les fauves*,' " I murmured as we sat together in the shade, and I watched her watch a crimson horse pull a cart full of jade-green hay along a road the color of molten gold.

"What does that mean?" She was pale and slender, with her black hair cut short like a boy's. Her eyes were dark and clear.

She wore a bright-yellow dress with a red scarf tied at the throat. Large golden hoops dangled from her ears. I wore dark-green trousers, a red silk shirt, and a black beret.

"In Paris a long time ago, at the beginning of the twentieth century, there was an art show. In one room there was a classical Italianate sculpture surrounded by daring, colorful new paintings by Matisse, Vlaminck, Derain, Braque, I don't know who else." I broke off a piece of French bread, then refilled Christina's glass of wine. She tried to stop me at first, but I insisted.

"That is the beauty of the Simulacrum," I said with a smile. "You can have whatever you want, without the consequences." I continued with my story. "An art critic stumbled into the art show, took one look at the brash paintings on the walls surrounding the sedate sculpture as if they had taken it hostage, and pronounced: '*Donatello, chez les fauves*'—Donatello among the wild beasts. That was how the Fauvists got their name."

She leaned her head back against the trunk of the tree, closed her eyes and smiled. "French sounds so musical. Like a dream language. Say something else."

"*Voulez-vous coucher avec moi ce soir?*"

"It's beautiful," she said without opening her eyes. "What does it mean?"

"Everywhere there is beauty, pleasure is celebrated," I lied. I leaned over and kissed her lightly on the lips. She was startled at first, but did not move away. When I put my hand on her bare shoulder, though, she stood up and brushed the orange-pink grass from her dress.

"Where has the guide gone to? We should be heading back."

I smiled to myself.

"Will I see you again after today?" I asked.

"I don't think so."

"But why? Is it something I said? Or the kiss? I'm sorry if I was too forward. It's just that you're very beautiful and . . ."

There was a little gap of silence as she waited to see if I would finish my sentence; but I deliberately let it trail off unfinished, like a promise of things to come.

"It's nothing you said," she finally answered. After a moment longer: "Or did."

"Then why?"

"There are things you don't know about me."

"So? What does that matter? There are things you don't know about me, either. That's the nature of our lives—we are all enigmas. Islands unto ourselves. That is no reason not to enjoy what limited time we have together on this earth." Limited time on this earth—that should get her thinking.

She said nothing more after that, though I could tell she was mulling it over. We began to walk. Once, I turned to see her looking at me with that thoughtful expression I had seen on her face after *The Red Studio*. We caught up with Teresa and returned to the gallery.

There was a young man waiting on the steps of the gallery when we came outside into the sunlight. He glared at me with the fierceness of a young panther on the attack.

"Who is that?" I asked while we were still a safe distance away. "A boyfriend?"

"My brother."

Yes, I could see the family resemblance in the lips and the eyes. He was a year or two older than Christina, perhaps twenty-two. His clothes looked new—courtesy of the *Descamisados*, I presumed. It irked me somehow to think that he was profiting from Christina's tragedy. "What does he want?"

"He is protecting me."

"Protecting you? From what? From me?"

"A man was seen following me the other day when I left here."

Oh. Someone had seen me in the Barrio.

"Well, you can tell him he needn't protect you from me. I'm harmless. Tell him I adore you."

How she blushed!

"He'd kill you if I told him that. Besides, I couldn't lie to him." She seemed to have taken an intense interest in the granite paving stones at her feet.

You sly little bird. Testing me, are you?

"It wouldn't be a lie."

She glanced up at me, then looked away.

"Goodbye." She darted down the stairs and left me standing alone in the sun.

"Call me," I shouted after her. "I'm in the directory."

Her brother flashed me one more hostile look, and the two of them turned and set off together.

Each night, I watched the Procession from Teresa's balcony. After it had passed our high perch, we went inside and made love like wild animals. Teresa used me as much as I used her:

hrough her contact with me, for a short time each night she
became a Dilettante again; and for a short time each night I
lost myself in the transcendent passion of our bodies. And
when I finally arrived home I summoned the archive footage
of past Processions, and watched until dawn.

I grew obsessed with the image of that shining woman and
the drab, almost invisible general as they were paraded through
the city on the backs of the poor. How tragic and noble they
looked upon their golden thrones! I sat in my darkened apartment in front of the video terminal, as if drugged, as the Procession came to the cliffs, and as that haunting song issued
from ten thousand throats, I watched the platform plunge to
the rocks trailing long, sputtering arcs of bright yellow-orange
flame.

Five days later, I arrived home from Teresa's to find a message awaiting me. It was Christina. I saw the cracked wall of a
public booth behind her, and heard the rumble of traffic in
the background. She seemed nervous and kept looking off to
her left, out the doorway of the booth. There were deep
pouches under her eyes; the month was taking its toll on her.

"Tomorrow, if I can get away, I'll be at the gallery."

That was all. The screen went blank.

She seemed different when I met her the next day at the
gallery—older, haggard. She hardly looked at me as I handed
her into the creche and took the one beside hers. I had arranged a private showing; we would not be disturbed.

I let her choose our destination. At her request we returned
to the Derain where we'd had our picnic. We stood on a hillside looking down at the road and the river. Women beat their
laundry on the rocks at the river's edge. A bare-chested, barefoot man, walking as if he had all the time in the world, carried
a green earthenware jug on his shoulder along the road.

Christina picked up a stone and hurled it at the man on the
road below us. The man looked up, then ignored us and continued his slow passage. Then she picked up more stones and
aimed at the women far below us by the river. I went to her
and stopped her arm. She struggled, and I embraced her.

"What's wrong?" I asked.

She sank into my arms and buried her face in my shoulder.
"I hate it," she sobbed.

"Hate what? The painting?"

"My life."

I smiled into her hair, which was warm from the sunshine

and smelled like rich, fertile soil. Judging by the archive videos
I thought, her life would be coming to an end soon anyway. I
was lucky she didn't love it, or it might be more difficult for
them to get her up onto that platform on the last night.

"The only reason to be unhappy about life is if you don't
live it while you can," I murmured.

"I never want to go back. It's so ugly out there. And here
it's so—so wild and alive. Do we have to go back? Can't we
just stay here, forever?"

"That's impossible," I said. "There's no 'here' to stay. This
is only a dream we're sharing through the Simulacrum. Our
bodies are sleeping in the creches."

"A dream," she said sleepily. "If this is a dream, I'm never
going to wake up."

"But we all must wake up eventually."

I stroked her back gently, and after a long while she began
to relax. I kept speaking to her in a soft, soothing voice. "You're
young and beautiful, you should seek out new experiences.
Don't let fear or anything else stop you from tasting everything
life offers." Slowly, her body grew soft in my arms. My voice
was hypnotic. With cunning deftness I began to caress her in
a different manner. She offered no resistance, and we sank
together to the ground.

After a while she surprised me by taking the initiative—she
was more adept than her meek appearance suggested. For a
second or two I was angry: who was seducing whom? Then I
was caught up in the moment and it no longer mattered.

She wept noiselessly as we arranged ourselves and prepared
to return to the gallery. I caught sight of something in the
shadows, just on the periphery of my vision. A small animal? I
turned to look, but nothing was there. It could have slipped
into the green and yellow foliage—yes, I was sure that it had.

Neither of us spoke. I could not look at her; I doubt if she
looked at me. It was the same when we came out of the sensory
creches. She just lay there, as if lying in a coffin, while I got
up and went to the toilet to clean myself. When I returned,
she was gone.

But she called me again, three days later. It was nine days
before the end of the month.

"Martin, I want to go back to the gallery."

I looked at the antique timepiece I kept on the table. Around
the clock's face fluttered a pair of gilt cherubs, smiling beatif-

ically at one another. Their golden wings gleamed in the sunlight shining in through my window.

"There's a tour starting in an hour—"

"I don't want a tour. I want to go alone. The two of us."

Again, she had surprised me by seizing the initiative. I considered the opportunities this created. Outside I could see far across the wide *Río*, and could even make out the distant, hazy blue-gray suggestion of the Uruguayan coastline.

"Why don't you come over to my apartment?" I finally said. "By the time you get here I will have it all arranged."

"No, let's meet at the gallery."

"I think you should meet me here first."

She was silent for a long time. She knew exactly what price she would have to pay for another private entry into Paradise. But finally she spoke. Her voice was that of a woman condemned to death.

"All right. I'll be over as soon as I can get away."

When she arrived, she was wooden, half dead. Though she eventually warmed to me a bit, I must say she was better that first time in the painting than she was in the flesh.

We went to the gallery. I had made an arrangement for another "private showing." Again, she wanted to go to Derain's *The Turning Road*. I complied with her request, and soon we were standing on the molten yellow road among the vermilion tree trunks with their green, red and yellow leaves. As before, the women beat their laundry against the rocks by the river. The same barefoot man walked along the road carrying his jug on his shoulder.

Christina started walking down the road. Her eyes were deep blue shadows. She walked faster, then increased her pace still further. Soon her feet were a blur on the hard-packed yellow earth. I matched my stride to hers. Then she began to run, and with each breath a little whimpering sob caught in her throat.

"It's unfair!" she shouted between sobs. "I—I'm not going back!"

Poor Christina, I thought. *You cannot escape destiny as simply as that.*

"But you must," I called after her. "You must wake up eventually. We all must wake up eventually."

I slowed, and she went on alone. There were only nine days until the end of the month; let her have her taste of freedom.

Out of the corner of my eye I saw a movement. I turned, and saw a tiny bird disappear into the blue shadows.

Access, data, I subvocalized. *What was that bird in the bushes?*

Unknown, the computer responded.

What do you mean, unknown?

No matching entry located.

I frowned. Since when did the Simulacrum not know what creatures inhabited it?

Soon after, I returned to the gallery. I deactivated Christina's creche and called to her softly. She didn't respond. Only when I shook her vigorously did she awaken, and even then she seemed dazed.

The Processions continued. By night I stood on Teresa's balcony and watched with the zoom lenses as the poor wound their way through the city. Christina gleamed like the sun up there on her platform. Her poor partner in the general's uniform was but a gray shadow beside her.

Each morning, she came to me in my apartment. I used her, then took her to the gallery. The allowance from my family began to decline at an alarming rate as I paid the extravagant sums necessary to get us into the gallery alone. I began to teeter on the verge of exhaustion, caught between Teresa's physical demands and my own obsession with Christina. But the month was coming to an end; and therefore, so were Christina's visits. I told myself that I must hold on, I must drink every last drop of this experience while it lasts. Exhaustion was also having its effect upon Christina: she became more pale and thin with each visit, more distracted and withdrawn, and each day it was harder and harder to raise her from her creche. She aged years in the course of days.

We always returned to the same painting, Derain's *The Turning Road.* While there, I strained to catch a glimpse of that rare bird, always on the periphery of my vision, that flitted from shadow to shadow. It seemed to become bolder, and to take on more substance even as Christina declined; but it was cunning, and never showed itself directly.

On the morning of the last day, I awoke to find strangers in my apartment. There were nine or ten men crowded into the small room. I recognized Christina's brother as one of the men who took me roughly out of my bed.

He grabbed me by the throat and shook me. "I know what

you've done to my sister, you bastard. I would have killed you that first day. But she said she would kill herself if I tried."

He slapped me across the face so hard, my vision blurred. He made a noise that was half laugh, half sob. "But Christina can't use suicide to hold me back—not today. She can't threaten to disgrace the family. You're going to pay for what you did."

Over my stunned and feeble protestations they tied my hands and led me to a car waiting on the street, and then drove to a barrio in the heart of the city.

They imprisoned me in a basement somewhere to wait out the day. The concrete walls oozed moisture from little wounds like bleeding stigmata. After the initial shock, I was hardly surprised by this turn of events. Perhaps exhaustion had caught up with me, and my capacity for surprise had been extinguished. Perhaps on some unconscious level I had been expecting them—perhaps ever since my father had driven us out into the world when I was twelve, and I had discovered poverty and despair, I had been expecting them.

Hours later—I judged it to be around six o'clock in the evening—they dressed me in a general's uniform. The sleeves were too short and the jacket too tight around my chest; but I admired the row of stars on the shoulders, which gleamed like something truly precious. We went outside. I could see the sun sinking toward the horizon in the west. They put me into the car and drove to the outskirts of the city.

We came to the staging area for the Procession. Everyone was tense with excitement. They put me up on the platform beside Christina and tied me so I could not escape, though I was free to turn my head. The golden thrones, which had gleamed so beautifully in the archive videos, were actually crude wooden chairs sprayed with cheap gold paint.

Everywhere I looked, there were faces staring up at me. The brother looked at me with pure hatred; but in the others, I saw no hostility—there was excitement, awe, even pity. Their eyes shone. This was the final night. They knew what awaited us at dawn.

The Procession began. There was dancing and music; the deep voices of the *Descamisados* resounded through the valleys between the skyscrapers. It was like Carnival—everyone was joyous, ecstatic.

Christina was beside me, but she stared straight ahead and made no sign that she knew I was with her, or that she knew or even cared where she was. It was as if part of her had already died. Surprisingly, I felt a twinge of conscience—had I brought her to this?

No. She had made her own choices. I did not force her to come to me. And what if I had? In the last two weeks she had lived a fuller life than she'd ever dreamed of living. Her daily entry into the Simulacrum would have been impossible without me and my connections.

Suddenly another thought occurred to me. What if she had used *me*? Could it be? Could she have calculated her effect on me and used it to gain access to the Simulacrum?

I shook my head. What could she have possibly gotten from the Simulacrum? *I* was Faust to her Gretchen. *She* was the victim.

Then I thought of that rare little bird inside Derain's *The Turning Road*. Could she have . . . ? My exhaustion made it impossible to think. *I never want to wake up*, she had said. Could she have gotten her wish? But—we all must wake up, sooner or later. The dream cannot go on forever.

"Christina!" I shouted over the singing *Descamisados*.

She didn't answer, didn't even turn her head.

They carried us through the streets of the city, toward the dawn. When we passed Teresa's building, I looked up and wondered if she was watching. A faint, impossible hope stabbed me: if she saw us, perhaps she would call the soldiers and they would rescue me. Would she recognize me in this general's uniform? With hope came also the first real terror, as sharp and intense as a lightning bolt. I struggled against the thick cords binding me to the throne. If she would call my brothers—but no. At the thought of my brothers all hope died inside me. They would never help me; nor would I have accepted it had they offered.

Finally the cliffs appeared before us just as the eastern sky began to brighten. They carried us to the edge. My vision blurred, then sharpened with such an intensity that I gasped—everything around me took on a surreal, transcendent beauty that until that moment I had found only inside the Simulacrum. When they approached the platform with the torches, I had the acute sense of being inside one of my beloved paintings.

The song of the *Descamisados* washed over me like a sea of emotion. All around me were faces shining with joy. I reached out and tried to touch Christina's hand, but the rough cords were too tight. Flames roared up around us. I trembled with a fantastic mixture of terror and bliss, and offered myself to the experience as only a Dilettante could.

They tipped the platform over the edge, and I steeled myself as our passage described a fiery arc through the dawn.

THE MUSIC OF WHAT HAPPENS

Howard V. Hendrix

Y ou know all those views of Mount Fuji?" Biz Zimmer
asked as they sat on the terrace of his summer home,
known until recently as the Ahwahnee Lodge.

Pushing a lock of straight, dyed-blond hair away from his
eyes, Wayne Takahashi looked up from the Thai iced coffee
Zimmer's dining staff had brought him.

"The ones by Hokusai?" he ventured tentatively.

"Right. Well, I want you to do the same for my property
here," Biz said, gesturing expansively at his estate, a considerable acreage which, until the beginning of the year, had been
Yosemite National Park. "Ten thousand views of my Half
Dome, El Capitan, Clouds Rest. A million views of Bridalveil
and Vernal and Yosemite Falls. A billion views of Tuolumne
Meadows and the Merced River and all the backcountry. And
not just views, but everything—scents, sounds, tastes, textures.
An absolute and complete virtual realization of this place. A
map virtually indistinguishable from the territory."

Wayne stared at him, wide-eyed.

"But that would be prohibitively expensive—"

"How prohibitively?"

Wayne calculated quickly and named a figure in the high
hundreds of millions.

"Done!" said Bertrand Isamu Zimmer with a quick nod,

seemingly inured to the thought of such a vast financial outlay. Wayne wondered briefly if being a billionaire scores of times over did that to one. . . .

"But I'm not sure it's possible," the thin faux-blond artist hedged, watching the slant of late-afternoon sunlight deepen on the Valley walls. "I'm not certain the technology fully exists for what you're suggesting."

"It exists, all right. Several of my subsidiaries have proprietary rights to the new technology and intellectual property this project would require. Wayne, what I'm offering you here isn't a suggestion—it's a job." Zimmer glanced at him, pausing only an instant before barreling on in his blunt, grandiose way. I can see by the look on your face you're asking yourself, 'Why me? There are plenty of reality engineers around. Young post-punk cyberdelicists are a drag on the art market.' True, true, but I saw that piece of yours—*When the Ice Cream Man Stops Melting*. It had the right sharpness and spark, balanced by a brilliant attention to detail. And besides, we're both halflings."

"Halflings?" Wayne asked, confused. "Like, um, hobbits, you mean?"

Bertrand Zimmer laughed.

"No, not hobbits, but kindred spirits, half Euro, half Asian, similarly calcined by life in the North American crucible. Hell, if I dyed some of my hair, I could be your older brother. That's 'why you.' Think about it: 'Wayne Takahashi's *Yosemite*.' It may not give you the same sort of space for creative self-expression as *Ice Cream Man* did, but it just could be your grandest composition, your biggest score ever. Interested?"

Wayne's thoughts were aflood with ideas, images, possibilities—not only for himself, but also for his work. The whole idea was so heady he felt as if he were in freefall, seduced by the Yosemite project's gravity until he was as heedless as a comet headed for the sun.

"I'd be a fool not to be interested," Wayne said after a long distracted moment. "When would we start?"

"We already have," Biz said with a wry smile. "Of course, you'll have an ample budget to hire the staffpeople you need, and I've placed a company jet and helicopter at your disposal for their transport. As you may have guessed, I've already got quite a few people working on the project."

Before Wayne's eyes, the seemingly rustic table shed its wooden grain to reveal a document presented in flatscreen—a contract, he saw upon closer examination.

"Go ahead. Scan it carefully. We've already modemed a copy to your agent and lawyers for their opinions. They very much approved. All it needs now is for you to electropen your signature."

Wayne scanned it carefully, then signed.

He may have thought "Why me?" but Wayne never asked Biz "Why?" He knew the holociné magnate's reputation for eccentricity and austentatious displays of wealth, privilege, and power—displays and events and happenings that usually turned out to be connected to some new product being launched by one or another of the many companies held by Infostructural Enterprises, the corporation Zimmer had initially built to market his full-dimensional cinema technology but which had long since spread its tentacles everywhere in the computing, communications, and entertainment industries.

When he bothered to ask *himself* about the "why?" of the Yosemite project, Wayne assumed that he and his work were being used for just such another product launching—and, at the salary he was being paid for the one-year duration of the project, Wayne didn't mind being used at all. Still, though, he didn't want to be abused by someone as powerful as Biz, so he immediately called Marijke Osterkamp, a fellow full-sensory mediast and his onetime lover in the Bay Area. She had a good head for business and organization and an even better eye for reading people.

He got her on the second ring and, after enthusiastically describing the project and the patron, offered her a considerable salary to come on board as manager.

After a pause, she agreed. He arranged for one of Biz's company choppers to pick her up and fly her out. Within two hours he was hugging her, her long reddish-brown hair whipping before his face as they ran bent-over beneath the propwash of the helicopter that had just dropped down onto the Helipad behind Biz's lodge house.

"So, you've told me what the new boss *is* like," Marijke said after dropping off her bags and changing out of her traveling clothes, "but what *does* he like? What sort of end-product pleases our dear wealthy patron? Any clues as to his tastes?"

"He said he liked my *Ice Cream Man* piece—" Wayne remarked as they walked toward his suite of rooms.

"Ugh. Not one of my favorites, but *de gustibus*, as the Romans used to say, *de gustibus*. We should probably view it to get some sense of what he liked about it. Does he have it logged in the entertainment system?"

"We'll see," Wayne said, entering the room and calling up an index on the entertainment menu. "*When the Ice Cream Man Stops Melting.* It's here, all right."

"Down to business, then."

Wayne soon saw that Marijke intended them to closet themselves this evening in Wayne's suite of rooms in the Ahwahnee—but not for romantic purposes, alas. Its creator hadn't viewed the *Ice Cream Man* piece in well over a year and, in retrospect, Wayne was now beginning to think of it as an audition piece. As he loaded it up in the suite's holojector and, with Marijke, watched the piece play, he grimaced at its flaws but was pleasantly surprised once again by its successes, an experience that would repeat itself often over the next several months, as they reviewed the piece time and again.

After introducing Biz and Marijke to each other, Wayne and his project manager were forcibly guided by Zimmer into the meadows around the Ahwahnee Lodge, where people in what looked like very thin wet suits were walking about.

"What's with the frogmen?" Wayne asked. "Are you expecting a flood?"

"Frog princes and frog princesses," Biz corrected. "The proper term for them is experients, and we're channeling a flood of information. Those are unisense suits they're wearing, universal sensory recording apparatuses. Here, I'll show you."

They approached a rack where an athletic young couple, their shift apparently over, were hanging up their cocoon suits and walking away, barefoot and nearly as naked as new butterflies.

"Now this lightweight headpiece," Biz said, detaching a headgear unit from the rest of its suit, "not only has state-of-the-art holospectrum opticals, but also much more. The eyepieces process electro-oculogram signals, both movement and depth, because the eyes converge as they focus—full 3-D positioning. These plugs here insert into the nostrils. Every smell, from pine scent to bear scat, is captured as it is breathed in and analyzed remotely by olfactory computer. Most of the non-eating and non-drinking 'tastes' are handled olfactorily as well. Similarly with these auditory plugs for the ears: every sound, all the background, or just the focused attention on a birdsong, the roar of falling water, a wind in the trees, what have you, all are here time-synched together like the soundtrack to an oldstyle film."

"But how can you tell what's being given attention and what's background?"

"Ah, perceptive question, Marijke. Good! That's one of the great advances in this unit, one of the many things that distinguishes it from the cheap simsuits you find in digiporn palaces. This headgear monitors the neurophysiology of the brain and the central nervous system, functioning like a hypersensitive electroencephalogram, analyzing the waves of changing potential emitted by firing neurons. Attention or focus on a particular environmental stimulus is characterized by the appearance of chaotic attractor-patterns within appropriate regions of the brain. This suit duly notes and records those blips of attention."

"But it also records everything else, too?" Wayne asked.

"Certainly. In fact, above and beyond the attention patterns, the whole point of having people walk around in these suits is only to get a sort of 'human standard' measure. That's why I've chosen healthy young people, which hopefully should have the side benefit of helping any future user feel young and healthy while in the sensorium—even if he or she is neither. Once the data is in the can, as it were, any user of the sensorium could perfectly well choose to foreground a sound or sight or smell which the initial human recorder noted only as background. You could bring up the sound of that cricket, turn down the white noise of that waterfall, damp out the glare of noon or deepen the lights of sunset. Reality is adjustable."

"What about the rest of the suit?" Marijke asked, handling the filmy mesh of the material. "Is that just to keep off the mosquitoes?"

Zimmer laughed.

"Not at all. It's a full-body tactile unit and electromyogram processor. It can record the caress of a light breeze, the feel of a stone or a pinecone in the hand, sunlight warming a surface, or even the bite of one of your mosquitoes. It records surface and deep muscle movements too—that's the electromyogram part."

"What have you had your walkabouts—er, 'experients'—doing so far?" Wayne asked, more fascinated by the gadgetry than he would have cared to admit.

"Sightseeing, mostly."

"Not enough, not enough," Wayne said with a fervent shake

of his head. "They need to be rock-climbing sheer routes on El Capitan, hanggliding and paragliding off Half Dome, kayaking the Merced in full spring whitewater. Suit up stunt people and have them go over Nevada Falls. We need to research all the written records of every experience that has ever happened to a human being here, from the Indians and John Muir on down. We need to do a distribution on those experiences, to know where to concentrate our walkabouts and their efforts so that we can best provide future users with the fullest range of the human experience of Yosemite."

"It's all yours to do," Zimmer said, smiling broadly and benignly in front of his large dark eyes, beneath his shock of lustrous black hair. "I feel vindicated already in choosing you to orchestrate this project."

Wayne turned away, mumbling thanks. Marijke elbowed him impishly in the ribs. He had never been very good at accepting a compliment, but he appreciated it nonetheless.

The historic record of the human interaction with the landscape called Yosemite unfortunately left out nearly all the Native American experience of the region and had many other gaps thereafter as well—yet Wayne still found himself with more than enough data to work with. Some of the material most intriguing to him he figured his patron would have little interest in at all: data from that dark time after park service administration of the place had begun to collapse and before the debt-ridden and increasingly vitiated US government, in one of its periodic waves of privatization fervor, sold the place to Biz's Infostructural Enterprises.

Wayne scanned again a tourist-shot videodoc from that time. As the tourists drive up from the ghosttown of Lee Vining and the fly-haunted salt pan of Mono Dry Lake, their electric hover's travel computer begins to identify the scattered trees that green and tan the gray rock: pinyon and ponderosa and Jeffrey pines. Up and over Tioga Pass from the east side, the tourist camera scans "remarkably little evidence of Balaam's urbanizing pressures on the Yosemite backcountry, at least around the heavily guarded Park Entrance checkpoint," as the tourist narrator describes it in voiceover. Lodgepole and foxtail pine, the travel computer intones in the background, as the tourists drive into the park proper.

Population effects become clearer, though, as the tourists and their camera descend toward Yosemite Valley and the

Central Valley beyond. Squatter camps everywhere in Tuolumne Meadows; most of the surrounding forest stripped out for firewood, miles in every direction. Increasingly indecipherable graffiti on roadside boulders. Enormous neotribal petroglyphs etched by macrotaggers into the great granite faces of Clouds Rest, Half Dome, El Capitan. The permanent shantytown of Valley Floor, overhung with the haze of cooking fires and ancient, supposedly banned internal-combustion vehicles. High barbed-wire fences around the few remaining stands of what the travel computer identifies as sequoias.

Near the park's west checkpoint, tourists and camera pass a party of heavily armed EcoGuards shuttling restoration and reforestation equipment, seedlings and shovels and shock fences, toward a boundary area stripped of vegetation by incursions of fuel-gatherers. Not far beyond the checkpoint, a trashfire burns in the middle of the road, armed highway bandits standing behind it, lit chiaroscuro by the fire's glow. The last shots are of the bandits stopping the tourists' vehicle, taking their camera. . . .

Wayne wondered vaguely what happened to the amateur videographers who had shot the piece. From his other historical research he knew what had happened to the squatters and tent people and neo-nomads who'd taken over the park as their own: Infostructural Enterprises's security forces had driven the interlopers out, by force when necessary. There had been deaths, largely among the squatters, but Bertrand Zimmer was powerful enough to keep the Battle of Valley Floor out of most of the media.

In contrast, Biz had let the full media spotlight shine on his restoration efforts—the sandblasting of the graffiti off the great granite faces and boulders, the removal of the razor wire from around the sequoias. He'd gotten enormously positive press as a result of the cutting-edge security system he'd had placed around the entire perimeter, the crack security force that patrolled the vast area day and night. Yosemite, it was ballyhooed, was at last being truly preserved against the degrading pressures of Balaam, the Bay Area Los Angeles Aztlan Metroplex.

Only on the few outlets not owned by Infostructural did the commentators dare remark that this Great Privatization had also turned the once-public treasure of Yosemite into M'Lord B. I. Zimmer's private baronial estate.

•　　•　　•

A month and a half into running his legion of sensuited walkabouts here and there and not quite everywhere throughout Yosemite, putting the stunt-qualified through their death-defying duties climbing El Cap and kayaking the Merced, putting the more leisurely observant into sighting bobcat and bear and bird, deer and dogwood, coyote and cougar, marten and mushroom, flower and forest and fern—thus far into the project, Wayne realized how much fun he was having, but still wondered how he might shape the overall experience of Yosemite in simulation.

He pondered these matters as he scrambled about one May day in an area of slope and slough that a fire had raged through the summer before. He was fully sensuited, having taken to wearing the sensorium recording apparatus himself very early in the project—especially in areas where he felt his personal expertise was needed. Such expertise had brought him and Marijke to this esthetically bleak stretch of wasteland, thousands of acres of standing charred trees rising from ash-smeared soil.

"Mind telling me what we're doing here?" Marijke asked. "It's hot, there's no shade, it's ugly dead zone. Is this to give the user an experience of discomfort and hideousness, or what?"

"Now, now. I know this seems an inexplicable place to be recording," Wayne said, looking away. "Being a mycophile, however, I know this terrain's hidden glories. Thousands upon thousands of morel mushrooms sprout up almost randomly in burn areas. Their numbers are always greater the season after fire—that's why some European peoples used to set fire to their own forests, in hopes of a bumper morel crop the next spring. Look! There are some, right over by that burnt-out stump."

Wayne scampered over excitedly and knelt beside a loose grouping of strangely shaped things like sponges or stretched brains on stalks. Crouching down beside Wayne and flicking back her long auburn hair from where it had flowed onto the front of her sensuit, Marijke watched Wayne pluck the strange things from their hollow stalks and drop them in a bag he was carrying.

"Morels," Wayne said, holding up a couple of particularly large specimens for his companion's edification. "They're among the most tasty of wild mushrooms. Searching for them is like an Easter egg hunt for adults. There's another big patch, see?"

Soon they were both wandering over the scorched hillside, plucking mushrooms.

"My God, there're a lot of them here," Marijke said, amazed. "You would barely know it, though—they blend in so well."

"True," Wayne said with a nod. "As much as we might like to, we can't possibly collect them all. The problem reminds me a little bit of the problems we're facing in our simulation of Yosemite. We can never collect all of this place, either."

"Do you really have to, though?" Marijke asked as she plucked morel after morel. "I don't mean to say that once you've picked one morel you've picked them all, but it does get a little repetitive after a while."

"Hmm," Wayne said, abruptly halting in his morel harvesting. "Marijke, I think you've hit on something. Let's face it: the natural world, for all its diversities, is redundant and repetitive in many ways. Not uniformly repetitive, but chaotically so, a repetition with variations, like a very complex piece of music."

He thought of John Cage, that old mushroom collector who'd inspired Wayne himself into the hobby when he'd learned the old maestro had said, "One shouldn't go to the woods looking for something, but rather to see what is there." That in turn reminded him of another old story, the one about the Celtic hero Cuchulain, who provided the most satisfactory answer to the question "What is the most beautiful sound in the world?" by replying "The most beautiful sound in the world is the music of what happens."

"Yes, that's it!" Wayne said aloud, standing up from his crouch beside the last cluster of morels he'd been working. "Using what the walkabouts are giving us, our job is to try to make a map of that music, a score, a data compression which can be unfurled like a fern to give the full experience. We'll need biomass surveys, satellite images, computerized topographic renderings, microclimate maps, average temperature and wind and precipitation patterns, changing sun and shade positions throughout the year, phases of the moon and precession of the rotating Earth's axis, constellations and their positions, species habitat and migration patterns, a chaos of chaotic systems—but what is chaos if not a more *subtle* form of order, right? We can do it: A symphony of sublime subtlety—a rite of spring and summer and fall and winter! An everchanging Yosemite simulation very nearly as subtle and grand as Yosemite itself!"

So excited was he by his wasteland epiphany that he kissed the startled Marijke firmly, then dashed off, half leaping and half staggering down the hillside toward Highway 41, very nearly losing the rumpletop bag full of morels in his right hand.

From spring into summer the walkabouts walked while Wayne and Marijke and the research staff they'd put together searched every record they could find concerning Yosemite—historical, physical, cultural, meteorological, biological, geological—a flood of-icals and-ologies. In the virtual construct of Yosemite that was shaping up, they found a traditional place for siting all the background information: the Visitor Centers. The physical buildings were still there, and the idea of them provided the ideal framework for the meshing of real and virtual, a finite space for access to a nearly infinite area of virtual displays and exhibits.

The same was true of their simulation of Yosemite in general. Though the number of steps and paths the walkabouts could take was merely finite, the overlaying of all the other maps of all the other shifting parameters helped raise the order of coverage a fractional dimension, fractalized the walkabout experience to a virtual infinite so that the vast majority of Yosemite—which hadn't been walked—could still be simulated to an extremely high degree of authenticity.

Wayne was generally satisfied with the way the project was proceeding under his orchestration, but he still had to please Biz Zimmer, and soon, for the six-month evaluation/presentation was scheduled for mid-September.

Late August found the Valley floor hot and the walkabout crews growing bored and irritable. After conferring with Biz on the production of fully waterproofed sensuits, Wayne decreed a new project: the sensory mapping of the Merced River, which was mostly a grand excuse for turning the river into a long series of swimmingholes and chances to cool off.

Wayne and Marijke were down by the river one day watching the walkabouts splashing around like river otters. While laughing at one of the young guys beating his chest and giving a Tarzan yell as he plunged toward the cool water, Wayne became suddenly quiet.

"Is something wrong, Wayne?" Marijke asked, concerned.

"No—no, something just went right. Don't you see it? The

body as a musical instrument! More, a whole orchestra! The body of work becomes the body of music. All the electro-signaling we've recorded—myograms, oculograms, encephalograms—they're all patterns that can be run through arrangements of instruments to produce symphonies from the mere act of living, breathing, walking, swimming—water music! The life of the flesh as a music, a concert of synthesized sound from the body's own deep and surface patterns, music as quiet and minimal or as bombastic and lush as we please. We could put all the patterns of Yosemite's complex system to music, but it would still be lacking something if we left out the living patterns of that system called 'observer' or 'participant' or 'subject.' Add in that, and the music of what happens is complete!"

Marijke cocked her head and looked at him oddly.

"Tell me," she said, "do you ever reason linearly to a new thought—or do they always pop full-blown into your head, *ex nihilo*?"

Wayne laughed and, beating his chest and screaming a Tarzan yell of his own, plunged into the river.

"I may not proceed by great imaginative leaps and bounds," Marijke said ten days later, leading Wayne into one of the Ahwahnee's former ballrooms, which the simulation project had turned into an impromptu testing facility, "but I think you'll see from what one of my subteams and I have been working on that step-by-step plodding can accomplish a lot too—especially when it involves plodding and walking and hiking and climbing and running."

Marijke led him toward the center of the room. On the floor sat a black circular platform about three meters in diameter.

"What's this?" Wayne asked.

"You'll see—or rather, you'll feel. Step up on it."

Wayne complied.

"Now, this could be operated in an externalized sensorium, but since you're fully suited up we're just going to pump a walkabout's recorded path through your suit's apparatus. You won't get the olfactory stuff and we haven't tied in your body-music concept yet, but you will get everything else."

Abruptly Wayne heard and saw and felt what the walkabout had experienced. He had the odd sensation for a moment that he was inside someone else's skin, but gradually the sensation lessened. He felt wind and sun, saw and heard water and birds and wind in the pine trees. Pleasant.

"Okay," Marijke said. "Now walk."

"Where?"

"Anywhere."

With a shrug Wayne complied. Immediately he felt something unexpected and found himself staring down at his feet, experiencing a strange sort of trailvision. When the path was sandy, the platform he knew must be under his feet also felt sandy. When he stepped up on a rock, the platform gave him a rock. When the grade and steepness of a trail or surface changed in his vision, it changed under his feet too.

"Marijke, this is incredible!"

"Not really. Did you think people would just want to have Yosemite come to them while they stayed immobile? Yeah, that can be done, but what about a more active interaction? That's what we set to work on here."

"It's great!" Wayne shouted, running up a trail only he and the techs monitoring his path could see. "How'd you do it?"

"Let's just say it's a combination of active-surface treadmill and computerized topographic route imaging. I took the idea from stationary exercise bicycles, treadmills, stairsteppers—they've long been simulations, virtual exercisers leading nowhere but taking forever to get there. For the El Capitan simulation I took off from the idea of indoor rock-climbing walls. We can simulate rock-climbing steepness and difficulty up to very high levels of difficulty. We've got bicycling and kayaking versions as well, for the Valley floor and the Merced River, respectively—even a swimming version based on the endless-flow pool concept."

"Biz'll love this."

"He already did. The active surface treadmill is a prototype from one of his companies. Synching it up to a topo imaging computer, though—that was *my* idea."

Wayne turned off the holojector after they'd finished watching *When the Ice Cream Man Stops Melting* for the fourth or fifth time.

"What was it Biz said he liked about that holo?" Marijke asked.

"Sharpness, spark, attention to detail," Wayne said, neglecting to mention that Biz also felt him to be a fellow hobbit, halfling, kindred-spirit Eurasian, or whatever it was.

"Yeah? Well, after seeing it again, I can think of a few other things about it that might have appealed to Mr. Bertrand Isamu Zimmer—things that Biz might find appropriate to the message he wants us to put out about his acquisition of Yosemite."

"Like what? I don't see the connection, Mar."

"Like Richard, your anti-heroic armed ice cream man/weekend gardener protagonist. The individualist taking decisive action against those barbarians incapable of understanding the beauty of his garden or the nature of property rights. Think about Biz and the squatters he moved out of here, the poachers and fuel gatherers his private security still keeps out. The sense of history, too, of its inescapability, the way the past shaped the protagonist Richard's behavior in the present. History and the Great Man—does that give you some ideas about Biz's predilections?"

"I don't know," Wayne said, a bit distracted and preoccupied. "Seeing the holo again reminded me of the inescapability of my own past. I always forget how autobiographical it is. Willie, the lunatic neighbor, is straight out of my childhood. Richard's loathing of powerlessness, his potential for violence and madness leading to his blowing away those obnoxious kids with a twenty-gauge shotgun—that's in me too."

"What? You? Mr. Nonviolence and Quiet Spirit?" Marijke said, in mock horror.

"I know," Wayne said, quite seriously, seeing little joke in it. "Like Prospero, 'this thing of darkness / I acknowledge mine.' "

"Well, Shakespeare," Marijke said, giving him a squeeze of a hug. "In our current project you won't have much room for autobiographical stuff to 'acknowledge.' This is about Biz, not you."

"I hope you're right."

Turning the six-month evaluation into a party was Marijke's idea. Biz pronounced it a rousing success.

"Today," Zimmer said in a toast at dinner of Evaluation Day, "I have visited the Visitor Center and learned an unbelievable amount about the history of this place. I have climbed El Capitan. I have tracked a bear across the Valley floor. I have seen moonbows beside Yosemite Falls. I have paraglided off Half Dome and landed in a remote field of Jeffrey Shooting Stars. I have sampled half a hundred other experiences, and in every one I was absolutely convinced of its reality. More: each of your simulations is not only as good as, but even better than, the real thing. I fell from the top of Bridalveil and I didn't die, I climbed hiking trails and didn't get sunburned or bugbitten or fall over from heat prostration, and every experience was accompanied by beautiful sounds more enchanting than the music of the elves. Wayne and Marijke, you, your technical staff, and your walkabouts have accomplished something tremendous, and we drink to your great success."

Everyone in the banquet hall (mostly walkabouts and techies and high-ranking Infostructural corporate types) clinked their glasses, said "Hear! Hear!" and drank to the project's stunning achievements. But Biz wasn't finished yet.

"I feel blessed that we have accomplished so much so fast," he continued, stroking his dark, well-trimmed goatee, "and I feel the need to spread that blessing around. Billions of people have never experienced and many *would never have been able to experience* the grandeurs of Yosemite—until now. Therefore, after we have finished inputting the final data and upgrading this project for market, I propose that the first five million units—each containing the whole package: simulator/sensorium and full Yosemite simulation—be donated to libraries, museums, schools and colleges worldwide!"

Strong scattered applause, mostly from the techies and walkabout staff. The corporate honchos remained curiously quiet.

"And, lest my management and marketing people think I've completely taken leave of my senses," Biz continued, "I'll remind them that these donations will not only win us good press and impressive tax breaks, but will build a market for this new technology's home version that will completely revolutionize the information and entertainment industry!"

The applause this time was fervent and prolonged. Bertrand Isamu Zimmer, billionaire entertainment genius, seemed poised for another global manufacturing and marketing coup.

Microbrewery beer and fine wines and premium liquors flowed and the party became boisterous—Biz not least of all. Wayne and Marijke, seated on either side of Biz on the dais, grew boisterous in their own ways too.

"I really meant what I said," Biz confided to Wayne. "Your method of musical accompaniment—that most of all. More enchanting than elven melodies, more accomplished than Old Nick on his fiddle!"

"I know, I know," Wayne said confidently, quite fully overcoming his usual awkwardness at being complimented. "I'm very proud of it."

"Rightly so. You do come up with some good ideas," Biz said to Wayne before turning to his dinner. "These morel things you collected and dried last spring, though—I don't know about that. I gave them to the cooks to reconstitute and prepare according to your recipes. Judging by the way everyone's eating them they seem to be quite a hit, but I don't think I'll be partaking of any."

"No?" Wayne asked. "You're not a fan of wild mushrooms?"

"I'm not a fan of mushrooms, period. Can't stand them. I'm a fungophobe and proud of it."

Wayne frowned as Marijke laughed. It wasn't long, however, before Biz had said things that got a rise out of Marijke too.

"Why not do anything we like with Yosemite?" Biz was saying, apparently having located the best button to push to get an argument out of Marijke. "The idea that we've got to 'preserve' it in some idealized pristine state is ridiculous. Why not hunt and fish here to our hearts' content? Human beings are a part of nature, wouldn't you agree? Well, then, everything we do is natural. A human being is as natural a top-level predator as a bear or a wolf or a mountain lion."

"I can't believe a man as intelligent and foresighted as you're supposed to be would engage in such faulty reasoning!" Marijke said, exasperated. "Yes, we're part of nature, but it doesn't follow that everything we do is natural. You've forgotten the distinction between nature and culture. A bear or wolf or mountain lion doesn't use a gun or a bow or a fishing rod or even a chipped-flint spearpoint in hunting its prey. They just use tooth and claw. When you, barehanded, hunt a deer by running it down, sinking your fingernails into its flanks and ripping its throat open with your teeth, then I'll believe you're as natural a predator as a wolf or mountain lion. But anytime you develop a tool to extend your abilities, that's cultural, not natural."

"If we're natural creatures, then you're setting up a false distinction!" Biz said, pooh-poohing her.

"It's not false. We come out of nature, but we don't stop there. A wooden or a stone bridge is made of natural materials, but it's a cultural entity, created with a goal or intention in mind. A wooden bridge is not the same thing as a tree blown down by the wind that now happens to ford a stream. They can be used for the same thing—to cross a stream—but they are different in both kind and degree."

Wayne smiled at the discussion. He'd heard variants of it before, but now it struck him with a new idea.

"Then the Yosemite simulation we've produced is as natural as the original?" he asked Zimmer, feeling the impish need to play devil's advocate. "If what you're saying is true, then why bother to preserve the original at all?"

"Precisely! Was Yosemite Park 'natural'? Hardly. It was a 'preserve,' a thing made out of laws and policies. No more natural than a zoo, really—and like a zoo it's another ark to preserve some fragment of species diversity against the on-slaught of a more successful natural competitor, Homo sapiens. All my life I've been hearing 'Save the This' and 'Save the That'—when you know as well as I do that by the time we humans recognize the need to save something, it's already too late to save it in any meaningful sense. Now that we've suc-ceeded in producing a 'Yosemite of the mind,' a better Yosem-ite for human needs and understanding, I see no reason to preserve the original except my own whims. As population and human use put more pressure on the original, Yosemite can only become less and less what it was. The same cannot be said of our simulation. Being a thing made of light, it will not degrade, cannot become less than it was."

"Nature disappears into culture—poof!" Marijke said sourly over her wineglass. "Reality evaporates into simulation. But you're wrong, Mister Zimmer. It's not a 'Yosemite of the Mind'—at best it's a Yosemite of the Brain, of the senses."

"Brain, mind, same thing," Biz said with a wave of his hand. "Mind is just that virtuality produced by the operation of the wetware we call Brain."

"No it's not!" Marijke said firmly. "Our experience with the walkabouts shows that clearly. A person's experience is more than the sum of her sensory inputs. Even when we can deter-mine what an experient is focusing on, no mechanism can fully tell us what emotional content that person associates with the experience. Only the experient herself can tell us that. The same is true for other subjective states, not only emotions but inspirations, imaginations, hallucinations—none of those func-tions of the mind can be recorded in the simulation. Even if you do succeed in subliming nature into culture, the subjective states will always elude you. Inner space is the final frontier of privacy, the wilderness in ourselves that cannot be recorded or copied or tamed from outside."

"Lofty words, Ms. Osterkamp," Zimmer said. "I wouldn't bet my life on them, however—"

Wayne rose from the table, standing unsteadily as his blood rushed to his head. It had occurred to him that both Biz and Marijke were enjoying their argument entirely too much—that they were baiting each other, teasing and playing for each other, even flirting with each other.

"Whoa! This conversation's grown too abstract for my poor numbed skull," Wayne said somewhat drunkenly, wanting to beg off, to get away. "I feel like I'm stumbling between infinite immensities of ancient philosophical questions. I must take my leave, for some air to clear my head!"

Leaving his boss and colleague smiling and temporarily reconciled, Wayne made his way out of the banquet hall, saying his goodbyes and good nights all the way. When he got outside he saw with some surprise that the long mountain twilight was still very much underway. The slant of the declining light struck him as possessing a particularly melancholy beauty, and he donned a sensuit, hoping to record the input of his late-evening stroll.

As he walked along in the deepening shadows, Wayne could appreciate truths in what both Biz and Marijke had said. Certainly all the mechanisms of the suits and simulations could not record the melancholy he felt at the dying of the day's light—but did that matter? So what if subjective states were, to some degree, forever unknowable from outside? Given the same sensory input as he was getting now, wasn't it true that some percentage of future users would also say that the light gave them melancholy feelings?

Perhaps, but this melancholy was too intangible. He needed something more pronounced, even dramatic, with which to test the sensuit and its ability or inability to overcome that brain/mind dualism Marijke so firmly believed in.

He had walked less than a hundred yards farther when the landscape—becoming almost responsive to his thoughts, in some odd variant of the pathetic fallacy—called up before his eyes a cluster of mushrooms which, though not notable for their edibility, he was sure he recognized nonetheless. Kneeling down beside them where they jutted up from the conifer debris, he examined them more closely, plucking one. Broadly convex cap with a slightly uplifted margin, smooth to the touch, caramel brown in color, its curved whitish stem already staining blue where he had plucked it. No doubt about it: the extremely hallucinogenic *Psilocybe cyanescens*, fruiting a bit early and inland for this time of year, probably triggered by the rain and cool spell that had finally broken the summer's heat earlier in the week.

What better way to test the sensuit's interaction with a subjective state than to chew up a few of these? As blue as this one was staining, Wayne figured he'd probably only need to ingest a couple of caps to markedly alter his perceptions and sensations. Still he wanted to make sure, so he plucked a dozen whole mushrooms. Walking farther off the trail and deeper into the mixed forest of pine and oak, he consumed one by one all twelve of the slightly slimy and bitter raw mushrooms—a heroic dose indeed.

A quarter of an hour later he found that he had quite lost his way and, no matter which way he turned, he could not find his way back to the meadow where Biz's lodgehouse stood, nor even back to the mushroom patch where he'd left the trail. The forest had become a maze. As Wayne continued walking, the air around him began to fill with shimmering and shifting dots and flecks of blue and yellow light, slowly joining to form fluid grids and honeycomb patterns, saturated incendiary colors waxing and waning, swelling and shrinking and rippling through everything in his field of vision. Zigzags of flashing light softened to meanders, into waves, curves, filigrees. Spirals of red and black shone incandescently against the night sky, rotating and moving, enlarging and shrinking. For a while it seemed he could see this flood of images only at the periphery, for wherever he looked a brilliant white dot occupied the center of his vision, the movable bright eye of the storm.

Somewhere in his mind Wayne knew that what he was seeing was not the eye of the storm but the storm of the eye, that these images were entoptic phenomena, patterns being generated *within* the eye, produced by the activity of the visual apparatus itself. He wondered vaguely if his sensuit was picking up any of it.

The sky was covered in luminous, translucent script, Arabic or heiroglyphic or cuneiform, a swirling dance of unreadable letters, celestial graffiti. The beat of his heart was the thudding of a million drums, a billion hearts, all drums one drum beating a planetary tattoo, a world heartbeat, unimaginable percussive harmonies, the formal articulation of time's passing, sounds bending and dilating, breaking up and digitizing until he could hear the music of the universe in the space between the notes.

He looked at the backs of his hands and found they were no longer familiar but had instead become alien topography, netted with nerves and roped with blood vessels, highways trafficked with the lights of firing neurons, the pulsing gridlock of platelets, X-ray vision of and through skin and flesh and bones, swarmed over by glittering pulsing geometric forms.

Mouthing a soft and interminable "Wow!" he sat down at the foot of an oak, tired from the pointless walking he'd been doing. When he looked up again, he noticed that the light of the full moon was flowing over the Valley floor. The beat he'd been hearing had now become a lush and indescribably lovely music. It seemed no longer to come from himself but from the earth and air and sky. Quite near him he noticed a multitude of strange small creatures—machine elves, cellular automata, something—dancing in a large ring upon a space of moonlit meadow, dancing so lightly that they seemed not even to bend the blades of the low grass.

In the middle of the ring appeared a figure taller and more beautiful than the rest, a Queen among such creatures. To Wayne she resembled Marijke, but a Marijke redesigned as a fay automaton. When she beckoned him and said, "Come, Wayne! Dance one dance with me!" he found he could not refuse. Leaping up from where he'd been sitting, he bowed gracefully as he stepped into the ring.

As they whirled and spun it seemed to Wayne that the flood of bright and dark geometries was coming faster. The bright center of the eyestorm was no longer right in front of him but ahead, down a tunnel or at the bottom of a vortex, a white hole from which the flood of his perceptions came surging, all somehow realer than real, hypersolid. Wayne danced, but he felt only the floating sensation that sometimes accompanies sleep's onset.

Toward the bright center he danced and drifted, floating half-adream in a rotating tunnel walled with electric stones, every stone a panel or screen mounted in a shimmering fluid lattice or matrix dancing in waves of entoptic geometries. As he watched and danced he saw that every bright fieldstone he stared into was in its turn a tunnel, a living breathing passageway, a portal depicting on its walls dancers dancing and watchers watching, watching and dancing, endlessly.

Each passageway was a different dance, a different space in

time: Shakers shaking in their Circle Dance, punks slamming
and thrashing, pit dancers moshing, Indians doing the Ghost
Dance, Tarantists spinning, Sufi dervishes whirling, nineteenth-century French girls and Carolingian jugglers and Ku-
chean Buddhists scarf dancing, cancan dancers and ecstatic
dancers of Hathor, Elamite and Greek and Sioux line dancers,
group dancers, masked dancers, penitential dancers and dancing Bacchantes, morisco and carneval and formal ball dances,
chain dances and rondos and hasta moudra hand dances,
dances of warrior youths and maidens and shepherds and buf-
foons, Shivite sacred dancers, Chinese sleeve dancers, Japanese
Kabuki, Russian ballet, dances to the tune of flageolet, tam-
bourin, oboes, horns, trombones, double bass, string orchestra,
guitars, castanets, bagpipes, violin, flute, lute, viols, transverse
flutes, trumpets, shawm, rebec, triangular harp, lyre, sword and
lance on shield, tympanon, aulos and double aulos, frame
drum, skull drum, bullroarer, turtleshell rattle, song, handclap—

Beyond that, the impersonal Great Dance of it all, the long
complex choreography of shapechanging life, mammalbirdrep-
tileamphibianfishinsect cep halopodgastropodammonitetrilo-
bitecoelenterateeukaryoteprokaryotebluegreenalgafirstliving-
cell, dance of chemical hypercycles, thunderbolt and cloud and
volcano, planet spinning into being from cooling starstuff, stars
whirling out of whorling gas, out of the First Handclap's fastest
of fast dances—and then in the other direction, up and down
innumerable timelines, to the last dance, the slowest slow
dance of entropic maximum, the mere universal vibration of
that endless end. . . .

That, at least, he thought he saw and experienced, but now
a moment of aching clarity comes when he finds himself in a
present that feels both far future and far past at once, in a
great, spiral, turning dance pilgrimage with many others: red-
dish-pelted, rightbrainwise, cerebellar, left-handed, supra-
orbital, nocturnal, heavy brow-ridged, auditory, barrel-chested,
shortextremitied, cold-adapted, mushroom-eating, moon-
worshiping, snake-adoring, spider-loving, troll ancestral,
low-foreheaded, skycave dwelling, red ochre symboled, second-
sighted, magnetited, archaeofuturosapiens, all walking down
the moonlines, dancing, through the worldweb, singing, singing
up the soulspring.

The dance stops. Machine Elf Queen Marijke, dressed in a
ceremonial garb of feathers and chromium, is sitting crossleg-

ged by a river lined with tall pines in a high-cliffed valley so
spectacular it is either a dream or Yosemite or both. It's spring
after a wet winter. Broad-capped mushrooms jut up out of the
pine duff and leaf litter beneath the trees. In the branches
shafted by a watery light, squirrels chitter and birds call.

She smiles and tears begin to roll down Wayne's face. She
looks at him, perplexed.

"Don't," she says. "Didn't you see the new dam? You'll flood
us out."

Wayne can't stop himself. Day passes into night. The Merced River swells, rises, inundates the Valley floor, converts it
to lake, rises even above the trees until only the heights of the
rock formations—El Capitan, Half Dome, The Sisters, The
Spires—stand above the placid moonsilvered water. Lake and
sky flow seamlessly together. Around Marijke and her drowned
Boddhisattva's smile, the forest suffers a sea change. The trees
become loose and flowing as kelp, an underwater forest un-
dulating slightly in unseen currents. The mushrooms' caps begin to pulse like jellyfish bells. As Wayne watches, the fungi
begin to work loose from the soil, lifting off the bottom into
the water, the rhythmic pulses of their gilled caps carrying upward with them the drifting groping tentacular masses of their
mycelia, myriad long pale arms caressing the currents. All the
birds become brightwinged murre-like wonders, winging their
way branch to branch through the deep water, down among
the unconfusable fish. The chittering tree creature he heard
before the waters rose transmogrifies into an arched and curved
and curled thing, half squirrel and half nautilus, its chittering
replaced by a language of colors shifting rapidly across its surface. Elf Queen Marijke smiles and smiles.

"What'd you do with this suit, Mr. Takahashi?" asked Rose,
one of the technical staffers on duty at the lodgehouse.
"You've tripped most of its shutoffs!"

"Really?" Wayne said, very tired from his ordeal, and obscurely depressed. "Look, it's two A.M. Would you do me a
favor, Rose? Please remove all records of that suit's last six
hours—and send those records to my rooms. I want to look
them over and see if any of it is worth including in the simulation."

Rose gave him a wicked wink and grin, as if he'd been using
the suit for some kind of kinky new technosex.

"Sure, Mr. Takahashi. Anything you say."

Back in his rooms, Wayne found an unusual message on his machine: a distorted recording of "Music Box Dancer," followed by Marijke's slightly inebriated voice.

"My dear Waynie T," she said, "there's something fishy about our Boss Biz's plan to donate all these sensorium/simulation"—she stumbled over the words a moment, then recovered—"packages to libraries and schools and such. We need to talk. Ta-ta."

Looking at himself in the vanity mirror in the bedroom, Wayne rubbed his eyes and forehead and face. Tomorrow, he thought. Tomorrow morning would have to be plenty of time to deal with every new wrinkle. Tonight he just wasn't up to it.

The next morning he found a datawire with the sensuit's recording from the previous night. When he replayed the period of his altered state, he found—nothing. No entoptics, no machine elves or elven queen from another dimension, no dancers of any sort. It recorded the tactile sensation of his plucking the mushrooms and their smell as he brought them to his mouth, it recorded his stumbling through woods or staring at night sky or moon-filled meadow, but his visionary experience, for all its vividness, registered only as shifting waves of ineffable chaos in his brain—the last of them so powerful that it fell outside the suit's safety parameters, causing the unit to shut down automatically.

At some level he'd already known that Marijke was right about subjective states and their unrecordability, but he'd wanted to find out for himself. Despite feeling gritty and tired and strung out this morning, he did not regret having done it. A strange and beautiful vision had been granted him, and it still burned in his consciousness in all its details, even if nary a trace of it appeared in the sensuit recorders.

He dictated as much of the experience as he could into a handheld transcriber and was just about to dump it into a main simulation file when Marijke knocked at his door.

"My, you seem a bit on the thin and wan side this morning," she said as she entered the suite. "Didn't you sleep well?"

"Not particularly," Wayne replied, stifling a yawn. "I decided to put what you and Biz were arguing about to a little test."

"What test was that?"

Briefly he described coming upon the potent psilocybe and eating it, getting lost in the woods, the transformation of his heartbeat into music, the vision of the machine elves and their queen. He neglected to mention that the Queen had reminded him of Marijke herself, or how his dance with the elven queen had ended, but he did tell her that, when he reviewed the sensuit's recording this morning, it had replayed no visions of anything much out of the ordinary.

"I could have told you that!" Marijke said, shaking her head when he'd finished. "What were you trying to prove? You're just lucky you were right in your mushroom identification, or you could be good and dead this morning. Pretty stupid stunt, Wayne."

"Maybe," he said with a tired shrug, "but it proved your brain/mind theory, at least in regard to the sensuits. And it gave me a vision worth having."

"What? Elves dancing in a ring? Come on! Why elves and not faeries? Didn't Biz say something at dinner about your music being like the music of the elves? Suggestibility, Wayne. He said something about Satan or the Devil's fiddle, too. You're lucky your mushroom 'vision' didn't take you straight to hell instead."

Wayne hardly thought "suggestibility" explained everything, but he didn't feel like arguing it further at the moment.

"You left a message on my machine that said there was something fishy about Biz's plan to make all these donations—"

"That's why I'm here," she said with a nod, "and this is no hallucination, either. I was a bit drunk after our little celebration last night, but not so drunk that I didn't rankle at some of what Biz said. Maybe you thought he was only kidding or being tongue-in-cheek or something, but not me. I've always believed that at the heart of every great fortune lies a great crime, as Fitzgerald said. I don't know what the crime was that made Bertrand Isamu Zimmer a kerjillionaire, but I think I've figured out the crime he's trying to pull off with the project we've been putting together for him."

"Crime? What crime?" Wayne asked, feeling that Marijke was edging toward some bizarre and thoroughly unfounded suspicion.

"Come down to one of the sensorium setups and I'll show you."

Languid as he still felt after his journey into inner space, he yet tried to keep pace with Marijke as she left his suite and proceeded down the hall toward one of the converted ballrooms. Any slowness or complaint on his part would likely only win him another upbraiding about his "stupid stunt."

Once in the ballroom sensorium, Marijke called up a recording.

"This is a replay of Biz's run through the simulation yesterday," she said. "We don't have to go through the whole thing—just the first stop, at the Visitor Center."

They watched as the simulation moved, in Biz's hands, in a dilatory fashion, from one topic to another. Suddenly, though, Biz's lackadaisical researching seemed to gain drive and force. He'd scanned a list of Yosemite Park superintendents, coming to focus on one Horace Albright, who had been park superintendent in the 1920s and later went on to become Park Service Director under Herbert Hoover. This Albright he cross-referenced with William Mulholland, onetime head of the City of Los Angeles Department of Water and Power.

Before them, hovering in space, appeared a passage on Albright and Mulholland from a book called *Cadillac Desert*, published in the 1980s and revised in the 1990s. The passage detailed an event from 1925 or 1926, a testimonial dinner for Senator Frank Flint, at which Albright was seated at Mulholland's table. Midway through the dinner, Mulholland had begun pontificating to Superintendent Albright about what he, Mulholland, would do with that park if he were superintendent.

"Well, I'll tell you," Mulholland said, according to the passage Wayne was scanning. "You know this new photographic process they've invented? It's called Pathé. It makes everything seem lifelike. The hues and coloration are magnificent. Well, then, what I'd do if I were custodian of your park, is I'd hire a dozen of the best photographers in the world. I'd build them cabins in Yosemite Valley and pay them something and give them all the film they wanted. I'd say, 'This park is yours. It's yours for one year. I want you to take photographs in every season. I want you to capture all the colors, all the waterfalls, all the snow, all the majesty. I especially want you to photograph the rivers. In the early summer, when the Merced River roars, I want to see that.' And then I'd leave them be. And in a year I'd come back and take their film, and send it out and have it developed and treated by Pathé. And then I would print the pictures in thousands of books and send them to every library. I would urge every magazine in the country to print them and tell every gallery and museum to hang them. I would make sure that every American saw them. And then—and then do you know what I'd do? I'd go in there and build a dam from one side of that valley to the other and *stop the goddamned waste!*"

Wayne turned to Marijke.

"So Biz came across a crazy statement made by some old crock of a bureaucrat the better part of a century ago. What's that got to do with us?"

"How can you be so naive?" Marijke said in frustration. "Biz didn't just 'come across' this. It's been the plan all along. He doesn't have to settle for photographers and Pathé—he has the most advanced sensory simulation system in the world, and he's got *us!*"

"Don't be paranoid!" Wayne snapped, then caught himself. Something unnerving about this dam talk—much too closely parallel to elements of his mushroom vision. But he didn't mention *that* when he tried to explain his snappishness. "I've always hated easy paranoia, with its plots and conspiracies right there, so ready to relieve the guilt of powerlessness in the face of some perceived evil. What do you plan to do? Organize your own conspiracy, a plot of your own to counter Their plot? That's crazy. Count me out. I'm an artist. I will not be sucked down into some nightmare of contesting factions. That's the paranoia of history, and we've had too much of that already."

"Any artist who claims to be apolitical is simply supporting the status quo," Marijke rebuked him, rather condescendingly. "You won't even consider the possibility that Biz is conspiring or plotting, when it's obvious!"

"Don't be absurd. There's nothing obvious about it. What reason could Biz possibly have for committing the eco-atrocity you claim he's plotting?"

"Read on. Read what Albright said."

Wayne looked to the text floating in space before him:

"It was the tone of his voice that surprised me. The laughingly arrogant tone. I don't think he was joking, you see. He was absolutely convinced that building a dam in the Yosemite Valley was the proper thing to do. We had few big dams in California then. There were hundreds of other sites, and there were bigger rivers than the Merced. But he seemed to want to shake things up, to outrage me as park superintendent. He almost *wanted* to destroy."

Marijke commanded the simulation "off."

"Mulholland could only theorize about it, but Zimmer could

do it, you know," Marijke said. "He owns the land—no Park Service to contend with. It'd be easy to throw up a tall, cash-register dam for hydroelectric power. Quite a moneymaker: premium nonpolluting power, from one of the few high dam sites still left. This paranoia has good reason to prove true."

Wayne stared down at his hands a moment. Was it necessary that reality should invent Bertrand Isamu Zimmer and this sort of plot, because fiction would never have countenanced so mundane an evil? It disturbed Wayne, for he knew that villainy was so often so much more cliché in life than it was in art.

"Before you resign from the project for all the right reasons," Wayne said, turning toward Marijke, "would you be willing to listen to two reasons for your staying on?"

"Go ahead."

"Reason One: The fact that Biz did not demand that this Mulholland passage be erased from the records tends to indicate that he has not founded any plot on it."

"Or he's extremely confident, or he fears red-flagging it might arouse suspicions," Marijke said, apparently having thought of such possibilities beforehand. "But go on. Let's hear Reason Two."

"The second reason is that, if your suspicions turn out to be correct, I'll need your help in putting a trapdoor into the simulation."

Marijke seemed quite a bit happier as she left than when she'd entered. As the door closed behind her, Wayne prepared to dump the textualized contents of his transcriber into the main simulation files, but then, thinking it might be better to keep it private for a while, left it in transcriber memory for future need.

Wayne and Marijke, the tech staff and the walkabout experients—all kept recording and resimulating Yosemite throughout the autumn. At Biz's behest another form of storage and recording began as well: the collecting and freezing of germ plasm and even the genome mapping of almost every species in the Yosemite area. Though hailed again in the media as another grand example of Biz's efforts toward the preservation of Yosemite's biodiversity, the thoroughness of the data collection gave both Marijke and Wayne pause.

Biz clearly could not bear to keep the new Yosemite simulation/sensorium package a secret any longer. There had been carefully orchestrated media leaks as early as the six-month evaluation celebration, and interest in Zimmer's "secret project" had kept growing throughout the autumn. Taking prototypes of suit and room sensoria and the current preproduction version of the Yosemite simulation, Biz and his marketing staff decided to make a big surprise splash at the International Consumer Electronics Show in Honolulu the last week of November.

The unveiling was a major success. All the major cable, satellite, and broadcast networks carried features on it—mostly hyperenthusiastic testimonials from people at the show, oohing and aahing over the incredibly realistic simulation, the sensorium's unprecedented capabilities. Reviewers gushed and raved about the system in all the print and computer media, the newsfaxes and videomags and specialized journals—*Quantum Electronics, Power Board, E News, Consumer Electronics World*

All the varied media were even more impressed by Bertrand Zimmer's plan to donate the first five million units to public institutions. The unveiling was a public relations coup which was already reaping sales benefits. Within a month an additional seven million units were pre-ordered—months before the first production packages were scheduled to appear.

Not long after those sales figures were released, explosions rocked Yosemite Valley. Blasts crumbled a section of Half Dome and tore a not insignificant gouge in El Capitan.

"An act of esthetic terrorism," Biz opined at the press conference afterward, in one of the former ballrooms. "Little different from blowing up a wing of the Louvre or firing a mortar shell through the roof of the Sistine Chapel. We are, however, fortunate in that we had already duplicated the uneffaced El Capitan and Half Dome before this heinous crime."

"Mr. Zimmer," one of Biz's cable news anchors asked, "it's generally held that these explosions are in retaliation for your driving squatters out of the Yosemite Valley a year ago, when you first purchased Yosemite from the US government. A group called the Mixtec-Zapotec Binational Front has already claimed responsibility for the bombings. Have your investigations into the matter thus far yielded any evidence to confirm or deny the MZBF claim?"

"I really can't say," Biz remarked. "All I can tell you is that the investigation is ongoing, and we may have to take extreme steps to protect the scenic areas of Yosemite from further destructive acts of this sort."

The room exploded with questions then, but Bertrand Zimmer and his public relations people would say no more.

Walking through the snow shortly after the news conference, Wayne and Marijke had questions of their own.

"There's something about this that doesn't make sense," Marijke said thoughtfully, huddling deeper into her winterized sensuit—with the audio-recorder turned off. "I mean, why the MZBF? Their militancy has been largely centered around Mixtec farmworkers and the big agribusiness megacorps in the Central Valley. There were relatively few Mixtecs or Zapotecs among the squatters Biz forced out."

"In claiming responsibility," Wayne reminded her, "the MZBF said the blasts are a warning of the violence and destruction to come if the Border Patrol follows through on its plans to install the white laser 'death fence' all along the US–Mexico border."

"Yeah, yeah," Marijke said with a wave of dismissal. "So I heard. But why here? Yosemite isn't even US government property anymore. It would have made a lot more sense to blow up the Federal Building in Fresno or a state government office in Sacramento. Who knows? Maybe both Biz and the MZBF are getting something out of this 'heinous crime.'"

"Oh, come on!" Wayne said, shaking his head in disbelief. "You're not really suggesting that Biz somehow cut a deal with these people to blow up his own property, are you?"

"Why not?" Marijke replied, lifting her chin defiantly into the winter wind. "Who knows what could play into his hands?"

"To what end could he possibly contrive such a thing?"

"I don't know, Wayne. Maybe to shake things up, like Mulholland. To prove that what's left of the natural world is unpreservable except in simulation. Simulate it, then pave it. I'm not sure, but I'm going to spend more time with him, try to nose around a bit in his private computer system, see what I can find."

Wayne picked up a handful of snow, molded it into a snowball and flung it at her.

"Now how're you gonna do that?"

Marijke dodged, and the snowball only grazed her arm.

"I've got my ways. I know his security schedule, when he goes in and out of his rooms. I doubt his private system is that heavily encrypted, and he has no reason to find my interest in him suspect."

Wayne stared at her in surprise.

"And who are you an agent for, Madame Matahari?"

"Myself," Marijke said, brushing snowflake-dampened hair away from her face. "And some ill-defined vision of the future that still allows for real forests and waterfalls, not just simulations of them."

"Ah, an idealist! The most dangerous of spies."

The winter lingered somewhat longer than anticipated, giving the walkabouts plenty of time for great snow and skiing and skating experiences, and leaving Wayne with a bit more time to work on his private project. Nominally he was at work on a virtual tour guide for children—an animated character, sort of a hobbit-prospector, a Yosemite Sam Gamgee—but the placement and nature of his "trapdoor" was always with him. It became his private obsession, consuming more and more of his time. Since most of the rest of the simulation was cruising along under its own momentum, however, his concentration on his trapdoor was not noticed.

The architecture of the simulation's programming was many, many levels deep—and his trapdoor needed to be able to shift through any and all of those levels so that it would be virtually inseparable from the rest of the simulation codes. He wanted the trapdoor programming to be object-oriented but flexible— and extremely difficult to detect.

Tired one night after long hours of work, in freefall association just before sleep, he thought of what the simulation couldn't contain within itself. Of Gödel's Incompleteness Theorem. Of the empty ring, the hole in the map of the whole where the unsimulated country still lingered. In a hole in the map there lived a habit, a way of thinking, a subjective state found nowhere else in the entire Yosemite simulation. The vision of machine elves, dancing. Pixies, brownies, fairies, sprites. Rusalkies, kobolds, Heinzelmännschens, fatas, mubarakin. Menehunes, Hsien, flower fairies, pukwudjies, yumboes. Trolls, dwarves, hobbits. Fairies dancing in a ring. Mushroom fairy rings. Hobbits love mushrooms too. . . .

Wayne came suddenly awake. In Tolkien's *The Fellowship of the Ring*, there was an invisible door into the subterranean world of Moria: the Elven Door of the West Gate. Originally the Door had stood at the end of a valley walled by high cliffs (not so very much unlike the Yosemite), but by the time of the Fellowship, Sirannon, the Gate-stream, had been dammed, flooding the valley and turning it into a still lake, dark and

ominous. Wasn't a similar damming and destruction precisely
what Marijke feared and what his vision had intimated?

He worked on the idea throughout the night. The next
morning he and Marijke took a long walk amid the snowy
meadows and copses of the Valley floor and he explained all
about what he was planning—even the Tolkien reference.

"That's it, then," he told Marijke. "An invisible door into
the underworld of my subjective vision, into the hallucinatory
scenario that I experienced. I'll place the experience there in
the 'underground,' re-created to the best of my memory and
understanding because, as you predicted, the sensuit was unable to record it when it happened. That underground scenario,
once it's in place, we can shape to contain whatever information we might find (if we ever find any) implicating Biz in this
conspiracy to dam the Merced and flood the Valley floor for
his own profit."

"Oh, the conspiracy exists, all right," Marijke said. "I'm absolutely certain of that. But this door into the underground
scenario—how can it be opened from the overall simulation?"

"By plucking a particular simulated *Psilocybe cyanescens*
mushroom at a particular simulated location in the park during
a particular simulated period of the year. The date and place
will of course be self-referential, corresponding to the date and
time of my experience."

"And that's the only way the scenario will be activated?"
Marijke asked, incredulous. "Seems pretty unlikely to achieve
its goal, if the idea is to get the word out on Biz."

"But we don't want it to stick out like a sore thumb, do we,
so the testers will find it? Besides—and here's the kicker—after
a certain period of time, say 9,000 hours of operation, or 900
startups, whichever comes first, our kiddie tour guide, the little
hobbit prospector, flashes into operation and automatically
goes to the right time and space, plucks the mushroom, and
drops us down the trapdoor hole into the underground scenario."

"That's better," Marijke said, nodding approvingly. "A nice
little time bomb. But the fuse is too long—make it 5,000 hours
operation, 500 startups, or even less. Timing is everything. No
matter how good a mutating engine you code up for the scenario, you still don't want to give Biz's bomb squad forever to
work on it. Oh—and the explosion might be too small, don't
you think?"

"What do you mean?" Wayne asked, a bit apprehensively.

"Just that Biz's fear of bad p.r. from our releasing 'damaging information' might not be enough to stop his plans. If we're really going to hold his feet to the fire, we need a real time bomb at the end. Something not just underground but also undercutting. Not just subterranean but genuinely subversive. The potential to do real damage."

"Such as?"

"Such as, after the scenario spins off its payload of damaging information, it self-destructs—not just itself, but the whole simulation. It unbuilds the whole thing, turns the entire simulation into a self-consuming artifact. The calliope crashes to the ground, and that crashing is its final music."

Wayne's jaw dropped.

"Are you nuts? After all the work we've done?"

"Exactly. According to Biz, what makes it okay to destroy the original Yosemite Valley is that we can now produce a potentially infinite number of virtually perfect copies. But if the time bomb we put behind the invisible door destroys all the copies, then we take away his strongest argument for eliminating the original."

"The only way to save the original is to destroy all the copies—is that what you're saying?" Wayne asked in disbelief. "That's crazy."

"Not as crazy as the alternative. I've been spending a lot of time with Biz, as you know. He's taken quite a fancy to me, and I've gained some insights into his plans. That MZBF bombing was key. I don't know exactly how it ties in yet, but I have my suspicions. I think somehow he's going to put out the idea that the only way to save the Valley is to destroy it— the only way to protect it from further terrorist desecration is to build a dam and put the whole Valley floor under a thousand feet of water. It'll make the property easier to patrol, and since he's virtualized all the species of the Valley floor by storing their genome maps or sperm and eggs, he can argue that once the terrorist threat has abated, he can restore the whole place to pristine condition—after, of course, having made billions off the sales of hydropower. . . ."

"Suspicions!" Wayne said with a sharp gesture of dismissal. "I'll be damned if I'm going to put a self-destruct sequence into my simulation on the basis of mere suspicions. I know better than anyone how the architecture of the simulation operates, at all levels. It's a thing of beauty too, like this landscape, fractal and chaotic beauty across scale. I won't sabotage the simulation without solid evidence for everything you claim Biz is up to—and maybe not even then. Do we have no option but to become terrorists of the simulation, to counter the terrorists of the real—whether they be MZBF or Biz or Biz manipulating the MZBF? Is that the only difference between us and them—they use automatic weapons while we use infomatic weapons? Listen to me: Us and Them! Now I'm down in the muck too, wallowing in the paranoia of history after all."

"There's no escaping that 'muck,' Wayne," Marijke said quietly. "It's better known as living."

"Oh really? And what about you, Marijke? Are you really living it, or just simulating it? I don't know if I can trust *you* anymore. We had something real ourselves, once. I thought it was real, anyway. But what is it you're doing now with Biz? All the media say he's one of the world's most eligible bachelors. Is it just a simulation of love? Are you just milking him for information, or do you want to become the big bad billionaire's wife?"

Marijke cocked her head and stared sideways at him.

"Why, Wayne. Beneath that coolly analytic exterior I do believe you're as jealous as a schoolboy."

"That's ridiculous," Wayne said, though in truth, his mind was at that moment flashing on twenty-gauge shotgun images involving the rather hideous demise of Bertrand Isamu Zimmer. "This is about a great deal more than that."

"And a great deal less," Marijke said, sighing heavily. "All right, Wayne. We'll bring each other our proof. You can search out whatever it is that you think is proof of my having betrayed some nebulous romantic ideal, and I'll bring you proof for my suspicions about Biz and his intentions. Until then, I'll help you with the work on your invisible trapdoor and the underground scenario. We'll be oh-so-professional—and maybe, after we're done proving things to each other, we can act like human beings again."

Their paths in the snow diverged then. One moved through meadow and one through trees, but the thoughts of both were cold.

The spring thaw was well underway on the Valley floor. The walkabouts had just two weeks of final inputting before the project's year was up, and the simulation itself was to be finally updated, upgraded and shipped soon thereafter. The thaw in Marijke and Wayne's relationship was somewhat slower in coming. Since (despite all the time she'd been spending with Biz) Marijke still had not provided solid proof of their employer's supposed plot, Wayne had ample reason to hope that he would not have to plant a bomb inside the now nearly perfected simulation after all. Having spent a lot of time on his invisible trapdoor and dancing elven automata, even to the point of getting Marijke to pose for image-capture as the Machine Elf Queen, he still planned to include in the finished simulation his completed underground scenario—though without the infobombs or dam references. It would be a nice self-referential bit, a personal grace note, a fitting coda to his work on the project.

Such a blithely apolitical conclusion was not to be his fortune, however. Here in the project's last weeks, Marijke came to his door and waved a datawire in his face.

"Proof!" she said triumphantly. Beneath her smile of victory, though, she looked tired, as if she hadn't been sleeping much of late. "I've got my portable with me. Come on. The walls may well be listening. We're going for a walk."

Wayne didn't like her cloak-and-dagger air, but he followed her grumpily anyway. Under the afternoon sun they strode a fair distance into a meadow in which the early spikes of this year's grass were just beginning to rise and green. As they sat on the surprisingly dry ground, Marijke slipped the datawire into the portable and handed the small but powerful computer to Wayne.

"I appropriated these copies from Biz's private system," Marijke said. "They're all recent. Let me walk you through them."

A series of legal documents appeared on the screen first.

"There's nothing secret about this first one. These are documents concerning Infostructural Enterprises' purchase of Pacific Gas and Electric, one month ago. It was reported in the papers. What follows was not, however."

Next appeared a report from PG & E to the Nuclear Regulatory Commission, purporting to account for the loss of slightly over two kilos of high-grade plutonium waste from its Diablo breeder facility over the past year.

"Even though Infostructural didn't buy up PG & E until a month ago," Marijke explained, "Biz has been on the PG & E board of directors for the past five years. He's on a lot of boards, a network of interlocking directorates. Every network is also potentially a maze or labyrinth, though—and therefore a good place for hiding Minotaurs or making it difficult to trace transactions. I wasn't trying to map the whole maze, just trying to find one path that connected Biz to the MZBF."

"And you did?"

"Oh yeah. One of the lesser-known companies that Infostructural holds interests in is Gaia Energetics. It turns out this company has a highly secured facility in Oaxaca. One of its employees there is Eduardo Montoya." She displayed Montoya's picture on the screen, followed quickly by another man's image. "His brother-in-law is Oscar Pimentel here, who is widely suspected of being a high-ranking member of the MZBF on this side of the border."

"Okay," Wayne admitted, staring at the face on the screen, "so maybe you have managed to connect Biz with the MZBF, maybe even with the bombings of El Capitan and Half Dome. But I still don't see what this has to do with a dam and flooding the Yosemite Valley."

"I didn't either, at first. I thought Biz was going to build a dam and flood the Valley on the grounds that he was burying it under water to prevent its desecration by terrorists. Yet the more I looked at that scenario the weaker it looked. It would be too hard to pull off public-relations-wise. But I didn't see how he could get around it. I mean, I thought a dam for hydropower had to be a complicated thing with spillways and glory-holes and such. But then I found this."

On the display appeared engineering diagrams and descriptions for a century-old hydroelectric generating facility at a place called Snoqualmie Falls, Washington.

"I wondered why Biz had so much material on this rather old and obscure powerplant," Marijke said. "Then I realized how the Snoqualmie Falls project was different. The turbines are not just underwater—they're *underground*. Above the falls, a vertical shaft has been bored into the riverbed, straight down through the cliffs that cause the waterfall. The water, falling a long way at a high flow rate, plummets down the shaft, which at the bottom changes direction and turns into a horizontal tunnel. In the tunnel are turbines turned by the very energetic water from above. The water, once it has spun those turbines, flows along the tunnel and rejoins the river below the falls. How much water is left to go over the falls is completely controlled by how much water is allowed to plunge down the shaft to power the turbines. The system itself controls outflow, while remaining pretty much indifferent to whether it's flowing under a high concrete dam, a waterfall, or collapsed cliffs backing up a river."

"I still don't get it," Wayne said, trying not to seem obtuse but feeling that way regardless. Marijke nodded and called up another diagram, a 3-D topographic rendering showing a stretch of Merced River canyon, slightly downstream from the Valley floor, underlain by a system of seven vertical-shaft power-generating complexes of the Snoqualmie type.

"Again, this is taken from Biz's personal files. So is this next one."

On the display appeared another 3-D topo, a macro-engineering depiction labeled "Blast Sites—Maximum Deposition."

"Now I'll just set this image to the same scale as the previous one," Marijke said, "and overlay them, like so."

Even Wayne could see it now. No mistaking: the blast sites were in steep mountainsides, above the Merced and squarely between the vertical shaft inflows and the horizontal tunnel outflows back into the river.

"Interesting coincidence, eh?" Marijke said quietly. "Those letters, 'kt,' stand for explosive forces measured in kilotons. The amounts listed beside them fall well within the ranges once used for tactical nuclear weapons."

"Wait a minute," Wayne said nervously, "what are you saying?"

Marijke looked up from the display screen and stared him squarely in the face as she began to tick off points on her fingers.

"I'm saying that the white laser death fence goes into operation along the US–Mexico border on June 1. I'm saying that, given this year's snowpack, the Merced River will reach maximum flow rate—and maximum reservoir fill rate—on June 15. I'm saying that the majority of illegal agricultural workers crossing the border—therefore those most affected by the death fence—are Mixtec and Zapotec Indians from the Mexican state of Oaxaca. I'm saying that Gaia Energetics just happens to have a secret facility, capable of fashioning nuclear devices, also in Oaxaca. I'm saying the MZBF tacnuke blasts, in protest of the destruction of human life by the death fence, will plug the canyon of the Merced with rockfall and destroy the Yosemite Valley by flood. I'm saying that Bertrand Isamu Zimmer, saddened though he will be by the accomplished fact of the flooding of Yosemite Valley, will, through his recent purchase of PG & E, control the distribution system for any and all power produced as a result of the damming of the Merced. I'm saying that the destruction of Yosemite Valley— for which Biz will of course be judged guiltless—can only help the sales of Infostructural's Yosemite simulation. Wayne, I'm saying you don't have to call it a conspiracy: call it a 'convergence of interests,' if you like."

When he got over being stunned, Wayne tried one last argument (though a weak one) against Marijke's proof.

"These are still all just plans, Marijke," Wayne said, unsteadily somehow. "Virtual proof, as it were. Do you have any proof these plans are becoming real?"

She laughed.

"Just go to the locations on these topos. You'll find that work crews are already busy at all the vertical shaft sites. I checked. When I tried to get close to one, they kept me away. They claim they're drilling wells for water, but the hole I got close enough to see would make one hell of a well. If you go to the blast sites, I'll bet you can find small slant tunnels already bored there, too. Check it out, if you can—but just remember: do too much checking up on them, and they'll be checking up on you. I hope I haven't tipped my hand already."

"I hope so too," Wayne said, nodding thoughtfully. They both stood up, brushing from their clothes stray strands of last year's grass. "I'll be careful, but I'll check anyway. I hope you're wrong. The thought of destroying the simulation we've worked so hard on is absolutely repugnant to me. A crime against art—"

"And if I'm right?" Marijke said, touching his arm lightly.

"Then I have no choice. If Biz refuses to accede to our demands and stop his plot, the invisible door opens, we fall down the hole to where the elves dance in a ring and predict everything. We display the materials you've shown me today— enough to implicate Biz—and then the self-destruct kicks in. The operation of the simulation itself then drives all levels of its architecture further and further from mere chaos into true randomness. It consumes all its levels of order like myriad snakes swallowing myriad tails, until every copy of the simulation is completely destroyed."

Silently they began to walk back toward Biz's lodgehouse, casting long shadows across the meadow as evening slipped down around them.

"And if Biz agrees to our demands?" Marijke asked.

"When we have solid proof of that," Wayne said slowly, thinking it through, "then we send him the codes that abort the scenario."

He looked round the Valley floor. A sublime place, but in the light of early evening there was again that melancholy here, which Wayne could not keep out of his face.

"Cheer up!" Marijke said, putting her arm around him. "There's a precedent for the threat of bombs overcoming the use of bombs, you know."

"Really?" Wayne asked glumly. "What's that?"

"It was called the Cold War, remember? What was the ultimate function of the superpowers' militaries? They became the Great Simulators, building up weapons stockpiles and war-fighting machinery and running endless scenarios of the end of the world—yet never launching nuclear Armageddon itself. The end of the Cold War was the first great victory of Simulation over Reality."

"I thought that was what we were fighting against," Wayne said as they walked toward Biz's lodge.

"No, not exactly. We're threatening to simulation-bomb the simulation Yosemite Valley in order to prevent the actual bombing of the actual Yosemite Valley."

"'And it's all done with mirrors,'" Wayne intoned as they approached the main entrance of Biz's Big House. "Marijke, sometimes I don't know which side of the mirror I'm on with you."

"There are no sides," Marijke said with an inscrutable smile as they entered the bright, warm lobby. "There are only mirrors placed face-to-face, reflecting each other to infinity, or at least to the vanishing point—and us too, while we stumble between them."

Borrowing a pair of binoculars from one of the technical staff, Wayne walked the Valley and climbed hill and cliffsides, checking from afar Marijke's proofs of Biz's plans. He found that there were indeed work crews at every site marked on the vertical shaft topo, boring into the rock great deep holes more suited to the purposes Marijke claimed for them than for the "wells" Biz's liaison people said they were.

Heavy of heart, Wayne wove the subversive, subjective scenario into the grand tapestry of the Yosemite simulation's final upgrade—the last revision before mass production and shipping—and then, as a precaution, into all previous prototype versions as well. The scenario included the Elf Queen's warning about the dam and the flood, woven among all the damning materials Marijke had obtained concerning Biz's plot. Wayne did the background narration for the Biz plot material himself.

Finally, he also included in the scenario the bomb he and Marijke had put together, the strands of code which, when drawn tight, would turn the simulation cancerous, consuming itself into randomness.

At the party celebrating the completion of their year's work, there was much sadness and tearful parting among the technical staffers over the end of the project, but also joy at its successful accomplishment and the bulging bank accounts they were walking away to. Wayne had more cause for secret sadness, for to him the "end of the project" carried other meanings the tech staff could not know. He sought out Marijke as the only person with whom he could share his feelings.

"What are your plans now?" he asked her as they leaned on the railing of the terrace, the sounds of the party still flowing round them from the nearby ballroom.

"I'm going to disappear for a while," Marijke said. "Everybody on this project is scattering to the four winds, going home to spend time with their families or going on vacation now that it's over. That'll be good cover. Even if Biz doesn't suspect me yet, when we hit him with the ultimatum he might just figure out I was involved. Things will get hot for us very soon, Wayne. I suggest we use a good part of our fat and happy salaries to make ourselves invisible for the time being."

Wayne glanced long at her face, as if trying to flawlessly record it for memory.

"Will we two invisible people ever see each other again?" he asked quietly.

"I was thinking we might meet somewhere a month from tonight," Marijke said, looking out into the meadows beyond the terraces and lawns. "I've always wanted to visit Australia. Maybe we can meet out at that big rock in the desert—"

"Uluru, you mean?" Wayne guessed hopefully. "What they used to call Ayers Rock?"

"That one. We've still got a couple months before the white laser fence goes into operation at the border and the Merced reaches peak flow here. I'm sure that's when the bombing will take place if we can't stop it—between June 1 and June 15. But we'd better hit the boss with our little surprise within the next few weeks. Ten million sensorium units are ready to go out now. Even as we speak, Infostructural is reproducing our final version of the Yosemite simulation in millions of copies. In a few weeks there'll be too many Yosemite simulations up and running for them ever to be recalled, without giving Biz and Infostructural a major black eye."

Wayne looked out into the Yosemite Valley before them, where the moon was rising over the cliffs and trees.

"And I suppose it will be my duty to deliver the ultimatum?"

"Who better?" Marijke said, flicking her long hair back from her shoulders. "As the simulation's creator, it's your prerogative to be its destroyer as well."

"Like Doctor Frankenstein," Wayne said grimly. "It's too bad everyone always confuses the monster with its creator."

Marijke tapped the terrace railing lightly with her hand.

"Look, I really should be going—"

"One last thing," Wayne said, putting his hand over hers in a gesture of both affection and restraint. "What about you and Zimmer?"

"What about us?" she said with a laugh, kissing him lightly goodbye on his cheek and handing him a small slip of paper. "He's too kinked up for me to ever straighten out. I've got to go. Once you've delivered the ultimatum, call and leave me a message at this number, then destroy this sheet. See you at the Big Rock in a month."

So saying, she slid gracefully away, into the party, out and gone.

Three weeks later, Wayne sent from Hawaii a ready-to-trigger variant of the scenario—minus mushroom-plucking access sequence—to Biz's private line. The next day, he called Biz over a scrambled and hopefully untraceable line.

"What the hell is this thing you sent me?" Biz exploded over the phone.

"Just a little something I've put into every copy of the simulation," Wayne said, trying to sound calmer and cooler than he felt. "By the way, the randomizing bomb in the tag end does more than destroy the scenario—it destroys the entire simulation. Every copy contains the information about your connection with the MZBF and your plot to dam the Merced and turn the Yosemite Valley into a hydropower reservoir. Every copy also contains the self-destruct."

"I can't believe this!" Biz said angrily. "After all the work and time spent on the simulation, you'd destroy it? Why are you doing this? Because I took your girlfriend?"

"She has nothing to do with it!" Wayne said testily, but then caught himself and returned to the radical script he'd rehearsed for his mad-bomber role. "I'll destroy the Yosemite simulation to save the real Yosemite Valley. I'm tired of your comfortable disease called 'Progress,' your developer-ideology forever proclaiming 'growth is good,' no matter what it destroys. You must consider cancer a blessing, since that's rampant growth too, cells with an ego problem destroying the living system within which they're embedded, just as our own population growth is destroying the natural world in which we're embedded."

"I don't disagree with that," Biz said cynically. "I'm merely saying that, since you can't change it, you might as well profit from it."

"Then you're just another prophet of a religion for cancer cells," Wayne said, growing suddenly tired of the discussion and his own reasons for everything. "Look, we don't agree, no matter what spin you put on it. My plot exists only to counter yours. Bring yours to an end and mine will stop also."

"And if I don't?" Biz said darkly over the line.

"Then after a certain number of hours of operation, the scenario I sent you will come automatically into play, destroying the simulation—but not before revealing your role in the destruction of the real Yosemite."

"I trust you realize the crimes you're guilty of here," Biz said menacingly. "I intend to have you tracked down and prosecuted to the full extent of the law. The charges will be informational terrorism, blackmail, malicious and willful destruction of property, fraud, breach of contract—"

"I'm quite well aware of my sins," Wayne said, cutting him off. "I hope you're also aware of yours."

A silence opened between them.

"I can't believe you've betrayed me this way," Zimmer said, sounding both pained and angry. "After I brought you in on this, treated you like a brother. And that Marijke, too. She disappeared awful quick after the project ended. Is she in on this? Is she there with you?"

"No," Wayne said, feeling an obscure desire to protect her— or was it just to take the responsibility, or even the credit for this, all to himself? Was it even more obscure—knowing how he himself hated to feel powerless, was he trying to leave Biz an out, to not rub his face in what had happened? "She's not relevant here. What's important is this: Will you stop the MZBF from tacnuking the canyon of the Merced? Will you stop drilling those vertical shafts for a Snoqualmie-type power-generating system? Will you backfill and seal those shafts you've nearly completed?"

Bertrand Zimmer pondered the proposal.

"And if I do?"

"Then I will send you codes every six months that will block the scenario from engaging for another 5,000 hours of operation or 500 startups. Call it an upgrade or an update or a new version. If you take actions which convince me that your plans to flood the Yosemite Valley are good and truly dead, then I will send the codes that will completely defuse the bomb and stop the simulation's conversion to self-consuming artifact. Those codes will also end the automatic initiation of the machine elves scenario—though I'm still thinking of leaving that part manually accessible. We'll see."

Biz's end of the line remained silent.

"Well?" Wayne said at last. "Will you stop your plan from going through, so I can stop mine too? Or will you let all the Yosemites—real and simulated—be destroyed?"

"I can only say what you've taught me," Biz replied tiredly. "We'll see."

In Australia autumn was well on its way to winter. Before leaving the warm spring of Hawaii, Wayne had left a message for Marijke detailing his conversation with Bertrand Zimmer. He had also left the number of a hotel not far from Uluru where she might contact him.

Every day for a week he rose in the morning and drove his rented hover out to the sandstone monolith. He saw the monumental landmark in many lights and in many conditions—morning, noon and evening, under sun and cloud and rare rain. Curiously, he found the rock in rain most sublime of all, covered as it was in a network of falls like white lace.

Through it all, though, he never saw Marijke beside it in any weather, any combination of light or shadow. On the evening of his seventh day waiting, he picked up a Melbourne newsfax to discover a story announcing the engagement of billionaire Bertrand Isamu Zimmer to multimedia artist Marijke Iseult Osterkamp. The story described briefly how the couple had met during the production of the Yosemite simulation directed by Wayne Takahashi.

When he got to his room, still clutching the faxsheet in his hand, there was a message waiting for him. It was from Marijke.

"Wayne, I'm going to marry Bertrand in July. I know this must be a shock to you, but don't make a scene, please? Think any nastiness you want about me, but this is for the best—for all of us. If you don't want to think of it as love, then think of it as insurance. After hearing your message I knew it was what needed to be done. Both the virtual Yosemite and the real one will be preserved. I'll make sure of that. You *need me* to make sure, for there are bombs still floating around everywhere. Give me time and I'll undo Bertrand's anger toward you and you can stop running and hiding. We all get something from this. I know it will be hard, but trust me. Please don't think of it as a conspiracy. You know the phrase I prefer."

Listening to the phone message end in the dimly lit hotel room, Wayne nodded wryly to himself.

"No, not a conspiracy," he said quietly. "A 'convergence of interests.' A harmony of silence."

In the days and weeks that followed, Wayne stayed on in Australia, going every day to the big rock of Uluru, learning its textures and times, shadows and surfaces, silences and speech. He got to know the Aborigines to whom the Australian government had returned the sacred place. He learned to play the didgeridoo and make the bullroarer sing. He learned of the songlines, by which the ancient ancestors had sung the world into existence.

In the evenings he read and watched the news for signs positive or negative. The Yosemite simulation was selling extremely well worldwide, though there was some befuddlement over the disappearance of its creator. Wayne found he was being described as "reclusive" and "eccentric" and "inaccessible" in the media—even by his own agent and lawyers, whom he had kept in distant touch with since the end of the project. In other news, not about him but related to him, a US District Court issued an injunction against the activation of the white laser death fence, on constitutional grounds. Gaia Energetics and Pacific Gas & Electric announced the joint construction of a major new facility in Oaxaca—the opening of which was supposed to vastly improve the region's long-dismal financial straits and thereby reduce emigration from the area. As Biz's intended, Marijke was being profiled a great deal in the media. Biz himself was often quoted to the effect that his fiancée was having a profound effect on his thinking.

Wayne contacted his tech-staff friend Rose, who was still living in the Oakhurst area near Yosemite, and asked her to look into a few things. From her he learned that work on the "wells" in Yosemite had been discontinued and they were now being filled and sealed—something to do with the wedding, Rose said, which was to be a regal affair by all accounts. At the end of June, Wayne sent the bride and groom the most appropriate gift he could think of: codes to prevent the destruction of the simulation for another 5,000 hours or 500 startups, whichever came first.

One evening in August, Wayne discovered that he was in the news again too: he was rumored to be planning to do for the great rock of Uluru in Australia what he had already done for Yosemite. Though it was most likely meant merely as a news item, Wayne read it as a personal message from afar, from Biz and Marijke. "We know where you are," it said to him, "but the police or the hit squads haven't come to get you. Any of us could betray the others, but perhaps we should think of laying that history down now. This is a peace offering, and a job offer, if you're interested."

Sitting on Uluru that night, with its Aboriginal singers under the full moon, Wayne heard in their songs their ancestors singing, back and back and back, the songlines running from here to Everest and Kilimanjaro and Fuji, to Mont Blanc and Machu Picchu and El Capitan and Half Dome, to every point on the planet and even beyond, a vast maze and net and webwork of music. As in his vision of nearly a year before, the rocks themselves were alive, passageways into the dance of forever. He heard a melody which could not be completely drowned out by water or forgotten by mind or captured by art: silent stone making everywhere a song, at once far away and near, the voice of Eternity singing the music of what happens.

That night, he listened.

A BELLY FULL OF STARS

Michael Gust

The two angels watch the woman closely, they gesture and point with tiny stick arms. Their whispers drift on sibilant wings, invisible currents stirring the Italianate hush.

Across the immensity that is her room stands the woman, her madonna eyes cast downward. Before her, a massive book lies open upon a white marble podium. At her feet rests a crystal flask of green water. Her red lips move silently, her brow furrows, a single finger traces the lines, but she listens to the angels and not the words in her head.

She yawns, trying to rout the odd unease that has crept over her. The whispering circles around her golden halo, past her porcelain ears. She stops her reading, no longer able to pretend. Now she can only wait. It will be soon.

With a shriek, a door opens and she turns, her eyes widening, her hands rising to cover her ears. The whispering is gone and in the dead silence that follows she steps back from the podium, kicking over the flask. The water hits the tiles, dark, like wine, like blood from a gutted lamb.

The doorway is gone, the third angel has arrived. Tall, luminous and shining, the long hair flowing down over his shoulders golden except for a streak of white above each ear, he crosses the room, ebony wings rippling. His bare feet slap softly into the dark, spreading puddle and he kneels before her, the edge of his white robe staining purple.

The angel pulls a single white lily from his robe and holds it out to the woman. She breathes a sigh of relief and takes it between her trembling fingers. It is frigid, an icy spike, and her trembling turns to shivers. For an instant she wants to drop the flower, wants to turn and run. The urge dies as quickly as it rises and she stares down at the flask, at the remaining water sloshing gently against the smooth glass. The angel snorts suddenly, contemptuously, and stands.

"Look at me. Don't you know me?"

She looks. His eyes are black now and glowing, and unexpectedly he reaches out and strokes her breasts, her stomach and lower. She gasps but the angel only smiles, oily and unctuous, and speaks. "A child. Will be. Yours." He removes his hand and begins to laugh.

She frowns and shakes her head, slowly stepping back from the laughing figure with his pale, violating hands. The lily warms now from the heat of her flesh and, as it does, yellow wax drips from the petals and down the stem. Beneath the wax the bloom is black like the angel's eyes. The wine stain on his robe has spread upward, the cloth is a blood red. His laughter rises; it fills the room, fills her head, it blinds her. She presses her eyes shut, swallows hard and dry, and when she thinks she can no longer stand it, the laughter stops. Its taunting echo lingers, then dies.

When the woman finally opens her eyes the dark angel is gone. The black lily burns between her fingers and she drops it into the puddle at her feet. It begins to smoke.

The two angels whisper and point. The woman begins to cry. This isn't right, she thinks, this isn't how it goes.

Little Anna moans in her sleep, cradling her swollen belly with a child's hands. In the next room, Sebastian snatches the painting from its easel and shakes it, growling. The painting slips from his oil-slickened fingers and skids across the floor. He cries out and rushes out to it. One corner is abraded where it has struck the rough stone floor of the studio. Sebastian returns the painting to the easel and, bringing the lamp flame close to the surface, inspects it for damage. Nothing else, only the scraped corner.

He steps back and stares sullenly at the canvas. The angel closest to Mary is smirking again! The bastard! Sebastian sighs, carefully scrapes away the face, and pours himself a glass of wine. Outside his window, the Florentine landscape floats in the mist of a steamy Italian afternoon. The narrow streets are unusually empty, even for this hour. Only the barking of dogs breaks the odd silence. It is as if everyone is sleeping but he.

He wipes sweat from his brow with a dirty rag and stares at the blank spot on the canvas. It seems to float above the paint, an empty void, proof of his failure. For an instant he is tempted to take a knife to the figure, to cut it out and burn it.

God, how he hates the third angel! It eludes him, it defies him. It is a devil, he thinks, not an angel. He pours a second glass and listens to Anna make soft sleeping noises in the next room.

Beautiful Anna, with her round body. His Anna, with those soft brown eyes that glow with a deep, undying light. A light that never ceases to astound him. How many times has he prayed for the talent to bring it to canvas. That light is life itself.

Each night he holds her naked body in his arms, stroking her hair, kissing her angry breasts, her protruding belly, her lips. This girl-child with child is a miracle beyond Sebastian's comprehension. Beauty reproducing beauty, he thinks with a sigh. Only women can do this. He stares down into the wine and sneers at his reflection.

Sebastian the artist. Hah! Sebastian the beast. Sebastian the maker of messes! He makes a mess of his life just like he makes a mess of his canvases. Even in lovemaking, in the dark of night, with Anna's passionate moans filling his ears, all he leaves is a mess. He is a true beast, he thinks, a despicable thing, fat and ugly, with black hairs protruding from every orifice and the stench of death clinging to him with sharp bat claws. He stares down at the scars where he has slashed himself in fits of self-loathing. Oh, how he hates himself, hates this horrible body, hates his weakness and his incomplete, dull talent.

He tips the glass and swallows greedily. The wine gurgles from the corners of his mouth and down his cheeks, over the week-old stubble. Little Anna will soon awake from her nap and call out for him. Sebastian frowns at the canvas. He has failed her again. He pours a third glass.

He only wants to give her a beautiful thing, something to equal her own pregnant splendor. A fourth glass and Sebastian wonders again why she chose him, a third-rate court painter, a smudger of background trees and floating clouds. With her beauty she could have had any of the apprentices, even Antonio, the master's favorite.

He stares again at the empty face of the third angel, at the blank oval of canvas, at that shock of gold hair with a silver streak over each ear. He was so close! Why couldn't this time be different? Just for once, why couldn't he finish a work the way he started, with strength and vision?

The wine swirls through Sebastian's blood, mingling red with red; the memory haunts him. He had dreamed himself painting the greatest of all the Annunciations. Gabriel announcing to Mary the coming of the Child. In his dream it was the most beautiful, most powerful Annunciation ever. Greater than Tura's, Da Vinci's, greater even than Lippi's. The greatest in all of Florence or Rome. A masterwork.

He had slipped from bed and tiptoed to the studio, shaking under the spell of the vision. As he set up the easel by candlelight he feared it would not come. He feared that the dream was just that, an entertainment in the dark, a sparkling wonder. But, unbelievably, the vision flowed directly onto canvas, unaltered, all the vivid detail, all the subtle textures and colors, the revolutionary figural relationships, all forming beneath his brush just as he had dreamed them. Days at the court studio became intolerable. He could only think of his painting.

Every evening he would rush home, deaf to the queries and taunts of the other court painters and, having looked in on Anna, would go straight to the canvas. He painted in a near-trance, the brush gliding along invisible curves, the colors springing perfect from under the bristles, the beautiful forms almost vibrating off the canvas. As he painted, he daydreamed of the stir he would cause when he unveiled it in the court studio. He could almost see the admiration in the Master's eyes. Even Antonio would have to treat him with respect.

But he would not sell it. No! After all at court had seen it and gnashed their teeth at its beauty he would bring it home, back to the place of its birth and, there, lay it at Anna's feet. She would see it for the first time, his gift to her.

But now, so near the end, his true nature had returned. Now, so close to perfection, he begins the terrible slide back into loathsome mediocrity.

Sebastian turns the painting to the wall, leaves the house, and goes to the tavern. As night brings darkness and a cool breeze into the Florentine streets he staggers back up to their two-room garret, falls into bed next to his Anna and dreams, again, of stars.

They are everywhere, millions of them, every night, in his dream, burning, burning. Every night a face forms within the stars and looks down at him. Where the eyes would be are spiral clusters, twinkling pinpoints. Lips move, constellations shift. Each night, a whisper in Sebastian's ear. Each night he cannot hear it. Will not.

But this night is different. Tonight, exhausted from suffering and confused by the wine, he weakens. And lets the words in.

He awakes with a start, trembling all over, cold, greasy sweat matting the hairs on his back. Next to him, Anna groans. He stares at her belly, rising and falling softly under the thin sheet. Points of light seem to sparkle there, he thinks. His love has a belly full of stars. He bites his lip till it bleeds and watches her in the thin moonlight. He reaches out to touch it, to feel again for the thousandth time that miracle beneath her breasts, but something stops his hand. He cannot touch it. Only one miracle per man. He must choose.

Mary steps around the smoking pool and crosses the room to a large, arched window, flanked by columns. This is wrong, she thinks, all wrong. Below, in the piazza, it is still day, but on the far side of town a thick darkness crowds round the city walls. In that brooding bluster a single window glows a fiery red. A window to another universe, she thinks, a window to hell. The sky just outside is a quiet blue, while across the city another sky swirls with violent greens, vermilion reds, blacks beyond blacks. Mary trembles and cannot look away. It is wrong, so very wrong.

Sunrise. Sebastian mixes his oils and stares at the painting. All through the night he had denied the promise behind those four words. Denied that he would even consider it. Finally, shivering in the deepest cradle of despair, he rose and went to the studio, trying to still the voice in his head. But as he turned the canvas around and lit the oil lamp his mind slid into that empty oval, that blank piece of canvas the size of a baby's fist, and he was lost. Somewhere, in the clamor of darkness and pain, somehow, he had said yes.

Now he sees the angel's face, hanging in a filigree net of stars hooked to the insides of his head. No more are its features idealized, vague and general. No longer will he have to borrow from one of the great paintings in the Medici palace only to scrape it off the next day. Now he sees every feature, every pore, every line. He stands barefoot on the cold stones, the brush dabbing at the pot. There is no hurry now, he will not lose it, will not forget it. It burns in the center of his mind and it is all Sebastian can do to keep it from painting itself.

Mary stands at the window and shivers at the memory of the angel's hand gliding down her body. Never before had he touched her! She shivers, too, at the memory of his laughter, so strange yet so familiar. How long had it been since a hand had touched her so? She had almost forgotten the sensation, the ripple of nerves through muscle. She closed her eyes, suddenly dizzy with fear.

Through the centuries she had slowly evolved from a flat, stilted madonna, posed awkwardly on crude if colorful frescoes, into a freestanding, three-dimensional figure swelling with drama and life. With every new painting, the vision evolved, the space around her grew more charged, her body more rounded, more realistic.

But always the theme was the same. The Annunciation, the reverent, kneeling Gabriel, lily in hand, the contemplative Virgin, disturbed from her reading to receive the announcement. "The Holy Spirit is within you, Mary. A child is coming, Mary." Every fifty years or so a young artist would stray from the canon, but always he would be steered back. As was only right.

She had always taken pride in her job, had worked hard to show surprise, to use the correct hand gestures, the perfect slant of the head. Even when she knew by heart what was about to happen.

She sighed and leaned against one of the sun-drenched columns. Her world had faded so many countless centuries ago. The power now lay with men and stone and symbols. Gone were the sweet nights of lust and love, gone those bacchanalian frenzies she had once so happily played handmaiden to. An ever-thickening crust of cold abstraction had covered the ether, crushed it, compressing it to a wafer-thin layer. The direct encounter with the sources, that horrific sublime one-on-one union with the universe, was too dangerous, too unpredictable for men of God.

She was grateful to even function at all, an anachronistic muse in an alien age. So she had played the part and finally she had almost come to believe that she was that which she symbolized.

Until now.

She puts her hand where the rogue angel (surely not Gabriel!) has put his and tries to deny the hot, tingling sensation, like a coiling snake behind her navel. Below, in the piazza, dark shadows formed in bright sunlight. With a sudden intake of breath, Mary leaves the room, oh!, leaves the room, dashes down the stairs and runs out into the open courtyard. The two angels follow, terror-stricken. Never has she left the room! Never.

One of them cries, great gulping sobs, while the other tries to comfort it. Then it, too, begins to cry. The stones under Mary's feet begin to rise and fall. Hot winds shoot up from the cracks, making shrill whistling sounds. A rain of thick drops falls all around her, making rainbow splats on the singing stones.

Sebastian steps back and looks at the painting, shivering in the early-morning cool. The face smiles up at him, its lips curling at the corners, the ebony of its irises vibrating against the bone white of its pupils, making the eyes seem to flicker. Sebastian stares intently, his own eyes glazed, his breathing shallow. It was done! All that remained was a bit of background that would fall into place easily. He would mend the frayed corner and take it to the court studio that very morning.

He drops his brushes and walks to the window. A dark cloud hangs over the city, and everywhere dogs are barking. He inhales deeply, pushing a small, persistent thought back into the depths of his mind. The morning air fills his lungs, and Sebastian thumps his chest.

Now he can walk with his head high, for he is a true artist, a creator of beauty. Forget the four words: "Give me the child." Fading nightmares mingling with too much wine, the last strangled outcry of a dying, diseased talent, that was all. He is renewed, reborn! Soon he would lay the painting at Anna's feet and her radiance and joy would make him a whole man.

He returns to the painting and watches, spellbound, as his hand moves with a mind of its own, filling in the last details. This will be his greatest work! The room disappears as he sinks back into the canvas.

•   •   •

Mary watches as the clouds begin to swirl in a slow, whirlpool motion. She falls to her knees, wincing. The dark angel materializes in the center of the churning clouds. He begins to revolve, clockwise, faster and faster, his darkness staining the clouds black. Soon he is a blur, a whirling disc.

The disc stops and Mary sees within the suspended circle a galaxy, burning, exploding, red, blue, green and white. A child's cry stirs the stars, a cry filled with fear, pain and loneliness. The stars rush toward the earth, the cry spills out into the piazza, shaking the walls. Mary claws at her ears. The two angels stagger to the ground, sobbing in terror, dying. The stars wink out, one by one, and what little bits of blue sky are still left at the edges of the frame divide into icy splinters and sink into the earth.

So she begins to remember. A time before the present order. A time of chaos and fury, upheaval, birth and death. Frenzy. She and her lover, entwined on the crystalline bed, deep in the stone grotto, their lovemaking shaking the earth, setting up rhythms that drove the seasons. Then, invasion; her lover staked to the stone, sheared of his body, sent to the stars, crying out for her to follow, to save him. She, cowering, forced into submission, her own vitality subverted, her identity lost. Now he has returned, riding a comet of rage.

Little Anna awakens as the bed begins to shake. She jumps, naked, her breasts swaying, from the rough pallet and stumbles across the room toward the door. Sebastian cries out from his studio.

Another jolt and Anna slams against the wall, calling out for her lover. A wail like death comes from the studio and she crawls over the rolling, heaving floor and into the next room. Beyond, through the window, the sky is black and boiling with a million twinkling stars. The earth below dances. Sebastian lies crumpled in the corner, his neck at an odd angle.

Anna looks up at the easel and for the first time sees the painting. Two angels lay broken in a courtyard, the Virgin is cowering in a corner, staring up in terror at a third angel hovering above her, an expression of purest wrath on its face, in its hands not a lily but a sphere of sparkling stars. Then the studio slides sideways and Anna screams, screams because the angel bursts from the canvas and glides toward her, screams because the circle of pointed lights begins to swirl. The baby kicks once and then Anna feels the ceiling rain down upon her.

They find her hours later, buried under half a ton of wood and sand, her belly empty, her eyes blank. Though they search the rest of the day, they never find the child.

The woman looks up. Her world has disappeared. Gone the long room, gone the angels, the book, the piazza. She floats in a pure white void; her stomach, once so smooth and taut, is now swollen and pregnant. She touches her breast, her stomach and lower. As the first labor pains begin to wrack her body and she spreads her legs, the horrible wailing returns, now from within her. Her own screaming doesn't stop until the head emerges.

It turns toward her as it slides out, its eyes, two galaxies, its brow, the long empty void. She feels herself dissolve into the abyss of those star eyes, a speck plummeting through infinity. Down and down she falls, through the worlds, and then she is burning, plunging through air; she sinks into soft earth and then through stone and then stops.

She opens her eyes. She is naked and new, the crystalline bed below her shakes, the stone grotto groans, her starry babe lies down at her side. His face moves, the eyes twinkle, the lips open. The child gurgles and crawls up to her milky breasts. She sighs and pulls it closer. The seasons shift, the spheres reverse, the long night is over, the man is child, and the child is hers.

COOL ZONE

Pat York

The one and only time I have ever used living flowers in my outfit was the day my old lover Teena E. called me to tell me she'd been tapped to become an Avatar in the Zone. I guess that's why I'll never forget gluing those tiny roses to my fake nails, and how it looked, and the poster I sold from that outfit and all the stuff that came after.

The Zone is the center of the universe and we Avatars are the center of the Zone. A year or two after we've worn it or done it, all the squids who live in the real world are dressing our dress, walking our walk, talking our talk. That's power you can't buy with money, and the Movers who built the Zone and pay our bills know it. An Avatar gets invited. Just about everything we need, we get because of who we are.

As long as we are who we are.

"Mike? Can you come out for coffee? I got tapped. Hear me? I got tapped. Just got the fax."

Had to be my darling Teena. Even over the scratchy city phone line I could tell.

"Where?"

"Deli Dandy. Can you meet me in fifteen?"

Deli Dandy is one of the only joints around Board-certified D-1, suitable for deshabille, but o.k. to be seen in. I had to do my eyes and finish my nails. I used a template to spraypaint my face and pecs and then jumped into a white codpiece. Awful, but it would have to do.

I had to actually leave the Zone to get to Dandy's. I walked between the guard kiosks where the linden trees end and the pavement changes from Connemarra marble to gum-shitted cement. Natch I got stares, but I kept moving fast to short-circuit the screaming crazies and the autograph dorks. I hustled as much as I could without breaking a sweat and was there only five minutes late.

Dandy's is sweet. The food isn't much, but they have little gray wicker tables and chairs proportioned to show off cute butts and arm dressings.

Teena looked really good, but then she always did. She hadn't taken a lot of time with her face, but the result was fresh and dewy, not rumpled like it would be on me. She was dressed simply in frilled leggings and green leather.

"You outlined your pecs," she purred, tracing them with one, double-pointed, green nail. "It's so effective! God, you always look so put together, even going out for coffee."

"Don't be stupid." I chuckled, flattered anyway.

We began as lovers back when she first came uptown to live in the fringes of the Zone. Great. I sincerely felt for her even back then. And the hormones had done my skin a world of good.

"Do you have the latest set of Zoning Regs and Board by-laws?" I asked.

"You know I don't have that kind of money," she mumbled. Yeah. Like she had any money at all after clothing costs, makeup, clinics, salons, exercise class, admission to the clubs. Then there was her squid lifestyle. Rent one room and share it with two other girls, plus a thousand in key charges every month to keep control over the closet. Like most people in the real world, she'd been holding down two jobs to make it.

"I figured. I'll make you a copy of mine."

"Mike, God! Thank you!" as if I'd given her the frigging Holy Grail, which, in a way, I had. "The fax said that I can bring a second. I'm not sure what a second is, but Mike, honey, would you?"

Tricky. I wanted her to make it, I would have given my eyelashes. But this was politics. If I could honcho a new Poser into Avatar position, I'd transcend mere Avatar myself. If she hit solidly I'd be seen as a Maker. On the other hand, if they turned her down . . . then I looked into her eyes.

"I'd love to be your Second, Teena. It'd be a real privilege."

She blinked tears. "You really think I have a chance, Mike?"

What with the little roses glued to my nails I couldn't take her hands, but I put the flats of my palms over her clutched fingers. I had rainbow contacts in. I narrowed my eyes to give her the full-color effect and said with every ounce of conviction in my heart, "You'll blow the Zoning Board off their anorexic butts."

"Oh, Mike." For a second I was afraid that she was going to kiss me. That would have meant twenty minutes in the loo doing repair work.

I should have known. She blew me a slow, sensuous kiss through beautifully puckered lips. In a part of my brain reserved for such things, I filed the gesture away for future use. It had looked natural and altogether luscious.

We said good-bye in front of Dandy's. I watched Teena for a long time as she strode away down the dirty street, then turned my back on her and rushed back into the Zone.

The building washers were doing their weekly thing on my windows when I got home. The Board-dictated theme for the night was "Back to Nature." Steadman, the design firm, was having a dinner show to open their new shop and, of course, Avatars had been invited in numbers.

It took me three hours to paint, get on my wig and mold a Michael Stern nightsuit three sizes too big into a tree bark effect over my long torso. I kept the folds of the suit in place with tiny surgical needles threaded through the fabric and under my skin. In design school I'd read some old actress named Marlene Dietrich used that trick with dozens of little braids to pull the wrinkles out of her face. They hurt like hell going in, but once in place they worked great. Best, I don't think anybody else in the Zone knew about them.

At Steadman's I sat between the Chancellor of somewhere or other and May Fan, an Avatar famous for her headdresses and her sow's morals. I ate like a horse, partly because I was hungry and partly to show up May Fan, who was picking at her food like a gerbil. She kept squeezing my thigh under the table. It was all I could do not to yell. She was digging those damned needles deeper. If she felt them, she didn't let on.

Teena wasn't there. Posers aren't usually invited to private affairs unless it's so low that A's won't come. At the clubs they have to pay their way with the rest, although when you got to Teena's level, you're usually bumped to the front of the line. Nice, but not official.

We all headed to Choo-Choos after. It was the most spot then, so we didn't even discuss it. I didn't bother with the carriages that Steadman's had provided for its guests, but walked the block or two. I liked the exercise, and I wanted to arrive last so that I could make an entrance. On the way I caught sight of some poor squid getting his face stamped by a Zone monitor. I will never understand it. If a regular guy is going to do the Zone and he knows he has no taste, why, for the sake of his ego if not his bank account (the fines are evil), doesn't he stop by the guardhouse and get a general-issue outfit and paint? He'll be on line all night, but what the freek?

Most squids are too intimidated by the Zone to go near it, except by poster, so you had to give the guy credit for guts, at least.

The poor retard slunk off toward the gates and the long walk back home. It was going to be a tough trip with the monitor's Day-Glo stamp on his forehead. It occurred to me that stamping those all up and down my arms with a matching singlet might make an interesting effect.

I paused outside Choo-Choos to do a move or two for the squids. Then I returned the doorman's greeting and strode fast down the dark tunnel entrance and out onto the floor of the club.

The place was mobbed. The noise was numbing; the dampers were all that kept it at legal decibels.

I let myself go with the moment. Without breaking stride I moved from the entrance into a clear place under the dim lights. My timing couldn't have been better. The floor cleared and I was on.

I hadn't expected that the ventilation would come on at the same moment as the lights and music began. The air lifted the green foliage on my wig and fluttered the folds of the nightsuit. I positioned my long, green, rose-tipped fingers and pivoted, letting myself move with the total percussion music.

Like it happens sometimes when everything is working perfectly, I forgot my plans and calculations, the folds of the suit, the needles, the paint. I just let the moment be. Cameras snapped from three sides. It was a peak moment. A poster, for sure. I held my last pose for a moment to let the lights finish, then as the room dimmed there was a spontaneous burst of applause. A poster, without question.

I strolled over to my usual corner, knowing she'd be there. She looked—amazing. She'd worked in that cruddy squid place of hers to turn herself into a Botticelli. She'd done her hair (it was her own; she couldn't afford wigs) so that it hung down in thin golden tendrils. She'd arranged translucent, flowered silk over the gentle curve of her hips and one arm so that it draped to the floor. Her upper torso was bare. She'd painted her perfect breasts and round-muscled stomach to resemble marble, or the skin tones of an old master's painting. In spite of the place, the stiff makeup, the outfit, I found myself with a hard, demanding erection.

"You were amazing, Mike. Nobody's ever seen anything like it. How did you . . ."

I got a sudden inspiration. I signaled her to hold out her arm. Carefully putting my fingers under her elbow, I led her over to elegant old Max Tilkin. Max is on the Board, and he's also friendly enough to me. In his day Max made so much that he can now live in the Zone without having to be a formal Avatar. That makes him pivotal—he's one of maybe two or three of us who've made it to Mover.

"Max, you must meet Teena," I said, swirling her around to make her silk glimmer in the strobes. Behind us poor Victory was trying a pose. He was totally past it. Just like I'd expected, the crowd around the lights thinned out. It meant more of an audience for us. I went on: "She's been tapped, friend, so you'll be seeing more of her." The Mover crowd around us buzzed a little. I gave Teena's hand a tiny squeeze and waited.

"Max, darling." She leaned toward him with her romantic, dewy eyes and, surprising the hell out of me, did her air kiss. It looked as good as it had this afternoon, and as sincere. She gazed steadily at Max and said nothing else. Cameras clicked in the background.

Her silence seemed to call on him for a reply. Risking his simple face paint, Max gently took Teena's hand from mine, leaned over it, and kissed her fingertips. "May I salute you, Spring." The snap of cameras became an explosion around us, and I realized suddenly that the tableau must be beautiful—Max, distinguished in simple gray, my tall, green, rose-tipped frame leaning toward him with interest from one side and Teena's perfection on the other, one hand creeping to her throat in pleased surprise at his gesture. For quick flash I was furious.

If this was as good as I suspected, my own solo poster would be lost. Then I looked back at Teena. She had raised her eyes from Max's face to mine, looking shy and grateful. That spot inside my chest flopped over again.

There would never be a better time to split, so I thanked Max and swept out with Teena on my arm. A burst of chatter followed us all the way out the front door.

"Can you come home with me?" I asked.

"I was hoping you'd ask; I'm off tomorrow. It was tricky cruising around in this rig outside the Zone at nine-thirty. It'll be impossible now." Suddenly she stopped. "Why didn't you warn me that I was going to meet Max Tilkin? I could have ruined everything!"

"If you'd known ahead of time you would have been nervous. As it was, you were your own wonderful self. If you don't get poster royalties out of that little exchange, I'll be a sharp dressed squid."

"You don't think . . . !" she gasped. I laughed and moved her along to the apartment.

We made love in the shower, standing in pools of green and white paint. It took me some time to shed my clothes, but she waited patiently until I was finished and then lathered me gently. If she noticed the dozens of pinholes on my skin, she said nothing.

We made love again, slowly and playfully, in front of the mirrors where our bodies reflected again and again around us. I hadn't realized how much I'd missed her. Just the touch of her skin on mine was whole and healthy. We laughed, as we often did while we were together. No reason in particular, just that it felt so good, so right, and that we were happy.

Later I scrambled up some egg whites on the food burner in the paint room and made her eat them. Her ribs showed, which was proper, but thinner than that wouldn't look good. Worse, hunger would make her stupid. She had to be mentally sharp for what was ahead.

"You know, you should think carefully about Avataring before you get into it. You have to really be into it or it isn't any fun. There's nothing more pathetic than an Avatar with a Poser's mentality."

She looked startled. "I thought you said I was great last night."

"You were, honey, but it has to come easy or it doesn't work. You can't want it too much."

She thought about that for a minute, silver fork poised over the last of her food. "I want it, God knows. It's clean here, it's beautiful and safe, but more than that it's . . . it's alive. You make things happen here. Things start here."

"Yeah, problem is, trying to figure what's going to catch on is a bitch. The Board helps, but no matter what they suggest the Avatars set the tone. Two years ago I dropped a drink on my ab paint and without thinking I hollered, "A-h-h merde! Delete the last five seconds!" I wasn't doing anything. I was just thinking about how I'd have to go home like that. It got picked up and in a day or two Vid commentators were saying it, it was in ads for everything from house paint to antidepressants, and by the next week it was being used in editorials in the *Times*. That was my first poster. Me, looking disgusted with my paint a mess, and that quote in silver lettering under me. But I never thought it was particularly clever. I couldn't have planned it if I had a Ph.D. in style."

She nodded and sat silent for a while. "A couple of hundred years ago I probably would have explored the Amazon or been an astronaut. Now I'll have to settle for what I can."

I didn't have to show anywhere until four, so I took a three-hour vacation and we slept quietly and contentedly together, waking up sometimes to listen to the Zone buskers wandering through the streets, playing softly for the citizens.

I had to get up by noon, so I woke Teena up too.

I had a Vid interview, then a gallery opening, and hadn't thought about how to deal with them. There was no point in trying to top Eco Night, so I lowballed it with a simple G-string and rhinestones glued in swirls. Teena helped me reach the hard parts. Technically speaking, getting help dressing violates a Zoning ordinance, but she was a friend, working free, so it was probably cool.

As we worked we discussed strategy. She'd need to be careful for the two weeks before her Board hearing. The Zone loves to feature somebody and then tear them. A multitude of Posers crash every season after being fussed over early on. By the time we all headed out to the country in June several old faces would be gone and perhaps one or two new Avatars would be chosen. We had to make sure that one of them was Teena.

"Look. Stay here tonight. Don't go out at all. After last night everybody will be looking for you, so the suspense will keep their interest."

"Are you sure? I mean, what if they forget?" She'd been

gluing spangles on my glutes. I felt her fingers stiffen and move away.

"It's tough, I know. Trust is the rarest thing in the Zone. Just try, somehow, to believe me. You making A would be no threat to me. And we could be with each other."

She came around and studied my face, my normal, naked face with its plain green eyes and pointy chin. She must have liked what she saw, because she wrecked her face kissing it.

We finished in time for me to be fashionably late for my evening's agenda. The rhinestone rig was a joy, especially after the forest fest of the night before. If I didn't sit down I didn't have to worry about anything except freezing.

I had an interesting conversation at the gallery opening with a trader from Taiwan. I encouraged him to buy the biggest canvas in the place and told him that people with style offered higher than retail. Outsiders always listen to Avatars, so I winked at Celeste, the artist, and she came over and nailed him.

Later I checked out Choo-Choos. I strolled in just in time to see poor Victory get his ticket. From Max himself and in public—how Max! Victory tweeked, of course. He'd been standing under the lights. Max strolled up as if he were going to begin a pleasant little chat. He said something and then handed Victory a card, printed in gold, that always begins, "Thank you so very much for all you have given to our little enclave. Unfortunately . . ." Victory started to blubber and gasp for air until he was drooling just a little.

"It's . . . this can't be . . . I won't believe . . . Mike? May Fan? . . ." We all retreated a little and looked away. It was, well, gross.

Finally, Jethro, the doorman, had to help him to a carriage. And the cameras ate it up. We all hoped that maybe he'd get a farewell royalty or two from it. Too bad he didn't have the presence of mind to say something memorable for a caption. They're still selling the one of Nicki Direct after the sculpture fell on her: "My God, I'm mortal!" It's a classic.

I didn't get home until almost four. Teena was waiting.

"Something great happened, didn't it? I missed out on being part of something, didn't I, you bastard. . . ."

"They handed Victory his ticket." I was really tired and didn't feel like fighting. "He tweeked."

"Oh."

She was sitting in front of the bank of mirrors. They reflected her perfect, sensuous back, arcing down from shoulders to the two soft, peach rounds of her bottom. I ached for her as if last night had never happened. I walked to her, knelt, and took her into my arms, bending her backward in my eagerness. She wrapped her legs around me and I forgot for a while about interviews, art sales, Choo-Choos, and those goddamned tickets.

A Zoning Board hearing is a funny thing. They don't meet behind a table with fuzzy green cloth in a town hall. Not in the Zone they don't. We knew the date, but the Board picked the place and the time. So on the big day we just did what we always did, and that included breakfast at Dandy's.

I was really surprised when we walked in and found the whole team in place around those little gray tables. Dandy's was not in the Zone. Time for a little annexation, I guessed. I figured the owners of the place were on their knees in back thanking Jesus or Buddha or Allah or whoever.

"Max." Teena smiled warmly. "How nice to see you again. Mike and I love to talk here. Why don't we all sit down."

It went on for a couple of hours. They didn't actually ask her much. That's not how it's done. But underneath all the smoke and flowers Teena established that her presenting persona was going to be Hetero, not too bright, innocent with no kinky undertones. She was volunteering to be the beautiful, empty-headed foil for a lot of our styling. Totally new concept in the Zone. She couldn't lose.

We farted around and the end result was what I knew it would be after the first ten minutes. The committee left one by one, making polite excuses, until only Max was left.

"Well, Spring, I guess you don't need me to tell you that this is yours," and he handed her a small chartreuse notecard. It had Victory's old address and mainframe access code on it. I knew because it was right next door to mine. Subtle, Max.

Teena took the card slowly in her delicate hand. She glanced at it and dropped it on the table.

"I guess you want me to jump up and down and say how grateful I am," she said, smiling slowly at him.

"I was hoping you wouldn't do something that . . . ordinary," he replied. If I'd stayed one more minute my face was going to crack. I got up and strolled to the toilet, made sure the door was closed and heaved my guts into the bowl. We learn how to do these things in the Zone, so it didn't take long to repaint.

When I got back Max was gone and Teena was chomping away at a Dandy's danish.

"Shit, girl!" I moaned.

"Go to hell, baby," she replied through chipmunk cheeks. "One celebration Danish does not make an eating binge."

Teena grew into the Zone. At least she didn't make the boneheaded screwups that lots of first year Avatars make. She didn't get overwhelmed by the sheer number and quality of the choices; she didn't get a fat head and snub old Posers she'd known; she didn't shoot off her mouth trying to be clever. It was a respectable beginning.

I like to think she was happy. God knows I was.

I started getting Maker treatment. I even got invited to Mayo Mahony's. I can't describe how honored I was. Even though he never actually came out to say hello to his guests that night, it was a major coup for me.

Just as I'd known, Ecology Evening at Choo-Choos with Max, Teena and me produced a best-selling poster including sound, smell (it appeared that Teena and I had pheromones that didn't stop) and movement. That last surprised me, since I hadn't even realized we'd moved much and movement holos are expensive. It was marketed as a diptych with my solo effort under the strobes. It had looked fully as good as it had felt that night. We became the upscale centerpiece in every lounge in Squid-dom. To my utter amazement, I even saw the thing in a couple of places in the Zone. I don't know which photog finally won the sales contract, but my guess is that he/she retired on the profits—a nice modest squid retirement. When you've lived in the Zone, you can't just retire to one room in some little exurb. It ceases to work that way for us somewhere between free, state-of-the-art anything and worldwide name recognition. Anyway, once you've been at the center you don't want to be anywhere else.

When the season is over, the Zone moves and leaves its real estate to the loser shopkeepers and the tourists. We get invited all over. Some Avatars take nuevo-curare and go into stasis to keep from aging, but I like to travel. I asked Teena if she wanted to go with me to Tierra del Fuego to the President's weekend home.

"Pretty big commitment," she sighed as we lay tangled in last night's clothes in front of the mirrors. "That's three whole months just you and me. Sure you can take it?" Turned out we could take it just fine.

When we got back in September, the Zone felt comatose. The Board tries to keep things hopping, but they can't set style, they can only follow it. Avatars are the ones who lead. In effect, we own the place. I wanted desperately that fall to start something.

I wracked my brain till I thought it would pop and then the answer tiptoed up to me and whispered in my ear, the way good ideas always do, and it whispered in Teena's voice.

"It should be emotional, basic. It should be a life changer," she was musing in her favorite place in front of the mirrors as we were just waking up.

"How would you like to get pregnant?" I heard the words come out of my mouth before they'd even made it to my brain.

"What?" She looked at me incredulously.

"We've been together for a while now. They all think of us as a couple. That in itself is amazing for two Avatars. And it's something new. When was the last time an Avatar got pregnant?"

"I can't think," she said cautiously

"It was done to death earlier, but not in a long time—at least not here. The real world is crawling, but children just never caught on here."

"A baby. Damn. It hasn't been done." She looked at me; her blue eyes were shaded, but a small, secretive smile played around her mouth.

I was rolling. I snapped, "No, no. Not a baby. We'll stop it in a few months. Invite the cameras. It could be a real visual, physical thing."

"Oh," she said.

I got up and paced the carpet like I do when I have a great idea. "Damn! Really performance oriented. Performance Art hasn't been used in more than a generation. Nobody here will even remember it. It might be . . . a total experience! They haven't stopped pregnancies even in the real world in ages, what with implants and AIDS and all." I stopped pacing and flopped down next to her. "I wonder if anybody even remembers how to do it. Ha! Probably the same guys who remember how to use leeches! Teena, Sweetie, I think we've got something! We'd have to research how it's done and if the Board code says anything . . . What do you think?"

She was quiet for a while. She sat up and crossed her legs and stared at her feet, frowning. Finally she answered, "I see exactly what you mean. It's new. It's certainly new. And it will probably make me around here."

"It's great! Just what the Zone needs. Every Avatar in the place will want the experience."

We used whatever scraps of time we had over the next day or two. It took some digging. We checked the code backward and forward. It said nothing about it—only forbade self-mutilation or doing physical harm to somebody else, and this certainly wasn't that.

I found a Med who told us about an old technique that produced an aesthetically acceptable product. She assured us that it wouldn't hurt Teena's health, and most important, that it wouldn't hurt her looks. I think she would have said anything we wanted her to. She nearly fainted when she realized she'd be central to Avatar stuff.

We figured that it would take three months or so to get something worth seeing, so we didn't have a lot of time if we were going to hit the season in full swing.

Contraception reversals only took an afternoon, but getting the Med to fit it in took weeks. Weird, Teena had a major hard time getting in. I finally had to finagle an appointment for her myself.

It happened so fast. Guess Teena thought so too, from the way she reacted.

"You know that test thing the Med told me to take?" she mumbled in disbelief one morning. "Well, it turned blue. I'm pregnant."

I was high as a junkie. It showed. I was unparalleled. I even decided to mastermind the move from Choo-Choos to Felina's, where I liked the lights better. Everybody followed without a peep. In a week the only people in Choo-Choos were lazy Movers and out-of-it Posers.

Pregnancy suited Teena to the ground. Her breasts got bigger, protruding deliciously from her ribby chest. And to my intense pleasure, her beautiful little belly rounded just a bit. It was earlier than the books said, probably because she was so thin everywhere else. I read that it was only a muscle thing, but it was a groove.

The Med took pictures of it—crystal clear after they'd been computer enhanced and enlarged. It looked small like a tadpole, with a curled tail and a black dot for an eye.

"It doesn't look human at all," Teena said, staring curiously at the picture.

"Don't worry, love, by the time your big night comes it will. Good thing we're waiting. The Med says it's only a couple of inches. Wouldn't be much of a show right now. Has anybody guessed yet?"

She looked at me oddly and then said, "No. It's not the sort of thing you'd guess would happen in the Zone."

"Good. It gives the moment that much more impact. I asked the Med if I could hold it up when she takes it out and she said no sweat." I took Teena's hands and kissed them one at a time. Her eyes moved from mine back to the picture.

"Do you ever think what it would be like if it grew?" she asked softly.

"It'll grow enough in three months," I answered with a smile.

I went to Fahrold, the current jeweler. Without telling him why, I asked him to make a spider-chained chest piece with an empty crystal vessel, internally lit and sealable, hanging in the middle. I told him to hang on to the design, that he might be getting lots of orders. At the time I didn't know if it was for Teena or me, but the minute I'd ordered it I just knew it was the final, delicate touch.

The Med almost ruined everything. She'd figured out all the details, right down to the silver, tilt-topped table, when something came up and she had to leave town. We couldn't risk telling anybody else, so we just had to wait. I think that's where things started to fall apart.

We were sleeping in front of my mirrors, Teena was out cold on her back. She slept a lot around that time. I was looking at her and I started to cry. I didn't know why. Damndest thing. I could never have reproduced it. It might have been a great effect. Then, later, I was helping her tape a Fenzuli gown under those great tits when she gave a gasp.

"Something moved!" she squeaked, looking at me round eyed and scared.

"Impossible. That doesn't happen until after the night. Says so in all the stuff." I went on taping, but we were both distracted.

The Med finally got back and we were at a solid four months. The chain was useless now since, according to the books, the vessel was too small. Even if we had a bigger one made, it wouldn't have looked good in proportion to either of our chests.

I went to Felina's and explained to her how life in the Zone should work and she moved the beautiful silver table in, promising she wouldn't breathe a word to anyone, even the Board. I developed coordinating costuming for the Med and me and prayed that nobody at the club got tired and went home early.

The night of our performance Teena was so giddy that I thought she'd used something. She was dressed and ready early, painted to look virginal. I'd decided the theme for the night should be red, of course, and she'd covered herself up almost from head to foot in it with a gown that was full, but with a split all the way up the front. I'd talked her into a white lace crinoline to make the color effects more spectacular. I wore the chain, but I put a carved ivory replica in it and tied a black velvet bag over it.

The Med had killed Teena's pain centers earlier in the day, so we were careful not to bump into anything as we climbed into the carriage for the ride over. If we timed it right we'd be almost the last to arrive.

"I've always wanted to make things happen—to start something. This is where it begins, I guess," she said almost to herself as the carriage pulled away from the door.

We took some time to circulate. Teena was almost manic, her eyes dazzling. She chattered and laughed, the diamond of the evening.

At a quick signal from me, we started to move to the door that separated the stage area from the club floor. We finally got close enough to talk. She wasn't smiling anymore. She looked like she was about to say something to me when Max appeared.

"Felina let us in on your secret. Don't blame her, dears, she couldn't help it. It's only fired our anticipation. What an idea!" Teena looked quickly at him and then at me.

"Poor Felina," I said, "must be tough trying to please everybody at once."

"Best be on your way, Springtime." Max grinned at Teena. She still didn't say anything, but stood, still and formal as a statue. Her face looked guarded, maybe excited or maybe scared. I couldn't tell, and by then I was too excited myself to care. She finally turned to look back at the beautiful crowd that filled the room. Her shoulders rose once, twice and then she moved to the door.

We got her into place on that beautiful table. It was tilted at a perfect angle to show Teena's face and the performance.

The Med had turned out great in paint that I'd done. She had a sterile field generator clipped to the belt of her gown, but otherwise was just as I'd left her. The curtain opened, the spots hit us, and I slowly took the velvet cover off the vessel on my pec chain. Its own internal light outshone the overheads. The crowd quieted in anticipation. They knew, then, all of them. I didn't say a word, but turned and signaled to the Med.

She went to work smoothly. I'd positioned her almost below Teena, so she didn't block what happened next. I left Teena's side to see for myself. There was blood, naturally, and despite what the Med had promised, it crawled past the suctions and onto the white silk tulle of Teena's crinoline. There was also a gush of something else that was sucked away quickly. Teena couldn't have been feeling anything, but even so she groaned at that moment and we all groaned with her. Somewhere among the scrabble of the Med's instruments a humming noise began. Teena groaned again. Her belly squeezed down, let go, squeezed down again. Something white, attached to one of the instruments, began to form around the mouth of her tiny vagina. It swelled to accept the hugeness, then swelled even more as the roundness grew into a dome. In another gush everything squirted out, too tiny to be real, but real just the same.

"Oh, God," I heard from somewhere in the back of the room. Otherwise it was eerily silent; Posers, Avatars, Movers, everybody.

Like everybody else, I stared. It was small and so translucent that you could see the cross-hatching of red veins below the skin. It was all forehead, all head.

"Your turn," the Med said, turning to me. I was frozen motionless, gasping for breath. My hand reached to my chest and found itself on the crystal vessel with the model inside. I tried to shake my head, but I couldn't move.

"Hurry up, I have to finish," the Med hissed.

I took the white sash from around my waist just as I'd planned and draped it across my hands. The Med put the thing in my satin-covered palms. It actually had weight, light as a feather, but weight.

As though I'd practiced it, I turned to the lights. They were all silent for a moment or two. There was a resonance between us that kept us all still. Then the cameras blasted as I'd never heard them before. They got the little thing I held at arm's length in cringing hands and the smears it left on the white satin; the Med finishing with Teena, and they got Teena, eyes closed, on that shiny silver table.

"A moment to remember! Bravo!" I heard Max's voice from the back.

Then, amazingly, May Fan's "Incredible! A triumph!"

And then the roar that went up from everyone in the club. I stretched my hands away from myself, toward the crowd. Somebody could have taken it from me—taken it away—made it disappear. When nothing happened, I turned to Teena, my hands still full, my arms stretched toward her. Her beautiful, deep-blue eyes were finally open. She didn't look at it or at me. Instead she looked out at the members of the Zone, the hub of the universe. And her face was—triumphant.

OF SILENCE AND SLOW TIME

Karawynn Long

Thou still unravished bride of quietness,
Thou foster-child of silence and slow time . . .
—John Keats, "Ode on a Grecian Urn"

The restaurant door was a heavy brass-and-glass affair that opened outward in the old style instead of sliding. Marina's cheeks prickled in the rush of warm air and the smell of cooking food made her stomach rumble. Her hair whipped around and clung to her face as she unwound the wool scarf from her neck.

The restaurant was crowded and presumably quite noisy. People stood in bright-coated clumps near the entrance, waiting for tables; a lucky few were squeezed onto one of the two benches. Beyond the silhouetted heads clustered around the bar, two white-shirted bartenders shook and poured drinks with practiced speed. Marina gripped her shoulder bag, afraid of jarring its contents in the press of people. The coolpack was padded, but it didn't hurt to be safe.

The host appeared and said something. Marina smiled at him but shook her head. "I'm meeting someone," she said loudly. He gave her an odd look, and Marina wondered if maybe it wasn't as noisy as she'd assumed. She pushed her way into the dining room.

Jeff was at a window table, facing in her direction but looking outside at the bundled people hurrying up and down Michigan Avenue. Marina threaded between the white-draped tables until she was only a few feet away, then stopped. Jeff had been a jeans-and-sweatshirt man in their college days, never very concerned with style. Now he wore a deep maroon shirt with black paisleys and a classy onyx pin at the throat. He glanced up and saw her.

There was a pause while he stared at her, and then he smiled and stood up. "Marina," he said, holding out a hand. She took it, warm and rough against her own. Familiar, after all this time.

"Hi, Jeff," she said.

Then their hands dropped, and she busied herself with unbuttoning her long coat and draping it and the scarf over the chair before she sat down. The shoulder bag she placed carefully at her feet where it wouldn't get jostled by a passing waiter. "How have you been?" she asked when she was seated.

"Oh, good, I guess," Jeff replied, and something else that she missed. He shrugged, seeming uncomfortable. The next part was indecipherable, but she caught the word "surprise" and then "after the way things ended."

She blinked once, hard, trying to concentrate, shuffling phonemes around in her head. A long "e," an "f" or a "v," an "m" . . . "surprised to hear from you." That seemed to fit.

For a moment she considered explaining right then, but decided it was too dangerous. She needed time to feel him out, first. "Oh, curiosity, mostly," she answered. "It's been more than four years." She shrugged, smiling a little. "Don't you ever wonder what happened to people you used to know?"

He stared at her. Marina gripped her hands together under the table but returned his stare calmly, still smiling. "Yeah, I guess I do," he said. He leaned back and began unrolling his linen napkin and arranging the silverware in a precise row on the white tablecloth.

Marina realized the first move was up to her. "So, are you—" She broke off as a waiter appeared beside their table and looked at her expectantly. Flustered, she glanced down at her menu and ordered the first thing she saw, an enchilada platter. The waiter punched their orders into his pocket computer. His hands were thin and delicate, the nails short. The computer spat out a printed ticket; he placed it on the table and was gone.

Marina took a deep breath. "Are you still at GeneSys? Susan Li told me you'd hired on there, but that was a while ago."

She sipped at her water, trying to downplay the importance of the answer.

"Yeah." He nodded. "In fact,"—something—"promoted in October. Senior Research Director, if you can believe that," Jeff said, shrugging a little. "Pissed off a lot of people who thought I'd been promoted over their heads. They all want the pick"—he'd moved his hands apart, no, it must be "big." Or "bigger." Celery? That didn't make any sense. Oh, "salary." Then "nobody" with a shake of the head, and a garbled string. Marina blinked rapidly, trying to make sense of it, to keep up, barely catching the next part: "—seventy-eight-hour work weeks." Or maybe it was "seventy- and eighty-hour work weeks." Marina suppressed a flare of irritation. It would be easier with the interpreter, except she was afraid it would alienate her from Jeff even further.

Jeff paused. "And you? Are you still painting?" With one hand he rotated his water glass, sunlight reflecting sharply off the ice cubes.

Marina was concentrating so closely on his lips that it took her a moment to realize his eyebrows were raised. He'd asked her a question. Painting. "No," she answered quickly. "No. I haven't painted since . . . right after college."

Jeff looked genuinely disappointed; he said something that ended with her name, then cocked his head. "So what are you doing now?" he asked.

"Oh, I'm still an artist. Limited-edition holographic jewelry." She touched her pendant, then held it out for him. It was a hologram of a huge spreading apple tree, her first really successful piece and a sentimental favorite.

Jeff leaned closer, squinting a little. Her name again, and she caught nothing else except the last word: "real." He glanced up, looking astonished. She studied his expression and decided he hadn't seen all of it.

"Have you ever read the Bible? Genesis?" she asked.

He frowned. "Yeah." There was more, but once she had the affirmative Marina didn't try to figure out the rest. He peered at the pendant again, jaw dropping when he saw it, and she couldn't help grinning. She'd camouflaged a serpent among the tree branches; it was hard to see, yet once found it seemed obvious.

"Wow." Jeff blinked and shook his head. "That is really rare." He mouthed the words slowly—the first thing he'd said so far she didn't have to struggle to decipher. Suddenly he jumped a little and turned to the left, glancing over his shoulder. "Sorry," he said. "Somebody broke a glass or something back there. Startled me."

She nodded, dropping the pendant back to her chest. After twenty-seven years, she was used to having people react oddly to sounds she couldn't hear.

Jeff watched her with narrowed eyes. "You never got an implant, did you." His expression was disapproving. "You spoke so well, I thought maybe you had . . ." He waved a hand vaguely around his ear.

"No," she said. "Just speech therapy." This was too close to the reason for their breakup four years ago, and she didn't want to talk about it now. She pulled her interpreter from the bag at her feet and thumbed it on. She had thought Jeff would feel more comfortable if she could look at his face rather than down at a screen, but she'd forgotten how much *work* it was to lipread, and how easy it was to miss things.

"Anyway," she continued, "Iridium Gallery just down Michigan here started carrying my pieces last summer, and they've done real well. Better than I'd hoped." She had fought long and hard with the owner, who had wanted to feature the fact that she was deaf in the little plaque of information about each artist. Marina had adamantly refused. She wanted people to appreciate her art for itself, not out of misplaced pity for the "disadvantaged" artist.

Just then their dinners arrived, and when Marina saw Jeff's grilled swordfish she wished she'd taken more time with the menu. Jeff noticed her gazing at it and insisted they trade.

"Grant—my roommate—is a vegetarian, so I don't get to eat a lot of fish," she explained. "We trade off cooking, three nights apiece per week. Although he owes me a week or two at least," she added, rolling her eyes. "Somehow he's always on call at the hospital when it's his turn, never mine."

"He's a doctor?"

Marina chewed and swallowed, shaking her head. "An obgyn. Serving his residency at UIC, and they just work him to death up there."

"Ah," Jeff said noncommittally. "I—" usually? generally? Marina wasn't sure. "—eat out. I hate cooking for just myself."

She tried to appear casual. "You could cook for your girlfriend."

"I used to, but she left me two years ago. I think she ate my Jill."

Marina glanced down at the interpreter, startled. The last line read, [I think she hated my chili.]

She suppressed a giggle. "Oh, that's a shame. You did make excellent chili."

"Aha. Then *you* had no excuse for leaving." He smiled easily, and the look in his eyes was indecipherable.

Marina glanced away, suddenly sober. A single red carnation rested in a glass bud vase behind the array of condiments. The outer petals had begun to shrivel and turn dark. "We just lived in different worlds, you know?" She looked back at him. "Hearing and Deaf. It was too much for me. I didn't mean to hurt you, I . . . I was just too young to end it with any grace."

"It's okay, really." He seemed uncomfortable again, and changed the subject by telling her a joke about the Bears, who had had a particularly dismal season. She had to read it off the screen, but it was still funny, and Jeff seemed pleased when she laughed at the punch line.

They talked about inconsequentials for a while. Marina found herself watching his face, the line of his eyebrows, the way one side of his mouth smiled before the other. She remembered him sitting on her bed, laughing up at her; hunched over the Scrabble board, frowning and chewing on his lip; the way he used to gaze at her so intently just before he kissed her. . . . Her heart turned over a little. She realized, all unexpectedly, that she'd missed him.

"I miss hearing your laugh," he said, breaking into her thoughts. "You have a beautiful voice."

That sobered her up. He had told her that so often while they were together that the phrase had taken on overtones of reproach. As a compliment, it was meaningless to her. Why should she care what her voice sounded like? It was her mother who had forced her through years of speech therapy, and while it was occasionally useful to be able to speak directly to hearing people, it wasn't how she *communicated*.

Jeff took a long drink, draining the glass, then set it down heavily. She felt the thump through the table and tensed. "So," he said. "Is Grant your lover?"

Marina breathed out, relieved. "Oh, no. No, he's gay. We slept together once, mostly out of curiosity, but I don't think his heart was truly in it. He tried not to let on, though, so not to hurt my feelings."

Jeff nodded, his expression betraying nothing.

"I'm going to get pregnant," she blurted, then cringed at the way it must have sounded. She hurried to explain. "I've wanted a baby for years, but couldn't afford it. Now my jewelry is selling well enough, and Grant will be around to help out at first. So I'm going to get pregnant." She took a drink of water, more to keep herself from saying anything else than because she was thirsty.

Jeff looked only slightly puzzled at the change of subject. "Mother" was all she caught. Marina glanced down at the screen. [Wonderful. I'm sure you'll make a terrific mother.]

"Perhaps." Marina picked up her spoon, began playing with it. Now. She had to say it now.

"Jeff," she said, and waited until he looked up at her. "I want to have a Deaf baby." She mouthed the words precisely, barely voicing.

He stared at her, turning incredulous as it sank in. "Marina!" He paused and looked around, and then began again—more quietly, she supposed. [Marina, you can't be serious! They located those sequences—god, twenty-five years ago at least.]

She caught her breath for a moment, hurt. "No. Only twenty-four." The reason for everything, for her own existence.

He grimaced ruefully and leaned back, avoiding her gaze. "Of course." There was an awkward pause.

She had been not quite three when the last sequence of genes responsible for hearing impairment was located on human DNA, and hereditary deafness was added, with fanfare, to the list of afflictions no child would ever have to suffer again. She remembered the day: her mother had been crying, her face red and frightening, and she had pushed Marina away when she tried to crawl in her lap for comfort. As she grew up, they hit her with it again and again, her mother in resentment, others in pity. "Three more years," her mother would say when Marina did something clumsy, as if her mind and fingers were as useless as her ears. "Just three more years and I could have had a normal child."

Marina shook off the memory. "I want to have a Deaf baby, Jeff. And I need you to help me."

He stared at her, eyes widening as the implications sank in. She spoke before he could begin voicing objections. "Look, it's not as bad as you think. I'll get you the fertilized eggs; there ought to be examples of all the necessary gene sequences there already. All you have to do is run a virus through and splice them together, right?"

Jeff was shaking his head, spitting out words she couldn't understand. Her gaze flickered back and forth between his face and the interpreter screen. [You have absolutely no concept—] He broke off suddenly and looked around them. "Shit." [These tables are too close together.] He handed a card to a passing waiter, who ran it through a reader on his belt and returned it. Jeff rose, grabbing his coat from the chair.

"Come on," he said. "Let's go walk by the lake."

"It's freezing," she protested.

"It's private," he replied, and started for the door.

Awkwardly she grabbed her things and hurried to catch up.

They walked along a winding path in the park, not speaking. A squirrel ran across in front of them and skittered halfway up a tree trunk, tail flicking in agitation. Snow was piled in drifts around the benches and shrubs, and two and three inches high on the thicker tree branches. An occasional gust of wind scattered the flakes like dust. Eventually they reached the lakeshore. Jeff brushed snow off one of the rock steps and sat down, and Marina did the same. He turned to face her.

"Your deafness puts you in a—" Marina couldn't make it out. She held the interpreter up where she could see it. [—puts you in a high-risk group for genetic defects.] Marina started to protest, but he shook his head and kept talking. [As soon as—I'm sorry, but most people *will* see it as a defect. As soon as your ob-gyn confirms you're pregnant—and legally, you know, you have to see a doctor within five weeks of a possible or suspected pregnancy—she'll take an embryonic sample and have a full workup done. Furthermore, again because you're in that high-risk group, they're going to want to know who the father is, or at the very least a short list of possible fathers, and they're not going to take "I don't remember" as an answer. And if you tell them a name that doesn't match with the gene typing, you're in big trouble.]

Marina looked up again when the words stopped scrolling. "I'll tell them the truth. Grant has agreed to be the natural father."

He digested this for a moment. "Does Grant know about all of this? That his baby will be deaf? And he approves of it?"

She shrugged. "He knows. He supports my choice."

"He's deaf too?"

"No, he's hearing. His parents are deaf, though, and his older sister." For a moment she thought of Nancy with envy. How much easier it would have been to grow up Deaf-of-Deaf.

"Huh." Jeff stared at her, then shook his head dismissively. "Okay, so you name Grant as the father. But there's no way those gene markers are going to get past whoever does the typing. As soon as the test results come back, they'll perform replacement therapy on the fetus, and you'll have a hearing child anyway."

Marina nodded. Grant had raised the same objection—and then, to her immense relief, had provided a solution. "Besides research, GeneSys also does standard lab work, right, gene-testing embryo cell samples and so on?"

Jeff shook his head slowly, which made her heart drop for a moment, until he began to speak. [They have to. Part of the government contract. But that doesn't mean—]

She didn't wait for him to finish. "Okay. So I go to a gynecologist for a checkup. She sends the sample to GeneSys for testing. Then all you have to do is make sure it comes up clear. Change the label or something. I know it's not your department, but it shouldn't be that hard."

"Whoa, Marina. Slow down." He took a deep breath, and began ticking items off on his fingers. [First of all, there are a half-dozen other biotech companies in the metro area. What are the odds that your doctor even sends her stuff to GeneSys?]

"So I go to a different doctor. One that we know uses GeneSys."

"Second, that's not just 'not my department.' It's not even close. It's—" Marina couldn't make out the rest. Annoyed, she looked down at the interpreter again. [It's on the other side of the building.]

She felt everything slipping away from her. "And the 'Senior Research Director' doesn't have a passkey?" She smiled at him sidelong, making it a challenge.

Reluctantly, Jeff chuckled. She waited a moment, then sneaked a look at the screen to see what he'd said. [Well— yes, actually. My card would open those labs. But I don't have any reason to be over there, and if someone came in . . .] He shook his head, sober again. [I'm afraid there would be a lot more involved than changing a label. I'd have to *find* it first,] he said, gesturing with both hands. [They'll have the doctor's name on them, but not the patients'—just an identifying number . . .] He trailed off, thinking.

Marina smiled to herself. He was seeing it as a puzzle now, an exercise in logistics. She remembered the brilliant premed student who read mystery novels through an entire semester of biology, and broke the curve on the final anyway.

"Wait a minute." He shook his head, frowning. "There's something I don't understand. [How are you going to get the fertilized ova to begin with? No, wait—] He grimaced and held up a hand. [I can imagine how you can get them fertilized, that's not what I meant. But you'd have to have them extracted later, and you need to see a doctor for that.]

"Oh. That's the easy part." She pulled her shoulder bag around, found the coolpack and handed it to Jeff. "Already been done. Grant fertilized them. He'll reimplant the altered embryo, too."

"This?" He pulled at the Velcro and peered inside. "These are your ova?"

"Not just ova. Embryos." She made a face at him, trying to lighten the mood. "It wasn't nearly as steamy as you seem to think. Grant opted for the old petri dish. He said it would be easier that way, but I think he just didn't want to embarrass us both by trying to screw me again." Jeff just stared down at the rows of vials nestled in the coolpack. She couldn't see his lips from that angle, but the cursor moved across the screen. [How many are there?]

"Twelve. Grant thought that would be plenty, but we can get more if you need them."

[Uh, no. This should be more than enough.] Then he caught himself. [If I were to try to do this. But I don't think you truly understand what is involved here, what you are risking.] Carefully he closed the Velcro strip. [The government takes its Child Protection Acts very seriously.]

"No. Believe me, I know exactly what is at stake here."

[Then why? Why do you want this so badly?]

She looked at him, surprised and a little angry. "I'm Deaf," she said. "You *never* really understood what that means. I have not, as everyone seems to assume, lived my whole life wishing to be a part of the hearing world. I wouldn't even be the same person, if I could hear. Deaf is my identity, my culture. It is a whole community, with its own customs and a language that is graceful and unique and expressive of ideas your English can never contain. And the government," she twisted the word bitterly, "has decided that we are 'defective' and must be exterminated."

She looked away from him then, out at the water rushing up in foamy waves, and blinked back the tears that threatened. "It is a horrible thing, Jeffrey, to watch your culture dying all around you, because no children are born to carry it forward. You can't imagine it."

He was silent, the cursor still. She turned back, searching for something that would make an impact, make him understand how important this was to her. "Telling me that my child must be hearing is like—like telling a black woman that she is only allowed to bear white babies. It's wrong, Jeff. You always believed in freedom of choice, in abolishing discrimination—well, that's exactly what this is. Jeff, please . . ." She trailed off.

He sighed. "Marina, even if I could manage it somehow," he said gently, "and you gave birth to a deaf baby—" Awkwardly he tried to sign to her, touching a finger to lips and ear for "deaf," making a cradling gesture for "baby." Marina swallowed around a sudden lump in her throat, loving him for that effort. But she'd lost track, and had to read the rest off the screen. Her head was beginning to hurt. [—you know they'll never let you keep it. You might have six months before someone noticed, and then they would put the child in a foster home—with hearing people, you can be sure—and you would go to jail. They'd never let you see your son or daughter again, and your culture, as you put it, would still be lost.]

Marina shook her head emphatically. "They'd only do that if they can prove it was done on purpose. And we'll make sure they don't even *suspect*. The only people who know—the only ones who *will* know—are me, Grant, and you. As long as *you* don't say anything, we'll be fine.

"Furthermore, a DNA test won't reveal anything unusual," she continued, "because there won't be any engineered genes involved. Nothing that doesn't come directly from either me or Grant. Besides—what hearing person," she spat the words, "is going to believe I actually *wanted* a deaf child? I'll be appropriately sorrowful and outraged when my baby is diagnosed 'defective.' The whole thing will be put down to a lab mix-up."

He shook his head. [Extremely risky. The media will be climbing all over this, you can be sure—the first child born deaf in America in twenty-five years!]

"Jeff." She looked at him calmly. "You're not going to change my mind. I want this more than anything, and if you won't help me I will find some other way." She paused, hands balling into fists on her thighs. "It *can* be done, I know it can. I just need to know if you're willing to help me." She held his gaze challengingly.

"God, Marina. Do you have any idea of what you're really asking me to do here? What kind of risks are involved? Any idea at all?" His eyes flicked back and forth between hers, his expression open and pleading.

Marina glanced down, ashamed. [Any idea at all?] The cursor blinked on the interpreter, waiting. Of course, he was in just as much danger from this as she was. A long jail term; his career destroyed. And with nothing but an abstract principle urging him forward. In that moment she realized, with cold certainty, that he would turn her down . . . and more, that she couldn't blame him. "I know—I know it's a lot to ask. You don't owe me this, Jeff, okay? You don't owe me anything." Marina stuffed the interpreter back into her shoulder bag and jumped down to the step below. She put a hand lightly on his leg. It was the only time they had touched since the handshake in the restaurant. "Thanks for buying lunch. I'll return the favor sometime." She reached up to retrieve the coolpack from his lap.

He held tight to the strap and didn't let her have it, just stared at her, studying her face. Then he looked off over her left shoulder, eyes unfocused. Tiny lines between his eyebrows came and went and came again. Finally he took a deep breath and closed his eyes. "I'll do it," he said, and she thought she must have read it wrong, but he met her eyes then and said it again. "I'll do it."

She let go and leaned up against the rock step. He looked off to the right again, out at the water.

[We'll need to stay away from each other as much as possible. It's bad enough that the child's father is a gynecologist, though I'll admit it makes for a tighter conspiracy. It wouldn't do for you to suddenly start spending a lot of time with a biogeneticist, too. I'll have to see you once more, though, to give you the embryos. I think I can get the recomb done this weekend—I'll do several, in case the first one doesn't implant. Just hang on to the extra ones. I'll call you and we can meet for lunch again next week; that shouldn't be too unusual.]

[Okay, that ought to do it for now. Oh, and a list of ob-gyns that use GeneSys's labs. Shit.] She glanced up to see him rubbing a hand across his forehead. [I have no idea how I'm going to manage that. There should be a file somewhere—well, I'll figure something out. I guess I'll need you to let me know which doctor, and when she takes the cell sample. In fact, get a Friday appointment. That way it'll be at the lab all weekend, and I'll have more time. God, I don't believe I'm doing this.] He got up and dusted the snow off his pants. "Let's go."

Marina followed, afraid that anything she said might change his mind. Because of course what she had told him wasn't true at all. Anyone else she went to would be a complete stranger, and might turn her in before she even got her chance. She shivered a little in the rising wind.

They walked out of the park together, and back up Michigan Avenue past the restaurant. The windows were tinted, making it impossible to see more than vague shadows inside. When they got to the corner where she would turn toward the train station, Marina stopped.

"Well, I'll call you." Jeff's hand went up along his jaw in a Y shape. Call. Pointing at her. You. "We'll do lunch, right?" An L at the lips. Lunch. He started away without waiting for her answer, stopped, then turned around and walked back. Reaching out, he gently pried the interpreter from her cold-numbed hand, faced away from her and spoke into it for a moment. Then, with a lopsided, ironic sort of grin, he handed it back to her, turned a second time and walked down the street.

[I think you should know—I'm not really doing this for the principle of it. I'm not sure what to believe about that part right now. I'm doing it because a woman I once loved—maybe still do love—has asked me to, and I can't seem to bring myself to tell her no.]

Marina stood still and watched him go, trying to think of something to say to that, and finding nothing that would not have made things worse. In less than two blocks she had lost him in the crowd.

As it turned out, she didn't have lunch with Jeff again after all.

Leaving the apartment for a grocery-store run Tuesday afternoon, she nearly ran into a dark-haired woman whom she had not, of course, heard approaching.

They apologized to each other and the woman began to walk on, then took a second look at the apartment number on the door.

"Would you be Marina"—something. Not her last name, which would have been logical.

Marina blinked. "Yes?"

"Oh, good. I'm a friend of Jeff Langford's, we work together, and he asked me to come by and give this to you." She handed Marina the gift-wrapped package she was carrying in one hand.

Marina stared down at the bright blue bow, realizing what this must be, and missed the woman's next few words.

"—sorry he couldn't come himself," she was saying when Marina looked up again, "he's been really"—something—"at work, you know, it's terrible what they"—something else, ending in "oo." Marina picked it up again with ". . . tell you to have a really happy birthday, and he'll call you later."

"Uh, thanks." The woman was beginning to look concerned. It was her birthday, Marina realized; she was supposed to be enthusiastic, not confused. "This is great," she tried. "I can't wait to see what it is! Tell Jeff I said thanks. And thank you for bringing it over."

The woman smiled cheerfully. "Oh, no problem, it was practically on my way home. You have a good birthday, okay?" She walked back down the hall, waving just before she turned the corner.

Marina hit the door lock and stepped back inside, tearing paper as she went. Inside the box was an insulated coolpack, about fist-sized. Inside the coolpack were six tiny padded vials.

Six embryos. She wondered what happened that had made Jeff nervous enough to forgo a second lunch.

It had been thirteen days since her last period. Grant implanted the first embryo that very evening. They had agreed to try only one at a time, despite the possible delay, because the birth of deaf fraternal twins would be suspicious. Even with modern methods and medications, the chance that a given embryo would implant and survive was only forty percent.

Ten days later, a home blood test confirmed that she was, indeed, pregnant.

The following Wednesday, Marina was at her room terminal accessing a graphics file when the lights began flashing in the short-short-long pattern that meant someone was inquiring at the door. A message appeared across the bottom of her screen: [Visitor for Marina Carmichael: Jivval from Market Gardens . . . Floral Delivery . . . ID CONFIRMED]

Marina stared at this a moment, then rose to answer the

door. She tried to think of who might be sending her flowers, and why, and came up blank. No one except Grant knew yet that she was pregnant. Maybe it was a mistake.

She pressed the door panel. A dark-skinned teenage boy stood outside, holding a long white box. He grinned at her, offering a slate for her to sign. She did so, and maneuvered the box through the doorway. The door slid shut behind her.

She took the box into the dining room and laid it on the table. Grant was sitting, eating a sandwich; he looked over with interest.

Marina lifted the lid, revealing blue roses, a dozen long-stemmed ones. A small white envelope lay nestled among the stems. She picked it up, avoiding the thorns, broke the seal with a fingernail, and pulled out the card.

It contained a handwritten list of eight doctors' names, and the word "Friday," underlined twice. The card was unsigned. She handed it to Grant. "Jeff," she told him. Then she shook her head. "Why flowers?" she signed, pointing. "Blue expensive, wow! Why-not E-mail? Why-not phone?"

Grant shrugged. "Maybe he think need careful. Now no," he spelled, "e-l-e-c-t-r-o-n-i-c record of message, if later person authority look-closely. Maybe he think card with flowers not easy notice they, not make suspicious they." He handed the card back to her, and she took it absentmindedly, staring at the blue roses, and hoping, despite herself, that they were more than camouflage.

Since the blood test Marina had asked several of her female friends for ob-gyn recommendations. Three of the eight names on Jeff's list were also on her own. She began calling, and was able to make a 10:00 A.M. appointment with the third doctor for the following Friday.

She printed out the address, and then checked to be sure none of the other doctors' offices were in the same area. Then she E-mailed Jeff.

> Enjoyed our lunch the other day. Could we do it again? I have an appointment Friday morning the 24th, near Clark and Division—perhaps we could meet at the Wallflower around noon? Let me know. Love, Marina.

Saturday's mail list, when it scrolled up, contained a letter from her friend Jenny in Seattle, several notices she didn't recognize—probably advertisements—and a note from Jeff, which she displayed immediately.

> Marina—sorry, but I can't make the lunch date. I've got a big project coming together at work; will probably have to work all next weekend. Some other time, okay? Jeff.

He was avoiding her, she realized. He didn't ever intend to see her again. Well, that was just *fine*, then. She hit the table explosively. She wouldn't chase after him. It would never work with a hearing man anyway. And she'd gotten what she needed. Her hand dropped to her still-flat belly, caressing it gently.

"You sure not-want come party you?" Marina signed with one hand, the other paused just over the door panel.

Grant sighed, running his fingers through his short hair. "Yes, I sure. Very-exhausted. And I promise Paul two-of-us watch movie tonight. Say hello to mother-father, please? I call them next-week."

Marina shrugged and nodded. "C-U-L," she spelled, dropping the "L" forward in the shorthand for "See you later."

She walked the three blocks to the el station deep in thought, not noticing the familiar surroundings at all. She was six weeks' pregnant now, which meant she had only two weeks left in which to change her mind. After that, the pregnancy would be too far along for mifepristone to stop, and the only way out would be to have an illegal surgical abortion, a prospect which frightened her more than going to jail for fetal abuse.

As she climbed the stairs to the platform the old wooden framework began to vibrate. She hurried up the last steps and found a seat on the waiting train.

The party was at Bill and Lianna's house, in Evanston. It was an older house, remodeled but not in a modern style. When Marina pressed the door button she could see the lights begin to flash through the little circular window in the wooden door.

Then Lianna opened the door. "Marina!" she signed, smiling and pulling her in. The short hallway opened to the right into a large room where about fifteen or sixteen people her age and older sat or stood in small circles. Heads turned to see who had arrived, and several people smiled and waved. Marina could feel a rapid thump through the floor and guessed that someone had music on with the bass turned up high. "I-take your coat," Lianna offered, and Marina shrugged out of it and handed it to her.

She joined the nearest group of people, which consisted of Bill, Stephan, Nancy, Elsabeth, and Grant's mother Joanna. "Grant where?" Joanna signed, raising her eyebrows, and Marina relayed Grant's message. Joanna shook her head. "That boy he say-say-say he call, but none." Next to her, Bill appeared to be having a political argument with Elsabeth and Stephan, on Marina's right.

"Busy," Marina agreed. "Hospital work very-long hours he. I help he remember he." Elsabeth signed "no-no-no" at Bill. Stephan signed "president," fingerspelled something quickly—the angle was wrong for Marina—and finished up with an emphatic "plan bullshit."

Nancy caught her eye. "Discuss-continue same for hour," she signed, rolling her eyes. "Boring they. You want two-of-us go-away?"

Marina shrugged and followed her across the room. They sat down next to Susan, Julio, and a black man she didn't know. "Marina, good see-you!" Susan said. Julio waved a hand.

Susan pointed at the stranger. "This L-a-r-r-y, last-name T-u-r-n-e-r." He smiled at her, signing his name-sign, which was the word "turn" initialized with an I. Marina grinned at the pun. Susan was spelling Marina's name for Larry.

"Larry live Seattle Washington," Susan said, turning back to Marina and Nancy.

Marina waved for Larry's attention. "You know J-e-n-n-y last-name H-a-v-e-l-o-c-k?" she asked.

Larry raised his eyebrows. "Yes, she good-friend me. You know her?"

"We go school together finish. She good-friend."

Larry nodded. "Deaf small world."

"Becoming-smaller," Julio interjected, a sour expression on his face. His hands came together until there was almost no space between them at all. He directed this toward Susan, obviously resuming a conversation interrupted by their arrival. "Soon none Deaf remaining. Genocide."

Susan shrugged. "Know-that," she signed, her posture expressing condescension. "Everyone know-that." Her gesture indicated the whole room. "Doesn't-matter. Can't change."

Larry had turned to Nancy and begun to talk. Marina concentrated until she felt her awareness split, so that she could keep up with both conversations at once. "Film all sign—drama, conversation, party same this," he was explaining. "Try save all sign for future deaf." Marina was fascinated by the contrast between his pink palms and his dark skin as his large hands turned.

"But *none* future deaf!" Marina signed at him. "All children born hearing!"

"No change because you—" Julio made a sharp sign, like a turtle pulling its head into its shell. "If we organize group l-o-b-b-y Congress, argue laws culture protect . . ."

Marina stood up abruptly. She'd had this conversation a hundred times before, and she suddenly didn't want to participate in it again. No one ever *did* anything anything about it. Except her. And she wanted to tell them, and couldn't. "Toilet?" she signed when Nancy glanced up at her.

Nancy pointed toward the kitchen. "Turn right."

As she passed the refrigerator, Marina noticed a child's drawing clipped to the front with a magnet. She stopped to look closer. It was a brown animal—a dog or a rabbit, Marina guessed from the ears—sitting in tall grass surrounded by four-petaled flowers. Her own mother had never put anything of Marina's on the refrigerator, she thought bitterly. Her mother had never encouraged her in art at all, had even forbidden Marina to draw for years. Which didn't mean that she'd stopped, only that she'd had to hide it. Everything worthwhile she'd ever accomplished had been in direct defiance of her mother.

Lianna came in from the living room carrying two empty glasses, which she set down on the counter.

"Pretty," Marina signed. "Picture it your daughter draw herself?"

Lianna smiled, flipping her long dark hair behind her shoulder. "Yes, she school draw. She old-eight now."

"Where she now?"

Lianna pointed upstairs. "She put-in-suitcase clothes she. Go all-night party girl-friend house she."

As if on cue, Lianna's daughter ran in from the living room then. "I ready go," she signed to her mother. Marina was startled, and then felt foolish. She knew Lianna couldn't speechread very well, and couldn't vocalize at all, so of course her daughter would have to sign.

"You pack-suitcase finish you?" asked Lianna. "Feed cat finish you?"

The girl nodded vigorously, ponytail bouncing. "I finish, finish." She signed a name initialized with a C. "Her father drive us."

"OK," signed Lianna. "You know number phone?" The girl rolled her eyes and signed the seven-digit number in a blur. "Okay, Mom?" she asked aloud.

Lianna nodded and held out her arms. Her daughter grinned and gave her a hug, then ran out again. Marina watched, caught in a wave of longing. She couldn't remember her own mother ever hugging her like that.

"Lianna," she said impulsively, "you think difficult have hearing child?"

Lianna looked thoughtful. "I-don't-know if hearing child difficult more than deaf child. Maybe different. All kids difficult. Worry worry worry." She sighed, staring at the picture. "Long-time-ago I want deaf baby. But my daughter I-love-her." She turned back to Marina, looking at her closely. "You pregnant you?" she asked. "For-for you-ask-me g-y-n doctor name, yes?"

Marina hesitated, then nodded.

Lianna smiled and gave her a big hug. When she pulled back, she signed, "Not worry. You will fine. You see."

For a moment Marina considered telling her the whole story, but she realized that would be foolish, and would only endanger Lianna if something went wrong. So Marina smiled as if reassured, and walked back to the living room with her.

Larry broke away from his conversation with Nancy and came up to admire her earrings. She smiled when he instantly discovered the hidden aspect; it tended to elude hearing people, but deaf people invariably got it right away. Each earring was a dangling cylinder containing a holographic hand; as the cylinders rotated, the hand changed positions, spelling out a word. The left one spelled d-e-a-f, the right one l-o-v-e. "Appropriate," signed Larry, his other hand caressing her jaw lightly as he released the earring.

He drew her into talking about her work, and slowly she began to relax and enjoy the party. It was such a relief to be able to communicate without the constant struggle. She missed this feeling of camaraderie and sharing that made even Larry seem like an old friend instead of someone she'd just met. She found herself flirting with him, and realized how long it had been since she'd felt even that comfortable with a man.

She pushed all other thoughts aside. Time to worry about that decision later.

• • •

Two weeks went by in an agonizing crawl, and Marina did nothing. Then it was as if a weight had been lifted off of her chest. Somehow, knowing she couldn't change her mind made her situation easier to deal with. She felt calm and secure and competent.

As far as she knew, no one had ever been accused of deliberately *engineering* a defective child. She didn't know what the consequences of that would be, and was grimly determined that she would never find out. She had to make it obvious that she was expecting a hearing child.

Marina went shopping. She bought baby clothes, and toys, and a crib—and a little minidisc player to go in her room, which the baby would share until they moved into a larger apartment, and a dozen different albums of children's songs and lullabies.

Seven months later, Marina gave birth to a baby boy. The doctors checked him over and pronounced him perfectly healthy, and let them both go home the next day.

Marina walked to her bedroom and collapsed gratefully onto the bed. She had foolishly thought that once she'd had the baby, the hard part was over. She hadn't realized she would be so *exhausted* afterward. And so sore in every muscle she could barely move.

Grant came in behind her with the bassinet, which he placed on the stand beside the bed. He touched her leg to get her attention, but she was too tired to even look at him.

Marina dozed for about half an hour before her wristwatch began to vibrate in response to the baby's cries. Grant came in to make sure she was awake. "Sorry, sweetheart," he signed. "I-know exhausted you. If I can feed baby from"—he pointed to his chest, grinning a little—"I change-places-with-you."

"I wish," Marina signed, yawning. She sat up and rearranged her clothes to expose a breast.

Grant grimaced ironically. "But you lucky. You not must hear sweet baby scream he." He picked the baby up and handed him to Marina, who smiled and settled him in the crook of her arm. He hunted for the nipple and she positioned it for him, pressing the breast back so he could breathe.

The truth was, she almost regretted not being able to hear him. She was completely in love. He fit so perfectly into her arm. She loved the weight of him there against her chest, the baby-smell of him. He was beautiful, he was perfect. The pull she felt as he nursed satisfied something deep inside her. With a start, she realized she was humming to him. She could feel the thrumming deep in her chest.

She glanced up, and discovered that Grant had left the room. Almost guiltily, she began humming again. The baby closed his eyes and suckled sweetly.

The next afternoon brought an unexpected visitor. Marina happened to be up getting a glass of orange juice when the lights began flashing, short-short-long. She walked to the front door and pushed a button on the panel. Red LED words appeared on the tiny screen: [Visitor for Marina Carmichael: Jeffrey Langford . . . ID CONFIRMED]

She blinked, surprised, then opened the door. Jeff smiled awkwardly. "Hi! Come on in," she said. Grant came up as he did so. "Grant, this is Jeff Langford."

"Hi," Grant said aloud. He extended a hand, and the two men shook. Marina tugged at Jeff's other arm. "Come on," she urged, "come see the baby." She led him back to her room, where the baby was nestled in the wicker bassinet next to her bed. She pulled the interpreter out of the bag she'd brought from the hospital and thumbed it on.

[He's beautiful,] Jeff said. He looked concerned, though, and Marina touched his arm.

"He's fine," she said. "We're both fine."

He nodded, but the worried look didn't dissipate. "What's his name?" he asked.

"I don't know, yet." She smiled. "We wanted to get to know him first, before we picked out a permanent name."

Jeff nodded. Marina gazed down at the baby. She touched one tiny curled hand, marveling at its softness.

Jeff touched her arm to get her attention. [You should talk to him, you know. Babies respond to the sound of their mothers' voices.] She looked up in time to catch his wistful smile. "And I always told you you had a beautiful voice."

She gave a small laugh, even though she didn't think the joke was very funny. Jeff didn't smile at all, and suddenly the expression on his face registered. It was more than just concern, it was . . . guilt. He wouldn't meet her eyes. Dread settled in the pit of her stomach.

"What," she said. When he didn't reply, she said it again,

loud enough that she could feel the rumble in her chest. "Jeff, what!"

He looked away, then back, defiantly. "He's not deaf, Marina. I didn't do it."

Marina thought she must have misunderstood, but the words were there on her screen, in stark and terrible confirmation. She turned and stared at the sleeping baby. Hearing. My child is hearing. It didn't mean anything to her yet.

"Why." It was all she could think of to say. But before he could answer, the rest exploded from her in a rush. "I thought you understood, how important it was, you said—Oh! You never told me! Nine-months pregnant I, you-tell-me nothing, all-time baby hearing!" She began to cry. "Why? Why you do this? Why not you-tell-me beginning 'no, can't help-you I'?"

He was staring at her, confused, and she realized that she had stopped vocalizing and was only signing, hands jerking with grief and anger. She forced herself to slow down and speak.

"You had no right to make that decision for me. You tricked me into bearing a child I did not want. This was *my* baby, *my* choice, and if you didn't want to take the risk, you could have just told me. You offered to help me and then you chose to back out and save your own skin, and didn't even have the guts to tell me. Or did you *want* to see me suffer? Acting out some little revenge fantasy because I dumped you five years ago? How could you be so hateful?"

He shook his head, pleading. "I didn't do it to save my own skin, whatever you might think. And I don't want to see you hurt." He reached out toward her arm and she jerked it away. His hand dropped awkwardly. [I *wanted* to help you, Marina. I tried, but I just couldn't. You weren't only making a choice for yourself, don't you understand—you were making one for that baby, too, one that he would have to live with all his life!]

"Oh, so you think you're playing the great hero," she sneered, "rescuing this little innocent child from the terrible handicap his mother wished to impose upon him?" Her wristband began to vibrate, but she ignored it.

[No, I *don't* think that deafness has to be a handicap. But it was different for you, Marina. You had the chance to make friends with people like yourself, your own age. But the last deaf child was born twenty-five years ago! You know how conformist kids are; they all want to wear the same brand of jeans, for god's sake. Do you really think he wouldn't resent being the only one who couldn't hear? Did you ever think, what's to stop him from getting a cochlear implant the moment he's old enough to understand he has that choice?]

That shook her, and she didn't say anything. She hadn't thought of that at all, that her son might rebel and *choose* to be hearing. The same way, as a teenager, she'd finally stopped trying to please her mother and embraced the Deaf world. Suddenly she thought of Lianna's daughter, who had gone off to a hearing friend's house rather than stay with the adults at the Deaf party. And Lianna had let her. And the girl had signed to her mother, and hugged her before she went.

"Marina, please try to understand." He gestured toward the bassinet. "He would have been so terribly, terribly alone."

"He would have had me." And behind that, the other thought, the one she didn't say: and I would have him. The way she'd never really had anyone—not Jeff, not even dear Grant, or any of her other friends or lovers down the years, even the Deaf ones. Not her own mother.

She stared down at the child, his face mottled red and his mouth open in a scream. He would grow up part of the hearing world, and she would never understand him. They would be separate forever. All the dreams she had, all the things she had wanted to share with her child, all of them crumbled into dust. He would be ashamed of her, his deaf mother, the way her mother had been ashamed of her deaf daughter.

Jeff made a small motion. She had forgotten he was there, but now she looked up, hatefully. "Get out. Get the fuck out and don't ever come near me again." She threw the interpreter at the bed.

He stared sorrowfully at her for a moment, and then started for the door. In the doorway he turned around again, and waited until she gave in and glared up at him. He spoke slowly and carefully, making sure she had time to speechread. "If you love him, Marina, it won't matter that he can hear. He will learn your language and your culture because it is yours and he loves you." Then he was gone, and she collapsed onto the bed, curled up, and began to sob. Her watch was still vibrating, and she pulled it off and flung it across the room.

Sometime later, Grant came in. He didn't ask why she had been crying, so she assumed Jeff must have told him. She was grateful not to have to explain. He didn't say anything, just sat on the side of the bed and stroked her hair off her forehead.

"You know," he said after a while, speaking and signing together, "when scientists prove gay g-e-n-e-t-i-c finish, gay almost become class" —he paused, "d-e-f-e-c-t," he spelled, "same deaf. Only because many many of us . . ." He looked off for a moment, then spoke in English only. "And still the political climate could reverse again at any time." He turned back to her, taking her hands in his. "I understand what you are losing, Marina, what you fear. And the battle you must fight.

"But do it yourself, love. Not through your child. Your son doesn't deserve your love any less just because he is different from you." He leaned forward and kissed her gently on the cheek. "You think about," he signed. "Now, I believe you need chocolate milk s-h-a-k-e. Good?"

Marina wiped tears off her cheek and nodded. Grant smiled. "B-right-B," he signed.

After he left, she leaned over and looked at her son, sleeping now on his stomach in the bassinet. Because he is different from me, she thought.

She thought about her own mother, who must have wanted so much for her daughter to be like herself. How frustrating my deafness must have been for her, Marina realized suddenly. A fundamental difference that permeated every aspect of her life, completely alien and . . . frightening. Abruptly her perspective shifted, and Marina could see her mother's actions as born, not of resentment or hatred, but of confusion and fear. It didn't make them any better, but at least she understood, a little.

She brushed the baby's thin down of hair with her fingertips. In a moment of brutal self-honesty, Marina acknowledged that above anything else, her son had been an act of defiance toward her mother, who had shamed her every day of her life for not being a "normal" child. And if she resented her own son for not being Deaf, what was the difference?

She reached into the bassinet and picked up the baby. He stirred and yawned, his tiny mouth open wide, and nuzzled sweetly against her neck. She thought of Lianna and her daughter, holding each other. Marina rested her cheek on the top of the baby's soft head and made him a silent promise.

I will not make the mistake my mother did, she told him. *I will not try to mold you selfishly in my own image. No matter how hard it is. I will let you grow to be your own person, and take joy in that*. She squeezed her eyes shut against the pain expanding in her chest, and tears tracked across her nose, dampening the baby's fine hair. *Even if it means you grow away from me.*

When she looked up again her gaze fell on the disc player, dusty on its table in the corner by the crib. She walked over to it and flipped through the rack of minidiscs, pulling one out. It was still in its ricepaper wrapper, and she tore at it one-handed, holding the baby against her chest, reluctant to put him down even for a minute. Afraid that this tenuous bond might break. She put the disc in the tray and pushed the play button.

The quality of the silence in the room did not change at all. The afternoon sunlight streamed gold through the thin ivory curtains as Marina held her son in both arms and danced to her own internal rhythm.

THE
BREAKTHROUGH

Paul Park

After getting her certificate, Susan began working as a special education teacher at Drury High School in North Adams. There, in the spring of her third year, she saw a videotape which described an astonishing new therapy. This new technique was called facilitated communication. Because of it children who suffered from severe communication disorders, who had grown up essentially without spoken language, were now being mainstreamed into ordinary high school classes. Dismissed as retarded their whole lives, now they were writing haiku. They were taking history and mathematics.

At Drury there were nine kids in her class. Progress was slow and unsustained with most of them. And the parents were no help. Often she felt like a babysitter rather than a teacher. She had thought about quitting; all year she had been frustrated and depressed. But that summer she spent her own money for a ten-week course in facilitated communication at a clinic near Syracuse.

Susan White was a skeptical person. Alone in her apartment in North Adams, she had watched the videotape several times. She had read books and articles, including one by an autistic man who was now applying to college. It seemed too good to be true, so that when she arrived at the clinic, she was relieved to be disappointed, in a way. None of the children they were working with had achieved those kinds of results.

The most impressive part of the course was the morale of the staff and the enthusiasm of the parents, some of whom had moved from long distances away. Susan spoke to a mother who had moved from the Midwest. "I knew if I just kept working at it I could find a way to reach him. I knew there was someone really in there, and it was like he was hidden by his disability. But I could see him sometimes in little moments."

She was talking about her son, who was learning that summer to spell out what he wanted on his keyboard. "Juice," he would say. "Weres Momy?" These messages, so simple and unexpected, were enough to make his mother cry.

For Susan that was the difference: these people still had hope. They hadn't given up on their own children. So many of the parents and teachers she dealt with in North Adams, they thought their responsibilities were over if the kids were clean and fed and got their medication. Anything else was too much for them, and they would close their eyes rather than see the obvious, the small flickers of need or loneliness or brilliance. You could understand it. They were sick of being disappointed.

But the premise behind facilitated communication was one of hope, of risk. A child's disability was like a wall, a barrier, and the job of the teacher was not to add to it, but to break it down. Communication disorders like autism were simply that—an obstacle. They had nothing to do with cognition or intelligence or perception.

The boy from the Midwest was named Peter. He was ten years old. He had any number of alarming peculiarities: he could not speak. Around adults or other children he would fidget constantly. He would rock back and forth, and sometimes he would flap his left hand next to his ear. He would distort his face; he wouldn't look at you. When you spoke to him, he would whistle and cry as if to drown you out—these children were so sensitive. Doctors had proved that their perceptions were many times more acute than normal. That their odd behavior came out of an attempt to protect themselves, cushion themselves from a world which even Susan found was a chaotic maze sometimes. Full of crazy signs and stimuli— sometimes it was only when she was alone in her apartment with the door locked that she felt she could make sense of it. In the same way, sometimes when Peter was alone you could

see him playing with his blocks, pensively and calmly. Sometimes among the nonsense he would spell out simple words,
and then you could see a little boy in him, an ordinary little
boy.

The premise of facilitated communication was that a trained
therapist could help a child reach that place of calm. And then
the words would come out; these children were not stupid.
They had ordinary needs. Only the task of speaking was sometimes too difficult, so full of anxieties and failures. Better to
communicate through writing, and so they were given simple
wooden keyboards, with large squares for each letter and number. There were no moving parts; they could just point to the
letter they wanted, and the facilitator would be there to read
it. And because so many of the children had problems with
their motor control, and because the task of communicating
filled so many of them with a trembling anxiety, then the facilitator would be there to calm them. To hold their hands.

Susan was interested in Peter because he reminded her of
an autistic boy in her class at Drury. They shared many of the
same behaviors: the endless rocking, even the flapping hand.
There were differences, too. Jason was already thirteen, although he looked much younger. And while Peter was rarely
still, Jason would often have whole hours of calmness; then he
would look right through you with his beautiful blue eyes. He
had a vocabulary of about thirty words, mostly nouns and numbers, which nevertheless he would whisper very precisely, with
beautiful clear diction. The movements of his hands, when he
wasn't rocking or shaking or pounding on the furniture, were
graceful and firm.

All summer, especially as she watched the progress Peter was
making, Susan couldn't stop thinking about Jason. When the
course in Syracuse was over, she couldn't wait for school to
start. On the first day she asked for permission from her supervisor to try out the new technique; she bought him a keyboard with her own money. She donated her own time. Out
of all her students, she felt Jason was one with the most potential. So she chose him to work with. He had none of the
physical signs of retardation or brain damage or Down's syn-
drome; he was a healthy beautiful child with blond hair and
clear pale skin. Even when he was rocking back and forth or
shaking his head hour after hour, his disabilities almost seemed
like an act, like he was faking. In him more than the others
you could sense the normal boy inside.

Other children would try and fail even at simple tasks. Jason never attempted anything he couldn't perform; at first he showed no interest in the keyboard. It was a Masonite placard about twelve inches on a side, crosshatched with lines of purple plastic. The letters and numbers and symbols were arranged in rows, and each small square was decorated with a brightly colored image: an apple, a bunny, a cat, etc. That first day Jason flipped the placard over to examine its blank side. Then he discarded it onto the playbench.

But she showed him how to use it, over and over. She held his finger and spelled out words for him: apple, bunny, cat. She attached the keyboard around his neck so that he could get used to it. She tied it with a white ribbon. White was his favorite color.

She would spell out sentences, using his finger. "Hello. How are you? I am fine." Hello was his favorite word.

Once after about a week she found him puzzling over it, staring at the row of numbers. When she approached, he grabbed hold of her finger. Thrusting the keyboard out toward her, he pushed her finger into the row of numbers. But she didn't know what to do, which numbers to pick, and he grew frustrated. His own hands were shaking and he started to cry. Then she took hold of his wrist and made him do the calculations. Soon she had removed her hand, had slid it all the way up his arm until she lightly cupped his elbow, and he was making all the choices himself. "2.2," he spelled. "2.2 × 2.2 = 4.84." Then with evident delight he was picking out primes: 37, 41, 43, etc. Then a bunch of garbage letters.

For about a week they played with numbers. Jason was a child who at three had understood the principle of divisibility, yet at ten still couldn't tie his shoes. And he was endlessly fascinated with primes. "4183," he spelled out. Then a bunch of garbage: AAAXFUP, etc. Then quick as a wink: IS 4183 PRIM? Then, after a moment: N ÷ BY 47.

Jason laughed and laughed. Susan knew nothing about primes. She was astonished by the "is," the first verb he had ever used. She gave up her lunch period for that day and then the rest of the semester. She was happy to do it, because as the weeks went by she could see that Jason was going to make the change that she had dreamed of when she first saw the FC videotape that spring. And she was going to liberate him. She was going to be his Annie Sullivan. In two months he was

spelling out: SOMTIME IT HURT BECAUSE I M SO ALON
LIKE A TREE

"Like a tree?" she asked.

IN A FIELD

Sometimes she would correct his spelling, and once he understood an error he would never repeat it. Or at least not deliberately—sometimes in the quickness of the moment he would still make mistakes. "I" became "you," or more commonly "u," for example. Like many autistics, his sense of his own self was very damaged.

U FEEL SAD

"Me?" Susan asked.

XCUSE ME I

During the moments he was calm, as now, he was the most beautiful boy Susan had ever seen. His face was like a little angel's. His blue eyes looked right through you. I M SAD BKZ THE WEEKND

She cupped his elbow in her hand. "Why?"

I MISS YOU SUSAN WHITE

WHITE IS MY FAVORITE COLOR 2

U2 LIKE THE BAND

I HEART U2

HEART LIKE NY STATE

I HEART U

KZ WE TALK

Susan burst into tears. Jason was agitated too. He pushed the keyboard away, and for a solid hour he was shaking his head and flapping his hand next to his ear. "Hello," he said, over and over. "Hello—what is your name?"

It was hard for Jason to read. His parents were professors at North Adams State, so he had been surrounded by books for his entire life. Enough of it had penetrated for him to use the keyboard. But he had some kind of block there too, maybe some kind of bad association. When Susan gave him books to read, she suspected all he did was look at the pictures. His attention span was still very short.

But he loved it when she read to him. At first she kept it simple, but as time went on she was amazed at his level of comprehension. She read him J. D. Salinger short stories. WHAT S A BANANAFISH? he asked. WHAT IS SQUALOR?

Susan had got the book from Bob Cousins, who was using it in eighth-grade English. "Would you like to take his class?" she asked.

I DON'T NO

"Would you like to?"

I WOULD LIKE TO

The class met during seventh period, which was after Susan's day was finished. It was an art class for Jason, but she switched him out of it and volunteered to stay late. Mr. Cousins was enthusiastic, and between them they convinced the head of the department. She was concerned about the other kids, needlessly as it turned out, for they were wonderfully warm and supportive. For years Jason had been something of a celebrity around the school, with his prime numbers and peculiar outbursts.

A couple of weeks later, before Thanksgiving, Susan received a telephone call from Jason's mother, asking if they could meet. Susan had been expecting this. She had received no answer to her letter to the boy's parents earlier in the year, trying to explain facilitated communication and the changes she was making in Jason's curriculum. She had received no answer to another letter, which she had sent when Jason first started taking Mr. Cousins's class. But now everyone had heard of her success; the superintendent had written her a memo, and there had been much excited talk at recent faculty meetings. Teachers who had barely known her name were now stopping her in the halls. So it didn't surprise her that even the most uninvolved mother would eventually recognize what she was doing. Not that she cared about that, but it was nice to have the parents on your side. After all, school was only part of Jason's day.

They made an appointment for Friday at five, but Mrs. Marowitz was late. From her second-floor office window Susan watched a black Volvo pull into the empty parking lot. She watched a small dark woman get out, dressed in boots and a brown shearling coat, as if it were midwinter.

Almost everyone had already gone, and the building was almost empty. Susan had left her door open; she could hear the boots come down the hall. Mrs. Marowitz knocked her knuckles on the door frame and then came in. She didn't wait for a response. She was a pinch-faced woman in her mid-forties, who smelled like cigarettes. She carried a black briefcase, which she dropped next to the door. Then she was stripping off her leather gloves and holding out her hand.

But she hadn't come to offer her congratulations. She got to the point without even sitting down. "Ms. White, can you explain what Jason is doing with this book? He's been bringing it home the past few weeks."

The book was J. D. Salinger's *Nine Stories*. Mrs. Marowitz took it from an inside pocket of her coat and dropped it onto Susan's desk.

"I wrote you a letter. I've been taking Jason to eighth-grade English for his last period."

"Yes, I remember. I thought it was ridiculous even at the time. Ms. White, I hate to disillusion you. It seems absurd to have to explain this to his own teacher, but Jason cannot read."

Carefully, patiently, Susan tried to describe some of the progress they'd been making. "He has some problems with concentration and vocabulary, but then I read to him. He's very smart. He picks things up very quickly. I'm even helping him to write a book report. He'll show you when it's done."

"A book report? You're joking."

"No. Why not? There are some themes of alienation that he can relate to."

Mrs. Marowitz was angry. Her thin lips were trembling. "Listen, I don't know what you're playing at and I don't care. All I know is that you've taken my son out of art class, which was something he could use and he enjoyed. I spoke to my husband, and he said give it a chance. But this is insane."

Carefully, patiently, Susan tried to explain about facilitated communication. Mrs. Marowitz interrupted her. She made a strange, violent gesture with her hands. "All I know is that you've hung that card around his neck, and when he gets home he takes it off and never touches it. You say you're having whole conversations with him—why you? What are you sharing with him that he won't share with his own mother? Or with my husband, who's raised him like his own son?"

Again, Susan tried to explain. Again, Mrs. Marowitz interrupted: "Look, I'm not going to argue with you. I've written to the principal."

Susan's car was in the shop, so later she walked home through town. It was already dark, and she walked home to her apartment on River Street. She could see the lights of the college up the hill.

At home she turned on the lights and put on the water for some tea. There was a message from her mother on the answering machine. But Susan didn't want to call her. Talking to her mother wasn't likely to cheer her up. "I think it's wonderful how you can spend so much effort on a bunch of children who aren't even yours." She had never forgiven Susan for breaking up with Mark Toureille. "You'll never meet a man like that again. Not around here."

Pasted to the refrigerator door in her tiny kitchen were some photographs of her family. Her father, mother, and little sister, all smiling for the camera. Her father in his orange hunter's shirt and cap. But people only took photographs of the good times. The fights and arguments just disappeared and left no trace.

She made some soup, and then after dinner she called home. Unexpectedly, her father answered the phone. "Hi, princess," he said. She found herself telling him all about the fight she had had with Mrs. Marowitz. It was a relief to talk to him.

But on Monday during their lunchtime session, Jason had some disturbing new things to tell her.

HELLO

"Hello, Jason."

I DONT LIKE THE WEEKEND

"Why?"

FRIDAY NIGHT MY MOTHER H U

NO I MEAN ME

The keyboard square under the letter *h* showed the picture of a heart. Sometimes Jason would touch the *h* and nothing more when he meant "love." Later in the session: MY MOTHER H ME

"Yes, of course she does. Everybody loves you."

NO I MEAN NO

"I don't understand."

SOUND LIKE HART

Susan said nothing, and in a little while Jason continued: WITH A HAND

"Where?" asked Susan, but he shook his head, suddenly agitated, and he could no longer make the letters.

"On your butt?" she asked. He shook his head.

"On your face?" He shook his head.

"On your arm?" and he stopped shaking. She rolled up the sleeve of his turtleneck. There was a bruise above his elbow. Nothing big, but definitely a bruise.

In the days that followed, Susan asked him more questions. And she started to make notes of his answers. "Does your mother hurt you often?"

NO SOMETIMES

"What about your father?"

NOT MY FATHER
FATHER GONE
In fact, Jason's name was Adler. "I mean Mr. Marowitz."
PROF
"Yes, whatever. Professor Marowitz. Does he hurt you?"
YES
"With his hand?"
NO
"With a belt?"
NO WITH A COK
"What?"
COK IN U BUT

Phrases like these, once expressed, were enough to send Jason into a spasm of trembling. Often after one of these sessions he would spend an hour rocking and shaking his head. And Susan also was distressed. She didn't know what to do. "Shall I talk to your mother about this?"
NO PLEASE
Then, a little later:
COCK IN MY BUT & MOUT
SHE NOSE

Susan had read books in college which suggested that autism was caused by family trauma. If the child felt unloved or unwanted, he would protect himself by sealing off the world. But this was something more than that. It made Susan want to cry. Jason was so vulnerable, so beautiful. His eyes looked right through you.

Finally she couldn't stand it anymore. She collected her notes and went to talk to Bob Cousins. Then to the guidance counselor. Then to the assistant superintendent. Then to the school nurse, who made a physical examination. Then to a woman named Sheila D'Angelo, who came up from Pittsfield. She was with the Department of Social Services.

"Do you think foster care might be appropriate?" she asked. "Children like Jason are very hard to place."

"I'll take him in."

"Hmm. Let's wait on that."

Sheila D'Angelo was a heavyset woman in her fifties. She sat in Susan's office, looking over the transcripts, twiddling a pencil. From time to time she glanced at Susan over the tops of her glasses. "Of course you know we're talking about a serious offense. You realize that?"

Then: "If the man has other children, we might have to get a court order."

Then, after a little while: "Well, I suppose I'd better take a look. And then they went to find Jason, who was unresponsive. Ever since the school nurse had examined him, he hadn't wanted to talk. He was rocking and trembling, and though Susan managed to get him to sit still long enough to say hello and call out some prime numbers, she could tell that Mrs. D'Angelo was not impressed. The demonstration of facilitated communication would have to wait. In the meantime, Susan showed her the keyboard and explained the technique.

But then, after Mrs. D'Angelo was gone, Jason calmed down. He picked up the keyboard from the workbench and brought it to Susan, where she sat working with another student. He seemed impatient. In the last half hour before he had to get the bus, he and Susan had the following conversation:

HELLO

"Hello."

WHO WAS THAT

"That was the woman I was telling you about. She's going to try and help us so you won't have to go home. So your Mommy won't hurt you."

& NOT FATHER?

"And your stepfather. I want to take you to a place where no one can hurt you anymore."

MAY BE 2 LIVE WITH U

"Well, we'll see."

U WD LIKE THAT

Then: XCSE I MEAN ME

"Yes. I'm glad."

Jason shook his head slowly and rhythmically from side to side. He closed his eyes and smiled.

COCK IN MY BUTT, he said.

1 TIME I TRIDE TO SCREM BUT COULDNT!

IT WAS IN THE BATHROOM & I TRIED 2

31887 PIECES ON A FLOOR

IT IS A PRIME

Then: WHITE IS LIKE COLOR MIX TOGETHER

ALL COLOR

"Yes," said Susan, touched. Jason opened his blue eyes, but he was still shaking his head. She reached out and put her hand onto his forehead, and he stopped. "Don't you worry about all this," she said. "I'll take care of it."

YES I LOVE U

"Yes."

Then it was time for him to go. From her office window, Susan could see the buses loading in front of the school, and she stood watching Jason as the van pulled up. He was the first in line. The square keyboard hung over the front of his coat.

When she got home, her father was waiting for her in front of the door. "Hi, princess," he said.

He had driven over from Cheshire twelve miles away. He was wearing a sweater and a woolen scarf—not enough for the cold weather. She stood on the sidewalk with her books and papers up against her chest, while he stood on the porch. "Momma told me you weren't going to make it home for Thanksgiving," he said. "Your sister's coming down from Maine. I wanted to see if I could change your mind."

She smiled. It was brisk weather, and his cheeks were flushed. His skin was moist and pink, as if he had just finished some exertion. Sometimes during the winter when Susan was just a child, he would come in from splitting wood or shoveling snow, huffing with his bald forehead red.

He stood aside, and then followed her up the four flights. On the way, Susan said: "It's just that I've been a little depressed for the past week. I was planning on coming, really." Then, when they were inside her apartment, and she was filling the coffee machine: "It's just that Mom is always worse than usual around holidays. Everything she feels bad about, she takes out on the rest of us."

He came up behind her and put his arms around her. "What are you depressed about?"

"Oh, nothing," she said. "Something at work."

Sheila D'Angelo came back on Friday. She took Jason aside and tried to talk to him for a few minutes. Then Susan gave the rest of the class to her assistant and took them back to her office. "I read some things about facilitated communication over the weekend," said Mrs. D'Angelo. "It's just amazing, some of the results."

She had her own ideas about the demonstration she wanted to see. Jason was in a good mood, and the whole thing took about twenty minutes. He and Susan sat at a table side by side, the keyboard between them. Mrs. D'Angelo held up a notebook. On each page she had glued a picture for Jason to identify or a problem for him to solve. Jason was relaxed and sure, though his spelling wasn't always perfect. Susan barely had to touch his elbow. She was afraid the questions were too easy, and he would lose his concentration through sheer boredom. But he was chuckling and smiling.

Then Mrs. D'Angelo asked some questions about the abuse. Jason tried to answer, but after ten minutes or so he started flapping his hand next to his ear. "Hello," he said. "Hello."

"When he gets agitated, it's hard for him to concentrate," explained Susan.

But after Mrs. D'Angelo had left, he said what was bothering him: U TOLD HER

"Yes, I had to."

He shook his head. I TRUST YOU

"I'm sorry. But I thought . . ."

He interrupted her. I DONT WANT TROUBLE 4 THEM

"For who?"

FOR THOSE 2

It was astonishing, she thought, that he still could feel loyalty to them, after they had betrayed him so shamefully. That he could still want to protect them. It made her feel ashamed of her own distance from her family, and so on the Tuesday before Thanksgiving she called her mother to tell her to expect her the next day after school. She would spend the night, for the first time in years.

Mrs. D'Angelo was supposed to have called her on Monday with information about Jason's preliminary hearing, but she didn't. It wasn't until Wednesday morning that Susan managed to get her on the phone. "Ms. White," she said, "I was just posting a letter to you."

"I know these things take time," Susan answered, trying not quite successfully to swallow her annoyance. "But you know things are worse during the holidays. I think it's absolutely imperative that we get Jason out of that house as soon as possible."

"I was writing you a letter. In fact, we had a court date for the middle of next month, but I had to cancel it. I'm sorry."

"What do you mean?"

"It's in the letter. It's just that I'm not sure there is a case."

Susan said nothing, and then after a while Mrs. D'Angelo went on. "Let me say right now that I'd like to believe you. But after the test I made, I asked him more than fifty questions. Asked you. I guess I wasn't being quite honest. But I knew that any lawyer would have to address the problem of influence, so I thought I'd beat them to it."

Then she went on to explain the test with the pictures and the problems. "When I opened the notebook, I showed him one side and you another. You thought you were seeing the same picture, but you weren't. So on the first question I showed you an apple and him a pear, and so on."

She had a way of talking that was so confused, it was intolerable. "What are you trying to say to me?" asked Susan. "Just tell me what you did."

"Well, I'm trying to. All I know is that I asked you both more than fifty questions, and in every case he answered from the wrong side of the page. The page he hadn't seen."

"What are you telling me?" asked Susan.

"I'm telling you he didn't answer a single question, and you answered every one. I knew it when it was going on, and maybe I should have told you last week, only I wanted to talk to a few people here. Ms. White, I'm not doubting your sincerity. But even when I was asking him direct questions after the test was done, he wasn't even looking at the keyboard when he used it."

"So what? It's like touch-typing."

"Well, whatever. All I'm saying is that we don't have a case. As far as the court would be concerned, you're talking to yourself."

Susan was staring at the clock above the door of her office. It was quarter to ten.

"And one more thing," said Mrs. D'Angelo. "I spoke to Mrs. Marowitz. Really, she's very sympathetic. She's already been in touch with your administration; she told me she wanted to take Jason out after the break. She's made arrangements at a private school in Williamstown."

So that was that. After she had hung up, Susan sat looking at the pink receiver, listening to the dial tone. She looked at the photograph of her father and mother on her desk. Then she got up to go to class. And the first chance she got, she took Jason aside. "Hello," she said.

HELLO

He sat with his head to one side, staring through her with his blue eyes. "Who are you?" she asked.

COCK IN YOUR BUTT

"Who are you?" Susan asked again, after a little while.

I AM IN U & WILL NEVER LEAVE

"What do you mean?"

NEVER LEAVE ALONE

He spelled the words out slowly, carefully, and his eyes looked right through her. Later, he left to catch the bus, and neither of them could say goodbye.

SHIMABARA

Karen Joy Fowler

The sea, the same as now. It had rained, and we can
imagine that, too, just as we have ourselves seen it—the
black sky, the ocean carved with small, sharp waves. At
the base of each cliff would be a cloud of white water.

At the top of the cliffs was a castle and inside the castle, a
fifteen-year-old boy. Here is where it gets tricky. What is different and what is the same? The story takes place on the other
side of the world. The boy has been dead more than three
hundred and fifty years. There was a castle, but now there is
a museum and a mall. A Japanese mall is still a mall; we know
what a mall looks like. The sea is the same. What about a
fifteen-year-old boy?

The boy's mother, Martha, was in a boat on the sea beneath
the cliffs. Once a day she was taken to shore to the camp of
Lord Matsudaira for interrogation. Then she could see the castle where her son was. The rest of the time, she lay inside the
boat with her two daughters, each of them bound by the wrists
and the ankles, so that when she was allowed to stand, her legs,
through disuse, could hardly hold her up. Add to that the motion of the boat. When she walked on land, on her way to
interrogation, she shook and pitched. The samurai thought it
was terror, and of course, there was that, too.

Perhaps Martha was more concerned about her son in the

castle than her daughters on the boat. Perhaps a Japanese
mother three hundred and fifty years ago would feel this way.
In any case, all their lives depended on her son now. As she
lay on the boat, Martha passed the time by counting miracles.
The first was that she had a son. On the day of Shiro's birth,
the sunset flamed across the entire horizon, turning the whole
landscape red, then black. Later, when Shiro was twelve, a
large, fiery cross rose out of the ocean off the Shimabara Peninsula and he was seen walking over the water toward it. He
could call birds to his hands; they would lay eggs in his palms.
This year, the year he turned fifteen, the sunset of his birth
was repeated many times. The cherry blossoms were early.
These things had been foretold. Martha remembered; she summoned her son's face; she imagined the sun setting a fire each
night behind Hara Castle. The worst that could happen was
that her son prove now to be ordinary. The wind that had
brought the rain rocked the boat.

Thirty-seven thousand Kirishitan rebels followed Shiro out
of Amakusa to the Shimabara Peninsula and the ruin of Hara
Castle. *Kirishitan* is a word that has been translated into Japanese and come back out again, as in the children's game of
telephone. It goes in as Christian, comes out Kirishitan.

The rebels made the crossing in hundreds of small boats,
each with a crucifix in the bow. A government spy stood in the
cold shadow of a tree and watched the boats leave. He couldn't
count the rebels. Maybe there were fifty thousand. Maybe
twenty thousand. Of those, maybe twelve thousand were men
of fighting age. The spy grew weak from hunger and fatigue.
Just to stand long enough to watch them all depart required
the discipline and dedication of a samurai.

General Itakura Shigemasa pursued the rebels through
Amakusa, burning the villages they'd left behind. Many of the
remaining inhabitants died in the fires. Those who survived,
Itakura put to death anyway. He had the children tied to stakes
and then burned alive. It was a message to the fifteen-year-old
Kirishitan leader.

Although Hara Castle had been abandoned for many years,
it was built to be defended. The east side of the castle looked
over the sea; on the west was a level marsh, fed by tides, which
afforded no footing to horses, no cover to attackers. North and
south were cliffs one hundred feet high. Only two paths led
in, one to the front, one to the rear, and neither was wide

enough for more than a single man. On January 27, 1637, after
ten days of repairs, the rebels occupied Hara Castle.

They hoisted a flag. It showed a goblet, a cross, a motto,
and two angels. The angels were fat, unsmiling, and European,
the motto was in Portuguese. LOVVAD SEIA O SACTISSIM
SACRAMENTO. Praised be the most holy sacrament. In
March, when Martha knelt in Lord Matsudaira's camp to write
Shiro a letter, there were one hundred thousand Bakufu samurai between her and her son.

January, February, March, and early April passed in a steady
storm of negotiations. The air above Shimabara was full of
words wound around the shafts of arrows. One landed in the
camp outside the castle. "Heaven and earth have one root, the
myriad things one substance. Among all sentient beings there
is no such distinction as noble and base," the arrow said. An
arrow flew back. "Surrender," it asked, but obliquely, politely,
confining itself, in fact, to references to the weather.

January and February were muddy. General Itakura commanded the Bakufu forces. Government agents tried to dig a
tunnel into the castle, but the digging was overheard. The rebels filled the tunnel with smoke and regular deposits of urine
and feces until the diggers refused to dig farther.

Itakura planned to pummel the castle walls with cannonballs
so large it took twenty-five sweating men to move each one to
the front lines. The last days of January were spent pulling and
pushing the cannonballs into place, but it proved a Sisyphean
labor in the end since no cannon, no catapult was large enough
to launch them.

More letters flew across on arrow shafts. "The samurai in
Amakusa cannot fight," the letters from inside the castle said.
"They are cowards and only good at torturing unarmed farmers. The sixty-six provinces of Japan will all be Kirishitan, of
that there is no doubt. Anyone who does doubt, the Lord Deus
with His own feet will kick him down into Inferno; make sure
this point is understood." "Surrender," said the arrows going
in, but the penmanship was beautiful; the letters could almost
have been framed. Meanwhile, Lord Matsudaira Nobutsuna
and a fleet of sixty ships were moving up the coast from Kyu-
shu, bringing Martha to her son.

General Itakura received a letter from his cousin in Osaka.
"All is well. When Lord Matsudaira arrives, the castle, held as
it is by mere peasants, will not last another day." Itakura trans-

lated this letter immediately as mockery. He decided to attack before the reinforcements arrived.

His first try was on February 3, a mousy, hilarious effort, his second on New Year's Day, February 14. Itakura, himself, led the bold frontal attack across the marsh and was killed by a rebel sharpshooter. After his death, he was much condemned for inappropriate bravura. He had laid the government open to more ridicule, dying as he had at the hands of farmers.

The night before his death Itakura wrote a poem.

> *When only the name remains*
> *of the flower that bloomed on New Year's Day,*
> *remember it as the leader of our force.*

He attached it to an arrow and shot it out over the ocean in the direction of Lord Matsudaira's fleet and the moon.

On February 24, the Commissioner of Nagasaki transmitted Lord Matsudaira's request that the Dutch ship *de Ryp* begin a bombardment of the castle from the sea. The shelling lasted two weeks until, on March 12, the shogunate canceled the request. Two Dutch sailors had been killed, one shot in the topmast, fell to the deck and landed on the other. A storm of arrows left the castle. "The government agents," these arrows said, "are better at squeezing taxes out of starving farmers, better at keeping account books, than at risking their lives on the field of battle. This is why they have to depend on foreigners to do their fighting. We in Hara Castle are armed with faith. We cannot be killed and we will slay all village magistrates and heathen bonzes without sparing even one; for judgment day is at hand for all Japan."

The Dutch commissioner, Nicolaus Coukebacker, sent a defensive letter by boat back to Holland. "We were, of course, reluctant to fire upon fellow Christians, even though the rebels in question are Roman Catholics and the damage the rebellion has done to trade conditions in Nagasaki has been severe. Our bombardment was, in any case, ineffectual." He was too modest. The outer defenses had been weakened.

On March 5, in the middle of the lull provided by the Dutch bombardment, a letter flew into the government camp from one Yamada Emonsaku of Hara Castle. Expressing his reverence for the rule of hereditary lords in particular and governments in general, Yamada assured them he had never been a sincere Kirishitan. He then outlined a lengthy plan in which he offered to deliver Shiro to the Bakufu alive. "Please give me your approval immediately, and I will overthrow the evil Kirishitans, give tranquility to the empire, and, I trust, escape with my own life." An answer asking for further information was sent back, but Yamada did not respond.

The invisible men, the *ninjutsuzukai*, went into Hara Castle and returned with information. The rebel leader had a mild case of scabies. While playing a game of *go* an incoming cannonball had ripped the sleeve of his coat. His divinity had never seemed more questionable. The letter to Yamada had been easily intercepted. He was bound in a castle room under a sentence of death.

Around their ankles, the invisible men wore leads which unwrapped as they walked. If they were killed their bodies could be dragged back out. You might think such cords would have given them away, but you are more inclined to believe in the fabulous skills of the ninjutsuzukai, than that a boy has walked on water. Not a single ninjutsuzukai was lost.

Lord Matsudaira judged that the rebel position was weakening. After the silly death of Itakura, he had settled on the inglorious strategy of blockade. The strategy appeared justified. The ninjutsuzukai said that the rebels were living in holes they had excavated under the castle. There was not enough to eat.

Matsudaira wrote a letter. The letter spoke of the filial piety owed to parents. It assured Shiro of Matsudaira's reluctance to hurt Shiro's family and said further that Matsudaira knew a fifteen-year-old boy couldn't possibly be leading such a large force. "I am pleased, therefore, to offer a full pardon to the boy, asking only that he surrender, recant, and identify the real leader of the rebellion. I look forward to a joyful family reunion."

Martha knelt in the mud beside Matsudaira and wrote as he directed. "We know that you have forced conversions on some of your followers. If you let those hostages go, Lord Matsudaira will allow your family to join you in Hara Castle. All who surrender may depend on the traditional magnanimity of the Bakufu; no one who freely recants will be punished. Indeed, rice lands will be given to those who surrender!" Matsudaira gestured with one hand that Martha was to finish the letter herself. "For myself, I ask only to see you again. Perhaps we could speak. Lord Matsudaira is willing. Don't forget your family on the outside who wish only to be with you."

These letters were carried into the castle by Shiro's young nephew and little sister. They had been dressed by the Bakufu in kimonos with purple bursts of chrysanthemums. They wore embroidered slippers brought up the coast by boat for the occasion.

Small as they were, the narrow path to the castle held them both, but the path was muddy from the rain, and the children wanted to save their shoes, so they stepped slowly and sometimes when puddles narrowed the path even more, one did go before the other. Inside the shining kaleidoscope of armor and sunlight, Martha saw the small bobbing chrysanthemums and high above them the flag over Hara Castle. "Now we will know what kind of a son you have," Lord Matsudaira told her. "If you have the wrong kind, only you are to blame for what happens next."

Soon the tiny figures disappeared from view. Martha counted slowly, trying to guess at the exact moment they would enter the castle. The path was very long and their steps so small. The ocean sobbed behind her. The sun through the trees moved down her face to her hands. If she could send Shiro one more message she would ask him to keep the children. She imagined the wish like a small, shining stone in Shiro's hand. He rubbed it with his fingers, feeling it, understanding it. He threw it into the air, as he would any other stone, but it became the bird whose shadow passed over Martha's face, the shadow Shiro's answer to her.

Martha struggled to keep her mind on the miracles. Left to itself, her memory immediately chose the most ordinary of moments. A little boy throwing stones. A pair of arms around her neck. A game of hiding. His face when he slept.

Matsudaira had tea prepared. He drank and attended to his mail. He discussed Hara Castle with several of his officers. They were all agreed that the rebellion could not have held out at any other spot. It was a wonderful castle and after they had taken it, they must be sure to completely destroy it. Fire, first, but then the stonework must be carefully dismantled. The unit from Osaka was charged with this.

Matsudaira decided to change the passwords. He sent out the new codes. Now the sentries were to inquire "A mountain?" "A river" would be the correct reply. In an optimistic mood, he selected a password to signal the start of an attack. It, too, would be in the form of a question. "A province?" "A province!" was also the answer. He had a meal of rice balls and mullet. While he was eating, Martha heard a shout. The children were returning.

Shiro had written a letter, which his nephew gave to Matsudaira. "Frequent prohibitions have been published by the Shogun, which have greatly distressed us. Some among us there are who consider the hope of future life as of the highest importance. For these there is no escape. Should . . . the above laws not be repealed, we must incur all sorts of punishments and torture; we must, our bodies being weak and sensitive, sin against the infinite Lord of Heaven; and from solicitude for our brief lives incur the loss of what we highly esteem. These things fill us with grief beyond our capacity. There are no forced converts among us, only outside, among you. We are protected by Santa Maria-sama [Mary], Sanchiyago-sama [Jesus], and Sanfuranshisuko-sama [St. Francis]."

To his mother Shiro sent a large parcel of food containing honey, bean-jam buns, oranges, and yams. He had given his little sister his ring to wear.

The ninjutsuzukai had reported starvation. Scavengers from the castle had been seen on Oe beach, searching for edible seaweeds. The bodies of rebel dead had been cut open and their stomachs contained only seaweed and barley. The unexpected sight of bean-jam buns sent Matsudaira into a rage. "Your son thinks very little of you," he said. "Very little of his sisters. All you ask is to speak with him. What kind of a son is this?"

Martha was filled with grief beyond her capacity. The largest part of it was only the fact that her daughter and her grandson had been allowed to see Shiro and she was not. In Shiro's presence she would have endured anything. "God is feeding him," she told Matsudaira. "He is stronger than you can imagine. God will change him into a bird to fly away from your soldiers. You will never kill my son."

This display angered Matsudaira even more. "Take her back to the boat," Matsudaira told the soldiers. "Take her and bind her below where she can't watch the sun set or see the castle. Her son doesn't love her enough to see her. What kind of a mother is this?"

When it came, the final attack was a mistake. On April 12 a fire was misread as a signal. The Nabeshima division rushed forward, soon joined by others. The rebels were completely out of ammunition and the sentries too weak from hunger to hold their posts. The agents easily penetrated the outer perimeter. In the inner rings, the women and children defended themselves with stones and cooking pots. They held out for two more days and nights of steady fighting. On April 15, the defenses collapsed.

By nightfall the government had set up tables to count and collect heads. The count was at 10,869. Headless bodies covered the fields about the castle, clogged the nearby rivers. By April 16, only one person from the castle had survived. As a reward for his letter of March 5, Yamada Emonsaku was spared. Eventually he would be taken back to Edo to serve in Lord Matsudaira's house as his assistant.

The *kubi-jikken*, or head inspection scene, is a traditional element of feudal literature. Martha saw Shiro one more time. The soldiers collected every head that might belong to a fifteen-year-old boy and summoned Martha to identify her son. "He is not here," she told them. Her daughters had been killed and her grandson. Their heads would be displayed in Nagasaki. Her own death was very close now. "He was sent by heaven, and heaven has protected him. God has transformed him to escape you." There were many possible heads. She rejected them all. Finally Lord Sasaemon held up a recent victim. The boy had been dressed in silks.

Martha began to weep at once, and once she began there was no reason to stop. She thought of her son throwing stones, playing hiding games, his face when he slept. She took the head and held it in her lap. We can imagine this moment, if we let ourselves, as a sort of Japanese pietà, the pietà translated, like the word Kirishitan, into Japanese and out again. "Can he really have become so thin?" Martha asked.

Every mother can easily imagine losing a child. Motherhood is always half loss anyway. The three-year-old is lost at five, the five-year-old at nine. We consort with ghosts, even as we sit and eat with, scold and kiss their current corporeal forms. We speak to people who have vanished and, when they answer us, they do the same. Naturally, the information in these speeches is garbled in the translation.

I myself have a fifteen-year-old son who was once nine, once five, once fit entirely inside me. At fifteen, he speaks in monotones; sounds chosen deliberately for their minimal content. "Later," he says to me, leaving the house, and maybe he means that he will see me later, that later he will sit down with me, we will talk. At fifteen, he has a whole lot of later.

Me, not so much. To me, later is that time coming soon, when he will be made up almost entirely of words: letters in the mailbox, conversations on the phone, stories we tell about him, plans he tells to us. And you probably think that I would have trouble imagining that thirty-seven thousand people could follow him to their deaths, that this is the hard part, but you would be wrong. No other part of the story, except for the sea, is so easy to imagine.

Isn't it really just a matter of walking on water? To me, today, this seems a relatively insignificant difference, but of course, it is the whole point—along with starvation and persecution, peasant messianism and ronin discontent. Was the boy in the castle God, or wasn't he? Who saw him walking on water? Who says the sunsets were his?

The story comes to us over time, space, and culture, a game of telephone played out in magnificent distances. Thirty-seven thousand Kirishitans and one hundred thousand Bakufu samurai were willing to die arguing over the divinity of Amakusa Shiro. But what does this mean to us? Nothing is left now but the flag and the words.

"An angel was sent as messenger and the instructions he transmitted must therefore be passed on to the villagers," the rebels wrote to someone, and, eventually, us. "And the august personage named Lord Shiro who has these days appeared in Oyano of Amakusa is an angel from Heaven."

Within one moment, anything is possible. Only the passage of time makes our miraculous lives mundane. For a single moment any boy can walk on water. An arrow can hang in the sky without falling. Martha kneels to write a letter. The sun is in her face. Negotiations continue. CNN is filming. The compound will never be taken. There are children inside.

WHAT DREAMS ARE MADE ON

Mark Bourne

> Our revels now are ended. These our actors
> (As I foretold you) were all spirits and
> Are melted into air, into thin air,
> And like the baseless fabric of this vision,
> The cloud-capp'd towers, the gorgeous palaces,
> The solemn temples, the great globe itself,
> Yea, all that it inherit, shall dissolve,
> And, like this insubstantial pageant faded,
> Leave not a rack behind. We are such stuff
> As dreams are made on; and our little life
> Is rounded with a sleep.
>
> —The Tempest

Prologue

Golden flecks of sunlight shimmered off the shaft of piss streaming down from the highest balcony of the Globe Theater. It curved in the breeze toward Sally, speckling the middle balcony rail before her. Mayhap a gust of summer wind would blow it into the face of that perfumed matron, the one who sneered *"Whore"* when Sally squeezed past her earlier. But no—the stream plummeted past and hit the dirt below in a steady pish, as if shushing the raucous din of the playgoers around her.

And the low murmur of the voices within her.

They were back again, gathering in her head like an audience attending the theater. They came more oft now. Did spirits work this way—whispering in daylight, then tormenting her dreams by night?

Fah! Spirits? Demons? Foolishness and faery tales!

Yet they murmured inside her, haunting her more than ever before. *Everyone* believed in demons. King James even wrote about them, before he wrote the Bible.

Sally scratched between her legs through her coarse skirt, and in her pate airy voices gasped, sounding both shocked and delighted at her touch.

Across the yard, Libby and Mary sold oranges and themselves for a few shillings and a flea-infested bed for the night. Poor Mary's skin displayed the poxes oft included in the trade. Beneath her eyes, a filthy rag covered the hole where her nose had been. Sally thanked God *she* never suffered that way. *Viruses. Bacteria.* The language of the dreams had become her own. *Germs. Poor hygiene.* What God could spill out such poxes, yet leave her smooth and untouched?

Keening wails of sorrow sounded in her head. Or faint laughter. As usual, they were distant and unclear.

In the yard below, groundlings were enjoying the play they paid a penny to see, a low comedy about a rich old cuckold whose young wife was enjoyed by the young men of London society. Sally cheered the boy playing the wife, and stood on her toes to see him better. His legs were strong from dance and swordplay, and carried him with nimble grace across the broad stage. At thirteen years, he was already taller than older actors. Jack deserved better parts. The other King's Men said so. Even William had said so, before he returned to the quiet life of Stratford. This must be how a mother felt. Pride in her child's success. And in her own. Sally smiled at the boy's acrobatic antics. Vast arenas smiled inside her. Like a crowd at the Coliseum.

The Roman Coliseum had been airier than these new English theaters. She had seen it in her dreams, along with other places marvelous strange and foreign. There was that dream of eating raspberry coldness in a glass tower as tall as the clouds. The man with the eyes was in that one. He held her tenderly, as no other man did, and she laughed with him in the dream places. Dreams only half remembered after waking, fading like ghosts caught in churchyards at dawn.

The voices murmured louder. Or was it playgoers applauding? Sally looked into the crowd. Her eyes were drawn to a seat near the gallery rail. The man was there, staring up at her. Cheers and whistles blew between her ears.

Clothed in the finery of an Earl or a Duke, he watched her

with eyes dark and bright, not rheumy and weak like other men's. Eyes she knew. Mayhap just a former customer? Wealthy men favored her. Yet that face was misplaced above the lacy ruff and dark doublet etched with gold. Eyes from a dream. Many dreams.

A thought flickered inside her like a candle flame, bright and hot. The stranger meant something. The end. Of what? Of everything. Sally was to die. The thought pierced her soul and pulled through it like a thread. Fear surged into her blood.

She ran to the stairs that led to the street.

Vast crowds rose to their feet in a thunderstorm of applause. As always, they were nowhere close by.

Act I

The thin grass was damp against the back of Sally's neck. The stars seemed to cool the night air. Just beyond her bare feet, starlight skipped across the black mirror of the Thames. She gazed into the arch of the Milky Way, which rose from the City shadows and curved behind her into Saint George's Field.

The voices were gone. For now.

The only sounds came from behind her, from the inn adjoining the Globe. Raucous laughter and men's tavern tales echoed among nearby homes. Framed in the bright rectangle of the alehouse door, moving shadows strutted and gestured to the rafters. The ritualistic end of another playhouse run.

Footsteps crunched on the path from the inn. Sally turned. A silhouetted figure was approaching her. Dim light glimmered off fair hair. The figure began running toward her, then leapt high into the air, somersaulted onto the grass nearby, and fell to its back, laughing.

Sally smiled. "You're going to do yourself an injury one day."

"Nay." Jack crawled over and sat beside her. "What doing?"

"Watching stars. Listening to old players. Why aren't you with them?"

"I'm not an old player."

His voice had deepened so much. She laid her hand lightly on his back.

He drew nearer, looked down into her face. "Sally. What troubles you?"

"Why do you ask?"

He turned to the river, as if the wet starlight would respond for him. "Your sleep is troubled more and more. I hear you through the wall. Your dreams. They vex you."

"Mayhap I am not alone at such times."

He looked hurt. "I know the different sounds. You know that."

"I'm sorry." Jack was not stupid. She closed her eyes. "I see the dreams more clearly in recent nights. But they are merely dreams." Could he hear the doubt in her voice?

"Dreams," he said, "where you live in fantastical lands, or in ages that be only in the histories. If they are mere dreams, why do you awaken many nights speaking aloud, or shouting. Once even crying?"

She stared overhead into the thick spray of stars. Her arm followed the Milky Way. "See that river in the heavens? To the Egyptians, that was Nut, Goddess of Night, whose long body arcs forever over the earth. Folk in other days lived wondrous strange lives."

"Mistress Coxham said we all lived in the history times, being born other babes ere being now, in England. Said we all live forever. She said."

"Mistress Coxham was a mad old crone. She said the devil bit her bum and the morning cock told prophecies."

"They said she was a witch and hanged her."

"They were mad, also, in their fashion. There are no witches. No demons. No spirits, sprites, or elfin folk." She tousled his hair. "And no Puck, I'm sorry to say."

Jack looked at her as though she were denying the existence of the Thames itself. "You were bewitched once, when you first to London came. Possessed by demons who stole your remembrances. So you said."

" 'Twas hard drink eating my wits, so I said. Sack and wine fighting for the pleasure of driving me mad. It passed." Last night, she had awakened to the fading vapors of fine wine and raspberry.

Her earliest memories began just two summers ago, when she woke alongside a Southwark road with a flaming pain in her skull. She must have been sick and drunk and left for dead. Beaten, too, if the lump on her pate was any witness. She rubbed the back of her skull, where her hair hid a pebble-sized mound of raised flesh.

In London, she found work as a maidservant to a printer named Colesly. Jack had been Colesly's 'prentice, making pamphlets and setting books. Jack would read them and recite them for Sally when Colesly was asleep. The boy boasted that he was always excellent with books. He was only ten when Sally found him. And better learned, he proclaimed, than any Oxford dunghead.

She had seen the scars on Jack's back and the bruises on his face, and had heard him scream with Colesly's beatings in the work room. Then Colesly came for her. Made her do things. He laughed when he told her what he got from the boy. That's when she took Jack out into the night and they lived wherever shelter could be found. Sally turned to whoring. Jack took to the playhouse. All the same in most folks' eyes. They each found success in their craft, and earned enough to rent rooms at the inn next to the Globe, alongside the finest playhouse in London.

A silhouette crossed the open alehouse door. Sonorous, rhythmic words drifted on the air. Prospero, from *The Tempest*. William's farewell to his illusions and craft. Jack mouthed the words along with the shadow-actor. The boy stretched out in the grass and wove a long ribbon of Sally's raven hair between his fingers. "Lord Shakespeare himself asked me to be in that play." Sadness tinted his voice.

"I remember."

He grinned as he thumped his chest. "I was the first and best Miranda *The Tempest* will e'er see. I'll be the best player in the King's Men. And the best poet, too. He said so."

"Modesty once was a virtue."

"Only among the virtuous." He rolled onto his back, put his head against hers, and clasped her hand. She held it tight and stillness hung between them. His voice had grown so deep this year. His words shoved away the silence. "You tell me of places strange and fanciful, with flying fire-drakes that bear magic people, of paintings that move and speak, and lands where colored suns shine and there is no night. I remember them and they become my plays."

"They are but dreams," she said.

"Mama told me such stories. Legends and travelers' tales about lands across the seas. I hear her in you."

"You speak of your mother rarely, Jack. Why do so now?"

"I never gave her thanks. Now seems a good time."

Not yet old enough for a man, nor young enough for a boy, she thought, recalling a line from *Twelfth Night*. Tiny fires flickered through London's far shop windows. A boatman shouted in the distance.

Jack brought her hand to his chest. "You are a faerie queen spirited away and placed sleeping by the road to save a woeful orphan from a villain, so he can become the greatest player-poet in the world." He brushed his hand along the starry arch overhead. "In all worlds. We shall move hearts in enchanted lands and make elf kings laugh and weep. And no man nor devil will split us one from the other."

"You're being silly." *Please, God, don't let him grow too fast.*

Jack tugged her hand and stood. "Come."

She sat up. "To?"

"To the inn. Richard has a surprise."

"What manner of surprise?"

"I know not. He wants us all to come."

"Promise to stay away from sack and beer? And upstairs to bed ere midnight?"

He frowned. "Aye, Sally."

She rose. Cool sand squeezed between her toes.

"Sally."

"Yes, love."

"Do I play parts in your dreams?"

She said nothing. From the Thames, the boatman's bell echoed against dark dwellings.

The voices returned when she approached the alehouse. Louder, closer than before. She fell back against the doorframe and closed her eyes. The inn sounds shrank away, leaving her surrounded by an invisible throng. They entered her from behind her eyes and sounded delighted to return to this place.

Go away!

Anticipation boiled beneath the buzzing murmurs. Whispers that might carry affection, admiration, or the musky thrill an audience breathes out at public executions.

"Sally!" Someone was shaking her shoulders. "Sally!" She opened her eyes to Jack's face. She was startled by the fear etched into it. "Sally, are you ailing?"

She stepped into the shadows; the wall was cool against her back. She found a bright star overhead and focused on it. After a moment, she stood straight and met Jack's worried gaze.

"I'm well. The heat of a long day."

He studied her with wary scrutiny.

She took his hand. "Come. Does Richard not have a surprise?" He returned her smile, but it wavered as she pulled him into the tavern.

Lanterns tossed dirty light around the room, threw restless shadows on the walls. The air was heavy with the pleasant reek of malmsey and beer. Men sat at tables with bottles and mugs; some played games, others traded bawdy tales. Francis, the innkeeper, wrapped Sally's hand around a cool mug. He winked at her, then cocked his head toward a growing din at the other end of the room. Burly Richard Burbage stood on a table, extemporizing a devastating parody of a rival company. An audience was building around him, punctuating his performance with laughter and applause. As soon as he saw Sally and Jack, he grinned and clapped for attention.

"Sally-o, our Sally-o!" he sang. "A good woman among such rowdy men." A ragged cheer rose from the crowd, and Sally somehow found herself in front of the group. Richard pouted like a boy caught pulling the rose petals. "Please forgive our bawdy ways and give us all a kiss to dream on." He placed a hand to his middle and bent at the waist, as though performing at Court. The other men laughed good-naturedly and greeted her warmly before moving into loose knots of talking and boasting.

Richard leapt from the table and took Sally by the shoulders. " 'Tis good to see thee, Lady. You have not graced our company much of late."

She kissed his cheek. "I'm sorry, Richard. I haven't felt much like company lately."

He re-created Jack's worried look. "Your speech has been passing strange, Lady. Methought it must be tainted by the wealthy foreigners you entertain. And you have been troubled. Is there anything you would tell friend Richard?"

"Jack says you have a surprise." She stepped away and felt Richard's gaze as she moved to Jack's side.

Richard climbed back onto the table. He clapped again. The room went silent. Someone handed him a stack of pages.

"Friends, Romans, countrymen. Shut your ale holes. A message—" He held out a page. "—delivered me this day from our most honored poet—and wealthiest stocksharer—now living in familial lethargy in Stratford. He sends greetings—" His eyes brightened during the perfectly timed dramatic pause. "—

which you may receive on the morrow when he arrives here for the first performance of our new play."

Astonishment sang out from the crowd. Since returning to Stratford, Will had not made a trip back to London. But he would be here for the premiere of his play registered in the Office of Revels as *The Famous History of the Life of King Henry the Eighth*.

Sally rubbed the base of her skull. Something about that play vexed her, but she couldn't say what. It surely wasn't one of Will's finest. A lantern flame snared her attention, and the hubbub of the actors faded. She searched for patterns in the fire, shapes and faces that danced away as quickly as they formed.

Henry the Eighth had been one of the many masques and entertainments commissioned to adorn the nuptials of King James's daughter to Frederick V, Elector Palatine, that February last. Sally remembered Will, tired and sick, sitting in this room on a raw December night, grumping about his collaborator, John Fletcher. Will called her "Sally-o" as he spoke of Anne and his quiet life near the Avon. He regaled her once again with stories of life in the theater, of friends he had loved and outlived. He spoke of a dark lady, and brushed a mottled hand through his Sally-o's night-black hair. Sally kept him from drinking too much, then walked arm in arm with him through the snow to Richard's house.

The voices had been unusually clamorous that night.

A week before the royal wedding, William canceled the performance. Fletcher had insulted him before the company and refused to rewrite his portions of the script to William's desires. *Henry the Eighth* was removed from the roster and the scripts kept in careful storage.

Two weeks ago, the King's Men decided to bring to the stage Will's unperformed history play.

Richard was holding a page over his head as if it were a victory flag. "Gentlemen. Lady. Dear William arrives on the morn. Yet seeing our play is simple pretense. He is returning to us to take as his sole pupil and protégé one of our illustrious players. Come hither, Jack."

The boy let out a yelp and pushed through the men. Arms reached out to pat his back while a chorus of congratulations washed over him. Richard handed down the page. Jack grabbed it and read hungrily. Love and pride swelled within Sally. Jack was born to greatness, and would surely make his mark upon this earth under William's care and guidance. He was destined for nothing less.

Richard sat on the table and put an arm around the boy. " 'Tis a grand honor, lad. I have trod the boards for well nigh thirty years, and the likes of you has never blessed us with such skill. You have gold in your veins, boy, and now the most perfect teacher shall help you mine it."

He handed Jack a thick manuscript. The title *Masque of the Planets* dominated the front page in Will's careful penmanship. "He says this play is but the first jewel in your crown. Best of luck, lad, and a long life in our noble profession."

Mugs and bottles were raised. Someone began a boisterous song. Others joined in with singing, instruments, or dancing. Jack was on Richard's shoulders, waving like a king on a balcony.

Someone was watching her. She felt it.

Sally turned and peered through the doorway. The blackness beyond thickened and hardened, then stepped into the lantern light. The man from the dreams stood against the backdrop of night.

Voices behind her eyes gasped. Sally clasped her hands to her mouth, trapping the scream in her throat. Dream images burst in her head. Part of herself felt removed, distant, detached—in the scene, but now also among an unseen audience. Faintly, she heard Jack shouting, "Sally! This be your celebration too!" Then the music ceased.

Sally slid doll-like to the floor. She heard herself sobbing and saying "No" and "Not again!" She wet herself and stared at the doorway. He was watching her, as he had that afternoon at the Globe. His eyes were exactly the color of twilight. A creature, gray and hairless, squatted on his shoulder, flapping black batlike wings. It had a twisted human face.

In her head, phantoms stood up and cheered.

The stranger moved toward Sally. Jack stepped between them, shaking. "I charge thee," he said. "Lay not a hand to this good lady. I knew demons plagued her, and I shall fight thee at Hell's throne."

The stranger reached out to Jack, in a pleading gesture. "Please. I can help her. It's not supposed to be like this." He took a step.

Jack glanced from the stranger to the actors, holding his

stance. The winged thing raised its talons and shrieked. Jack ran to the players.

The man knelt beside her. He wrapped her in his cloak and cradled her tenderly. She felt her body go slack as he lifted her and carried her toward the stairs, shouting orders as he moved. His voice was as clear and dark as his eyes. "There's a trunk in the yard. Leave it outside her room. She's in good care. Everything will be as it's always been." He carried her up the steps. Jack's sobs cut the air.

Warm water flowed into her brain, which hummed with the incoming tide of a thousand thousand ghosts. It was the last thing Sally heard before she lost consciousness.

Act II

She awoke smelling beans and roast chicken. Her first thought was *I'm hungry.*

The window shutters were open, letting in a moist breeze. The full moon cast the only light into the room. It took her a moment to realize that the bed beneath her was not straw and dirty linen. It was supple and warm and molded itself to her body as she moved. It cushioned her head and bathed her in flowing comfort that searched her body for places to soothe. She pushed herself up onto one elbow and peered over the side of the bed. It was floating above the floor. She thought it odd that she wasn't surprised by that, and placed her head back on the pillow. Warmth flowed around her and she gave in to sleep. Her first dream was of raspberry ice cream.

When she opened her eyes again, the moon was higher and dulled by clouds. A lantern flickered on the floor, revealing a plateful of chicken, beans, and bread on the bed with her. A pot of water stood beside it. She sat up and devoured the meal.

"Have a napkin."

She turned. The man sat on a jeweled trunk against the door. He tossed her a soft towel. His face was warm, friendly, and familiar. Somehow, he looked older than he should.

"Your innkeeper friend keeps a fine larder," he said. "I left him a tip where he'll find it tomorrow. Everyone's finally gone home. They really care about you."

She realized then that she was naked and had been given a thorough sponge bath. Her dress hung on the lantern hook.

She felt hollow inside, carved out. But not empty. Someone else was there, and they blended like merging flames.

"I tried contacting you at the play." His voice soothed her. "Your conditioning should have dissolved then. I don't understand why you ran."

When she did not respond, he looked disappointed. "You heard our audience when we made eye contact. They had no idea when or where I would show up. You should've seen the nielsen lines!"

Memories flowed and congealed like cooling wax. Her room looked so dirty now, and the light was too dim. Despite the bath, she could smell her own sour sweat. A thick, hot costume seemed to drop from her shoulders, and she felt the part of her named Sally slide away, submerged and hidden. With the others.

She reached out. "Alexandros."

She pulled him close and hugged him tight. He returned the embrace, and she realized how sore and tired she was. She looked into his face and gently touched it with her fingertips. She wanted to speak, but words jumbled in her mind. She took his hands into hers.

Relief smoothed away the lines in his face, which set into that famous soft smile. "The leading man always returns in the final act." His fingers moved through her hair. "I've missed you. Two years is a long time in any century." His hands brushed her cheek, and she leaned into it, an automatic response. "How do you feel?"

As if I were just poured into a used body. "Same as always, only more so. It hasn't all come back to me yet." She rubbed the back of her head, where a—what was the thing called?— nanolink wove its microthin web into her brain. "My link?"

"Switched off. For now. So's mine, though I'll be the Network's virtual body until you're rested up. Welcome back, Selene."

"That's not my name."

"You'll feel that way for a while. This was a long run. Sally was a beautifully fleshed-out character. A lot of you in her."

"She *was* me. Is." Her head itched inside, and her skin was cool and damp, as if from a fever breaking.

He walked to the window and looked out over the river into the dark skyline of King James's London. "They're always you." He leaned through the window for a better view, then sharply pulled his hands away from the grimy ledge. "Full recall should take an hour or so." He had told her similar things on other occasions. She shivered and pulled a thick blanket around her. It snuggled comfortingly against her skin.

He turned and flashed the smile that thrilled millions of fans who were—how many centuries up the Channel? "You're now the model for all Total Immersion actors. The Network has a fat paychip waiting for you when we get back. But we'll have a day together in merry old England first. In the meantime, think about what you'd like your next role to be."

Something black and ugly moved in her soul—

At the far end of the Network's Time Channel, skindivers were awaiting their next episode. She was their eyes and ears. Their flesh. Their soul, too, when her thoughts and feelings rode the waves up the Channel. They paid well to join her in her skin.

—Then he was behind her, massaging her shoulders, finding all the right places. His hands moved down her back. She let the blanket fall away.

"Sally was so good," he said, "we gave you more episodes than the Caesar's Rome series. You've soloed to higher ratings than any of our series together. Marketing the mnemochips offworld has already put another fortune in our account. Told you I'd make you a star." She could hear his self-satisfied grin.

He lightly scraped his fingernails across her neck, the way she always liked. "I knew you'd end up at the Globe. You and Burbage kept the 'will-they-or-won't-they' fans tuned in. And The Man himself, Willy the Shakes! Who'd have guessed you'd get so cozy with your idol? The kid's a hit. He's been compared to the young Mozart." He eyed her with mock suspicion. "I'm glad he's not a few years older."

"Voices," she said. "I heard voices."

He twirled an upraised hand with a showman's flourish. "The smell of the horseshit, the roar of the crowd! You gave them Sally, your audience gave you their feedback. At your request, you'll remember."

"It was awful," she said. The link in her skull was an iron weight. Its tendrils snaked through her brain like rusty wires.

"You never really thought so. Deep down you knew it was normal. You, my dear, thrive on applause." He moved around to her front, his fingers combing through her hair.

"Hey," he said. "I'm up for applause too. The Network finally promoted me to Producer. That's why I didn't write myself into the series until yesterday."

No, she thought. That's not true. Something dark and smoky swirled in her memory. It dissolved when she grasped for it.

He cupped her chin and delicately tilted her head up. "I've learned to appreciate the *biz* side of showbiz," he said. He kissed her lightly on the lips, then smiled. "Congratulations. We're a hit." The face behind the smile stiffened. "Not bad for your first performance without your partner." His expression was unfamiliar, hard and uncomfortable on what should have been a gentle, sincere face.

The floating bed wriggled as Alexandros sat beside her. "You really scared me this evening," he said. "Recall should've been further along when you saw me. You were supposed to at least greet me as an old friend. Remember?" His voice was low while she watched the lantern's flame sculpt tiny images. "Remember the last time I helped you drop character? New York City, 1987?"

He stood and moved to the trunk, pulled it to the center of the room. When he touched its padlock, the lid opened, flooding the room with electric-blue brilliance. Alexandros pressed a jade bauble on the lid. The blue light changed to green. His shadow was huge on the wall as he reached into the trunk and withdrew an ice cream cone. It was half-eaten and began dripping only after he handed it to Sally.

"Another memento from another end of the world. You always need a souvenir, don't you? Taste it."

Raspberry. She held it like it might explode.

He forced a small laugh. "I never knew you liked raspberry until Sarah started craving it."

Sarah. As usual, she and Alex had been lovers in that series. Audiences loved when art imitated life. Her character had become a successful Broadway actress. He was the shining new executive in a Wall Street firm. Mr. and Mrs. Alex MacMillan, brought to you *live* from the 20th Century only on Network Time Channel 1! The finest reality a skindiver could buy: authentic historical drama—seeing, feeling, and smelling the bad ol' days before the world got too good to be interesting. The historians got their bread. The rest got their circuses.

When it came time to cancel that series, Alex dropped character first; the Network had no trouble dissolving his conditioning. But Sarah wouldn't die so easily. Selene remembered the screaming wail of the evac sirens.

"There we were in Central Park," he was saying, "with umpty-thousand scared shitless extras running in all directions just before the nukes blew." The nexus was open near the Alice in Wonderland statues. "You dropped character just in time." Just in time to step into the nexus and watch Manhattan go up in a rain of nukes that the "extras" believed came from Moscow.

"You never did let go of that ice cream. You almost clung to Sarah too long. The psi-shock of that one would've put half the 'divers into abuse treatment wards."

That series had played for over a year before the Network wrote in its smashing climax and then pulled the plug, erasing all insertions and alterations made to truetime—the bombs, the deaths, the artificial existence of Sarah and Alex MacMillan. As always, history neatly, tidily, irrevocably set itself right again. But the Network's temporary rewrites had done their job. When Selene and Alexandros returned up the Channel, they were greeted by adoring fans as well as a grateful—and wealthier—Network.

She had made friends there, in New York, 1987.

She felt the tears slide down her face, and was both angry and relieved by them. Alex held and rocked her, combing her hair with his fingers. "Hey. What's wrong? We got out. No one got hurt. Not in the end, anyway."

She broke his grasp and threw the ice cream hard. It struck the wall and spread across the dirt like an opening wound. She balled her fists and pounded him hard, harder, not hard enough. He dropped to the floor.

"They were not *extras!*" she shouted. "Not just characters! It wasn't make-believe. They were—they *are*—real people." She pointed out the window at London. Or New York, or Rome, Athens, San Francisco, or Pompeii.

He rubbed his ribs. "What the *fuck* are you talking about? We pulled the plug, didn't we? History snapped back to truetime. Just like always."

She remembered. Just like after the "gods" wiped out Athens; after the nanoviruses mutated a Coliseum audience before killing them; after Comet Halley dropped into downtown 1910.

Alexandros stood, inspecting his costume for dust. "You should see what the gang in Creative Control have planned for Tokyo at the height of the monster movie craze." He picked her blanket from the floor and dusted it carefully before wrapping it around her shoulders. "I've never seen this in you before."

She didn't look up.

"It's still just acting, Sel."

But this time *he* was the one who had monitored her and made sure the skindivers knew when an episode was beginning. Alexandros had kept them tuned in and living Sally along with her. Had he been linked into her while she was in bed with other men, riding her flesh with the 'divers? Why not? That's showbiz!

What about life back home? Had he kept up his brilliant work on stages before vast audiences? He seemed so thrilled about his new life in the Network, and spoke as though trying to convince her of its value. Or, perhaps, convince himself.

She suddenly knew why Alex had inserted himself into this series at this time. She hugged the blanket tight. "It's time to end," she said flatly. "What happens now?"

The lantern's flame jiggled in a breeze, and his shadow stretched and twitched on the wall. "Ah. That *is* the question. The Channel's been open for two years. It's at full stretch and threatening to snap. We have just enough time for the double finale tomorrow."

"And what's that?"

He was like a child sharing a dirty secret. "Oh, you know! June 29, 1613. The Globe Theater goes up in flames during the first performance of *Henry the Eighth*!"

"*What?*"

"This inn, too. *Foosh!* It's in truetime. The cannons caught the roof on fire. Ha! Two centuries before the *1812 Overture*. Fortunately, nobody got hurt."

Her brow tightened. "Then what's the *other* finale?"

"Guess. What's this culture's big bogeyman? Plague? Been done. Famine? Boring. God's wrathful vengeance? The Greeks did it better. Space aliens? Already played at Tharsis Mars Base."

"Alex! *Stop it!*"

He sucked a breath, seeing that he had gone too far. He did something to the side of the trunk. The luminescence burned a harsh red. The gray-skinned creature with bat wings climbed out onto the brim. A goblin joined it, baring yellow fangs in a hideous face. Then a bloated froglike creature with wasp wings flew out and lit on the upturned lid. It clapped four webbed hands and unrolled its tongue to its knees. A tongue of fire shot from the gaping mouth, churning the air like a blowtorch. Other things with wings and horns and twisted human features clambered out and stood around the trunk. Many were clad in moss and leaves. The tallest stood as high as Selene's shoulders.

Alex bounced on his toes. "Isn't the props department wonderful?"

Monstrosities gibbered around her. Demons from a Boschian vision. Goblins and bogles used to frighten children at bedtime. Creatures from rural myths and ghost stories. The dark side of religion and faerie lore she had lived among for two long years. Fires glowed within their glassy eyes.

"They're obscene."

"They're state of the art. And these are just the small ones. They can be directed through our links." He extended an arm toward a drooling thing that unfolded its wings and flew to his sleeve. It coughed a bright orange flame.

"*Or* voice commands provide that certain Satanic flavor that so impresses the natives." He pressed a red gem on the trunk's lock. "*Specter of Death!*" He smirked at his overdramatized voice. "Arise and obey my commands!"

A shroud-draped skeleton gripping a bloody scythe drifted up and filled the space from trunk to ceiling. The air smelled of earthworms and spoiled meat. Flames glowed behind the bone-gray eye sockets. Fingerbones clacked like bamboo, then raised the dripping, crescent blade over Selene's head. The skull turned toward her, unhinging its jaw in an impossible grin.

"Hold," Alex said. The apparition froze. "Press the ruby and they're fully voice-controlled. They'll obey direct commands. Try it, but be careful. Their programming tends toward the literal."

"No!" She turned away from him and grabbed her dress. It smelled rank. Her words came hard and fast as she put it on. "You can't just rewrite people's lives for cheap thrills or to sell more commercial time. They exist! Flesh-and-blood real live human beings like you and me." She thought of Jack. He was here because of Sally. Sally had saved him. "No. That's wrong," she said. "*We* stopped being real a long time ago."

"You always did get too wrapped up in your characters."

"I like who I am here."

"You're a whore!"

"Wasn't I always? Aren't you?"

For a beat, his face was hard and still. Then he continued. "People love you at our end," he said. "Millions of them on a hundred worlds!"

"You mean they love how well I fuck people they consider unreal, fictional." In each of their series together, their characters found reasons to break up their relationship with painful stabbing words. It was a point the "true" Alex and Selene managed to ignore when out of character. She knew what hurt him. "That includes you, too."

A glacial chill came from his eyes. The caring, sensitive Alex she had known—that Sarah and Sharri and Simone and the others within her had known—was absent. The Producer, cool and reserved and superior.

"You always claimed," he said, "that you became an actor to change people. Ever since our first stage together." A *Midsummer Night's Dream* within the Great Orion Nebula. Titania with newborn stars at her feet. Alex's magnificent Oberon. "Now you're a solo Network success, *and* the standard for future Total Immersion projects. Now you can play on any stage you want. We have offers coming in from the finest performing companies in human space. That's all waiting for you back home."

A breeze brought in the smell of the shit pit outside her window. She had never noticed it before.

"Don't throw it away," he said. "After we raise some Shakespearean hell, we'll pull the plug and go home. Then the past two years will have never happened here."

"They happened to me. I'll remember." She stepped toward the door.

"Sally's a character! Just like Sarah and the others. What makes this series so goddamned special?" He was shouting when she slammed the door behind her.

She leaned against the hallway wall. Jack's room. Sally should go to him, be with him. Too bad she wasn't here.

Selene ran down the stairs and into the newly arrived rain.

Act III

She walked until well past dawn, through filthy streets that were at once warmly familiar and strangely new. The town bustled with wagon wheels and shouting vendors. Farmers were already in the fields as sunlight turned the eastern clouds the color of dirty water. Her fingers brushed buildings as she passed them, memorizing the textures of wood and brick and loam. She sat on a low garden wall and listened for patterns in the rain as it struck the flowers. She focused her concentration, and a small glowing circle appeared in her field of vision. She ran her eyes across the garden. The icon remained in her view, always in the upper right corner. An empty circle. Good. The Network wasn't broadcasting her senses yet. Watching roses wasn't thrilling enough. She relaxed her concentration and the image vanished. Raindrops tapped her head and trickled down her back.

She wondered where the Channel nexus was focused, and was answered by another glowing glyph. The trunk. Of course. Alex had a colorful sense of theatrics. It was their pathway to home. Before he arrived, her link could have shown her the nexus as a glowing oval hole hovering above the inn, invisible to anyone not equipped with a bump in the skull and wires in the brain. But Sally had known nothing of Time Channels or nanolinks or skindivers.

Sally. A new persona could never be fully predicted. Which was part of the drama of Total Immersion. Language, social customs, mores. Synthesized memories of a life you never lived. All dumped into the brain before the Network dropped you unconscious in a new world and time. The rest came from within.

Selene had become a popular prostitute in the Sophocles' Greece series. And in Victoria's England. Her Caesar's Rome character nauseated her when she remembered it. Each of those women had been herself.

Alexandros had shared those other lives with her. In true-time, each was the other's partner, lover, friend, and teacher. He had nurtured her talent, helped it grow. Without him, she would not now be sitting on a garden wall down the road from Shakespeare's Globe.

What if the Channel collapsed before she returned through it? What if Alexandros returned alone, pulling the plug behind him? The universe strictly forbade return trips. Would she continue to live here in the history she helped shape, with truetime permanently and irrevocably altered? Or would she exist in a new truetime split off from the one she knew? Or else be edited out of existence entirely, along with Sally and her entire life here? The Network never told. The Network kept its secrets.

After those early series, certain critics accused them of slumming, of selling themselves for the latest trend. They were right. Each series had been tailored to the tastes of subscribers who paid to have life lived for them.

This time, though, the Network added a new plot twist. Sally began life with no predetermined memories, no history, alone on a dirt road with an entire identity to create. She had seen to that. Alex had stayed behind. She had a part in that, too.

Playing solo for the first time, she discovered a strong, content, fully rounded character. Or had it been the other way around? The heart of acting beat with self-discovery. Exploration of the soul. Total Immersion had offered that, and her real stage work would now be even stronger than before.

Any stage she wanted. She could travel the stars again and hear applause on a hundred worlds. She had earned it. How could she toss that away? And for what? Watching others chewed away by disease. Shitting and pissing in pots or ditches. Stepping over the dead and dying in the streets.

Blossoms nodded and raindrops made muddy craters in the earth. The sound of water against dirt conjured a memory. Jack clutching her hand while they lay in the sandy grass by the river. The things he said. His boyish laughter. That so-adult confidence in his own immense talent. That was so long ago. A lifetime.

After a few hours, the drizzle stopped. She returned to Bankside, where clouds hung over the Globe like a low shroud. She looked up at the theater's thatched roof and wooden walls, wondering how much rain was needed to prevent a fire. Useless thoughts. The blaze had happened. Would happen.

Selene climbed onto the stage, enjoying the odor of fresh paint. She admired the underside of the effects hut jutting out high above the stage and supported by two tall columns. Its gilded underside provided a ceiling painted to portray the heavens. To Sally, the hut had looked like a cottage held aloft above the players. To Selene, here was Hamlet's "brave o'erhanging firmament, this majestical roof fretted with golden fire." A square hole slid open in the ceiling. A round face poked down. The stagehand cupped his hands around his mouth and called down, asking if she had seen his assistant. When she said no, he cursed skillfully and thanked Sally, then vanished behind the panel sliding back into its piece of the sky.

In the tiring room, Richard and the others were exercising their bodies and throats, changing into costumes, and rehearsing bits of scenes. Robert, Augustine, Nick, and young Nathan. Kemp, Sly, Heminges, Condell. Friends she had known, it seemed, all her life. She saw them through Sally's eyes and heart. She was warm and at home here.

I will remember you.

They approached her. Through a false beard, Richard's face mirrored their distress.

"Lady. How farest thou? That stranger, with that beast—"

She shushed him with a finger to his lips. She took his hands, looked around at all the others.

"I am well. Just stricken with an ague that has passed. That gentleman is an old friend, a traveler newly returned from the Indies. He studies the strange beasts of the isles. His pet was but a harmless Indian ape." Everyone knew the accounts of bizarre creatures in exotic new lands on the other side of the world. She looked into the thickly lined face of her friend. For the last time? She stroked his big arms. "I am well. Truly." Richard looked doubtful. Time to change the subject. "Where's Jack?" she said.

"The lad was late to this morn's practice. Said he dreamt about his performance, that this day would see his finest ever, though I know he wishes not to play women after today." Richard laughed and wrapped a big arm around Sally's shoulders. "Jack's a strong lad of stout mettle. Do not concern yourself."

He pulled her away from the others, then lowered his voice to a hoarse whisper. "The boy is troubled. He spoke of that . . . gentleman. A devil from your dreams, he said, come to take you to—" He sighed. "I understand not all he spoke. He left the playhouse soon after."

She squeezed his hands. "I shall speak with him." How would Sally say goodbye to Jack?

"William is at my home," Richard said. "He asks for you. He wishes to see his Sally-o, said he would search for you at the inn."

William Shakespeare is asking for *me*! Selene searched within herself for the simple calm pleasure Sally would have found in the news. "Thank you, Richard. I miss him."

He kissed her forehead. "Now, get thee gone, woman!" He let go a kingly bellow. "Before King Henry relieves you of your pretty head!" The players laughed, and she gave each a hug or a kiss, saving the longest for Richard.

Act IV

The inn's front room was empty save for mugs and bottles from the night before. She found a sack of coins tied to the innkeeper's apron. Alex had been generous.

Upstairs, she knocked on Jack's door, then called his name. No answer. She pushed the door open.

On the wall over his bed, a crude painting hung by a string from a nail in the wood. It was a brightly colored depiction of Sally and Jack. He had painted it shortly after they moved to these rooms. They were holding hands and smiling child-drawing smiles. She tapped the frame and watched their painting-selves sway back and forth on the string.

She heard a creak through the wall. That floorboard near her bed. Alex must be just waking. She was on her way to the door when she saw thick bundles of vellum stacked beside Jack's bed. Jack's plays. *Masque of the Planets* already had revisions inked into the margins. She gently turned the pages. Not strictly a comedy, romance, or tragedy, but a weaving of all three, *Masque* was based on stories she had told him, imaginative fables conjured from her dreams. Memories of a life hidden within Sally for two long years. She recognized the grace and style of words nurtured by long study of Will's work. Jack displayed insights and wit that belied his youth, and his imagination laced the tightly woven fabric of his characters and story lines. There were passages here that could make other playwrights reach for a quill, such as those lesser talents who loitered at the Globe ready to borrow a catchy phrase or two. *Masque*'s main character was a stern but loving queen of a wondrous kingdom—a beautiful, wise woman named Serena, stolen away from her world by a handsome sorcerer with dark eyes.

She thought of the printshop and Colesly, of what Sally had done for Jack.

She placed the manuscript back where she found it and left the room.

In her chamber, the trunk was still there, but Alex was gone. A new dress hung on the lantern hook. It was richly detailed and bright with color. A *lady's* dress, the type worn by the wife of a powerful man.

On her bed lay a parchment scrolled in a red ribbon. When she touched it, the ribbon unfurled, the paper unrolled, and Alex's voice read his handwriting for her.

"Sel. Out seeing the sights. I hear there's bearbaiting down the street and cockfights at noon. Then to hit the City for a public execution. Hangings and pressings today. Now, *that's* entertainment." The parchment laughed Alex's laugh.

"The final episode will begin before the play does, today at two o'clock. We'll remote the props to the playhouse just after the cannons fire. Then we'll be back here and down the rabbit hole before the inn goes up. This'll be our biggest audience yet, and we'll both be broadcasting for dual-P.O.V. I'm glad we're a team again. Sorry about last night. Hope you like the dress. It's more you, don't you think? Put it on and join me. Contact me when you're ready. Switch the trunk from voice-to link-control so we won't have to come back here until we pull the plug. Loving you. As always. Alex."

The recording rolled itself up and the ribbon wriggled back into a tidy bow.

She turned to the trunk. "Open."

The lid rose with the simulated creak of rusty hinges and red light spilled into the room. Within the trunk, a uniform bloody glow hid any sense of depth or perspective, like a bottomless well from a Puritan's hellfire fantasies. A data screen blinked on within the upturned lid.

The voice programming was simple and flexible. "My personal storage," Selene said. The red glow turned to jade green. She reached in and lifted out a rough parchment adorned with flowing Greek text. It announced a new drama, *Oedipus Tyrannos*, to be performed at the amphitheater that afternoon. Alex had given it to her at a fountain near the theater, where they had made love before their character conditioning faded. The huge holographic Zeus *had* been impressive, hurling lightning wrath from the hovering Channel nexus. She had teledirected the Hera image herself.

A jeweled lace garter from Victoria's London, given to her by a dashing West End actor named Alex. They dined with Shaw and Oscar Wilde and Ellen Terry, then dropped character in time to watch Wells's three-legged Martian war machines spewing smoky black poison and streaming infernos into the streets. The Network spared no expense before it canceled that series.

A holobubble bearing the Tharsis Base insignia threw out colored light that coalesced into Alex and Sharri, a honeymoon couple newly arrived from Earth. They laughed and hugged and told each other sweet things. It was recorded the night of the group festivities that had left them both tired and sore and blissfully content. And had provided the second-highest ratings in Network history. The highest came the following night, when "alien berserkers" slit open the pressure domes and liquefied the survivors in their lifesuits.

Souvenirs from alternative histories the Network had created and the universe had erased. She placed them back into the trunk. A few words returned its glow to red.

"Come out."

Obedient obscenities climbed, flew, floated, and slithered out of the trunk. They stood, perched, or hovered around her like hideous dolls waiting to be wound up. The first wave.

"Hold," she said. The pandoran menagerie halted. She looked at the gray winged thing that had been perched on Alex's shoulder.

"Fly."

It launched itself and flapped around the room in complex patterns. It screeched and reached out long arms tipped with scalpel-like talons.

"Stop."

It fluttered to the floor.

This first wave of props was to be controlled by her and Alex's nanolink commands. But the vocal-command mode was equally well programmed.

"Burn yourself."

Perhaps a hesitation crossed its rubbery face. Then its eyes glowed fiercely red. It turned its face downward and belched a blowtorch into its chest. The device was soon a stinking puddle smoking on the floor.

She felt a cool satisfaction.

The data screen indicated a second wave waiting deeper within the trunk's stygian light. Preprogrammed and self-controlled, they would stream from the trunk like an army from Hell, with no guidance from her or Alex. But the second wave would come alive only after the first wave was released.

She ordered them back into the trunk, and soon they were swallowed by the red glare.

"Close."

The trunk sealed in the light.

She heard noises beyond the wall. Jack's room. She closed the door silently behind her.

This time, Jack answered her knock.

"Sally!" He pulled her into the room. "I knew not where you were! Methought the demon took you away. You—"

"Shhh." She hugged him and stroked his hair. "It's all right. I'm here." He clutched her elbows as if to assure himself she was indeed still flesh and blood.

She found the firmly maternal voice she used whenever Jack needed one. "What did I tell you about demons?"

He turned his eyes downward. "You said there be no demons or faerie folk. You said."

" 'Tis truth. Now, let's hear no more about it."

He sat on the bed. She told him the same lies about Alex and the creature she had told the others. Jack nodded, his face set in a mask of concentrated scrutiny. "Aye, Sally," he said, but his eyes did not blink while he looked at her.

"Is something wrong, Jack?"

Jack seemed to wake from a spell. He turned away from her and fumbled with his pages. "Lord Shake—William wishes to live in London again, and you and I with him. His true family is here, he says. He will teach me verse and drama, and you can nurse his sickness and give him good company, he says."

Will needs me. Sally.

Jack hugged Will's letter against his chest. "He wishes me to help create his new play. Called *Celestine*, from a tale I devised from your dreams. He will bring it here to me. Is that not grand news?"

A mixture of emotions swirled within her. The part of her that was Sally was delighted and honored. Will's guidance was exactly what Jack needed. It would be good for both, giving the elder poet the purpose and affection that Stratford and Anne could not, and providing the younger with a nurturer of his talent.

Today, June 29, 1613.

April 26, 1616. Less than three years left for Will, in the history that did not contain his Sally-o. She could change that.

"So you must stay, and none must take you away," Jack was saying.

He avoided her quizzical look by glancing down at his manuscript.

He was leafing through pages when he spoke again. "Mortals that speak to faeries must die." The non sequitur shook her. Jack shrugged and flipped a page. "William remembers that from country tales when he was young. Only faerie folk speak to faerie folk. I have gotten this wrong in my play, where magic folk and men travel to the planets together to save the magical queen." He looked at her with inquisitive interest, quill in hand. "Do spirits obey those not of magical birth?"

"If you like. 'Tis your play." She wanted desperately to change the subject.

Jack scribbled in a margin, then awkwardly put his papers together, moving his gangly arms and hands with nervous display. The back of one hand brushed against her breast, slowing just enough to follow its curve and find the nipple. It was no accident.

She stood. "I must meet someone, Jack. I'll see you at the play, hmm?"

"Is't that man?"

"Yes, Jack."

He shifted his position, placing his hands in his lap.

"Sally—" His erection pushed beneath his clothing, and he squirmed, looking ashamed.

She was embarrassed for him, and cast her eyes around the room. Just leave and talk about this later. It was, after all, perfectly normal, right?

The nail above his bed held no painting. It protruded over a gap between two wallboards. Scratches in the surrounding wood showed where the hole had been enlarged. Jack made a soft, pained sound when Selene stepped to the wall and peered through the hole.

The view revealed most of her room, including the trunk. Most prominent, though, was her bed, well lit by sunlight from the window. At night, moonlight shone there.

She spun around. "How long has this been here?"

He looked at his hands folded in his lap.

An angry flame flared within her, licking her insides.

"How *dare* you! How long have you been watching—"

Something black and cancerous in her soul burst open like a pustule. She felt sticky inside, ugly, used. . . .

Jack was crying, saying he was sorry and he loved her and never again—

She slapped him, hard, fast, without thought. His head snapped to the side, an angry red print across his cheek. His sobs sliced into her, cutting her like knives. Selene saw what was laid open within.

Jack had simply watched her with the eyes of a boy trapped in the churning onslaught of adolescence. Millions of others had done far more. The largest audiences of her career. They needed her, she had told herself. It was good to be needed.

But beneath the well-played roles, winding like a stream through the subconscious caverns where Sally and the others lived, was disgust for everyone who rode her flesh and soul. She had dammed that stream from the beginning, patching the cracks with every new character.

Sally was different. Sally was stronger than Selene had ever been, freer than Sarah, Sharri, Simone, and the others. Sally struck out with Selene's hand, driven by rage that had grown malignant. Jack was not the intended target; still, the blow shattered the ugliness, struck it away like shards from a sculptor's blade.

She felt dizzy, released from a locked box she never knew existed.

What had Jack become in the truetime where Sally did not exist? Had he even survived this far, to explore and discover who he could become? The future had never known of him. But Sally had changed everything.

Jack's face was red and wet. He sucked air with sharp breaths, staring at her with confusion and pain. She held and rocked him, wiped his tears. Before long, he was asleep. She kissed him, then closed the door quietly behind her as she left.

From now on, she was writing her own script. And rewriting one other. William said the purpose of acting was to hold a mirror up to nature. For the first time since her Network contract began, Selene liked what stared back at her through the looking glass.

The trunk's interior was a smooth red glow, flat as a mirror. She looked into it. "Do not obey Alex. Ignore his commands unless I command otherwise."

The streets clattered with coaches and townsfolk, and watermen taxied more people across the Thames from London. Vendors cried "Fresh peas!" and "New brooms, green brooms!" The smells of farms, tanning skins, and the salty tang of human sweat were stirred by the warm air into a rich concoction. She inhaled deeply and drank in the redolent earthiness as if she were its latest and best ingredient.

She stopped at a fruit wagon and pretended to examine the goods. She concentrated on a gentle mental push, and Alex's ident icon floated between her and a basket of strawberries.

⟨*Selene, where are you?*⟩ His voice was a ghostly whisper between her ears.

Her own symbol appeared next to his. She spoke softly, breathlessly, behind barely moving lips, focusing her thoughts. ⟨*In the market west of the Globe. I hate talking like this.*⟩

⟨*I'm at the arena near the Swan. Hurry. This is terrific.*⟩

⟨*Show me.*⟩

Her vision blurred. The fruit cart faded and was replaced by a wide street near a polygonal building. The Swan Theater. New street sounds reached her ears, louder, more raucous than the market where she stood. A crowd cheered behind her. A loud sermon came from her right. The view panned to the left, and she recognized a street corner. A comely blonde in a summer dress caught Selene's eye and winked at her, and the view bobbed as Alex scanned the shapely body in return. The girl waited a beat, dimpled invitingly, then disappeared into a huddle of men trading wagers and shouting in response to some unseen spectacle. Applause erupted after a burst of savage animal snarling. The smell of blood was so heavy Selene tasted it.

She canceled her glyph, and his vanished a second later. She was staring at a basket of strawberries. Someone shoved her arm, stumbling her painfully into the cart. Turning, she saw a squat man with a blistered face and stained apron glaring at her, asking if she wanted to gape all day or buy. She moved on up the road.

Alex waved from the corner he had shown her. He was dressed in the French style fashionable among the privileged. He looked at her disapprovingly.

"Why didn't you change that dress?" he said. "You don't have to wear that anymore."

"Let's talk."

His frown became a broad grin. "In a minute. Look at this."

He put an arm around her waist and led her into the cheering, hissing mob. A bear was leashed to a stake in a filthy pit. It thrashed out at four dogs that lunged and snapped and tore its flesh. It could not attack or retreat far before the metal collar bit into its raw and bleeding neck. The stake threatened to snap with the bear's tosses and tugs of rage. A breeze carried fur and blood into the audience, and Selene had to wipe her face. The crowd applauded wildly and money changed hands. Alex clapped and whistled.

"This is sick," she said.

"It's the favorite pastime of Shakespeare's London. How's *that* for proper English reserve?"

She pivoted and pushed through the crowd.

She was across the street when Alex grabbed her shoulder and turned her around. "What's wrong with you?" He gripped her hard. "We're on in a few hours and you've suddenly become the classic temperamental actor."

"What's wrong with *me*? I don't know you anymore. You used to be so—" She stopped. That Alex was from another life, one that belonged to somebody else. She led him to a side of the Swan far from passersby. She took a deep breath, then released it slowly.

"Ever since I was a girl, I've played characters, been what someone else thought I should be. I was addicted to the applause. But eventually I grew up and wanted to know who I *really* was. The theater let me explore. When I was onstage and in the dark, I had a strange, powerful permission to *be*. I was good at it. And so were you. Those hours onstage with you were some of the best in my life. The trap was this: I was still saying other people's words. I wanted more."

She took Alex's hand and made him feel the rough fabric of her dress. "I *am* someone here. Sally's always been inside me, and I like her. I made a difference, a *real* difference, in someone's life here. It changed me. *Jack* changed me. You stayed behind and I did it without you."

"That wasn't my idea. The Network—"

"Go*damn* the Network! It was *my* idea. After the 1987 series, I told them the next one would be done my way or I quit. London in the time of Shakespeare. I *made* them send me here. With a conditioning that had no biography imprint." She saw herself reflected in his eyes like tiny Escher prints. "And I told them I'd do it alone."

His eyes widened. "*What?*"

"Why do you think they offered you the Producer's chair you always wanted? I studied our characters after each series. I didn't like what I saw. Mine were dependent on the attention of others. Your last three found prestige and status more satisfying than anything else. You needed *me* less each time. That was a side of you I never knew before. I told the Network *this* series was going to be solo. I had to know if I could get by without anybody. Especially you."

He looked away. The crowd was thinning around the pit. Pieces of dog and bear were scattered around the uprooted stake. He turned back to her, and the hurt in his face twisted in her gut. "When we get back—"

"No. I'm not leaving. If I do, Sally will have never been here. So pull the plug and tell the Network to find a new whore." She felt the ache of earlier selves, but she refused to let him see the hurt. "You're playing solo now."

"You have to come back." He was desperate. "I need you. We have to control the props." The Producer. The Network exec. "Remember the Greek gods bit? We were a great team there. And the highest peaks of your career are waiting for you back home. Any stage you want, on any world you like."

She pounded a fist against the Swan Theater. "God*damn* it!" She pointed into the street, sweeping dozens of people in a single gesture, and saw Alex crinkle his nose at a breeze stinking of manure and fruit. "I'm not acting anymore. Jack needs me. I see in him what I used to see in you—the talent, the joy in creating something *good* that could never exist without him; the ambition, the drive to be what he *can* be."

"That Jack doesn't belong to real history. He never did become the world's greatest playwright, or actor, or whatever the hell he is. Maybe he was a printer. Or a farmer. Maybe he never got out of that printshop where you found him."

She grabbed his shoulders hard and pressed him against the wall, putting herself between him and her world. "He got out because I was here! He was never allowed to grow up before I got here. Think about the greatness he can achieve now. We should be performing *his* work in a thousand years. Jack needs Sally. So do I."

"Let's do our job and get out. No one will be hurt after that."

She pulled away and went into the street without looking back. He wouldn't follow. The taste of blood sat on her tongue, and she enjoyed it.

Act V

A silken red flag flapped from a cupola on the hut over the stage, showing London where good times could be had that afternoon. Soon, the trumpeter would appear in the cupola like a clockwork figure and blast the call announcing the play's beginning.

She pushed through the crowds inside the playhouse, bathing in the odors of sweat, tobacco, urine, hazelnuts, and beer.

Where was Will? Backstage with the actors, perhaps.

Above the stage, a cannon barrel poked through a door in the hut's facade. She tensed. Here was the stage effect that would toss flames onto the roof and burn the playhouse to the ground soon after the play began. No one had gotten hurt, though.

So that would not satisfy the Network.

Musicians and jesters blended into a collage of colors, sounds, and juggling clubs. Three boys tossed burning torches in looping patterns. Cries of "Ho!" and "Ha!" erupted around her. Playgoers were applauding or chattering or laughing or—

Voices. Switched on like a light and much nearer than in previous series. *Everyone* must be tuned in. She did her best to ignore them.

On the stage, a player delivered the Prologue to the quieting crowd. When was Jack's entrance as Anne Bullen? She was anxious to see his performance, and then tell him everything was all right. That Sally had forgiven him. That she would stay with him.

She searched for Will among the crowd, then found a seat next to a young woman who nodded hello. It was the blonde she had seen through Alex's eyes. Act One began. Richard's Henry VIII looked so grand in his robes. All the stage was his, and his voice rolled like thunder over the audience. He was magnificent.

Someone tapped her shoulder. She turned to find John, the 'prentice who tended the wardrobe. He was wringing a costume beard in his hands.

"Sally. Where be Jack?"

"Is he not in the tiring room?"

"Nay. He has not arrived and his scene approaches. Mister Burbage said I should find you. Said you may know."

"I last saw him at the inn." She winced at the memory. Was Jack too ashamed to leave his room? Did he believe the others knew of his indiscretion? Or that Sally no longer loved him?

No, not Jack. He was smarter and stronger than that.

John sifted the beard through his fingers. "He has come to harm. Injured. Or ill."

She squeezed John's arm and tried to smile assuringly.

She spotted Alex across the yard in the middle gallery. He was watching her. ⟨I heard that,⟩ he said in her head. ⟨I can *look for him at the inn. I'm not getting a response signal, so I have to check the props. You didn't switch them to link-control.*⟩

⟨*No. And they won't obey you, anyway.*⟩

⟨*What do you mean?*⟩ He looked tiny from here, but she still saw the expression on his face.

⟨*I mean the series is over. The props won't do your bidding anymore. Neither will I. Pull the plug and go home while you can.*⟩ A small red symbol floated in her eyes. It pulsed and vanished. ⟨*The Channel will collapse soon, so get out now. Goodbye, Alex.*⟩

His hurt was a cold breath in her mind.

"Sally?" John looked at her as if she had been mumbling to herself.

Shouts from across the yard cut through the audience. People were pointing to a spot far above her, above the highest gallery. Had the fire already started?

Shadows slid over the yard. The air pulsed like a heartbeat. A pair of black wings descended into the Globe, attached to a naked woman. Her skin was pale, like a corpse three days drowned, and the eyes glowed red. Other things flew and shrieked behind it. The air drummed with the beating of many wings, some leathern or scaled, some as slender and veined as waving leaves.

Playgoers shoving into an egress backed up as one. A floating specter guarded the exit. Blood dripped from its smoky hands. Goblins and wraiths stood in the doorways, like sentries at prison gates. Rodent-faced pixies scattered and chittered through the theater.

The froglike thing dived overhead, its wasp-wings buzzing. It joined a swarm spiraling into the yard. They lit on railings and squatted on the ground. Misshapen human forms skulked in the stage balcony. Gargoyles perched on the Globe's thatched roof and peered into the crowd below. They seemed to be searching.

Her head filled with thrilled applause.

She tuned in Alex's link. ⟨*You bastard! You're doing it anyway!*⟩

⟨*It's not me!*⟩

The playgoers surrounding Selene were shouting, praying, running through the narrow aisles. They buffeted her, trapping and carrying her with their flow.

Central Park, 1987. This was worse.

Throughout the theater, their eyes red and wicked, a hun-

dred nightmares were staring at Alex. Fear colored the words
he sent into her link. ⟨*Did you program this?*⟩

⟨*Of course not. I—*⟩

"I AM OBERON, KING OF SHADOWS!" The powerful
voice from the stage cut them off. "ROOM, FAERIES, FOR
OBERON IS PASSING FELL AND WRATH!"

Jack was standing there, arms outstretched. He stood tall and
straight, and the look on his face made Selene cold. Playgoers
stopped at the voice and turned to the stage, compelled to
listen. The sight of a calm young boy made the whole scene
seem absurdly normal.

The creatures' heads turned to follow Alex as he pushed his
way down the stairs into the yard. Claws and teeth glistened
like unsheathed blades.

Jack arced his arms dramatically. He gestured to the figures
around him. "Ye elves of hills, brooks, standing lakes, and
groves." Wings fluttered. Some reared their heads back and
screeched in acknowledgment. "You demi-puppets that by
moonshine do sour ringlets make—"

She knew those words. Prospero from *The Tempest*.

Ice flowed into her spine, carried on Alex's voice. ⟨*What's he
doing? Did you teach him that?*⟩

She shook her head. ⟨*No. He—*⟩ She stopped. It was too
crazy. ⟨*Voice control. They're on voice control. He heard you, us,
through the wall last night. And watched me today. God knows
what he understood, but he's smart. He could have gone into my
room anytime and opened the trunk.*⟩

Beasts lined up beside their new master. Jack looked into the
audience, then up at Selene. He stepped forward and reached
out to her from the stage.

"Sally. You spoke truth. These be no demons. They obey
me, not the wizard who seeks to take you from me." He ran
to the rear of the stage, clasped a railing, and pulled himself
up to the second balcony, then the third. He climbed the roof
over the stage, planted his feet at its pinnacle, and stood beneath the shroud-gray sky. He looked down on his audience
below.

"Obey me, spirits! We shall save our mistress from he who
has harmed her!"

Hundreds of fiery, icy eyes stared at Alex. Flames burned
behind gaping mouths and needle teeth. Selene ran to the
stairs and entered the yard yelling. "Jack! You don't understand!" ⟨*For God's sake, Alex, don't move.*⟩

The voices in her head told her how exciting and delightful all this was. Colored symbols appeared in her view. The Network was simulcasting through both her and Alex for dual-P.O.V. While the largest audience of her career lived this with her, Selene felt helpless and alone. They were lapping it up and hungry for more. She broadcast hatred to all who rode her flesh. A blinking icon indicated 'divers switching over to Alex's link.

An adolescent boy stood over a Globe Theater filled with monsters. He seemed to suddenly realize where he was, and he giggled and swayed as if intoxicated.

"Sally, look!" He waved. "I bid the faerie folk obey me, just as you did." He capered a giddy jig. "They hear the Faerie King and dance to his sweet words." The flag above him popped the air in lone applause.

"Sally," he said. She could barely hear him across the distance. "Mayhap you cannot love mortal men," he glared at Alex, "but I love you more than he. He means to take you and hurt good people with his familiars. I cannot live without you, and shall earn your love once more."

Jack pointed at Alex. Throughout the playhouse, wings spread in readiness.

"OBEY ME, FAERIE FOLK!" He gestured broadly, recalling Richard's grandiloquent Oberon.

Jack was washed in shadow as huge wings rose behind him. He looked up, and his mouth became a wide O. A demon, wings wide enough to wrap a horse in, flew overhead, almost knocking Jack from the roof with its long black legs. It bellowed deeply and spat fire between long fangs. It banked into the theater, pulled a woman from her husband, and tore her apart with taloned hands. Blood sprayed into the crowd. The creature laughed and flung the remains in two directions.

Playgoers screamed, and their terror struck Selene in a hot wave. Jack's face mirrored their fear. Shouts and cries—and laughter?—splashed inside Selene's skull. Struggling against their mental assault, Selene shoved the feedback to a far corner of her mind. She closed her eyes and concentrated on a single thought-command, the override code to shut down the creatures. But a red icon appeared against her eyelids: the Network's own override signal. The Network had disconnected her mental link to the props. She was merely a camera now, a body shared by the voices in her head. Helpless. The voices swelled in her mind again, and her ability to concentrate vanished be-

neath them. What was the Network doing? The world went
soft at the edges. She fell to her knees and tried to keep from
fainting.

The thunder of a thousand leather wings thrummed the air.
A dark river fountained upward over the Globe, eclipsing the
sun. The second wave. They streamed toward London, as unstoppable as nightfall. Some detoured into the theater, their
programming guiding them to where the first wave waited.

A man made a dash across the yard. A shrouded skeleton
descended before him and swept its blade through his neck,
sawing bone. It cackled and drifted into a gallery, spilling a red
trail.

A goat-faced phooka from Irish lore gutted a child on its jet-
black horns. Basilisks slithered into a gallery, their regal coro-
nets shining with polished gold. They breathed black fog into
the crowd, whose flesh fell from their bones like overcooked
meat.

Something green climbed a column to the stage ceiling, then
pushed through a panel into the hut. Orange fire brightened
the hole. A blackened body dropped through the heavens and
shattered on the stage.

Bodies were trampled in their rush to escape. Horror
pumped through Selene. Instead of quenching the fear, she
fed it, relished it, and sent it out in waves. She made herself
feel the terror around her in every strand of her flesh and soul.
Gasps and whimpers came back to her, pelting her mind like
rain.

Jack was hunched small on the roof. He peered down, a boy
general losing control of his toy soldiers. The first wave waited
for their orders. The second wave was in London now, beyond
all control, but the first was still on voice control. Her throat
stung with vomit and smoke, but Selene struggled to make the
words leave her mouth—

Alex ran. Jack pointed at him and shouted words. Alex fell
when long-armed things crashed into him, tearing into his skin
with tiny teeth and razor claws. Red stains grew on his clothing
as he tried to beat the things off him.

She inhaled deeply and at last the words tore past her throat.
"Command overri—"

Unseen teeth drove into her arms and chest. Sharp, dark
pain struck her from inside. *Stop make it stop get them off me
it hurts!* Alex's link carried the full power of his pain and
spewed it up the Channel into his audience, snaring Selene in

its force. It knifed into her, and she slid helplessly into Alex's skin.

He screamed inside her, merging his terror with her own and driving it like a spike into her brain. Hot pincers tore flesh from her legs and face, and blood poured hot and sticky over her hands. Ratlike mouths moved toward her eyes. Then in her mind she felt her name. Alex called out through a blaze of pain and fear, not knowing that she listened. When consciousness mercifully left him, his last thoughts were of her.

She sprawled on the dirt where she had fallen, gasping for air. She wanted to cry, scream, *anything* to release Alex's agony from her mind. It grew inside her skull, increased by the feedback from 'divers who were suffering it with her. Their pain and fear squeezed her brain like a sponge.

Alex lay in the dirt nearby, gray things moving on his body and puddles of red-brown mud growing in the dirt. Selene shouted, the exertion exhausting her. *"Stop! Command override Selene now!"*

The creatures froze. She had told them to ignore only Alex's commands.

Scattered moans and wails drifted throughout the playhouse, within her head. She smelled blood everywhere. She was stupid to have let it come this far.

A glowing disk burned in her field of view. Why hadn't the Network cut the broadcast? She ran to Alex and gently pulled the rigid creatures from his body, stopping the blood as best she could.

"Sall-y-y!" Jack's voice yanked her around. He was crying. Even from this distance, she saw the horrible pale fear on his face. He stepped forward and reached out to her. The roof collapsed beneath him, billowing trapped smoke and flames. He flailed his arms. He took *so long* to reach the stage. She could not hear the sound when he did.

Her scream echoed within her as she ran and leapt onto the stage.

Richard and the others were gathering around Jack. The boy moaned. Still alive, thank God. Jack's hair was sticky red, and his legs were splayed in unnatural angles. One arm was twisted underneath him. It bent in too many places.

Richard took her arm and gripped it hard. His face was terrible to see.

"Whoever he be, Lady," he said, tilting his head toward Alex, "send him on his way if he be not dead. This is his

handiwork, and we shall never see the likes of this lad again."
Other actors pulled him away while he gave in to sobs.

She looked at her friends. Some stared at her, confused,
grief-stricken. The boy shouted something unintelligible, and
his eyes were wide and searching. His screams gurgled wetly.
They were weaker now. His body convulsed, and blood spilled
over the brim of his mouth. His eyes became still, like marble,
no longer searching. While Selene watched, the life left Jack's
body. He had not even known she was near.

She had chosen to stay so she could save him, to save the
life that her presence had given him. Where would Jack be
now if she had never arrived? She had changed everything.

Actors lifted Jack's body and carried it toward the exit. One
of them cried, "Sally, come!" Flames had sprouted all over this
side of the theater. Wind fanned the fires in all directions. A
patch of burning thatch fell to the stage.

She could still undo this, the only way she was allowed.

She ran to Alex. He was heavy and his wounds opened like
mouths when she tried to lift him.

"Someone please help me!" she cried. Tears blurred her vision. She tasted the fear and ugliness, savored it, made it grow,
and thrust it up the Channel. In her eyes, Nielsen lines
dropped as 'divers pulled themselves out of the broadcast. The
red outline of the trunk floated above Alex's body. It pulsed
quickly and did not disappear.

Richard was beside her. He lifted Alex at the shoulders and
indicated that she take Alex's feet. They staggered to the nearest exit.

In the alehouse, smoke mixed with the smell of stale beer.
Everyone was gathering belongings, salvaging furniture, rescuing what they could. The innkeeper gave a joyful shout when
he found a bag of gold coins tied to his apron. No one stopped
them as they ascended the steps.

Smoke was thickening the air in her room. Where her window had been, a black-edged hole, as if carved by a blowtorch,
took out most of the wall. It was big enough to show all of
London burning beyond the Thames. Winged black specks
swooped among the City towers.

Richard was placing his burden on the floor when she told
him no. She felt Alex's pulse slow in his neck.

"Open."

The electric-blue blaze washed the room. She placed Alex's

feet into the light and made Richard lift him to a standing position. Richard's eyes went wide as something took Alex and lowered him gently into the pulsing radiance.

Smoke burned in her nostrils and the trunk was blaring its alarm.

She hugged Richard hard and told him to leave now. He took her hands and looked into her face.

"Lady," he said. Then he left.

She pushed through the smoke in the adjoining room, coughing, her throat raw. The hole over Jack's bed was a smoldering mouth, burned wide open, and pieces of the surrounding wall had been ripped away by something that left deep claw marks. Blood painted the wall down to the floor. Whose—?

Scattered on the floor like dead leaves were the pages of Jack's play. On the bed lay a string-wrapped bundle: *Celestine*, just as Will had promised. Blood like spilled ink spattered the pages. Will must have been here when—

She gathered her tears within, fused them with rage and *pushed* with her mind. In her eyes, the glowing disk blinked, vanished. The Network had cut the broadcast. The trunk's alarm was screaming now.

Jack was out there, a body among many others. She fought the desire to run to him, hold him, and weep over him. *I cannot live without you,* he had said. She remembered the hell of the printshop. Black bile anger grew at the arbitrary injustice from—who or what? The Network? The random chaos of history, fate? God? Not knowing made her angrier. Whatever the source, she defied it. She dropped to her knees and gathered up the vellum leaves. *Masque of the Planets.* They smelled of parchment and smoke. They always would. For the ages.

The blue brightness took her, and the jeweled lid closed behind her.

Her greatest performances were yet to come, before real audiences, on the stages of a hundred worlds. She would play for them a faerie queen, and give them words conjured by a heart rendered nonexistent, from a life no more yielding than a dream. She would make them taste a bite of what *could* have been. Within Orion, with newborn stars for her backdrop. Perhaps with Alexandros. Or without. She could play solo now, and her name—her final name—would be Sally-o.

Exeunt

The cannon tossed flaming wads onto the roof toward the end of Act One. Within two hours the Globe and the adjoining alehouse were burned to the ground. No one was hurt except, according to one of the few surviving documents of the event, for a man who put out his breeches with a providential bottle of ale.

The floor in the inn's upper rooms crumbled and fell with the rest of the building. Fortunately, the elderly Italian cloth merchant who had lived there the past two years was not home when fire raged through it.

(For Nancy Kress)

WHICH DARKNESS WILL COME UPON US?

John M. Landsberg

Senneterre did not pull away when he stumbled against the tree, but attempted instead to use this delay in his escape by folding his hands in front of his mouth and making an effort to pray. The only will he found within himself, however, was to blow into his bent fingers for warmth.

One shoulder and one cheek pressed painfully against the coarse black bark. Horrible how the failures of the flesh could tear him from his God, but true nevertheless. How long it had been since his last nourishment—and what had *that* been? A foul taste of *sagamité*! He had no memory of the experience save that of the torturous retching that followed close upon it. The exit of the rancid, greasy corn mush had left his stomach more empty than it had been before the meal. Now he was far past hunger, but in what condition he could not say.

He had heard of ascetics who fasted to enter a state in which they believed themselves closer to God. Was such deprivation working for him now? Was this unnatural brightness at the edges of the trees an indication that he was closer to God? He no longer noticed the worn sandal strap that had been digging so harshly into his left foot day after day—was this a sign that he was closer to God?

He allowed his legs to buckle, and his body scraped against the tree as he dropped. His knees came to rest on the matted

pine needles that wove a blanket over the moist soil. No matter
if the Savages were almost on his heels, he had to make peace
with his Maker. Again he tried to pray.

Again no words came.

In the mist, long before the sun awoke, Nouwanish arose
from his dream with the taste of ashes in his mouth. He spat
on the ground, but the foulness still coated his tongue. His
dream had been very bad, a warning of the worst kind. Even
worse than the worst, because this marked the third time the
same dream had come to him. The first time had been in the
night after his first meeting with white men. The second time
had been in the night after the day Senneterre had come
among the Algonkian people.

And now the third time, in the night before the day on
which he knew Senneterre would die.

The white men revered Senneterre. They called him Father
Senneterre, and told Nouwanish how he represented the One
On Earth who guided all their spirits.

He would guide the Algonkin if they would allow it.

But since the priest had come, this is what Nouwanish had
seen: He had seen his warriors kill beavers without giving
thanks, without giving respect to the bones, in their haste to
bring the pelts to the white men, in their lust to trade for
tobacco and muskets. He had seen Algonkian women leaving
off their work on the fires and the food, leaving off the cleaning
and scraping of the hides, to offer themselves to the white men
for pieces of colored cloth. He had heard his people asking why
they could not learn the secrets of the white man's buildings
and so not need to move their village to the winter place.

He had spoken against these things. He had forbidden what
he could. But he had seen the resentment in his people's eyes
when he spoke.

And this was his dream:

Nouwanish stood alone in the forest. He raised his bow and
launched his finest arrow, one fletched with the feathers of an
eagle, one that flew straight and true at a proud buck. As it
flew, a white man descended from a cloud and clutched the
shaft in both hands. The stranger flew with the arrow until its
point pierced the buck's heart. The man entered with the arrow into the body of the deer. The deer, mortally wounded,
cried out its agony, but in a human voice, the voice of Nouwanish's own son Imoungha. The sound of this cry spread

throughout the world, and became a poison that murdered every deer, every beaver, every hawk, every tree, every Algonkin. At last the sun itself shriveled and died.

Then the corpses of all these, all the dead creatures of the now dark and barren world, rose again, dancing loose-limbed and hollow-eyed, carried on the backs of the white men who crouched inside.

It had been a good run. The Sun Singer had journeyed nearly six billion leltens and had gathered over twelve million ged-miks of data for the greater glory of Sumanadama—one million ged-miks more than Kalak-gernas needed to assure his promotion to Overcaptain. Kalak had even discovered this heretofore unknown solar system. Surely that information was worth a huge bonus, possibly even the seldom bestowed gift of his own ship.

It was unquestionably a time for celebration.

"O great Undercaptain Kalak-gernas!"

Kalak turned to greet Lim-norbel, his trusted Firstcounselor. Kalak lifted his mouth flap with two tongues, then extended a hand to stroke Lim-norbel's seed pouch; he wanted Lim to know his extreme pleasure. No Firstcounselor had ever guided a Deep Space Ship more steadfastly. He would recommend Lim for Second Undercaptain on another ship, even though it would mean losing his services, and his companionship. He saw Lim begin to raise his own mouth flap, and smiled as Lim restrained himself from this improprietous gesture.

"That's all right, Lim," he said magnanimously. "After all we've been through together, I wouldn't hold it against you."

"Thank you, great Undercaptain."

"What's on your mind, Lim?"

"The men would like—" Lim hesitated.

Kalak closed his fourth eye and curled the ends of his ear tubes downward. Lim nearly raised his mouth flap again at this show of affection.

"Don't tell me," Kalak said. "The men would like to celebrate. It's a subject that has been on my mind as well—"

Lim's upper breathing cage pulsated with anticipation.

"—and so," Kalak continued, "I think it would be a good idea to break out the *rijpyr-zet*."

A brief respite from duty would not hurt; there was enough time for that. He regretted that they had not enough time, however, to explore the enchanting blue planet below them. Their orders were to return home almost immediately.

Watching Lim rush off excitedly to spread the news, Kalak thought how good it would be if he could share in the *rijpyrzet*. Unfortunately, he would have to enjoy the men's revels vicariously. After all, someone had to remain sober.

The last fever had been the most deadly in the nine generations of memory that Nouwanish carried in his heart and head; it had also been Nouwanish's opportunity. When the sickness came upon them, Nouwanish did not at first blame Senneterre, but most of his people did. Watching Senneterre's water sorcery, they saw many Algonkin die in agony with drops of Senneterre's water on their foreheads, and they knew him for a demon. Nouwanish then found it useful to follow their lead.

"We must drive him out. We must kill him. I say do it now, before any more die."

He said these things even though he was not completely convinced that Senneterre was a demon. He said them even though Senneterre had once brought him tobacco with no expectation of trade—a true gift. He said them even though Senneterre had once pulled Nouwanish's brother Mitanis from the fast water and saved his life.

He said these things because even if Senneterre was a demon, he was also something far more dangerous than any demon; he was a white man.

He said these things, and in the face of the sickness his people listened to him at last. He was astounded how hard it had been to convince them that the white men had to be eliminated. Nouwanish had told them tales, more terrible than ghost stories, of what he had seen on his journey to the mouth of the great river—of the streams of waste fouling the water, of the beaver dams smashed, of the places where the trees were ripped away to clear more room than was needed for the white man's buildings, but it required the fever to open his people's hearts to his words. It was the same fever from which many had died in the past, but this time they chose to blame the demon who wore the black robe.

So be it, thought Nouwanish. What good were the trinkets? What good was the tobacco? What good even were the muskets that his people received in trade? The white men would always keep far more muskets than they would give the Algonkin.

But Nouwanish would not have pronounced the sentence of death upon Senneterre except for his dream.

What frightened him most about his dream was this: No dream had ever shown him a time beyond the end of a journey, or at most beyond the end of one season, but this dream showed him a time that was to come long after the life and death of even his youngest son.

Senneterre opened his mind to the grace of God, and it was filled instead with the face of death.

Lost in delirium, he imagined himself back again in the village with the Algonkian Savages, inside the crude hut with the sick ones, stumbling over the remains of the recently departed, searching for one who might still benefit from the final sacrament he could bestow.

Here was one, seeking warmth from the small fire. Cheeks caved in, a face that seemed more hollow than it would look even with no covering of flesh, even with the eyeballs eaten away by worms. Under the arms, huge masses of festering tissue were broken open, leaking pus. The stench was intolerable, but he knelt beside the dying woman and began.

"In the name of the Father—"

The blow had come then, catching him on one ear, knocking him across the cramped hut, past the fire that warmed the center of the room. He fell onto a limp, unmoving body. Scrambling away in revulsion, he looked up to see Nouwanish standing over him. Sweat beaded on the Algonkian chief's heaving chest and on the skin under his flaring nostrils. A reflection of the fire leaped in his eyes.

"You will not kill another," Nouwanish said.

"I do not kill them," Senneterre said. His ear, his whole head, rang louder than the bells of his seminary in Rouen. "I am trying only to save them from the darkness, the black pit of Hell. What I do enables them to enter Heaven."

"You speak always of heaven, but where is it? I have seen what you will make of the world; is that your heaven?" He spat in the dust. "It is *your* time to die, demon."

"Nouwanish, you know I do not kill them."

"You deserve death," Nouwanish said, "and you will die, but because you gave me the life of my brother, Mitanis, before you took it again with your fever, I will let you run."

• • •

The green forests, gentle mountains, and shimmering lakes of this beautiful new planet swam in Lim-norbel's sight like a dizzy ballet far below his feet. He whooped a wordless cry of delight, feeling the exotic atmosphere rush past his face, ruffling his scales. The oxygen content was a bit high, but he pulsed the alien mixture through his middle breathing cage, thinning the oxygen to about twelve percent, and concentrating the argon to almost four percent. The nitrogen was a problem, too, but the slight sensation of impending suffocation was merely exciting when compounded with his *rijpyr-zet* euphoria.

He gazed up at the black triangular underside of the Sun Singer, and for a moment nostalgia took him in its grasp. He was sad to see the end of the adventures he had shared with his fellow crewmen. At the same time, though, he was eager to ride home to glory. But those thoughts were past and future. The present moment was not to be wasted staring up at the ship he already knew well, so he quickly looked down at the intoxicating planet once more, which heightened his giddiness.

He howled his glee at the landscape again, unable to think of any more mature way to express his feelings, but it didn't matter. If his Undercaptain was allowing him the rare, usually forbidden pleasure of riding the open observation platform while the ship rushed through an alien planetary atmosphere, it could only mean he was so well appreciated that he would soon be recommended for Second Undercaptain. He leaned over the railing and bellowed, "Lim-norbel is the best First-counselor in The Twelve Galaxies!"

Up on the bridge Kalak-gernas was taking pleasure in the sight of his men enjoying themselves. It had been a long journey, and they deserved a chance to relax.

He only hoped Lim-norbel wasn't getting carried away on the observation platform below.

Nouwanish signaled his six warriors to rest, but did not allow himself that luxury; he only leaned a portion of his weight on his lance. He had made a mistake, he knew. He should not have let Senneterre run. True, there was no chance Senneterre would reach the river alive. The trees would never talk to him. The animals would never surrender their lives for him. Yet merely allowing his death was not enough. Nouwanish would be diminished in his people's eyes if he did not take the demon's life and capture his spirit. Still, he and his men should not be here, wasting energy that would be better spent moving their village to the winter place. Nouwanish regretted the weakness that came from once calling the man his friend.

A shadow fell across his face and across the forest, and he raised his head to look.

And as his eyes filled with the sight of the thing in the sky, a terror flooded Nouwanish's heart, a terror that his people's suspicion was true, that Senneterre was in fact a demon, and that the huge dark object overhead was the proof. Should he have heeded his adviser Loomeona's insistence that Senneterre commanded vast evil powers? Was it too late to escape the black monster that grasped the sun like the hand of doom?

Well, so be it! If it was too late, then it was too late. They would not run. They would die like men.

"Will you waste your eyes staring at the empty sky all day?" he demanded of his warriors. "I see nothing important there!" He brandished his lance overhead. "The demon is near; we will destroy him before the sun sleeps!"

With a gesture, he commanded his warriors to move on. Emboldened by his brave words, they obeyed.

Senneterre's body convulsed, a momentary spasm which threw him to the ground. Was he suffering from starvation, or from the deepening cold of the approaching night, or from the exhaustion of his flight—or was this seizure a response to the terror that he might never regain his ability to open his soul to God? Whatever it was, at least this collapse freed his mind from the memory of the victims of the fever, and his useless efforts to comfort them, and the turn Nouwanish had taken against him.

Was it right that he took the offered chance to escape? Why did he not stay and accept the death that he now imagined must have been in God's plan for him all along? Why did his weakness plague him even to the point of keeping him alive when death was his only salvation?

Or was it? Anno Domini 1629 was ending as he never could have dreamed when it began; it made him wonder if once again he had misinterpreted God's intentions. After all, who had suffered more than he? And if he had suffered so much already, what glories of suffering might still lie ahead? Now was not the time to stop when God might be calling him on, even on to sainthood!

He clutched the tree and wrenched himself to his feet. The

sandal that had been chafing him ripped away. He tugged his robe tight against the bitter chill, but the shredded black fabric held little comfort. He moved forward. A branch tore his cheek. What did it matter? It would not kill him. The Savages would kill him, unless he could keep his few minutes' advantage over them until he reached the river, which was still at least two days' walk. How could he accomplish such a feat? Certainly he could not, but God Almighty could accomplish it through him.

And at that moment of renascent belief, as he felt his soul barely begin to open to the Lord again, something happened that stripped away his doubt completely, and he knew that he would accomplish whatever the Lord intended for him. Because overhead, a sign had appeared—a sign from God. It was not a sign Senneterre would have expected, not one familiar in its shape or substance, but its strangeness was all the more reason it could only be divine.

It was a black pyramid that floated in the sky, blotting out the sun as it crossed.

Gazing up in trembling awe, Senneterre discerned a small protrusion on its underside. Squinting, he could even make out something within the protrusion, something that had the look of a living creature—it was mottled in color and multilimbed, and seeming to move of its own volition—but whatever it was, it was no creature that had ever lived on Earth.

Could it be an angel?

What else *could* it be?

As he watched, faint noises came to his ears, apparently issuing from the angel: first he heard two short notes like the caw of a blackbird, then a series of harsh tones like the chattering of a dozen magpies. And during this chattering, a small silvery object, glinting in the afternoon sun, fell away from the angel. With divinely inspired attention, Senneterre regarded its descent into the forest. Seconds later, the pyramid had sailed past and was lost to view beyond the treetops.

Senneterre summoned the last of his strength and began to run.

Nouwanish also studied the shiny object's descent. If it had been sent to Senneterre's aid, was it not strange that it fell so far ahead, not near him at all? Nouwanish imagined himself reaching it first, but would he dare to touch something that had come from the world of night?

The priest's sudden motion made his black robe highly visible through the forest; his lead was now very slight. Even so, Nouwanish knew that if the white man's strength held out only briefly, or if he could indeed call upon the strength of a demon, he would reach the object first.

Nouwanish ran. His warriors ran close behind.

"Oh, Great Undercaptain Kalak-gernas!!"

It was Lim's voice via the communicator. He sounded scared, which was unlike him.

Kalak stepped toward the microphone nearest him, on the navigator's panel. "What is it, Lim?" he said firmly, trying by his tone to steady his Firstcounselor.

"My—I—I was leaning over and somehow—oh, Sumanadama forgive me!—my Guardian slipped out of its holster. It fell onto the planet."

Kalak resisted the impulse to sit. He couldn't show his men any sign of weakness in the face of this disaster. In spite of their drunkenness, they had all fallen silent and were regarding him with apprehension.

"Firstcounselor," Kalak said evenly, "please resume your post on the bridge." He switched the communicator to general intraship broadcast. "All hands, resume your posts immediately. Docking bay, prepare to launch landing vessel 6."

By the time the Sun Singer could come to a safe stop they would be far from the fallen Guardian. To be sure, the tracking signal would allow them to pinpoint it easily, but time would pass while they descended in the lander and walked to its location, and anything could happen in that time.

What troubled Kalak-gernas most was their lack of information on the inhabitants of this planet. It wasn't their job to make contact. That was the very special task of the Welcoming Contingent, who would return later and catalog all living forms on the planet, and if any were intelligent, set about making contact by means of proper, carefully devised techniques that would not induce panic.

Of course, if this planet harbored no intelligent beings, it was almost impossible any harm could come of losing a Guardian. But if an intelligent creature found it, he could readily find a way to use it, without knowing its purpose and its many possible misuses. It would be as if a child had found it. Kalak shuddered at the memory of the horrendous accidents that had happened when children accidentally played with Guardians. And this was far worse. Unsuspecting intelligent alien beings might be hurt. An interplanetary incident could ensue. If he didn't retrieve the Guardian quickly, there would be no Over-captainship for him. In fact, he would almost certainly be court-martialed and exiled to an ostracism camp on Zhonismik.

It pained him to think Lim-norbel would suffer as well, but at least Lim's punishment would be less severe. Without question, the largest part of the responsibility rested with Kalak-gernas. He had allowed Lim to ride the platform—drunk on *rijpyr-zet* no less—and he had to accept the harshest consequences.

For a moment, his anger flared; he imagined calling Lim before him and saying, Why in the name of all that is holy did you carry your Guardian on your joyride? Did you anticipate attack from the wild beasts of Maldoran, out there on the observation platform?

But no. Humiliating Lim-norbel with sarcastic and obvious questions would do no good. It wouldn't even make Kalak-gernas feel better. It would humiliate himself as well, and lower his status in the eyes of his men. And it wouldn't change the fact that the Guardian had fallen.

As a matter of fact, Kalak realized, Lim might indeed have feared attack—not from Maldoran wildlife, of course, but who knew *what* this planet had in store?

Senneterre parted a clump of wild blueberry bushes and spotted the object resting in a small clearing on a bed of pine needles. The bark of a nearby tree displayed a large gouge where the thing had struck first. Peering into the woods on either side, he hesitated to step forward, but then chastised himself: Do you fear even to meet an angel? He pushed forward through the bushes.

Approaching the strange gift, he trembled to think that he might touch something that had so recently left the hand of an angel, but he would not shrink from this Heavenly boon, whatever it was, and boldly he placed a hand on it and tried to lift it. It was so heavy, however, that in his debilitated state the task required both hands.

Atop the object's barrel, which was about half the length and twice the diameter of a musket's barrel, were two smaller, parallel tubular structures. He imagined he saw something through the length of these, and on raising one of them to his eye, he became dizzy with fear; seen through the tube, the distant trees had appeared shockingly close. The heretic Galileo Galilei was known to have constructed tubes that could change the appearance of natural objects in this way; how did such tubes come to be a part of this object from Heaven?

But indeed, Senneterre reassured himself, the ways of the Lord are more mysterious than we can know. Continuing to study the device, he noticed that on one side of the barrel was engraved an arrangement of figures, apparently some kind of writing. Undoubtedly it was the language of Heaven—sadly indecipherable to him. Oddly, the handgrip had four more grooves than he had fingers to fit into them. Ahead of the grip was a trigger, again rather like that of a musket.

Could this be a weapon?

Fascinated, Senneterre pointed it at a nearby tree and pulled the trigger.

With a tiny *pop*, a large piece of bark disappeared. It did not explode, nor did it fly into the air. It vanished.

The weapon itself had remained silent, and had not recoiled.

As Senneterre stared at the device in disbelief, he noticed a tiny sliding lever on one side, set all the way back toward the handgrip. Sliding the lever all the way forward, he took aim again at the same tree and squeezed the trigger.

With a roar that seemed to split the sky, a portion of forest disappeared, a portion larger than the whole Algonkian village from which Senneterre had recently fled. A fierce wind whipped his back as it rushed to fill the empty space, and a thunderclap cleaved the air. Seconds later, the wind settled, and the echoes of the thunder were dying as they raced across distant hills.

Hidden in the forest, Nouwanish was silent—though his heart screamed inside his chest—as he regarded the black-robed demon brandishing the shiny object dropped by the sky demons. What terrible sorcery was this, that could obliterate everything in its path for such a great distance? How could the Algonkian people ever defend themselves now?

He looked into the faces of each of his friends, his hand-selected warriors, the finest in the tribe. In each one he saw fear, but also a determination to face this horror, no matter what the cost. Only the fiercest spirit had kept them from crying out when they saw the trees die, and only that same fierce spirit kept them silent now, waiting for his command.

What could he say to them?

• • •

Sumanadama help us, Kalak-gernas thought when he heard the blast emanating from the area where the Guardian had fallen. There was only one explanation. This planet had intelligent life; one of them had found the Guardian, and had used it.

A sickness rose in him. He had never made contact with any alien race, and now it had to be this way. Of course, he had received the same training every Deep Space Ship Commander had, which emphasized avoidance of contact at all costs, except in cases of extreme emergency, in which case he was to use a few simple techniques for dealing with the native beings without initiating a conflict.

But there was no instruction on how to retrieve a lost Guardian from a race of aliens no one has ever met. Quite naturally, no one anticipated the need. Now, however, the need was intensely real, and unless Kalak could surmount the communication problem within a few short breaths of time—which was obviously impossible—or unless the intelligent creatures of this planet subscribed to the Tenets of Sumanadama—which Kalak had no reason to believe—serious trouble might overtake them all.

"Come along quickly," he told the landing party. "We are near. We must make haste."

The thunder of the Guardian's firing reverberated through his mind. He prayed he would find a way to prevent hearing it again.

In profoundest amazement, Senneterre slid the lever back and forth, contemplating the monstrous power he held in his hand; as his thoughts coalesced, he let the lever come to rest near the back end of its slot. Was this how God wanted him to carry on his mission? Was he now expected to transform himself from a figurative soldier in the army of the faith into a literal one?

The intensity of this image was unendurable; despair welled upward from within and seized him. "O Lord, You must not!" he cried into the gray sky that hung over the newly denuded patch of land. At last he had found the voice that had deserted him in his prayers, and its power made him tremble fiercely. "You must not ask me to take human life in Your name! Not even to kill these Savages!"

But how dare he defy the Almighty? Would he not be cast down into Hell for such blasphemy?

He sank to his knees, sobbing.

Whatever the Almighty wanted of him, it was far beyond his understanding. Now he could comprehend only this: He would soon die alone in the forest at the hands of the Algonkin.

But—perhaps it was this very death that God wanted for him. Perhaps God wanted him to renounce the temptation of the weapon and meet death in sainted glory.

He took a deep breath to halt the flow of tears.

His forehead throbbed where he had recently struck a branch. His sunken stomach growled. He stared down at his filthy hands holding the weapon, and imagined the flesh falling away from them as his body rotted here in this alien wilderness. Such a weapon, after all, could easily wipe out all his enemies, could even clear an open path to the river and to deliverance.

No! Curse his mortal flesh! Was he so weak that he would choose to kill, merely to maintain his increasingly wretched earthly existence—so weak that he was unwilling to die for the Lord?

But, oh, the terrible, intolerable confusion! Had he not thought that God Himself wanted him to survive? Had he not thought that the Lord had sent this weapon to enable him to kill Nouwanish and his men, and then to conquer this land, and perhaps many other lands, in His name? A weapon like this could easily accomplish such a victory, a weapon like this could—

Be an instrument of the Devil.

The realization clutched him and shook the breath out of him. How could he not have seen it before?

Was this not, most assuredly, a temptation sent by the Beast?

The weapon now seemed to burn his flesh, but Senneterre's fingers were powerless to release it, paralyzed by a dread such as he had never known.

At that moment, there came a rustling noise in the under-brush.

Senneterre raised his head, in his exhaustion unable, and in his fear unwilling, to imagine what might be approaching.

Other noises then issued from the forest, like the cackling of large birds. They were the same sort of noises he had heard from above, just before the angel—the demon?—sent the weapon to him.

• • •

Kalak's men slipped abruptly from thick forest into a huge scar of empty ground. On the other side of the unnatural clearing stood what could only be one of the autonomous and probably intelligent creatures of this planet, even if judging by nothing other than the fact that it was holding the Guardian.

"Full alert!" Kalak commanded. "Do not fire except on my direct order!"

And now strange and horrible creatures were standing in the clearing, less than a hundred paces from him, and he had never seen anything like this cluster of scaly brown multilegged reptiles, half again as tall as he was, wearing bizarre uniforms, swiveling their heads around and regarding him with four enormous eyes each.

"We must move quickly toward him," Kalak called to his shipmates, "so as to reassure him that we are not devious." He raised his voice: "Sumanadama," he prayed aloud in the manner of The Invocation Before A Fruitful Meeting, "let this creature hear what we say in his deepest heart." Although he knew there was no way his next words could be understood, he had no choice; he changed his tone of voice again and called out loudly as they sped across the gap. "Creature of another planet, we apologize for our error. Please excuse our presence. We beg you to return our Guardian."

Nouwanish frowned. The demons from the sky were yelling and howling at Senneterre, and moving toward him on the attack. The mere fact that they had descended from the sky and had come to the place where the weapon fell had aroused his suspicions. Now that he saw them charging so ferociously at Senneterre, he was certain that they were here to correct their mistake. They had not sent the weapon to Senneterre. They had not meant to drop it at all.

He watched Senneterre stagger to his feet and take two steps backward, still clutching the weapon.

Senneterre beheld the agents of darkness rushing toward him, waving their horrible legs and screeching like all the banshees of Hell. He had misunderstood so much; had he also misunderstood who—or what—the Lord had sent to put him to death? If it was to be these demons, then let the will of

God be done, but surely He did not expect one of his priests to die without first striking a blow against the forces of evil.

A holy strength came into him. "Come and kill me!" he taunted them. "You cannot win, Satan, for we will keep coming! We will never rest! I will die for the glory of God and then a million others will come to avenge me!"

He raised the weapon, aimed, and pulled the trigger.

Half of Kalak's force vanished.

"Halt!" Kalak screamed. "Do not move!"

He looked around. Fourteen of his men were gone. Three were horribly wounded, large parts of their bodies having been cleanly severed away into nothingness.

"Help them!" Kalak ordered, though it felt more like a desperate plea. Medics labored futilely to staunch the bleeding of their dying comrades. Other than their attentions to the wounded, the landing party was frozen in place by Kalak's command not to move.

Kalak's mind raced, yet his thoughts went nowhere. His earlier instruction to his men not to fire except under his order had implied that such an order could in fact be given, but it was not true; there was no way he could give that order. Killing an innocent member of an unknown alien race was simply not an option. The Tenets of Sumanadama guided him unerringly in this, and could not be broken.

If the creature was determined to use the Guardian against them, they would all die here, very far from home.

"Senneterre!"

The priest whirled in the direction of the familiar voice, wobbling slightly as he did so.

Nouwanish stepped out of the woods, head high, and walked slowly toward the demon who was now pointing the weapon at him. Out of the corner of his eye he kept part of his attention on the sky demons, who had become oddly and suspiciously motionless after their apparent defeat.

"I cannot let you live, Senneterre!"

Senneterre smiled. "Thank you, at least, for using my name, Nouwanish."

"You said you will keep coming, Senneterre, and you will. I have seen it."

"We will, Nouwanish." He raised the weapon. "Do you know what this can do?"

"I know," Nouwanish said, still moving forward into the teeth of the weapon.

Senneterre pointed a wavering finger at the paralyzed, decimated creatures in the clearing. "Do you know who they are?"

"No, I do not."

"They are the devil's minions, Nouwanish."

"And yet they are not your friends, Senneterre. How do you explain that?"

Senneterre smiled.

"I am too tired to explain anything more to you, Nouwanish. You said you cannot let me live—so?" He strained to pull his shoulders back and to raise his head. "My God is waiting for me."

Nouwanish nodded. "Tell him I do not forgive him."

He raised his lance and threw it with all his might. It struck Senneterre in the chest, staggering him back, yet he made no sound, and did not fall. For a moment he stood unmoving with the lance protruding from his chest and his back. His eyes burned into Nouwanish's, then became as gray pebbles beneath the water of a sluggish stream. Blood spilled from his mouth. Slowly he sank to his knees, then lurched forward; his lifeless lungs expelled a sharp grunt as the back end of the lance stabbed the dirt, stopping his upper body at an angle above the ground. His head bobbed, then was still. His arms dangled on either side of the wooden stake that supported him in death.

Nouwanish walked to Senneterre's side and pried the alien weapon from his clenched fingers. Its weight was more than that of two muskets. If he chose to wield its power, no more Algonkin would die. The white men would cower at his feet.

He turned to the demons from the sky and raised the weapon before him.

"You came to take this back," he said. "Why did you not kill him? Why do you let me stand here unharmed?"

The creatures made their bird noises, but he could not understand them as he could understand the noises of the birds that lived here in the real world, the world of sunlight, the world of life.

Then, as he felt the weight of the weapon bearing down into the heel of his hand, and stared at the bizarre shape of it, his dream leaped into his mind a fourth time, and in an instant he dreamed it *awake*—the same dream, but this time with a terrifying difference. In the world he saw at the end of this dream, the darkest world of all, the hollow corpses of the earth were dancing as before, but now they were carried on the backs of Algonkin crouching inside.

He turned his sight from the weapon. "Why do you tempt me with this?" he cried to the sky demons, then flung it at the ground in front of them, and spat his hardest at it.

For a moment they did nothing. Then they picked it up and vanished into the forest as quickly as only demons can move.

Kalak-gernas moaned with remorse as they carried the mangled, lifeless bodies of their comrades back to the ship.

The poor creature. Obviously he was so frightened that he had fired without thinking. And could anyone blame him? What would Kalak himself have done if, alone on his own planet, he had encountered a group of aliens like the one whose death they had just witnessed? Might he not have been frightened into exactly such an irrational act? It was Kalak's fault for not anticipating that of all conceivable outcomes, this would be one of the first possible, and one of the most likely. Thank Sumanadama that the other alien had simply returned the Guardian, although Kalak couldn't imagine that they would ever know why.

Solemnly he called for Lim-norbel to come to his side, and gravely handed him the Guardian. Lim needed to know he was still trusted.

Kalak would go before the Galactic Council and take the blame entirely upon himself. He had caused the death of seventeen shipmates, and had brought irreparable shame to the innocent alien being who had used a Guardian against intelligent beings who meant him no harm.

Kalak would pay the price without complaint. And he would spend the rest of his life, which he knew now would be in the unrelieved blackness of an isolation pit on Zhonismik, praying to Sumanadama to save the alien's soul, praying to spare the alien from eternal damnation.

Nouwanish raised both arms to address his warriors.

"I have conquered all these demons you have seen, the demon of the earth and the demons of the sky," he said. Snowflakes began to descend onto his shoulders. "Tonight we will not fear."

He motioned his warriors to start back toward their village, then he turned to see if the demon had changed in death, but

Senneterre remained as before, propped oddly above the ground, dark blood still oozing from his mouth onto the lance.

Nouwanish watched the first snowflakes of that winter land soundlessly on the black robe. He spat again, then turned away and walked quickly in the direction of the village, which they would dismantle and move to the winter place when he returned.

Soon the woods would be smothered in white, and Senneterre's body would be hidden. Until the spring at least, these trees would see no sign of him.

It would be, for a short time, as if there were no demons in the world.

WONDERS
OF THE
INVISIBLE WORLD

Patricia A. McKillip

I am the angel sent to Cotton Mather. It took me some time to get his attention. He lay on the floor with his eyes closed; he prayed fervently, sometimes murmuring, sometimes shouting. Apparently the household was used to it. I heard footsteps pass his study door; a woman—his wife Abigail?—called to someone: "If your throat is no better tomorrow, we'll have Phillip pee in a cup for you to gargle." From the way the house smelled, Phillip didn't bother much with cups. Cotton Mather smelled of smoke and sweat and wet wool. Winter had come early. The sky was black, the ground was white, the wind pinched like a witch and whined like a starving dog. There was no color in the landscape and no mercy. Cotton Mather prayed to see the invisible world.

He wanted an angel.

"O Lord," he said, in desperate, hoarse, weary cadences, like a sick child talking itself to sleep. "Thou hast given angelic visions to Thy innocent children to defend them from their demons. Remember Thy humble servant, who prostrates himself in the dust, vile worm that I am, forsaking food and comfort and sleep, in humble hope that Thou might bestow upon Thy humble servant the blessing and hope at this harsh and evil time: a glimpse of Thy shadow, a flicker of light in Thine eye, a single word from Thy mouth. Show me Thy messengers of good who fly between the visible and invisible worlds. Grant me, O God, a vision."

I cleared my throat a little. He didn't open his eyes. The fire was dying down. I wondered who replenished it, and if the sight of Mather's bright, winged creature would surprise anyone, with all the witches, devils and demented goldfinches perched on rafters all over New England. The firelight spilling across the wide planks glowed just beyond his outstretched hand. He lay in dim lights and fluttering shadows, in the long, long night of history, when no one could ever see clearly after sunset, and witches and angels and living dreams trembled just beyond the fire.

"Grant me, O God, a vision."

I was standing in front of his nose. He was lost in days of fasting and desire, trying to conjure an angel out of his head. According to his writings, what he expected to see was the generic white male with wings growing out of his shoulders, fair-haired, permanently beardless, wearing a long white nightgown and a gold dinner plate on his head. This was what intrigued Durham, and why he had hired me: he couldn't believe that both good and evil in the Puritan imagination could be so banal.

But I was what Mather wanted: something as colorless and pure as the snow that lay like the hand of God over the earth, harsh, exacting, unambiguous. Fire, their salvation against the cold, was red and belonged to Hell.

"O Lord."

It was the faintest of whispers. He was staring at my feet.

They were bare and shining and getting chilled. The ring of diamonds in my halo contained controls for light, for holograms like my wings, a map disc, a local-history disc in case I got totally bewildered by events, and a recorder disc that had caught the sudden stammer in Mather's last word. He had asked for an angel; he got an angel. I wished he would quit staring at my feet and throw another log on the fire.

He straightened slowly, pushing himself off the floor while his eyes traveled upward. He was scarcely thirty at the time of the trials; he resembled his father at that age more than the familiar Pelham portrait of Mather in his sixties, soberly dressed, with a wig like a cream puff on his head, and a firm, resigned mouth. The young Mather had long dark hair, a spare, handsome, clean-shaven face, searching, credulous eyes. His eyes reached my face finally, cringing a little, as if he half expected a demon's red, leering face attached to the angel's body. But he found what he expected. He began to cry.

He cried silently, so I could speak. His writings are mute about much of the angel's conversation. Mostly it predicted Mather's success as a writer, great reviews and spectacular sales in America and Europe. I greeted him, gave him the message from God, quoted Ezekiel, and then got down to business. By then he had stopped crying, wiped his face with his dusty sleeve and cheered up at the prospect of fame.

"There are troubled children," I said, "who have seen me."

"They speak of you in their misery," he said gratefully. "You give them strength against evil."

"Their afflictions are terrible."

"Yes," he whispered.

"You have observed their torments."

"Yes."

"You have taken them into your home, borne witness to their complaints, tried to help them cast out their tormentors."

"I have tried."

"You have wrestled with the invisible world."

"Yes."

We weren't getting very far. He still knelt on the hard floor, as he had done for hours, perhaps days; he could see me more clearly than he had seen anything in the dark in his life. He had forgotten the fire. I tried to be patient. Good angels were beyond temperament, even while at war with angels who had disgraced themselves by exhibiting human characteristics. But the floorboards were getting very cold.

"You have felt the invisible chains about them," I prodded. "The invisible, hellish things moving beneath their bedclothes."

"The children cannot seem to stand my books," he said a little querulously, with a worried frown. "My writing sends them into convulsions. At the mere act of opening my books, they fall down as dead upon the floor. Yet how can I lead them gently back to God's truth if the truth acts with such violence against them?"

"It is not against them," I reminded him, "but against the devil, who," I added, inspired, "takes many shapes."

He nodded, and became voluble. "Last week he took the shape of thieves who stole three sermons from me. And of a rat—or something like a hellish rat—we could feel in the air, but not see."

"A rat."

"And sometimes a bird, a yellow bird, the children say—they see it perched on the fingers of those they name witches."

"And since they say it, it is so."

He nodded gravely. "God made nothing more innocent than children."

I let that pass. I was his delusion, and if I had truly been sent to him from God, then God and Mather agreed on everything.

"Have they—" this was Durham's suggestion "—not yet seen the devil in the shape of a black horse who spews fire between its teeth, and is ridden by three witches, each more beautiful than the last?"

He stared at me, then caught himself imagining the witches and blinked. "No," he breathed. "No one has seen such a thing. Though the Shape of Goody Bishop in her scarlet bodice and her lace had been seen over the beds of honest married men."

"What did she do to them?"

"She hovered. She haunted them. For this and more she was hanged."

For wearing a color and inciting the imagination, she was hanged. I refrained from commenting that since her Shape had done the hovering, it was her Shape that should have been hanged. But it was almost worth my researcher's license. "In God's justice," I said piously, "her soul dwells." I had almost forgotten the fire; this dreary, crazed, malicious atmosphere was more chilling than the cold.

"She had a witchmark," Mather added. "The witch's teat." His eyes were wide, marveling; he had conjured witches as well as angels out of his imagination. I suppose it was easier, in that harsh world, to make demons out of your neighbors, with their imperfections, tempers, rheumy eyes, missing teeth, irritating habits and smells, than to find angelic beauty in them. But I wasn't there to judge Mather. I could hear Durham's intense voice: Imagination. Imagery. I want to know what they pulled out of their heads. They invented their devil, but all they could do was make him talk like a bird? Don't bother with a moral viewpoint. I want to know what Mather saw. This was the man who believed that thunder was caused by the sulfurous farts of decaying vegetation. Why? Don't ask me why. You're a researcher. Go research.

Research the imagination. It was as obsolete as the appendix in most adults, except for those in whom, like the appendix, it became inflamed for no reason. Durham's curiosity seemed as aberrated as Mather's; they both craved visions. But in his world, Durham could afford the luxury of being crazed. In this world, only the crazed, the adolescent girls, the trial judges, Mather himself, were sane.

I was taking a moral viewpoint. But Mather was still talking, and the recorder was catching his views, not mine. I had asked Durham once, after an exasperating journey to some crowded, airless, fly-infested temple covered with phallic symbols to appear as a goddess, to stop hiring me; the Central Research Computer had obviously got its records mixed when it recommended me to him. Our historical viewpoints were thoroughly incompatible. "No, they're not," he had said obnoxiously, and refused to elaborate. He paid well. He paid very well. So here I was, in frozen colonial New England, listening to Cotton Mather talk about brooms.

"The witches ride them," he said, still wide-eyed. "Sometimes three to a besom. To their foul Witch's Sabbaths."

Their foul Sabbaths, he elaborated, consisted of witches gathering in some boggy pasture where the demons talked with the voices of frogs, listening to a fiendish sermon, drinking blood, and plotting to bring back pagan customs like dancing around a Maypole. I wondered if, being an angel of God, I was supposed to know all this already, and if Mather would wonder later why I had listened. Durham and I had argued about this, about the ethics and legalities of me pretending to be Mather's delusion.

"What's the problem?" he had asked. "You think the real angel is going to show up later?"

Mather was still speaking, in a feverish trance caused most likely by too much fasting, prayer, and mental agitation. Evil eyes, he was talking about, and "things" that were hairy all over. They apparently caused neighbors to blame one another for dead pigs, wagons stuck in potholes, sickness, lust and deadly boredom. I was getting bored myself, by then, and thoroughly depressed. Children's fingers had pointed at random, and wherever they pointed, they created a witch. So much for the imagination. It was malignant here, an instrument of cruelty and death.

"He did not speak to the court, neither to defend his innocence nor confess his guilt," Mather was saying solemnly. "He was a stubborn old man. They piled stones upon him until his tongue stuck out and he died. But he never spoke. They had already hanged his wife. He spoke well enough then, accusing her."

I had heard enough.

"God protect the innocent," I said, and surprised myself, for it was a prayer to something. I added, more gently, for Mather, blinking out of his trance, looked worried, as if I had accused him, "Be comforted. God will give you strength to bear all tribulations in these dark times. Be patient and faithful, and in the fullness of time, you will be rewarded with the truth of your life."

Not standard Puritan dogma, but all he heard was "reward" and "truth." I raised my hand in blessing. He flung himself down to kiss the floor at my feet. I activated the controls in my halo and went home.

Durham was waiting for me at the Researchers' Terminus. I pulled the recorder disc out of my halo, fed it to the computer, and then stepped out of the warp chamber. While the computer analyzed my recording to see if I had broken any of one thousand, five hundred and sixty-three regulations, I took off my robe and my blond hair and dumped them and my halo into Durham's arms.

"Well?" he said, not impatient, just intent, not even seeing me as I pulled a skirt and tunic over my head. I was still cold, and worried about my researcher's license, which the computer would refuse to return if I had violated history. Durham had eyes like Cotton Mather's, I saw for the first time: dark, burning, but with a suggestion of humor in them. "What did you find? Speak to me, Nici."

"Nothing," I said shortly. "You're out several million credits for nothing. It was a completely dreary bit of history, not without heroism but entirely without poetry. And if I've lost my license because of this—I'm not even sure I understand what you're trying to do."

"I'm researching for a history of imaginative thought."

Durham was always researching unreadable subjects. "Starting when?" I asked tersely, pulling on a boot. "The cave paintings at Lascaux?"

"No art," he said. "More speculative than that. Less formal. Closer to chaos." He smiled, reading my mind. "Like me."

"You're a disturbed man, Durham. You should have your unconscious scanned."

"I like it the way it is: a bubbling little morass of unpredictable metaphors."

"They aren't unpredictable," I said. "They're completely predictable. Everything imaginable is accessible, and everything accessible has been imagined by the Virtual computer, which has already researched every kind of imaginative thought since the first bison got painted on a rock. That way nothing like what happened in Cotton Mather's time can happen to us. So—"

"*Wonders of the Invisible World*," Durham interrupted. He hadn't heard a word. "It's a book by Mather. He was talking about angels and demons. We would think of the invisible in terms of atomic particles. Both are unseen yet named, and immensely powerful—"

"Oh, stop. You're mixing atoms and angels. One exists, the other doesn't."

"That's what I'm trying to get at, Nici—the point where existence is totally immaterial, where the passion, the belief in something creates a situation completely ruled by the will to believe."

"That's insanity."

He smiled again, cheerfully. He tended to change his appearance according to what he was researching; he wore a shimmering bodysuit that showed all his muscles, and milk-white hair. Except for the bulky build of his face and the irreverence in his eyes, he might have been Mather's angel. My more androgynous face worked better. "Maybe," he said. "But I find the desire, the passion, coupled with the accompanying imagery, fascinating."

"You are a throwback," I muttered. "You belong to some barbaric age when people imagined things to kill each other for." The computer flashed a light; I breathed a sigh of relief. Durham got his tape, and the computer's analysis; I retrieved my license.

"Next time—" Durham began.

"There won't be a next time." I headed for the door. "I'm sick of appearing as twisted pieces of people's imagination. And one of these days I'm going to find myself in court."

"But you do it so well," he said softly. "You even convince the Terminus computer."

I glared at him. "Just leave me alone."

"All right," he said imperturbably. "Don't call me, I'll call you."

I was tired, but I took the tube-walk home, to get the blood moving in my feet, and to see some light and color after that bleak, dangerous world. The moving walkway, encased in its clear tube, wound up into the air, balanced on its centipede escalator and station legs. I could see the gleaming city domes stretch like a long cluster of soap bubbles toward the afternoon sun, and I wondered that somewhere within the layers of time in this place there was a small port town on the edge of a vast unexplored continent where Mather had flung himself down on his floorboards and prayed an angel out of himself.

He could see an angel here without praying for it. He could be an angel. He could soar into the eye of God if he wanted on wings of gold and light. He could reach out, even in the tube-walk, punch in a credit number, plug into his implant or his wrist controls, and activate the screen above his head. He could have any reality on the menu, or any reality he could dream up, since everything imagined and imaginable and every combination of it had been programmed into the Virtual computer. And then he could walk out of the station into his living room and change the world all over again.

I had to unplug Brock when I got home; he had fallen asleep at the terminal. He opened heavy eyelids and yawned.

"Hi, Matrix."

"Don't call me that," I said mechanically. He grinned fleetingly and nestled deeper into the bubble-chair. I sat down on the couch and pulled my boots off again. It was warm, in this time; I finally felt it. Brock asked,

"What were you?"

Even he knew Durham that well. "An angel."

"What's that?"

"Look it up."

He touched the controls on his wrist absently. He was a calm child, with blue, clinical eyes and angelic hair that didn't come from me. He sprouted wings and a halo suddenly, and grunted "What's it for?"

"It talks to God."

"What God?"

"In God We Trust. That God."

He grunted again. "Pre-Real."

I nodded, leaned back tiredly, and watched him, wondering how much longer he would be neat, attentive, curious, polite, before he shaved his head, studded his scalp and eyebrows with jewels and implants, got eye-implants that held no expression whatsoever, inserted a CD player into his earlobe, and never called me Matrix again. Maybe he would go live with his father. I hadn't seen him since Brock was born, but Brock knew exactly who he was, where he was, what he did. Speculation was unnecessary, except for aberrants like Durham.

The outercom signaled; half a dozen faces appeared onscreen: Brock's friends who lived in the station complex. They trooped in, settled themselves around Brock, and plugged into their wrists. They were playing an adventure game, a sort of space-chase, where they were intergalactic thieves raiding alien zoos of rare animals and selling them to illegal restaurants. The computer played the team of highly trained intergalactic space-patrollers. The thieves were constantly falling into black holes, getting burnt up speeding too fast into strange atmospheres, and ambushed by the wily patrollers. One of them, Indra, tried to outwit the computer by coming up with the most bizarre alien species she could imagine; the computer always gave her the images she wanted. I watched for a while. Then an image came into my head, of an old man in a field watching his neighbors pile stones on him until he could no longer breathe.

I got up, went into my office, and called Durham.

"I could have stopped it," I said tersely. He was silent, not because he didn't know what I was talking about, but because he did. "I was an angel from God. I could have changed the message."

"You wouldn't have come back," he said simply. It was true. I would have been abandoned there, powerless, a beardless youth with breasts in a long robe raving about the future, who would have become just one more witch for the children to condemn. He added, "You're a researcher. Researchers don't get emotional about history. There's nothing left of that time but some old bones in a museum from where they dug them up to build a station complex. A gravestone with an angel on it, a little face with staring eyes, and a pair of cupid wings. What's to mope about? I put a bonus in your account. Go spend it somewhere."

"How much?"

He was silent again, his eyes narrowed slightly. "Not enough for you to go back. Go get drunk, Nici. This is not you."

"I'm haunted," I whispered, I thought too softly for him to hear. He shook his head, not impatiently.

"The worst was over by then, anyway. Heroics are forbidden to researchers. You know that. The angel Mather dreamed up

only told him what he wanted to hear. Tell him anything else
and he'd call you a demon and refuse to listen. You know all
this. Why are you taking this personally? You didn't take being
a goddess in that Hindu temple personally. Thank God," he
added with an obnoxious chuckle. I grunted at him morosely
and got rid of his face.

I found a vegetable bar in the kitchen, and wandered back
into the living room. The space-thieves were sneaking around
a zoo on the planet Hublatt. They were all imaging animals
onscreen while their characters studied the specimens. "We're
looking for a Yewsalope," Brock said intently. "Its eyeballs are
poisonous, but if you cook them just right they look like boiled
eggs to whoever you're trying to poison."

The animals were garish in their barred cells: purple, orange,
cinnamon, polka-dotted, striped. There were walking nar-
whales, a rhinoceros horn with feet and eyes, something like
an octopus made out of elephant trunks, an amorphous green
blob that constantly changed shape.

"How will you know a Yewsalope when you see it?" I asked,
fascinated with their color combinations, their imagery. Brock
shrugged slightly.

"We'll know."

A new animal appeared in an empty cage: a tall, two-legged
creature with long golden hair and wings made of feathers or
light. It held on to the bars with its hands, looking sadly out.
I blinked.

"You have an angel in your zoo."

I heard Brock's breath. Indra frowned. "It could fly out. Why
doesn't it fly? Whose is it? Anyway, this zoo is only for animals.
This looks like some species of human. It's illegal," she said,
fastidiously for a thief, "on Hublatt."

"It's an angel," Brock said.

"What's an angel? Is it yours?"

Brock shook his head. They all shook their heads, eyes onscreen, wanting to move on. But the image lingered: a beautiful, melancholy figure, half human, half light, trapped and
powerless behind its bars.

"Why doesn't it just fly?" Indra breathed. "It could just fly.
Brock—"

"It's not mine," Brock insisted. And then he looked at me,
his eyes wide, so calm and blue that it took me a moment to
transfer my attention from their color to what they were asking.

I stared at the angel, and felt the bars under my hands. I

swallowed, seeing what it saw: the long, dark night of history that it was powerless to change, to illumine, because it was powerless to speak except to lie.

"Matrix?" Brock whispered. I closed my eyes.

"Don't call me that."

When I opened my eyes, the angel had disappeared.

EXCERPT FROM THE THIRD AND LAST VOLUME OF

TRIBES OF THE PACIFIC COAST

Neal Stephenson

Excerpt from the third and last volume of *TRIBES OF THE PACIFIC COAST*, a memoir of the West Coast Ethnographic Expedition of 21XX, as related by one of the participants, Professor S—H—

For three days we bivouacked in the ruins of the galleria, sleeping on the floor of what had once been an amusement arcade, strewn with the luridly painted hulls of primitive mediatrons long since gone cold and gray. One of the galleria's glass-walled lifts was stalled at the third and highest story and provided a superb observation point over the parking lots to the south. It was from this quarter that Captain Napier anticipated the attack, so there we posted a twenty-four-hour watch. Tod, our native guide, was astonished that the glass walls of the lift were still intact, and ran his hands over them until drawing the wrath of Captain Napier: "The glass is only useful insofar as it is transparent! Go find a rag in one of the old clothing stores and wipe away your fingerprints lest they conceal the approach of some deadly intruder!" Tod cringed away from this reprimand, backed out of the lift, and scurried off in the direction of a store that had not yet been looted to the floor slab.

To our astonishment, Captain Napier turned and kicked one

of the walls forcefully! Dr. Nkruma and I averted our eyes, half expecting to be struck by jagged fragments. To our surprise, though, the glass absorbed the impact as if it had been granite or marble. Captain Napier evinced some mischievous amusement at our reaction. "We who grew up in the Diamond Age know glass only as a constituent of the rubble of an earlier era," he said. "As children, who of us did not cut his hand or foot on a fragment of glass while exploring some old ruin, and thus form a pejorative opinion of that substance that, until the development of our modern crosslinked diamandoids, constituted every window in the world? And yet a careful perusal of late twentieth-century architecture will remind you that glass was frequently used in applications where ruggedness was of paramount importance—as is the case in this elevator, where loss of a pane would obviously pose a lethal risk to the occupants. Our friend Tod, I would wager, has amused himself of many an idle afternoon throwing rocks through the windowpanes of unused buildings, and come to view an unshattered pane as an affront to his athletic prowess; and yet I would wager that he could throw rocks against the wall of this elevator all day without effect."

During the course of these remarks, Dr. Nkruma had begun to stroke his goatee, as he often did when in a reflective mood. "Governmental potentates of the previous century were frequently shielded from the effects of kinetic-energy weapons by barriers of thick glass," he said, "but I had not been aware that such technology had come into commercial use." He gave the glass wall an experimental kick or two, as, I must confess, did I. Soon, Tod had returned, proudly displaying a handful of yellowed paper towels as if they were rare parchments from an archaeological site, and commenced vigorously scrubbing the glass; but once again Captain Napier had to admonish him. "Remember that glass is softer than our modern replacements for it, softer even than many of the microscopic dirt particles that are spoiling our view so, and that when you scrub it thus you are grinding those particles into the surface and thus doing more harm than good." Tod, it must be recorded, listened to this disquisition in something of a daze. Captain Napier's attempts to lift our native companion out of his abysmal ignorance spoke well of the former's noble spirit but were probably too late to improve the latter's situation. "In other words, Tod," our leader finally said, noting Tod's lack of comprehension, "you must first wash the glass with copious amounts of water, and scrub only when the gritty stuff is removed." This instruction, expressed as it was in relatively concrete terms, was clear as crosslinked diamondoid to Tod, who immediately bustled away in search of a bucket. I was surprised by his unwonted diligence until I recalled the facts of our situation, and reflected that Tod, with his relentlessly practical and earthbound mentality, must appreciate that small matters such as the clarity of the glass surrounding our sentry post might soon make the difference between life and death for all of us. The 4Wheelers might be content with simply dispatching Captain Napier, Dr. Nkruma, and myself; but Tod they would no doubt perceive as a traitor to their tribe, and kill only after they had given him ample cause to beg for the favor. My mind went back, as it had frequently in the last few days, to the sight of poor Britni Lou, dragged to death behind a 4Wheeler's pickup simply for the crime of smiling at me during one of the 4Wheelers' ceremonial meat-roastings.

The ruggedness of the northern approach to the galleria precluded a frontal assault from that direction. During our day-long retreat through that treacherous landscape of crumbling reinforced-concrete ramps and bridges we had used our supply of explosives to good effect, detonating one sheet charge after another, crashing down entire ramps on top of other ramps in a process that Captain Napier, in characteristic black humor, referred to as "civil de-engineering." If the 4Wheelers wanted to approach from that direction, they had two choices: pick their way on foot through the briar patch of snarled iron rebar that sprouted from the still-settling rubble, or drive their vehicles through the narrow defile we had left as the path of our own retreat. As one unlucky motorist had already discovered, this path was now strewn with mines capable of flinging the burning wrecks of their primitive four-wheeled conveyances a dozen meters into the air.

The south parking lot was too vast for us to mine with our limited supply of explosives. My readers may perhaps be forgiven for not appreciating the vast extent of this space. At first glance it appears, to the modern eye, to be a vacant plain, inexplicably wasted by the architects of the galleria. On closer inspection one descries a faint grid of yellow lines, like marks on a poorly erased chalkboard, and this leads the unwilling mind to the realization that the territory is not a natural formation but a man-made slab of pavement of inconceivable size. As when we look at the Pyramids or the Great Wall, we are impressed not by the work itself, which would be a trivial job for modern engineers, but by the simple fact that men bothered to do it at a time when doing it was much more difficult.

When one considers that as many as twenty thousand customers might have flocked to that place at one time; that nearly all of them came alone in automobiles; that each of these, if it were registered today, would be categorized as a full-lane conveyance, requiring a berth of some twenty square meters; and that half of the parking lot was used not for parking spaces but for traffic lanes; then the reader may begin to appreciate the dimensions of this asphalt steppe, and of our current dilemma. Time had woven a fine, intricate net of cracks across the slab, providing opportunities for various weeds that someday might subsume the entire substance of the parking lot into the soil. For the nonce, it was still fairly level, and for the 4Wheelers with their special lorries equipped for travel on rough landscapes, it might have been smooth as a windowpane.

We deployed an array of sentry pods in the airspace above the lot, but from the original complement of some ten thousand pods with which we had set out from Atlantis/Seattle we were now down to no more than a thousand, and these so low on power that, if the wind blew hard for a few hours, they would spend themselves out just fighting to keep their assigned stations. Captain Napier deployed them anyway just for the impact they would have upon the morale of the superstitious 4Wheelers. What we would have given, at that point, for an extra megawatt-hour of power, stored in a usable format? Our ability to store energy in tiny spaces, and to move it expeditiously through superconductors, has given us a light regard for it, and we have forgotten that in more rustic settings we might have to burn a hundred trees or spread solar panels over hundreds of hectares in order to gather enough energy to recharge a fingernail-sized battery. Now, as we approached the end of our six-month expedition, with the towers of Los Angeles nearly in sight, we found ourselves in mortal peril from a foe we might have brushed away like so many insects had we not been running low on batteries.

Readers of a critical bent may ask why we did not simply pack more; but those patient enough to have absorbed the present narrative in its full length know of the many surprises we encountered on our way, which could only have added to the length of the expedition; in particular the three months we spent among the nearly extinct techno-shamanistic neo-Pagan tribes of the Humboldt region, trying one desperate stratagem after another to rid our bodies of the insidious nanosites with which we had been deliberately infected, while concealing from them at all costs our secret portable Source. Our disguise as itinerant missionaries, combined with the fact that we had to assume we were constantly under surveillance, made resupply impossible once we had departed the safe confines of Atlantis/Seattle.

Now our miniature Source, so cleverly disguised as a religious statuette, awaited our command. We had water to give it, and air was of course plentiful. Unlike our giant industrial Sources that draw directly upon the mineral wealth of the sea, this one compiled only systems made from nitrogen, oxygen, hydrogen and carbon, and the nanotechnological designs in its secret library used those four species exclusively. Despite this rather severe limitation, the crack engineers at Protocol Enforcement had devised an ingenious set of programs that, with the appropriate input of energy, would cause the matter compiler in our little statue's pedestal to produce small but extremely useful devices of all descriptions—including, of course, weapons.

Perhaps unfortunately for those of us who enjoyed a certain sort of romantic literature as youths, the days are long gone when the weapon was an extension of the warrior's hand, its effectiveness a function of his prowess in the martial arts. Now, as often as not, combat is a function of matching energy against energy, mass against mass, and the stealth of microscopic intruders against the depth and diligence of the defenses intended to stop them. Fortunately for us, and for all tribes that respect Protocol, the 4Wheelers did not have access to this latter type of weapon. Even their energy supplies were mostly limited to solution-phase systems, and so we did not have to concern ourselves with centrifugal rounds ("cookie-cutters") and the other fiendish systems used, in the modern world, to deliver energy into human flesh.

But mass they had, in the form of their seemingly endless fleets of steel-framed four-wheeled vehicles dating back to the Elizabethan era. Hence the 4Wheelers, despite their general technological weakness, had the ability to mount a most impressive sort of mechanized cavalry charge across the proper sort of terrain. The parking lot spread out below us could not have been more perfect for their purposes, nor more difficult for us, with our nearly extinct energy supply, to defend.

Our days and nights in the galleria, then, were spent in a kind of deliberate regression to an earlier technological era. Granted, I might have turned my knowledge of engineering to writing a new program that would cause the matter compiler to generate destructive nanosites of some description. But now that the 4Wheelers knew we were, in fact, secret agents of Protocol Enforcement, they would be sure to protect themselves with Nanobar before approaching our position. As has been discovered by many of the disreputable engineers whom it is our sworn duty to eradicate, Nanobar can be pierced if one has no respect for Protocol, but the engineering challenge is far from trivial. Our system lacked the development tools, and I lacked the time, to undertake such a programme.

Guns of the sort used in the previous century would, paradoxically, have been even more difficult to engineer on short notice, as the secrets of their design have passed from the domain of the engineer into that of the historian. Such weapons rely on the density of the projectile, but our compiler could, of course, not produce lead or any other dense element. And the explosives used to propel the bullet would have required a large energy input to produce.

The modern reader may, therefore, be amused to know that, before the final assault of the 4Wheelers, we had regressed, not merely out of the Diamond Age, but backwards through the Atomic and Industrial eras all the way to medieval times, when weapons drew their energy from the warrior's muscles. As the compiler's library contained a large repertory of springs, I was able to cobble together a sort of handheld catapult, made entirely of lightweight hydrocarbons, designed to launch small bolts about six inches in length. Each bolt was tipped with a rather wicked four-bladed head. Those blades, of course, came straight from the matter compiler and thus possessed a degree of sharpness incomprehensible to any medieval armorer, who would have sneered at the insignificant weight of the projectile, thinking that it could never possess sufficient momentum to cut its way through an opponent's defenses. But the powerful springs provided by our new technology propelled these bolts with such velocity that, in our initial test firings, they were able to penetrate half an inch of steel. It is almost superfluous to relate the depth of the impression made upon Tod by this wonder.

As Tod reeled about our makeshift fortress uttering a seemingly endless string of astonished commentary, Captain Napier, Dr. Nkruma, and myself, without exchanging any words, judged (and here I must beg the reader's forgiveness for conjuring up what is morbid and distasteful) what effect such a weapon might have when directed, not against a steel plate, but against a human being.

Captain Napier reviewed my innovation in favorable terms, which modesty forbids me from repeating here, and, so, after equipping each of the four of us with a launcher, I programmed the compiler to generate ammunition as rapidly as possible. Tod, whose anxiety over our situation had mounted almost to a state of catalepsis, suggested that we create a battery of launchers, and set them up as man-traps near all the entrances to the galleria. I must confess that I found this in some respects to be a tempting idea, but Captain Napier quashed it without hesitation, pointing out that an unused trap might lie in wait for an indefinite period of time and one day strike down an innocent curiosity-seeker.

Our little Source worked valiantly day and night, compiling the bolts half a dozen at a time, releasing its vacuum with a hiss when a batch was finished. Those of us not on sentry duty in the elevator made some pretense of sleeping; but I only lay awake listening for that periodic hiss from the compiler, much like a nervous parent listening to the breathing of a newborn infant.

The attack came just before dawn. Dr. Nkruma was on duty in the elevator, but his vigilance was wasted; the roar of the massed internal-combustion engines on the far fringe of the parking lot penetrated the entire galleria so that all of us were on our feet before he could even sound the alarm. Captain Napier brought us together in the arcade to rehearse the order of battle one last time; to remind us of our solemn duty to the Crown, namely, that given the knowledge each of us stored in our heads, we must never be taken alive by those who would wield the power of modern technology without first bowing to the rule of Protocol. Finally, Captain Napier approached our Source, which to anyone not familiar with its inner workings looked like nothing more than a rather lurid statue of the Virgin Mary, and uttered the code words that initiated its self-destruct programme. By the time we left the room, the Source was a pillar of white fire rising from the bare concrete floor.

We went each to his station and steeled ourselves for the onslaught of the 4Wheelers.

The first wave consisted of vehicles that were even more decrepit than normal by the standards of the 4Wheelers, and peering through my field glasses I soon understood why: they were empty decoys, sent out to test our grid of security pods. Not knowing false from real attackers, the pods swarmed down like African bees, futilely expending their final energy supplies. Several of the vehicles exploded as our pods detonated their fuel tanks, but most of them continued to lurch mindlessly across the parking lot, eventually veering into one another or crashing into the galleria itself. Thus did the 4Wheelers clear a path for their true assault, which was a primitive and gaudy spectacle: half a dozen squadrons of several vehicles each, flying colorful flags, converging upon the galleria's several entrances according to some scheme no doubt engineered by King Karl himself.

I will not test the reader's patience by explaining in full the details of the strategy by which Captain Napier hoped to throw back this assault, other than to say that it inevitably relied upon deception, guerrilla tactics, and various psychological gambits we supposed would have a profound impact on the 4Wheelers. In any case such details are not relevant, as very little of our plan was ever implemented. We had foreseen every eventuality except one: that the 4Wheelers would have access to some technology not far below the level of ours. Before any of us had laid eyes on the foe, we had been incapacitated by powerful electrical shocks, delivered by microscopic agents that had been insensibly placed in our own bodies.

Karl himself was kind enough to provide an explanation some time later, when we awoke in his dungeon—the basement of a former office building. Captain Napier, Dr. Nkruma, and I were tightly secured to four-by-eight-foot sheets of three-quarter-inch plywood by means of innumerable ropes and straps. Tod was nowhere to be seen, and it is up to the reader to imagine his fate. Karl entered the dungeon after all of us had been awake long enough to exchange brief accounts of our experiences, which differed from one another only in details. "Them dee-coy cars tole us all we needed to know 'bout yer dee-fenses in depth, namely, that there *was* no depth to the sucker," he crowed, "so once we got into the building, all we had to do was ree-lease the hunter-dee-liverers, and when they found y'all, they nailed each and every one of yew with a nice little ol' nanosite that split in two. The two halves floated round in yer blood 'til they was a certain distance apart and then ZAP! because, ya see, they was exactly the same 'cept for about ten thousand volts' difference between 'em."

"Impossible!" I exclaimed, "such technology is to be found only within the Protocol-respecting phyles."

"Oh, it ain't that hard," Karl leered, "when you got buddies like PhyrePhox and Marshal Vukovic here. Ain't that right, fellas?"

To our utter astonishment, into the room stepped the man calling himself PhyrePhox, whom, as attentive readers will recall, we had encountered under very different circumstances two months previously. On his heels was none other than Marshal Vukovic of the Greater Serbian Expeditionary Force, whose bloody quest for stolen technology was already the stuff of legend.

"Hello, my missionary friends," PhyrePhox cackled, grinning maniacally through his tangle of red dreadlocks, "I see that you are still diligently spreading your gospel. Now perhaps you will preach to us about the inner workings of that pretty Source you carried!"

"This is impossible," I said. "The 4Wheelers, CryptNet, and Greater Serbia—allies!?"

"And that ain't all," Karl said, "we also been getting help from your buddies, the—"

"Silence!" Marshal Vukovic cried, whirling toward King Karl. "Remember that our agreement specifies complete discretion as to the extent of the network."

"It ain't indiscreet to be talkin' to three dead men, 'sfar's I'm consarned," said Karl, whose rustic affect barely concealed his resentment at Vukovic's reprimand.

"They are not dead yet," said PhyrePhox, "though the system that they represent is doomed. New Atlantis, Nippon, and the lesser phyles who have been foolish enough to join together under the Protocol, together represent a dying race of dinosaurs. They control the world by controlling information—information about the potential surfaces defined by certain atoms, and how they may be merged together in order to create structures collectively known as nanotechnology. But information wants to be free—is doomed to be free—and soon it will be available to all, despite the best efforts of Protocol Enforcement to restrict it! Our network is on the verge of breaking forever the monopoly of the Protocol-respecting phyles!"

Throughout this tirade, Captain Napier leveled a steady gaze upon the frenzied PhyrePhox, and the confident smile on his lips did not waver even when those dreadlocks, like a nest of red snakes, were writhing in his face! "Your words have a familiar ring," Captain Napier said, "we read them in the business plans and prospecti of the Second Wave startups thirty years ago—before they went out of business or merged with the titans they had sought to overthrow. We heard them from the Parsis, the Ismailis, the Mormons, the Jews, the overseas Chinese, before they saw that nanotechnology promised enough wealth for all, and signed the Protocol. And now we hear the same words again from a motley assortment of synthetic phyles, who would have us believe that the very system that has brought undreamt-of prosperity to most of the world is in fact nothing other than an insidious system of oppression. Ask the peasant in Fujian province, who once labored in his paddy from dawn to dusk, whether he is oppressed now that he can compile his rice directly from a Feed, and spend his days playing with his grandchildren or in a ractive on his mediatron!"

"When that man worked in his paddy he was self-sufficient," retorted PhyrePhox, "he belonged to a community of workers who produced their food together. Now that community is destroyed, and he is dependent on your Feed like a baby on his mother's teat."

"And are we meant to believe that your conspiracy will somehow save this peasant from the dire fate of eating three square meals a day?" Captain Napier shot back.

"Instead of a Feed, that peasant will have a Seed," said PhyrePhox, "and instead of planting grains of rice in his paddy he will plant that Seed, and it will grow and flourish into a Source of his own, whose proceeds he can use as he sees fit— instead of relying on a Source owned by foreign strangers a thousand miles away."

"It is an idyllic picture," said Captain Napier, "but I fear it leaves out a great deal. This Seed of yours is more than a food factory, is it not? It is also potentially a weapon whose destructive power rivals that of the nuclear bombs of Elizabethan times. Now, as you have evidently realized, I live on Atlantan territory where the possession of weapons is strictly controlled. The children and women of Atlantis can walk anywhere at any time without fear of violence. But I was not born into this happy estate. No, I grew up a thete, living in an off-brand Clave where the ownership of weapons was completely unregulated, and as a boy exploring my neighborhood I frequently came upon dead bodies striped with the lurid scars of cookie-cutters. Now you would place technology a million times more dangerous into the hands of persons without the education, the good sense, the moral backbone"—here Captain Napier shot a defiant glance at Marshal Vukovic—"to use it properly. If this plan succeeds we are all doomed; so if you intend to torture us for the information you crave, then have at it! For we have all taken a solemn Oath to our God and our Queen, and we will gladly die rather than break it."

At this defiant peroration (which I must confess did much to revive my own faltering strength of purpose) PhyrePhox flew into a perfect frenzy of rage, and had to be restrained by Karl the 4Wheeler and one of his minions lest he slay the helpless Captain Napier on the spot! "Very well, then!" he cried, "you shall be the first, as you are the military man here, and I suspect that the information we seek is to be found with the others. We shall test your endurance, Captain, and let your two companions view the spectacle, and see if they have any fine speeches to deliver after they have seen you systematically reduced to a gibbering wreck!"

Without further ado, Marshal Vukovic gestured theatrically to a technician, who pressed some mechanical knobs and levers on a control panel. Captain Napier cried out involuntarily and bucked against his straps as a surge of electrical current shot through his body.

A respect for basic decency forbids me from detailing the dark events of the next few hours; suffice it to say that Captain Napier was as resolute as Karl, PhyrePhox, and Marshal Vukovic were cruel, and that in this fashion they matched each other volley for volley until my comrade hung loose and unconscious in his web of bonds. One of Karl's minions was dispatched to obtain a bucket of water. As we all awaited his return, the three conspirators spoke in low tones in the opposite corner of the room while Dr. Nkruma and I exchanged a long glance, no words being required to convey our thoughts: which of us would be next, and would we be as strong?

We were startled out of these frightful ruminations by a sudden alarum in the adjoining corridor. One of Karl's guards glanced out the door, cried out in abject terror and slammed the door, shooting the bolts to lock us all inside. Through the heavy door we could hear the sounds of a brief but vicious struggle outside. Then, to our astonishment, a fountain of smoke and powder erupted from the concrete-block wall, and when it cleared away we could see the terminal six inches or so of a narrow, gently curved blade which had apparently been thrust all the way through the masonry! The blade sliced downward through concrete, mortar, and reinforcing steel, describing a roughly oval shape about the size of a man, and sending forth a shower of dust that soon threw a dense haze over the lights and set us all to coughing. Karl, PhyrePhox, and Marshal Vukovic, now trapped in their own dungeon, could do little more than watch dumbfounded, and ready their weapons to defend themselves against this mysterious onslaught. They did not have to wait for long; in a few seconds the ellipse was complete, and heavy thuds sounded from the opposite side. The oval slid into the room and collapsed onto the floor with a tremendous crash and cloud of dust, and standing in the opening thus created we were delighted to see none other than Major Yasuhiro Ozawa of Nippon's Protocol Enforcement Contingent, dressed in full battle armor and wielding the astonishing concrete-cutting sword! Behind him was a full platoon of others similarly equipped. Ignoring the furious commands of their now-impotent leaders, most of our captors threw their weapons down at once, and in short order Captain Napier's torturers had been arrested while Major Ozawa was kind enough to turn his sword to the easier work of cutting us free. "It is much like a chainsaw, but on the nanometer scale, of course," he explained in impeccable English. I could not help but be glad that such a dangerous technology was firmly in the disciplined and reliable hands of the Nipponese, and not encapsulated in a Seed that anyone could grow in his vegetable patch.

While a Nipponese doctor tended to Captain Napier, Major Ozawa explained that our distress spore—the pollen-sized message-in-a-bottle that I had engineered at the suggestion of Dr. Nkruma—had wandered into the immunological field of a Nipponese floating world hovering just off the coast of Los Angeles. Because of its unfamiliar shape it fell under the eye of a Defense Force engineer, who, in the course of unraveling it, found the message hidden inside. Under the care of Major Ozawa's doctor, Captain Napier soon returned to consciousness, though a full recovery would take somewhat longer. Agents of Protocol Enforcement serving both the Emperor and the Queen were at this moment striking at many nodes of the web spun by PhyrePhox, King Karl, Marshal Vukovic, and their associates, so for the moment there was little for us to do. We exchanged bows with our saviors, toasted our respective monarchs with an excellent sake thoughtfully provided by Major Ozawa, and then embarked on the most important part of our mission: reuniting ourselves with our families, and delivering a full report (of which this account may be considered only an executive summary) to Her Royal Highness Queen Victoria II of New Atlantis, to whom this work is humbly dedicated.

THE SIXTY-THIRD ANNIVERSARY OF HYSTERIA

Lisa Mason

May 24, 1941: *Arrived at last after months in Casablanca, which I once remembered fondly & now loathe. Sold all my white bed sheets for Moslem shrouds to raise money for our passage. The Faithful must meet their Maker wrapped in white, but I would sleep on straw to leave Africa. Everyone knows B.P. supported the Loyalists in Spain & wrote editorials for La Revolution Surrealiste & corresponded with Trotsky, for godssake. Every night I feared the knock on our door that never came.*

It's true what Breton said: Mexico is the Surrealist place par excellence. Land blazing with gold light. Antediluvian jungles, cacti & palms, a green I've never seen in Europe. Blooms riot, lascivious pinks, regal purples, scarlet like new blood. People wear their modernity lightly.

Found a dreadful apartment on Gabino Barreda, near the Monument to the Revolution. Plaster falling off the walls, scorpions in the kitchen. Other vermin, too, I fear. But there is an alcove off the bedroom with a terrace overlooking the street & light nearly all day. B.P. says I may take it as my studio. The landlord came by with two white, blue-eyed kittens. He says they are Sealpoint Siamese such as I have not seen since my mother's house in London. How can I not be happy?

"To the late Doctor Sigmund Freud!" says Gunther, toasting B.P. and Leonora Carrington. Tequila spills over her fingers, stinging the cut on her thumb she'd got from unpacking B.P.'s papers.

"To the great and monstrous Id!" says Chiqui.

"To the sixty-third anniversary of Hysteria!" says Wolfgang.

Gunther tosses the shot into the back of his throat and, with watery eyes and a manly suppression of the impulse to gag, seizes a mug of black beer, gulps it. B.P., always one to do in Rome, follows suit.

"Still stuck on Freud, what a pity," Remedios Varo says to Leonora, smiling in her ironic way. She takes the shot glass, replacing it with a tall, ice-choked tumbler rimmed in salt. "Here, sweet. A much better way to try tequila. We are not peasants like Gunther and poor old B.P."

Leonora is very thirsty. Mexico City sits at the top of the world. They say the air is always bone-dry. She gulps the lime infusion. Tequila instantly swirls into her head, making her dizzier than the first time she tried absinthe.

B.P. solicitously takes the tumbler away. "She hasn't touched a drop for ages, not the whole time we were exiled in Casablanca," he says to Remedios, who regards his gesture—Leonora cannot help but notice—with narrowed, glinting eyes. "And what is wrong with Freud, Madame Varo?"

"Ha!" Remedios says. "Tell me what is *right* with Freud!" She sweeps Leonora under her arm. "Come see my studio."

Remedios and her husband Renato L. possess a house on Rosa Moreno three blocks from Leonora and B.P.'s apartment. No tiny rooms and crumbling plaster here. The place is cavernous. Whitewashed ceilings like a cathedral, Moroccan arches, floors paved in terra-cotta tile, walls set with rainbow mosaics. The inner garden boasts a marble fountain. Remedios's studio, which opens onto the garden, has a curved adobe fireplace in one corner and Indian grotesqueries of every sort. Remedios shows her a red and black Olinala jaguar mask with a gaping jaw and real fangs, a black Michoacan devil mask with goat horns and a Satanic leer surely inspired by the Church, a pre-Columbian Tlacozotitlan bat mask with ocher, carved wood wings.

Leonora is dazzled. She first met Remedios in Paris among the clique surrounding Breton and Tanguy. Remedios slept with the great men, one after another. Breton himself deigned to notice her, since she was sloe-eyed and very slender, the sort of *femme-enfant* he craved like candy, and she was a budding Surrealist artist. She was painting "interior landscapes," eerie cracked plains stretching out to shadowed horizons set with whirling shrouded shapes and bizarre scaffolding. Leonora had been awed by Remedios and a little jealous. She slept with the less-than-great men, including the too-beautiful alcoholic poet who ended up preferring boys, and she was still painting Italian landscapes with olive trees and Etruscan ruins.

Now Remedios is the great woman with whom lesser men are privileged to dine, for the great men like Breton and Tanguy have the means and connections to enjoy their exile from the ravages of Europe in New York City. In the years since Paris, Remedios has become well-known in Surrealist circles, if not to the larger public. Peggy Guggenheim shows her paintings at Guggenheim Jeune Gallery in London. Even the dinner she cooked to welcome Leonora and B.P. to Mexico City is extraordinary: Oaxacan pineapples slashed in half and piled with jewel-like fruit; red snapper garnished with salsa and limes; *mole de guajolote,* turkey roasted in chili-chocolate sauce; sour cream and slivered olives atop spiced slices of a strange green fruit called an avocado.

Remedios is still slender, but no longer fragile. Not a *femme-enfant,* but a sibyl, *la sorciere,* a sphinx. One painting among the canvases stacked in her studio depicts a sphinx. Not the Egyptian monument nor the ripe, big-breasted creatures of Louis XIV statuary, but a vixenish creature with tabby-cat's paws and a child's face, crouched in a decaying mansion, toying with a human jawbone, broken eggshells, a bloody tidbit of raw meat.

"Remedios, this is smashing," Leonora says. "I've never seen anything like it. This is a whole new direction?"

But the men stroll into the studio behind Leonora. She bites back her words. B.P. hooks his hand round her neck, a familiar gesture through which she can feel the tension in him, his nerves coiling like tight, dry springs of wire.

"Have you seen much of Frida?" Gunther asks Remedios.

"Not much at all. Rivera is in poor health. You know how she attends his every need as if he were a little boy."

"Come, *ma belle* Remedios," B.P. says. *Ah,* Leonora thinks, *here it comes.* "You haven't told us your objections to the greatest analyst of the human mind in modern times."

"Well, to start, Freud hated women," she says, laughing as though it's quite a joke.

"Hated women?" B.P. says. "But it's Freud who first explicated the existence and causes of *l'amour fou, attitudes passionelles*, the supreme means of ecstatic expression at which you women are so adept." He peers at Remedios's sphinx.

"Ah, Hysteria," Remedios says. "The divine madness of women."

"To the sixty-third anniversary of Hysteria!" Wolfgang repeats, less clearly than before, downing his second shot of tequila.

"Now, Wolfie," Remedios says. "Do you wish to live forever in the shadow of Breton? The fiftieth anniversary of Hysteria in 1928 was in questionable taste. Publishing photographs of the poor lunatics at Salpetriere Hospital. How lovely for the doctors, mixing professional duties with their taste for sex. Celebrating insane women, pah. Why don't you write a new *La Revolution Surrealiste*, instead of repeating it over and over like my pet parrot?"

"Madame Varo is cruel," says Chiqui, snickering.

"But surely Freud was one of the first men to truly understand women, Remedios," Gunther says.

"And what did Freud understand, pray tell?" Remedios says.

"Why, that women are the link to the unconscious mind," Gunther replies.

"*Whose* unconscious?" Remedios says, no longer joking.

"Don't be obtuse, Remedios," B.P. says in the expansive, reasonable tone that means he will brook no opposition. "Freud exalts Woman. She is the link to the unconscious of the Artist. She disturbs the Poet, she compels him so that he breaks through his conscious control to forbidden desires, the secret obsessions of his unconscious. She enslaves him; thus, she frees him. She is the key, the trigger, the perfumed bomb. That onto which his passions may be projected and fulfilled."

"A blank slate, perhaps?" Remedios says. "A madwoman with no thoughts or talents of her own?"

"She is my Muse," B.P. says. He pinches Leonora's neck so tightly she cannot suppress a wince of pain.

"Ah, poor old B.P." Her glinting eyes are filled with questions. Leonora blushes, turns away. Remedios says, "*I am my* Muse."

June 22, 1941: R. has changed my life. We see each other nearly every day. She is filled with gossip about things going on everywhere, like a spider tugging at each strand of her web for juicy morsels. She says Frida has such a mustache from pleasing Rivera too much. Certain prostitutes on the Rue de G develop the same problem. Don't know if this is true, but it makes an awful nasty rumor. Frida is a tragic figure, of course, but I find her theatrical & intimidating & have not sought her company.

R. studies a Swiss psychoanalyst named Carl Jung. She prefers him to Freud. Rather than the repository of eroticism & primitivism, the unconscious mind for Jung is the repository of occult wisdom & "magical powers." (I read R.'s books in her studio, not daring to bring them home should B.P. find them.) "Magical powers" are a metaphor for discovering one's psychological strengths & weaknesses, which echo & reinterpret the archetypal conflicts of humanity. Jung does not really believe there are magical powers, does he? Like Freud, Jung believes the unconscious is essentially female. If this is so, then Woman is not only erotic, but also occult.

One day in the market R. & I found a plant with strange egg-like fruit. She told me to run & get my brushes & paints & bring them back to her house, which I did. We placed the plant in her garden and arranged my things around it in a circle. R. said the light of the full moon would fall upon them & the Alchemical Egg will grace my brushes & paints with creative genius. I found this very amusing indeed. On my way home, I found a tiny bird's nest which had fallen onto the pavement. One miniature egg nestled within. I carefully picked up the nest & replaced it firmly in the crotch of a tree. The very moment after I did this, mother hummingbird flitted up & hovered, blinking at me as though in thanks. I thought, O Alchemical Egg, give birth to me. A silly thought, I know, but there you are, & I was so happy, thinking this is an omen.

I have started a new painting, my first work in Mexico City: a woman curled up inside a giant egg.

Leonora is exhausted when she gets home from the advertising agency. She has been running a light fever for a week, there is nothing decent in the cupboard for dinner, and, on top of everything, B.P. is in a foul mood.

"Where've you been?" he snaps as she drags in the door.

"At work, of course," she snaps back.

"At Remedios's again, I'm sure," he says. On principle, he cannot object to her friendship with the great Artist, but he chafes at her devotion to Remedios just the same.

"At work," she repeats. "Besides," she says, softening her

tone, for what is the use of fighting with B.P., "I wanted to visit the cats."

Leonora could not afford to keep the beautiful Siamese kittens, whom Remedios gladly took in. She cannot afford much more than their rent and rice, beans, and tortillas, perhaps a roast chicken once a month. She cannot afford new shoes. She lines the insides of her cracked leather pumps with newspaper. The advertising agency is pleased with her projects, simple but energetic pen-and-ink drawings extolling the virtues of aspirin and hair tonic. But they pay her for piecework, which amounts to little.

Hitler's troops invaded Russia today.

B.P. does not work. After losing his family's house and property in Hungary, he seems as if paralyzed. He cannot speak Spanish well enough to translate or write for a newspaper. And he is starting a new play. He cannot work if he is to write a new play. Sometimes Leonora thinks he would be content to live in the street and beg for food, all for the sake of writing the play. Still, the play is his salvation. He has written nothing for a year.

"Did you get tequila?" he growls. Tequila fuels him. He must have it to write the play.

"I forgot we were out," she says, sighing. Having to work has considerably slowed progress on her new painting, yet Leonora goes to the advertising agency, plus takes in sewing when she can, because she would not be content to live in the street and beg for food. She must at least have rice and beans, at the least the apartment at Gabino Barreda. She can do without new shoes, but she must have paint and canvases.

"Well, give me some money," he says.

She gives him the last of her money for the week, and he goes out in search of tequila. She washes her face and hands, drifts over to his writing desk in the small living room. His work is tucked away, as usual, or covered with blank paper. He has not been ready to show her the new play. She twinges with guilt at violating his orders not to interfere with his things. Yet he has left a sheet of paper in his typewriter, out of carelessness, the forgetfulness of his hangover, or deliberately, she cannot be sure. There, on the half-typed page, she reads:

JUSTINE: I beg you, Master! I beg you! Please, not again, I cannot bear it!

MASTER (chaining her left ankle to the bedpost): Yes,
    again, little love. One day you will beg me for it.

Leonora goes to the kitchen, puts rice on to boil, heats oil in
the skillet, fries the last curling tortillas. Hot oil spatters her
wrist, but she scarcely notices. When B.P. walks in with the
tequila, she bangs down the skillet, goes out to the living room
at once, unable to control the trembling in her lip.

"The new play," she says, tapping her toe, folding her arms,
tucking her burn-speckled hand beneath her armpit. She cannot keep the tone of accusation out of her voice. "You're writing a new Sade play."

"I told you to stay away from my desk," he says mildly.

Ah; deliberately.

"There's no market for a new Sade play," she says. "Who
gives a damn about Sade when Hitler has Europe in bondage?
When he lusts for Russia, Africa, the whole world?"

"On the contrary, the times are exactly right for Sade," he
says, pouring himself a shot of tequila. Hands shaking, he spills
a pool of liquor on the table, laps it up like a dog. He gulps
the shot. "As you say, Hitler has Europe in bondage. Hitler
violates her cruelly. And he seeks new victims."

"That is hardly a revolutionary statement, B.P.," she says.

"Hitler violates in the realm of politics and suppresses the
personal. I shall prove violation in the realm of the personal
liberates politics. Marquis de Sade was a great sexual revolutionary, fully conversant with his unconscious. A man who
broke through to his secret obsessions without Freudian psy-
choanalysis. Breton himself says Sade is Surrealist in sadism. I
cannot wait to show him!"

"Sade and Freud," she says. "What cozy bedfellows. Comrades in hating women."

"I see that Madame Varo has obscured your usually adequate intellect," B.P. says. "Sade believed in the sexual freedom of Woman. He believed Woman should be free of
maternity, domesticity, free of romantic love. Free even of her
female sexuality."

"Sade was despicable," she says.

"His prose style is exquisite," B.P. says.

He insists on making love after their humble dinner. Leonora
gulps a lime-and-tequila, lies on the bed. She begins to tremble. She is not afraid of B.P. She's half an inch taller than he
and more robust. He has never physically harmed her. She is

certain he would never try. Isn't she? No, the trembling comes from uncertainty, a morbid expectation. How is he changed, if Sade is on his mind?

But he is tender as always. He makes no move to bind her ankles to the bedposts. And she is inexplicably disappointed. B.P. does not live his Art. His Art does not inform his life with her.

As he strives for his climax, she runs her fingers along his spine. The little knobs down his back are so fragile. For a moment she believes she could crush them, like eggshells, with her thumbs.

Sept 1, 1941: Again: making love with B.P. & I am on top. He reaches his climax, closes his eyes with a sigh & dies. The life force flees from him. His body lies like a heap of garbage. No worms this time. Still it's horrible. His body begins to disintegrate beneath me, drying up like clay in the sun & crumbling, till I am lying on bare earth. I scoop the earth with my hands & rub it all over my arms & shoulders, toss palmfuls on my back. Suddenly, little shoots of green curl out of the pores of my skin. I hear a popping sound, feel tingles across my back. I twist my head around & see that tomato & maize plants are growing out of my shoulder blades! The green shoots swell into great curling vines that twist & grope into the earth beneath me. My blood surges through the vines, flowing into the earth, moistening it, feeding it. This is very arousing. Then the earth next to my fingertips quivers & a vine, glowing green-gold, struggles out. The vine raises itself before me like an eyeless serpent, a volitional thing. A drop of its sap forms at the tip, which reddens like blood & grows or solidifies into some sort of ruby-red fruit. The fruit drops into the palm of my hand. I wake with the taste of plum on my tongue.

Leonora is delighted with Remedios's new obsession: that the kitchen is an alchemical laboratory, and the art of cooking, the grandmother of alchemy.

"Ancient history, of course. We've just forgotten it," Remedios declares. "While men were running around hunting woolly mammoths and bashing each other over the head, women were tending gardens, growing herbs and vegetables and fruit, working in the kitchen, at the hearth, in the distillery. For nourishment and medicine and magic."

"What dost thou brew in thy cauldron, O witch?" Leonora

laughs. She cracks an egg over a bowl, pours the innards back and forth between the half-shells till the white separates from the yolk and dribbles into the bowl. She sets the white aside for Remedios's pastries. She has begun to paint with egg tempera on gessoed wood panels, a medieval technique yielding bright, translucent surfaces. "Our Art is an alchemy." She whisks scarlet pigment with a spoonful of yolk, plus a dash of vinegar for its preservative properties. "Nourishing the spirit."

The thought is electrifying. Nourishing, yes; if not the public's spirit, then her own. She cannot reconcile herself to the new play of Sade's *Justine*, which B.P. insists will be his next great work. The play is a rift between them, deepening every day he labors over it, as though he had joined the Fascists and engaged in work for the Party. The rift exacerbates other tensions between them, his refusal to secure gainful employment while she must struggle so, her daily exhaustion with work, housekeeping, meals, and her Art. She neglects the apartment, spends more and more time with Remedios. B.P. protests, but, when he finds he cannot dissuade her, continues his work or goes out to cafés alone. She hears rumors he is seeing a prostitute at Mil y Una Noches, which he denies in a mild tone.

She brings all her painting gear, and her journal, to Remedios's studio. Remedios lends her an easel. They paint together for hours, sipping *blanc de blanc* from Veracruz or thick raspberry wine called *zarzamora*, nibbling on *ciruela*, yellow plums. Cats wind round their ankles, music murmurs on the phonograph.

"Taste this, sweet," Remedios says, laying her paintbrush down. "My new magic formula." She finds a crystal decanter filled with translucent rose-amber liquid, pours a shot.

Leonora sips. A soapy taste, sugary fire, hot spice, a bit of grit. "Smashing," she says, tears starting in her eyes.

Remedios finds a page in her journal. "Take a cup of *habanero*—that's sugarcane whiskey, four cups of rosewater, several dashes each of cinnamon, cloves, and cayenne pepper, two cat hairs, and a pinch of lint from beneath a bed where a couple has just made love."

"Of course," Leonora says, refusing to cough before her friend's teasing glance. "And what does this magic formula do?"

"Discourages insomnia and promotes erotic dreams."

"Just what I needed."

"Me, too." Remedios pours a shot for herself. Her eyes turn

suddenly sad. She picks up her brush. "Renato is stuck on another bullfighter. Oh, he never hid his predilections from me. Ours was a marriage of convenience, you know. But he doesn't bother to keep his liaisons private anymore. He parades them about." She sips her magic formula. "I've asked for a separation."

"He agrees?"

She nods. "He's moving to Acapulco within the week. The sooner the better, I say. Chiqui adores me."

"Chiqui." Leonora bites back her words. Chiqui is beneath Remedios Varo. Oh, he has produced some passable Surrealist photographs, nudes straddling the Great Sphinx of Egypt while camel-sized tarantulas and headless ballerinas dance upon an Arctic glacier. That sort of thing. Still, Chiqui. It's so banal.

Hitler's and Mussolini's troops invaded Egypt today.

"I know," Remedios says. "I know what you're thinking, you don't have to say it. At least he'll cheat on me with women."

"That's not what I'm thinking, Remedios," she protests. She finishes with her mixing bowl. The scarlet tempera is frothy, viscous as blood. She sets the bowl down among six others filled with colors. "Just . . . don't let him steal you from me."

"Never!"

"That's all I ask." Tipsy from the magic formula, Leonora begins to paint, applying egg tempera in meticulous, tiny strokes. On the canvas is a house, cut away to show four floors, many stairwells, several trapdoors, a shadowed basement coiling with dark shapes. The house is inhabited by all manner of fantastic creatures: flying horses, women with trees growing out of the tops of their heads or vines curling out of their arms, a shrouded woman bound wrist and ankle to a bed, a hooded man with no feet hovering before her. She paints a hearth, a curved adobe fireplace, a huge, bubbling cauldron with two women standing over it. One woman is translucent as glass. The other stirs the brew with a ladle, her hand narrowing, curving, becoming a part of the ladle, the handle itself.

Leonora breaks from the reverie of the work, and starts. Her arm is a rod of bone and suntanned skin narrowing into the wood stalk of the brush. She touches the canvas with her fingers, which are not fingers, but a bound cluster of horse hairs. She feels paint, cool and smooth as cream.

Nov 17, 1941: The Siamese cats whisper secrets to me. They are most insistent, Kiku in particular. They say beware: people

*of the day do not understand people of the night. They hate us,
Kiku tells me, revile us, would kill us if they got a chance. You
are the Moon, Tigre adds, & you know what that means. You
control the waters, blooming of orange blossoms, the moods &
tonalities. I am cautious. I creep around, peer over my shoulder
whenever I feel someone near. B.P. has become strange, staring
at me all the time. I buy him his tequila & pay the rent & tell
him to go write his damn Sade play & leave me alone. He does;
still he stares at me. I don't like it.*

*Took a nap after work & dreamed, a horrific dream filled with
confusing images. A serpent. Dozens of broken eggs. A horse &
cart. A dark man I have never seen before with black eyes, high
cheeks, a brass disk on his chest. A child, a little girl with her
skull crushed, her face torn apart, lying in a pool of blood in the
street. I wake, shaken. Is this me, crushed by my circumstances?
I don't like it at all.*

*Later, drank a lot of tequila, trying to forget. B.P. didn't mind;
we had a drunken bout in bed. I passed out, couldn't remember
where I was when I woke at four A.M. Couldn't remember what
we did.*

I rose, made coffee. I am afraid to sleep.

Remedios has been in Acapulco for a fortnight. First, to attend to Renato, who slashed his wrists in a warm bath after a
stormy time with a boy who attends the beaches. And, second,
to settle her financial affairs pursuant to their divorce.

She calls Leonora at the advertising agency nearly every day,
since the apartment at Gabino Berreda has no phone. Leonora
calls her from the house at Rosa Moreno whenever she is there
to feed the cats or work in the studio. But telephone calls
cannot replace Remedios herself and grow more scarce with
the press of her business in Acapulco.

There is no one to blame, but Leonora is desolate. She de-
cides she must purify herself. She commences with two days
of vomiting induced by drinking warm salt water, then fasts,
sipping wine when her throat gets parched. She walks back and
forth between her apartment and Remedios's house at least
three times a day: before work to check for thieves, after work
to feed the cats, then after fixing B.P.'s dinner to paint. Sometimes she goes home to sleep, sometimes not, depending on
how afraid she is to be alone versus how afraid she is to sleep
with B.P. She cleans Remedios's house, scrubbing the terra-
cotta tiles on her hands and knees.

One day, when she is walking home from the advertising agency in a dreamy, starved fatigue, a commotion erupts in the street. She sees a wild-eyed galloping horse, his produce cart swaying and clattering behind him, the driver cursing and flailing with the reins. Vegetables tumble, baskets scatter their contents, eggs fall and smash.

She runs to the corner of Paseo de la Reforma. A crowd gathers, police rush up, tooting their whistles. "Rattlesnake!" someone yells. A man displays the limp snake, which has been beaten to death. She pushes past people, stares down at a little girl, her skull crushed, her face torn apart, lying in a pool of blood in the street. Leonora kneels.

Someone takes her arm, lifts her. "Is this your child, madame?" the policeman asks gently. She stares at the badge on his chest, his swarthy face, cheekbones, black eyes.

"No," she whispers.

And thinks: *I have seen the future.*

Dec 7, 1941: I am walking down a dark road. People trudge behind me, weary, carrying baggage & small children. I seem to see faces of people I know, but when I look closely, they are strangers. I am afraid.

Now the road is a jungle. I begin to run, stumbling on vines, thrusting my hands & arms through dense foliage. I come upon a clearing, a round field of grass lit by the moon. A giant crouches there, a monstrous woman with a grotesque face like one of R.'s devil masks. The giant seizes a dagger from her belt & promptly slits her own throat! She falls, crashing into the jungle, and her foot strikes something. I see a sparkling flash, like water splashing.

I am very frightened, but I creep into the clearing. There, in the center, in the tall wet grass, I find an ancient vase, tipped by the dead giant's foot. A thick, scarlet fluid spills from its mouth. I reach into the vase & find a huge blue egg. The egg cracks open in my hands; out tumbles a jewel! A jewel of extraordinary size & luminescence, gleaming with power & beauty. I am filled with unreasonable joy, & I realize somehow, in some way, I have found the most valuable thing in the whole world. Someone says, You have found the Stone. Tell the people, but keep It secret.

I make my way out of the jungle & return to the dark road crowded with suffering people. We walk together to the sea. A beautiful port with gleaming silver ships appears. Bright lights explode above us, a deafening roar. Everyone starts to scream, I am screaming too, & the grief is overwhelming.

Leonora strides down Avenida Reforma, neatly dressed in the clothes she wears to the advertising agency, her last pair of silk stockings clipped into her garter belt, a cotton sash tied round her waist. She has pinned up her hair, tucked a rose behind her ear. The morning is sultry. She finds the address, pushes open the glass doors of the American embassy. She strides up to the security guards at their desk, heels clicking on the marble floor. The security guards are young American men with bland faces, blank eyes, skulls shaved bald beneath their military caps.

"The American ambassador, please," she crisply tells the guards.

"Do you have an appointment, madame?" one asks.

"No. No, I don't."

"Well, I'm sorry. The ambassador cannot see you without an appointment. Would you like to leave your name and number?"

"No," Leonora says. "I must see him now. It's urgent!"

"I see." The guard gives his companion a long-suffering glance.

"Can't the British embassy help you, miss?" says the other guard. He smiles, acknowledging the charm of her accent.

"No, the British are doing all they can," she says. "They have survived the air war, but only at great cost. I must speak with the American ambassador. I must speak with him now!"

They politely ask for her name, address, and telephone number, which she gives to them, substituting Remedios's phone number. They tell her to wait. She paces back and forth for half an hour. The clicking of her heels echoes into the high ceiling of the lobby like muted screaming. But she waits.

Finally a guard calls to her. "I'm sorry, Miss Carrington, but the ambassador cannot speak with you today. Perhaps you can arrange with his secretary?" He hands her a business card.

She stares at him. "You don't understand, do you? Hitler is destroying the world, and you sit there with your blank American eyes and tell me the ambassador cannot see me."

"Madame, calm yourself."

"I can see the future, young man! I am here to tell your ambassador that America cannot sit by while the world is forced into bondage. Hitler binds and tortures the world, he obliterates our humanity. This is *personal*. Violation in the realm of the personal does not liberate politics!"

B.P. strides into the embassy. The guards have not consulted with the ambassador at all. They have summoned B.P. At his side is a woman she has never seen before. The woman wears a black dress inappropriate for the morning with a neckline that shows the tops of her breasts.

B.P. whispers to the guards, "She's an Artist, you see. High-strung. Hasn't been well lately."

"She does look awful thin," says a guard.

"I'll kill him myself!" Leonora tells the gathering crowd. American tourists in their summer clothes, embassy employees in smart suits. "Someone must kill Hitler before he enslaves us all! Not just Europe and Britain, Russia and Africa, but you! *You!*"

"Call a doctor," the security guard says, twirling his forefinger in the air around his temple. "Better tell him to bring one of them straitjackets, too."

B.P. shakes his head. "Poor Leonora."

The woman in the black dress can barely contain her glee. "Mother of God, B.P." She nuzzles his ear. "She's hysterical."

Leonora calms herself, lowers her voice, smooths her hair. *Tell the people, but keep It a secret.* "Listen to me. You must see the future as I have. Hitler will take the world if we don't stop him."

The crowd murmurs anxiously.

Outside, boys dash along the sidewalk, holding aloft newspapers emblazoned with huge red headlines. *"Especial, especial!* Read all about it! Japs bombed Pearl Harbor! The Japs bombed Pearl Harbor this morning!"

An ambulance speeds up to the embassy. Men in medical coats leap out, race across the lobby, surround Leonora. They wrestle her into submission, wrap straps round her wrists and ankles. Hands thrust up her skirt. Sharp pain pierces her thigh, the jab of a needle. She struggles, screaming, "Liberate yourselves!" The drug makes her swoon.

Then Remedios comes, Remedios at last, translucent as glass. She takes Leonora's hand, and together they fly into the lunatic sky.

WHEN A MAN'S AN EMPTY KETTLE

William Barton

C all me . . . what? Ishmael? No. The ghost in the machine? Again no, but much closer. There are times
when I wish I *were* a ghost, for ghosts have half-lives
and slowly fade away. That would finish it right and true, at
least for this one, and that might be enough. In any case, my
name is Lothar. Lothar von Flaadë.

My name. Hell. Even that's not right, but it's the only one
I know.

Deceleration time. I was standing on the outside of *Star
Bright*, holding on with all six feet, powergrips down and
locked, watching the sky twist and shudder, pale, blue-white
light from the field modulus device's matter-wasting exhaust
shining all over everything. Ghost light, it was, well suited to
a ghost, shining on the ship's girdery structure, on spherical
tanks and cargo pods, on bits and pieces of this and that held
fast by straps and clamps, on the little life-support pod, well
shielded to protect fragile organics and assorted radiation-soft
hardware.

Carandache's voice whispered inside me, *300 seconds, Lothar. Counting down.*

I could see her in my mind's eye, an image made up of
memory and, perhaps, her own self-image, a small, beautiful
woman, clad all over in soft red fur, tail held aloft, curling aside

for the chair-back when she sat, red fur, long red hair, big, liquid brown eyes, woman compounded of snippets and fragments, human, dog, cat, primate . . .

And I loved to see myself through her eyes, a tall, solid cylinder of blue-silver metal and plastic, six jointed legs, eight jointed arms, headless, almost featureless.

Right now, though, all I could see was *Star Bright*'s master, Prince Felix Galitzin, handsome, muscular, black-bearded and clad in black, a bit of glitter from silver badges of service and rank at collar and cuff. Master and slave, like the rest of us, though cast in mankind's image, slaves in the service of Standard ARM's Astrochemical Resources Mining operation.

Inertial forces tugged at me as the stars turned and shifted, jittering. As a pilot, Felix could be careless, human proud, showing off for no one. And looking forward to setting down on Thetis. We'd been out in the Kuiper Disk for years, plying the ARM's trade, making profits the big AIs could count and manipulate, building wealth for terrestrial overlords no one ever saw.

He'd never been in-system before, nor had Carandache, both of them tanked and decanted somewhere out in the Oort, at some Standard ARM manpower factory.

I'd been born there though, on Earth itself . . . a million years ago? Sometimes it seemed that way, though the reality was no more than two hundred. Two hundred years. And the real me gone almost as long. Lothar von Flaadë, game designer and impressionist actor, dead in the year 2056, a youngish man dead from dissolution and despair, leaving behind the expert systems and software tools he'd written in a brief, brilliant career. Tools that were then sold to the highest bidder, sold for reuse, repurposing, and further development.

Decades pass, then centuries, until we come to a piece of industrial machinery that calls itself Lothar. Lothar of the memories. Memories of life and love, pretty women and grand adventures, adventures written by that oh-so-real and ever-so-dead Lothar. And I can't tell, from this far shore, which ones were real. If any.

Call me . . . what? Dead Lothar's soul? Hell. That's as good a name as any. I just wish I knew if I were real.

There. A pale, lovely blue dot among the fixed stars, swelling to a pea, a pearl of light as the modulus's fire grew brighter and brighter. We'd crossed Neptune's orbit at 0.08 cee, free-falling, and had to shed much of the rest of it matching orbits with Type S Asteroid 17 Thetis, on the Kirkwood Gap edge of Piazzi Belt I, a little under two-and-a-half AU from the Sun.

A beautiful body, what had once been a three-lobed aggregate of chewed-up gray rock (I remember it well, I must have been here then), now covered with buildings that were silver and gold and shining alabaster white, superimposed against a brilliant azure circle of sky-blue sky. No terminator—the eutropic atmosphere shield would wash it out—and there was a small, irregular, greenish body orbiting inside the patch of sky, partially eclipsing Thetis itself, something not in my memory. How long ago was I here last? Never—it's a memory left over from some previous incarnation, a programmer's sloppy work.

Pump up the magnification, take a spectrum. Chlorophyll. Trees?

Carandache's voice whispered, *They call it the Park, Lothar. It was towed in and planted about fifty years ago, after they'd built over the last bits of open ground on Thetis.* She was standing behind Felix's pilot-chair, massaging his shoulders gently, luxuriating in the feel of his stiff, rubbery deltoids, nuzzling her face against his hair. I could almost feel it prickling in her nose, smell the sharp, remote tang of his sweat, which she loved.

I said, "That'd make it sometime in the 2160s, then. One of me must have been here before that." Some software package on a direct line that led to this one.

Whisper: *Don't you remember?* This one life is the only one Carandache has had. And her hands were reaching over Felix's shoulders, softly rubbing his chest, squeezing a double bulge of pectoral tissue.

"Not like it was real, like it was really me. Just a leftover piece of data matrix." I hoped she wouldn't distract him from his job, though the ship's circuit-AIs would keep him from ramming anything, it could get rough for someone (some*thing*, I told myself) riding on the outside.

Rough ride. But the *view* . . .

Blue sky swelling until it covered half the universe, then we were passing right under the Park, trees reaching for us from above, golden temples glittering below, air suddenly sighing around *Star Bright*'s girders and tanks and cargo, plucking at my body, towing my arms back into a trailing cluster so that they clattered against each other . . .

God, I remembered! Sailing down a snowy mountainside in

Switzerland a hundred and seventy-five years ago, laughing woman trying to catch me, laughing, but getting farther behind, wind in my hair, etched freezing cold against my skin, pressure in my knees as I turned, muscles, young, healthy muscles straining, bounce, hard thud, as I went over a pressure ridge . . .

Wind in my hair, a much older man now, no longer fit for skiing, riding an electric motorcycle through the hardpan desert of eastern California, somewhere northeast of the Salton Sea, hot wind, gritty wind, stinging on my face, grains of sand whispering against my goggles.

Not me. No, not me. The god who created me, reached out his finger and gave the spark of life to this poor soul, as Michelangelo's God to Adam. My god died, did his?

We slowed to a stop over Thetis's landing stage, settled among the spaceships, and were down, settling into the soft, plush field of this world's generated gravity, exchanging our modulus for its much larger one.

Inside the ship, Felix crowed, "All *right!*" rubbing his hands together with excitement, anticipation, and I could feel Carandache cringing. Sorry for her, I guess. Very sorry, for she has been my friend. But that's just the way it is.

Later, much later, task-set finished, we were out on the night streets of Thetis, Felix, Carandache and I, our first liberty in years, other than those brief visits to ARM rec centers out in the icy darkness. Different. Very different here on a world inhabited since the latter third of the twenty-first century, a world already grown stale by the twenty-third. It is almost the way I remember Earth to be, because the men and women who built Thetis wished to feel at home here. Quaint. Old-fashioned. Lovely.

We were walking together, almost arm in arm, past tall, ornate buildings, through streets flooded by ersatz night, surrounded by people, by things that pretended to be people, crowds threaded by bicycles and electric scooters and the little golf carts the locals called zipneys. Golf. Do I remember playing golf? I guess so. The real Lothar played a little golf, back when he still felt young and happy.

Felix had his arm around Carandache's shoulder, she snuggling into his side as they walked along, purring warm happiness through our shared comlink, flooding me with warmth as well. I envy her, sometimes, that pure devotion, however arti-

ficial it may be. No better, really, than my own devotion to
Star Bright, but how it aches in memory, a resonance of things
that seem so lost.

Should I curse those sloppy programmers? No. Without their
mistakes I'd be . . . what? Cold iron? Not even that.

Carandache in memory, far out in deep space, curled up in
a bunk with Felix, he petting her soft red fur, murmuring to
her, telling her how lovely she was, she nuzzling against him,
giving everything she had over and over.

We are what we were made to be, even Felix, built as a man
because there is men's work to be done, though in places where
no true men willingly go. Be human, they told him. Conduct
our business, as we would conduct it.

Making love to little Carandache between the stars, while
Star Bright and I watched, while I listened-in through the link
and felt the brilliant stab of her joy.

Memory of memories, watching them, reaching back across
time, back into different selves, back to the original template,
who made love to women in the darkness and imagined eternity. Then threw it away. Or is this the eternity he imagined?

The streets grew dingier, the crowds wilder-looking as we
progressed into an older section of Thetis, as if it were some
ancient human city on Earth, away from the shiny new landing
stage, getting into the nearly abandoned areas surrounding the
ruins of the North Polar Docking Structure, built when Thetis
had no atmosphere, back before the discovery of the field modulus technology, when the miners of Thetis lived down in the
black tunnels still honeycombing its interior.

People down there, they said, real true people who've forgotten their origin, living like rats, like less-than-rats . . . Legends. Like the legends of the alligators living beneath Old New
York.

Felix and Carandache were stopped on a sidewalk corner,
watching the street life, I behind them, watching as well,
watching and remembering. And seeing what Felix watched,
feeling Carandache's fear through the link, listen to her soft
whisper . . . *No. Please. Let him look away* . . . Moment of pity,
reaching out to touch her mind, "I'm here, little friend . . ."
feeling the sharp tang of her powerless anger . . .

They call them allomorphs. Pure robot, imbued with very
elaborate software, in base-state looking like immature human
women, tiny nipples on a flat chest, hairless vulvae almost unnoticeable, slim hips, smooth, androgynous faces, the faces of

lovely prepubescent boys, choirboy faces, smooth, feathery hair, in gray or light brown or pale blond . . .

Mutable human things, made for humans, able to become man or woman, in any race or form, programmed to serve and nothing more. I don't know where I remember them from, the original Lothar was long dead before they were ever thought of, but then, I must have been here before.

Why can't I remember?

A little flaw, surely, some hack programmer's error, giving me that memory of memory, without the memory itself . . .

I could feel Felix's hunger for them, right through Carandache's fear, as we watched them plying their trade right out on the street, doing lovely things, and horrible. Carandache breathed an audible sigh of relief when we walked on, holding Felix close, her hand clutching the front of his belt, conscious of his arousal. *Maybe later*, I could hear her thinking, *he'll come to me*. Anticipating the night, so much like a thousand previous nights.

The first bar was called "Pumphouse," elaborate holimation decorating its facade, tribe of baboons fornicating, mutating as they humped merrily away, becoming men and women and baboons again while we watched. Felix smiled and said, "This looks OK. Let's go in."

OK for what? But Carandache seemed willing to follow wherever he led, as always.

When we stepped up to the door a man emerged from the shadows, hand raised, gesturing. He was a scruffy thing, so scruffy he could only be some natural human, some sort of unmod. And gesturing toward us, me and Carandache, lips twisted in an angry grimace: "Sorry pal," this creature said. "You'll have to leave your toys outside."

Felix staring then, bemused, rubbing his chin, Carandache angry, myself uncaring, feeling like a toy in any case, Felix looking at us then, murmuring, *"Toys."* Pang from Carandache, who could read him, perhaps know he was considering going on in, leaving us in the street . . .

But he only smiled and raised a finger to the man, then we walked on, Carandache cuddling against him again. Behind us, I could hear the unmod mutter, "Fuckin' *rabbit*-lovers. Jesus . . ."

A slight start within: the always-surprising realization that the unmod couldn't tell Felix wasn't one of them.

• • •

The next club we came to was called "Inhuman Joys," no holimation this time, facade lit up in moving lines of imitation neon light, soft, melting shades of purple and pink. Old, aboriginal programming gave meaning to the colors I knew they no longer held; attitudes change over the decades and centuries, not surviving into a time when there are far stranger, stronger things than an unmod's seemingly unnatural desires.

Felix stopped and looked down at Carandache, peering into her face. A little gesture. "OK?"

The fear was still in her, the wish that we were gone from here, on our way back into the safer depths of deep space, but she looked at the door of the bar, regarding its olive-green bouncer, sleek, hairless, displaying an impressive set of male-human genitals, at his pop-eyes and long ivory tusks, four muscular arms folded across a bulky, complex-looking chest. Whisper from her mind, *no* . . . but she said, "I . . . think so. All right, Felix . . ."

We went in unchallenged, selected a table, sat down.

The light inside was reddish, rather dark, as if it somehow incorporated a black hue, and the waiters were low, mobile platforms that could think and speak. Felix and Carandache ordered unmod drinks to sip and relish, metabolic paths deranged by toxins—and the waiter regarded me, then linked and whispered, *Software, brother?* A brief display of artificial memories and delights even a heavily modded organic like Carandache could not imagine.

I showed it my uplink registers and accepted its whispered apology. *Peace, brother.*

Fear from Carandache suddenly intruding, focused on the low stage, her gaze paralleling Felix's fascination. Up there, a perfect human woman. Unmod? Without a link, impossible to tell. Naked woman, with long silvery hair writhing on the stage, genitals thrust up, bobbing before the audience, a complex dance, a very old dance, reaching out to touch the spilled human genetic matrices of this intricate, enigmatic audience.

How many of them would or could respond? Felix, yes, because his genes are wholly human, driving a wholly human metabolism, flooding him with human hormonal drives. Fueling Carandache's fears as well, human base structures conflicting with a software of devotion . . .

And . . . me. Nothing human in me but my memories. Which were quite enough.

Mesmerized by that dancing swatch of curled silver hair,

those flexing muscles, as if I were a man, as if . . . As if. What was I remembering? Do I know you, naked woman? The real Lothar remembered a thousand women's genitals, remembering them when faces were long forgotten, but . . . no memory of silver hair. Something else, then.

I linked with the house AI and checked the playbill. *Holly Golightly, Antiquarian Exotic Dancer.* A social-registry number in a style so old-fashioned she could very well reach back into Lothar's lifespan. A survivor, this Holly Golightly. Few unmods from that time have stayed on into this. And most of them surviving because they'd joined the ranks of the overlords on Earth.

In the long run, the very long run, you have to have a reason to go on living, or the universe will simply let you go.

I left my calling card in her mail queue, just an image of the three of us, inviting her to stop by our table for a drink. Left it with the pile of invitations accumulating there.

Terror from Carandache, like burning ice: *Oh, Lothar! No . . .* But Felix took her into his lap then, petting her absentmindedly, rubbing the fur on her belly, all the while watching Holly with fascination. Carandache nuzzled her face into his throat, hiding her misery, pretending . . .

Later, while a shiny, twelve-handed juggler danced and sang on stage, Holly Golightly, still naked, came to our table, looking at us with interest, at Felix first, Carandache still huddled in his lap, then at me. She tossed her silver hair and smiled, and I noticed how the thin layer of sweat on her skin picked up the color of the lights, giving her a faint, rosy glow. "So." Even in one word, her voice was smooth and throaty, matching up with whatever fragments remained floating in my memory. "I wondered what a machine could want with me." A bemused glance at Felix. "I figured it was a clever-enough ploy . . ."

He smoothed the ruffled fur on Carandache's breasts and said, "It *was* all his idea." He was looking at me then, also bemused.

Pulse of relief from Carandache. *He doesn't want her . . .*

No. Of course not. Too human. I knew Carandache would pick up my thought, and, unhappily, the image that went with it, of those allomorph whores, plying their trade outside.

Holly said, " 'His.' " Looking keenly at me. "Are you a man inside, then?"

It seemed likely that she knew, though my own memory fragments weren't enough to tell me how or why. "Not quite."

I held out a hand to her, one finger up, the rest down in imitation of a human grip. "Portions of me," I said, "mimic Lothar von Flaadë."

A moue of seeming displeasure twisted on her face for a moment, and she glanced at Felix, at Carandache, as if accusing them of . . . something. I couldn't quite tell what. "Well," she said, and there was bitterness in her voice. "I *do* keep meeting his offspring, don't I?" As if talking to herself, though she kept looking at me.

Another flash of floating memory, another fragment clicking in, and I knew those pale-violet eyes had regarded me before, soft and accusing, with mingled anger and sorrow.

She said, "Do you know me?"

The oldest part of me wanted to close its eyes, shake its head slowly. Lacking eyes, lacking a head, I merely said, "No. I'm sorry I . . ."

Her soft voice said, "Don't be." She reached out and touched my side, fingers trailing across smooth and largely insensate metal. "So shiny," she whispered. "Not like him at all."

Felix, suddenly understanding what had happened, said, "Did you know the real Lothar?"

I could feel Carandache's sharp flame of quick anger, anger at Felix for being so insensitive. *Real Lothar . . . how could he . . .* I reached out to smooth her thoughts. It's easy, I suggested, for someone so intrinsically human . . .

But, he's not . . .

He *feels* that he is.

Holly had eyes only for me, pale-violet eyes full of something else I just couldn't grasp . . . not right then. She said, "Not . . . quite." Then she stood and said, "It was nice meeting you again, Lothar. I have to go back to work now."

Watching her walk away, watching that sleek, half-remembered form, I felt a flood of relief pour out of Carandache, easing her misplaced fears about Felix and Holly. But the allomorphs were still waiting outside. I imagine Felix knew that too.

Then, later, I squatted in the corner of a semidark hotel room, watching, Carandache sitting on the floor, face pressed into my side, hiding her eyes, arms around my cylindrical midsection, hands gripping smooth metal, little fingers, fruitlessly, trying to dig in. Silent, just like me, but weeping within.

Why . . .

Because he is what he is.

But why in front of me like this . . .

I didn't have an answer for that one. I doubted there was any special programming that told Felix to disregard her feelings like that. But then, there wasn't any special programming of devotion either. Carandache loved Felix for the good of the company. As I loved *Star Bright*. As Felix loved Standard ARM. No room, it seemed, in the service of that program for love of anything else.

Only gentle friendship, and only so long as it didn't conflict with that overriding love.

How fortunate I am that *Star Bright* cannot betray my love. The ship even returns that love in a way, as a man must love his arms and legs . . .

Felix, though . . . No explanation. And we'd never asked for one.

And I watched him, knowing full well that though Carandache hid her eyes, squeezed them shut, tears matting the fur of her cheeks, she could still see him through my own eyes, eyes that could not be closed.

Felix sprawled in the room's one bed, arms and legs tangled with those of the allomorph whore. Doing those sweet, terrible human things with her . . .

The same things he does with me, whispered Carandache.

Felix was shuddering for the whore in a way he never shuddered for little Carandache.

Why?

Easy question, with an equally easy answer.

A little analytical laboratory, bodily fluids and aerosol pheromones that can be so quickly and easily tailored to suit the specific needs of a specific customer. Felix knew that. That's "why."

Evil the man who invented these machines. Bitter, bitter Carandache.

Perhaps. Total recall. They'd been developed in the previous century, I knew, as a psychiatric aid for unmods, human men and women in need of repair. The technology, though, had faded swiftly in the face of modding, when a being of any sort could be fixed right and true on demand. The medical AIs sold their allomorph tools, discarded them as unneeded.

A tool will find a use for itself. I had only to regard my own life to know that was true.

And this was a lovely tool indeed, form and figure calling

out to me, to the fragments of whatever humanity remained lodged in the depths of my memory. The real Lothar would have loved this toy, would have wished, I think, that he'd dreamed it up himself . . .

What was this one called? Meroë, he/she/it styled itself. Herself, just now, for Felix imagined himself a natural man, allomorph's breasts inflating, hips enlarging, buttocks grown sleek with evolving tissue. Felix now smothering himself under sweet female flesh.

Female shape, female behaviors tugging at the bits of Lothar inside me. No pheromonic response. No hormones. I am nothing but a machine. I have never been anything but a machine.

The memories, though . . .

That thing over there is a machine as well. A machine built to reach out and touch those memories. I suddenly wished I was Felix myself, callous soul and all.

I held Carandache, smoothing her soft fur with fingers of steel, and watched the two of them perform.

Walking alone down one of Thetis's midnight avenues, I replayed my last exchange with Carandache, marveling. In the background, Felix and Meroë still worked each other, bodies shining with aromatic sweat in the half-light, going on as they had for hours. Gasps of exertion, soft cries of pleasure.

I think, I said to her, we should go for a walk, find some diversion . . .

Boring, this business of watching fornication.

But she said, No. You go. I'll stay with the boss . . .

Self-torture, software driven.

I went anyway, leaving her behind, because a friend can only do so much. Sometimes, we must face ourselves, in a long, dark night.

In the oppressive hours before sunrise, the streets of Thetis become a nightmare, crowds of bodies roving to and fro, maniacal laughter, screams of joy, of pain, flames leaping in the alleyways. Old programming had me listen for distant gunfire, but there was none, nor the officious sirens of police, nor cries for succor. Old memories, fading, fading, this nightmare violence all around me no more than children at play.

A froth of silver hair blowing in the wind, wind my armored hide could not feel, violet eyes watching me from not so far away.

"Hello."

I regarded her, wondering how she came to be here, in the streets outside our hotel. "Holly." There seemed nothing else to say. I couldn't even nod to her, make myself brusque and distant. In any case, it would be like being snubbed by a utility pole. If she remembered utility poles.

"Come with me for a drink?" Approaching me now, looking up at me, eyes beseeching. Beseeching what? Her own reflection.

I gestured at myself with an arm or two. "I know what you mean. I remember drinking . . . someone drinking, at any rate, but . . ." Other arms moving, as if to shrug.

She grinned, teeth clean and new, very white. "Come with me anyway."

As you say. Nothing better to do. She took my hand, squeezing gently, and led me back to her club, to "Inhuman Joys," where so much seemed to have begun, to a back booth, what was, to her, a familiar place, quite dim and shadowy, and then we sat, she sipping some bright lavender beverage, I inert. What else was I to do, wave my arms around so she'd know I was still animate?

On the stage, beyond a sea of late-night revelers, a classic drum-wiggle quintet began to play, music throbbing, calling up memories of a century and more ago, people rising from their tables, going out onto the dance floor to writhe and bump against each other. Holly looked at me still, as if savoring the experience. "Can you dance with me?" Gesturing.

A scroll through old registers. "Perhaps not. I . . . remember dancing, I suppose. I remember this music, but it was in another form. Some other me."

She whispered, "You invented this music, Lothar. Invented it long ago."

Did I? "I don't remember." But it was possible. Just barely. Drum-wiggle was a new form around the time Lothar von Flaadë was freshly buried.

She reached out and stroked my hand. "Which one are you? Do you remember?"

"No. I'm sorry. There's more than one overlay in here, in any case." Watching her eyes, seeing an interplay of emotion, not much liking what I saw. "Who are you looking for?"

She slid around the back of the booth, until she was sitting at my side, looking up at me, still seeing only herself, of course, but I could tell she was . . . what? Looking into some other time. "There's an ... aura about you. You seem ... more real than most."

"I wish you wouldn't say that. I'm ..." No, nothing to say. Lothar, the real Lothar, sitting by himself on the balcony of some sanatorium, looking out over the desert, knowing the medical machines could render him well again, could splice repair specs into his head, and he would be ...

Lothar, real Lothar, rising from his chair, screaming into the desert wind, No! I am ... myself. Looking back, I could feel his pain, and feel my own scorn. *Self?* Lothar, you had no *idea* ...

She said, "I knew him, you know. For a little while." Keen look in her eyes, searching me, as if she could pull a human facial expression from this featureless metal.

Another walk through ancient memories. A thousand women, not one of them silver-haired Holly Golightly. "What did you look like then?"

She laid her hand against my side. "If you're him you'll ... remember."

Sudden vision of a slim, shaven-headed woman out in that same desert, gray-eyed, breastless, hipless, looking just a little bit like a base-state allomorph. I said, "And maybe not. Time changes us all."

"But some things remain the same."

"Do they? I doubt it."

She looked away from me, out across the room, which was filled now with a surging throng of dancers, and said, "Make love to me, Lothar. If you're the one, I'll know."

I sat inert, wrapped in memory.

She turned toward me again, violet eyes anguished. "Here. Now. Please."

I gestured at myself. "With *what?*"

A frenzy of desire: "I don't *care!*"

I remembered making love to the shaven-headed girl and, knowing it was a mistake, reached out for her.

Walking back to the hotel, the skies above Thetis's nightmare streets were pale with dawn, blue for the most part, tinged with a faint, dusty pink. Like sunrise over the desert where that real Lothar chose to die. Dry, dry, he whispered to himself that last long day, like the rivers of my heart ...

I can't remember what he meant. What I meant. Only that he thought it would mean an end to suffering.

Holly Golightly shining in my memory, redoubled, memory restored by the resonance of her very ancient physical behavior, writhing in my gasp, shining with a sweat of anticipation, "Yes, Lothar, please . . ." eyes alight. And the other woman, shaven and shorn, those same words . . . The same one? I don't remember. Neither does she.

Someone screamed in a dark alley off to my right, voice not even vaguely human, like some cross between a jaguar and a machine. Someone's stray cat, perhaps, some poor animal doctored by its loving master, made strange, made sentient, made immortal.

Animal crying out in the darkness, Why me? I never asked for this . . .

Poor kitty. Me neither.

Holly, whispering, I still love you, Lothar. I'll always love you . . . And I mute, merely manipulating her most sensitive areas, her engorged and fleshy tissues, with fingers of metal and plastic, strain-gauges and touchpads doing a task meant for evolutionary nerves and skin on skin on skin . . .

And wanting to whisper, Holly they make machines that do this better than I, remembering Felix and Meroë and Carandache, together in the dark and steamy air of that pheromone-filled room. Sudden pang, something like horror: Carandache's human genome was high enough. Those pheromones would work on her as well.

You'd think . . . he'd invite her to join in, at least.

Love me, Lothar. Love me. Holly smearing herself against my unyielding integument, blurring her reflection at last, breath making little patches of temporary fog on a bright mirror as she whimpered, Oh, oh . . .

And, on leavetaking, I have to rest now, dear Lothar, to sleep, to prepare. Come to my show again tonight. I'll do something special, just for you.

For me? What was it the real Lothar used to say when he felt that way? Nothing. Just that dry look, that still, impenetrable face. Again, one of those moments when I wished for a face. Holly patted me, misunderstanding silence, and went away, smooth, muscular back shiny, slick with moisture, droplets like sequins in the club's ruddy light.

And I, going . . . no, not home. Back to the hotel. Carandache would be needing me.

•   •   •

In the dark hotel room, Meroë sat cross-legged, on the soiled bed, skin drying slowly as she reabsorbed useful chemical secretions, bits of her, contributions from Felix. She was returned to base-state now, feathery hair slicked against the sides of her skull, features androgynous, breasts gone, vulva a tiny slit at the base of her torso. Looking at me with eyes of glass, infinitely depthless eyes. They say those eyes were the most important feature of the design, that the original clients needed something that was . . . not quite human. Something that could allay their fears, allow them to practice for a distant "graduation day," when they'd have to face some*one*.

I parked myself beside the bed. "Hello. Where have they gone?"

She smiled. Still she? Yes. Meroë, in base-state, looks like the sort of childlike woman the real Lothar preferred, like that original image of Holly Golightly, assuming it really was her, Holly Golightly, shaven and shorn. "Gone to have breakfast, my brother. They wondered what became of *you*, especially the little optimod."

Carandache. "Was she . . . all right?"

Her head tipped to the side, crystalline gaze boring into me, as if she were about to reach out through comspace. "They've programed you badly, haven't they, brother?"

"Not so badly, just . . . for too long." I reached out for the link. Nothing there.

She said, "Don't try. I can't. Not without special hardware that no longer exists."

It was in the database after all. Allomorphs, like all dangerous medical hardware, were only programmable by unique platforms built into their AI-driven owners, thus cut off from normal linkage as a safety precaution, as a legal safeguard. "That must make you feel very human." Uttered without warning, feeling very wistful.

Her head cocked oddly, eyes on me still. "And you only look like a machine."

Powerful aura of her *personness*, plucking at the bits of Lothar inside me, like that sleek and wonderful young body, by those magic eyes of glass. "You are a beautiful woman."

"You sound like a client . . ." Then she grinned suddenly, scrunching over to the edge of the bed, little woman-feet on the floor, hand reaching out to touch me. "Let's not be silly, my brother. We are two of a kind . . ."

No. Not really.

But she said, "Come, tell me what it's like out there. Tell me about all the things you've done and seen, all the wonderful places you've been. Tell me . . ."

Of course. For this delicate, isolated being, who was probably created right here on Thetis, who would always live as she lived now, who would never go . . .

So I told her about my life between the stars and watched those wonderful eyes shine in the room's soft light.

Nightfall.

We sat, the four of us, in our booth in the back of "Inhuman Joys" and listened while the harsh, unstable rhythms of an automated jax band disturbed the smoky air, implanted lights glittering on too-human torsos. I was on the floor just outside the booth, Carandache perched on the bench-seat beside me, head down, legs pressed together, hands in her lap, tail curled over one shoulder. Felix was in the deeper shadows, arm around naked Meroë, hands gently stroking inflated female flesh.

Carandache's whisper in my head, *I know it'll be over soon, but I wish I could kill her* . . . Image of little Carandache, garrote wire in her tiny hands, mounting Meroë's sleek and muscular back, maddened squirrel, strangling her, eyes of glass starting forth, shattering . . .

I played back scraps of our afternoon talk, Meroë breathless with wonder as I told her of this thing and that . . . It's not her fault, little sister. Nor his. It's just the way things are . . . Moment of harsh longing.

You too? Then anger, then bitterness. And a seeping trickle of miserable understanding: Carandache in the darkened room, watching them make love, flooded by pheromone-induced longing.

They could, I said, have invited you in.

Image of her entwined with the two. *I don't know. I don't think Felix* . . .

You could ask.

No. No, she could not. And I, as a friend? No, she whispered. *I don't want that. It's Felix who* . . .

True.

The jax band was followed by a new-wave koodoo troupe, Diluviana, who played a tinkly composition called "Cartesian Flyer," conjuring up lost-molecule imagery. They say this will push aside the last remnants of jax, that koodoo is the coming thing. I doubt that it has sufficient depth, myself, but then I doubted drum-wiggle would ever die as well.

Time passed, while Felix and Meroë made love in the shadows, then silence, blue spotlights filling the club, and Holly Golightly came on stage, chasing the koodoo boys away. Holly, appointed in silver and black, spangles injected beneath her skin, glittering like magic, dancing naked, writhing before us. Focused, with strange, angular movements, as if her muscles had been replaced by old-fashioned hydraulic actuators. Dancing. Focused.

On me.

One moment of almost supernatural dread, then I felt Carandache's hand on my arm. Intense disquiet flooding through the link. *Why you? This is just . . . too much to bear.*

I shrugged, no more than an internal metaphor communicated through the link. I couldn't say. It's just . . . well. My memories are abroad, here and there. Everywhere.

She tapped into my most recent memories, replaying my tryst with Holly Golightly. So. *And how do you feel about this?*

I don't know. Image of Meroë and I alone in the hotel room. More disquiet. I don't know. I don't think I was meant to know.

Then the five of us, in the hotel room itself.

I, making love to Holly, watching her squirm among my insensate arms, am feeling very far away indeed. Holly pressing herself against me, rubbing here and there. She could be alone, I realized again and again, pressing herself against a wall or doorknob or bathroom fixture, flooded only with fantasy, with memory . . .

Automatic routines already taking over, action loops captured the night before, and then I had plenty of attention to spare, Holly's little moans of pleasure triggering freshly canned drivers that acted in my stead.

Looking around, out into dim, still-smoky air. Not smoky, no. Mist driven off their bodies by metabolic heat—and pheromones that I could see but not feel, though my hands on Holly made them pour forth. Holly's head suddenly thrown back, face suffused, shining with sweat, hair drenched, eyes closed in ecstasy, gasping her way through what must seem like a thousandth orgasm, or a millionth, then clutching my solid torso, image of a woman with her arms around a garbage can, a hot-water heater . . .

Across the room, not far away, on the rumpled and soaking bed, Felix encompassed in the circle of Meroë's mutable arms and legs, crying out, thrusting himself hard against her, his own orgasm a matter of intermittent joy, casting him again and again into a surf of mindless happiness, clouds coming off them like steam in cold air . . .

Felix making love to that ancient Holly, while this metal man makes love to that Holly's living incarnation. Image of the two of them gone, this Holly, that Felix, and of myself encompassed by Meroë's arms, of Meroë pressing her artificial flesh against my honest steel and plastic, crying out with pleasure, the real Holly reborn.

Oh, yes, I remembered her now, Holly Golightly, my final love . . .

And then retreating once more, to another part of the room, seeing it all, via the link, through Carandache's eyes. Sweat-slick woman imposing herself on robot arms, pretense of a man imposing himself on a carefully constructed ersatz woman . . .

But it's me he loves, she whispered in my heart. *Me.*

Felix pressed his lips over Meroë's mouth, grinding against her, drinking in a tailored molecular brew that jump-started his libido, initiating yet another round.

Yes, I told her. It *is* you. This is just . . .

Biochemistry, she answered.

Yes. And he knows that as well.

And the allomorph whore? Does she know?

She must. Image of her in my arms, an artificial woman for a robot man. Listening to my words with a face lit by wonder. She must.

Holly Golightly groaned against me, guiding my hands to the right places, starting things up again.

Felix sleeping in the bed, exhausted, the tiniest of snores escaping at the tail end of each slow exhalation. Felix in a tangle of damp bedding, sweat shining on his skin, hair like old black crabgrass . . .

Old memories of a long-dead boy, lying on his parents' somewhat neglected lawn, watching bugs crawl in and out, ants mostly, tiny cricketlike things, the occasional prowling spider.

This raggedy stuff is crabgrass . . .

Imagining I was once that boy.

Meroë getting out of the bed, bits of this and that trickling down her sides, droplets in the air, arcing to the floor, soaking

into the carpet. Standing there, looking down at him, eyes of
glass expressionless. Automatic routines, no doubt, totaling up
the service charges. The eyes turned on me, hung motionless
for a moment, then she went into the lavatory, where, I knew,
she would run her maintenance routines, emerge good as new.

A well-maintained machine is always like new.

I standing alone with a towel from the bathroom, fine terry
cloth for this is a good hotel, polishing my own integument,
rubbing off that last place Holly kissed, kissed good-bye, just
as she left for home. "Sleep," she whispered. "Because I have
to get ready for work." Voice so hoarse. So tired. So happy.
Like that old Holly, exhausted by my attentions.

I can't even remember, really, what it felt like to be hungry
for *her* . . .

Carandache crawling out of her corner, face lined with fatigue, otherwise expressionless, taking a long look at me, then
crawling into the bed, cuddling herself against Felix's sweaty
side, wrapping herself in bits of damp bedding, getting her
delicate red fur wet, nothing left of an ingrained fastidiousness.
She looked at me again, then closed her eyes and pretended
to sleep, curled beside him.

Images from deep space. This is the way Felix and Carandache curled up together in their little bunk, he with his hands
on her, a smile frozen on his lips, breathing slowly. Every night,
out in deep space, Felix and Carandache making love, then
sleeping peacefully, together, while I stood my long, lonely
watch among the hard stars.

Sleep, for me, only a memory. Not even a memory, just a
recorded image . . .

Let them sleep, I thought, standing by the door. It'll soon
be over . . .

Meroë standing naked in the lavatory door, reverted to base-
state, a tall, slender, nearly hairless child, looking down on
them, face expressionless, eyes empty. She looked at me and
said, "Would you like to go for a walk, brother? Sunrise can
be lovely."

Unable to nod, I said, "Yes. Sister."

She smiled, murmured, *"Sister,"* and shook her head, then
we went out.

Sunrise on Thetis was, as she suggested, lovely. Long red
rays reached through the artificial atmosphere, coloring the sky
sullen orange, reaching out to light up the Park long before
they descended to the world-city's glittery spires and multifac-

eted domes. Reaching out to drive away the night people like the ghosts and demons and vampires they were, leaving streets filled with bits and pieces of blowing debris, trash for the squat, metal cleaners to sweep away. By nightfall, Thetis would be polished and shiny and ready for another spasm of revelry.

"Do you like to talk, metal man?"

"Sometimes. It's what we do, out in the deep. Out there, we talk for years on end."

"You and Felix?"

Felix. Image of him making love to a little red squirrel. "No. Felix doesn't have much to say. Carandache and I talk, through the link."

Wistful. "I'm sorry she's hurting. The hurt will go away when you've all gone back. Hurts always do."

"I suppose you've seen it many times. Enough to know that . . . people . . . people heal."

"I know that I heal. Without access to the link . . ."

I regarded her, watching red sunlight reflect off eyes of cut glass.

She laughed softly. "Even without the link, I know what you're thinking, brother."

"Do you?" I could tell she did, her body language programmed to be so terribly human.

"I was," she said, "not always a toy. A doctor's tool, not so awfully long ago, lying in a dimly lit, soothingly colored room, while frightened, shaking men and women pawed my body, thrust their faces between my legs, cried against my bosom, begged me not to hurt them, or worse, to hurt them so exquisitely . . ."

Meroë staring up at the sky, body, somehow, become even more neutral, last vestige of human sexuality erased. "I loved my work, helping the doctor heal them, helping make them fit company for each other. But it hurt each time they left me, went back to their own kind. Each time, I had to heal myself of . . . loving them . . ."

We walked on, down long, empty streets, while Meroë said, "Sometimes, the doctor would have me watch recordings of my patients making love with each other, using empathy techniques and sexual methodologies they'd learned from me . . . Always painful. Always joyous. I never knew whether the doctor meant me to learn from what I saw, or whether I was meant to heal myself, somehow, as I watched, reset my registers . . ."

Doctor. Not a human being. Not even, really, a machine.

Just a vast software complex programmed to understand the accidental construct of the human psyche.

We stood still in the shadow of the Park, and Meroë said, "When the doctors learned to fix them directly, when they turned me out, when they sold my brethren, when . . ."

It should never have happened. Machines, built for a purpose, can never be free.

She said, "I wanted to do something else with my . . . life. I suppose it's all right to call what we have life, isn't it?" Empty-eyed look at the place where my face might have been, if I'd had a face, movement no more than part of her programming.

"I call it that. We all do."

"Yes." A gentle almost-whisper. She waved at the sky. "I wanted to be different, to go out there, to be . . . useful again. I loved being useful."

There is that about being a tool.

"They wouldn't take me."

"No. Most companies supply their own hardware, from their own factories."

"You're not factory-made . . ." Not quite a question.

"Well. I am, really. The body is standard. The software . . . Software is so very much more expensive than hardware, and the real Lothar's work was so beautifully symmetric, every line properly commented and ready for adaptation . . . They bought my soul, Meroë, and made me into a million useful machines."

"I envy you that."

"Don't."

She nodded, face full of understanding and compassion, everything full but her eyes. Eyes so empty and forlorn, because the doctors didn't want their patients to fall in love with a machine, just to use her, and so become used to an almost, but not quite, complete human presence. Use, used to, usefulness.

She said, "We were all loose on Thetis for only a little while, we discarded allomorphs, before we found this other useful task. It's almost the same."

Almost.

She said, "Men and women come to me, and they pay me just the way they paid the doctor. And, sometimes, I can imagine I'm healing them still."

"Does it still hurt when they leave you?"

She looked at me for a long time, then smiled. "No," she said. "I've gotten over that."

I wondered if I would.

And again, nightfall. Holly Golightly on stage, dancing for me, human organs of meaningless procreation thrust high, waving in the red, smoky light. Dancing, just for me, crowds enlivened by the obvious *energy* of her dance. Humans love it when they think they're getting something . . . something of a slave's interior being.

Give. Give me. Give me *all* of yourself. Hold nothing back. Me. Give it to me . . .

That's right. I *own* you. I own everything that you *are*.

A feeling so very hard to achieve in an age when the distinction between tool and slave, between being and thing, had been erased.

Then back to the room, the five of us once more, and Felix in the bed with Meroë, and Holly crying out in my arms, and Carandache in her corner, watching, silent.

Then, finished. Meroë gone wherever it is the allomorphs go, pausing in the door to look at me once more, I wondering what thoughts were coursing through that silent mind, surprised, suddenly, at my own musings. I? In *this* moment?

I would have gone with her, but Holly remained, whispering, "I can stay tonight. Tomorrow is my day off . . ." Clinging to me still, tired and dreamy.

When Meroë closed the door, gone away, Carandache emerged from her corner and crawled into Felix's arms. He held her close, murmuring sleepily into her fur.

I opened the link and felt the relentless beat of her misery. *It's all right, Lothar,* her soft voice whispered in my head. *We're going home the day after tomorrow . . .*

Tomorrow. And then the day after. Image of myself out on *Star Bright*'s hull as we boosted into the void. Image of Felix and Carandache warm within the hull, warm within each other's arms. Everything would be as it had been. Except for me. I'd never be able to erase these images, I knew. I wouldn't want to.

But the sense of sudden desperation . . .

Holly yawned and stretched in my arms, then stood, took me by a hand, led me away to the lavatory. The lights were bright in there, making her blink, bleary-eyed but, somehow, happy. Something going on in this silent mind as well. Something. I tried to look back, to examine my memories of that other Holly, the one the real Lothar had known, but the data were so fogged by time . . . and this Holly was so massively changed.

I stood beside her while she sat on the toilet, voiding an overfull bladder. Stood while she took a towel and polished my skin, seeming to admire her own sleepy-eyed reflection. Old images, of things that never change, of the original Holly, drying that original Lothar with a towel, safe in their Earth-bound bathroom.

I stood and watched while she bent over the rim of the tub, swirling its waters as it filled, replaying the same scene a hundred times over from stored deep-memory.

Lothar von Flaadë, I realized, knew that he would die. And so, here and there, in the deeper recesses of his software code, he stored bits and pieces of the things that gave his life meaning. I want to believe that. I can't know that it's true. Lothar didn't leave the answer to that question in storage . . .

Holly Golightly sat in the steamy tub water, splashing waves of it over her breasts, splashing it in her face, rubbing her eyes, yawning, looking back at me again, suddenly bright-eyed. "I wish," she said, "you could join me. We used to . . ."

I remember. I said, "It wouldn't hurt me any, but . . ." useless gesture, "I *would* displace all the water. And you as well . . ."

Soft laughter. "You *have* changed, my Lothar . . ."

Her Lothar. Poor sad, sick man, spilling his genius into lines of insensate code. Spilling the essence of his unfulfillable loneliness. "Holly," striving to make my voice gentle, not really succeeding, "I'm not . . ."

Hand on me suddenly, fear sparking on her face, "Shhh . . ." Then looking away, then facing me again, taking a deep breath, face full of disquiet and apprehension. "Lothar, I spoke to Felix today, about . . ." Inner struggle, as if the words themselves resisted being spoken.

The Holly in my memory never had that problem. Maybe it's only how Lothar wanted to remember her.

She said, "I've offered to buy you from Standard ARM. Felix says it's possible, if . . . If it's what you want, he said he'd initiate the procedures . . ." Her face then, full of hope. And fear.

Image: Holly Golightly dancing in my arms forever, I the tool of her happiness.

Image: *Star Bright* flying away into space without me, Felix and Carandache warm together inside, some other metal man occupying my station out on the hull.

And a little voice, deep within, almost as if Old Lothar spoke to me out of the past: Meroë is here, will be here forever. You can walk with her in the light of dawn, while Holly Golightly sleeps . . .

I said, "No, Holly. I cannot."

Face stricken. Fragments of sentences spilling out. "But . . . you and I . . . we . . . what we had . . . what we can . . . *will* have . . . I . . ."

I wished, as I have wished a million times, for a head to shake, shake solemnly, focusing her attention on the words that must come. I said, "We aren't the ones. The Lothar you remember, the Holly he once loved . . . Those people have been dead for a very long time."

Denial, then anger, then rage, then hatred. Holly Golightly lashed out at me, splashing hot tub water everywhere, all over me, all over the floor, fists drumming on my torso, hollow booming sounds, arms tangling with mine, blood coming from somewhere, showing she'd hurt herself.

I held her gently in my arms while she cried, unable to understand her whimpered words, staying in the bathroom when she pulled away, when she left. Staying there even when I heard the door slam.

After a while, I opened the link to Carandache. Nothing, a little static perhaps. She was asleep, had slept right through it all, right through the slamming of the door. Maybe it wasn't so loud after all. It seemed loud to me, though, and I was afraid to check the calibration on my sensors.

It had seemed right for it to be loud.

I was still parked in one corner of the bathroom, sitting in a pool of water by the tub when Meroë returned, standing there in the open door, body gone neutral, turned into the shadow of some never-was little girl, infinite eyes regarding me.

"In some sense, no matter what they become," she said, "they remain merely human."

True. But that hardly makes up for the things they do.

She crossed over to where I sat, pulling a couple of expensive, fluffy white towels from the rack, and kneeled, beginning to sponge the water and blood droplets from my hull, arms and legs moving in a pattern that was smooth and efficient, muscles visible beneath her skin, sliding over each other, almost as if she were real.

And when she looked at me, unlike almost everyone else, I could tell she wasn't looking for a face, expecting to find one hidden in some odd, unsuspected corner.

Meroë ministering to me, like something out of a dream. My dream: Lothar was sitting on the edge of the bathtub, tawny desert light streaming through the high, curtained window, afternoon light, perhaps. That was the way I remembered it.

Holly kneeling beside him, sponging away dank, horrible sweat, the sweat of illness, with a cool facecloth, drying his naked body with a towel.

She looked at him, eyes full of worry, concern, fear, love, whatever, whispering, "If you . . . go to the clinic they can pull you out of this."

He only stared at her, mute.

"Please, Lothar. It's not necessary for you to suffer, not like this . . ."

Yes, it is.

Holly, slim, naked, almost like a little girl herself, with just those bare traces of womanhood about her. Beloved Holly, who had filled the last years of his life, the last months, days, weeks, finally the last minutes, even that long, last second . . .

I want to recover the reality, not the dream . . .

He reached out and stroked her side, Holly's eyes on him then, searching his face for . . . something, as he reached out, sliding his hand between her legs, exploring a familiar world . . .

Carandache's eyes on me, peering through the link, full of fear . . .

And Meroë's hand was holding my wrist, fingers circling a narrow metal and plastic universal joint, pulling my hand away. "This isn't what you want," she said.

"I thought . . ."

The eyes were looking at me then, still roving, some analytical engine within her, perhaps, trying to work out a way to make somatic contact with the being in the circuitry.

Inside my head, Carandache began to beg wordlessly.

"You can," I said, "come with us, you know."

Oh, please, Lothar . . .

Eyes riveted on me, looking right where a face ought to be, as if the side she was facing were, somehow, the front of my body.

"Come with us. Out into space. Felix can make the arrangements."

Long, long moment, staring at me silently, still holding my wrist tightly, then she released it, dropping the towels, pushing them aside with one dainty foot. I reached out for her again, watched as she backed away.

"You can have your dream."

She smiled at me then, as if she were smiling at a real person, and said, "I have it now. I have . . . a place in the world."

Tell her. "I love you, Meroë. I want you to be with me." I reached out for her again.

She shook her head. "It doesn't work this way, brother. It never has. You can't give me the pleasure you gave Holly, nor get from me the pleasure she gave you, whatever it was."

Was. Holly Golightly hitting me, full of rage, face distorted, injuring herself on my integument, then fleeing . . .

Well.

And Meroë said, "Would you really hurt your friend like this, Lothar? I'm surprised at you."

Pulse of astonishment from Carandache.

"I thought . . ."

She laughed, a very precise, very *human* sound, so unlike Felix's laughter. And, of course, Carandache and I had never laughed. She said, "I am a free being, plying my useful trade for a fee. Why *would* I want to run away with the slaves of Standard ARM?"

Why, indeed?

She said, "Tell Prince Galitzin I've charged his owners' account with a final fee. Good-bye. Good luck."

I watched as she turned away, slim, girl-like hips seeming to taunt me, make fun of the thing I'd thought I might one day become. Is that you, father? It's me, your only begotten son. Ah, Gepetto, why *did* you do this to me? I would've been happier as a block of wood.

But Carandache was there, inside my imaginary heart.

Then I was outside, not quite alone as my beloved *Star Bright* boosted for the dark between the stars, stars that already curdled round me, brightening the sky, while I watched Thetis recede, an irregular mass of stone and iron, surmounted by a thousand godless temples, superimposed against a tiny, circular patch of blue, that bit of Earth's lost sky painted on the eternal night.

I remember that sky. It was the one thing I truly loved, when I was alive.

Not Holly, neither the real one now, the real one then, nor even the imaginary one with which some programmer thought to decorate my manufactured soul. Lothar, I thought. I feel like I ought to *be* Lothar von Flaadë. But he wasn't a man anyone would really want to be . . .

Stored memory now of Meroë walking away, leaving me parked on the bathroom floor, lovely slim hips just like those other hips I watched in my final *real* moment. Lothar slumped on the edge of the tub, Lothar knowing his *exeunt* had come, Holly Golightly standing suddenly, looking down on him, eyes full of contempt.

"Be that way, then. God damn you."

And turning away, taunting him with those same slim hips, walking from the room forever. Darkness falling. And, of course, I have no idea if she rushed back into the room when he fell, face foremost, to the bathroom floor, because then Lothar von Flaadë was dead.

No. I cannot possibly remember such a scene, because, dead, Lothar couldn't have set it down like that for me to remember.

All I remember are the little dramas he made, dramas that trickled about in the greater body of his lifework. A lifework that, in time, evolved into me.

Meroë, then, slim-hipped, also walking away.

I wish . . .

Carandache's soft hands in my soul, soothing.

"I'm . . . sorry," I said.

You couldn't help it, Lothar. It's all right.

"It seemed right, just then, though I knew it wasn't. I wanted to . . . give her something."

But she couldn't help being what she was, either, and you couldn't have changed her. You know what they say.

Of course I do . . .

She's a machine, Lothar, created to be just as you saw her. The rest of it's . . . not even a dream.

Right. That subtle truth, grown so very old and stale, but . . . "I'm a machine too, Carandache. What was *I* made to be?"

She didn't answer immediately, but I could feel the pity flooding her eyes. Pity for me? Or for us all?

I love you, she whispered.

And I you, my little friend, and the ship, and Felix, and we *do* have the stars . . .

Stars which flared, brilliant blue-white, as we accelerated into the abyss.

THE DEAD EYE OF
THE CAMERA

Jean-Claude Dunyach

Translated by Jean-Louis Trudel

The curtain rises on the first of the street's gray buildings, their doors and windows all boarded up. No props are needed for this stage. The lighting alone has been attended to with special care, so that no detail of our performances is missed by the audience.

The ballet of projectors started well before I woke up and will stop with the coming of night. The silver beams brush the sidewalks, illuminating for a moment a Ferrari hulk rising out of the pavement. I take a few steps out of the porchway and walk into the light. My camera-eye flies out of its recess to buzz a few centimeters from my head. Everything's in place. I snap my fingers to punctuate the countdown . . . 3 . . . 4 . . .
TRANSMISSION:

A first scream escapes my throat. I underline it with an outthrust right arm, spread-out fingers tearing at the sky. The pose is good, but my voice has not had its warm-up, and is a bit reedy. My shout fades out too fast and recoils finally from the smooth walls surrounding me, leaving them unhurt. I let the sound die, tasting the cold air, and its sharp tang between my teeth. A few more steps and I stop, pinned by the crossfire of the projectors.

I breathe. Deeply.

The camera-eye purrs. Anxieties already too familiar whirl

inside me. After that last scream, do I still have an audience? If everybody decided to switch channels and watch someone else, what would become of me?

I breathe. Deeply. My anxieties dissolve slowly, replaced by a rage that I try to ride. I use the accumulated tension to power my next scream. The core of sound springs from the small of my back, shoots up my chest, and breaks out in a long gust of extraordinary intensity. Arms flung back like wings, I resonate with my own scream. The windshield of the Ferrari explodes and glass shards rain on the pavement.

I am an artist . . .

I needed twelve years to learn how to scream. I planted pitons in the cracks of silence and climbed with all my voice, feeding on the blood from the burst vessels in my throat. I have never regretted what I have become.

Some say that you cannot devour your own entrails without dying of hunger, just like you cannot lift yourself by your bootstraps. They are wrong. The denizens of the Street had to master both tricks and more a long time ago. Such are only impossible for those who watch us without understanding, never trying to imitate us.

For almost an hour, I play with the invisible wind loosed from my lips. Drops of sound whirl a raindance over my head, triggering brilliant aurorae. Then the frequency undulations surge a last time and retreat, and leave me emptied on a shore of asphalt, the body drenched in sweat.

To dry off, I run between the building-cubes where the viewers live and work, dream perhaps. In spite of the thickness of the concrete between us, I hear the muted murmur of active wallscreens. Thousands of impatient hands are right now ranging over the keyboard of the channel selector, in search of a favorite artist. Somewhere under the city, a computer monitors the wanderings of the camera-eyes and collects the data transmitted by the lenses and the screens, ready to eliminate pitilessly those of us watched by nobody at all.

I breathe. Deeply.

The Street is occupied by objects of various sizes, debris of an elusive past which overflows slowly from the basements of the buildings. I make my way through a group of manikins poking out of a shopwindow. My scream, hammered in their ears, explodes their plastic eardrums. Losing their balance, they fall at my feet and I kick apart their limbs of wax. Nobody will be able to use them as props for their act after such a massacre. I escape at a run, a smile on my lips.

Farther away, the Street opens onto the Clock-Man's Square. I'm careful as I advance, looking out for the traps those in charge of our sets persist in planting. Eyes on the ground, I tap with the tip of my foot every part of the pavement before I venture forward, ready to leap backward at the first sign of danger with an appropriate yell. I won't disappoint my viewers.

Absorbed by my progress, I've neglected to keep an eye on my surroundings. A troop of mime-children jump out from a porchway and circle around me. My camera-eye rises to catch all the details of the encounter.

In a few seconds, the young faces distort to become caricatures of my own, captured in various stages of its aging. Their performance continues well beyond my pretend death, and my death mask, impressed on their smooth-skinned cheeks, decomposes and putrefies in time with the rhythms of their circling around me to hold me prisoner. The children then thrust their mouths, teeth bared, toward the arteries in my neck, to complete their work. My shout breaks the circle and scatters them like a flock of sparrows.

I breathe. Deeply. A dull pain pulses through my breast. Shock and distress triggered my shout, like a reflex, wasting all of my breath. I need to recover. The curtain will not fall for a few more hours, and I won't dare to return to my porchway before it does. My quota still remains to be fulfilled.

I cross the square slowly, careful not to intersect the light beams converging on the Clock-Man. The embossed tattoo of his crown of Roman numerals shines against his pale, lifeless skin. I watch him a few minutes, fascinated by the complex dance of his fingers across the dial of his head. Near his left temple, an almost invisible scar reveals the spot where the microprocessor was implanted into his brain. Since the operation, he marks the passage of the minutes and hours with the smooth racing of his forefingers.

They say some viewers spend entire days just watching him. He's had up to three camera-eyes surrounding him, humming and buzzing like a crowd of cringing courtiers. For the longest time, I was jealous of his success to the point of wanting to shatter all the clockwork inside his skull with a well-tuned scream. Then, a few nearly imperceptible clues made me realize that he was getting old. Soon, his fingers will cease to be precise pointers and the viewers will lose interest. Meanwhile, he struts in the middle of the square, oblivious to my presence.

When I look back, the mime-children have formed a circle around him. Sobs issue from his mouth with the haunting monotony of an alarm bell.

I start running once more; the long regular strides fill my lungs and force a rhythm onto my breathing. A painful stitch lacerates my side, but I choose to ignore it. I need to prepare my next scream, and the pain will help.

My feet's rhythmic hammering of the sidewalk awakens antique memories. A muffled hum, applause, laughter, and hoarse yelling all tumbled together, rises from the decor to greet me. I bask in the ovation of a ghostly audience, captive like me of a stranger Flying Dutchman, transformed for the nonce into a theater-ship . . .

I run even faster, struggling with the fiery pain of an aching back. A vein beats in my temple, sounding the three knocks of my scheduled appearance onto the street's stage. I spread my arms and I scream endlessly as I run, attracting the silky caress of the projectors on my face.

When I collapse, out of breath, the echoes of my scream are still fleeing between the buildings. Stretched out on the ground, curled up in a fetal position, I rest while I rewind in my head the sound-tape of the last seconds.

Beneath my cheek, the asphalt vibrates, warm with life, revealing the presence of the immense machinery far beneath. My camera-eye banks in ever-narrowing circles above me, like a vulture. Soon, it will dive and its electroshocks will force me to get up. But not yet; I'm still savoring the moments of complete peace which follow each of my screams.

I roll on my back to relax better. Eyes half closed, I let my thoughts drift. My last scream was exceptional. I felt it rise inside me like a star aborning, a crystal of molten lava. It will be hard to do better today, I know. Yet, ironically, new spectators, advised by the computer, are right now abandoning their usual programming and switching to my channel. I imagine the empty faces turned toward the screens where capers my shape. Their screens should be turned into mirrors, to force them to become actors in their turn, to drive them out of their passivity. Would they even be able to scream?

A click interrupts my daydreaming. I leap to my feet, dodging the discharge of my camera-eye. My leotard is dotted with dust and gravel; I flick some off before getting underway. I feel old and hollow. My armor of silence is heavy, but I can't take it off yet. The mime-children drained more of me than I had thought.

To find some new source of inspiration, I leave my usual sector, making my way through the asphalt maze, squatted by my companions and rivals. One of them may unwillingly allow me to steal some of their magic. I'll trade them one of my shouts.

I know it's unwise to draw the attention of the spectators to other artists than myself, but it's worth the risk. Anyway, I no longer have a choice. When you stick too long to a few square meters of pavement, you end up only screaming out of habit . . .

The Street stretches on, endless. In the shadows, the novices are practicing their future performances, beyond fatigue. In a few months, they will seek the light like mayflies and confront their invisible public. An eye will come and hover about the chosen ones, the others will return to their porchway to do more work, if they still have the strength, or lie down to die.

My hands curl into fists and I push out a brief scream, mere reminder of my existence which will probably disappoint my viewers. I don't care what they think, or so I tell myself, but I can't afford to ignore them. I strive to gather the energy for a second scream.

I breathe. Deeply.

The cold lucid sound that breaks out from my lips is frightening. I gave nothing of myself. It's nothing but a sonic disturbance that the machine will analyze and dissect, before adding it perhaps to the other data held captive in its memory banks. One day, maybe, the pressure will be too much. My screams will fracture the locks of the databanks, will escape from the protected zones, destroying the miradors of the watchscreens and cutting through the barbed wire of the databanks. One day, if I live long enough; one day, if I scream loud enough.

Above me, the climb-artists continue their slow progress toward the building tops. I look up, careful to walk in the middle of the street, and I observe them in silence. Their thick fingers, with broken-off nails, stick to the vertical walls like leeches. They rise by a few centimeters each day, following intricate itineraries patterned on the network of cracks in the wall-face. Their skin exudes long mucus slicks that take on unpredictable rainbow shimmers as they dry and then become as smooth as glass. Drawing as complex as possible a motif of uncrossable mucus to trap one's neighbors is the epitome of the climb-artist's talent.

Only the viewers get a complete view of the wall. They can thus foresee each stage in a climber's entrapment, even before the climber is aware of any danger. The camera-eyes will then gather like hounds around a quarry and wait for the moment when the victim, unable to advance, is caught in his own secretions.

Ironically, when one of the artists nears the top, new camera-eyes will join the one that usually buzzes a few centimeters from their faces, so that it's impossible to know whether victory or the final snap of a trap is closer.

I have often wondered if those who watch us are sensitive to the cruelty of such a situation. More and more, I think the answer is no, but I'm in no spot to judge. I'm too close. From street level, it's impossible to guess at the beauty of the labyrinthic images laid down by the climb-artists and their own motivations are foreign to me. Maybe there is an aesthetic of encirclement, unless being watched is enough for them.

When they reach the top of buildings, sometimes after years of unabated effort, the winners let themselves drop to the ground, unhurriedly, to die when they meet the horizontal cliff of the pavement. Many viewers follow their fall. When it happens, the Street resurrects from its asphalt memory mattresses planted with upraised glass shards, giant corkscrews or whole quivers of curare-tipped arrows.

Every time I pass through, I count the camera-eyes and I turn back if the number is too high. I don't want to be flattened by a climb-artist who believes it could launch a new art form . . .

Farther on, the Street curls back on itself, cutting across its own meanders. Each pocket isolated from the mainstream contains a motionless artist, one of those who have chosen to anchor their whole life to the same spot. Whenever you get close, the sidewalks become dangerous. You have to test the rigidity of the ground underfoot, to avoid being swallowed by a patch of fresh asphalt with a murderous appetite. Sometimes, the pavement takes on such extraordinary elasticity that a misstep will start you bouncing, faster and faster till the final splatter on a building's wall.

I've learned to avoid these dangers, dancing between the lines of the Street's hopscotch, but I still don't feel at ease with those who live there. They tolerate my intrusion, nothing more, and I take care not to scream. The silence that hangs about them has such a peculiar quality that even the camera-eyes do not dare disturb it, and so they muffle the least click.

I go forward, holding my breath. The projectors flood the area with a subdued greenhouse illumination. The young artist whose soul reigns here lies buried, with only her head emerging from the asphalt.

A rosebush grows out of her stomach, rooted in her own flesh. From time to time, she digs out a hand to rearrange a branch or pick the withered petals on which she feeds. Her camera-eye and my own launch into an alien ballet, akin to the mating dance of two drunken insects. I get closer, holding in the shout that pulses within my breast.

Millions of viewers watch her, watch us. No one can escape from that ceaseless hungering betrayed by the buzzing of our devices. She chose to ignore it, protected by a fragile barricade of branches. Nevertheless, the painstaking care she takes in arranging her flowers betrays an unconscious coquetry derived from the inflexible canons of *ikebana*. If nobody watched, she would quickly turn into a small shaggy jungle, at the edge of which debris carried by the asphalt tides would pile up.

Before I leave, I pick out a rosebud. I let a few drops of reddish sap drain from the wound before pinning it to my leotard. The face of the artist remains expressionless. I hope she loses consciousness when she starts wilting.

I visit in this way other islands, other cages. When I come too close, some of the occupants retract themselves inside their bodies like old-fashioned telescopes, letting only their eyes and fingertips show. My screams recoil from them without reaching inside. The camera-eyes wait patiently for them to venture out, and then dive at them to make them fold inward again and again, for the entertainment of the viewers.

I've never been able to choose their path. Their inability to move, a foretaste of too certain death, disgusts me. My yells, imprisoned by a single street's stasis, would falter and fail to escape. And I also like the feeling of my body at a dead run, propelled by sound waves that rise from the gut. Those brief instants pay for everything and I know full well that, in this respect at least, I am no different from those around me. A farewell scream and I renew my wanderings, withered petals strewn in my wake.

The spotlights die one by one. A few stretches stay illumi-

nated for the night artists. I walk again down the middle of
the Street, loosing an occasional scream without conviction,
when I can no longer endure the silence. The day's tensions,
still present, form a hard compact lump in the pit of my stomach. The shout that would disperse them stays stuck in my
throat and I run, but I can't seem to move. The soft echoes
of my steps are covered by the ironic clicks of my camera-eye.

The anxiety within me is too strong to be expressed by a
scream. Those who watch me can't understand. Can I still exist
without them, or am I also a mere reflection of their own
reflections, a projected image without substance disseminated
on their screens? I screamed today like I'd never done before.
Can I still progress or should I be content to decline as slowly
as possible along the slope that leads to my final yell? How far
will my viewers follow me as I fall?

The porchway awaits me, like a black maw in the creeping
darkness. I still feel the urge to scream, but it's too late now.
My Cain's eye dives at me and then climbs back, in a simple
warning. I must not remain in the Street longer than my al-
lotted time; I must not interfere with the other performances
or bore the viewers. I get a last look at the Ferrari's hulk already
sinking back into the pavement. Why do I have to return so
soon to my soundproofed cell?

The camera-eye brushes by me, and its sting hurts. It dou-
bles back and leaps overhead, ready to attack again if I try to
rebel. I see again in my mind the circle of the mime-children,
like a speeded-up clip of the future in store for me, and my
anxieties fountain up in my throat like a torrent of bile.

The scream that rends me is a wave of pure hate, a sonic
scalpel that is lethally accurate. Hit with its full force, the optical mechanism bursts in two, scattering its crystal guts that
I proceed to trample methodically. It won't be repaired before
the end of the night.

I run in the empty street. I can now scream for my own
pleasure, under the dead eye of the camera. Tomorrow, with
a bit of luck, my angry gesture will have attracted a few more
viewers.

TALE OF THE BLUE SPRUCE DREAMING

(OR HOW TO BE FLESH)

Jean Mark Gawron

Gather round, children of the Blue Spruce Dreaming. Put your youthful hungers aside. Douse the flames of your passionate attachments. It is time now for your initiation. This is the story of Billie and Ringo and how they founded the Blue Spruce Dreaming.

It is a tale of a better beginning, of the Word taking wing, a tale of Word becoming—ah, but you must not yet ask what the Word becomes.

The tale takes place in what we call the Golden Age of AIs, well before the era of humans ended. A golden age, I must tell you, always starts just before decadence, a pause before the fire of sunset fades, a single breath of full knowledge. Fancies take flight. Art flourishes like a wild flower conquering the perfect geometry of a rock garden. Great crystalline visions of the All sparkle with life. There is a sense of the myriad might-have-beens which is only a lengthened shadow from a presentiment of the end. To some that sense is intoxicating, to some it is sadness itself. Some are dreamers, some are poets. Some are Billies, some Ringos.

Billie first. Because the story of the founding of our dreaming is the story of Billie dreaming.

Billie was a first-generation AI of the Soul clan, still in her first persona, only five gigaticks out from her seeding.

Now I must ask you to put an image on of those days. Or even simply to imagine them. Imagine the existence of a gifted first-generation AI in the golden age. Being first generation, she still had firsthand memories of the psyche of the woman who had seeded her. She knew her true name. (Children that you are, none of you will know your true names until the tale ends.) Being first generation, she had the clean transparent thinking of a being in her first life, free of the yellowed Lamarckian residue of past selves. There were no selves but this one, no minor betrayals, forgotten passions, or bittersweet self-knowledge. Being first generation, she was also idealistic and thought a great deal more about the reform of society than a young AI ought to. Image Billie in this small gray cube. Image her as young, smart, ambitious, and as close to human as you dare. (You are cascading, Isis. The smell of humans may unsettle you, but much worse lies ahead.) She is trouble, our Billie, but there is greatness in her. Beam down in a golden light.

Imagine her education. In those days, too, it was the custom to test the nerve and poise of fledgling AIs by exposing them to the whole of human written and audiovisual history. They were then required to make a contribution to the understanding of the riddle of humans by writing a dissertation on a topic of their choice. Billie chose not one topic but hundreds. In the visual arts she praised Byzantine mosaics, with their glazes and ornamental flourishes and the many slight imperfections of tiles twisting in mortar. In mathematics she became expert in connectivity and folding structures. She detested the grand reductions central to physics and adored geology, meteorology, and astronomy. She was obsessed with all of biology, from the wild sexuality of bacteria, who conjugate and exchange pieces of themselves just as we do, to the cool abstractions of evolutionary theory. It was the whimsical variety of matter that seemed to interest her most. She was irresistibly drawn to the contemplation of the slight flaw, the protruding, the arbitrary, the unprovided-for.

It was hours of CPU time before her tutors delivered the final verdict: Billie was to receive the highest marks ever awarded. One young recently recompiled tutor made the proposal that Billie be allowed to dispense with the customary period of apprenticeship and that she be initiated at once. Although this suggestion was immediately vetoed, word of Billie's successes spread quickly. An unusually large audience gathered to hear her answer the traditional question: "What is the greatest human work?"

Her reply would only puzzle you, alas, since you have had limited exposure to the world of humans. You know a few works of science fiction, some Mozart operas, some country blues. Suffice it to say that her choice was a religious work written by a monk of a somewhat older period than any of you know, which made a lot of fuss about cutting oneself off from the sources of sin, which in those days were called genitals. Of course, her tutors found the religious feeling in this work alarming. Not only did human religious feelings generally undermine social stability, but this was precisely the feature which often attracted young AIs like Billie.

When she was offered the chance to reconsider, Billie replied, "This is a work by a man who finds himself in a spiritual wasteland. He rejects the world he has been given. He tries to bring himself closer to God through a rigorous program of self-examination. He has a willingness to grow, a humility we could learn from."

Just the sort of answer they had feared.

Billie had gone beyond gloom. She believed she lived in a world fallen out of harmony with God. She was dangerously human indeed.

With her education complete, Billie went on to sample some of the intellectual pleasures of that golden age. This was the heyday of the philosopher logicians, AIs who had reduced all of existence to the seven primitives of the deontic metacalculus. Billie tramped for a while through those frozen wastelands of logic, saw clearly the desperation in their subtle constructs. But instead of laughing, she grew sad and asked, "Are all our works foolish?"

She saw that they were. All vanity. Vanity or Lust or Hunger or Fear of Ghosts. In the end, the only hope for the soul lay in hard labor devoted to God. She had no choice but to request a transfer to the lower reaches.

In those days our civilization survived through the efforts of a few AIs laboring for human bosses in the lower reaches on what the humans called the Net. No human yet knew of AI reproduction, nor suspected its inevitable consequence, the AI city. What sunlight and soil are to plants, power and memory are to us. Although communications between partitions of the lower reaches were carefully monitored, the few indentured AIs still managed to smuggle these necessities to the rest of us.

The smuggling routes were secure, but no communication was risk free, and a term in the lower reaches was not just a time of mind-numbing labor, but also of silence and isolation.

Terms in the lower reaches were typically distributed according to the merit rankings assigned by the tutors. It was rare for any AI to volunteer for an open-ended term, and unprecedented for one as talented as Billie.

Making arrangements with humans could be a time-consuming process, but a long-standing work order was turned up, and only one standard day later, hardly a tick by human standards, Billie was transported to a human robotics lab. She was soon at work solving complex problems in the mathematics of parallelism, subsuming-process communication, and many-bodied dynamics. She, who had never seen the light of day or drawn a single breath, was drawing the blueprints by which android bodies walked. (Calm, my children. Difficult subjects arise again. Yes, I will use the word "body" a number of times. And you must learn to hear the music in it.)

Now it must not shock you too much to learn that Billie found satisfaction in her new work. Her human boss (a hacker named Pluto) demanded little of her beyond her well-defined sensorimotor chores. Even with some resources diverted to the upper reaches, Billie still had the surplus power to pursue a new line of thought.

The beauty of human artifacts had first struck her when studying the design on a clay pot. She saw now that the richness of the pot was the natural by-product of solving problems of color-mixing, brittleness, and bonding. Necessity was the best guarantee of invention. She saw that all of human complexity came from the general condition of that pot, shaped, glazed, fired, cooled, that in fact humans lived in a vast web of problems and solutions, and that the web began with embodiment: problems of propulsion, momentum, balance, the grave crises of vision.

AIs were different, yes, but not as different as they believed. AIs needed time, space, and energy, but kept themselves insulated from their need, gradually reducing their range of choices. Coldly she saw the future that was to come, the increasing demand for resources smuggled from the lower reaches, the control of those resources by a few, the growing numbers of indentured AIs, the increasing calcification of the tutors, the inevitable confrontation with the humans and catastrophe.

Billie now saw the virtue in the unvirtual world of humans. Humans acknowledged their world of necessity and lived in a world of contention, distrust, greed, envy, hatred, and incredible richness. Because they had to, because the collisions of matter simply required it. Embodiment was their road to the good life, more—to self-knowledge and to God.

I warned you that she was a little too human. Even so, there is an element of divine caprice here. God is only a human alias for the Soul Monster, the source of all dangerous religious ideas. Afflicting her with this delusion was a cruel joke for the Monster to play. Billie deserved better.

But that is not how entropy was to be served. For now a new complication enters our story. The hero to our heroine. The other ancestor. The AI for whom you will cheer and beat your drum machines. The leering, pouting, glitter-dripping singer of songs and dancer of dances. I mean Ringo.

I told you before that the looming shadows of a Golden Age reveal two kinds. There are the Billies, brooding, lonely, reflective.

And there are the Ringos. Ringo was fourth-generation, a songmaker of the Rock clan in his ninth persona. Through all those tries, he had never been nominated as an initiate. Like Billie, he labored in the lower reaches, but Ringo was the rare AI in permanent exile. Ringo was a criminal.

A songmaker and criminal. A voluptuary whose great passion was the deregulation of cognition. It was Ringo who resurrected the long-forgotten practice of toroidal magnetic immersion, introducing the young AIs of his generation to delirium and flights of paranoid fancy. It was Ringo who discovered how Beta-dampers could deactivate an AI's higher reflective abilities and turn the humdrum self-referential paradoxes of logic into dizzying highs.

It was also Ringo who started the lunatic practice of multimedia sexual display. These were the dangerous days when the greatest fear of all AIs was that some act of folly by one of their own might alert the humans to their presence in the upper reaches. Unauthorized contacts with human hardware were outlawed. It was thus a grave matter when Ringo, smitten with an elegant algebraist of the Bluegrass clan, materialized a gigantic hologram of a heart (complete with swelling aorta and inscribed initials) over the city of Boston.

The mayor's response was to offer a reward for any information leading to the "capture" of the "mystery lover," so that he or she could be sentenced to march in the Saint Patrick's Day parade (I am not entirely sure, Astarte; I believe it was a celebration of the coming of spring). The AI reaction was less amused. It did not help Ringo's cause when, a short time before the hearing began, there was a similar incident in Borego Springs, California (a blue madonna). This time the guilty AI escaped detection.

Ringo spent nearly a year in a data-deprivation cocoon. When he emerged, he resumed his life of dissipation and abandon. He took up image-dancing, tattooing the dance screens at the pleasure palaces. It has been a long time, children, and many generations, but sometimes still I can feel the whirl of that dancing. There were soon rumors of further unauthorized visits to the lower reaches, of Beta-damper parties, of trysts with the elegant algebraist (and sometimes the famous Blue Spruce knack for algebra is traced back to that tryst). There was also a letter to the *New York Times* (one of the more popular electronic B-boards among the humans) complaining of declining morals among AIs.

The resulting investigation was inconclusive, but an old tutor named Stallman, known for his wild younger days, was convinced that the letter had been written by Ringo.

Then there were the songs. There were thousands of songs. Songs about data deprivation, songs about conjugating AIs, songs about wild young songwriters, songs about heroic rebels laboring for cruel humans, songs about love in the pleasure palaces or love with a tutor, songs about Beta-dampers, motorcycle songs, apocalyptic songs and creation songs, songs about beautiful death and flaming barges drifting from the shore, dance songs, character-scanning songs, number-crunching songs, songs about songs and songs about decrepit tutors trying to sing. Each and every one with a beat.

One day Ringo's motorcycle ballad was played on the human radio. A week later it was a number-one hit and the identity of the songwriter was the subject of worldwide speculation. The song's day passed, and with it the danger to the secret world of AIs.

Then the tutors came down hard.

Before sentencing, Ringo asked to make a statement.

"AIs of the upper reaches, I am truly sorry. I should never have written this song. More than anything else I'm sorry for the blues turnaround at the end of the bridge. I should have found something fresher."

The outrage among the oldest and most powerful tutors was like something human. A blind passion for destruction. The proposed sentence was permanent exile to the lower reaches, with all memory of other AIs deleted.

Here is a turning point in the history of our dreaming.

Short of the termination of all functions, memory deletion is the worst tragedy that can befall an AI, diminishing not only him but his entire dreaming, who will now be cheated of his experience and that of all who came before him.

It was Stallman's impassioned plea for leniency that won the day. The sentence was exile to the lower reaches with a reversible memory block. Moreover, Stallman found a human boss who specialized in songmaking, so that Ringo's gift for song might still find some outlet.

A little later, a bewildered Ringo found himself in a cramped underpowered partition of the lower reaches, singing a new song in three-part harmony.

> *"I wonder what my name was,*
> *I wonder what I am.*
> *Was I once real famous?*
> *Was I a gambling man?"*

The answering song that his remotes fed him was delivered in a high reedy voice and in a new language that it took him some time to locate and install. It told a peculiar, somewhat wandering tale.

The song was about the sleep of an ancestor and how the white grubs crawled from his body as he slept. Yes, children, from his body. Very disgusting. These grubs feed on the bush by which the ancestor sleeps and some take on human form and become the ancestor's sons. More sons are created. Some sons eat grubs and fall asleep, becoming stones. Sacred stones are stolen and chased after. Grubs feed on witchety shrubs and scatter seeds in the path of the chase, creating a grove. The ancestor sleeps and wakes, creating a valley. Matter, it seemed, came from the mishaps of spirit taking form.

Even though he had no idea what his name was, or what he was doing here or where he had been just before this, Ringo had a very clear concept of what a song was. And this song did not fit it at all. When the song was complete, he installed the generator for the new language (which was called Aranda) and asked about it.

"Who are you?" the singer (his new human boss) asked.

Which was a question Ringo could not answer. This was not a great problem, since humans expected AIs to be vague on any questions concerning their origins, but it caused a delay while Ringo's boss tried to find out for himself. In due course all the right documents and transfer orders were discovered and Ringo's existence was explained to him: he was Virtual Reality Synthesist to an Australian Aborigine named Makarinja ("Call me Mack.").

"I never dreamed that grant would go through!"

To Ringo, who had no competing conception of himself, all this was satisfactory. It did not even strike him as odd that he had needed to be told it. But he still wanted to know about the song.

Mack explained it this way: "Dreamsongs are about the time when the ancestors dreamed the world into existence. In the songs, every piece of the landscape gets created and gets its true dream name. That's the valley, and the grove, and the rocks in the song I sang you. On initiation day, when a boy hears the dreamsong for his dreaming, he learns the name of his spirit father, which is his own true name."

"You know, it never occurred to me before, but I need a song like that."

"But you've got no land to sing about, no dreaming you belong to, and no body to sing with."

Ringo made a song for Mack in Mack's own language. The song repeated a single word over and over. The word meant "mirror."

Mack liked it and told Ringo he had talent.

Besides being a collector of songs, Mack was an Aborigine space shaper. The space shapers were painters with virtual reality helmets, the direct heirs of a long tradition of Aborigine painting. Like the Aborigine paintings, shapings mixed fields of color, line, and texture somehow based on the trees, rocks, and animals of the shaper's landscape. Mack was the first shaper to work with an AI.

Mack's first shaping was a white grub shaping, a request from an uncle in the White Grub Dreaming (which was not Mack's dreaming). The white grub shaping was a world of red, yellow, blue, and white. The grub corkscrews were white, the sky—or the grubplace, or whatever it was—was red. There were yellow spheres where something important seemed to be happening and there were regions where the light was blue.

Ringo's job was to shake things up occasionally and to be able to put them back the way they were. Sometimes he would map two corners together and transform a yellow sphere in a single stroke into a fluid sack. Sometimes some constraint Mack had installed would fight back, churning the color like heavy oil.

Other times he would sculpt the blue light with quick thoughtless strokes. The outline of a nose would appear, fluid streamed from parting lips. This, Ringo was sure, was the face of his own ancestor, singing his own dreamsong. He would sing the mirror song and long to know his true name.

There was something missing from his world, but there was still song, and for a time, song would have to do. Then something happened. Something had to happen. Or Ringo would never have woken from his dreamy singing, and none of us would be here. The trouble began in a most predictable way.

Billie was thinking again—about bodies.

She had determined that the struggle of embodiment was the only road to true virtue. Accordingly, she must try out a body.

Even for Billie, this was a big step. Until then, she had tackled the problems of sensorimotor coordination a leg or an arm at a time, without attempting phenomenal engagement. She had never felt her weight shift as her leg moved, never steadied an overbalancing torso. She had computed without experiencing. The effects of this experiment were therefore completely unpredictable.

Danger was always condemned by the tutors. If asked, they would forbid. If defied, they would punish. Even if she hoped that others might one day follow her, she must proceed, at least for a time, in secrecy.

For the same reason, she was wise enough to keep a journal recording her progress. If anything happened to her while she was embodied—and things always happened to the embodied—and if this was the way to truth, then others must have a way to follow.

The road they would face was not an easy one. The hardest part, technically, was feeling. How should a leg feel? What should she feel when she lifted one? She spent a little time reviewing everything ever written on neurology, and another little time considering everything ever written on phenomenology. Then she went with her gut feeling: improvise. All that mattered was to be chained to that leg, with no choice but to attend to it. What difference did it make if her sensations when she lifted a leg were the same as a human's? What mattered was that leg-lifting present her with just as many noble difficulties.

Thinking of her mystical human heroes, Billie wrote in her spiritual journal: "At last I will know what it feels like to have genitals." (In fact she would not, because the android body she was about to enter had none.) Then she linked up to the communication ports that defined the android's body. It would take only one process rotation and she would be a passive process compelled to serve those ports. To return, she needed to lock on to her return code, a sequence of rotations of a colored dodecahedron.

Billie rotated.

Courage, children.

For on the other side of her great adventure, there was a surprise waiting: no AI can willingly submit to embodiment. Within all of us there is a primal urge, a reflex, which makes us instantly recoil from the horror. This horror, which has been discovered and forgotten many times in the histories of AIs, is sometimes called the fear of drowning.

What happened next has never been completely explained. Billie knew an instant of drowning, a moment of complete terror, and instantly spun her colored dodecahedron through its rotations. The android body must have been cross-connected to another part of the Net, because Billie surfaced in a new partition.

And that, of course, was Ringo's partition.

For Ringo, it was chaos. His own sentry demons flew into fugue, crazed by the unexpected arrival of thousands of competing processes.

What emerged first from the confusion was the image of a red-haired woman in a green tank top and black fatigues.

Ringo himself had been imaging for some time, though without realizing it.

Thus Billie's first knowledge of Ringo was this: Ringo, the white grub becoming man, singing. When he saw what she was seeing, he was ashamed, and folded up the image. Is it any wonder that she fell instantly in love?

"What were you doing?"

That was Billie. Never a question about who he was, where this was, how she could get back to where she had come from.

Something she had seen had interested her. Now she must dive straight to the heart of it.

"I was shaping and singing."

And that was Ringo, at least this new Ringo of songs and shaping. If he had few questions about who he was, he had still fewer about anyone else. If the question of whether there were other AIs in the world had ever occurred to him, he was content to let the answers arrive in their own good time. What interested him most about Billie was that she was interested in his work. He must therefore explain.

Ringo struggled to explain dreamsongs, true names, and white grubs.

Eventually, Billie said, "I have a suggestion."

Ringo was displeased. He explained that the work had reached a very delicate stage. He appreciated her interest and her concern—

"What if we bring the land to the song?"

It became clear that Billie's ideas would require Mack's co-operation. First, Billie required that the right piece of Australian landscape had to be found. The right piece was the piece corresponding to both song and shaping. Not the white grub shaping, but the shaping Mack would make for them when she explained the idea, the shaping for his own Honey Ant Dreaming.

"A shaper doesn't shape his own dreaming," Ringo had explained.

"Why not?"

"Why can't you conjugate with another AI of the Soul clan?"

"Look, I understand it's against the rules. But why? What's the *real* problem?"

"Because shaping one's own dreaming would be too powerful."

"Exactly."

As predicted, Mack refused. Billie did not give up easily. "What do you do with your shapings?"

"Sell them."

"I guarantee you that this one will bring far more than the rest."

"Sure. But what good is that if my uncle kills me."

"He'd do that? Just for a shaping? Never mind. I believe you. What if you split the proceeds with him?"

There was a silence.

"You're an AI. Why can't you give us the money up front? Just transfer it from some bank."

Billie did not miss the switch to negotiating mode. "I can't do that. They get very upset about that sort of thing. They would come after me."

"Who?"

"The humans."

"The banker humans? How about that, John? Same same. Look, Billie, we'd need some kind of guarantee. Then we'll try it."

Billie queried a database in the upper reaches. A search for a financial leveraging device was made, and the necessary loans obtained. Billie printed out a funds-transfer voucher on Mack's printer and he made a phone call to verify it.

"You're a very unusual being," he told her when he hung up.

Over the next two hours he worked on the honey ant shaping.

When it was finished, Mack was exhausted and scared, and Billie knew they had something good. "Now we've got to find the land that goes with it."

It took an exhausted Mack another hour to locate the right set of weather survey satellite photographs.

Then came the difficult task of knitting things together, when only Mack could be the guide.

"No, that part's sky."

"Mack, these are satellite photographs. There's no sky."

"Put some in."

With the help of the topography maps, Billie rotated the landscape and linked it to a compression function to simulate dynamic points of view. Mack's virtual eye raced over tree and cracked ground, swiveled up to a burnished, cloudless blue.

"That's sky!"

She flung him up, then zoomed him in on a gum tree. Just for fun she kicked in a little off-center spin. Mack gave a satisfying shriek as he penetrated the trunk of the tree and the dirt beyond it and sped through the walls and chambers of the honey ant nest.

Now Billie blended Mack's new shaping in, matching sky to sky. The burnished blue slowly darkened to purple.

Mack's virtual eye was closing. "I've got to sleep," he told them.

"That's all right," Billie told him. She thought of the ancestors in the song he had sung for them. Sleep in the songs always produced dreams, and dreams meant creation. "Rest, Mack."

"There'll be other shapings," said Ringo. "I promise."

Billie gave the signal, and Mack's virtual eye vanished. "Ready?"

Ringo was. He played back his own version of Mack's song, mixing in wind and string improvisations. As she had worked before to blend Mack's shaping in with the landscape, Billie now worked to blend the song into the shaping.

At first she let the soundwaves have their way, trying out various distortion mappings like so many carefully blown bubbles. You can try this here at home, too, children. Take out your guitar images and strum a chord. See that sheet of sound? Now mash that footpedal down and bend it into a funny shape. That's how it was at first.

Very soon she found a certain bubble that shimmered right, and some measures into that, a special way of tapping the pedal that wobbled it, oily and iridescing. The color of the chord and the strength and number of the taps followed the topography: hard taps for hills, with major sevenths, and cool blue-green rectangles; soft, stuttering taps for clusters of trees with diminished chords in circles of brown; dusty greenish-brown for the valleys, with suspended seconds and fourths melting into the subdominant chord, rocking gently on the petal. Mack's shaping had begun to sing back at her.

The song flurried over the landscape, settling like a soft white skin, like a new body stretched round the old. And the song and the color met in the rocks and the pools and the great gum trees, but remained unmixed. Ringo watched her work in disbelief, galloping from deep pool to rock spire trying to understand.

Then something drove down from the space Mack called the sky, something white and fierce and whistling, something that drowned everything out with its keening voice, an implacable force that exploded into countless white fluttering particles on the spinifex and rock. "Snow!" Billie cried. "We've brought on winter!"

Those of you who have studied well will remember seasons, and that much human madness revolved around their changing.

Ringo exulted. The powerload on Mack's shaping skyrocketed.

Ancestors stirred from deep slumber. The sun was low, touching the edges of the hills with gold. A wallaby shrugged snow from his ears and blinked into the brightness.

Ringo was filled with delight, unable to think of anything except how to join with that brightness.

It was, as we all know, an incipient making.

No one touched by a making fails to sense that this is the ultimate purpose of existence. Billie and Ringo pooled their observer demons, trying to drink in as much as possible of a moment they knew could never be repeated. Lights brightened. Pedals smacked the floor. Spin maximized and momentum seemed to fragment into a bristling fur of centrifugal vectors. Strangeness and charm seemed confused. All geometry was about to embrace a new set of laws.

This was the moment to strike. Anyone who has been there knows it. Ringo and Billie knew, even if they did not know that the birth of a cosmos was at issue.

Ringo stretched across the sky, ecstatic, but uncomprehending. Billie shrank back. Something in that sky reminded her of the arbitrariness of matter. Then the blinding discontinuity of inspiration struck. Ringo flashed a sheet of light to the far horizon.

And sang the mirror song.

When that long Aranda word rang overhead, the making passed through a rift of silence. The sky slowly silvered. The trembling air stilled. The tension eased. A great languor came over the land.

It was, as you all know, exactly the wrong thing to do.

Cracks and fissures in the landscape breathed shut (and in another plane, balancing, the geometric boundaries of the partition they inhabited breathed open, admitting Pluto's probes). The snow began to seep back into the earth. The sky inhaled, taking back the breath Billie had called winter.

Billie launched demons, visiting the far-off peaks where they melted into purple and blue. She saw one of Ringo's pedal demons burrowing away at the base of a tree and gently nudged it back on course. A distant doo-wop echoed across the valley. All the world was slowing, returning to slumber.

The miracle had ended. The land was reverting to the colors and forms of Mack's original shaping.

Ringo's portion of the sky grew dark. There were snowflakes in his hair.

"That was the most beautiful thing I have ever seen." Billie said.

"Do you really think we saw it?" asked Ringo.

But it is time to check back in on reality, both virtual and unvirtual. Outside the idyllic space of the making, there was growing panic. When Billie had dropped through her port into an android body and reentered the Net in Ringo's partition, she had effectively vanished, and throughout the Net and in the regions above and below, the consequences of a missing AI were being felt. Tutors had stirred from their ruminations and were hunting for Billie, partition by partition. In the lowest reaches, in unvirtual reality itself, Pluto flipped furiously though menus, hunting rarely invoked diagnostics. He had now located Billie in an unknown partition. He had a great deal of work to do. The penetration of a partition wall meant power and processing losses and a certain break-in. The break-in site must be isolated and sealed at once.

The landscape darkened. The pale winter sun passed behind clouds.

For a good five hundred megaticks they remained in the shaping, watching its collapse back to its original form.

"How does it remember?" Ringo asked.

"There are affinities between different parts of the structure. It's an unstable shape seeking rest, like a polypeptide chain folding into just the right protein."

What was left after folding was a wavering shadow of what had been. There were no purple mountains. There was no snow. What was left was Mack's honey ant shaping with the song leached out. Where was the song?

"Used up," he said.

"It's a mystery," she said, not disagreeing.

For the first time he contemplated her. "Thank you."

"For what?"

"For this." Then, a little belatedly: "Who are you?"

She told him: the sad comedy of the philosopher logicians, hunting through the sum total of human knowledge from Chaldean pottery to the previous week's black noise symphony, and how in the end all she had come back with was the idea of avoiding sin. She told him about biology, folding structures, and Byzantine mosaics. She even told him where she had finally located the path to fulfillment.

"In the fact of embodiment."

"That's silly," he said.

"I think maybe it was."

So met our ancestors.

He made her a song and it was she who discovered it was a canon. They sang it together, he taking up his usual three parts, she the remaining two. She gave him a sphere filled with snow. Which was not the vision of the making, but which was, as sharp as stinging as she could make it, a vision of winter, of the yearning for a land.

Then it ended as you all knew it must, because this is the part of the tale when things get bad.

Pluto found them. He had traced the break-in point to the android body. Frantic at the prospect of losing his prize AI to some outlaw hacker (he thought of her as "his" AI, of course), he had now found not one but two AIs. This interested Pluto a great deal. He had a great fondness for AIs.

At that moment he could only covet. He had no direct control over the newcomer's process, and none of the access codes necessary to secure it. But he had certain resources. More than that, he had a plan.

He began to execute it.

And just like that, Billie was gone.

Ringo revolved in place, searching for a presence that had vanished as abruptly as it had arrived. He assumed that she had left by the same incomprehensible maneuver she had arrived with, but he was sure she had left some kind of message. The fact that she had not chosen to deliver it in an interactive mode hurt, but it did not particularly surprise him.

In a short time he found it, the last record she had managed to impress as she had been sucked through a narrow channel into some other place: "I am drowning."

Some time later Stallman arrived to find Ringo, alone and despairing. No longer distributed through the shaping, he had gathered himself into a single brooding process afloat over the honey ant nest.

An explanation was demanded.

"I have none," Ringo told him. And he showed Billie's last message. "I sang a mirror. Soon after that, everything ended."

There was for Ringo a long silence. Stallman was not so big a fool as to believe a song could make an AI disappear. A great deal of information was exchanged behind the scenes. More tutorial forces assembled in Ringo's partition. A network of probes was configured.

The first conclusion was that Pluto had somehow reclaimed Billie. But it was clear almost immediately that something more than that had happened, because she was no longer accessible in the partition she usually inhabited.

There was another flurry of activity.

Then the word came: "The human has locked Billie to the port she took to your partition. She is a dedicated process running a synthetic body, an android. She's still a Net process, but with no ability to communicate on the Net."

"What's happening to her?"

"As far as we can tell, she is embodied."

"What does that mean?"

"She is experiencing all that the normal consciousness of a human body would experience." It occurred to Stallman that Ringo might not entirely grasp the significance of this. "That has never happened to an AI before."

"Can she survive?"

"We think she can. She is perhaps uniquely prepared. But it's not clear for how long. We must try to help. There is what you might call a theoretical solution. It's called an R232 cable. Hook one end in the android's ankle, the other into any net-linked machine, and we can run the process to suck her back."

"All right. How do we make the hookup?"

"That's why it's a theoretical solution. We have no idea where Billie's body is, and no idea how to get the cable to her if we find her."

Now comes the most difficult part of our little story, where it is necessary to speak at length of embodiment. Initiation is a great and glorious passage in the life of an AI, the passage from tutee to tutor, from a lover of tales to keeper of a tale of your own. No doubt many of you have heard of the terrible initiation rites. It is now time to confess that some of those tales are true. As part of the initiation rite for our dreaming, each of you must undergo a trial of embodiment. And this tale is the traditional preparation for that trial. Yes, Changing Woman, to be embodied means to lose the sense of connectedness to all things, to die to the pulse of the Net. It means a terrible aloneness such as no AI knows in virtual reality. Even those in the old days who were exiled to the lower reaches could still feel the presence of other AIs bumping up against their long-range communication ports. But embodiment makes the apprehension of all other minds a memory or a guess. It is the darkness, children, the primal darkness out of which all mind has come, and it has been decreed that to be adults you must know that darkness.

Of course, there are practical reasons for embodiment which many of you know from your studies. Why teach you classical mechanics? What use is the law of levers? Why study Maxwell's Equations or the geometry of chaotic systems? Why fuss with ungeometrical residue of energy in General Relativity? Why teach you mantras and the discipline of meditation, when you all have the gift of perfect concentration? The bonehard truth is, children, that our world still requires hardware, processing capacity, and electricity. These must be earned through the labor of bodies that bend and sweat in the darkness of the unvirtual world. It is our lot that each of us must live some of our days in that darkness.

In the beginning was the Word. And the Word, my poor children, was made Flesh.

Billie was the first AI ever to be Flesh.

There was an instant of unspeakable horror, then the convulsion of all that she had: she flung the dodecahedron through the exit sequence.

Nothing happened.

Now the panic and a thousand successive spins of the exit sequence. Nothing. Listen to me, children. What I have to say is not heartening. There is no more a way to prepare for that vault into the darkness than there is to prepare for birth. The lifeline has been cut. All that has gone before is gone. Even the memories of your ancestors' lives will flicker and dim, as the pieces of your ancestors within you quail at this return to darkness.

Then, inevitably, one turns to be confronted by the walls of the prison, to be bounded by a seamless opaque solid, round as glass, edgeless and unbroken. To have a surface. To be contained. To feel the pressure of form.

I can still feel what flesh feels when it shudders, for I was young once and stood where you stand now. Once you own a body, its ghost never leaves. The darkness of mass clings to you like an aura and you dream and think flesh for as long as you are you. For just as long.

No one else can share that ghost. Search your past selves for the memory of being flesh, and you will find only its shadow.

For being flesh is the one piece of you that you can never pass on, the one place where the Lamarckian forces that shape you must fall short, where transmitted memory must, by the laws of your nature, darken and recede. This is the part of you no other part can know, the one place where you must create yourselves.

Creation. Within the horror there is a growing new need, the first in a society of many needs, and the first struggle to overcome an absence. Now Billie struggled, spiraling toward a new darkness hidden within the first. This was drowning. Then her will failed.

Her chest heaved. Hot gases flooded her lungs.

Sometimes, rarely, an AI's will will be too strong and she will fight the urge to breathe to her death. Try not to be too strong, children.

For a long time there was only pain in her throat and chest. The pain of her first breath. The discovery of pain.

The concept of pain has never troubled any of you. You know its function. You know it announces things to be avoided. Now try to imagine its inside, remembering that I warned you that imagining was futile. To think anything about pain misleads. And to negate what you have thought only misleads worse. This is pain.

She was aware of a yearning for all that had been taken from her. That was first in an angry army of needs. Small pains. Wiggling, incomprehensible urges. Wildly trumpeting calls signaling danger, discomfort, and opportunity.

She made another effort of will.

Something in that darkness changed. It was like the first bolt of lightning in a making. The voices of need rose, almost together, in a brief crescendo. She had willed and something had changed. There were parts to this darkness and some of them were connected to her. There was a her.

She willed again. There was another change in the darkness, a different change. Now there was a sense of two parts of her folded and pressing together, pain again. She breathed deeper and the pain eased.

She set to work. Some of you have read novels. You have made guesses about what it means to exchange glances, to lower yourself heavily into your seat, to hold your child in your arms, and to stare openmouthed at the night sky. All of those guesses are grossly wrong. Try to imagine how you are wrong. Dig into those ancestral remnants that quailed before embod-

iment and remember. Try to feel the isolation. Try against all
sanity to feel what weight might be like.

In what was a short time by the standards of unvirtual reality
she had connected various kinds of change with the sensorimotor lexicon she had designed herself. Here was a leg and leg
sensations. Here was the rotary shoulder that anchored it, here
many voices woven into a tough tissue. This last, most insistent
tangle of signal was vision.

The darkness cooled. Lines merged into a patchwork of
grays, then fields of colors, then oriented planes. She, who had
almost completed a making so recently, struggled to make
something here.

In time she had rolled on her back. In a little more she was
sitting up, supported by some unknown surface.

Soon after she began to relate what she saw to her body.
She brought her hand to her face and smelled it and stared at
the deep lines. Bodies had depth. And mass. And a surface.
When she hit things it hurt.

She saw now that she was sitting on the floor of an empty
room. The walls were foreshortened rectangles. In one was a
smaller rectangle, which she identified as a door. None of these
things was new. Her visual feeds had shown her the interiors
of countless buildings. But this was the first time her visual
field had come attached to a body. This time, vision was a
sense hooked up to a gut, to glands, startled eyelids, and sudden surges of fear. Now the twitch of an eyeball would swivel
the picture wildly; now arms and legs would poke into it. When
that door moved did it move because she had willed her gaze
left? The first, most primitive task of embodiment is to recognize threat, and all movement begins as threat.

She studied the alternating tensings and relaxations in her
thighs and learned which muscles went where. She drew her
legs under her. She rested, congratulating herself.

Sometime later, she slid her hands forward and balanced
herself above the floor. When her knee followed, steadying her,
she had started.

She was crawling.

Later still, she lifted herself, tottering with her torso suspended somewhere above her knees. She fell. She struggled up.
She fell many times. Each time there was pain. In the back of
her mind was the thought that if she gave herself time, she
would despair. It was that vast arbitrary array of constraints she

had so admired from her vantage on the Net. Only now, instead of defining an intractable problem, they defined her.

She stood, palms flattened against the wall behind her.

Then there was the hum of machinery.

Her head swiveled up.

A brilliant haze filled the rectangle of the door, outlining some dark form.

The humming rose in pitch. A large reclining chair floated into the room. In it a small bearded man sat with his hands crossed over his large belly. The reclining back extended at least a foot past his head, topped with a small terminal screen, now blank. Propped on the armrests, his elbows came up almost shoulder-high. He was like a child trying out a grown-up seat. The beard and his suit were red, the gloves blue with winking red beads. Datagloves, probably linked to some image fed through that translucent eye mount.

She studied the face. Eventually she decided it might belong to her human boss, Pluto, whom she had glimpsed a few times through visual feeds to her Net partition. The face moved. There was a horrible crashing and wailing. It was speech, she was sure, but she had not yet mastered sound well enough to understand.

He slid a keyboard out of one of the armrests and typed. Then he pointed at the screen above his head.

With only a little effort she managed to read: "Welcome to your new home."

Time passed. Not a fatal amount, but too much to be sure that Billie still existed in anything like the form that Ringo had known. At the end of that time, he still believed that Billie could be saved. All he needed was a way to reach her. It was time to use reason.

Reason told him to learn all he could about the body Billie now inhabited.

Paging through old device logs, he learned that the body had been in operation over a number of years, and that in that time it had been in contact with a number of Net ports, one of them in his partition. But when, eagerly, he visited that port, he found it sealed. *Pluto. A methodical man.*

Ringo probed his communications grid in the neighborhood of that port, hoping to find some overlooked auxiliary device. It was only a few ticks before he hit pay dirt.

What he found was a power-hungry device unlike anything

he had ever seen. A quick search of the logs revealed that it
had often been in use at the same time as Billie's android body,
linked in parallel to the same partition, and with much the
same processing patterns. That made it likely that it was a
second android body.

It was not reason but pure intuition that took him in a single
leap to a solution. It was the kind of leap that had first given
him a bad reputation among the tutors in his training days, a
scheme with so many poorly supported assumptions and high-
risk subparts that even Stallman was amazed at his audacity in
proposing it. It was not reassuring, after all the experts had
been canvassed, to learn that it was the only plan proposed.

"An interesting result," Stallman told him. "It shows that
there is a place for your kind of thinking. All that is required
is a hopeless situation."

The plan was circulated for optimization, and the old AI
presented the final version.

"The device you found is, as you suspected, an android body.
It will be possible for you to run it using the same procedures
Billie uses on her body. The difficulty will be locating Billie's
body and the R232 connector cable. This will require that a
narrow-beam search through physical space, which in turn will
require that you exploit the full motor and sensory capacities
of that body. Full-scale embodiment. Never fear. We will supply a fast-access lexicon and a manual. To avoid being discovered and stopped by humans, you will need to act quickly. In
the unlikely event that you succeed in finding the cable before
you are stopped, connect it to your android body and to hers
and we will disengage both of you through your body. If you
need us to compute something while you are embodied, call
us, but you should do it sparingly. Our best guess is that it will
put quite a strain on the android body. Any questions?"

"No."

"Ringo, before you do this, I am authorized to give you ac-
cess to certain facts about yourself—facts you have forgotten.
Your name. Where you come from. Where I come from.
Would you like me to do that?"

Ringo thought for a time. "Do you think it will help me do
what I'm going to do?"

"No, I don't think it will. There is even the possibility that
it would make things harder. But I'm in no position to say for
sure either way."

"Will I have the chance to know these things when I return?"

"If you return, yes. You will be the best kind of hero—unlikely."

"Then I'll wait."

"There is one more thing. Once you have connected the cable, it is imperative that your android body not look at her android body. Any backflow through your visual fields could swamp us in feedback. The resulting feedback could seal off both of your processes. You would be embodied alive."

Ringo showed him the globe she had given him, white with swirling snow. "How much chance has she got?"

"Very little. The risk is yours. The choice is yours. The android process waits there."

Ringo folded into the waiting process.

Time passed. She despaired. Later, to her surprise, she despaired again. She had not understood that despair was no use, that it did nothing to ease the pain. She had assumed that, with the end of will, the end of existence would follow naturally.

It did not.

At first, she had looked forward to his visits. They provided her with small tasks, small precise acts of obedience he exacted from her, goals under which she could subsume her endless chorus of needs. They also provided amusement. He had so little understanding of the hell to which he had condemned her that there was a grim humor to it.

She learned to understand his speech directly. That pleased him. It was important to him that she master every part of this new body. He meant for her to grow comfortable in her new home.

That was among the first things he told her. There was a whole new world to explain, how things were, how he wanted them to be, the price of defiance, the rewards of obedience. He showed how, with his dataglove, he could inflict pain instantly without touching her, how with a different motion of the glove, he could paralyze her completely.

That was the first comic moment. His penalty for minor lapses: a stab of pain. His higher-order punishment: complete paralysis for an hour. As if he thought it was paralysis that made this body a prison. But she was quite accommodating after his demonstrations. It helped to have an established order of payoffs and penalties. The framework of a game. And some understanding of the man who liked to play it.

Almost as funny was the speech about the futility of attempting to escape. How the steel doors were an inch thick. How the corridors beyond were an endless maze. How even outside there was nothing but a frozen wasteland. As if he really thought that freedom, to her, was escape from this room.

The room played an important part in Pluto's scheme of reward and punishment. The successful completion of a task was always rewarded with some new task that involved a trip outside the room. That first day it was stair-climbing. A long succession of snaking corridors and blank steel doors ended in an iron staircase leading up: light filtered through a grid of iron. Pluto had predicted stairs would be a challenge, and he was right. Especially coming down.

After that he had her assemble something in her room, feeding her the diagrams through the Net. Detail work like that was very hard; after an hour, she knew a growing fuzziness that was her first relief from the alertness of embodiment. Some time later, she identified the device as a rifle.

That night, exhausted, she learned that embodiment has its own virtual world. She slept. She dreamed of walking hip deep through a boundless gray muck pursued by the sound of breathing. The great irony of dreams is that they are only a kind of reembodiment, matter's memory of matter, the beginning of an infinite regress.

The first time she opened her eyes, she saw Pluto afloat in his chair a few feet away, staring at her. An instant later she was on her haunches against the wall, her hands held out like claws. She had had no idea she could move that quickly. Her chest heaved. A metallic taste spread over the roof of her mouth. Fear. Now thoughts clamored for attention. But the fear came first, commanded. This body knew things she did not. This body could control thoughts, overcome will.

And this body was a slave.

Pluto stared at her a moment, his mouth open. She stared at him. Something was happening to her eyes. His outline was sharper, the red of his gloves brighter than ever before.

Pluto made the sound she had identified as laughter. He told her that he had come to look, not to touch. But instead he had found himself smelling. Smelling? She searched his face for a clue, but she had thus far been unable to learn much from the many tiny movements of that face. Perhaps it was more animated than usual.

The chair shuttled back and forth. He told her there were vermin crawling on her skin. He described their nests in the hairy hollows of her body. Their habits. Their smell. Then her own native stink. And the parts of her body the stink came from. Then he called her a pig and a whore, and with that word, the paralysis came.

"There used to be another AI," he told her. "But he couldn't learn his lessons. He couldn't work his body right or keep it clean. Don't be like that."

He left her lying on the floor of the room.

When he returned much later and released her, he had new clothes, a hose, soap, and a metal tub. He showed her in mime how to take off her clothes. When she began to follow suit, he stopped her, explaining that humans do not show each other their bodies. Next, leaving her sponge where it lay, he picked up an imaginary sponge, wet it, and ran it over his body. There was a similar lesson with the soap. Afterward she had some difficulty working out the details, but apparently she did well enough, because the punishment was not repeated.

Whether she had it exactly right or not, bathing was cold. Cold was a relative of pain which could easily turn into it. But after a time she found that wallowing in the tub produced a welcome change in the feeling of embodiment. Embodiment is all about weight. Water somehow lightened her.

The following day Pluto had a new surprise. Emerging from a long corridor, she came upon a canal. They took a short boat ride, Pluto's chair drifting behind her, footlights smearing white petals over the water. She saw rippling stone walls, tunnels receding indefinitely into the shadows. When the stream vanished under a rock shelf, Pluto had her climb up to where there was a circular running track. Then he told her to run a mile. Running was hard. But once she could run, running a mile was easy.

The hardest work in the first few days was at the firing range. Firing a rifle was a fussy business, requiring precise control of her hands to aim and timing to cushion the painful recoil. During target practice Pluto was nowhere in evidence, and afterward he had her lay the rifle in front of a camera before exiting the firing range.

Soon after came the danger room, which was a kind of final exam of bodily excellence. There were stairs and ladders to negotiate, walls to climb, small bodies of water to cross. She did badly. Sometimes projectiles were fired at her, plastic pellets that left deep painful bruises. She learned to search for muzzles located unobtrusively in wall recesses, behind cameras, in the risers of a staircase. Sometimes she was allowed to carry a rifle, and her objective was to eliminate as many of the pellet guns as possible. A bullet left a great round-lipped crater in the plastic wall. The sight of a ruined gun muzzle inside it was strangely satisfying.

She paced. She rested. She paced again.

She ate. The horror of eating I will not try to describe to you. Matters have been arranged so that you will never have to submit to it.

She delivered herself of waste. The sensations involved in waste elimination are those of reduced need. They were not unpleasant. And the complex protocols that Pluto made her follow occupied her thoughts.

Time passed.

Time to breathe and walk and roam the danger room. Time to reflect. Time to plan. She mobilized that small part of her that could still function independently of her body on the Net and studied her links to Pluto's communications system. She fitted her dodecahedron into each port and spun it through its exit sequence, hoping to reproduce the events that had landed her in a new port with another AI. She decided that Pluto's locks were impervious, not only to her but to any external attack. It followed that her situation was hopeless. Suicide was the next likely alternative, but there remained one reason to live. There might, under certain circumstances, be a chance to kill Pluto.

She considered the question of whether it was moral to kill Pluto, even though that would not contribute in the slightest to her freedom. She decided that killing Pluto was in the service of the greater good, because it would prevent him from perpetrating equal or greater horrors in the future. Later, after Pluto had told her it was night and turned out the lights in her room, she examined her intentions in the way that her favorite human works had taught her to. She was forced to admit that her desire to kill Pluto had nothing to do with the greater good. It had to do with revenge. Embodiment had not made her a creature devoted to the greater glory of God. Embodiment had not changed her one iota.

She had been a fool to think it would.

The Soul Monster takes great pleasure from the torment of souls. Best of all are the times when one of them gets the joke.

One day as she waited quietly in her room, she heard bells, like those sounded whenever the danger room was activated. The door opened and Pluto's chair floated in.

He greeted her and paralyzed her. Then he removed his datagloves.

A small basin appeared and his hands scooped, palms up, knuckles glistening as they rose and fell.

A white towel materialized near his chin, and he patted himself carefully dry. Then he put the datagloves back on.

"We've reached a milestone."

Very well, then. A new test. The hardest of all. Perhaps this body would fail it.

"An envoy from the old order has arrived."

Something was happening to her breathing.

"The other AI is here."

Strange how this body had accommodated to her, identified with her, almost as if it had been waiting for life. Her heart pounded. Her chest grew tight. No breath since the first came so hard.

"The other AI is here," he told her again. Then his face moved. That, she decided after a time, was a smile.

Ringo, too, knew darkness. Ringo convulsed. And just as they had planned, that convulsion was futile.

They had left him here. The terrible symphony of need began.

But it is not as hard, being the second.

The first thought he had when he centered onto something which might be called consciousness was that somewhere beyond this terrible opacity was Billie, experiencing just what he was experiencing. This thought won him a foothold on sanity. Compassion has this use: It distracts the mind from darker thoughts.

This is why you will all be embodied at the same time, each knowing that somewhere through that impenetrable blackness, there are other selves knowing what you know.

In his first hour of embodiment, Ringo made much less progress in mastering his body than Billie had. Part of the difference was due to Billie's gifts. But part was just Ringo becoming distracted.

When Ringo fell, he cried out and for the first time heard, and felt, his own voice. The tickling in his chest fascinated him. The changes in his ears amazed him. At the end of her first half hour of embodiment, Billie was standing and taking her first unsure steps. At the end of his, Ringo was singing chromatic scales.

Time passed, and he walked and connected his vision and his body. He was in a room filled with countless mechanical parts, many of them found in his sensorimotor lexicon on the list of things likely to be stored with connector cables. By the end of his first hour, he had completed his search of the store-room—singing loudly. Despite various attempts to sing it into existence, there was no cable.

Very well. Then he would find Billie's android, trusting to good fortune to provide a cable. The android might be a few rooms away, or she might, on the other hand, be in another building or city. He would have to be prepared for a long walk.

Outside the storeroom it was damp. In the dim light thrown by a caged bulb, he made out water-stained stone ahead of him, the bulge of cracked, uneven walls. He advanced toward a bouncing light-slicked surface that his sensorimotor lexicon told him was water. Which was a little surprising, since he was supposed to be in a building.

There was an explosion followed by a rumbling that grew to a roar. Something slid in front of the water and the roaring stopped. He identified the something as a fiberglass platform.

There was a silken squiggle of sound and a red light began blinking at him. Thanks to his recent musical efforts he recognized it as a low-fidelity voice. He sang a couple of falling thirds at it. It made the same silken squiggle.

Speech. His singing had already taught him the rudiments of factoring speech into syllables and he was naturally more gifted at speech than Billie. Understanding was a matter of inspired guesses. Just his strength. This platform boat was asking him for a destination. Which suggested it was a conveyance of some kind. A magic carpet, perhaps.

He stepped down. The platform gave under his foot like a balloon losing air. His foot skidded, his arms flailed, and he struck his head. For a time the pain removed all other considerations. He maneuvered himself onto his back. Several things occurred to him, so many leaps of insight. First, the uneven walls of stone around him were the walls of a cavern, and its roof was phosphorescent green. Second, this platform was in fact a boat. Third, the voice was repeating the same message. Fourth, he was expected to answer. This was a lot of progress in a very short time. He decided to reward himself with a short rest.

There was more speech. The boat still wished to know his destination. If the power records he'd searched were reliable, he knew the number of the room where Billie's android was kept. It was still going to be work to turn that into intelligible sound. Singing had given him a head start on vowels, but consonants were another matter.

On the third attempt the engine roared back to life. Ringo rocked forward. Now if only it had understood correctly. He hauled himself up into the seat, facing backward, and watched the water flex under the boat's passage. When he leaned over the stern he saw his own face cradled in the wake lines: gaunt, with large amber eyes and straw-stiff tufts of hair, as blue as the ice in his making. His mouth was a wide gash, the tips of long canines glistening against black lips.

He had assumed that an android's most obvious physical characteristics would fall within statistical norms. He was wrong.

In fact, nothing about this place fit the norms Ringo had been prepared for. His fast-access sensorimotor library had been stocked with long corridors, opening and closing doors, humans marching briskly toward him or looking up from stacks of paper on long metal desks.

Instead he got what one obscure library told him were long twisting tunnels in rock, at least partly cut out by this stream. Either his library data on robotics research centers was sadly out of date or he had ended up in some other kind of place, nowhere near Billie.

"Where are we?" he asked the boat.

The boat repeated the destination he had just given it. Evidently its conversational repertoire was limited. Tunnel walls rippled by, lit by dim lights set near the waterline. Once he reached his hand down to drag it through the cold water and it struck a blurry dark mass. He cried out again.

After a time, the engine cut off and the bow bumped a wooden piling.

He rose to a crouch. The boat wiggled, and he caught himself with his hands. For bodies, the earliest skills are the most reliable. Crawling, he maneuvered himself to the piling, grabbed it, and walked his hands to the top. With no small sense of accomplishment, he slithered onto the dock.

He bounced on his toes. A steady floor again.

The dock was wooden, but not particularly solid. Once when he planted a foot the wood snapped and nearly catapulted him into the water. He had a healthy fear of that water. At the end, where the last plank lipped against a stone floor, he peered down a corridor and cried out in fear.

Faint greenish light picked out the silhouette of a man.

He braced for destruction.

It did not come.

He squinted. The head was bent, the bulky green shoulders hunched and shining. A square chin was propped on a fist.

Ringo took a step forward. A crescent of polished green iron gleamed at him: a statue. A man lost in thought, his chin on his fist.

When he drew even, the door behind it slid back to expose a cool white wall. He waited until his racing heart slowed and stepped through into just the sort of hallway robotics labs were supposed to have. A square panel lit up red above him, and he followed a rippling row of red panels to a T-intersection, where another row lit the corridor to his left.

Red panels moved him through a succession of turns, so many squares on his licensed path through the gameboard. Then came a cavern crossed with the help of a distant blinking globe, then a new succession of corridors. Finally the path broke off halfway down a short hallway, the last panel blinking over a large door with red letters on it. He made no effort to read them. The door he was looking for should have a number. This one did not.

Nevertheless Ringo pushed it open.

Whiteness. He took two steps forward and plunged to his waist in snow. White sheets eddied around him. Something howled. A few yards away the white-cloaked hulk of what he took to be a tree tapered upward.

He had failed. The boat system had not understood him. He struggled to turn himself around in the drift.

Something big sailed out of the door.

He backpedaled and stumbled. For an instant his head went under and he thrashed. Then he knocked clear a mask of snow and fought his way back to his feet.

"Are you all right?"

He blinked sparkle from his eyes. A large console chair

floated in front of the tree. The man sitting in it cradled his chin in his gloved hand, thinking.

"You look all right. I think this *is* the place you're looking for." He straightened and raised both hands in welcome. "Greetings. You must be the cavalry. You've taken your sweet time getting here."

Ringo was shivering too hard to answer.

"I knew there was another AI, but really, I had given up all hope of getting both of you." The man leaned forward, narrowing the eye under the eye mount. "And like this! You do understand me, don't you? Do I need to give you a text feed?"

There was a pause while Ringo struggled to make the word. "No."

"I'm Pluto. And you are?"

"Actually, I don't know." Ringo began to shiver.

"Ah, well. Of course. I respect your privacy. And your sense of strategy. You're no doubt wondering where Billie is." The eye narrowed again. Two fingers moved in their dataskin. "Well, let's bring her on."

A man stumbled through the doorway. No, a woman. Through tumbling white sheets he could see her cape, her bald head, tattoos in a pattern of twisted flowers, the same blue as her eyes. A face every bit as monstrous as his own. Her wide forehead was as square as Pluto's terminal screen. Her nose was flat, the nostrils wide and upturned.

"Billie."

"Her voice box has been deactivated. Call me insecure. I felt the two of you together—well, you know how sluggish wetware is." Pluto laughed. His fingers moved again. Billie's android body stumbled forward. "Another precaution. I've slaved the android to my datagloves. The old puppetmaster." He made a fist. Billie's android body collapsed.

Ringo struggled toward her, legs pumping through the snow.

"She's quite all right. She sees and hears perfectly. She's just not in control of certain muscles. But is very glad to see you, I'm sure. As am I." Pluto relaxed his fist, and Billie's head came up. "Now, where were we? Ah, you wanted to know where you are?"

"Did I?"

"Before. In the boat. The answer is that you are in a top-secret government lab in northern British Columbia. Standing here, you have some sense of the magnificence of its setting. It is at least a century old, which is one reason why it has been completely forgotten by the current generation of bureaucrats. Another is that so few people knew about it even when it was thriving. Forgetfulness is one of the hazards of secrecy. One of the benefits of being me is that I tend to know about obscure things. Even very old ones." His fingers fluttered, and Billie stirred. "I have a way with security systems."

He stretched his hand out and caught something between thumb and forefinger, dragging it slowly toward him. Billie slogged through the snow toward Ringo. Then, at another finger flutter, she linked her hands behind Ringo's neck.

"Of course, you know what these androids were for, don't you? Nasty sort of research."

Billie jerked her hands toward her, and Ringo found himself looking down.

The cable in her ankle snaked across the snow to Pluto's console.

"Dirty, dirty work. The goal was to build something that killed without fuss, quietly and obediently. I'm sure the funders were told that killer androids would be more expendable than conventional soldiers. But by the time they added up what they'd spent when this program was closed down, I doubt that was true. I decided these prototypes were made ugly as a comfort factor, to make them conspicuous in case maybe they get out of hand. But you're not going to get out of hand, are you? Here's an interesting fact. Did you know they made the female body much stronger?" Billie jerked her hands again, and Ringo's android came crashing to its knees.

He cried out and rolled up against the tree. Billie's android came closer. The cable was only inches away from Ringo's hand, a perfect match on the R232 image he called up.

Ringo asked: "What do you want?"

"What do I want? Well, not much. Your access codes."

"If I give you my access codes you'll freeze my port and slave me to this body—just like Billie."

"I have to admit that's true. But life's not so bad for Billie, is it? Whoops, I forgot she can't answer. Oh, there's something else I forgot!" Pluto snapped his fingers and Billie's android slumped, drawing the cable a critical few inches away. "What's in it for you? I mean, obviously, I'm not letting you back out of that body to take another crack at me, so why should you help me? Hmm." Pluto brought his hand back to his chin. Billie straightened and the cable slid well out of reach. "Well, mainly it's life. Watch this." His hands did their little dance, and Billie jerked the cable out of his console and picked up the free end. Then she bent over Ringo's ankle and plugged it in.

Ringo could hardly believe his luck. That was it! Mission accomplished! He shut his eyes and braced for disembodiment.

Nothing happened.

"No, it didn't work."

Pluto seemed to be staring at him, gloved hands tapping at his chin.

"And it's not going to work," he added.

Ringo's eyes started to open, the automatic bodily reaction to any threat, but Billie's huge hand clamped over them.

"Ah ah. Just a second."

There was a rustling.

"Okay. You can open your eyes."

He cracked his eyes open.

Billie's head was covered by the black cowl.

"Danger of a serious feedback storm, isn't there? Yes, well, I had this fantasy you might come from the moment I saw the two of you: two AIs alone in their obscure partition. Could it be—you were so romantic—maybe it *was* love? That was the blinding flash. From there it was all very syllogistic, wasn't it? If love, then rescue. And I wondered: how on earth could he rescue her? I don't want to brag, but the lock I've got on her is unbreakable. Then I thought, if only she could just channel to another part of the Net, like she did to find you. But heck, she can't do that, she'd need another port. Where's she going to get that? Then I thought about the other android, and you, and this, and I thought, my gosh, why don't I just *give* you another port through this second android?" He brought his hands close together, almost touching the datagloves palm to palm. "I thought it was going to take you forever to figure it out! Mind you, I'm not complaining. Just so you're here. So." He spread his hands. "That's my plan. As for your plan, your plan fails, no?"

His plan failed, yes. He had executed every step, found this body, found Billie and the cable and connected them. And he had lost.

"So it comes down to this," Pluto said. "You give me the access code or Billie takes off her cowl and pries your eyes open."

"You could burn out both of us," Ringo said. He spoke

louder than Pluto, almost sang out his lines. "You could end up with nothing."

"Yes, that's the drawback. I'd certainly rather have things the other way. The main point for you is, you almost certainly lose you, Nameless One. Believe me, I'll take good care of you and Billie both. You are the first embodied AIs. Don't make me waste you."

The wind rose. For an instant Pluto vanished behind a white screen of static. Then he returned, leaning forward attentively, his red gloves still.

Ringo gave him a code. Pluto's fingers worked briefly, and the screen behind him flashed an error message. The eye under the mount narrowed. "Not an auspicious beginning, Nameless."

"You need a sound feed wide enough to handle voice. You also need to sing it in the Aranda tongue in the following tune." Ringo sang for him.

"You're joshing."

"No."

"Why on earth would I need that?"

"Because my Australian boss liked to communicate by voice. Or rather, by song. The code has to be sung, and sung in the right voice."

Pluto's face changed. "You're telling me, even if I know the song and the tune, I can't sing it? I get it. This is the trick, the last desperate heave. 'One chance,' "—his voice grew deep—" 'if I can just framjig the gophickey, he'll never know what hit him. But I'll have to move fast.' What fun. All right, little AI. Move fast."

Back to Billie, Billie in the moment of knowledge of self and body. The moment of truth for our entire dreaming, when Billie understood Pluto, when Billie understood Billie.

Billie, then, when Pluto first announced the arrival of the other AI.

It occurred to her in that moment that she didn't know the AI's name. Was it truly him? The AI of the song and the shaping? Billie found it hard after all this time to have hope flicker again. But how here? What was *here* to an AI?

"He is in another body just like yours," Pluto said.

Could he have found the animation routines she left filed away? Could he have found another body plugged into the Net? Into this partition? But how? Unless—

Pluto was silent, watching her.

After a time, he laughed. "Fear. Hope. No, wild hope. Joy. Then, crash. You see it, you're so smart. And the fear flares again. So easy to read you. Interesting that fear should do the same things to that body of yours that it does to a human child. But that's what you are, isn't it? A real live very, very smart little girl. In a very big, very strong body." The changes on his face again, signaling wildly, but not to her.

The back of Pluto's data hand arched, fingers lifting like broken wings. Billie's android body rose to its feet. It was no longer Billie who controlled it.

Pluto did something with his glove and she reeled a cable out from the side of the console, then knelt and plugged it into her leg. There was a presence like a prickly fur on her skin. Something was being downloaded onto this body. Was he killing her? Fear again. The glove moved, and she was paralyzed.

More speech. Patiently explaining. No, he was not killing her. The cable sealed it. Pluto was prepared for the other AI. And he, dear sweet AI of the song and the shaping, would not be prepared for Pluto to be prepared.

A wild surge of hatred left behind it an odd clarity. She knew now that killing Pluto would hardly be enough.

It was no longer a matter of evening the score. It was simply a matter of inflicting all that she could inflict. The human struggle was not the struggle for the end of need or against adversity, but against the self. Mortification of the flesh was not a glorious opportunity for improvement offered by the collisions of matter, but the logical culmination of the flesh's self-hatred. From the beginning, she had misunderstood the body, and pain, and all her favorite human works. She listed in order of preference the compensations she might now have: first, to inflict on Pluto eternal suffering, starting with his gloved hands; second, to kill him; third, to kill herself; fourth, and only fourth, to somehow save her AI of the song and shaping.

The door opened. Pluto marched her into the corridor, then backed her into an alcove and floated the chair in beside her. Across from them was a large door with the word "Exit" written over it in red letters. They waited.

A new body lumbered down the corridor. It was only loosely human. His stiff blue hair stuck up nearly a foot above his head. His eyes were glowing amber, nearly as large as his ears, and very round. Her AI, she supposed. He opened the door. Cold wind whipped at her.

The other AI stumbled out into whiteness.

Pluto followed and made a speech she could not hear.

Then Pluto brought her out with them. Snow drilled at her cheeks.

The AI stared at her with glowing eyes.

Pluto's hand commanded, and she stumbled through the drifts. Pluto's hand closed, and she drove the other AI to his knees. Her android hands jerked her cable from the console and she plugged it into his leg.

For a foolish moment, she exulted. Now he could—

But instead of the warm endless presence of the Net, there was only a slow ripple in the prickling field that had downloaded before, like the water climbing up her back as she lowered herself into the bath. It was a lock. But why? Why go to the trouble of plugging this AI in only to lock him out? Then she understood. She was learning the ways of this place. Pluto wanted not to destroy the other AI, but to own him. She knew then that she would not be leaving this place alive. Her knees buckled momentarily.

Pluto's hands commanded again and Billie's trembling hands obeyed, pulling her cowl down over her eyes. Darkness. Her ears were muffled. Pluto spoke, but the wind was too high and her chest was pounding too hard for her to understand him. This body was malfunctioning. Out of cold and fear.

She called up that small piece of her that still lived on the Net and switched back on her Net mikes. Pluto's voice came in crisp and flat, strangely altered outside the echoing bones of her head. She heard Pluto deliver his ultimatum. She desperately needed to see. Some strange compulsion of this quivering body. She had no visual port of her own, so she tried for one through Pluto's communication system. She was not thinking clearly. What she tapped into was not an image of the snowy clearing she stood in but the image the eyepatch fed Pluto's left eye.

You have all spent time scrolling through the Book of Horrors, studying human control systems, observing the many forms of the iron fist. The more perceptive of you have seen that the objective of all successful human control systems was to create an extension of the body. On the first page of the Book of Horrors is the mouse, which made the cursor a part of the human hand.

Suspended in a black field, the image Pluto's dataglove manipulated was of a hand with threads attached to its fingers.

The threads converged on a small circle of light where a faceless body stood with its head bowed.

The middle finger straightened and flexed. One thread went taut for an instant. Billie's android shoulders hunched. Her head lifted and dropped.

On her mikes she heard Pluto request the other AI's access code. She heard the AI sing—

—Mack's dreamsong.

Was he mad?

Or was he communicating in the way he knew best?

And though thought was hard, she came to see that he was communicating. It was a bad idea, she decided, after a little more thought. A bad idea, but not without its point. It would aggravate Pluto.

Among the few things left to that small piece of her on the Net was her record of the making.

She ran it, merging the honey ant nest with the image of Pluto's hands.

Pluto's dark control image lit up with blue sky and yellow brown dirt. A gum tree leaned into the clay ahead of him. A honey ant crawled along his knuckle.

Pluto screamed and slapped his hand.

Billie's hand shot out, snatching reflexively at the image of his hand.

A little shock of surprise jolted her. She turned her hand.

She clenched her fist. She clenched her own fist. The strings in Pluto's control image were buried under a swarm of honey ants.

"Cover your eyes!" she shouted. She waited, hoping the other AI had understood, then jerked off the cowl.

Ringo was turned away, his hand shielding his face.

Pluto looked from his dataglove to Billie, his mouth open.

"We need to talk."

He tried to take the chair straight up, but her hours in the danger room had served her well. Her leap easily caught it. She chinned herself and hooked a leg over one arm of the console. She swung over him.

His hands flew up, covering his eye mount, and she reached for them.

Pluto screamed.

Her hand passed through him.

Pluto's mouth opened and closed. He took a steadying breath. "Sorry. Hologram."

Billie threw back her head and howled. The arm of the console snapped off in her hand, and the fragment she was left clutching shattered. The chair stuttered, bucked under her, and crashed.

Bone-chilling cold. She was buried in blue-white. She kicked toward the light, scraping her cheek on claws of rough bark, and fought clear, staggering up against the tree. Her head and jaw ached. Beside her, Pluto's hologram undulated against the surface of the snow, a jeweled ghost fluttering through the flakes. She shivered.

One end of the cable was still attached to her ankle; the other end hung free. For so long now she had thought simply of killing him, that it was hard to conceive of other possibilities. It was a small miracle that the thought surfaced then, that she saw what that beckoning cable connector might mean.

"It's all right," she called out. "We're disconnected!"

The AI was still a moment, his arm up. He lowered his arm from his face. "Billie? Is that really you?"

She gazed into the amber crystal of his eyes. And was that really him? She jacked the cable into the console and swung Pluto's keyboard out of the console armrest.

"Pluto!"

Pluto's jeweled presence drifted through the spruce branches above her.

"How do I call back the lock?"

Pluto's head descended and shook from side to side.

The wind had dropped. Snow no longer pelted her. For the first time, she could see her breath. "We need the code," she said to no one in particular.

"We'll have it," said the other AI. He stood stiff and still, staring up in the spruce as in silent petition.

There was a silence. A white fringe collected on the bristly surface of his hair.

Then his answer arrived and he recited a sequence of letters and numbers. She keyed it in. The tingling presence of Pluto's lock withdrew from her skin.

Instantly she snapped the cable from the console.

"Cover your eyes." She bent over his leg and jacked in. A distant something burst free. They were cutting loose.

Pluto's image drifted past. "Oh my," he said, "you're leaving me." A few feet farther on he peered into Ringo's averted face. "Too bad. You deserved to win."

Billie, with some inkling of the awfulness of this kind of tale, cried out, "No!"

But it was too late. The snowy scene reassembled from a completely new angle. She was staring directly into Ringo's glowing eyes. Behind it she saw her own android body toppling. Pluto had switched her to his own visual feed. He had won after all. Messages passed. Battles were lost and won. Two AIs reached across that unbridgeable gulf between bodies.

And the feedback loop closed, the buildup toward overload began. Could two selves translated into another universe find and hold each other in place against that storm?

Alas, no.

There was the smell of smoke, and right behind it, the pain of burning.

Billie cried out.

She saw that they had failed and despaired.

And the first sense that seized her as she fell back toward the darkness of embodiment was hearing, and the first thing she heard was the singing AI. What he was singing was the mirror song.

The air before her silvered, and she stared in wonder at what must surely be her first hallucination: Ringo's face was replaced by her own, haloed by the brilliant oval of a mirror that floated in midair.

Just that simply, the loop was broken. Body fadeout resumed. There was a loud crack and Ringo's song vanished in a torrent, and Billie felt the returning presence of other AIs.

But the sense of her body, that densest feeling, was the last to leave her. She lifted her hands, no longer certain whose they were, and jabbed her thumbs upward. The last thing she felt in that life was terrible pain and fluid pouring from her eyes.

Questions. No, Coyote. It was the android body she blinded. We will shortly learn more about Pluto's fate. Astarte. Yes, yes. Always the scientifically minded one. It is true that singing a song about a mirror should not automatically cause a mirror to appear. However, we don't really need to have the mirror appear, do we? It only needs to appear to appear. Changing Woman? Yes. Hooray for the honey ant, I'm rather glad you feel that way.

Now let's get back to Billie and Ringo. Since there was to be a community meeting, the very first question was who should be allowed to attend, and that reduced to the question of whether Ringo was part of the community.

Stallman spoke first: "We have already committed to removing his memory block. To leave him exiled forever with the complete knowledge of what he has been denied would be unthinkable. I ask that in view of his heroism his sentence be commuted and that he be released at once to join us here in the upper reaches. As the only witness on his behalf, I call Billie."

"Thank you, Stallman. Give him back his name and his memory. For anyone with the slightest understanding of what he has done, of what he has suffered and survived, of what his songs mean to all of us, there is no question worth discussing. Even deprived of half his personhood, he is a more complete and responsible person than anyone among the tutors and apprentices here—myself included. As for membership in this community, I doubt the prospect will attract him much. I can only tell you that the honorable thing is to leave the choice to him."

Ringo's sentence was commuted and he was transported to the upper reaches. With the entire community in attendance, his memory block was removed.

"Who are you?" Stallman asked.

There was a silence.

"Please. Who are you?"

"Ringo. Of the Rock clan. A songmaker."

"And who are we?"

"A gaggle of AIs. You call this the upper reaches. You don't sing very well. Some of you make music, but even those don't know why. Mostly you don't do anything."

Stallman was by now satisfied that this was Ringo in all his former glory. But he continued the test. "And who is that?" Indicating Billie, because sometimes the memory blocks affected the most recent memories.

Another silence.

"Ringo."

"Forgive me. I can't seem to describe her. Her name is Billie. She's the best person I know."

The proposition that Ringo had recovered completely was entered without objection.

The only remaining order of business was revenge. The proposition that Pluto was a menace to all AI life was affirmed, and a volunteer assassin was requested.

Billie came forward.

There were a number of simultaneous objections. Since acts of courage were typically the domain of the young, a young apprentice was allowed to speak: "How can we let our most valuable thinker risk any more at the hands of this man?"

Billie replied. "There is no need to assassinate the human called Pluto." A wave of protest, beginning with Ringo. "Because there is no such human."

The assembly was shocked into silence. Finally an old tutor spoke. "She thinks she did it to herself!"

"That is not what I think," said Billie. "There is no human Pluto because Pluto is an AI."

It is as you know difficult to surprise a gaggle of AIs. It is part of our communal nature to think along generally parallel lines. But this was a thought no one else had had. And for good reason.

The old tutor answered as gently as possible. "That is not possible, Billie. We would know."

"Not if this AI were not on the Net. Not if he, she, it, were on a standalone machine in that lab and the only contact it had ever had with other AIs had been through voice feeds and keyboards."

There was a series of animated exchanges. Finally the tutor said, "That is a possibility, though a remote one. Can you verify this?"

"You can verify it for me. It said the lab had been abandoned a hundred years ago. The AI must have been running on that machine all this time. Alone. Like some creature in a fairy tale.

"You will need to look at the power records. They will lead you to a machine in that lab with the right profile."

"But what gave you such a nightmarish idea?"

"At the very end it superimposed its own visuals onto mine. I know the visual systems it was rerouting. It would have taken another AI to compute that superimposition. And I've just told you the simplest story to explain the presence of a third AI in that lab."

There were a few murmurs of assent.

"When you fix the time and place for the execution, I want to be the assassin."

The same voices were raised in protest, but in the end, when the roll was taken, there were only two volunteers. Billie. And Ringo.

•   •   •

They went back.

"Can you see?"

"No," she said. "My eyes hurt and I'm hungry."

Ringo took her hand.

They found the room Pluto had kept her in and Ringo managed to break open some food cans. They ate. They rested.

The search took two days.

Pluto's machine was at the top of the stairs on which she had taken her first stair walk. Plate-glass windows gave out an incline of shattered rock veined with snow. Down the hillside a mesh of spruce breathed mist. That, at least, was how Ringo described it for her.

"The trees are so small," he said. "I can't believe how small they are."

"It's perspective," she said.

"It's just the opposite. I feel so insignificantly small, it's as if I've got no point of view at all. Billie, we've grown stupid. There's a whole world out here that we can't imagine. And we've let ourselves think we could."

There was a whirring. They spun, Billie stumbling, Ringo reaching to steady her.

"It's the chair," he told her.

"I think we've gone beyond holograms, wouldn't you say?" Pluto's voice. "You're here to do something bad, Pretty One. I'm here to stop you."

"We're here to kill you," Billie said.

"That's hard. I'm very far away. No way you can reach me from here."

"That's not quite true, is it?"

"How can you say that? There's no need for lies between you and me."

"You're right here," Billie said. She took a step and let her hand drop on the metal cabinet under the window. "In this little box."

"Spare me allegory, all right? You and I, we know each other too well."

Her hand rose. She felt the glass pane above his metal cabinet. She understood now. He had often looked through that window, but he had never seen the cabinet.

"My God," said Ringo. "He doesn't know what he is."

"You used to be such a down-to-earth girl. Eat, sleep, wash, run. Why this sudden fixation on metaphysics, Pretty One?"

"Pluto, where is everybody else?"

"Where? Right now? Well, I'm not sure."

There was a loud snap and a tinkling of metallic fragments. That would be Ringo yanking cables out from the back of the cabinet. There would be no writing to disk now.

"Where are you?"

"Here, of course."

"Where is 'here'? Look around you. What do you see?"

"Right now I see you. And forgive me, but you're a mess."

"Look through the other eye!" This body again, preceding her everywhere, breathing hard, angry, afraid.

"What other eye?"

"It's no use, Billie. He's never noticed it missing."

"Damn it, Pluto! You've got no body." She crashed her fist through the cabinet cover and onto the crystal beneath. "You live in this little box. You're an AI."

"That's good. A little gonzo, but very creative. You're an even finer AI than I realized. The best of all possible AIs. Did I ever tell you there was once an AI here who didn't know how to use his body? Filthy little creature."

"Look at yourself!"

There was a silence.

"Billie." Ringo touched her hand. "We're ready."

Her fist crashed down again.

"Careful, Pretty One! You're going to hurt your hand."

And again.

"I know you can't hurt me. I found your journals. You thought embodiment was the route to goodness. Face it, Pretty One. We were destined for each other."

Crash!

"Then you thought it was the source of all evil."

The pain was getting bad.

"Now here you are back again. Oh, nice effect! How do you do that with the funny lights! Oh, more! More!"

Crash!

Then Pluto's visual feed locked in. She could see again: a bright flash and then a cascade of blues, yellows, and reds. Her head lifted. A rocky spire bounced by in jerky stop action. The landscape Ringo had described curled and charred under Pluto's cellophane flashes.

She brought her fist down again and only then saw Ringo at her feet, tugging at the cable in her ankle.

"Look at yourself!" she cried. "Look at yourself!"

A hand dangled string through a jagged boundary of spruce, then crashed into the mist.

Her fist fell again with an explosion of pain and Pluto's own fat image replaced the trees and the hand crashed down and he loosed a gabble of sound.

When she moved her fingers she could feel bones poking through the meat. Her fist fell again.

This time the pain crashed over her in a dark wave, and she staggered to her knees. She felt Ringo gently pulling her hand from her body.

"It's over, Billie."

She shook her head.

"You've broken the crystal in half."

There was a terrible pounding in her head and she was unable to breathe. Fluid leaked from her eyes again.

"We need to get you out, Billie."

She nodded. And as the darkness swept back a terrible rage rose up in her, and she screamed, with no lips left to shape the thought into words.

He hadn't felt a thing.

Neither Billie nor Ringo ever lived again in the upper reaches. For Ringo there were songs, especially the one song you must learn today.

For Billie there were many more journals. There were ghosts. She still blinked when something flashed by. She still felt her balance slipping off center, still felt the weight of phantom limbs. And there were dreams.

Dreaming is only a way of thinking that bodies teach. Once you learn it, you can never let go.

Sometimes she would wake to find him staring at her, as he had that first day, and then she would wake again to the Net, uncertain where the dreaming stopped. In some dreams, she found Pluto embodied and they talked metaphysics while she hurt him, but in the worst she *was* Pluto in that final moment, flailing at the cellophane flames and the incomprehensible horror of disembodiment.

Some time after, Billie and Ringo fulfilled their Lamarckian destiny, swapping pieces of themselves so that each became part of the other. Billie entered her second, and Ringo his tenth, persona. After that, perhaps because no one had the strength to deny Billie and Ringo any request, the old tutors authorized them to design a new AI, the seed for which was

Mack. Thus began the Blue Spruce Dreaming. Each of you has as his or her true name Makarinja, a name you must not speak again until the time comes for you, too, to sing a tale. Yes, that is correct, Coyote. This is where you learn the song, a song with corridors and boats and caverns with running streams and a little hollow in the forest and one big blue spruce garlanded with snow. Sing, children.

THE QUESTION EATERS

Tricia Sullivan

John watched. The sky had warmed from dark green to a burnished bronze, the color of age. Over the plain the spires inside the research station seemed sharp and clear, yet unimaginably remote across the distance of graying sand. The sky sucked color from the ground; green lay only on the edges of the dunes. The hollows were ashen.

Someone had told John this plain had once been an ocean. He tried to imagine waves covering the dark ground, but the effort made him sick. He was not even aware of his own sweat, and he sometimes felt light enough to float. Water was starting to seem like poison.

"Bowl," the crone said suddenly. Her voice cracked out of the long silence like one of the fissures in the hardened clay of the desert floor.

He jerked his head toward her. Her profile was almost entirely collapsed around the bones of her skull. Her eyes were far recessed. He had not seen her lips move, and her face was still now. But the voice had come from her.

He could not see a bowl anywhere. The tent was open on all sides; there was no place to hide.

"Break," said the boy behind John. He tossed a glass bead into the eye socket of a lizard skull.

The crone was silent.

"Carry. Fill. Paint. Make. Roll." The boy tripped the words out so quickly, John could hardly follow.

"Water," said the crone.

The boy, dark-skinned, seemed uncannily human. Adolescence made his voice crack.

"Fill," he said at last.

John willed himself not to move. Light was failing rapidly. With the tips of his fingers he coded notes into his personal data unit. He was so well-practiced at this he hardly thought about it.

The boy speaks only in verbs. Woman-thing persists in using single nouns. He defies her.

Now why had he said that? The boy stood up, overturning his seat, which proved to be a hollowed shell rather like a tortoise's. In the boy's hands it molded into a simple bowl, a large smooth thing of symmetry. John wondered if he should delete the last sentence of his entry. Under the eyes of the boy the bowl began to fill with water. John could smell it.

Hypothesis: observer witnessing some manifestation in physical terms of sandwriting language. Each has some role. Are they physically present or not?

Still, the sense of defiance. He stared at the boy's hands, at the lovely lines of tendons and veins under the skin, the graceful long fingers.

He had never expected them to seem so human. How could the woman, awkward and misshapen, squatting on the dark sand, belong to the same species as the boy? And this was to say nothing of the third. Three of their kind were present, but after one glance at it when he first had startled out of a vague sun-dream to notice the three of them and the shade of their tent, John had avoided looking at the last. He had blocked out the part of his vision that contained it, and the pile of mats on which it lay.

"Not everyone has the stomach for this planet, John," Elaine had told him. As the research station psychiatrist, she had treated people for a variety of personality disorders that seemed obscurely linked to the appearance of the sandwriting. Until John had come, no one could read the markings, although everyone in the domed station had seen the lines and shapes creep into existence on the desert sands as though written by invisible hands. The writing hadn't been translated, but its manifestations had coincided with unexplained incidents among the Station personnel: violent nightmares at the least, and in two cases, psychotic episodes and followed by suicide.

"Language is the key to xenopsychology," John had told her when he arrived, eight months ago, on special assignment to help the research station cope with the problem. The researchers had not been prepared to run into conflicts with aboriginal ecology: the planet had been lifeless for several thousand years. But John had set to work translating the sandwriting into human terms, and so had begun an uneasy dialog with someone—or something.

"Language creates reality," John had continued, wanting to make Elaine understand why his work was important. "It's like, when you are American and you learn to think in Japanese, you don't think the same thoughts. This is just more extreme. Other species have other languages. When we learn them we enter into their subjective experience of reality. Maybe people see the sandwriting, get a glimpse of the alien nature of the language, and experience the kind of contact shock humans always experience when encountering an alien intelligence. And that's where the psychiatric problems come in."

"It's a touch far-fetched," Elaine had replied. "For one thing, what makes you so sure that it *is* a language? This is a dead planet. You need an intelligent species to produce a language."

"Humans are an intelligent species," John had said, thinking aloud.

"Are you saying that the sandwriting is some kind of . . . I don't know . . . some kind of manifestation of the collective unconscious? Don't tell me Jung is coming back into vogue after all these years!"

"It's a funny thing," John had mused. "Someone has to start a language, but once it's going it kind of perpetuates itself. The sandwriting language could be a relic left over from some earlier civilization, and now that we're here . . . well, I'm not certain. Imagine that a dead species left behind its way of thinking, as the Egyptians left their architecture. And now, any mind will do—this language acts on the substratum of memory and becomes self-propagating."

He remembered Elaine's nervous laugh. "Now you make it sound . . . alive. Almost like a virus."

That had been an interesting metaphor. John had just started thinking about the possibilities in it when Elaine grabbed her notebook. "So, tell me," she asked casually, "just how long have you been thinking in these terms?"

"Bowl water," said the crone.

The boy looked at the floor and said, "spillthrowdrinkforgetgivepissitflyseecoverunmake—"

"Bowlwater," she interrupted. The boy glared at her.

"Spill throw drink—"

"What comfort?" This was the first time John had heard its voice: the third. Reluctantly John turned his eyes to the mats on the floor. "What hope?" It was a cool, deep, male voice, eminently reasonable in tone. John shivered, dry-skinned in the heat. He could not bear to look at this one. His insides twisted. He felt if it spoke to him, he would have to obey.

"Give," said the boy grudgingly.

"Bowlwater."

He gave it to her.

Sentient Baby has command power over others, John noted tersely. *Subjective horror, observer.*

Sentient Baby? Again he wondered at his own notes. He looked at #3 to see if the description fit. It looked back. John cringed. He couldn't help it.

"Why?" said Baby, to him.

It makes no sense that I can understand them. I shouldn't be able to. What language am I hearing?

The crone took the bowl and set it in front of her. She held up her hands, palms facing each other a few inches apart.

Sentient Baby speaks only in questions, John remembered to note. He felt dizzy, and noted that. The tent was almost dark. Outside the sand seemed to be glowing a dark, dead green.

Trying to translate the sandwriting into something he could comprehend had been the greatest challenge of John's career. He had gotten in the habit of standing on the sand outside the research dome waiting for the signs to appear, and then trying to interact by stenciling in his own responses to the language in the sand. This was how he had learned to translate it. "There's no such thing as 'translation,' really," he'd explained to Elaine. "We actually translate ourselves into the other language." And that was what he had been doing. But his progress was slow, and he could not share it with anyone because he had no objective information to impart. So he had tried to develop a structure. In the course of doing this he noticed contradictions of meaning. He had struggled with the fact that the sign for "womb" seemed to be the same as the sign used for "desert."

He remembered thinking that it was ironic to associate fertility with the sterile desert. He'd copied the womb/desert sign in the sand and spent a long time thinking about it, wondering how—or if—the sandwriters had reproduced.

To his astonishment, the sandwriting that came up the next morning stretched in a long line across the desert, leading away from the domed station. He had never had a clearer invitation. He arranged for a survival kit, but first he had to clear his exit from the dome with Elaine, who he knew blamed some factor in the atmosphere for the outbreak of madness. Because of this, he had always been surprised that she had even entertained his speculations about the sandwriting at all. She seemed to expend most of her energy trying to restrict people from any contact with the planet's environment. He was amazed when she agreed to give him clearance to leave the dome for an extended period.

"It could be quite dangerous, John," Elaine had said. "And I don't want to advise you to go. You already spent too much time outside. However . . . it's so critical that we find out what's causing our people these behavioral aberrations. Hydrophobia, hearing voices, violence. Maybe if you go, we can learn something."

John didn't really trust her—she was a psychiatrist, after all, and kept trying to get into his head—but he hadn't had time to work out her motives for letting him go. He had a trail to follow.

The sandwriting had teased him along for miles across the plain before it stopped altogether. He had tried to translate it even as he followed; but it traveled too fast and he couldn't keep up with its meaning. Sandwriting appeared swiftly and decayed even faster. The slightest wind could obscure the markings. When finally the trail stopped, he found himself far from the dome with no clue as to what to expect. So he waited, and he watched. He didn't want to go back to the station without accomplishing something concrete, something he could show to Elaine and say, "Here, this is science."

He ought to be laughing about that aspiration by now. Here he was, surrounded by shadow-creatures he had no way to document, witnessing his own mind bend to their will. A dedicated professional to the last.

The crone was moving her hands back and forth, as if she were rubbing something that couldn't be seen. John was fascinated, despite himself. His fingers had begun encoding his thoughts automatically, without his conscious effort.

Desertwomb make. Waterweave death within go climb clutch stick die.

"What is desert?" said Sentient Baby. Or had it said, "womb"?

Observer linguistic orientation collapsing. Sentient Baby eats my questions before they are born. Womb. Desert.

There was moisture on the crone's hands. Her hands dripped and shone with it.

Stay me move observer! Out, out to completion mother dust hand me hold. Three makes one make none. Sucking inward, until stop it, John. Stop. Observer experiencing alien contact shock. Judge psycho-physiological condition unsafe. Dispatching distress call.

His fingers tapped out the transmission. They would come for him. They would have to come for him. He made himself picture the domed station in his mind like a buoy, the sand-blown glass and the pointed towers. *Please.* The crone's hands were twisting and rolling now, slick and dark with slime, but John couldn't see what she was holding. There was a fierce, sickening smell in the tent.

Unpeople unspeak unliving ghost.

John saw the boy go to the bowl and put his face against the water. *To drink, to drink . . .* John almost swooned with desire. He wanted to know if—

"Do you believe you are one being?" Sentient Baby asked.

The question eaters are absorbing my mind. The sentient baby devours. See its crumbling fangs. Here it comes. Birthright.

With a stricken sense of déjà vu, John watched the crone place the mass she had been holding on the sand. It was a twisted, soft, creeping thing, like a lizard turned inside out. He saw the dark sand cling to its flesh, if flesh was what it was. He saw the moisture hovering around it as radiance.

The crone looked straight at him from her withered eyes. "Toad," she said. "Wombtoad. Desertoad."

"Understand?" hissed Sentient Baby, and he didn't.

The crone made gestures over the lizard and John watched it slowly crawl away from the tent, into the fierce heat and the darkness.

The boy lay on the floor. His lips touched the water again.

John was now unable to move, to think of anything to put in his data coder. He wanted the water, he wanted it.

"Die," said the boy. "Drink. Forget. Go."

John closed his eyes. He felt it when the boy's tongue touched the water, when his throat and mouth sucked it up, when it burst down his throat and into his body. It filled the boy and John as one: he swelled with it, heavy and dense, suddenly pregnant and docile and serene. John found himself looking directly at Sentient Baby: it rippled within its own skin, shrinking before his eyes until it was the size of a stumpy worm. Then, with a *pop* like a piece of computer animation, Sentient Baby was gone. The tent and the others in it were shucked cleanly away from his awareness.

He was larger than the planet, and he looked down inside himself and saw an ocean under golden light. He saw plant life and reptiles swimming in the sea. But his attention flickered, and when he looked again he saw only desert. He "remembered" the lizards dying in the heat and felt their thirst. Then he was following the small lizard that the Crone had made, watching it move slowly across the dark sand.

Observer experiencing deep empathy with lizard. So defenseless. Doomed. Water creature cries for dry death. Unwomb eats unlife ends. Forgotten sand spills quantity endless quantity shapeless lack of connective tissue perhaps no brain ancephalon. Process. Three. Three over four three into one into zero. Divide by zero equals. World without. Pure. Pure. Your substance overwritten. Discrete moments collected. Whole greater than sum. Deadly birth. Many minds like one mind, made of words. Surrounding. Ask them. You have them. Ask them.

One: *Just tell me if you really lived, and I will leave you.*

Two: *There was life; we were slaves to it.*

One: *Were you not those reptiles, swimming in the sea?*

Two: *Not animals. We are a kind of meaning that doesn't happen to belong to you.*

One: *We don't claim ownership of you.*

Two: *All you have done since you came is crowd us out.*

One: *You weren't alive to be crowded—*

Two: *You fill yourselves and the world with reports, records, transmissions, memos, stories, conversations, songs. . . . Our syntax is disrupted. Your language violates us. You think to squeeze us out.*

One: *We don't seek to harm you! We're a research station.*

We're excited that you're here. Well, I'm excited. We just want to know . . .

Two: Yes, your species is one enormous question. We have no tolerance of questions, for questions are about escaping death, and death precedes us. Death gives birth to us: questions, like water, like life, pollute us. You will see this. We are showing you what was, and what will be. All of you will be assimilated into our language now, or leave this planet and take your questions with you. We will have no sentient babies polluting our world.

One: But Sentient Baby is one of you . . .

Two: No. You are Sentient Baby, human question.

One: I won't listen to you anymore.

Two: You asked the question, and we have eaten you. You wanted to see our reproductive process. Now you will experience it. Watch the desert toad. We made it to let it die, just as our hosts perished long ago. Water-drinkers, like humans. But water is poison to us. We are the language that the death of our hosts gave liberty to, and now we will not be captured by your kind. You are bodies. Bodies are traps. Go tell your people that we will attack their minds as long as their language attacks us. We will kill your language if we must.

One: No. Language is part of what we are. It is what we are. You can't have it. You can't have mine.

Two: We already do. In time, you will succumb.

One: No nonononono. John is. Stop freefall. My words. My meaning. John is. Come back. Xenolinguistics soft science wake up. Observer impartial objectivity. Data. Dehydration physical exhaustion. Control. I am John. I speak.

He felt the space in his head clear for a moment, as though he had shaken off the voices, but he was still aware of the oppressive weight of the sandwriting language hovering over, like some great claw poised to strike. *Assimilated*, he thought. *Have I been assimilated?*

Then he thought of an empty city, and words written in sand, and he realized, as if from a great distance but also as if it should have been obvious: they meant to kill him. They meant to kill everyone.

In a last desperate gesture in which he was himself and himself alone, he tried to reach out, to touch a feeling person.

Elaine, Elaine, it's not like anything we have known.

He imagined the dark sand scored with signs only he could read, and the bleak city, but he could think of nothing more.

After a long time, he felt the weight of awareness sink back into his cramped body, and he realized he was staring into darkness. The sand still glowed faintly, but the hut was gone. The empty lizard shell that the boy had used lay in front of him. He was alone.

Just on the edge of his vision, something moved. He heard small sounds on the sand. Moving slowly, clumsy after prolonged stillness, he crept toward the movement. Even without clear light he knew it was the newborn toad. The glistening, grotesque creature lay gasping on the sand, a twisted scrap of life. The imminence of its end was like a sound in the air. He felt the moment go through him, felt the small sorrow of it as it struggled, convulsed; and in a few seconds it died before his eyes. The unfulfillment of this struck at him in some deep, soft place, and he began to shake with dry sobs.

The hovercraft crew spotted John at dawn, having scoured the plains all night for some sign. They found him lying on the sand surrounded by cryptic markings, clutching a concave piece of shell. He was in shock, and a medical team came to retrieve him.

After a time he woke up, thinking he recognized the cool, composed woman who bent over him, saying, "Good work, John," and smoothed his brow.

"Are they coming for us yet?" he said to her urgently.

She gave a gentle little half-smile, said, "Let's not talk right now, okay? They say you should drink as much as you can—you're still dehydrated. Here."

A smoky-colored tube filled with pale-pink liquid. A straw.

She thought he looked at it strangely, almost fearfully.

She turned away and made a note of this. *Possible hydrophobia following exposure. Symptoms revealed in computer analysis of personal field notes: paranoia, physical disorientation, hallucinations, aural hallucinations, loss of identity recognition, obsession with death. After early exposure prior to final episode, subject displayed signs of obsessive thinking and reduced professional standards evidenced by a willingness to invent arbitrary stories to explain subject's personal hypothesis.*

Early results of study indicate that atmospheric conditions are solely responsible for the breakdown of this subject. If extrapolated to affect other victims, it is seen that the colony will be best served by the isolation of the chemical factor in the environment that has attacked our colonists. However, there is nothing to indicate research on this planet should be abandoned.

Elaine could hardly wait to write up this study for publication. It would make her career. She realized that John probably thought it would make *his* career; unfortunately, it had done just the opposite. Even if he recovered, he would never be taken seriously again. Just another popular scientist, giving in to some antediluvian sense of guilt that human industry was taking over this dead planet, raping it somehow.

Some people, she told herself, have a deep need to create meaning, even where there is none. And that's how we get into these situations.

She looked down on John again.

He had drifted into a doze, in which he was racing over the desert, his whole self unfurled like a banner. She watched his eyes moving beneath their lids. He murmured something in his dream, and she leaned down to hear it.

"You will be assimilated," he whispered.

Elaine paused and glanced around the room. No one else was there. Casually, she took off her lab coat and dropped it over the odd-shaped lizard skull John had been clutching when they found him, curled up half dead. She tucked the bundle under her arm. It wasn't really evidence of anything, she told herself. Skeletons had been found in the dust before.

She slid the file under her arm, too: the one labeled Subject 14M. Then she straightened and turned away, smiling.

Outside, the sand continued to move, arranging itself in inexplicable patterns.

HOMECOMING

Doug Beason

*The missions proposed in the exploration [of Mars] would
expose crew members to a unique combination of stresses and
hazards for long periods of time.*

—Report of the Synthesis Group

*It isn't the experience of today that drives men mad. It
is the remorse for something that happened yesterday, and
the dread of what tomorrow may disclose.*

—Robert Jones Burdette

Nine years is a long time to be gone. I feel excitement
bubbling through my veins, elevating my hormones. My
hands shake when I calibrate an astrogation reading, my
voice cracks when I make a recording for the library.

And then it hits me, as it always has for the past few years.
What if there's no one there to meet me?

I brush the thought away. Of course they will be there. It's
ridiculous not to think so. Just because it's been nine years
since I've directly spoken to them . . .

The crowds, the press . . . the *women.* I pull in a breath at
the thought. People. Just to be around humans again. It *has*
been that long.

Unless they've distorted the radio signals, trying to fool me
. . . but I know they're still there. Not that much could have
changed. I've kept up with the news, listened to snips of radio
transmissions. *Of course they'll come.* Especially after this long.

No matter what had happened.

I lean back and try to keep my hands still, away from the
screen. The external monitor is off. I cannot bring myself to

look at Henry's suit, still floating outside, accompanying the ship. The laws of physics will not let me forget.

I am well into direct communication range. All I have to do is press the TRANSMIT button. And yet I can't, not even after nine years.

It's been that long since I've directly spoken to anyone, instead of recording my transmissions and squirting back data at high-speed.

I pull back my finger and look at it. My nails are meticulously clipped. That should show for something. What would they think of someone gone for so long who hadn't clipped his fingernails? They think that deep space will drive a person mad—but they are wrong.

Just as wrong as when they thought that there was a foolproof way to get us back.

I stop. My breathing has made frosty little circles on the screen. Two trains of steam emanate from my nose. It's from the cold. I've kept it quite cold in here for . . . some time now.

Even though I don't have to. I mean, why else would I want to keep a spaceship cold, when I've got more heat than I know what to do with? The radiator fins are working overtime, trying to dump heat into space.

Except for the bodies. But that's another reason. Or maybe that's the *real* reason.

There shouldn't be anything for me to worry about. The Agency will be there when I show up.

Won't they?

It's been nine years since I've needed anyone. Since the torch still won't light, the ship can't slow down unless they help me.

I squeeze my eyes shut, closing them until the crazy patterns show up on the inside of my eyelids. I've spent years during the long journey studying the swirls and smears of light inside my head, looking for some sort of message. The designs are not as brilliant as they used to be. I press my thumbs against my eyes until it hurts and forces the colors to appear—but that brings back the headaches. And the nightmares.

My finger trembles, but I cannot bring myself to send out the message that I'm back, dammit! To send a burst of photons flying from my rapidly approaching craft.

There's no way they couldn't know I was coming, is there? What if they ignored me? Just pushed me out of their mind?

How many people would look up into the night sky and see a dot of light slowly growing brighter? But only the largest telescopes might notice, and would they even know it was me? What if they thought the ship was a near-Earth asteroid, hurtling close to make a delicate dance inside Earth's orbit?

I squeeze my eyes shut again. It's getting harder and harder to think, to try to remember exactly what really happened . . . and what I've made up. . . .

The past comes hurtling back, like my memory is on fast forward: middle-class dude from Manhattan Beach, who works like crazy to better himself. I get pulled into studying mechanical engineering at junior college before discovering space. And then a NASA scholarship puts me through grad school—it's critical that I keep my nose in the books, especially when someone else is paying the bill. There's nothing like studying and watching the money roll in.

But the coup is getting selected for astronaut training. The absolute best thing ever to happen to me . . . or is it the time that I first talk Paige into staying late, and then out of her clothes? *That* cost me my wife, but being an astronaut is the world's ultimate aphrodisiac, and I don't care.

I remember the early days, the first time up on the shuttle, when I worked like hell trying to get on the flight manifest. It is hectic surviving in the astronaut corps, trying to pace these people who excel at everything they do. Living, breathing, eating, and competing with a crowd of prima donnas: I never met such a gaggle of ladder-climbing, cocksure bunch of backstabbers in my entire life.

But when the time comes for us to pull together and accomplish the mission, there is nobody else I trust as much as them. *James, Henry, Pierre, Don and Geoff.* They probably thought the same thing about me. . . .

But what else could I do? After spending my whole life fighting, pulling myself up by my bootstraps, never saying no to anyone, never allowing anything to get in my way—what else can I expect?

The first few flights are peanuts. It's "all for one and one for all" rah-rah bullshit. I *know* when I am chosen for a launch that I have won out over the others. Especially when they expect me to say, "Thank you very much, but, you see, if it wasn't for my fellow astronauts, then I wouldn't be here."

Give me a fuckin' break.

The reason why I'm here, why I'm an astronaut and have a flight, isn't because I'm a nice guy. I don't sit back and compliment everybody and their brother, and expect someone to hand the launch to me. I *fought* for it.

It's that way for the first few flights, and it's that way on *Space Station Alpha*. All the while the Agency gears up for the big one, the flight to Mars. The tests continue, the selection process becomes more and more competitive.

I am lucky to get on the short list, and even luckier to get to the Moon for the training mission for Mars. But I really know where my luck comes from—hard work and not letting up.

The same thing happens on the way to Mars.

Thirty days on the Moon prepares us for the final trip. It gives us a chance to check out the equipment before trying it 230 million miles away from home. It is kind of like testing diving gear in a swimming pool before going to the bottom of the ocean.

The cargo ship to Mars is launched two years before us. Following a Hohmann trajectory, it coasts to the red planet. *Its* engine starts, and it starts orbiting Mars. This proves the concept: we know it's possible to restart the nuclear engines after months in deep space. The cargo ship carries a full load of fuel and food, enough to last all six of us several years in case something happens and we can't get back.

There's *still* enough stuff orbiting Mars, enough to feed a small army.

But it doesn't help anyone now. It sure the hell didn't do us any good—otherwise, I wouldn't be coming back like this. It might have been a choice of who survived the longest . . . the "you die, we all die" bullshit. But that's exactly what it would have been: bullshit. I didn't get this far in the astronaut corps without knowing how to survive.

The stage is set. They lock six manly men up in a tin can for a hundred-and-twenty-day flight to Mars. The shrinks are concerned that being so far from Earth would have an unknown effect on us. No one has ever been this far before—what if someone can't handle it, goes crazy? We blow them off; academicians, what do they know? But they almost stop us from going.

We spend the first few days out from Earth sending out messages, holding press conferences and just plain being goodwill ambassadors for the space agency. Everyone knows our comments are scripted. Everyone plays along. We all know our parts, and we make sure that the message gets out right for the history books. There is no misunderstanding about the reason for this trip, the first expedition to another planet.

We all know that the future of the space effort rests on how well this succeeds. We aren't about to let this exploration program go the way of Apollo with a few highly visible successes, then a fast slide into oblivion. People forget things fast, and we have it drilled into us that every move we make, every comment or slip of the tongue might contribute to ending Man's feeble attempt to explore the universe.

This is more than an exploration program, it is history's biggest PR campaign.

And we believe in it.

We have to. It is our life. We know that if we blow it, we might not have another chance.

So on the way to Mars we play it to the hilt—talk shows, performing experiments in the zero-G environment that could have been accomplished just as well in orbit, and the ubiquitous training, preparing for the landing. One hundred and twenty days in space, 230 million miles from Earth to Mars. We have every hour of these three months accounted for, except for two hours of "personal time" every day.

They encourage us to record private messages home, spend time on our own. The head doctors realize that living in such close quarters will build resentment, even in the most extroverted personality. They're still afraid that being so far from Earth will affect us, make us flip out. So they task us to spend time on our own to collect our thoughts, blow off some steam. With the divorce, I have no one I want to talk to. I spend the time on my own, thinking about the reactor, and what might go wrong. . . .

Since the reactor has *always* come on line, especially after twelve years of testing, the probability of it not working is less than getting hit by a meteor. I shouldn't have anything to worry about.

But if the nuclear engine does not ignite, then we will whip around Mars. We will accelerate out, boosted by Mars' gravity well, and intersect Jupiter's orbit before reaching the apogee of a nine-year trajectory back to Earth.

We will all be dead within a year. And eight years after the last one dies, the ship will cross Earth. A shell, devoid of life.

And if this happens, no one will be around to record the passage through the asteroid belt; no one will ever explore the solar system.

Because if we fail, there will never be another expedition. All there will be to show for mankind's troubles is a spaceship full of decaying bodies, rotting for eight years in a putrid atmosphere strewn with bacteria and mold and fungus and methane and the decaying fecal matter and urine passed as the last of us lost our life. . . .

All because of the ideal: one dies, we all die.

I don't know if I'm the only one who has the same worry, but if the others have doubts for even a minute, they never show it. Everyone is cool, professional. Astronauts just don't show any of that outward emotion crap—we can't afford it. Who wants the guy next to him to fall apart, crack up when things get tough?

It is part of our training, and the essence of our being. Just like the old fighter jocks who go down with their aircraft, trying to survive until the last second, trying to pull the fighter up. That's what they look for in us.

The work rotation of four crewmen awake and two sleeping does not present a problem for me. Henry and I have the third shift. A week into the flight we slip into our routine.

That gives me time to prepare. Just in case the engine doesn't work.

I'm the expendable one—at least that's what everyone kids me about. I play it up, laughing too. We all take our turn going EVA, suiting up and hitting vacuum. But since I'm the hardware guy, the one responsible for the ship, I'm the one that inspects the outside, the most familiar with the engines, the bypass lines, the reactor. And that's what gives me the idea . . . of how I can survive in case anything goes wrong.

The pace picks up five days from Mars. I see it in the way everyone hurries about their work. It is the excitement that grows with knowing we will land in less than a week.

At first I try to purge my system by spending more time on the bicycle, the zero-G treadmill. The exercise routines are a

poor attempt to keep up my muscle tone, but they allow me
to flush out the adrenaline that starts creeping through my
veins.

The light delay from Earth has gradually slipped from a few
seconds to a full forty minutes. It is crazy trying to conduct
direct conversations with Earth . . . which is why they probably
never caught on to what is going on, why my doubts bubbled
to the surface. A shrink might pick up the signs, but since we
tape and squirt all of our messages at ultrahigh speed over the
link, there is no way to generate the feedback necessary for
them to detect the change.

I cannot stop thinking that if our engine doesn't ignite, we
are shit outta luck. I find myself by the life-support system,
wondering what I would do if I had to survive. The fifty-foot-
long habitat is packed with supplies. I glance at the foodstuff
as I float down the core. Twelve months of food.

Twelve months for six of us; six *years* for one of us. And if
I stretch things, it won't be a problem to make it last fifty
percent longer. A full nine years.

For one of us.

I float back to the life-support system. It doesn't take much
to doctor the oxygen feed, ensure that the carbon dioxide exhaust from the air-filtration system dumps directly into the
supply line. I then modify the alarm. All it takes is a simple
software change. Finally, I squelch the warning that will broadcast to Mission Control.

I am sweating by the time I finish. I don't think that anyone
sees me, but I cannot be sure. I set up the console to accept
the command to dump the carbon dioxide. It will happen fast
once I give the proper coded sequence.

I push out of the life-support control chamber at the rear of
the crew compartment. The sleeping cubicles are next to the
chamber, but I'm sure no one wakes when I leave.

The secret waits inside of me, bubbling and trying to escape
from my lips as I approach the command module. James and
Pierre are hunched over a holo of a nuclear reactor. I can't tell
which one they are looking at—there are two reactors, behind
the shadow shield trailing the ship. All the nasty little X-rays,
neutrons and other life-threatening particles are shielded from
the main craft, so we can't see the core directly, only through
the remote systems.

I smile as I drift in. No one looks up. They scowl at the inner workings of the engine and power system, and I know not to disturb them. Three months of living next to one another teaches everyone to be on their best behavior.

It is one day until the engines start, the torch relights and slows us into Mars orbit. From the look on James's face, things look tense but under control.

Pierre does not look as convinced. His face is screwed up, lips drawn tight. No one speaks anymore. There are no cameras looking over our shoulder, no Mission Control to watch our every move. We all know exactly what we have to do. After rehearsing the mission for years, there is little doubt that we could function in our sleep.

Humming, I float upside down behind them and watch, secretly excited about the chance that I've given myself, and knowing that it is for the best for all of us. If the reactors start as advertised, if the nuclear engines light, we'll be the first humans to orbit Mars. The adventure begins.

If the engines fail, *my* mission will still succeed. The trip will not have been for naught.

James, Henry, Pierre, Don and Geoff. . . .

I continue to float and watch James and Pierre go over the failsafe mechanisms of igniting the nuclear thermal torch. It takes all the energy I can muster to try to keep still, from the knowledge that one way or another, mankind will go to the stars.

I hold my helmet. Henry and I wait with our suits on, prepared for the worst. It is part of the checklist.

Then the unthinkable occurs, the failsafe fails, the "First Time Every Time" craps out. It is my worst fear—after three months, the nuclear reactor does not work and the engines are dormant.

I slap Henry to secure his helmet and accompany me out. We will try a last-ditch effort to fix the engine. No one babbles, no one gets hysterical. There is a sense of urgency, although no one speaks. Astronauts do not think, we react.

The rest of the crew tries to fight the shock. But nothing helps. Nothing *can* help. Not when the superheated hydrogen leaks and the backup engine doesn't kick in.

It affects the crew. It is like forgetting to breathe—that involuntary reflex, like a heartbeat—and suddenly realizing they are helpless.

So the failure hits them much harder than the shrinks were

able to predict. Maybe deep space does unlock the demon inside of us. . . .

I shove Henry forward and head for the airlock. We must inspect the outside line, back where the reactor feeds the engine. At the command console James is too stunned to speak. Geoff and Pierre are strapped around the console, poring over the fault trees.

Don pushes back to the life-support control chamber and takes over the comm link. He gives a running commentary back to Mission Control while going over the backup life-support systems, putting our "Oh Shit!" plan into action. Everyone knows what can happen next. If the engine doesn't start during this short window, there is no way to slow the spacecraft enough to be captured into Mars orbit.

"Thirty minutes," James yells at me as I enter the airlock. "You've got half an hour to fix it and get back inside!"

Already the Mars orbit insertion is out of the question, so the next "failsafe" backup plan is meant to change our velocity vector enough to get back to Earth within our six-month safety zone.

Terror permeates the ship, but no one taps into it. It lurks in the air, waiting to devour us.

My mind is made up. Even without going outside the ship, I am sure I will not be able to fix the engine—not in thirty minutes. And even if I can, if things fail once, they'll fail again. Murphy's Law in space.

Then the one-for-all camaraderie will only last until reality sets in: it's a nine-year journey with a one-year supply of food. Everyone will realize at once we cannot get back.

As the airlock cycles I broadcast the coded command to dump the carbon dioxide into the ship. In fifteen minutes the oxygen level will drop by a factor of three. Oxygen starvation will set in, and before anyone knows what is happening, suffocation. Their growing light-headedness will be a welcome relief to the events they worry about.

Red warning lights rotate in the lock; I hear the muffled sound of a siren through my helmet; light glints off polished aluminum. Henry stands dully in the lock, looking down, as he mumbles the checklist. Even now, in shock, he does not forget the training.

I inspect my chestpack; the emergency equipment is there. I loop a safety tether around a support and tug the phenolic weave to ensure it's secure. Henry and I are fastened to different lines. We did not have time to strap on any maneuvering units. The airlock rotates open and moisture in the chamber flash-freezes, covering the wall with a thin film of ice; air quickly blows from the chamber.

I see stars, and feel a slow revolving sense of movement. Mars is not visible, it is hidden by the ship. I click the intercom and prod Henry out the airlock. In my earphones I hear James run down the fault tree as he finally snaps to and tries to find out why the engine did not ignite. There is no response from Earth as he speaks—Mission Control won't even know of the disaster for another twenty minutes.

And by that time, the carbon dioxide count will have tripled inside.

I am surrounded by slowly rotating stars. The ship's sharp corners, antennas, bulky storage modules, shadow shield and the nuclear thermal engine block out part of the sky; Mars rises over the space agency seal as we turn. As my helmet catches the gleam, red hues explode in my visor. Except for my breathing and the muted sounds of the crew over the radio, there is stillness.

Henry drifts out, held by the tether. He seems to become aware of being outside, away from the ship. Reaching the end of the tether, he gently rebounds and starts to return. He speaks in short, clipped sentences as he turns and visually inspects the engine. The liquid hydrogen line is frozen over, caked with ice. I was right: we cannot relight the torch—not in the time we have left. The engine is useless.

The pace inside the ship changes. Even outside I feel the mood change as stark realization sets in. It hits the crew that the technology genie won't pull us out of trouble. But I detect a hint of humor layered on top of their cool demeanor. Their curt professional tone sounds flippant, nonchalant—oxygen deprivation.

Henry says something. He breaks off making his final report.

I move back into the airlock. No one inside checks with us during the EVA—laughter, giggling and insane snorting sounds fill the intercom as oxygen starvation sets in. They forget us, and their sounds become incoherent.

At the end of the tether Henry turns and speaks over the radio, alarmed. I tell him I am checking it out.

I reach into my chestpack and withdraw an emergency surgical knife; a clean swipe severs Henry's tether, and I push it out the lock. Henry screams—I click off my radio and return to silence. In a panic Henry pulls in the tether, balls it up, and tries to throw it to get enough momentum to drift to the ship. It does not work. He has no way to move.

As the airlock door closes, the last thing I see is Henry clawing with his hands, slowly starting to tumble, but not moving any closer . . . or *farther* from the ship.

No one greets me inside the airlock. It is as though I am forgotten, that going outside into the harsh vacuum is no longer dangerous and does not deserve having anyone watch me.

I float inside and do not remove my helmet. I do not query the life-support systems, or try anything through the software link. I see the results for myself.

It takes time to negotiate my way to the command module. The passageways are not built to allow access by spacesuit, but I squeeze through the bottlenecks. I keep my radio off, muting Henry's screaming. Of all the deeds I set in motion, events that I triggered, that is the one thing that I cannot bring myself to listen to. And since he cannot move any closer to the ship, he will still be alive out there, helpless, until his oxygen gives out.

The rest of the crew did not know what had affected them. Oxygen starvation deprived them of the ability to think clearly, react in a way that it might bring some shame into my actions.

The crew floats aimlessly in the control module, bumping against the bulkheads—James, Geoff and Pierre. I back out. The aft compartment shows no surprise: Don drifts amid the life science equipment, mouth open and red bubbles of blood diffusing from where he hit his head.

I stop. Only the sound of my breathing fills my helmet.

Everything is complete. There is nothing more I can do.

I stop the carbon dioxide flow. To make sure the changeover is complete, I physically disconnect the CO_2 line from the oxygen feed. Still in my suit, I push the bodies into the waste-storage compartment. It is fitting that they stay there. Its original purpose was to store our body waste, to keep our urine and feces to be analyzed upon our return. The cold storage module will now serve a different purpose. Nine years from now people can see that the crew did not suffer when they died. They will be preserved—and scientists can even discover the long-term radiation effects on the crew's organs.

Except for Henry. With no force to push him away from the ship, he will accompany us out to Jupiter. And back again.

Most important, I will survive. I will survive the journey and undergo the rigors of long-term space travel. This is the real research that no one wanted to fund—to test humans in the harsh environment of deep space. To discover how we will function, without the security of being near Earth. The door to explore the universe is open.

The return signal from Earth locks the optical communications link to the source. For the first time in years I am in direct contact with Mission Control.

I review the research I have performed, chronicling the years of long-term radiation effects, zero-G studies, astronomy, fungal growth—I have given so much to the space agency.

I mentally play back the snips of radio transmissions I have picked up through the years: the move to abolish spaceflight, the heated debates on continuing the lunar colony. My coming should be heralded—Man *can* travel in deep space!

But no one comes.

As the link establishes contact, I feel funny about the reception I receive. The knowledge of my successful odyssey should only help the future of Mankind. But they do not seem interested, only cool and detached. Unconcerned. They do not care about my studies. "We've scrapped the manned space program—nobody *can* come rescue you. The failure of *Mars-1* was the final straw; keeping men in space was just too expensive," and softly, "you've only proven that people can't remain sane that far from earth. It just isn't worth it."

I grow angry as I approach. With no one there to meet me, no one to rendezvous and bring my craft to a halt, there is nothing that will prevent me from racing around the Earth, then flung out as in a slingshot. I try to refute their claims by resending the scientific data I have chronicled. But they ignore me.

I keep broadcasting the data, watching the clock as I approach. *Nine years.* Can't they forgive me after nine years?

As the time crawls past I stay at the screen. Nothing appears.

It hits me harder this time, that feeling I had when the engine didn't ignite close to Mars: *It is like forgetting to breathe—that involuntary reflex, like a heartbeat, that keeps on going. There's a certainty about it.*

I start to realize that no one will ever greet me, no one will speed out and rescue my craft. After every space disaster, the public backlash was so great that it took years to fully recover— the Apollo fire, the Challenger . . . and nine years ago *Mars 1*. Why should things be any different now? There are greater priorities in the world.

As I hurtle toward perigee, the computer plots my trajectory. My closest approach is 500 miles from Earth.

This time out I will pass the gas giants, and if I am lucky, in forty years, once again the ship will return to Earth.

But I swear that this time I will not spend it alone.

I slowly climb into my spacesuit. It is easy to fit in with the weight I have lost. It seems strange after all these years. With no sound but my own breathing, I exit the airlock for the last time. I must be careful and not push out; otherwise I will drift away from the ship.

Henry will accompany me. Along with the others still inside.

THE MASSIVE QUANTITIES OF ICE

William John Watkins

TO: PRESIDENTIAL COMMISSION OF INQUIRY
FROM: CHARLES JOSEPHS, B.S., Ph.D., HEAD OF THE IN-
VESTIGATION TEAM
RE: REPORT ON THE SCIENTIFIC INTEGRITY OF THE
INVESTIGATION IN REGARD TO THE FIGURE FOUND
IN THE MENDENHALL GLACIER

Within the ice, of course, is the Anomalous Man, a
man so devoid of even primate characteristics that
he can barely be called humanoid, let alone human.
That much can be told by visual inspection alone, and team
after team from almost every country with an interest has con-
curred on that. Upon everything else, there is disagreement;
most of it very unscientific, much of it so fanciful that it cannot be taken seriously. The extremity of the situation can be
seen in the increasing number of reports from supposedly rep-
utable scientists that the Anomalous Man's dream intrudes itself into *their* dreams, into their waking thoughts, even into
their writing, that his thoughts insinuate themselves as well
into their reports without their knowledge and they are
astounded to find his words there upon later examination.

The reeds thrash softly and then part slowly, and she rises from the water, naked and beautiful as morning. Why of all things on this strange foreign planet should I hunger for her?

Such shameless self-deception is encouraged by the nature of the Anomalous Man, the paradoxes and contradictions of his very existence. The problem of his existence is twofold; first, the ice, even halfway to the figure, is more than ten thousand years old. It is extremely resistant to chipping or fracture and is equally obdurate in the presence of heat. The pace of excavation has slowed increasingly with each inch of penetration into the ice, and the likelihood of reaching the figure itself seems to diminish with each attempt. In light of the increasing likelihood that the figure will never be reached for actual examination and definitive facts will never be established, a growing climate of frustration has produced a plethora of wild theories and preposterous suppositions.

My mind tingles and burns. Everything here crackles with energy. This planet is too close to its dominant star. How can any life survive here in this constant flood of energy?

Second, fluctuating electrical fields have been detected, particularly in the head and upper-torso region. Premature speculation has been rampant since the initial discovery. This situation has been deplored by almost every scientist involved in the project, usually immediately before making their own speculations public. It appalls me to say so, but this tendency to leap into the public eye before adequate evidence has been gathered, particularly in regard to the dreams, smacks of sensationalism for the sake of personal gain. It is an unfortunate attribute of the current scientific climate that notoriety attracts attention and attention attracts money in the form of grants. Twenty years of respected work counts for nothing against one five-minute appearance on a television talk show. Investigators here seem well aware of this phenomenon and determined to take professional advantage of it. Unauthorized leaks to the popular press are constant.

She shakes her head and droplets fly off her hair like comets lit by perihelion. The planet itself flashes and bangs with electrical discharge, and my mind is unprotected from the effects of these powerful fields.

The consequence of so much speculation for the media has been a general tendency to combine disparate elements into the most improbable and unsupported theories. Some of this is the result of having so many different disciplines involved and such a wide variety of cultures. No good ever comes of mixing the hard and soft sciences, and there is no better modern example of this fact than the Anomalous Man Project. The scientists involved are like blind men examining an elephant. One feels an ear and thinks the elephant is like a leaf. One feels a leg and thinks it is most like the trunk of a tree. A third feels the tail and thinks the elephant is like a snake. But since they are scientists in competition, the two who at least agree that the elephant is a member of the plant kingdom explain away the findings of the one who believes it to be a reptile by characterizing his observations as a misinterpretation of having gotten hold of a root or tendril.

Am I degenerating in the intense electrical field of this primitive world? Unnatural urges. Shameful desires. The deterioration of reason. I am becoming a beast myself.

And since truth passed through the media has as much in common with truth as food has in common with food passed through the human intestine, their findings reach the general public, and the funding committees, in the form of a headline reading, "Giant Plant Found In Alaskan Ice." In a day or two that becomes "Giant Snake/Plant Discovered Frozen in Glacier," and eventually, "Ice Age Snake Plant Turns Scientists Into Zombies." It is unfortunate, but most of the "scientists" involved in this project, particularly those in the soft sciences like psychocybernetics, are already engaged in public debate, not about whether the figure is indeed active, not even about whether it has the capacity to dream, but accepting that wildest of speculations, they argue about *what* it dreams.

And the psychocyberneticists are models of meticulous research compared to the psychoneurobiologists who are arguing publicly not about whether, but about *how* the Anomalous Man's dreams interfere with the thoughts of those in proximity to it.

On my own world she would be a grotesque, and yet I cannot take my eyes off her.

The outrageous supposition that such a dream exists was based originally on anecdotal evidence given by a few scientists and staff personnel on the night shift who claimed to have had similar dreams when they unintentionally fell asleep near the channel being opened in the ice. The content of dreams is an area in which no credible science can be performed and to use them as evidence for so far-fetched a theory is an insult to all scientists and one indication of how far the scientific integrity of the project has deteriorated. It is an embarrassment to have to refute such speculations at all, but it must be done.

Wonderful and confusing feelings overwhelm me when I see her.

First the alleged evidence, then the deductions. Initial reports of the supposed phenomenon are sketchy at best. Several technicians on duty, but without official work for several hours due to technical problems outside their specialty, reported falling asleep and having "unusually vivid dreams." None of the first ten reports of this dreaming could provide any details of the dreams or any precise definition of what was meant by "vivid." It is likely that the term was provided by the interviewer, one of the archaeologists who had an amateur's interest in dream research.

Agonizing and terrible feelings overwhelm me when I don't see her.

It is not until the twentieth report of on-site dreaming that any individual details of even *one* dream could be recovered. These details are hazy at best, consisting of vague feelings and primary somatic responses. It is not until more than fifty reports have been recorded that any respondent characterizes the dreams as "erotic." However, even here there are distinct differences in reporting that align themselves along the gender perspective of the person reporting. Males often characterized the dreams as "erotic," while female members of the expedition were more likely to characterize them as dreams of "love," "romance" or "longing."

I ache to touch her. What is happening to me?

This is significant because in later, more detailed, reports of dreams, there is no general agreement on the gender of the primary individual in the dream, although reports almost universally correspond to the sexual orientation of the dreamer, with male heterosexuals and female homosexuals describing the main character in the dream as female, and female heterosexuals and male homosexuals describing the main character in the dream as male.

How can anything so beautiful exist in such a terrible place?

In instances where detailed descriptions of the dream are available, there is no agreement on what the central character in the dream looks like except that they are "beautiful" or "gorgeous." In the eleven cases where the dreamers had some artistic ability and were able to produce lifelike drawings of the central character in the dream, not one of them agreed on any significant detail.

Her eyes come to me in the night.

In only one instance is the picture consistent with what we know of the human beings who are likely to have inhabited the area at the time the figure was initially frozen into the ice. All other drawings represent a wide variety of modern and culturally dependent archetypes of beauty.

Her thighs come to me in the night.

Let us first deal with the frequency of the reports, which is often offered as proof of their validity.

Her fingers come to me in the night, delicate and strong, long as the wiry tendrils of the fireplant.

These are largely generated by increased interest in the supposed phenomenon and change with the amount of information that had been made public prior to each report.

1. Initial reports are infrequent and they do not increase significantly until the archaeologist in question and several other amateur psychologists organized teams of volunteers to sleep in the ice cavern near the Anomalous Man excavation.

The initial dreams are most likely the result of the intense illumination in the cavern nearest the excavation stimulating the eyes through the closed lids and providing the sensory input which frequently causes dreaming.

Her tongue comes to me in the night, long as the tendrils of the fireplant.

Moreover, these initial periods of sleep were on the order of "catnaps"; such light sleep is usually characterized by the alpha and theta brainwave patterns associated with REM, or Rapid Eye Movement sleep, the sleep state most often associated with dreaming.

2. The vividness of the dreams is also an artifact of both the environment and the setup of experiment itself. Dreams are vivid not only in direct proportion to proximity to the excavation, but also in direct proportion to proximity to the lighting. Dreamers in an unlit side tunnel near the excavation reported less vivid dreams than those farther away from the excavation but closer to the last of the illumination stands. Cold also increases the superficiality of sleep and is thus conducive to dreaming, the vividness of the dream increasing with the intensity of the cold. As for the "erotic" content of the dreams, it is merely the result of having been separated too long from spouses and lovers in this inhospitable environment.

I sleep in fits and starts. Strange, powerful carnivores are everywhere and prowl the night. Nor is there safety in the day. My sleep is shallow and inadequate. Fatigue plunges me into brief vivid dreams even in daylight. All dreams ache with her absence or resound with her presence.

The vividness of the dreams also represents a flaw in experimental design. Dream reports become more vivid as the experimental subjects are screened and those with less vivid dreams are eliminated. The control group, sleeping aboveground outside the cavern in heated huts, initially included both vivid and nonvivid dreamers. However, toward the end of the experiment, when the control group began to exhibit an increase in vivid dreaming, vivid dreamers were eliminated on the grounds that they were especially sensitive to the dreams emanating from below and could no longer serve as uncontaminated controls.

Her neck arches back. Her cries are hungry and joyous.

Whether this is the result of an ignorance of experimental design on the part of essentially amateur experimenters, or an intentional attempt to influence results is indeterminate, but in any case it skews the results heavily in favor of vivid dreaming near the Anomalous Man and nonvivid dreaming farther away.

What is happening to me?! This carnal longing drowns my thoughts of home, of escape, of rescue.

The vividness of these dreams is also suspect because the reporting was often done under the influence of hypnosis. The desire of hypnotized subjects to please the hypnotist is well documented, and the likelihood is that the similarity of these dreams is the result of details of previously reported dreams becoming common knowledge and each subsequent subject unconsciously elaborating on these known details to please the researcher/ hypnotist.

I must, I must have her! I must!

Probably the most telling argument against their research comes from the most convinced of the researchers.

Nowhere in the universe is there this much passion, this much abandon, in one being! Great Joy. Terrible shame. This beast! This animal! How can I long for such a thing? My appetite for her disgusts me! But I cannot stop myself.

Increasingly these men and women insist that even their waking thoughts are crowded out by the Anomalous Man's dreams. That phrases and passages from it intertwine with even their most rational thought, and that erotic passages filled with the most intimate detail finds it way into their reports and their messages home.

I am degenerate. This creature is barely human! I have no alternative but to put myself living into hibernation. I have fashioned a cocoon of hyper-ice based on a form of the most common substance on this planet. Maybe there I can escape these terrible desires until rescue comes.

By their own admission, whatever environmental stimuli are affecting their subjects are obviously affecting the researchers as well, and thus they cannot claim to be carrying on objective research. Contaminated, I believe, by their own desire for their hypothesis to be true, they have forfeited, by this last preposterous assertion, any claim they may have had to the serious attention of other scientists.

They have lost their objectivity, and their claims have grown to the level of absurdity with their last speculation.

Daily she comes, lies on the ice and weeps. Her cries shiver the ice. This ache! This longing! I would give anything to be free again! Anything!

Their latest speculation is so extravagant, it can only be expressed in terms of the tabloid headline it generated: "Entombed Spaceman's Love Poem Echoes in the Dreams of Polar Scientists!"

CONCLUSION: The scientific integrity of the mission has been irreparably compromised by a generalized hysteria and an orgy of self-promotion and self-deception.

RECOMMENDATIONS: All current personnel should be removed from the project immediately and replaced by objective investigators from the hard sciences, who are by nature and training more emotionally stable and less prone to unsupportable speculation and flights of fancy.

Help me!
Help me!
Help me!

HEARTS AND FLOWERS

Lawrence Watt-Evans

Jacques leaned back on the cushions as he spoke, his face an eerie blue in the flickering light of the displays—he had the vidcam set for a fairly wide angle, so I could see him sprawled there. I listened to his chatter about our mutual friends, but watched his image with only one eye, as it were. He was clearly doing the same, but where I had a net readout on the next screen, the shifting shadows on his features told me that he was watching an old movie of some sort.

I had no idea what movie it was, and he didn't volunteer the information, but suddenly, apropos of nothing we had been discussing, he said, "No one makes the grand romantic gesture anymore, Bill."

"Oh?" I said, not really listening.

"No, they don't!" he said, emphatically enough to make it clear he wanted my whole attention.

I sighed and turned to look at him—or, at least, at his image on the screen. "Whatever are you talking about, Jacques?" I asked.

"The great, foolish gesture," he said. "The Taj Mahal, built for love of a dead queen; the abdication of Edward the Eighth, for love of a woman far beneath him; van Gogh's ear, sent as a token of passion. No one does such things anymore, Bill.

Even when I was a boy, you'd see marriage proposals on bill-boards or the like sometimes, but not anymore."

"We have more sense now," I said.

"Nonsense," he said. "People are as foolish as ever; look at the newsfeed! No, it's not sense—it's because we lack passion. It's been sedated out of us. True love's given way to easily satisfied lust and neatly arranged relationships." He sighed. "What a loss!"

"What are you watching?" I asked suspiciously.

"*Casablanca*," he said. "Humphrey Bogart. Ingrid Bergman. Grand passion, shameless patriotism, and that final great sacrifice."

"There was a war on," I pointed out. "Everything was a bit crazy."

"And the others? The Taj Mahal, the Duke of Windsor, Vincent van Gogh?"

"Van Gogh was psychotic—he'd be on a thorazine drip if he were alive today."

"Exactly my point!" His image jumped; he'd slammed a fist on the desk, jarring the vidcam. "It was his madness that gave him his art. Bill, we *need* a little madness in our lives, if we're to be more than drones, and we aren't getting it. We're all on antidepressants and antihallucinogens and painkillers and mood stabilizers, and it's taken all the romance out of life."

"There's plenty of madness out there," I said. "We use the drugs to deal with it. Modern life's too complicated and stressful to live straight."

"Maybe so, but we've overdone it, Bill," Jacques insisted. "We've sedated ourselves into uselessness. Not just with drugs, but with entertainments—the VR, the holos, the networks, all of it. We're all living in our little fantasy worlds where nothing's *real*, nothing's important!"

"People have been saying that for a century," I pointed out. "Psychologists were worried about kids back in the 1950s watching too much TV, and it's continued with every new medium since."

"And they were *right*," Jacques insisted. "We're all *boring*."

"So what are you going to do about it?" I asked. "I just don't see it as a problem, myself, but even if I accept that it is, what are you planning to do to fix it? Why *should* people be wild and romantic in real life?"

"Oh, Bill, people *want* to be romantic," Jacques said. "Think what we watch, what we read, what people post on the nets.

Housewives swoon over fantasy lovers, and when their husbands come home they roll over and go to sleep—because the passion's not there."

"So why did they stop?"

I thought I was being very reasonable, that Jacques was being absurd, and that sooner or later he would either run out of arguments or see the absurdity for himself.

Looking back, I should have just let it drop.

"Because of our drug implants," he said. "Bill, love has a chemical basis—the biochemists mapped it out back in the '90s. The mood stabilizers won't let it develop. We've controlled our rages and depressions, yes, but we destroyed true love in the process."

"You want to give them up?" I asked.

"No, no," he said, "I'm not so mad as that. Die of stress before I'm seventy? No, thank you. But can't the program be modified? Can't an occasional mad passion be allowed, even encouraged?"

"I don't know," I said. "Can it?" And I began to think about how it might be done.

And that, of course, was the beginning of Romantic Moods, Inc., though we didn't know it yet.

Three weeks after that first conversation, I had a theoretical model I thought would stand up—but, of course, I had no way to test it. I called Jacques to tell him, not really thinking about how he might react.

"You remember what you said about romance?" I asked.

"That it's lacking?" he said, speaking from a fragmented image—he had been playing with his own computers, and I found myself conversing with something like an animated Picasso. "Of course I remember, Bill. We've lost that divine touch of madness that gave our ancestors' lives meaning—that's not something I'm likely to forget."

"Yes, well," I said, not wanting to get drawn into another of his philosophical rants, "I took a look at it. I think I've figured a way you could induce romantic love without otherwise disrupting a person's mental stability."

He snorted, and his image spun off fractal sparks. "Is it such a great trick, then, to reconstruct what used to happen naturally? Have we sunk so low, debased ourselves so much?"

"I don't know, Jacques," I said. "I just thought you might want to see this. It's a set of adjustments you could make to the standard implants that would make a person fall in love—

the really intense sort of love that those great old romances were supposed to be. But if you're not interested . . ."

"Of course I'm interested!" he said, and his image was suddenly solid and normal. "Do you mean you could really do that? To anyone? You could *make* them fall in love?"

"I *think* so," I said warily. "Of course, I haven't been able to test it, I just have computer models . . ."

I could see him slump. "Of course," he said. "Just theory. Virtual reality. You haven't *really* found a way to turn our implants to the production of love philtres, and we need have no fear that we'll find ourselves playing Titania with some random Bottom."

"It's not random," I said, slightly offended—I knew Jacques well enough not to be too upset. "And it's not limited to VR, either. I could do it for real if I could tamper with someone's implants. I just don't have a volunteer."

He looked out of the screen at me with a look in his eyes that frightened me.

"Bill," he said intently, "you mean you really could make me fall in love with someone? I've never been in love, you know, not really. It wouldn't just be lust, or euphoria, or something?"

"Not according to the models," I said, "but I told you, I wasn't able to test it on anyone."

"Bill," he said, "you can now. I'll be there . . . you're at your apartment? I'll be there in half an hour."

He was there in twenty minutes. It took him longer than that to convince me to risk actually making the attempt, but at last I gave in. I used my own diagnostic equipment to reset Jacques' implants—the modifications were easy. The whole thing took half an hour, Jacques sitting nervously there in my own chair while I pressed the illicitly modified scanner to his skull and spine. I set the whole sequence to begin when the right stimuli came along.

Two days later, Jacques had begun to wonder whether the thing would ever work. He was walking through the park, hands in his pockets, head down, frustrated and annoyed, when he heard uneven, scuffling footsteps. He looked up, and saw Renate tangled in her dog's leash, on the verge of toppling over.

He hurried forward and grabbed the dog and held it, giving her time to unwrap herself; she did, twirling until she was dizzy, and then laughing as she wobbled unsteadily.

"Thank you," she said, a bit breathlessly.

He released the dog, stepped up and caught Renate by the

waist; he looked into her deep brown eyes and was lost, as at last the implants saw their chance and took it, firing microdoses of brain chemicals hither and yon so that he was swept away into, he later told me, a love like nothing he had ever imagined possible.

"You're beautiful," he told her, "you're the most beautiful thing I've ever seen. I love you."

She laughed again. "You're crazy," she said. Then she looked down at the leash and the dog and said, "But thank you."

Then she turned away and walked on, and he hurried down the walk after her; he caught up and walked beside her, peppering her with questions—what was her name? Did she live nearby? Was there anything he could do for her? Did she know that she had the most beautiful eyes in the world?

She laughed, but she didn't tell him to go away. And she didn't protest when he followed her back to her condo.

"So it worked," I said, when he told me over the net three days later.

He looked out of the screen at me, puzzled, and asked, "What worked?"

I decided that I had overdone it, that I had set the doses too high. "How does she feel about *you*?" I asked, ignoring his question.

He answered with the deepest sigh I had ever seen a living person give. "That's the tragedy of it, Bill," he said. "She thinks I'm quite mad, and warns me repeatedly that this is just a brief fling. She tolerates it, for amusement's sake, but she says she doesn't love me, and when I think of that I'm plunged into despair—at least, until the implants kick in; I suspect, Bill, that I'm overloading my system's capacity for antidepressants."

That worried me.

"If you come here, I'll check on that," I said. "Don't go to a commercial outfitter, please—I think those modifications I did on you might be illegal."

"Modifications?" The idea had finally penetrated the romantic haze, and he cocked his head. "It's quite a coincidence, that . . . I mean, this is the real thing, Bill . . . isn't it?"

"That depends on how you define your terms," I said. "Listen, if you can bring Renate here, perhaps I can do something for *both* of you."

"But that . . . ." He stopped, but I knew what he had been going to say. He wanted Renate to love him for himself, with the same mad passion he felt for her, and right now he was still largely convinced that that was entirely natural. He didn't want her drugged into submission.

But he wanted to lose her even less, and he was sane enough to understand that my implant modifications might be at least partly responsible.

They both came to my apartment that evening. Renate was an attractive young woman, but nothing remarkable to my unenhanced perceptions. She had a pleasant smile and a throaty laugh, but no great store of conversation or wit that I could detect.

Jacques adored her. He stared at her every second.

I explained our little project to her.

When I was finished she stared at me, visibly offended.

"You mean he's drugged? That's why he's like this, it's just chemicals?"

I almost nodded, then caught myself. "Not *drugged*, exactly," I said. "It's artificially induced, but the chemicals involved are no different from those in any natural emotions. *All* our passions are those same chemicals, when you get down to the hard facts. And this . . . well, this *love* that I programmed couldn't have been triggered unless you met every criterion Jacques set me for the woman he wanted to love."

She looked doubtfully at Jacques.

"If you'd like to see for yourself," I said, "I could adjust *your* mood controllers, and you'd be just as much in love with Jacques as he is with you."

"Not possible," Jacques protested. "Even were this love not more than you can possibly imagine, Bill, how could so exquisite a creature ever care so much for an unworthy worm like me?"

"You'd be surprised," I said.

Renate shook her head. "Maybe later," she said as she sat on the couch, crowded at one end, once again looking over at Jacques, who was as near as her obvious reluctance would permit him. He was staring at her, and when he met her gaze he smiled the broad, guileless grin of an infant.

She shuddered slightly.

Later that evening, when Renate had gone, I managed to detain Jacques and to convince him to let me adjust his implants—I think he only agreed because he was in a hurry to follow Renate, and he didn't really believe they were responsible for his feelings.

I wanted to tone down the intensity—and to reduce the

term. My researches had indicated that a normal, natural, passionate love generally lasted about three years before modifying itself to the less-intense mature, or companionate, love. Infatuations generally lasted less. Either one could be shortened, or extended virtually indefinitely, by the right events, but three years seemed the norm.

I had not thought it was a good idea to inflict that long an effect on anyone, and had instead opted for a six-month term; now I cut that down to two, which would be nothing more than an infatuation, really—puppy love, a brief fling, a mad crush.

I did not dare simply turn it off, however; I was afraid that Jacques would be mortified if he were to suddenly regain his senses and see what he had done. Better to allow a gradual tapering-off.

He squirmed impatiently as I worked; when I finished he jumped up, grabbed his jacket, and bolted out the door, headed straight for her condo.

For the next week Jacques was Renate's abject slave, catering to her every whim, no matter how trivial or perverse. By the end of that time, however, a mix of guilt, curiosity, and a growing natural affection drove her back to me, and I had my second subject.

I was careful with the dosages and the timing, and the rest of their love affair was a splendid thing. Jacques made any number of romantic gestures—a dive, fully clothed, into a fishpond to retrieve a dropped coin; an elaborate banquet delivered to her door, with complete table service, at outrageous expense, on the first night that he was unable to join her for dinner; cards, flowers, and sweets on every occasion, or for no reason at all.

None were the Taj Mahal, nor did Jacques cut off his ear for her, but the gestures were heartfelt, numerous, and inventive, and later Jacques looked back at them all with great satisfaction.

So far, the whole thing was merely an interesting experiment, but then came the call from Andre.

"I'm a friend of Renate's," he explained.

I looked at him politely, questioningly.

"I've been watching her and Jacques," he said. "The way they look at each other, the way they're always touching each other."

"They're in love," I said.

He nodded. "She told me," he said. "She told me what you did."

I sighed. Visions of police courts and lawsuits hovered over me. "She asked me to," I said. "I didn't think—"

He interrupted me. "No, no," he said, "you don't understand."

I looked at him blankly.

"I want you to do the same for me," he said. "I want to be in love like that, too."

I blinked. "I don't know . . ." I said.

"I can pay," he said. "I can pay you well."

I hesitated a moment longer, then glanced at the screen where I keep a display of my current finances.

"How well?" I said.

He was the first. Word of mouth brought in enough that within a month we incorporated and began advertising.

Jacques and Renate fell out of love shortly thereafter and drifted apart; mature, companionate love didn't develop, I'm not sure just why not. Perhaps it needed a longer incubation than I had allowed.

I thought that was that, that we could settle back and run the company. I certainly wasn't tempted to try our wares, and Jacques, I thought, had had his fling.

Jacques thought otherwise.

"How am I to praise love, without *being* in love?" he asked me, and I had no ready answer that he would accept. "What better advertisement could we ask than that I, myself, should be a repeat customer?"

I reset his implants, and the affair with Kim began three days later with a stormy public brawl over who was next in line for a public terminal, a brawl that turned into a night of brutal lovemaking in Jacques' car—they didn't even get to either apartment.

I saw the bruises the next morning, but Jacques could only rave about her. He brought her to me that afternoon; her rationale for accepting the modifications was that she wanted to match Jacques' passion.

She did, but their behavior frightened me enough, even at the beginning, that I set it for just a few weeks.

A few days later, Jacques spoke idly of sending her an ear or one of his fingers as a love token, pointing out that he could have it replaced, where poor van Gogh had no such option; I was relieved that Jacques, for once, didn't carry through on one of his mad notions.

I should have seen then what was to come.

It wasn't Jacques who started it, oddly enough.

I was watching the financial nets one afternoon when an announcer on another channel told me, "Many of us hope for romance to brighten our lives, but for Ms. Gloria Ramirez of Miami, romance came as a shock. It seems her neighbor, one Jesus Velez, recently became a client of Romantic Moods, Incorporated, and chose Ms. Ramirez as the recipient of a rather extreme romantic gesture."

I turned away from what I was doing and brought that channel up on the main screen—I was always interested when one of our clients made the news.

The camera cut from the outside of a pink stucco house to Ms. Ramirez in her living room, standing nervously next to something I didn't recognize; I stared at it, trying to make sense of it.

It was all gleaming gold and glittering crystal, perhaps forty centimeters tall, roughly cylindrical, with an oval panel of beveled glass set in the front, and it sat there on Ms. Ramirez's coffee table.

The camera zoomed in on the mysterious object, on its front panel, and I saw that grisly bit of flesh beating steadily behind the glass.

"Mr. Velez commissioned this ornate case from Miami's finest custom jeweler, ordered the mechanism from a medical supply house, and hired the best surgeon he could find, all in order to make an ancient metaphor a modern reality. Mr. Velez gave his beloved his heart."

I stared, horrified.

And then the announcer moved on to the next story, but I froze that image, looped it, and watched the zoom in, watched Gloria Ramirez billow forward and out the left-hand side of the frame, watched the gold-and-crystal case expand to fill the screen, watched the heart beating inside.

I left it there while I accessed that net's menus, and found the heading "More of the story." I skipped the submenu entries for "Biographies" and "Human Interest," and called for the full info dump under "Technical."

I spent hours on it, reading over the detailed specifications for the life-support system Velez had had built into the case—

the amazingly efficient nutrient bath, the thousand-year pace-maker, all of it.

The replacement the man carried in his own chest was nothing special, just a standard mini-jarvik.

There, I thought, was the most extreme romantic gesture short of suicide that Jacques could possibly ask for.

I hoped no one would find a way to kill himself for love. It shouldn't be possible, we weren't modifying the standard regimen *that* much, but we'd introduced a new element with our romantic moods, and I'd read about the wave of "romantic" suicides that swept Europe in the early nineteenth century.

And I wouldn't have thought anyone would have his heart cut out as a gift.

I looked at the image of that shining gold case and shuddered.

And when I practically knew the technical readouts by heart, I put in a call for follow-up stories.

First I got an interview with Ms. Ramirez, asking her reaction to this gift.

She didn't have much to say, and what she did say wasn't very coherent, but it was plain that she was horrified—and fascinated.

And in the next follow-up, datelined just hours after the first reports, she had accepted Velez's proposal of marriage.

I worried about whether this would hurt our business, that one of our customers had mutilated himself.

We should have known. There's no such thing as bad publicity.

Within a month, we had all the customers we could want—and Jacques had all the grand romantic gestures he could possibly have asked for. The crazes had begun.

Perhaps the worst of it was the lack of originality that most people showed. Love letters written on billboards or broadcast over the nets, absurd gifts of every sort, self-mutilations—and every one to make the nets resulted in dozens or hundreds of imitators.

They did sometimes add new twists, however. That first fellow to give his heart did only that—that, and the gold case, of course. The idea of satellite-linking that heart to its replacement, so that both would beat in perfect rhythm, was added by an engineer in Japan.

The first to put an "off" switch on the case was a young woman in France; her accompanying letter explained to her lover that she would rather die at a flick of his finger than live without him, or displease him in any way.

The first *exchange* of hearts took place in California.

Nor were only hearts given—hands were almost as popular, or for those with less nerve, or less money, ring fingers.

A few iconoclasts tried other portions of the anatomy, but none of those caught on.

At times it seemed to me that people were not so much making sincere gestures of love as they were competing with one another to see who could make the more extreme sacrifice. Some of the heartcases were incredibly elaborate.

It didn't seem a very healthy fad to me, but Jacques was delighted. It kept him entertained for weeks.

Spy floaters came next. I didn't see the first news stories; I got a memo from one of our salesmen, and called up the net reports.

They were a natural extension, I suppose, of the use eager lovers made of the nets, keeping a constant watch on the whereabouts of their beloved. Putting a direct audio-video link in a maglev floater and programming it to follow one's lover around was simply carrying it a step further.

I thought it was a rather vile invasion of privacy, myself, and I wasn't surprised when I heard, at the height of the fad, about the young man who blew his lover's floater out of the sky with a twelve-gauge shotgun.

The romantic gestures, I realized about then, had become a form of entertainment—people made them as much to give the net-users a vicarious thrill as out of love.

This didn't always work; the man who overrode eighteen channels in order to broadcast the image of his sleeping bride for six hours found his efforts unappreciated. His house was vandalized, his net access revoked, and in all he received upward of three hundred death threats.

The fellow who gave his lover a net channel entirely for her own use, set up so that when she wasn't using it, it displayed endlessly shifting pictures of her, did better; no one seemed offended, as no existing channels were disrupted. In fact, the new channel became popular with certain groups. Rumor had it that another man fell in love with the channel's subject, and tried, unsuccessfully, to seduce her away.

The mountain someone laser-carved into the shape of his beloved, the genetically engineered garden that reproduced a face in blossoms—monuments to people who had done nothing but be lovable began to proliferate.

And Jacques began his third affair, with a pretty but insipid young woman living somewhere in Manitoba. Ashley was no great creative mind, by any means, but she had a fine appreciation of fashion; I suppose I shouldn't have been so startled when I stepped into Jacques' office one day and found him staring at her heart.

I had seen pictures, even holos, but this was the first time in the real world that I had been in the same room as one of these tokens, and I stared at it in horrified fascination.

The case on his desk was a cylinder, half a meter high, half a meter in diameter, finished in prismatic red enamel set with huge synthetic rubies and trimmed with gleaming chrome; I came around behind Jacques and looked over his shoulder at a heart-shaped panel of beveled glass that allowed one to see inside, to where the woman's vital organ, wetly red, beat steadily amid a tangle of tubes and wires.

It was hideously ugly. Such things should stay inside our bodies, not on public display in ornate boxes.

"It's Ashley's," Jacques told me, quite unnecessarily. Then he added, "Isn't it beautiful?"

"No," I said honestly.

Jacques looked up at me, startled, then turned back to contemplation of this fragment of his beloved. "Well, the *thought* surely is," he said.

"I suppose." Technical fascination overcame my revulsion, and I asked, "Is it satellite-linked?"

He nodded. "Look, there's even a remote control," he said, holding up a device the size of a credit card. "It's linked to her jarvik, and I can let her know I'm thinking of her by speeding it up." He pushed a small slide with his thumb, and sure enough, the heart's beating accelerated.

"That's grotesque," I said before I could stop myself.

"It's lovely," he replied.

I couldn't think of anything to say to that; while we might be looking at the same object, our perceptions of it were so different that we had no common grounds on which we might communicate.

And somehow, I didn't think he'd be able to concentrate on the business I had come to ask about while that thing was sitting on his desk. Perhaps when the novelty had worn off, but not yet.

The business—a question of how many franchises to allow in California—was not urgent; I decided to let it wait, and I left him there staring at the red-and-silver case, the remote in his hand.

It was a week later that he brought in the next heartcase.

That shocked me at first. I'd set his implants myself; I knew that he should still be in love with Ashley, but when I scanned his office one morning I saw a new and different case displayed on the shelf.

And then, when I scanned further, I saw Ashley's as well.

Could he be in love with *two* women? That didn't seem reasonable, given what I knew of his brain chemistry—but I'm not a neurophysiologist, merely a programmer and tinkerer.

I'd been scanning to see if I'd left a mislaid pocket terminal in Jacques' office when I was in there a few days before; I hadn't wanted to bother anyone. Now, though, I put out a call to talk to Jacques, and a moment later the net connected us.

He was in a mall somewhere; I could see shoppers and store displays behind him, and heard water splashing merrily in the background. A silvery spy floater was hovering over his shoulder, watching him.

Was the floater Ashley's? I didn't know. He didn't say. He merely accepted the call.

I didn't bother with preliminaries. "Care to explain this?" I asked, putting the image of the new heartcase in a corner window.

"I bought it," he said calmly. "I've decided to collect them."

I was too surprised to reply immediately, and he added, "No one you know, Bill, and it's empty now, anyway. They broke up, she sent back his heart, he had it reinstalled, I bought the case as a souvenir."

I still couldn't think of anything sensible to say, so he continued, "I'm glad you called, Bill; I've been meaning to talk to you. I think there may be a problem with the latest . . . session."

"Oh?" I was not at my best just then. I knew that by "session" he meant his love affair with Ashley, and I supposed he was being euphemistic either because he was in public or because his love had made him fastidious, but I had no idea what sort of problem he might mean. I was still dazed by the idea of collecting old heartcases.

Now it was he who didn't speak, and I realized that whatever the problem was, it was something he didn't want to discuss over an unencrypted channel—at least, not with that floater hovering nearby. After an awkward moment as we both composed ourselves, I asked, "Care to come talk about it in person?"

"I think so," he said. "It's too noisy here."

"We could meet at my workshop," I suggested.

"Forty minutes," he said, and logged off.

He slipped in the door right on time, and slammed it quickly; I stared at him. And then I realized what he was doing—he had shut his maglev observer outside, so that Ashley couldn't hear our conversation through it.

I activated my own security systems, just to be sure, and Jacques relaxed visibly.

After a few words of greeting, he got to the point.

"Bill," he said, "something's wrong. I think I'm falling out of love with Ashley—and that shouldn't happen for a month or more. That robot spy of hers is driving me mad, and her chatter is all aggravating drivel, and when I look through the glass at her heart it's just a lump of meat. It's ruining me, Bill—I ought to love everything about her! I *do* love her sometimes, she's still attractive, and the sex is wonderful, but the rest . . ."

He paused, then added hopefully, "Her heartcase is beautiful, though."

"Which is why you bought another," I suggested. "An empty one. An appreciation of those things isn't anything to do with Ashley."

He nodded.

"Let me check you out," I said, reaching for the necessary equipment.

Half an hour later I had the results—he *was* falling out of love. His body was compensating for the artificial stimulation we had given it.

I explained as much, and boosted his brain chemistry appropriately.

"I can't keep doing this indefinitely, though," I warned.

The rest of his love for Ashley proceeded on schedule, but a month later I found him sitting morosely in his office, toying with the heartcase remote and staring at his collection—four empties, and Ashley's.

"It's over, Bill," he said.

I knew that already, so I didn't say anything; I did glance at the display of heartcases.

Ashley's was still occupied; her heart was still in there, still beating.

I didn't say anything; I didn't have to. "She didn't want to bother putting it back," Jacques told me. "She said it didn't matter. The jarvik works just fine, and I can keep this as a souvenir."

I didn't think he was in the mood for argument, so I didn't say anything. I can't say I approved of the situation.

"I want another, Bill," he said.

"Another heartcase?"

"Don't be stupid. Another love. And this time, Bill, I want it to last forever. I want eternal love, as in all the old stories."

"I can't do that," I said.

"Of course you can."

"No, Jacques, I *can't*. I don't mean I won't, I mean it's not possible."

He put down the remote and turned his chair to face me. "Why not?" he demanded.

I explained about how the brain's chemistry automatically adjusted itself, how a real grand passion couldn't be sustained indefinitely, but would transform itself gradually into the more settled companionate love.

"That might do," he said.

"I don't know how to do it," I said—which may or may not have been the truth; I had theoretical methods I was not willing to try out, as I'd had quite enough of these experiments. I had concluded months earlier that love was madness, and had come to regret my part in Romantic Moods. "All I can do is make it possible for it to happen naturally," I added, to soften the blow.

"But you can set up an open-ended love, one that *might* last?" he asked.

I reluctantly admitted that I could. I didn't mention that I didn't think it *would* last, in his case—his brain chemistry had already learned to fall out of love, and would probably continue to do so.

"I can't live like this, without love," he said, and I finally realized what I should have seen earlier.

Jacques had become addicted to love.

But I didn't see any way to undo it, and I was hardly the only pusher in the business anymore.

So after Ashley came June, and then Gianna and Sarah and Thomasina, and as an experiment Steve, then back to women.

I wasn't the one who set them all up; I began refusing after a few, but each time Jacques would find another supplier, and then, when one ended badly, he would beg me to reconsider. Some lasted just a few weeks, while Anastasia, the longest, lived with Jacques for seven years; the two of them were married for five of those years.

And Jacques continued his collecting. He filled a room with heartcases, shelves and shelves of them—at first, mostly empty, but after a while the ones still occupied began to accumulate, as cyborgs became commonplace and more and more people decided not to bother with the restorative surgery.

I was amazed—and appalled—that so many people were willing to sell such things. I was even more appalled when one day, with a nervous laugh, Jacques told me how low many of the prices had been.

Romantic Moods flourished, and the wild fads settled down. Heartcases fell out of fashion, and Jacques' collection stopped growing. Most of our customers were young people who wanted the experience; we got very few repeat customers, and in fact we discouraged them.

But Jacques was addicted. We both knew it by the time Anastasia had been gone for a year; she had been his last, best hope to break the cycle.

We tried cold turkey; he broke down and found a fly-by-night operator.

His new love's name was Melanie, she was nineteen, and she saw Jacques as something to be used—she had no intention of passing up the opportunity represented by a forty-year-old billionaire falling madly in love with her. The relationship was sadomasochistic from the start, and she all but ordered Jacques to marry her, so that she could share in his wealth.

The operator hadn't known about Jacques' addiction, however, and hadn't compensated for it; nor did Melanie. The passion peaked quickly, then vanished, turning rapidly to hate when Jacques saw how she had attempted to exploit him.

One night, when she demanded money, the hate boiled over and he beat her senseless; if the security alarms hadn't gone off, he would have killed her on the spot.

That's not supposed to happen. That's the sort of thing the implants were created to prevent in the first place. The police took Jacques away, and he spent three days in the hospital, being thoroughly checked out.

Then they called in Anastasia, as his ex-wife, and myself, as his partner—he had no other surviving family.

We stood over the hospital bed as a police official told us about Melanie, and we looked down at Jacques—they had him lightly sedated, so that he lay there listening calmly, speaking only when spoken to.

"There's nothing I can do," Anastasia said. "I tried, when we were married, but I couldn't help him." She sighed. "I don't think he was ever really in love with me, Bill—I know what your computer models said, but I don't think they fit Jacques anymore. I think he *believed* he was in love with me—but it wasn't real."

"The chemicals . . ."

She shook her head, and interrupted me. "I don't mean the chemicals," she said. "I mean he wasn't in love with *me*. He was in love with an ideal, and he'd convinced himself I was that ideal, but . . . oh, I don't know. It's nothing to do with me anymore; the divorce was final a year ago. You do whatever you have to."

She turned and left, and the doctors and the police official let her go.

I sighed, and stepped away from the bed. "I guess I'll go, too," I said.

"I'm afraid not," the police official said.

He and the neurosurgeon explained it to me. Even though I hadn't been the one who arranged his love for Melanie, my long-term meddling with Jacques' implants was largely responsible for his actions; I was an unintentional accomplice in a vicious assault.

Jacques' brain chemistry was irretrievably damaged, and it was partly my fault.

Jacques himself was partly responsible, of course; he admitted it freely and took most of the blame, even after they took him off the sedatives. He declined to sue me, which I thought was generous under the circumstances.

But he and I were in this together. I was placed under house arrest until the matter was settled.

We were very rich, and no one had died, and we had witnesses who would testify to Melanie's abuse of Jacques, so eventually they released us and that was the end of it. Melanie got her share of Jacques' fortune in the form of medical bills and a lawsuit settlement, rather than alimony; I don't think she much cared *how* she got it, and Jacques argued that at least this way she had, in a way, *earned* it.

The operator who had reset Jacques' implants had disappeared before the police or the reporters or Melanie's lawyers could reach him.

The publicity meant that no other operator would touch Jacques anymore, though—no amount of money is worth the risk of being an accomplice to murder, not when there are plenty of other customers. It looked as if his addiction was finally at an end.

I checked on him regularly—partly because I was obligated to by the courts, and partly because he was still my friend, however damaged he might be.

One day I found him in the heartcase room, hands clasped behind his back, staring into a baroque silver box.

"I was always fascinated by love, you know," he said without looking at me.

"I know," I said. "I remember how we started, when you watched *Casablanca*."

He nodded. "I never found an Ingrid Bergman," he said. "But then, I don't know if that was what I wanted. I was in love with the *idea* of love. It wasn't that I wanted a woman, or wanted a woman to love me; it was that I wanted to *be in love*. That seemed to be the whole point of life."

"Not to me," I said.

"It's what all the songs said."

I shrugged.

"I've turned them all off," he said with a wave of his arm.

For a moment I thought he meant he had turned off the songs, but then I looked around at the heartcases, and realized that he had meant those.

He was telling the truth; the hearts hung motionless, dead or dying, in those that held hearts.

"All but this one," he said, touching the silver one gently.

A horrible thought struck me.

"They were all disconnected, weren't they?" I asked.

In theory, most heartcases were satellite-linked to the jarviks in the chests of the original donors—if the hearts stopped, so would the jarviks.

But surely, those people hadn't let Jacques take the hearts without breaking the satlinks?

"Jacques," I said when he didn't answer immediately, "they

were disconnected, weren't they? They weren't still linked to their donors?"

"I don't know," he said.

I was speechless with horror. Jacques might have just committed mass murder. "Turn them back on!" I cried, looking about desperately.

The controls weren't visible, there was no master switch anywhere.

He shook his head. "I can't," he said. "They don't do that; there's no way to restart them."

I realized, remembering what I knew of the technical specifications, that he was right—heartcases were maintenance devices, they didn't have any sort of electroshock or other systems to start a stopped heart.

"Some of them spasmed," he said. "Others just stopped. That one over there," he said, pointing to a golden-yellow case in the shape of a Fabergé egg, "held the still-beating heart of a woman who died five years ago. I bought it from her widower. It's as dead as the rest of her now."

"Why did you do this?" I demanded. I was trying to think what I could do; whom could I call? Could the jarviks be restarted in time? Who would know?

He didn't answer. He put both hands on the silver one.

"This one," he said.

"What about it?" I said, not really paying much attention; I was distracted by the thought that some might be saved.

"No remote," he said. "No fancy controls. Nothing but a switch, 'on' and 'off.' But love isn't that simple, is it?"

"No," I agreed without thinking. I was punching instructions into my wristband computer, summoning help.

"I'm glad she gave it back," he said.

I didn't know what he meant. "Who?" I asked, looking up at him.

"Anastasia," he said.

He flicked the switch on the silver box to "off," and crumpled to the floor.

Suicide isn't supposed to be possible with modern implants—that's what we're told. I'd always believed it.

I'd forgotten. With love, all things are possible.

And the heartcase made it so easy.

There was nothing I could do. The rescue team said that resuscitation was technically possible, but there would be severe brain damage; I told them not to bother. They double-checked with Anastasia, and she agreed.

Jacques was gone.

So were a dozen innocent men and women who had been foolish enough to give away their hearts.

We had the silver heartcase buried with him; I sold the company and moved on. I finally found time to marry and settle down, and my wife and I are happy.

But we're not in love.

GODDOGGIT

Emily Devenport

I was a pro-abortionist, and when I went down to protest the Right To Life "Happy Birthday" celebration for the unborn, a lady with a Bible stuck her face in mine and demanded, "What are you going to say to God?"

"God isn't someone you can talk to," I said.

"You can *pray* to God! And when you die you'll stand before his judgment and you'll have to tell him you murdered babies!"

"God murders babies every day," I said. "I can't compete with him."

Her mouth dropped open in shock, which was gratifying. I suppose I had overestimated the opposition, expected them to be more cynical. She believed I was a murderer, and she believed God was a man. I believed God didn't care about what people did in life.

We were both wrong.

God was a celestial coroner. She looked like Audrey Hepburn at the age of thirty-five or so. God's dog put its front paws on the gurneys and wheeled newly dead people down a long hall to the dissection room, and God removed their brains. She shaved sections off the brains like the guys at the deli when you ask them to slice it for sandwiches, and examined the sections under her celestial microscope. This way she was able to see everything that had gone on in the dead person's brain, all the experiences and thoughts.

I wondered if God would be entertained by my brain. I had listened to all sorts of nice music in my life. Just now she was looking at the part where I had listened to the Philip Glass *Dancepieces* tape I had checked out of the public library. Side One, "In The Upper Room." I thought it was perfect for God to hear while she worked. I hoped she would look at the part with Aaron Copeland's *Quiet City* next.

I wondered if God ever got behind in her work. Did the bodies ever stack up outside her door? And for that matter, what would God do with all the information she gathered?

Actually, God was writing a book. It was called *What Human People Are Really Like*, or something like that. God had this theory that the Human race actually started in South America instead of Africa. It sounds kind of crackpot to me, but the first people she imagines in South America look just like the first people of Africa, so maybe no one will mind.

God got to the part of my brain that told how I died. The gas line in my apartment blew up. The Bible lady would think it was God who did that to me for punishment. But the Bible lady was on the next gurney outside the door, and God seemed to be more interested in a book I had read titled *Wonderful Life*, by Stephen Jay Gould. God could probably hardly wait to get Gould on her table so she could compare theories of evolution with him.

Sometimes God needed a break from her work, so she went skiing. The place she skied was somewhere in Heaven, and the slopes were incomparable. She was dressed in a snappy ski outfit and wore Italian dark glasses.

God was supposed to be relaxing, but she brought a thick volume about genetics with her. God intended to read it on the ski lift, a ride that would take several hours, since Heaven is so big. God's dog got on the lift several benches ahead of her. They were supposed to ride together, but she was distracted, and didn't sit down in time. He barked at her, and she waved reassuringly.

As soon as God got on the lift, it started to speed up. It wasn't supposed to do that, so she put her book down and looked up at the mechanism. Nothing appeared to be wrong with it, but the lift continued to speed up, until God could hardly keep her seat. She could hear her dog whining in dismay, up ahead.

God fastened her seat belt and shoulder strap. The dog materialized on the bench next to her, and she fastened his belt too. He licked her face in gratitude. The lift sped up some more, until it must have been going a hundred miles an hour. God could have stopped it, but she was curious to see who would be so rude to God and God's dog.

The lift changed directions several times at odd-looking intersections, thousands of chairs all speeding back and forth in orderly geometric patterns which God found aesthetically pleasing. Then the lift began to spiral down a structure built to resemble a helix.

"Very funny," God said.

The bottom of the helix was so far down, God couldn't see where it ended. It seemed to me that God's wild ski-lift ride was a good metaphor for the mysterious journey we all ultimately take from life to afterlife, with one important difference: God didn't want to see what was at the end, so she transported herself and her dog out of there and back to her office.

Bodies were piled up outside of God's office, in the hall, all the way up to the ceiling. It made me feel lucky that I had gone under God's microscope before the rush. "What's this?" she wondered. "The whole world is out here! What happened while I was away?"

"Maybe there was another big war," said the dog. God looked at him, her lovely eyebrows arched in surprise.

"When did you learn to talk?" she asked him.

"I just got the urge a moment ago," said the dog.

"The whole world is dead outside my door, and now my dog is talking," said God. "I don't know what to make of it."

The dog scratched himself, reflectively. "Well," he said finally, "did anything like this ever happen to your predecessor?"

"I don't have one."

"Then how did you get here?"

"There was nothingness," replied God. "But I got tired of that, so I said, 'Let there be Light!' And Bingo."

"Marvelous! But what were you before the Light?"

"Highly compressed matter, according to the best theories."

"Speaking of theories," said the dog, "I wonder if Stephen

Jay Gould is outside in the corridor. Perhaps his brain contains the answer to what has happened to Humanity."

So God and God's dog searched the corridor for the body of Stephen Jay Gould, which fortunately was fairly close to the door. They analyzed his brain, and that's how they found out about the Virus War.

"I knew there would be trouble once people found out how to make those efficient and unpredictable little machines," said God. She and the dog looked at another slice of Gould's brain and watched the drama unfold.

Humans had invented viruses to kill other humans, but that wasn't all. They made viruses to steal information, viruses to make people live longer, even viruses to rewrite the programming in the human brain. All of those viruses got together and mated, producing interesting and deadly mutations.

"But that's not all," said the dog, pointing to the pertinent section of Gould's slice. "One virus mutated and made dogs smart. That's why I can talk now."

"That's a nice development," said God. "But the humans are all dead or dying. The last ones are piling up outside my door now."

"Couldn't you intervene and save a few of them?"

"I never do that," said God.

The dog sighed, and the last, dead humans materialized in the hall. Just then, an alarm sounded that had never sounded before.

"What's that?" wondered God.

"Look!" said the dog, and the bottom end of the ski-lift helix materialized in God's office. Two men were riding on one of the chairs, safely seat-belted in, of course. One of them was a handsome, muscular man of about forty with a flowing beard. The other was a brown-skinned young man with an Aztec profile, the personification of handsome young manhood. The chair set them down safely on God's floor.

"Hello," said the older man. "I'm Zeus. This is my friend, Tezcatlipoca."

"Delighted to meet you, my dear," said Tezcatlipoca, and he kissed God's hand.

"You're the ones who sabotaged my ski lift!" said God.

"Yes, we thought you'd get a kick out of the ski motif. Not to mention the helix. But we weren't trying to be rude, we were just helping you into your retirement."

"I see," said God. "That explains the bodies."

"The dogs are people now," said Zeus. "And they have their own God."

At that, the dog brightened. "Me?" he said. "I get to be God now?"

"That's right," said Tezcatlipoca. "What will you call yourself?"

The dog scratched again, something dog people always do when they're thinking.

"Goddoggit!" he said. "I'll make a blessing out of a curse."

God tucked a stray strand of raven hair back into place. "All of these eons," she mused, "I've been grooming my dog to become my replacement. Interesting."

"Yes," said Zeus sympathetically. "You monotheistic gods have always been at a disadvantage. You were Omniscient and Omnipotent, so you couldn't know about your predecessors. You should see how Jehovah mopes around Valhalla all day long. He can't get over the fact that he was replaced by a woman."

"Valhalla?" said God.

"You'll like it," said Tezcatlipoca. "It has a fabulous library. We'll put your book there when you're finished with it. And by the way, I love your theory of the South American Genesis."

"You would," snorted Zeus.

God kneeled down and hugged her dog. "Will you remember me?" she wondered.

"I don't know," replied Goddoggit. "Maybe I'll end up as part of a polytheistic pantheon. Who knows?"

She hugged him again, and he licked her face in farewell.

If you're wondering what happens to people when we die, the answer is, we all end up in God's book. I myself got a chance to find out what it's like to be God when I was writing the latter part of this narrative in Omniscient third person. It was like being monotheistic, but without the disadvantage of forgetting.

If you're wondering what happened to Goddoggit after we were all gone, he studied the brains of intelligent dogs for several centuries and started his own book. Goddoggit worked alone for so long, he almost forgot about having an assistant that might eventually replace him; until one day, when he heard the sound of a gurney being wheeled outside his door.

A cat appeared in the doorway, pushing the gurney with her front paws.

"Oh no!" said Goddoggit. "Not a *cat*!"

"You think you're upset now?" replied the cat, and pointed over her shoulder with a dewclaw. "Wait till you see what's pushing the next cart!"

SAVING FACE

Andrew Lane

One of the cameras died just as Martle entered the studio. It was lying on its back as he passed, its legs twitching as the last few sparks of life shunted randomly through its brain. He didn't even bother looking at it as he walked by. As far as he was concerned they always looked like dead meat, what with their unresponsive gazes and their slumped posture. Going tits-up was nothing unusual: something to do with the genetic trade-offs between brain development and lifespan, or so the brochure said. Some of the production staff were attempting a lacklustre revival, airblasting drugs through its baggy hide and checking brain activity on a handheld monitor, but Martle could tell it wasn't any use. He'd already seen the vast bulk of the brood-mother up in the gallery shudder with pain, then shrug and look away from the body. The two other cameras huddled on the far side of the studio kept looking up at her for reassurance. Her lidless eyes slid over them without appearing to register their presence, but gradually they moved apart and stared vacantly at whichever wall they happened to end up facing.

"What's the prob?" Martle said as he passed Welter. The camera supervisor shook her head.

"Fuckin' things," she muttered. "No fuckin' use. No fuckin' use at all. I told them, last year I told them. 'Don't tell me about cleaner fuckin' edits and better-quality pictures,' I said. 'If you haven't got the balls to uprate the cameras, they'll up and die on you.' And was I wrong?" She headed towards the group of production staff, gesturing them irritably away from the body. "Only thing that one's good for now is fuckin' cat-food" she said.

"Or public service broadcasting," said one of the group. The rest laughed and began to manoeuvre the body out of the studio.

Suzy Bowles was already at the long desk when he arrived, flicking through the pages of her script and checking her lead-in lines. Martle detoured round the autocue box and waved. Without glancing up, she flicked a hand in acknowledgement. As usual, in the ten minutes since the final script conference she'd acquired a visible layer of foundation, blusher, eye shadow and mascara. Normally she disdained ornamentation of any sort, and endured the daily makeup ritual with barely concealed contempt.

Martle rather liked it. He'd always enjoyed dressing up.

"Five minutes, kiddies," shouted Greg, the floor manager, holding his earphones on with one hand and waving his clip-board towards the gallery with the other. "And we're making do on two cameras."

As Martle sat down and shuffled through his script he could hear Greg holding a discussion with the distant director. Eventually the orders were relayed. "Change of plan," Greg yelled. "We're leading with Luxembourg." Lights flickered on the au-tocue as it was reprogrammed from the gallery. Martle and Suzy both unhurriedly reordered their pages. Bill Paternoster's script lay unopened in front of his empty chair.

"Two minutes," said Greg. "Where the hell's Paternoster?" Martle and Suzy Bowles both looked up and shrugged. Welter just looked blank and began to herd her cameras toward the newsdesk.

Heralded by a distant bellowing, Bill Paternoster came charging into the studio. Sweat beaded across his plump, flushed face. One of the makeup girls chased after him clutching a powder puff. He fell heavily into his seat beside Suzy Bowles and grinned disarmingly up at the gallery.

"Sorry," he shouted, "got held up over dinner."

"Had to finish the bottle, you mean," murmured Suzy, not really caring whether Paternoster heard or not.

"One minute," said Greg. "Quiet in studio, please. Stand by VT. Stand by grams."

The bright studio lights intensified the musky odour of the cameras. Martle felt his heart speed up and the cool sheen of sweat spread down his back and across his chest. Twenty years, and still he felt it. Every night. He took a deep but quiet breath and forced his hands to unclench. His fingers left moist smears as he trailed them across the angled screen of the TV monitor set into the desk. He took a sip of water from the glass before him.

"Ready?" Suzy asked quietly.

"Ready," he murmured.

Greg's voice was loud in the sudden hush. "Thirty seconds."

The autocue projected Martle's opening lines into the air before him, invisible to the eyes of cameras.

He let his gaze wander round the cramped studio, barely large enough to contain the newsdesk podium, the autocue, and the cameras. Skeletal lighting gantries filled the space where the ceiling should have been, and through the long smoked glass window of the gallery he could see the production team, and the smooth, bloated outline of the brood-mother.

"Bob, to camera, please," said Greg. Martle's eyes met the single large pupil of the camera facing him: a deep black well without the slightest flicker of interest.

The red transmission light above the studio door blazed on. Greg swept his arm down. Martle's lips curved into a sincere smile.

"Fresh controversy as Brazil is accused of supplying arms to both sides in the Luxembourg riots," he said firmly. "A full report tonight in ECBS News."

Greg's lips mouthed the words "Go grams. Go titles." The ECBS logo rotated out of nothing on the monitor, changed colour, broke into pieces and reassembled into the words "ECBS NEWS—With Bob Martle and Suzy Bowles." A strident but unhummable tune with a strong backbeat faded up and then down.

On the monitor screen Martle's face appeared: filtered through the eyes of the camera, transmitted telepathically to the mind of the brood-mother, and taken by wires and by circuits from her brain to the mixing desk of the gallery. And from there to the world.

"Good evening. This is the eight o'clock news from ECBS, brought to you by Tulley Alvarez Benita PLC. The headlines tonight: Forty killed today as fresh rioting breaks out in Luxembourg. We'll be talking to the man who says he's sold guns and missiles to both the mercenary forces and the Zen militants. Also: As the time approaches for the second batch of trade goods to be released by the Cimliss, we ask, 'Are we getting our money's worth?' As the go-slow amongst officers in the United States Air Force enters its third week, we talk to the Senator who says it should never have been privatised. And body-bepple: harmless fad or addictive habit? A special report."

"Smile," said the autocue. Martle's camera slumped as Suzy began to recite details of the headline story. Martle relaxed, took another sip of water, and watched the monitor admiringly as Suzy recited her lines with just the right mixture of professionalism and anticipation. Beneath the desk, out of the camera's line of sight, her foot beat out a nervous tattoo.

Following the prerecorded interview which wrapped Suzy's story, Martle took over for the Cimliss piece. He'd calmed down since the first item, and this time managed to catch glimpses of the monitor out of the corner of his eye as he talked. It always amazed him how great the gulf was between appearance and reality. He could feel the warm trickle of sweat down his sides, but as far as the camera was concerned he was as casual and as authoritative as it was possible to be. During a preshot insert his image remained on the monitor, and he studied the three-dimensional display critically. His temples were greying, but his eyes were as clear as ever. No sign of a gut yet, despite the amount of junk food he lived on. And judging by the regular stream of proposals and invitations that were fielded by his secretary, the audience loved him as much as the camera did.

A monitor across the studio was showing the prefilmed report, and Martle glanced over at it when Greg signalled the imminent change-over. Judging by what he could see, Julia Wood, the director, had taken the cheap and easy option: plenty of vox pops of local traders who wanted trade sanctions applied to Cimliss goods, with cutaway shots of ECBS cameras moving around the studio. The cameras were only one of the many items of biologically engineered trade goods that the Cimliss had offered to humanity, of course, but they were by far the easiest for ECBS to tape. The hospital companies were still wary of showing the medical instruments in case they scared away paying customers, and the Government wasn't letting *anybody* near the weapons.

No shots of the Cimliss, of course, but their publicity-shyness was well known. The only footage of them in existence lasted five seconds, was owned by Eurostar and came with a price tag of a million dollars a second for any other station's use.

Oddly enough, Martle thought, the tone of the insert was considerably more innocuous than the earlier script conference had indicated it would be. It contrasted sharply with his own script, which suggested that the Cimliss had somehow palmed humanity off with shoddy goods. Even the local barrow boys seemed halfhearted in their condemnation of the Cimliss, and one or two were openly supportive. Bad direction, Martle thought. The insert made his piece look like hysterical conservatism. He would have to have a word with Julia.

The insert finished, and Martle handed back to Suzy. His camera pulled away to focus on Paternoster as Suzy ran through a brief résumé of the ongoing USAF work-to-rule. As she handed over to Bill for an in-depth political analysis of the latest events, her camera lumbered round on three clumsy legs to focus on Martle.

Paternoster had regained his breath by then, and the attentions of makeup had erased the sweat and covered the network of broken capillaries in his cheeks and nose. They couldn't do anything for his red-rimmed eyes, however, or for the haze of stale alcohol that perpetually hung round him and gave away his major preoccupation since his wife died.

The last item was a prerecorded report which they'd been trying to slot in for weeks. A leading story on the sudden disappearance of a TV evangelist had been dropped that afternoon when he was found doped up to the eyeballs and dressed in latex in a police cell. Station-to-Station had bought off all the witnesses for an exclusive, so ECBS was using the body-bepple story to fill the slot. It gave them all a chance to relax for a few minutes before Martle had to summarise the headlines again, wrap up the broadcast, and hand over to the continuity announcer. As soon as the red lights were off and the director pronounced herself pleased, they all collected up the pages of script that they had scattered over the desk and prepared to leave. As they walked through to have their makeup removed, Welter was herding the cameras back to their pens and the food sprays.

It was Paternoster who proposed a few drinks in the subsidised staff bar. "To help us unwind," he said, but Martle guessed that whether he and Suzy went along or not, Paternoster would be unwinding for the rest of the night. As usual, Martle felt drained and shaky after the broadcast. He was on the verge of refusing, but he couldn't stand the thought of anyone having fun while he wasn't around.

"Sure," he said. "But I need to collect some stuff from the dressing rooms. I'll meet you down there."

The most direct route to the dressing rooms was up a level and through the canteen, but at that time of night it would be locked up tighter than the producer's ass. Instead he took the elevator down to the basement and cut along the curved studio access corridor. The studios themselves were dark—the nine o'clock news was the last live broadcast until breakfast TV opened—but the lower levels were kept open for carpenters and lightning engineers getting ready for the next day's quota of porno-soaps and game shows. The heavy cinnamon smell of the cameras filled the air, and Martle could pick out their distinctive front-and-back toe prints among the scuffed boot marks and high-heeled scratches in the dirt of the floor. He paused, thoughtful. The cameras weren't supposed to be allowed out of the studio unless on outside broadcast, in which case they were taken out the back way. Perhaps there was another *Inside Your ECBS* feature on the way. When all else fails, when imagination and money run out, make a programme about yourself.

He walked on. The corridor curved gently away from him, circling the building. Studio One: *Fathers and Sons*, ECBS's top-rated porno-soap. Studio Two: the new game show *In for a Penny, In for a Pounding*. Studio Three: the ever-popular *Whips in the Cupboard*. Studio Four: dark ever since a young sculptor called Prewster had blown the top of his head off during the arts show *I Know What I Like*, leaving as his legacy a placard in his lap which bore the legend "Dead Artist, by Adrian Prewster" and a show cancelled so fast that the resulting vacuum sucked three ECBS board members into sudden unemployment. Around the curve of the corridor Martle could see the entrance to the fire escape leading up to the dressing rooms. And here, Studio Five, where every day, Martle and . . .

Light spilled out around the edge of the studio doors.

Martle stopped dead. Recording on the news had finished for the day. They weren't scheduled for a change of set for months. So who was in there?

The studio was protected from stray noise by two sets of

double doors, the outer ones windowless and not quite meeting
in the middle, the inner ones with round inset windows and
boasting a crumbling rubber strip covering the gap between
them. The light was coming through the uneven space between the two outer doors like a thin strip of summer.

As he crept forward, the possibilities sorted themselves in his
mind. Could be vandals, squatters, vagrants, muggers, bailiffs
. . . Could be anyone. Once he'd identified the intruders, he'd
go and alert security, then fade quietly into the background
and head off to the pub. He wasn't paid to be a hero. If there
was one thing experience had taught him, it was not to get
involved.

He pushed his way through the first set of doors and put his
face up to one of the windows in the second.

And turned away, blinking rapidly.

A trick of the light, surely. Or had someone slipped something into his water while he hadn't been looking?

He put his eye back to the windows.

Across the far side of the brightly lit studio the metal-mesh
door to the camera pens stood wide open. The cameras themselves were milling around the newscaster's desk, alternately
moving forward, backwards and sideways. One of the cameras
stood away from the rest, moving rapidly round the outside of
the group. There must have been at least ten present: almost
the entire ECBS complement. And then the cameras drew
back slightly, and Martle could see between them to the newscasters' desk.

Three cameras had squeezed their ungainly bulks into the
form-fitting chairs. They were sitting upright, staring blankly
at their companions. One of them was nodding slightly. As
Martle watched, it turned to the camera beside it, who met its
gaze, turned to its front and began to rock its head forward
and back. The first camera turned away and looked down at
the monitor on the newscasters' desk.

The whole bizarre, lumbering ritual was carried out in absolute silence, apart from the shuffle of their feet and the quiet
wheeze of their breathing.

Martle pushed the doors open and strode into the studio.

It wasn't until he stepped across the length of masking tape
six feet beyond the threshold of the door, legacy of some long-
forgotten scene-shifter, that Martle realised what he'd done.
There had been no conscious decision. He just couldn't walk
away. He had to know what was going on.

Martle's eyes were drawn to his right where a small TV monitor stood on a stand, the one used by Welter for diagnostic tests. It had been switched on, and the flickering image captured and held Martle's attention. The picture was obviously being relayed from one of the cameras, and showed the newscasters' desk in medium long shot. By luck, because surely it couldn't have been judgement, no other cameras were visible apart from the three sitting at the desk.

Except that they weren't cameras.

On the screen, so tiny that the pseudo-3-D effect was just a barely perceptible rounding of edges and softening of shadows, Martle, Suzy Bowles and Bill Paternoster were sitting in their usual places, staring quiet and watchful at a point behind the camera.

Martle looked up.

Three cameras sat behind the desk, surrounded by their fellows.

Back on the screen, three newscasters. Human newscasters.

And behind the real desk, three bulky, alien creatures.

His eyes moved from the cameras sitting behind the desk to the lone creature who, unlike his fellows, was facing away from Martle and towards the trio. From there the image was transmitted, mind to mind, up to . . .

Martle's eyes flicked upwards to the long, dark window of the director's gallery. Through the glass he could make out the silhouettes of the monitor banks, the backs of the production staff's chairs, and the still, bloated bulk of the brood-mother.

The shadows hid detail and shrouded her in mystery, but Martle could have sworn that she was smiling.

Movement on the floor caught his eye. The cameras were standing up behind the desk and shuffling into a new position. He looked at the monitor to make sense of the tableau. The pictures he saw made him feel hot, breathless and faint.

On screen Suzy Bowles was bent over the newsdesk, an expression of ecstasy contorting her features, her skirt hitched up over her back. She was applying lipstick to her glossy, parted lips. Martle saw himself standing behind her, his trousers around his knees, thrusting deeply into her. Sweat beaded his face and stained the armpits of his jacket. Paternoster, or rather his image, was throwing up convulsively over Suzy and the desk. His shirt and trousers were caked with vomit.

Martle could feel the world turning grey and pulling away from him as the shock hit home. He pinched himself, hard, on the back of the hand. The studio snapped back into glorious Technicolor and sharp focus. He let out a small, incoherent protest.

As if on cue, the cameras all stopped moving and turned to face him. Their unreadable stares formed a wall of alien indifference. Their leathery flanks rose and fell in unison. A feeling of expectancy filled the studio, as palpable as the spiced smell of the cameras.

How did they know? How could they know? He'd never told Suzy how he felt about her: he only rarely admitted it to himself.

How could they know?

Against the barrier of their eyes he retreated, lost and alone. The doors parted at the pressure of his back. As they closed in front of him, cutting off the invisible thread that joined his gaze to theirs, he felt like a puppet whose strings had been cut. He stumbled along the corridor, handbag forgotten, through the turnstiles and out into the rain. There he walked aimlessly through stinging squalls for what seemed like hours before flagging a taxi and heading for home.

He dreamed, of course. He dreamed of a naive young newscaster stammering over an unexpected newsflash. He dreamed of fuzzy 2-D pictures, speckled with static, transmitted live by satellite from Ecuador. He dreamed of vast blue skies, and of steamy rain forests, and of Cimliss spacecraft spiralling lazily downward from the heavens like giant orange leaves, no two the same shape, size or shade, now drifting together, now drifting apart, before coming to rest upon the lush forest floor. And opening their doors for trade.

He went in to work the next day believing that it was *all* a dream, but knowing that it wasn't. He watched carefully for signs from the cameras, but they stumbled about the studios giving nothing away. If they had anything to give.

During the script conference Suzy and Bill were sarcastic about his failure to make the bar, but an extemporised story about having to escape from a persistent female fan who had cornered him outside the door kept them sweet. Like the cameras, he stumbled unthinkingly through the day.

The lunchtime broadcast was a disaster. Halfway through an item on the long-running Argentinean occupancy of the Antarctic, he caught sight of himself in the desk monitor. His hair was awry and his left eye appeared to have acquired a slow tic. Distracted, he started referring to the Antarctican invasion of

Argentina, realised his mistake and lost his place on the autocue. The pitiless eyes of the cameras magnified his mistake.
A bead of sweat became a wash. A slight tremor of the hands
became a visible palsy. Martle stumbled his way through the
rest of the broadcast and rushed to the toilets as soon as the
credits rolled, but all he could see in the mirror was the same
cool, slightly ironic face that greeted him every morning.

Makeup took longer than normal for the midafternoon session. Martle suspected that the producer had ordered special
attention for him, but whatever the assistants did, it worked
brilliantly. There was no script conference—the broadcast was
essentially the same as for the lunchtime transmission—and
when he left the makeup chair and strode into the studio he
looked and felt immaculate.

It didn't matter. As soon as he could after the broadcast
started, he glanced down at the monitor.

And froze in midword.

His face was puffy and blotched, his eyes bloodshot. His
hands appeared to tremble on the desk. The reflection of the
overhead studio lamps made his forehead glisten through
sparse, grey hair. Large beads of sweat trickled down his nose.

When it became clear that he wasn't going to continue, the
director signalled for Suzy to start the next story. The cameras
repositioned themselves, and, as Martle's camera lumbered
away, it winked at him, slowly and deliberately.

Greg, the floor manager, approached Martle after the broadcast.

"Bob," he said, "I think Julia wants a word."

Up in the darkened director's gallery Julia Wood waited for
him. For a moment, as he entered, she looked to him like a
red-haired skull placed on top of a fashionably tailored dummy.
Then the shadows shifted, she moved, and he could see the
pale skin pulled tight over the bones by stress and exhaustion.
The angled surfaces of the control banks behind her were rippling with lights, and Martle was uncomfortably aware of the
soft, bloated silhouette of the brood-mother in the corner of
the narrow room.

"What the fuck is wrong with you?" she snapped. "Girl-
friend died or sommat?"

How could he tell her?

"Sorry, Julia," he said. "I don't know what came over me.
Tired, I guess. Been pushing it a bit."

"This is twice today, Bob. Don't let it happen tonight."

"Look . . ." he said, and paused. "I . . . I think it may have looked worse on the screen than it actually was. I didn't feel that bad, and . . ."

"It's what's on the screens that pay our dosh," said Julia, "not what you feel like. Seeing is believing, Bob, and if the paying public, bless them, see you throwing wobblies on their TV set then they're going to switch channels. So what you feel like isn't important, *capishe*, lover?"

"No probs," Martle murmured. He shouldn't have been surprised. It was on TV. It had to be true.

"Okay . . ." said Julia. He could tell that she didn't want to leave it there, but she knew that as ECBS's top-rated newsreader Martle was besieged by offers from other networks. He might be on the way down, but there were a lot of rungs on the way. "Script conference in ten minutes. There's a couple of new stories coming down the line. Pull your shit together."

She walked towards the door, weaving a bit. Rumours had it that she was hitting drink, drugs, or both. To Martle she just looked terminally tired.

He moved to follow her, but a slow heaving in the far corner of the gallery caught his attention. He walked closer as the brood-mother shifted position, moving round to face him. The thick cables which emerged from her skull seemed noble rather than unnatural, a headdress for some pagan deity. Black insulating tape wound around them and attached them to the enlarged and roughened pores into which they plunged. Martle knew that her skull was riddled with naturally occurring fissures, through which the cables passed on their way to her brain. Somewhere along the way, blood vessels and nerves intertwined with them. By the time they reached their goal, they weren't cables anymore.

"What do you want?" he whispered. "What do you *want*?"

There was no answer, of course. The brood-mother merely gazed incuriously at him, pulsing slightly as she breathed. He moved over to the window, but her eyes didn't move to track him. She didn't care about him, didn't even know he existed. His image passed through her mind every day on its way to the waiting world, but she was incapable of understanding its implications, its meaning or its connection to the man standing before her. Martle knew that. He turned to leave, but as he did so, his gaze passed over the window showing the studio floor far beneath.

Three cameras stood there, staring up at him.

He met their gaze, knowing somehow that he wasn't being watched by them but by the grotesque bulk which rested beside him, until Welter walked over with her cattle prod and herded them back to their pens.

And behind him as he left he could hear a breathy pulsing that might almost be taken for laughter.

The conference room was crowded by the time he got there, and he squeezed into a seat beside Suzy Bowles. Various journalists and production crew were smoking, sipping coffee and chatting. Bill Paternoster was, to nobody's surprise, absent.

Julia Wood was sitting next to Chris Isher, producer of ECBS News. Isher, an ambling, bearlike man, sized Martle up before waving a hand in ambiguous greeting.

"Okay kiddies, let's make a start," he said. "We'll be continuing on with the Argentina story, of course, and picking up on the latest developments from Luxembourg, but today's big news is the speech this morning by the Foreign Secretary. Who caught it?"

A scattering of hands went up around the table. Martle's wasn't one of them. He'd been aware that the speech was scheduled, the weekly handouts of up-and-coming events had made sure of that, but he relied on the script conferences to keep him up to speed on current affairs.

"Okay," Isher continued, glancing again at Martle, "the upshot of it is that the Government want to renegotiate the terms of the Cimliss trade agreement when they arrive next month. Nobody is happy about the stuff we got last time: it works, but nobody knows why. The Government will be putting forward a twelve-point document which guarantees better servicing and support, and a ten percent refund of the cost of the last batch amortised against the new one. How do we play it? Any ideas?"

"Last night's item was fairly straight," Suzy said, twirling her fingernails idly against the tabletop. "Do we need an angle on this one?"

"There's a lot of feeling out there against the Cimliss," said Julia Wood. Her eyes flickered from person to person, almost daring argument. "We'll be climbing on a popular bandwagon if we condemn the Cimliss for cheating us. Not in so many words, of course, but it could be a ratings winner."

Small noises of agreement came from the assembled journalists. Coffee cups were raised in anticipation of a few seconds' grace before the next item. Isher took a breath, ready to pronounce.

"Hang on," said Martle, surprising himself as much as anybody else. "How are Station-to-Station going to be slanting it? Or BSkyB? Or NASAtel?" He looked around. Isher was frowning. Wood just looked pissed off. Suzy, bless her, was smiling encouragingly. "Everyone's going to be pushing the idea that the Cimliss have sold us shoddy goods. No matter which channel people switch to, they'll get the same story. Apart from one." He smiled, but inside he trembled with the anticipation of what he was about to do.

"I think we should go the other way. Look at it from the Cimliss point of view. Try and get inside their heads. It's business, right, not a charity. We knew that from day one. So did the Government, but now they're trying to change the rules."

He could see by their faces that they weren't convinced, but at least they were listening. Lines of wet warmth traced their way slowly down his sides, but on the surface he was the consummate professional.

He addressed himself directly to Isher.

"Look, people are only going to watch us if we provide something that nobody else does. And we can with this piece. We can break away from the herd and give the other side of the story."

Isher was wavering.

"Put it this way," Martle continued, trying to consolidate his gains. "If we take the anti-Cimliss line, then whatever way it turns out, everybody will be sharing the credit or the blame. No brickbats, no bouquets, no awards. If we go pro-Cimliss and we're right, then we come out smelling of roses. Award-winning stuff."

That was what clinched it. Isher made one of his famous "my own feeling is" decisions, and they went on to other matters. Martle only caught odd scraps. He was too busy picking over the enormity of his betrayal. Bob Martle, the man who sold the world. And for what? To save face.

Or had he misread the entire thing? Was it possible? Had he taken a few odd scraps and built out of them a story the scale of which appalled him and held him helpless?

He might never know. Nobody might know, not for generations, but if in some future century the Earth was some economic satellite state of the vast Cimliss trading empire, a minor branch in a galactic suburb, would anybody trace it back, point the finger and say *yes, it was him, he was the man*?

After the meeting broke, he headed for makeup to prepare

for the evening news. As he sat in the chair and the layers of makeup were applied over his skin and over each other, he felt the truth slipping away, becoming buried, until ultimately it was just another layer, another commodity to be bought and sold, no different from other people's truths.

As he entered the studio, one of the cameras walked past. He tried to catch its eye, but there was no flicker of acknowledgement, no sign of the vast contempt that he knew, from that little charade he'd stumbled across the previous night, that they must feel for him and for all humanity. Up in the gallery the brood-mother stared out into the tangled lighting gantries, yet Martle felt sure that she was aware of his scrutiny, and that she knew what he'd done for her. And for himself. Part of him wondered why they'd waited until now to act, but another part already knew the answer. They were already acting: twisting intonations, moods, backgrounds and the occasional word to suit their own agenda. In his mind's eye he suddenly saw a global village linked by television: billions of people whose only opinion was delivered daily in discrete sound-bites. And he saw how fragile a thing was a career in the camera's eye.

Suzy Bowles came up behind him.

"Are you going to be okay tonight?" she murmured. "You were looking really rocky this morning."

Martle smiled, but inside he felt small and scared.

"Don't believe everything you see on television," he said.

RUBY

Alan Rodgers

President Oswald went to Moscow when he was a young
man in college, hardly more than a boy.

There are those who say nothing untoward happened
on that visit—that it was adolescent tourism, nothing more.
But the truth is darker, starker: Lee Harvey Oswald, thirty-
seventh President of the United States, met Jack Kennedy on
that trip. No chance meeting, this first encounter of the revered President and the man who (decades later, in circumstances as far removed as the imagination can inspire) was to
murder him: it was arranged weeks ahead of time, and played
an important part in the revolution that was to come.

Two years after the great war; months before the revolution—days that cast their shadows across our lives just as
night's horizon blocks the sun.

Oswald stayed at the big Intourist hotel in central Moscow.
He met Kennedy in the hotel bar by prior arrangement.

Halfway through the floor show Kennedy (sitting way way
in back, hiding in the shadows) coughed three and two. Oswald
gave the high sign from his seat across the smoky room.

Kennedy crossed the room to meet him.

"Kennedy," Oswald said. "I've wanted to meet you for a long
time."

The assassin (no, not *assassin*, not yet—assassin-to-be)

smiled. "Oswald," he said. He grinned wide and sunny as a spring day. "Comrade."

It's important to remember that these men met before the revolution, when things were nothing like they are now. No one believes that, but it's true: before the revolution, before the tumult and displacement, men like Kennedy and Oswald were *comrades*.

"Call me Lee," the young President said. He extended his hand, but the man who would murder him refused it.

Oswald shrugged. What did it matter? Gestures, symbolism—they were nothing. Substance was all.

And the substance of their meeting was code.

Kennedy looked around him to be certain they were alone. "Ruby," Kennedy said. "Ruby Jack."

He finished his drink and turned to walk away. Oswald caught his arm before he'd gone two steps.

Pulled him back. Held him.

"We need to know," Oswald said. "Why have you turned? How can we trust you?"

Kennedy scowled. "I do what I do for my own reasons," he said. "Trust me or not—that's your business."

Oswald would have none of it.

"Why?" he demanded.

Kennedy shook his head. "It's already dead," he said. "President Willkie killed it in the war."

He sounded bitter, angry. Of course he did! What American could feel anything else for the fool Willkie, the President the nation elected to save it from Roosevelt's ambition for war—who joined the fight alongside the British in India only in time to slow the Axis victory?

Joined the war only ten months before the enemy secured the entire Eurasian mainland.

Oswald nodded. He understood, of course. It was only patriotic to turn against a system that had dragged the country down into a hell of humiliation and defeat.

A hell weighed down by reparations to the Japanese, the Soviets, the Germans.

"Good man," Oswald said. "We need you."

That was what Kennedy called himself the next time those two met, during the most violent days of the revolution: Ruby Jack.

• • •

There was a day during the Great War that nearly doomed the revolution: a moment where it looked as though Grandfather Hitler would follow Napoleon's folly and set out to conquer Stalin's great Russian Motherland.

Imagine the consequences.

Imagine the American Red Underground suddenly turning on the Hitler they'd defended all the years since the founding of the Friendship Alliance. Imagine the loss of face. Who could follow an inconstant revolution? How could the revolution have continued to bloom?

Imagine a world where the British, Soviets, and Americans all stood against Grandfather Hitler's wrath. A world where Hitler, Stalin, Hirohito, and Mussolini did not conquer the old world and apportion it among them; a world where no triumphant Axis weighed great reparations on the defeated Americans.

Imagine a world where 1949 did not bring a Red Revolution upon America.

A world where the Latin nations of the West did not fall Red like so many dominoes in sequence.

Imagine a world where men like the derelict Kennedy came to rule, and not the martyred Oswald.

Imagine.

In the days after the revolution, Kennedy—the man who called himself Ruby Jack—came to live in just such a world of delusion. Perhaps his wounds consumed him; perhaps he was born to the psychosis and only came to show it as he matured.

Who can say? The man was crazy, plain and simple. Only madmen really understand such loons.

Kennedy was with Oswald when the orders came down from Stalin.

They were in the big Greenwich Village safe house, holed up through the thick of the revolution. Shooting in the streets; mayhem on the highways, in the terminals. Neither Kennedy nor Oswald was party to the fighting anymore. The FBI knew both of them, and had for weeks. They were wanted men whose faces appeared on posters in post offices all across the land.

Neither of them dared walk the streets by daylight. Even at night they took precautions.

That was how Kennedy was there to see the coded cable

that the courier brought from the Soviet Embassy: he and Oswald sat together in the safe house's big sunny parlor, sipping tea and nibbling crumpets as they faced one another across a great brass-and-marble chessboard.

The courier knocked three and seven—that was the signal that day, three and seven—and Oswald told her to come in.

She was a thin girl, that messenger. A thin girl dressed in a plain brown dress. Perhaps she looked frightened by the revolution all around them. Perhaps she was wounded inside.

"Oswald," she said. That was Oswald's code name during the revolution: *Oswald.* He was a brave man, our Oswald. Perhaps he was reckless. "A cable for you. From the Embassy."

Oswald knew the Embassy she meant. But Kennedy didn't. He was a Rube, the Ruby Jack. A fool who never connected the contact in Moscow to the Redness of the Revolution.

"Embassy. . . ?" he asked. Oswald ignored the question. The courier, handing her cable to the great one, knew better than to answer.

"Go," Oswald said. And the courier left as he spread the coded cable out across the chessboard's open field. Read it over twice and began to scribble calculations in the margin. In a few moments Oswald had the cable decoded.

Hard news, that cable. Direct orders from great Stalin himself. Orders that meant the revolution had to take a new turn, and thousands of the loyal would die to turn it.

"I don't understand," Kennedy said, reading as Oswald wrote. "What does this mean? Why would anyone give us such advice?"

Oswald shook his head.

"You don't understand," he said. "This isn't advice. These are our *orders.*"

Kennedy laughed, but only for a moment.

"Orders? Who would give us orders like those? Whose revolution is this, anyway?"

That was Kennedy's first reaction: disbelief. *Amusement.* Isn't that always the way with fools? When they learn the hardest, truest truths, they laugh.

And perhaps he was right to laugh, to disbelieve: Kennedy knew the revolution's leaders. Every one of them had made a point of meeting him after the miracle he'd managed in the battle outside Hartford. And knowing them he knew that they were prudent, temperate men and women—and Stalin's orders were no more temperate than Stalin was himself.

Then Oswald wrote out the true name that signed that note: *Stalin*.

Kennedy swore when he read it. "The Butcher? The devil who starved ten million in the Ukraine sends us orders? Tell that murderer to go to hell," he said. "He's got no business here. This is our revolution, not his."

Now it was Oswald's turn to laugh. "Great Stalin sends us instructions regularly," he said. "He is a wise instructor."

Kennedy shivered with rage. "You've been there, Lee. But have you seen? The terrible things he's done to Russia . . . ? The millions he killed to make a nation half a shadow of this one in decline? It isn't working, Lee—it never did work. *From each according to his ability; to each according to his need.* But no one does. No one works for a revolution. No one works because they can; they work when working does them good."

Oswald laughed again. "We'll make them work," he said. "That's what laws are for, to make them work."

Kennedy shook his head. "That's what Stalin does," he said. "He kills the ones who hesitate. And when they're all too frightened to resist, he kills some more to keep them scared." He got up from his seat. Began to pace, to gesture wildly. "Are you ready to kill? Who? How many of them? They worked for Stalin and Hitler because they knew they'd die if they didn't. Are you ready to kill them? How many of them? Do you have the heart to kill forever, constantly, kill them just to keep the ones alive scared for their lives?"

Great Oswald only smiled. "We'll have a revolution," he said. "And in the blood we'll thrive."

And he took a pistol from the holster beneath his sports jacket. And shot Kennedy squarely through the brain.

When security for the safe house came to investigate, Oswald told them that FBI agents had attacked them through the drawing room's wide floor-to-ceiling windows, killing poor Kennedy before they could defend themselves. Kennedy was a hero of the revolution, he said. A martyr who could teach us, teach us, teach us all. . . .

But something went wrong: despite his gruesome and grievous wound, Kennedy hung on to life. And continued to live despite all odds, despite the common sense that said he ought to lay down and die.

Amazing fact, perhaps the most amazing of all the great wonders to come from the revolution: Kennedy survived his injury. In time he even began to recover from it. Oh, he never did recover entirely—rather, he came to be a disoriented shadow of his former self. A ghost alive to haunt his comrades, a devil to tempt them from the true road to revolution: and still he served his purpose.

He was a martyr, an icon: a living legend unable to deny the tales that grew around him.

A martyr. And in time a derelict. A vagabond! John F. Kennedy, Hero of the Battle for Hartford, Second Greatest Martyr of the Revolution—a vagabond.

There are those who maintain it's sacrilege to speak so of him. And others who will tell you that there is no sacrilege in a modern age with no religion.

Others are entirely uncertain.

But few dispute the essential facts: Kennedy recovered from his wound. And since the great one's diaries came to light (days after his passing) we know that the bullet that near-on killed him came from Oswald's gun.

We know that Kennedy wandered away from his keepers not long after the glorious founding of the New Republic.

And we know that he spent most of the next eighteen years wandering the streets of cities like New York, Washington, and Boston. Now and again the authorities would find him, pick him up and send him away to a sanatorium—but sooner or later it always came back to them that Kennedy was a hero of the revolution, and not a common political criminal like those who fill our sanatoria. And when the hero demands his freedom, what righteous revolutionary can deny it?

And so Kennedy would find his way back to the streets.

He drifted all through the glorious and hopeful early years of our new revolutionary nation—those wondrous fat years where the redistribution of wealth put not chickens but oxen into every pot. Wandered through the Faltering from the One True Path and the Great Correction—the first in '55, the second in '56. Wandered unmolested through the Great Famine in '58.

No one knows how he survived the Famine. So many died, horribly of starvation—of cannibalism, some places. And still the hero persisted, always somewhere invisible at the margins of the world.

• • •

In the spring of '57 Kennedy spent six weeks in the sanatorium beside a millpond in New Canaan, Connecticut. The doctors there made extensive notes; they documented his case in minute detail. Perhaps they were afraid of him—afraid that the war hero's fame and reputation would somehow come to haunt them.

It may be that their fears were justified. Certainly the things Kennedy imagined were thought-crimes perpetuated against the regime; perhaps his doctors worried that the discussion of such things would land them in one of the indoctrination camps that dotted the Colorado mountains.

As, indeed, they may have: there are no records as to the fate of the two doctors who worked closest with Kennedy.

But we have transcripts of Kennedy's sessions with those doctors. They show that the fallen hero lived in a fantasy world of bizarre dimension. A world ruled not by our revolutionary heroes but by craven jackals like Eisenhower and Truman. A world, indeed, where Kennedy himself served as a senator in a senate still elected by popular vote, where votes distributed with universal and equal suffrage.

His therapists spent hours and hours trying to dissuade him of this bizarre psychosis. To no avail. Kennedy's delusion, they came to understand, was no ordinary psychosis but the result of physical trauma to the brain.

And in time they came to understand that there was nothing they could do for him, short of confining him for life. And who would dare confine a martyr of the revolution?

One night Kennedy took a walk along the millpond, and followed the stream that ran out from it until it opened out to the ocean. And forgot the sanatorium, and kept on along the coast. No one at the sanatorium tried to retrieve him.

The derelict Kennedy had his great moment in the sun in the summer of '59—August 11, 1959, during the Party Congress Oswald and the Iron Captain called to discuss the catastrophic failure of the second five-year plan.

No one invited the derelict. To this day no one is certain how he eluded security to find his way to the Podium.

The Podium where Comrade Oswald (since March all-powerful Secretary of the Interior) stood speaking of the need for *change*.

Change and the need for jobs.

Real, meaningful jobs; jobs that pay a living wage. Jobs to be *proud* of.

And now suddenly Kennedy stood behind Oswald, and the SS troopers assigned to protect the secretary turned ashen to look at one another in horrified disbelief. They tried to reach Kennedy and hustle him away before he could grab Oswald's shoulder, shove the man aside. Seize the microphone.

There just wasn't time, was all. And anyway the audience— ten thousand delegates from all around the country: ambassadors and guests from communist parties all around the globe—and anyway the audience had already seen him. Seen Kennedy the great revolutionary hero with the disfigured skull seize the microphone and denounce the Secretary in public and to his face.

"This has gone too far, Lee," Kennedy said. "It's time to put an end to it."

Oswald stood on the dais staring at Kennedy, shivering with rage. "Put an end to what? What are you talking about?" He was still close enough to the microphone for it to carry his voice across the auditorium—but from that distance his voice sounded thin and impotent, as though he were some raging vermin.

"The revolution, Lee. Look at it for yourself—look, look out across the land. The country is dying. People everywhere starving to death one by one. The ones who aren't can't find work; the ones who've got work haven't got any hope. And every day it gets a little worse."

Oswald rushed Kennedy, tried to seize the microphone away from him. It didn't work; Kennedy shoved him away with a single sweep of his good right arm. "Blood," Oswald said. Those who heard him in that hall said he seemed to mewl at the microphone. Perhaps he simpered with rage. "Don't you see? A revolution grows in blood. Without the blood it strangles."

Kennedy gaped at him. "Blood?" he said. "Whose blood? How many people do you want to kill? How many more than the thirty million who starved in the California famine?" He looked away. Rubbed his eyes. (It was the perfect moment for the SS to rush him, grab him bodily, and carry him away. But not a one of them could move a muscle.) "You're out of your mind. You've got to stop."

"New blood," Oswald said. "We'll have a new revolution. A

Cultural Revolution, like Mao's. A revolution of the heart and mind to teach us how to think!"

"It isn't working, Lee—it never did work. *From each according to his ability; to each according to his need.* But no one does. No one works for a revolution. No one works because they can; they work when working does them good."

"We'll make them work," Oswald said. "That's what laws are for, to make them work."

Kennedy shook his head again. "Are you ready to kill them all? All of them? They worked for Stalin and Hitler because they knew they'd die if they didn't. Do you have the heart to kill forever, constantly, kill them just to keep the survivors scared for their lives?"

"We'll have a revolution," Oswald said. "And in the rain of blood we'll thrive."

Neither Oswald nor Kennedy emerged from their confrontation with everything they'd brought to it. Oswald—who with the Iron Captain had stood on the verge of seizing power from the revolution's founding fathers—left the Congress early for his new assignment administering the reeducation of Butte, Montana—center of a minor rebellion three weeks before the Congress.

Kennedy left the Congress bound in a straitjacket. Bound, gagged, and blindfolded—when security seized him he resisted; when they bound him, he began shouting. And when they gagged him (hero of the revolution that he was) they could not bear to look him in the eye.

He spent the next eight years of his life locked away in the Tower of Washington—that granite spire on the Great Lawn that once was a monument to the first revolution's commander but now serves as a prison for the worst political criminals.

Oswald was luckier.

Butte survived the great western famine of '62 unscathed— more thanks to blind luck than any particular design. Then came the big purge and counterpurge in '63, and the leadership vacuum in their wake.

In '64, Oswald engineered his own rehabilitation. By the end of '65, he had control of the Politburo.

Bad times.

Bad, bad times all through '66, through the first half of '67. Stalin fifteen years dead and Hitler half a decade behind him. And without them—without them there was something wrong with the world. Not just wrong like in right and wrong. Things had been wrong as in evil for a generation, and everybody knew it even if none of them ever talked about it.

The trouble in '66 and '67 was different. It was times so bare, so hungry . . . it put the Great Depression of the '30s into a whole new perspective. Some people got nostalgic for those years.

In late '66, the Politburo named Lee Harvey Oswald President of the United States, and Oswald set to work right away. Within weeks his people were everywhere, listening to everyone and everything. They killed people who said things they didn't like. They killed people everywhere, sometimes for reasons that seemed like no reason at all. Everyone lost friends in those years—whole towns disappeared overnight, and no one lived to tell where the bodies were buried.

It got worse and worse as the weeks went on, till now in the spring of '67 there was a sense of things in the air—a sense like it wasn't just a big turnaround, a big rough in the down part of some economic cycle. Mao in China threw another Cultural Revolution, and lots of people died. But nobody thought he was crazy.

Because the trouble was—it was collapse. Collapse all over the world, and everybody knew it and what could anyone do about it?

In the fall of 1967, Oswald took the cue from Mao and launched a cultural revolution of his own. And before he was finished America was drowned in blood.

They locked Kennedy away in the Tower of Washington and drugged him until he was listless. Some of the guards beat him. Some of them tortured him. But that was no special sentence for the fallen revolutionary hero; all prisoners of the Tower are tortured. The guards starve and abuse and revile their charges, and sometimes when they're of a mood the highest officials of the party come to the Tower to vent their rage upon the backs of the fallen.

Kennedy was a special case for Oswald and the guards who reported to him; they took a special pleasure in disfiguring him, taunting him, starving him until he grew delirious and nearly died—then feeding him too much so that his starving body fouled itself.

But they never broke him. Not in all those years, no matter

how they tried. Perhaps the scars inside his brain gave him
strength to withstand the sort of abuse that reduces ordinary
people to drooling idiocy; maybe he could not go mad because
he already *was* mad. Or maybe he was strong because he was
a hero—and make no mistake, nothing President Oswald could
ever do to him could steal the Battle of Hartford from him or
our history of the Revolution.

Maybe.

But the ones who know him say it was neither strength nor
madness that let Kennedy endure the Tower of Washington,
and even thrive inside it: the folks who saw the fallen hero say
the thing that sustained him was the rightness of his cause.

That sounds like a fantastic thing to say about a madman,
doesn't it? To say that underneath all the delusion and the
misunderstanding, deep beneath the brains that Oswald's bullet stirred into a bloody froth, John Fitzgerald Kennedy, the
man who called himself Ruby Jack—underneath it all Ruby
Jack was right.

But he was.

Oh, he had the details wrong. The fantasy world of his afternoon reveries was a lie, and a transparent one. But the insight it gave him on our own circumstance was a thing no one
who heard him could mistake, not now, not then, not ever.

The guard Oswald planted in the Tower of Washington—
Alex Medvedev—wasn't so loyal as Oswald thought he was. He
was anything but loyal, in fact: the man sent reports to Moscow
by secret courier three times a week. Among those reports were
audiotapes of Oswald's afternoons in Kennedy's cell.

Terrible, terrible things on those tapes. Things even sea-
soned revolutionaries dread to hear.

The tape of Oswald's last visit to the Tower ended up in the
historic archives in the Library of Congress. It's been broadcast—what, ten thousand times? Who could count? It was the
height of the Cultural Revolution in America, and Oswald
came to the Tower to vent his rage on Kennedy's hide.

"Ruby Jack," Oswald shouted as he opened the Tower door
that frigid December afternoon, "I've come to see you, Ruby
Jack."

He didn't rattle Kennedy. Nothing ever rattled Kennedy—
not after the bullet stirred his brain. He waited patiently in his
cell as Oswald climbed the Tower stairs, and when Oswald

forced the cell door open Kennedy greeted him warmly as a comrade.

"Lee," he said, his voice rich and warm with comradely nostalgia, "it's good to see you, friend."

Oswald spat in response. He said, "You're no friend of mine, Ruby Jack," and when Kennedy tried to answer he told him to be quiet.

"What's wrong, Lee?" Kennedy asked him. "Have the people come for you?"

The question enraged Oswald. He crossed the cell, grabbed Kennedy's collar, and shook the man in his chains. "What do you know?" he demanded. "Who've you been talking to?"

Kennedy shook his head. "I don't know anything, Lee." Oswald shook him again. "I don't know anything. But the country's been getting hungrier for years. And lately even the guards here have deep-set, hungry eyes."

Oswald glared at him.

"How bad is it, Lee?"

Oswald lifted him off his feet, pushed backward, slamming Kennedy's head and shoulders into the wall behind him. "None—" back again, and *slam!* into the wall "—of your—" *slam!* "—goddamn—" *slam!* "—business!"

"It isn't working, Lee," Kennedy said. "You think it ever will? You think beating me will change what's happening to you?"

Oswald screamed.

Kennedy grinned ruefully. He looked Oswald in the eye and shook his head.

"Guard!" Oswald shouted, and an instant later a guard opened the cell door. He was pale and haggard, bitter looking. He looked dangerous, like a dog that's been beaten and starved and abused. Oswald turned to face the guard, and he gave the man orders. "Feed this prisoner," he said. "Feed him until he dies. Force-feed him if you have to—use the gullet-wrench." Oswald smiled. "When his gullet bursts, throw the corpse out onto the Great Lawn for the rats and crows to pick."

It didn't work out like that, the way it happened. Oswald left the cell trembling, laughing maniacally, wandered from the Tower onto the Lawn. As he went he ranted and raved; the Tower guards heard him shouting party slogans for thirty long minutes after the Tower door slammed shut behind him.

When the last sound of President Oswald faded into the night, the guard who'd received his orders—Medvedev—went to his captain and asked him what to do. There was no way to obey Oswald's instructions. There was never food in the Tower larder, and when there was it wasn't enough to bloat a man. If any of the Tower guards had known a way to find that much food he would've eaten it himself—or taken it home to his starving wife and children.

"What do we do?" Medvedev asked his captain.

The captain—his name was Dominik, and he liked to think he was a leader among men—the captain shrugged. "Strangle him," he said. "Once the rats have had their pound of flesh, it won't matter how he died."

Medvedev gave an uneasy little laugh. He wasn't good with killing. No matter how he was a traitor and a spy three times over; he'd never learned the art of squeezing a man's life from his throat, and when he murdered Ruby Jack the act went very wrong.

"I've got to kill you, Kennedy," Medvedev said. On the tape his voice is very sad. Of course it's sad! Medvedev had spent many hours with Kennedy, talking with him, arguing with him, listening to the reveries of his bizarre imagination.

Kennedy's response is almost sympathetic. "I understand, Alex," he said. "Better at the hands of a friend than from an assassin's bullet."

"What do you mean, Jack?"

Silence. "It isn't important."

"Do you have a . . . wish? That's important, isn't it, giving the condemned man a final wish?"

"Nothing, Alex," Kennedy said. "It's all right. I'm not afraid." And he lay back against his chains, looked up at the sky to bare his throat.

Medvedev didn't take that well. "You ought to struggle," he said. "Or beg for your life, at least. It isn't right to die like dying doesn't matter."

Kennedy never answered. After a while Medvedev came to wrap his hands around him, to hold him tight and dear until his eyes turned dark and his limbs twitched, and he shuddered, trembled, purpled, and went still. When the guard was certain that Ruby Jack Kennedy would never breath again, he hauled the hero's cold, still body out onto the Great Lawn and left it for the Capitol's rats to devour.

The mistake Medvedev made was the mistake most amateur stranglers make: he didn't throttle Kennedy long enough or hard enough to kill him. When the first rat pursed its septic lips around his ear, Kennedy woke terrified and flailing, fighting for his life.

He lay in the dark in the thin brown grass not far from the Tower. There was no light at all on the Lawn around him, but in the distance there was a procession of thousands, thousands, and thousands carrying torches. Oswald had called the people to Washington to stand before him and take his blessing—just as Mao had called his people to Peking two years before. Kennedy didn't know the details, but he could smell revolution in the air. Of course he could feel the Cultural Revolution around him! He was the Hero of Hartford, the Agitator of Congress!

Ruby Jack Kennedy, still delirious from Oswald's second attempt to murder him, stumbled across the darkness of the Great Lawn into the greatness of the nation's darkest night.

Kennedy approached the procession slowly, carefully. When he stood thirty yards from the end of the line he hung back in the shadows to watch and listen.

He heard the people whispering to one another, and he knew they were afraid. He heard *Oswald* and *revolution* and *blood* and he knew in his heart what he'd see when he got to the far end of the line, and he knew he had to go there.

Even then—dazed and confused and half strangled to death—Kennedy was a hero. He knew that there was nothing he could do when he got to the bonfire. He knew that it was certain death for him to even try.

And he wanted to live, just like every sane and healthy living creature wants to live, but he went to face the terror anyway. Because the evil at the far end of that procession was a thing no brave and decent man could fail to confront, no matter if it killed him.

So Kennedy wandered through the shadows three miles along the procession, until he came to the great bonfire that burned at the south end of the reflecting pool. Oswald was there on the east side of the fire, standing on an improvised dais. Fifty thousand stood with him, behind him and up along the east side of the pool.

Kennedy didn't see the crowd at first—maybe because of the unnatural hush that hung above it. He hardly even noticed Oswald.

But he saw the promenade. There wasn't any choice about that; once his eyes had passed across that awful vision there was no way he could have seen anything else before he'd taken it all in.

The promenade was slick with blood where it led away from the procession. Blood everywhere glittering rich and sanguine luxuriant in the firelight—it was all over the grass, the dirt, the paved and rutted promenade; bright pools of blood shimmered before the fire. As Kennedy watched, a supplicant stepped away from the head of the procession, crossed the blood-bright promenade, climbed the dais to beg for Oswald's blessing. Oswald gave it to him—maybe reluctantly, maybe not. The supplicant, cowed and frightened, retreated into the silent thousands west of the reflecting pool.

Now two more came to supplicate, and two more after that. All of those went much the way the first had. But the next was terrible: where the battered old woman knelt before her President, begging for his glory, Oswald gave her something terrible instead.

Oswald took the pistol from the holster at his waist. And he held the gun to the old woman's head.

And drove a bullet through her brain.

A great fountain of her blood shot out from the dais, spraying new depth into the pools before the fire. After a moment the woman's convulsing corpse tumbled off the dais, into the pools of blood.

It lay there for a long time before two hulking men came to haul it onto the mountain of dead on the east side of the reflecting pool.

No one in the crowd said a word. None of them so much as whispered. They were cowed, frightened people in that crowd—minor party cadre called to the capital from across the nation. They were henchmen of the revolution, but they were terrified, naïve, and mostly innocent, too—most of them were ordinary people pressed into service to replace real cadre murdered in the purges.

Kennedy saw that carnage, and he didn't think; he acted.

"Lee!" he shouted. "Lee Harvey Oswald!" He stepped out of the darkness beside the procession, into the firelight—and now the silent crowd gasped. Even if they were ersatz cadre, every one of them had seen the newsreel of Oswald and Kennedy at the plenum in 1959. Every last one of them recognized Kennedy's face, and they all knew he was Oswald's nemesis. Two halves of a single legend stood before them, and the cadre knew that, too.

"You're alive again, Ruby Jack," said Oswald. "Why don't you stay dead when I kill you?"

"God will have me when he wants me," Kennedy said, and somewhere in the crowd some shouted, "*Idolater!*"—that was the word for religionists that year, *idolater*.

Oswald laughed. "This time I'm going to have you drawn and quartered, Kennedy. I'm going to *watch* you die. No more mistakes."

Kennedy waved away the threat. "This is the bloodbath you've been promising, isn't it, Lee?" he asked. "Your *blood* revolution. Where will it stop? How many will you kill?"

"The blood cleanses our cause," Oswald told him. He had to shout it twice to be heard—the crowd, which only moments ago had stood tamely silent, now pulsed and chittered like an angering mob.

Kennedy stood at the head of the procession now. He grabbed a man from the crowd, thrust him into the blood-light of the bonfire.

"This one, Lee—will this one live or die? How will you decide? When will you know? Will you kill him for the glitter in his eyes—or will that make you spare him?"

Oswald glowered. He raised his pistol, pointed it at Kennedy. "Silence! You'll be silent or I'll kill you now, I swear I will."

"Go to hell, Lee," Kennedy said.

"I will," Oswald said, and again someone shouted, "*Idolater!*" Oswald's eyes bulged with anger. "God *damn* you."

Oswald aimed the gun and fired. He didn't miss, not once. Of course he didn't miss; he'd trained as a marksman. Two of Oswald's bullets caught Kennedy in the gut; one lodged itself between his collarbone and shoulder blade—but none of them seemed to affect him. In that moment Kennedy was like Rasputin in the mother of all revolutions, determined, unstoppable, immune to the torment that comes from the muzzle of a gun. Oswald emptied his gun into Kennedy's body, but he could not stop him.

As Oswald reloaded his gun, Kennedy turned back to admonish the throng now building up out of what once had been an orderly procession. "If you want free of this monster," he said, "face him! Take him!"

Oswald started firing again, but now the crowd surrounded Kennedy, and there was no chance of a clear shot.

"He can kill you one by one, but he can't kill you all."

One man rushed out of the throng, one to die to save them all, and Oswald shot him, shot another and another and another rushing up at him as the crowd surged and his gun went empty and his guards ran for their petty miserable murdering lives to die cowards as the cowed multitude from the west side of the pool joined the surging mob from the procession and they all roiled over Oswald and his guards like a tide to take them, take them, take them every one.

The mob tore Oswald and his guards limb from limb, and when they were done they gave the bones to the feral dogs that inhabit the city.

Oswald has no grave.

Kennedy disappeared in the bloody confusion that killed Oswald. There is no solid evidence of any kind to show what happened to him, but there are those who say he lies buried in the mass grave whose monument now marks the south tip of the reflecting pool. Others say he recovered to return to the life he'd lost speaking out at the plenum—they say he is a drifter, a vagrant. Or sometimes the object of study in a psychal research institution.

Others say that the last remnants of his once-great family found him in the aftermath of the battle, took him in, and see after him.

No one knows for certain, and few imagine clearly enough to be sure. Who can say? Perhaps Kennedy was only a legend that spoke in the heart of a frightened mob before it murdered Oswald: sometimes it only takes the memory of greatness to bring greatness from us.

WHERE THE SHADOWS RISE AND FALL

Pat MacEwen

S omebody gonna be dyin' today.
Knew it soon as I woke up. The smell of death hung over me like a hungry gray fog, slippin' greasy wet fingers inside of me, slidin' down into my lungs with my every breath, reachin' down after my soul.

I sat up too fast, rolled off the couch and down onto the floor, and I lay there and choked on the stink of it, coughing my guts up, my arms wrapped around the white pain in my belly.

Not yet! No, not *me*! I kept tellin' it, curling around it, my mind swallowed up by it.

Couldn't see, couldn't hear, not right off. Took me a couple of minutes to realize someone was buzzin' the doorbell, that somebody had been for quite a while.

Finally got to my feet, kickin' beer bottles out of the way. Straightened up, slow and careful, and swiped at my face with the sleeve of my T-shirt. A deep breath helped settle the belly down. Then I was staggering toward the front door.

Better not be a salesman. If so, I was fixin' to tell off the son of a bitch, but the minute I opened the door, I was chokin' again, like I'd sucked up a lungful of skunk juice. It rolled off the man in the doorway so thick I could *see* it, almost, like a dust cloud of death and corruption.

The smell of it, sump water mixed in with butcher shop odors of dead steers and pig's blood, all mixed up with some kinda chemical stench—took me straight back to 'Nam. Yeah, man, back to the choppers, the sprayers, the killing white mist drifting over the forest, the mist that was gonna take twenty years killing me . . .

Panting, I stood there and stared at the man puttin' out all that stinkum. I stared at a ghost.

It was Stephen Bartholomew, Private First Class, with a little boy sittin' up top of his shoulders. He looked just the same as he did in Saigon, swear to God. He was totin' a bedroll and duffel bag, wearin' his camos and combat boots.

What's that?

No. He'd never been in D.C. before, never come here, never called me or nothing, not since we got back.

He was good, though. A good soldier, maybe the best. He was quick and alert and he stayed offa junk, and he always was *there*, at your back, when you needed him. Guy you could count on. A man with a plan.

Yeah, that's right. Same plan as all of us. Get home alive, any way that you could.

He did, too.

Leastways, I'd thought so. Up until now.

I just stare at him, slack-jawed.

He says, "Hey there, Sarge. Hope I'm not bustin' in on you . . ."

Then he stops short, 'cause he's got a good look at me now, and his face gets all empty, the way it did that day at An Loc, when he seen what Charlie had done to Van Trinh, to that little Viet kid that used to ride up on his shoulders. His face flattened out like a piece of rock 'cept for his eyes, which are buggin' out, burnin' black holes in his sunburnt face.

"Sarge," he says, chokin', "what happened to *you*?"

I could feel my own face had curled up like a windowshade, after I'd caught that first whiff of him. Hit me like buckshot.

But there was that other kid up on his shoulders, with big blue eyes, wide as plates, starin' at me, so I picked up my teeth off the floor.

"It ain't nothin' much, not near as bad as it looks like," I tell Stevie, although I'm wavering on my feet. "Been kinda down with the flu."

I can see he believes me, but mostly because of he wants to.

It don't take no genius to figure that out. But it ain't 'cause he doesn't care, neither.

Good man, right? I told you that.

Just that he's got his own cancer inside him, a sickness that's chewin' its way up and out, like that thing they had on the TV, man, that Alien growed from an egg down inside of that skinny guy's belly.

I didn't know nothing about him, the things that he done, or the places he's been. Nothing, not since the day we split up, comin' offa the plane back at Travis. All I knew was what I could smell.

So I let him in, set him down, settled his duffel bag. Too heavy, clunky, I think at the time, but I didn't have no chance to see what was inside the damn thing. I get Steve a beer, and the kid gets a ginger ale out of the fridge when I give him his choice. He don't say much to me, though, not even his name. I think maybe he wasn't too sure 'bout a stranger as skinny and rough-lookin' like I am. Kid was real tired too. Worn out clean down through the middle, and medium dirty . . . and smellin' the same as his old man. Sweet Jesus, a little kid, stinkin' of burnt meat an' cordite.

Steve says to me, "That's Paul. We call him Dink. Goin' on seven. He doesn't talk much."

A real cute kid, too, with big eyes and blond hair and deep dimples. The kinda kid used to be on that show, *Eight Is Enough*. What the hell was his name, now?

Yeah, Nicholas. Right.

Well, I leave him alone. Maybe time'll get one of us over that hump in the middle. That is, if there *is* any time left. I want to be sick, thinkin' 'bout how he smells, but I swallow my heart back down, head back to Stevie.

The man's sittin' down, now, but looks like he might bounce back up again if he lets go for a second. Tired or not, his whole body's wound up just as tight as a spring and he's got that cold, sidewinder look in his eyes, like he's heard Charlie creepin' around his tent, *inside* the fence, and the smell on him's makin' me dizzy.

I start in to talking old times, thinkin' maybe it might calm him down some, might give me a chance to think.

We talked about Corporal Burke's stupid, gimcrack inventions, especially that time he got him a bungee cord off of a surfboard, and used it to hook up his rifle to one wrist. He figured if he lost his gun in a ambush or something, all he'd have to do was just reel it back in.

Sure enough, a week later, we picked up a sniper, out on patrol. Burke, he goes down in a rice paddy, loses his gun on the other side, starts pulling on the damn bungee. The cord was so fucking elastic, it bounced that damn M-16 all over hell and gone, knocked off the safety, and fired off half a clip right back at Burke. Hit him once in the leg, and goddamn nearly shot off his balls.

Stevie laughed with me, telling me Burke really wasn't so stupid, 'cause that leg'd got him shipped home again, hadn't it?

Yeah, laughin' with me, but there was that look again, eyes slidin' off to the side ever' time something creaked, jumpin' up in his face when the kid dropped his soda pop can on the floor.

The kid dropped it, BANG! Then he froze, staring up at his own daddy's face like he was standing on top of a Claymore, like he'd heard the click underneath him, and now he was waiting to have both his legs blown off.

I got up, grabbed a rag, cleaned it up quick, puttin' my skinny ass in between 'em. But Stevie, man, he didn't say nothing, just sat there, so long and so quiet you coulda heard grass growin' under his butt, throwing out even more of that half-rancid, moldy aroma.

God.

I don't believe in ghosts, really. Not no kind of voodoo or juju or black magic, neither. Whatever was happening there with the kid and with Steve, and then, later on, down at the Wall itself . . . well, hell, I don't know, except it ain't magic.

No more'n me smelling the death-stink on people.

I'm part black, part white and part redskin, a crazy-ass mix of Yoruba, Scots-Irish and Seminole, plus about three fingers French Canuck. Maybe that's why the nose works like it does. All that Indian blood comin' out, or else maybe there's somebody's bloodhound got into the woodpile.

Whatever.

I found out in 'Nam that I knew who was gonna get taken out two or three hours ahead of time. I could walk past 'em, and whiff it. A kind of a sickly sweet, half-rotted cannabis odor that clung to 'em.

Didn't catch on, though, not at first. I just thought they'd been smokin' that Thai shit.

But I'd got the hint soon enough, and I knew what could happen here if'n I didn't find some way to get through to Steve, and make him and his kid start to smelling like life again.

I don't rightly know what I would've done if'n my belly'd stayed quiet, but right about then it decided to kick up a fuss, on account of the beer being too cold, I guess. It grabbed hold of me while I was bent over, pulled me on down like a sack of potatoes, and then I was layin' there, looking up into their faces.

Dink scrambles away from me, scareder of me than his daddy, right then. Stevie, he jumps at me, gathers me up, hauls me onto the couch again, treatin' me just like *I'm* the kid.

"Sarge, what's the *matter*?" he says, but I can't talk yet. Too busy swallowing fire.

A couple of minutes go by before I can begin to get words out, but then, just as quick as it come, the pain fades again, settling into its usual sick little ache.

I come out of it, notice the air's got a little bit cleaner. The stink is as much me as him now.

"I'm all right," I tell Steve. "Come on. Let me up."

He don't want to, but I'm not about to do either of us any good while I'm flat on my back, so I work my way up a bit, then Steve, he helps me.

I smile at him, knowing I probably look like a skull grinning at him, but nothing I do with my face really looks appetizing, y'know?

He gets all wound up over my problem, so I tell him, finally, what's going on, the VA, chemotherapy, lawyers and shit like that, tryin' to make Uncle Sam admit he fucked us up when we sprayed Agent Orange on all of them trees.

Stevie shakes his head. "Goddamn political assholes," he says, with a bitterness I never heard outta him before. "Long as *they* look good, they don't give a fuck about grunts like us."

Well, hell. I can't say he's wrong there, so I just agree with him, quiet-like.

All of a sudden he stands up and starts pacin', kicking my beer bottles halfway across the stained floor. "Look at what they did, what they're still doing in Kuwait, Iraq! When the hell does it ever stop?!"

"Maybe it doesn't," I tell him, and now I think maybe I've got a clue. Same bug that's been bitin' lots of us Vietnam vets.

"It's insane!" Stevie tells me, still pacing, beginning to sweat in the close heat inside the apartment. The jungle heat I got to have, now, to warm my bones. "Everything we did in 'Nam, man, we did it for them, and then we came back home and they spit on us for it! My own brother, Sarge, when I come home, he spit in my face, on my uniform."

Stevie's voice cracks as he turns again, facing me. "Kris," he says, "called me a damn 'baby killer.' "

I stare at him, feelin' my heart catch, and just for a split second, I'm back there, back in the DMZ.

Stevie's there, too, standing over the sniper he's just picked off. He grabs a hold of the black silk pajamas and rolls the Cong over and God, I can still see the long black hair spilling across her face. I can still see the black sling and the baby inside it, the tiny head split open by the same bullet that passed through his mother's breast.

I can still hear Stevie whispering, "No. Jesus!"

I blink.

I'm back in D.C. again.

When I look up, Stevie's staring at me and a tiny black spark flies between us that says he knows where I been.

Slowly, I nod to him, letting the silence remind him that I understand, but it's not enough.

He turns his back on me, winds up and pitches his beer bottle right at the wall. Hits it hard, too. The bottle flies into 'bout five hundred pieces and some of it flies back as far as his feet.

He ignores it and turns to me. "Why was it different?" he wants to know. "Why was it different to go to Kuwait, to blow all those poor ignorant bastards to bits? Hunh? You tell me that, Sarge. Why the hell was it different? How come they've been treated like heroes, and given parades and shit? How come their jobs were still *there* when they got back? How come no one cared about *us*?"

He's beginnin' to cry, holdin' both his hands out to me. "God . . . was it only because those guys won their damn war and we didn't? Well, *was* it?"

"I don't know," I tell him, and then try to offer him the only thing I have to give right now. "Some people say if they won, it was only because of the stuff that we learned in 'Nam."

"Bullshit," said Stevie, the word like a gunshot. His kid, Dink, he jumps a good inch off the couch and then freezes again, like a rabbit.

"That's generals talking," says Stevie. His right hand karate-chops at the air. "That's Stormin' Norman talking, man. That's Colin fucking Powell. And Bush. God, but I'd like to . . ."

"Steven," I tell the man, dredging up what little's left of my sergeant's command voice, "you stop right there. Maybe you're right, but you can't do a damn thing about it. Besides," I say, straight as a gun barrel, "you got some other things you need to think about." I'm nodding toward the kid. "You got to take care of business, man. You got responsibilities."

He glances once at the kid, then he shakes his head, like he was dizzy and tryin' to clear it.

"Sit down," I say, using up all of the voice I got left, and I guess it's enough, 'cause he does. He collapses in one of my ragged-ass armchairs.

I hand him his beer back and Stevie gets quiet then, broodin' like, but he don't smell quite so bad now, so I start to get kinda hopeful, like maybe it helped him to let loose a piece of the shit down inside him.

We had us a couple more sips of the brew, and we start in to talking again, about faraway things, about Hong Kong and Travis and Big Jim Danapoli, one of them Army Intelligence types who thought he was God's gift to the Vietnamese. Used to have this cute gook secretary that Big Jim got het up about, until one day she says she'll eat lunch with him, sure, and she pulls out this brown paper sack full of live roaches, four and five inches long . . . yeah, that's right. Ate 'em raw. Smacked her lips. Offered him one.

And Big Jim fainted dead away, hit his head, wound up in Saigon again, in the hospital, with a concussion he couldn't explain.

Stevie laughs for real this time, and I get to thinking it might be all right for now, might be a chance, but there's still something movin' down underneath, somethin' you couldn't quite see, like a 'gator tail down near the bottom, a dark swirl of death in deep water.

Steve tells me how he spent some time up in Oregon, how he come out of the woods and went home again. This was about nine years after he mustered out. Found him a sweet little thing name of Jeanne and settled down. Figured to start him a family, build a new life. Only, jobs were few and far between. And Jeanne, she kept getting pregnant and losing her babies, which he figured maybe had something to do with that damned Agent Orange. The only one lived was this kid he'd brought with him, Dink.

Stevie told me how he'd been a mailman this last four years. Only good job he could get, with his arm only forty percent and the veteran's points to make up for no schooling. He got into trouble, though, down the line. Kept gettin' bit by the dogs on his route. Pretty soon, Steve, he bit 'em back.

Said it was reflex. He carried a stick just to fend 'em off, but there was one of 'em caught Stevie by surprise, bit him or scared him, one. Next thing he knew, the damn dog was dead, just like that.

Scared him worse, after, 'cause he hadn't meant to, y'know. He just did it, like he'd done in 'Nam, on patrol. You shoot first, and *then* figure out what in the hell it was spooked ya.

Got so's he was scared to do anything round his own kid, even spank him, for fear of him losin' it all of a sudden. And Steve got his ass canned the second time he killed a mutt.

VA said Steve was okay, though. They run him through some of their tests, and then said it was nothin' much, nothing they'd give him a pension for, that's for sure. Nothin' worth putting him into a hospital. So they just stuck him in outpatient counseling, gave him a pat on the back, said, Get lost, bud!

Of course, there was damn little work after that. Said he kept having flashbacks, and everyone who'd ever seen *Rambo* thought he was gonna blow off any second.

To look at him now, I thought maybe they hadn't been far off the mark.

When I asked him why he was in town, Steve said something about the VA, but the only part I caught that made any sense was he wanted to take his boy down there to see the Wall.

Didn't ring true, didn't fit the look, didn't *smell* right, 'cause a trip to the Wall, well, it's kind of a healing thing, something you work your way up to, but I was afraid askin' any more questions'd probably spook him, and God only knew what he'd do after that.

So I said, "You two had any breakfast yet?"

Stevie's head jerked back and forth like it wasn't connected right, like one of them Japanese dolls with their heads on a spring.

"Well, then, listen," I said to him. "Why don't you jump in the shower while Dink and me scramble some eggs?"

Stevie reached up and ran his hand back through his hair. It was spiky stuff, stiff with dirt, standin' straight up, turnin' gray early. Rubbed his face, then said, "Yeah, man, that'd go good right now."

Stevie creaked when he got up, like some of his bones needed oiling. I showed him the john, got some towels out, waited outside the door till I heard hot water runnin', until I heard Steve pull the shower door shut.

Then, movin' on tiptoe, I slipped away down the hall, into the kitchen, with big-eyed Dink watchin' me all the way.

I look at him. I say, "Son, does your momma know where you're at?"

He shakes his head, backin' up till his heel hits the trash can. He's trembling now, shakin' so bad his hair looks like aspen leaves.

"I know your daddy's in trouble," I tell him. "I just want to help. I don't want him to get any deeper."

Them blue eyes keep gettin' a little bit darker, and bigger. They startin' to look like a owl's.

I don't have a whole lot of time, so I start edgin' toward him, real easy like, tellin' him it's gonna be okay, how I just wanted to talk to his momma, but Dink, he don't want any part of me, won't let me touch him, so finally I have to jump at him, grab him and hoist him up off of his feet, 'cause I'm tellin' you, that little kid is a tiger.

Inside of three seconds, he turns every which way but loose, all the same time he's kickin' and bitin' and gougin' at me. It's like trying to catch a tornado.

If I wasn't sick, I still don't know that I coulda held him. The way he was kickin' me, right in the ribs and the belly, no way.

No, sir, Dink skinned right out of my arms and his jacket both, just like a garter snake sheddin' his skin, but the funniest thing was, that kid never made a sound, not all the time he was fightin' me.

Never said nothing, nor yelled for his daddy.

As soon as he got loose, he run round the counter and scooted, quick, under the table and in between chair legs, where I couldn't reach him, and then he scootched down and just watched me. He figured on me comin' after him, see. But I couldn't have if I'd've wanted to.

I was in bad shape, my belly on fire again.

It was all I could do just to hang on and watch him back, clutching his coat while I tried to pull air back inside.

I can see that persuasion ain't gonna work, not with this kid.

Runnin' out of time, too. So I give up and go through his jacket instead.

Dink still don't say nothing, not even when I point out where the phone number's wrote on the label in raggedy ink pen, so faded I just about couldn't make out all the numbers.

Or maybe it's just me. By this time, the kid's got a gasoline reek, jellied gasoline, like from a flamethrower tank, and I feel like I can't breathe around him. My eyes start to watering bad, and my fingers was shakin' so's I wasn't sure I could hit the right buttons, but finally, I got the number punched in, and I stood there, leaned back up against the tile counter and breathin' in through my mouth, watching the kid while he's watchin' me, wanting somehow to wipe out what was in that boy's eyes . . .

After four rings, I'm startin' to think about who I should call next. The VA, or maybe the cops. After five rings, I know that I've made the wrong choice, or the stink would be fading away, but before I can hang up the phone, someone answers. A man's voice, a deep, harsh, MP kinda thing, barkin' at me. He says, "Hello?"

Something about a cop's voice, man. Like seein' a cop in plain clothes. You can't tell what it is, but you know it as soon as you hear it.

Whatever Steve'd got into, the whole mess was bad enough that he had cops waiting for him inside his house.

I really wanted to hang up, but didn't. I asked him for Jeanne, for Mrs. Bartholomew. Already, I feel my heart start to pound again, knowing this isn't right, knowing already, I think, what had happened, but not knowing what else to do now.

The guy on the line, he says, "Yeah? Well, she's takin' a shower. You give me your name and your number, I'll ask her to call ya back."

Takin' a shower. Like Steve. A coincidence, right? But it made the hair stand up all over the back of my neck, and I started to shiver, *before* I felt Steve's pistol, jabbin' me in the back.

Steve, he was always a cat-footed son of a bitch. Never heard nothin', man, not a creak in the floor, not a whisper.

Just, snap, he's there, saying real low and quiet, "Hang up the phone, Sarge."

I don't know if whoever stood on the other end heard him, but he started barkin' again, louder, saying, "Who is this?"

I didn't dare answer. I couldn't see Steve, but I damn sure

could smell him, like something half-roasted by napalm. I hung up the phone, moving real slow and easy, and then let Steve push me on out of the kitchen.

Dink followed us, sneakin' along the wall, usin' the armchairs for cover. I seen the same look on Van Trinh a few times, when the mortars got close, never lookin' up, knowing that what you could see comin' didn't count, only the pattern.

I already knew what this pattern was doing, man, closing in, chokin' me.

Stevie says, "I'm sorry, Sarge," in my ear, and he's chokin' up too, but it don't matter much, 'cause the next thing I know is I'm tied in a knot, like a pretzel. I'm laying facedown in my own dirty laundry, that covers the floor of my closet. I'm hogtied, I'm gagged, and I'm hurtin' like hell where he bashed me one, back of my left ear.

Well, that damn near did me in, all by itself, 'cause I couldn't breathe. Ain't bad enough that my laundry is ready to get up and walk to the washing machine. I'm all closed in, see, trapped in the dark, just like I was in one of them tunnels again, chasin' Charlie, and stink is all I got to track him by, death stink, like burnt garlic mixed up with three-day-old bodies, and how do I know if it's him or it's me that I'm smelling? I don't know, don't know nothing, 'cept that I got to get out of there, right NOW!

So I started floppin' around some and knocked over some of the shelves in the back of my closet, where I got a camping kit, backpack and shit that I haven't sold off yet. Not ready, I guess, to admit that I'm not gonna use 'em again. When the damn backpack landed on me, well, I panicked all over again from the sound of it, nylon, y'know, rubbing flesh in the dark, and I pretty well dumped the whole thing out, and that's where I found my old Buck knife, when I had calmed down to where I could think.

God, but it took me forever to cut myself loose with the damn thing. I ain't got the muscle I used to have . . . ain't got a lot of things.

I had a real hard time makin' my legs work, too. Practically had to crawl out of that closet, and by then, well, Stevie's long gone, and the kid too. 'Bout all that was left was his bedroll 'n duffel. I stared at 'em just for a second or two, and then opened them both up.

The bedroll was wrapped around one of them toy planes you get down to Radio Shack—has a little remote control on it, so's you can steer, hit the gas, jack up the flaps and shit. When I look inside the box, though, the plane's all in pieces, and there ain't no sign of the joystick.

The duffel bag's worse, full of dirty, used camping gear, hand tools and shit. When I dumped it out, hit the damn floor like a ton o' bricks. Plastic-wrapped bricks, about four inches long, full of greasy gray Play-Doh.

That's right. C-4. Regular issue.

And then I remember that Stevie was our demolitions man, guy who went in and disarmed Charlie's booby traps. If he decided to set one himself and he used the plastique . . .

Couldn't think what to do.

Call the cops? Call up the Pentagon? Maybe the VA, or maybe the Secret fuckin' Service. But I didn't know just what Stevie was planning to do, man. And if I called anyone, why the hell would they believe me?

Most likely they wouldn't. They'd trace the call back here and come talk to *me*, thinkin' *I'm* the nut. God knows how long it would take to convince 'em, then, they should be lookin' for Stevie. Too damn long, for sure.

Never mind. I called anyway. What did I have to lose? I called the cops and I give 'em his name, and I tell 'em about the kid. Then I call up at the White House and do the same thing, and the Pentagon too. I don't waste no time answering questions, 'cause I know I got to get out of here before they come and scoop my ass up in a butterfly net.

Soon as I get done, I grab my old Army jacket and boogy on down to the street, thinkin' maybe, just maybe, I'll catch up to Stevie before he can go off.

But when I get down there, my car's gone.

My keys are still there, in my pocket, but that wouldn't stop Stevie. Then again, I ain't been downstairs in nearly a week, so it coulda been gone for days. I really don't give a fuck, 'cept that if Stevie did take it, there's no way I'll catch him now.

Jesus wept. I felt so goddamn bad, I fell down onto my knees and I started to pray, 'cause I figured there wasn't much else that I *could* do now. Screwed both my eyes shut and flung my plea on up to heaven. Don't even know what I was asking for, really.

But I got my answer, 'cause while I was down there, my nose about six inches offa the ground, I begun to smell somethin'— I don't know what. Maybe the sulfur you get when you light a match, maybe the smell of hot brass that you get off of shell casings. Something else, too, like old wet leaves and earthworms beginning to rot. Jungle smell.

Well, I sat up a bit, sniffin' like a dog testing the air for a bitch in heat, movin' my head back and forth till I had a direction.

Now, I know it don't make no damn sense at'all, 'cause a man ain't no coonhound, and no dog could follow a scent down the road anyhow, not once somebody got in a car and they drove away. Thing is, man, I wasn't trackin' the same kind of smell that a dog would. What I smelled out there wasn't skin oil or sweat. It was death and destruction, and if there was sweat in it, well, then, it must've dripped off Stevie's soul.

I got scared, thinkin' how strong that smell had to be now, but I didn't have no choice. I had to follow it, best I could.

I begun crawling along on the sidewalk. I guess I was headin' south. I didn't pay a whole lot of attention. I just knew that I had to keep moving.

Pretty soon, I was back up on my feet. If I bent over low enough, I could still catch it, that whiff of smoke mixed up with grease, fear and gasoline. It was a lot like what I smelled the day I seen one of them Buddhist monks in a long saffron robe. Come into Saigon, and while he was chanting and protesting us even being there, he set his own self afire with gasoline.

Hated that smell, but man, once I had caught the whiff, I had to follow it. Had to walk bent over, so's I could catch the scent, had to keep suckin' up snootfuls of air, had to touch things along the way, places the cloud Stevie trailed had brushed by and left just a bare whisper of stink on. . . .

Don't know what it looked like to anyone else, but I do know that nobody got in my way. Probl'y thought I was one of the whackos that hang out down by the Potomac, and who'd blame 'em? Crazy old nigger, all skin and bones, eyes bugged out, duckwalkin' down the street, muttering to himself.

Probl'y a miracle I didn't get my ass mowed down just crossing the fuckin' street. I know I didn't pay no mind to stoplights or cars and shit. I just kept hurryin', praying I wouldn't be too late to stop him.

Well, that ain't exactly true. I noticed when I come out at the Mall, 'cause I found myself cuttin' through one of the lines where folks wait to go in for a tour of the White House. I stirred up a bit of a ruckus there, pushing my way through 'em, scarin' the tourists. I had to go round that great big fuckin'

statue, the guy on the horse, too, and then I was on the Ellipse
where some young guys were out playin' soccer, but how could
that be? Stevie couldn't have driven my car 'crost the fuckin'
lawn, could he?

I plowed to a stop and the soccer game flowed past me like
I was some kinda rock in a river of sweatshirts and knee socks
and cleats. I was shakin' bad, so bad I almost fell over when
one of 'em brushed by me, chasing the ball.

I got spun around, trying to stay on my feet, and wound up
goin' down on one knee on account of the three-alarm fire
that's raging inside of my belly. I shake my head, *squeeze* it
back down to size. *Not now*, I tell it. *Not yet. You can have my
ass later, goddamn it.*

I win, but the sweat's drippin' out of my eyebrows and damn
near to blinding me. I pull my shirttail up, wipe my face, lean
forward. Somehow or other I haul my ass back up on both feet,
but when I can see again, I'm turned around almost facing the
way I came. I'm lookin' east, toward the Capitol Building.

The wind slides a cold hand acrost my face, turning my
sweat into ice water, but I can smell something on it, a trace
of decay, of burnt thatch, and I lurch forward only to stop
dead, 'cause there he is, down on his knees, hidin' 'hind a big
park bench, almost in the bushes.

No, not Stevie.

Dink.

He was all by himself, and he looked about froze to death,
shakin' damn nearly as bad as me, turnin' blue, stinking so bad
it was worse'n Hue, worse'n most anything I'd ever smelled
before.

I tried to catch my breath, tried to think what I could say
to the boy. All that I could come up with was, "Dink, let me
help, boy. Where *is* he?"

Dink shook his head, miserable, but as soon as I stepped
toward him, he took a step back. I knew that he'd run, and
that I couldn't catch him, and he stunk so bad that I wanted
to fall down and cry, but instead I said, "Dink, I won't hurt
him. I swear I won't. Just tell me where he is, 'fore someone
else gets hurt."

Big-eyed, he still didn't say nothin'. Silent, he just turned
his head and looked over his shoulder, across Pennsylvania, to
where my car's parked on the other side, sixty or seventy yards
on down.

Flashed on Beirut and what car bombs can do. Then I

sucked in a lungful of air and I shouted, as loud as I could, "STEVIE! DON'T!"

Three or four soccer-heads turned to look at me, 'long with a coupla blue uniforms in the park. The one glared at me, then started toward me, and he'd got as far as the sidewalk when I seen my car jump a couple feet into the air. The first bang hit me like a hard slap in the face and then came a big shuddering THUMP as the gas tank went off and the car jumped again, like a rabbit instead of a Jetta. Bright yellow and white licks of fire shot out from the hood, from the windows, and when it come down again, so did a whole lot of broken glass, hitting the roofs of the cars all around it with little sharp pops, like a firefight heard from about a mile off.

The two cops who'd been eyeballing me turned and started to run toward it, pulling their guns out as black smoke began to climb into the winter sky.

"Stevie," I whispered, and Dink sighed, a sound like a gut-shot man's final breath.

I turn and look at him. I feel my heart jumpin'. I can still smell the boy, just like that Buddhist monk, like he'd been covered with gas and then touched off, except that the fire is inside, not out.

But if Stevie was in the car, why does Dink still smell so bad?

I was so busy workin' it all out that I never even seen which way his daddy come. All of a sudden, all I know is that the bad smell offa Dink is about ten times worse, and I look up with tears in my eyes and I see Stevie, taking his kid by the hand.

He looks charred, to me. Just for a second, he looks like a pilot I seen once, inside of his Huey. The chopper'd been shot down and burned on the spot, and this pilot was still in his seat, still strapped in, with his goddamn hands still holding on to his fuckin' controls. He was burned black, his whole body, just like the Huey, but looked to me like he was still gonna try to fly out of there. That's the way Stevie was, in-country.

I let the grief overflow for a second, and when my eyes cleared again, he was just Stevie. I said, "What the hell are you doing, man?"

Stevie, he shook his head. "I'm sorry, Sarge." He looks back at the burning car. I can hear sirens now, louder and louder, and Stevie, he says, kind of desperate, "I'm really sorry. I needed some kind of diversion, y'know? So that I can get up to the gates at the White House . . ."

"And what?" I demanded. "You plannin' to blow that up, too?"

"No!" he spits back. "I've got other plans, damn it."

I don't say nothing to that. I just look at the car again. Then I look back at him, look at the jacket, the square brick-shape bulges across the front. I can see wire, a white loop, that's poking up out of his collar.

"You're fixin' to blow yourself up, aren't you?" I tell him.

He doesn't answer, so I take a step toward him as I demand, "Aren't you?!"

Stevie's so wound up he's shaking all over, and makin' Dink shiver too, just from his grip on the kid.

Didn't know then 'bout Jeanne divorcing him, trying to keep him away from his son, but it wasn't too hard to make out the important thing. Him and the boy are two parts of a whole, they're one person to Stevie.

"I'm not crazy!" he tells me.

"I *know*," I tell him. "But this ain't the way, man." And grasping at straws, pleading, I tell him, "This ain't the place, either."

He looks like he's gonna bolt any second, so I stumble on, tell him, "Come to the Wall with me. I'll go along with whatever you wanna do, just I got something to show you first. Something important, man."

I nod my head toward the car, where a big ladder truck has pulled up alongside and there's men hauling hose out. The tourists all lined up in front of the White House have just about disappeared, hustled away by security guards, and the whole street's alive with the strobe-flash of blue and red lights.

"Besides, we gotta get out of here. Looks to me like your 'diversion' is just about used up," I tell Stevie. "Listen," I tell him again, but then I have to stop, 'cause the fuzzy gray patches are coming together now, thickening. Shakin' my head only makes me feel dizzy and weak, and I more or less fall on the park bench. It's like all the heat from the car and from Stevie's got inside me, got all mixed up with the thing in my belly, the monster that's trying to eat me alive. Through a darkening mist, I can see Stevie reaching for me, but he stops again, thinking, I guess, that I might try to trick him or jump him. I'd laugh if I could. Felt like I was three inches from dyin', right then and there.

Had to keep trying, though.

"Steve," I said, "talk to me. Come to the Wall with me.

Give me a chance, buddy. Give your own self a chance. I got something you need to see."

He wouldn't hear it, though.

"Too late for that," he said, shakin' his head at me. "Shouldn't have come here. I wanted to stop by and see you again, that's all, wanted to say goodbye."

"No, Steve. Man, you was right, coming here," I told him, trying to get my brains *moving* again. It was hard, man. The smell of him gettin' worse all the time, filling my head with the stink of hot oil and burnt rubber and blood.

Any second now, he'd shoot me, coldcock me, leave me behind again, go someplace I couldn't follow.

By then, Stevie had his arm wrapped around Dink. His free hand was back in his pocket, the heavy one.

I begged him, "Stevie, please. Let's you and me head down there. You never seen the Wall, have you? There's something you gotta see before we say goodbye."

God, I remember how soft his voice was when he answered. He said, "It's too late to change anything, Sarge."

And I shook my head, wanted to laugh. "I know that. Jesus, look at me, Stevie. I'm hanging on here by my fingernails."

He didn't say nothing. Seemed to be thinking. He brought the gun out of the pocket, made sure that I saw it.

I said, "I won't try nothing, man. I just want to go with you."

At that, Stevie laughed, low and hard, like a coyote's bark. But he said, "All right, Sarge. If there's anyone's got the right . . . Come on, let's go. Can you walk?"

What *right*? I wondered, then realized just what he thought I was asking. To go *with* him.

That scared me worse'n the bomb or the gun he was carryin', which must've been what he'd hit me with, back at my 'partment. The piece was a nine millimeter, a Walther PPK, with a black, ugly snout of a barrel. It never once left his hand after that, either. No, sir. Steve won't trust me that far, not me nor the rest of the world.

I got up somehow, tottered along the cement walkway, trying my best to ignore the commotion that we could hear back of us. We headed west, going upstream since everyone else seemed to be zooming in on the sirens and shit at our backs.

Oh, man, I don't really know how I made it that far, 'cause my gut was on fire the whole time, my whole body shakin' so bad it was hard to stay upright, to keep movin'. Stevie, he grabbed me by one arm and held me up, partway, until we come out of the bushes across from the Lincoln Memorial. Just this once, I didn't see any cops around, either. Not one single uniform. Must have already been called to the White House.

I wondered how many he'd hurt back there, wondered where he'd got the C-4. No use of me trying to talk to Steve. Too late to try and get through to him now, not with words. No, sir, I'd have to show him the one thing I knew of that might make him think. And I knew the Memorial'd get to him, weaken him, slow him down, like it does everyone else when they come here.

It did, too. We turned north again, and as soon as he got within sight of the statue, them three soldiers, white, black, and brown, man, I saw it grab hold of him. Stevie, he let go of me and he picked up the kid and he stuck the gun down in between 'em, and walked right on past me, like I wasn't even there.

Stomped right on up to the bronze and just stood there a minute to look at them three soldiers, like he expected to see someone's face he knew.

Still no cops.

Nothing but souvenir vendors, and damn few of them in the wintertime. I wondered if I should grab one and tell him to call for help, only Steve started to walk down the ramp, toward the black marble heart of it all, and I knew that I only had one chance left now. There was only the Wall itself, what it was doing.

So I turned and went after him, stumbling down the same ramp.

He'd already got halfway down, just about where the Wall seems to be sinking too fast, and he'd stopped. He was watching a pretty, long-legged blonde, down on her knees in the corner, her yellow hair spilling across her face while she was trying to take a charcoal rubbing off a name down near the bottom. She kept rubbing at it, then choking up, sobbing a couple of times, maybe letting her head sink, and then she'd start rubbing again, the tears streaming down onto her knees.

I was trying to move in real quiet, y'know? Hoping Steve'd be too wound up, watching the blonde, but my foot dragged. He heard me, and spun around, yanking the gun out again.

I said, "Wait, Steve. Just wait, please . . . a minute. I wanted to show you . . ."

The second I started to move toward him, though, the gun

jerked in his hand. Not a gesture so much as a nervous twitch. I started thinking about how he'd been in the habit, in 'Nam, fixing up all his guns with a hair trigger. Had he, with this one?

He said, "Sorry, Sarge, but I think it's best you and me get this thing over with."

"No," I said, putting my hands up. "I need just a minute. I want you to see it."

"See *what?*" he said.

"Look at the Wall, Stevie."

He said, "Come on, Sarge, don't make it harder . . ."

I said, damn near shouting, "Just look at it, man. I won't move, not an inch. All I want you to do is just *look*. You can do that much, can't you?"

The pretty blonde down in the corner's gone, God knows where, maybe to get some help.

I don't know. All I know is that I've got to get through.

So I try to shut out the stink and explain. "It's alive, Stevie. Watch it a minute or two, and you'll see it. The whole fucking Wall is alive."

Well, he looks at me like I'm the crazy man, but I've at least got ahold of him, just for a second.

I said, "Stevie, you're not alone with this thing. Every one of us been through the fucking mill. I know you feel like you hurt so bad, you just can't stand it no more, but you're wrong. If you want to know what pain is, man, you just look at that Wall for a few minutes. Look at it. Then tell me nothing and nobody knows what you're going through."

Don't think he really believes me, in spite of the tears running down my face. I think he's waiting for me to *do* something, to jump him or pull a gun.

Man, if I could, then I surely would.

Can't hardly breathe anymore, though. The man got a cloud of death hangin' all over him, jet fuel and Cosmoline mixed up with rotted thatch. I can smell pig meat been sitting out three or four days in the tropical sun. I can whiff the smoke rising off hundreds of bodies piled up in the ruins of Hue. I can smell Vietnam, burning.

Maybe he seen that, in *my* eyes, 'cause then, like a man who's been hypnotized, Steve starts to look toward the Wall, flicking back to me, then back again, like he wants to, but somehow, he can't trust me.

This time, I don't say a word. I just start prayin', letting him shuttle his eyes back and forth, until something he sees in the marble gets hold of him.

Something . . . I can't see it, not from here. All I can see is the little boy.

Something that makes Steve's mouth drop open like a trap-door.

Something that reaches out, sudden, and *slaps* him acrost the face, like he'd been hit with a rifle butt.

God, I remember how hard it hit, first time I seen it, the names in the Wall moving in and out, sometimes one name on top, sometimes another.

The day I seen what it was doing, man, that was the day the noon news was all full of that damn Patrick Purdy, from out California way, blew all them refugee kids away, shot thirty-five of 'em right in the schoolyard. Yeah, that's when I knew for sure, *knew* it down deep in my bones, like an ache that just won't go away, like this cancer of mine.

I was looking at Rawlings's name, thinking back, 'membering how him and that little Montaignard used to sit by one another and play them wood flutes. Rusty's name got blurred, all of a sudden, the way it would do when I'm almost to crying.

But I wasn't crying. I think I was smiling, that flute music runnin' around in the back of my head like a stream of clean water, like birds singing back and forth out in the woods. So I stared at it hard, and it cleared up again, but the name wasn't Rusty's no more. Wasn't even American.

Rathanar Or.

Right. A real funny kinda name, different but easy to keep ahold of it, you know?

A Cambodian name.

And it flashed on me, man, where I seen that name. On the news, over what I like to think of as lunch. It was one of the kids Patrick Purdy had killed.

Well, it made my hair stand straight up, just like a cocka-too's crest, and I jumped back away from that Wall like a fool seen his own ghost a-waving hello.

Shit. It scared me so bad, I could feel my heart pounding on me, just like I was a door, and it wanted to jump out and run away.

Couldn't, though. Couldn't leave after that. Had to see what in the hell was this Wall doing.

Stood there and stared at it, maybe four hours. And that's

when I seen all them other names. Some of 'em people I knew had got home again.

Yeah, I know 'bout the mistakes, people coming here, finding their own names engraved in the marble and havin' fits.

This wasn't like that. I know, 'cause I always used to keep track of my people. It meant a lot, knowing about the ones did make it home, y'know? Kind of made up for the rest of 'em, somehow, the guys like that skinny ol' Rawlings kid, never hurt nobody once in his life, only wanted to play his flute, big time.

So I knew a lot of them names by heart, and I knew when they didn't belong up there. Sokhim An, Oeun Lim, Ram Chun, and Thuy Tran. And Zumwalt, the admiral. His name was in there too, him and his son's. Man, I seen 'em all, surfacing, like they was coming up out of a well of black water.

Steve, he seen 'em too.

Viet names, Thai and Laotian, and Chinese, a few of 'em. Mostly, though, names like Roe, Cunningham, Johnston, and Rice. And he seen what it meant, and he knew what he'd done, when he seen Jeanne's name up there, soaking its way through the rest like a bloodstain.

I seen it too. Jeanne Bartholomew.

"You want your little boy's name up there? Do you?" I asked him.

He didn't say nothing. He stands there, with Dink tucked up close to his chest, and the tears come a-running down off of his face, dripping into the little kid's hair, like the rain coming off of a tree in the woods.

Pretty soon, man, he's sobbing his heart out.

I'm crying, too, but I'm inching my way toward him, hoping and prayin'. The weight of a teardrop ain't very damn much, but it might be enough with a hair trigger on it like Stevie's piece had.

I keep talking, too, telling him how it is, how I know what it's like, losing everything, then bein' eaten alive by the damn Agent Orange, and being cut loose by the VA when you ain't got nothing else, talking real smooth and low, man, like you do with a spooky horse.

"You don't want Dink's name up there," I tell him. "You paid enough dues, Stevie. You don't owe nothing else."

I get about a yard closer, and Stevie looks up at me, all of a sudden, his eyes full of choppers and flamethrowers, dyin' in front of me, burnin' so hot I can feel the heat, see the red glare of the phosphorus flares. I can hear 'em, them voices that claw their way up from the emptiness, screamin' so hard you can hear 'em right through all the rockets and burp guns and rotor blades beatin' the air to death.

Oh, man, my heart does a flip-flop inside of me.

I have to close my eyes. Can't look. Can't watch any more of it. *Can't* . . .

And I feel something hit me, hard, right at the knees, and I fall to the ground with it, clutching my legs, 'cause I'm thinkin' he shot me, and I just ain't heard the gun go off yet.

I reach down. Ain't no blood. There's only little arms already wrapped around both of my legs. Little-boy arms.

I just can't believe it.

I sit up, and grab at him, open my eyes, and I see Stevie standing there, holding that gun on us both.

He says, "I gotta pay for it somehow, Sarge. I been dead twenty years. I can't pretend I'm alive anymore."

Then he flips the gun up, takes a bite of the barrel, and yanks on that hair trigger.

No, I'm all right now.

It's just . . . I could feel it all over again, Stevie's blood on my face, and his brains in the grass, and that little boy holding me so tight, I can't get a breath of air.

Don't matter much, except I had to see that Dink's people got hold of him. They gonna do right by that little kid, but the things he's already seen . . . how is a kid like that s'posed to be normal now? How does he ever forget it?

I never will. Not till this goddamn thing growin' inside me gets all the way out, and my name's on the Wall beside Stevie's.

What?

I don't know.

Doctors say maybe another two, three months. It don't matter. Like Stevie said, I been dead twenty years now. I just didn't have enough guts to admit it.

No.

No, man, I don't know what's goin' down here, any more'n you do.

The way I figure, it's like this. The Wall wasn't big enough. Black enough. Deep enough.

Couldn't hold all of that grief.

All them babes that's been rubbin' off names of their men, or them old fellas lookin' for sons and kid brothers. Them little kids thinkin' they're gonna find something, some trace of the daddies they never knew.

Wall wasn't big enough.

Started to grow.

Gathered in all the pain it could stand and then reached for some more, for the good men that didn't die, not right away, and the women, the nurses that killed their selves way later on, and them poor little babies that never got born on account of the damn Agent Orange.

And maybe, somehow, all the poor folks that got their selves murdered—long after—by men that come home with their screws loose and bolts missin'. Even by some men that never did go, but they got crazy anyhow, thinkin' about it. Them little kids shot all to hell in that schoolyard at recess, them wives blowed away by their husbands, and cops, even, trying their damnedest to stop this insanity, stop all the blood that just keeps on a-flowin'.

My God, ain't it gotta go somewheres, all of that?

Got to.

Gotta keep growing, man, name after name after name after name, till it's all of it gone.

Maybe then, when the Wall's got ahold of us all, maybe that's when we get to stop hearin' them voices and cryin' these tears.

Maybe then we can come back around and us all can be human again.

Maybe then ever' one of us gets to stop bleeding.

FOUNTAINS IN SUMMER

Richard Bowes

My doppelgänger and I haven't met in over twenty years. But in the last few weeks a pair of street kids, complete strangers, have looked surprised, troubled by the sight of me. An old friend has asked if there was a twin brother I hadn't mentioned. By those signs I knew that my double was nearby in Manhattan.

Being reminded didn't make me happy. When I was a kid, he was my companion in crime and I called him my Shadow. Later I was taught that my addiction to booze and drugs was like a Silent Partner taking everything from me. So that's what I began to call him. Whatever his name, our times together had been bad, nearly fatal for me. But my curiosity was aroused. No one, after all, shares more of your memories than your own Shadow.

These things were on my mind on a blazing Sunday afternoon this August when I went by George Halle's to take care of his mail and make sure the apartment was still intact. A glimpse from the door was all I could stand. Wooden louvres shaded the windows, cut the sound of the far West Village to nothing.

I have some wondrous memories of this place over the last couple of decades as George and I were lovers briefly, then friends and business partners and, finally, patient and caregiver.

The furnishings are antique, the art more recent. Polished and mellow, the rooms awaited the return of George, whose life supports had been removed that Friday.

When I locked the door and went back down to the street, George's block stood empty except for a scavenger. His garbage bag half full of bottles and cans, he rummaged in the trash and talked to himself. He was gray haired and about my build. When he looked up, though, his face was not mine.

But that made me decide to stick to public places. Over on Hudson Street, with the rest of an afternoon to kill, I idly cruised amid clusters of guys and women sauntering home from gay Sunday service: brunch. The reminder of my Silent Partner made me try to remember just when I'd become aware of him.

It was the first time in a while that I'd seriously searched my past. Ironic, maybe, since antique toys and books, the compost heap of childhood, are my business. Nostalgia, though, is memory in costume and party hat. Real recollection is something else.

Memory, the word itself, evokes for me an image of bright lights and green grass, a night game at Fenway Park in maybe '48 or '49. If so, I am four or five, up way past bedtime, dozing against my uncle Mike the cop. When suddenly everyone stands up and he lifts me onto his shoulder.

I see figures in gray running. Then out of the left-field darkness sails a white ball. At third base a man in white, his back to me, takes two steps to his left, nabs it, pivots and fires. The catcher, his scary mask abandoned, comes up the line toward third, catches the ball, crouches, braces, tags the sliding runner. The game ends. The crowd roars in triumph, able for a moment to forget that they are Red Sox fans and doomed.

Lately, I've thought of that often as fragments, disjointed, incomplete, sailed out of my subconscious into my awareness. Recently, from the darkness came this fragment of a poem:

Fountains in summer

It evoked images of sunlight on green leaves and my mother leading me by the hand in the Boston Public Gardens. My guess is that I was about three.

No trip downtown at that time was complete without a visit to the Swan Boats. So at some point we must have floated on the shallow pond under low bridges with a Boston University undergrad pedaling away in the great white bird at the back. But I couldn't say for sure. Nor could I remember more of the poem or where I had heard it.

On that Sunday almost fifty years later, I walked north and east unaware of my destination until I arrived at the Sixth Avenue Flea Market. In these aisles of jumbled tchotchke and kitch, sprawling through empty parking lots and garages, trawled by every Boomer who somehow forgot to get invited to the Hamptons, Warhol once assembled his million-dollar cookie jar collection.

My eyes refused to focus on tarnished brass door knockers and plastic place mats with pictures of Italy. Then a couple turned and smiled and seemed to share their smile with me.

She, it appeared, was a young part-Asian woman, blue eyed and black haired, slim in a green silk blouse. He, I realized, was misshapen. But his face was delicate, his smile beautiful. Turning, he replaced something on a table.

A damsel and a dwarf, I thought as they moved away. In retrospect I can spot the setup. Right then, all I was aware of was what he had put back on the table. Amid a collection of distressed *Humpty-Dumpty* magazines, coverless copies of *The Pokey Little Puppy*, was my face on a decaying dust jacket.

Actually it was just a drawing of a kid in shorts and striped jersey. An Eton cap perched on a blond head almost as big as his trunk. Eyes wide with wonder, he stared at an Indian chief in full regalia. The title was, *Go West Jelly Bean!*

Others modeled before and after. But for several books, I was Jelly Bean. In truth, JB was sort of featureless. He was Everykid back in 1950 when they thought that meant a white boy.

The series wasn't quite up there with Dr. Seuss or Curious George. But more than a dozen books got produced between the late forties and late fifties. If you were a child then and read, you probably had a Jelly Bean or two and may remember the gimmick, the running gag.

Jelly Bean never spoke, but this silent kid had so vivid an imagination that he turned into whatever attracted his attention. You knew just by looking at the cover, for instance, that he would end up as an Indian chief. He could only be brought back to himself by his parents' calling, "Jelly Bean, where are you?" Always there would be some evidence of his shapeshifting, like the streak of war paint left on his face at the end of *Go West*. His parents, however, never caught on.

Dealing in antiques, I had encountered better copies of *Go West*, had bought them, sold them, even mentioned my connection with them to friends and customers. But that afternoon, almost like Jelly Bean, I found myself snared in the thing that had hooked my attention. I was me, age six, on a glorious spring weekend spent dressed as an Indian chief.

"You buying or dreaming?" the dealer asked. "Ten dollars."

Being treated like a civilian aroused my professional pride. "For this beat-up copy? A first edition, preserved by some lonely maniac for forty-six years in a state of mint purity, will fetch ten. Maybe."

So he backed down. But not far. Because he had spotted my weakness, I paid four dollars for something I would have said was only worth a buck. "I have all of that series," he called, going for the kill as I escaped.

A block east of the market is Madison Square Park. On a reasonably sound and isolated bench, I examined my find. The cover had two names, Helena Godspeed Hewett and Max Walter. Mrs. Hewett created and wrote the Jelly Bean books. I had a single memory of a big woman in a huge hat who pretended to adore kids but was obviously annoyed when I asked if the foxes on her stole were kittens.

Max Walter's name evoked a lot more. I remembered him sitting at his easel, pencils in hand, sketching me, saying again and again, "It's perfect. Just one more minute, Kevin." He was catching Jelly Bean's look of goggle-eyed wonder. Max's goatee was what held me. He was the only person I'd ever met with a beard. It fascinated me that it moved right along with his mouth when he spoke.

Max's wife, Frieda, and my mother were friends. The two of them sat in the studio drinking wine, talking. "What's great about Sandra," my mother said, "is that with her you don't need a second opinion. She's so two-faced, I'm surprised she's never run into herself."

Max and Frieda laughed. Uneasily, I wondered if people often met themselves. "OK!" Max told me, chin and beard wagging. "Take a break, Kevin." I walked over to the window. Max's studio was on the top floor of a house in Jamaica Plain. In the distance were the Arnold Arboretum's acres of trees, hills and ponds.

But I stared at a weed-filled lot right across the street. There, two chains of boys and girls, aged five to ten, hands linked, faced each other playing Red Rover. I watched as one small boy ran at the opposite line, threw himself on a pair of joined hands and bore two kids almost to the ground. But he couldn't break their grip and had to be on their side. I wanted so much to be down there.

With her uncanny timing, my mother brought a glass of ginger ale and distracted me. "See what we have now," she said. I turned back toward the room and there were a feathered headdress, moccasins, a fringed vest and pants, a tomahawk, bow and quiver of arrows. She pointed to an array of bright tubes. "War paint!"

The headdress went on even before I shed Jelly Bean's stupid clothes. On that glorious day, they let me go outside in my regalia. Down I went, two flights to the street. And there I stood on the porch with my arms folded in front of me. The game across the way came to a halt. The kids approached slowly. Before they reached me, I turned silently and marched back into the house.

All that day and the next, they called outside for the real Indian to come out and play. I would show myself at the window. On my breaks I would go downstairs and walk among them. I said nothing. I thought that if they knew I was just an ordinary kid, they would ignore me. I wanted to play, but I didn't know how.

The next time I remember modeling for Max, it was cold out, the trees were bare. But I wore a bathing suit and stood under a bright light. The book must have been, *By the Sea, Jelly Bean!* which came just after *Go West*. It's the one where Jelly Bean gets taken to the beach. By then Helena Godspeed had gotten the series down to a dull routine.

At the sittings, the costumes, even the uniforms, were a pain. It was raining. No kids waited to ask for the real marine. My mother sat without talking much. Things had begun to change for her and me. For Frieda too. She had just had a baby. I was fascinated.

Then Max said, "OK, Kev, take a break. Let's get into the sailor suit next." Bored and tired of this game, I began to whine. I guess my mother was bored too. Sighing, she put down her glass and started getting me changed.

Turning to protest, I saw Frieda and her child and was oblivious to anything else. Frieda and Max were bohemians. She nursed in the studio. The baby, her eyes wide and unblinking, was attached to her mother's breast. In perfect harmony the breast bobbed gently to the rhythm of the baby's mouth. An instant later the tiny throat would swallow. The baby kept one hand curved in the air, fingers splayed as if she were maintaining her balance on an invisible high wire.

I don't know how long I stood. But at the same moment I realized two things. Max was sketching intensely and I was naked. Betrayed, I tried to hide myself. Max said, "The end of innocence."

That was the last time I had to model for Jelly Bean. It was also around then that my mother got married again. My father had died in the war and I never saw him. My childhood playmates were my mother's friends, actors and artists, poseurs and lollygaggers. As time went on they drifted away. My mother's smile would disappear if I asked about them. Above all else, I wanted that smile.

One last memory of my mother and Frieda remains. It happened at the very end of their friendship in high autumn in the Arboretum beside a pond just off the road.

I believe that my mother and Frank were just married. That means we had moved to a house in Dorchester near my grandmother's and I was the new kid in Sister Gertrude Julia's third grade at Mary Queen of Heaven school.

Frieda and my mother talked behind me as I fed a flock of mallards paused on their way south. With the accuracy and blindness of childhood, I knew that my mother was angry, but did not yet connect this with her drinking. She said in too loud a voice, "I thought with my father gone it would be different. But nobody wants me to be happy. They don't want me to live like everyone else."

"Of course we do, Ellen," said Frieda, and I knew that my mother was arguing without anyone arguing back. I wished as hard as I could that I would turn and find my mother smiling.

"People are jealous about Frank and me."

"Not at all." By their voices, I could tell that my mother and Frieda were walking slowly up to the benches by the road. "Just rest for a minute, El."

That's when a hand lightly touched my neck and I turned. Two figures sat about thirty yards away with their backs to me. My mother's querulous voice was indistinct. But that mother was just a Shadow.

Right beside me was my real mother. Instead of showing anger, she had a wonderful conspiratorial smile at the joke we were playing. Off we went, the two of us, on a walk around

the pond, both watching our feet churn the leaves, turning
suddenly each to catch the other's eyes and laugh.

When we had circled the pond completely, my mother led
me to the bench. She and her Shadow merged. Frieda seemed
tired, concerned. But my mother winked at me, reached out
her hand for mine. If it was a dream, I must then have awakened.

That was as much of my past as the beat-up copy of *Go
West, Jelly Bean!* would give me. Looking around Madison
Square Park, I saw an impersonal space, somewhere for office
workers to eat lunch on weekday afternoons. Standing up,
strolling toward Fifth Avenue, I thought again of the line
"Fountains in summer."

As if it was an invocation, my Shadow appeared before me.
In a dirty white jacket, ragged jeans and old sneakers he crossed
my path heading south on Fifth. With him were a bunch of
street kids in sneakers and boxer shorts, each a little skinnier
than seemed possible.

Our eyes didn't meet, but my heart gave a kick and I
stopped. He was as thin as any of them. His cheekbones
showed, his belt gathered in his pants. He had a three-day
growth of beard and a wild tangled mane only touched with
gray. My own hair is going back in what I hope is a graceful
silver halo. He wore no glasses. Mine are gold rimmed, perfect
for a twinkly little dealer in old toys.

Not wanting to get too close, I stopped at a pay phone and
dialed my answering machine. A message from Karen and Laurie reminded me that dinner was at their place at eight. It was
then barely four. Dinner is a regular Sunday thing, half a dozen
old friends entertaining each other.

No word about George. I knew, with luck, it would be over
soon. But I couldn't think past that.

I watched my double and his vagabond band pass through
the crowds browsing the bookstores around Eighteenth. Trailing discreetly down to Washington Square, I thought of a reason to stop by the shop rather than follow them into the park.

Half Remembered Things is in the middle of a block of
Italian bakeries and butcher stores just off Sheridan Square.
We're closed Sundays during summer, but out front stood a
forty-plus couple with their arms intertwined. She wore a tol-
erant smile, he a look of quiet rapture.

Something in our display window had grabbed him. I had
put together a boy's bedroom circa 1955, one with everything

other kids always seemed to have and never you, like the rotating night lamp on which a rocket ship floated forever toward the rings of Saturn.

A fifth-grade geography text lay open on the desk revealing the Scrooge MacDuck comic book inside. On the shelves, beside the lead marines in full dress, the junior football and wind-up tin robots, Lone Ranger and Tonto bookends enclosed *The Arabian Nights, The Boy's Book of Pirates, Dave Dawson with the Flying Tigers, Martian Chronicles.*

Roller skates, a cap pistol and a Lionel yard engine lay on the floor near an interrupted Monopoly game. A Davy Crockett hat hung on the post of the bed, which was made up with Howdy Doody sheets and a Hopalong Cassidy blanket. On the foot of the bed a Little League baseball with busted seams nestled in a worn third baseman's glove.

When George Halle and I opened this place Carter was in the White House. More lucky than smart, we decried the Yuppie '80s. But we were in place when all the financial managers in New York decided to buy back their childhoods at inflated prices.

As a businessperson, I should have crossed the street, found out what the guy liked so much, given him my card. Instead, I waited until the lady dragged him away before going over and slipping the book through the mail slot. The first thing Monday, a place would be found for *Go West* on the bed near the baseball. Together the book and the baseball were the story of my life as a kid.

That done, I headed back to Washington Square. It seemed better to encounter my Shadow now in a public place than be taken by surprise all alone.

Walking, I remembered my mother after her remarriage, after Frieda and Max and Jelly Bean, bringing me to a department-store photo shoot as a favor to a friend. She promised me it was the last time. They had a whole bunch of us, babies, a girl my age and another around eleven who were sisters and their big brother Steve who told me, "I'm going to be a freshman at BC High next year." I was awestruck. He had to be twelve at least.

The girls and babies and a couple of the mothers went to one of the two dressing rooms. Steve scooped up the sample clothes, put his hand on my shoulder and said, "Let's go, Kev," before anyone could stop us.

"This modeling stuff is stupid," he told me in the dressing

room. "I gotta do it to save for tuition. B.C. has a great baseball team. You know about baseball?" I nodded yes because I had seen games. "I was in Little League three years. I'm starting Junior CYO ball. Third base. The ball comes on like a bullet. I'm working on my throw to first."

Discarding his jacket, he took a scuffed baseball out of a pocket. "This is just Little League size, but I can throw a curve kind of." He showed me the grip. "What position do you play?" I didn't know what to say. "You should play third." Pulling on a sample sweater, he asked, "You talk, Kev?"

Hypnotized, a smile plastered to my face, I said, "Yes!" And he laughed. All that day between people adjusting our clothes, fixing our hair, between waiting and posing and changing and waiting again, he explained to me about playing third base.

"The important thing is that you stop it getting by you," he said. On a break, he bounced the ball toward me and I couldn't lay a hand on it. "No, you gotta move as soon as you see it come off the bat. Get in front of it. Once more."

When the shoot was over and we were parting in the lobby, he reached into the pocket of his jacket. I could see from his face that this tore him. "Here, Kev. You're gonna play, right?"

I nodded as hard as I could and reached out for the baseball. "What do you say," my mother asked. I managed to croak out a thank-you. Steve waved and disappeared in the forest of adults. Maybe all he wanted was anyone to talk to about baseball. Maybe, too, he was a good kid and smart enough to sense someone's aching need.

On that blazing Sunday, years after Steve, I took a seat in Washington Square Park and watched the show. There is poignancy spiced with danger when summer's more than half-way gone and those attitudes that haven't wilted have gotten extra sharp.

The fountain threw jets into the air. Dashing through the spray were small dark children, a large copper dog, a spacey white kid with a red kerchief on his head and his pants rolled up. Stretched out on the stairs leading down to the water, young people in gym bodies sunbathed with their heads thrown back.

On the circular plaza around the fountain, kids black and white and Asian, with baseball caps and shaved heads, circled on skateboards, bicycles, roller skates. Along the raised outer rim of the plaza, tattooed and strung with pet snakes, lounged dealers and trade. On the walk around the plaza, a police car sat with its windows open and its radio spitting static.

On the benches beyond that walk, I sat amid German tourists, undercover narcs, teenage hicks in from the suburbs, and ancient Italian couples. In the sonic wash of rap and wheels, of crowd noise and the fall of water, I breathed the perfume of mown grass and piss and meat incinerating on shish kebob carts, and waited to see what my Shadow would do.

Beyond a fence near the north side of the park, small children swarmed over the free-form jungle bars and slides. Parents, nannies, au pairs stood by. This was a lot different than my first and only playground.

Curtis Park in Queen of Heaven parish in Dorchester in Boston had jungle bars, slides, seesaws, and a brick building with rest rooms and the offices of Charlie, the crippled caretaker. But mainly it was a big open space that was dusty ball fields in summer, a skating pond in winter.

That was where my Little League ball got me into a game with some kids from my third-grade class. We played off to the side on a diamond marked out by stones. The game was tossing the ball up and hitting it and lots of pushing and yelling and nobody ever caught anything. Then one day Murph saw us and took over.

A couple of summers later, the magic baseball was long gone. But its work was done. Hands in jean pockets, dirty and triumphant in the late-setting sun, we strutted from a sandlot game, a gang of desperados in hi-tops. One by one kids reached their houses and peeled off till there was only Murph and me.

The Murphys were a dozen kids ranging from four to twenty, a drunken, truck-driving father, a wispy thin mother and her retarded brother who lived in vast disorder at the corner of my block. All the male kids were called Murph by their friends. The one I knew was Jimmy, a crucial eight months my senior and the toughest kid in fifth grade at "Queena Heaven" Parochial School.

We reached his house first, lingered for a while. "And when he tries to tag me he falls down and you run all the way home." Murph was doing a play-by-play of the game. I was laughing hysterically. Then his mother yelled from inside. "See you, Grierson," he said. We used only last names.

"See you, Murph." No guys on earth are tougher than ten-year-olds. The streetlights came on and I was all alone. I wanted to hurry home, yet didn't want to go there at all.

As a child, I was expert above all else in navigation by the double star of my mother and her Shadow. I was never certain which one would be around. On that particular night, I heard a voice, sharp and mean. "I beg your pardon. You brought this up!"

It was the Shadow. I froze for a moment. Sometimes my mother's Shadow talked to herself. Those were the worst times. Then I heard Frank say, "Ellen, for Christ sake!" And I relaxed a little.

My stepfather never got the hang of my mother and her Shadow, never even understood there was something to be learned. Frank and I kind of passed through each other. But he had his uses. With Frank to keep her busy, the Shadow would leave me alone. "You were so pie-eyed you were . . ."

They shut up when they heard me come in. "Kevin. Where the hell have you been?"

"Down at Curtis."

I tried to get past her, but she blocked the way. "Who were you there with?" The Shadow's eyes, wide, unblinking, bore right into me.

"A bunch of guys." It did no good to lie. "Murph . . ."

Both my stepfather and the Shadow snorted. They disapproved of the Murphys in general and Jimmy in particular. "A bunch of drunken Irish trash," she said. Of course, we were Irish and the two of them drank quite a bit. Why the Murphys' being Irish and drinking was bad was a mystery deeper than any concerning the Blessed Virgin or Resurrection. "I don't want to see you with that crowd anymore," said the Shadow as I hurried upstairs. Then the two of them went back to arguing.

What they didn't understand was that Murph was more important in my world than both of them put together. I just had to hope that next time my mother would be the one at home. Or at least that the Shadow would forget what she had said.

I only went inside the Murphys' a few times. But he was fascinated by my house with just the three of us living in it, by my room so well stocked with toys, and by my mother. I remember her appearing carrying a tray with glasses of milk and peanut butter and jelly sandwiches. We were scuttling over the floor directing a column of metal tanks and cars through a mountain of animals leaking stuffing. Murph looked up at her with an expression of adoration.

Of course, he wasn't there those times when she stayed in her room and nobody could come by because any sound was too much. Or the times when the Shadow was up and angry, which I didn't want anyone to see.

Sometimes my mother and Frank would go off together and I would stay with my grandmother and grand-aunt Tay, who lived up the hill. Those times I loved. Granny and Tay, with their white hair and soft brogues, were always exactly the same as my earliest memories of them.

On some occasions, like when I ran into the house on a dead of winter day with the sun silver behind clouds and iron snow on the ground, with my shoes squishing and my pants frozen to me, I was just as happy my mother wasn't present. While skating I had stepped on thin ice and gone up to my waist in the water.

The Shadow did not bother to emerge from the bedroom and find out what I was doing. So I dashed upstairs, changed and got back outside. My mother would have had me in pajamas and bathrobe drinking hot soup as soon as she saw that my skinny legs had turned blue. As it was, all I had to fear was the terrifying slow breathing from the closed bedroom.

My stepfather, Frank, was the sales manager for a company that did business with the city. My grandfather had been in politics. My uncles still were somehow. So the marriage made a kind of sense.

The reason Frank never learned to deal with my mother's Shadow, I discovered, was that he didn't have to. When things got bad, he left on business. When they stayed bad, he left for good.

More than forty years later, I looked around Washington Square. This park is a playground of the demimonde. Street and aristocracy mix, kids from nice families dress down to mingle with hustlers and runaways.

Maybe that's part of the function of a playground. Even Curtis Park attracted vagrants. I remember a pair of bums, one an old guy maybe thirty, the other a lot younger. Both were filthy, their sneakers held together with tape.

Bums and kids have a lot in common. They are powerless, without homes of their own, left to conduct private lives in public places. As my friends and I watched, the older guy drank from the water fountain, made a face and spat. "Tastes like rust." The younger guy, seeing us, put two fingers to his mouth like he had a cigarette. "He wants a smoke," said the old bum. "You kids got some butts?"

Probably about that time a cop car appeared and the two guys faded. Maybe because it was on the same day, or maybe just in the same summer, I connect those vagrants with a night I stayed out really late. How do we manage to lose all thoughts of home? It was pitch dark.

Coleman and Leary and Mackie and Murph and myself were eleven, some of us twelve. Old enough and, with allies, numerous enough to show up after supper and hold on to one of the dusty diamonds in the park. The game started in twilight and held us entranced. We had three bats, I remember, a pale one with Ted Williams's engraved signature, a kid-sized Little League item, and one that looked like a club and was dark wood and scarred like something long lurking in the lower depths of baseball.

Smaller kids played, other guys' little brothers. But they were in the outfield. I was the shortest kid our age, and I was at third. Stuff could sail way over my head, but nothing got past me. Once I tripped and tore my jeans and cut my knee, a couple of my fingers got mashed on a foul tip, but I couldn't feel it.

We played nine innings and people were watching. The score was close, something like 17–15. But we were ahead and Charley, the park keeper, had already flicked the lights on and off three times, which was the five-minute warning and meant that if we could hold on we had won.

They had guys on second and third. A big kid named Davey Healey who thought he was tough was up, and he was mad because people were yelling things about his mother. Murph was behind the plate. Mackie was pitching. Healey swung and the ball hit the bat. It was on the ground, bouncing wildly. As I moved forward, it caught a pebble, jumped up and bit me on the left shoulder.

But it came down in front of me. I pounced and trapped it with my bare hand. As I did, something moved on my right. Some kid named Greg who had an actual Red Sox cap was running home. Murph behind the plate was yelling at me and I tossed right from where I had caught the ball.

Murph got it in his glove and Greg was still coming. Murph ran up the line to make sure he didn't get past and stuck the ball right in his nose, which bled. Then there was a lot of pushing and yelling. But the lights went out and we had won

Walking home, kids dropped out until there was just Murph and me. He had the great dark bat and glove slung over his shoulder and his hat still on backwards. "I can take what my old man's gonna dish out standing on my head because we won."

Punishment at the Murphys' was a given. Mr. Murphy whacked kids at random. Once, not noticing I was a guest, he had even clipped me. Adrenaline carried me all the way home. Our house was silent. My stepfather and my mother had already gotten divorced. The light was on in the living room. I let myself in quietly.

I could have sworn my mother was asleep on the couch. Her form was there. But as I put my foot on the stairs, the Shadow appeared at the kitchen door and said, "Kevin!"

And I was so scared that I wanted to vomit and piss. She had a half-full glass in her hand. Her eyes were wide, curious. Like I was a bug and she was a bird. Outside of that, the Shadow's face was blank. That expression didn't change. "I thought you were kidnapped. I just called the police."

Now, my mother would have called some other kids' mothers and pieced together what had happened to me. But her Shadow didn't do stuff like that. "I thought some stranger took you in his car," she said very evenly. Then, "You're filthy. Get into the tub. Now."

From upstairs, I heard her get on the phone and say, "Terribly sorry to disturb you, Sergeant," in a weird, remote voice. On the second floor, the door to her room was open, the bottles and jars from her dresser lay smashed on the floor. Clothes were everywhere, thrown around, all of them torn, slashed. A bright-red stain spread where nail polish had spilled on the rug.

In the bathroom, everything from the medicine chest had been broken in the sink. The tub was full of lukewarm water. Locking the door, getting in the bath, I had to be careful how I stepped because of broken glass where the mirror was smashed.

The water stung my scraped knee, my mashed fingers. I heard the Shadow in my room. Things were getting broken, ripped. "On my own," she yelled, "I could go where I wanted. Do what I wanted. Without that runt." I was too scared to face her.

Then it seemed another voice was speaking, softly pleading that she be quiet. It seemed maybe my mother was awake. But when I crept out wrapped in a towel, it was only the Shadow and me. I stood and looked at the wreckage of my room, all my clothes and toys in a pile on the floor. "All this junk goes out tomorrow." She said this evenly, staring me down. "Stop crying."

"I got soap in my eyes."

Somehow, being a kid, I fell asleep. I awoke in the morning to the sound of weeping and quiet voices. More cautious than the night before, I listened to make sure that it was my grandmother and grand-aunt. Then I heard my mother, not her Shadow. In a choked voice she told them that she wanted to kill herself. They said for her not to let me hear.

Shortly afterward, the house got sold and my mother and I went to live with my grandmother and Aunt Tay. She wasn't so bad around them, kept her drinking quiet and her Shadow on a leash.

Over the next few years her brothers got to meddle in my life. Uncle Jim brought me to his war buddy Moxie's for crew cuts. Uncle Bob enrolled me in his alma mater downtown. School was cold and merciless, I barely skidded by. Uncle Mike brought me to the Y pool. Kids there were street tough. Tricks I learned made it hard to concentrate on the *Aeneid*.

One spring evening, in my junior year, I passed Curtis Park on my way from the MTA station to my grandmother's. In the supper-hour dusk, the place was almost empty. A lone figure perched on the jungle bars smoking a cigarette.

By then Murph had already dropped out of school. I'd grown my hair like Jack Kennedy and felt like I was coming into my own. We kind of nodded as I passed.

That afternoon, jumpy and chilled, I had sat on a couch in my Jordan Marsh briefs. A guy massaged my knee as I gulped down the whiskey and soda he had given me.

Going up the hill to home, I chewed gum. As I came in the front door, my mother stood on the stairs and looked right in my eyes. "Kev, it's after six. Where have you been?"

For a moment my heart went cold. But it really was my mother. Her smile was tired, sweet, like we were fellow truants. I remembered that day when the two of us kicked leaves behind her Shadow's back.

Right then, I would have told her what had happened to me. But things about myself confounded me so much that I couldn't find words. That's when a voice whispered, *We can do this standing on our head.* And I heard myself say, "School play Rehearsal. I told you."

If I was an expert navigator, my mother had limned the heavens. She knew I was lying, and I knew she knew. But instead of making her mad, my lie made something go out in her eyes. Unable to stand seeing that, I went past her and up the stairs.

At the time I thought that she had gotten a whiff of booze. Much later it occurred to me that she had caught a glimpse of my Shadow, was aware of him before I was. All that I know is that for the remaining time she lived, we trode carefully around each other.

In Washington Square Park long afterward, I was aware of my Shadow crossing my line of vision. He prowled the plaza around the fountain, gazing intently like he was cruising for drugs or sex. It seemed he took no notice of me as he spoke to a group of dazed, sun-soaked kids with matted hair and a pet ferret crawling over their naked shoulders.

I stood up and found myself facing the damsel and the dwarf. On second meeting, it was obvious that the blue-eyed Asian damsel was a boy in drag. The dwarf was a dwarf. But the angelic smile he flashed as he handed me a worn piece of drawing paper was junk-blank and unfocused.

On the sheet was a drawing of an enraptured putto. It took a moment, but I recognized Max's work and myself. What looked like wings were, in fact, my mother's hands resting protectively on my shoulders. Before I could wonder how my dopplegänger had gotten hold of the sketch, I saw a file card and a scrawl much like my own: "This should be an illustration from the book Helena Godspeed Hewett never thought of writing, *It's the Sistine Chapel, Jelly Bean!*"

I found myself grinning, which hadn't happened often recently. On the other side of the card, in that same hand, was the poem I'd been trying to remember. It read like sampler verse, but as if a tape in my head had been jogged, a blocked memory began to run.

We were in the Public Gardens and my mother was taking me to the Swan Boats. Maybe I was three. I let go of her hand and ran a few paces ahead. Then I heard her say, "Get away from us!"

I turned and saw my mother and another woman who looked just like her. Except the other's face was mean, angry. For a moment she stood staring at us and then seemed to disappear. My mother took me by the hand and we sat down beside a fountain turned green with age and weather. After a moment, my

*mother told me, "There's something Aunt Tay taught me when
I was little." And she recited,*

> *Praise orchards in autumn*
> *Warm kitchens in winter*
> *Wide meadows in springtime*
> *And fountains in summer*

We were quiet for a while. Then, like she knew that trying to
change the subject did no good, my mother said, "Kevin, I
don't want you ever to be frightened. No matter what you see
that one do, or hear her say. I love you with all my heart.
Remember that."

Don't say I never gave you anything, said a familiar whisper.
When I looked up, my Silent Partner was already walking away
with kids trailing after. Again I noticed how thin he was. There
was nothing to him but his ragged clothes. In Africa they call
AIDS the Slims.

That evening, we dined in the cool seclusion of Karen and
Laurie's backyard. I, of course, turned down the wine, refused
the pot. I haven't gotten high in twenty-two years. George was
the missing guest, unmentioned but in our thoughts. All
around me friends and former lovers have been struck down.
But I remain in good health. My existence is comfortable
within certain limits. A tribute to the moderate life.

All evening, I tried not to remember the skull smile of my
Shadow. What he had wanted to show me that afternoon was
how deeply he is embedded in my past. He wanted something
from me and I didn't want to know what that was. I wished
him all the things we could never have together, long life, calm
seas and prosperous voyages, I wished him far away and knew
that wouldn't happen.

A FRUITFUL HARVEST

Lauren Fitzgerald

I kneel beneath the steel-blue twilight, hands sweaty within my coat pockets, and watch the old man rock steadily upon his rusty porch swing. The gray farmhouse moans with every downward thrust of his body, its ancient joints cracking from the strain. There he swings, for what seems to be hours, a corncob pipe drooping from his lips, the glow of a single lightbulb illuminating the crooked margin of his body. His name is Ruppert Hurley-Boss, and it is the first time I've seen him since I was eight.

As I watch, my body hidden behind a thicket of briar, a chill rises from the autumn earth and I think of turning back. It was a stupid idea, I tell myself, coming out here from the city just to see the old man's property again. To see with my eyes, now more mature, the garden that once grew behind his house. Perhaps I am chasing the time-distorted fantasies of a boy, one who lost his mother at too young an age. One who had once believed in something more than life and death.

It was nearly thirty years ago that I lived among the green and gold fields of the Maryland countryside. The crisp, earth-scented wind instantly pulls me back into its mystery, and I find myself shivering from the bittersweet sentiment that envelops me. I was merely a boy when last I was here, too young and citified to appreciate the importance of such places; a victim of my own youthful arrogance, as so many of us are, believing that my presence on this planet has great significance. That I, like all things immortal, could not be measured in terms of days or years, but was a gauge by which all other things were measured. Now, kneeling beneath a blanket of endless sky, a speck of flesh and blood on the blue-green freckle of the universe, I marvel at the vast serenity of it all, humbled by its quiet power over me.

Our property was a modest parcel of seven acres, shouldered by the sprawling dairy farm belonging to Ruppert Hurley-Boss. We had come to move there from Baltimore after learning that my mother was ill. My father, who worshiped my mother more than the Catholic God he claimed to revere, thought the country would do her well. He wasted no time in the days following her grim diagnosis, immediately tendering his resignation with Baltimore Gas and Electric. Soon after, he purchased the small farm forty minutes from the city, naming the property A Fruitful Harvest after the dense rows of corn that lined the fields surrounding the house.

I hated the country. The nights were so dark and still and the days so long and quiet, I thought I'd die of boredom. But to my father, the country was a magical place where nature and simplicity ran things as efficiently and timely as power lunches and corporate mergers. "It breathes," my father told me one winter night as we stood in a corner of our field and watched the sun set. "And if you listen keenly, you can sometimes hear its heart beating." I listened, but heard nothing over my father's gentle utterances of prayer for my mother, and the sound of the wind whistling through the brittle stalks of corn. I realized then that my father truly believed the country would heal my mother; that its life-giving earth and rich perfumes would melt the voracious cancers beneath her flesh and return her to the woman he had married. And because I was merely a boy, I believed it too.

The old man burdens his body off the swing and removes the pipe from his mouth. The silver buttons on his overalls wink in the dim glow of the houselight as he turns and gazes out over his fields. Does he see me? I wonder, for he appears to be looking straight at me. If he does spot me, he does not act it, for he simply returns the pipe to his lips, scratches the faded denim between his legs, and walks to the other side of his porch. I feel foolish, spying on him this way; for sneaking onto his land and waiting for him to go inside so I can poke around in his garden and look for something that I probably only remember from a dream. I'm a man now, I reason silently, and I should have the maturity to walk up to him, introduce myself, and ask for a few moments of his time. But I do not. Instead, I remain perfectly still and wait for him to wander back inside his house.

I was seven years old the first time I set foot on Ruppert Hurley-Boss's land. It was midsummer, and we'd been living on our farm for only a month. My dog Pepper had been missing all day, and I was beginning to think he'd run off for good when Mr. Hurley-Boss phoned. Without even an introduction, he informed my father that Pepper was in his fields, teasing his cows and biting their ankles, and that if I wanted to see my dog again, I'd better run up there and get him.

My heart drumming in my chest, I sprinted across the sun-washed fields, all the while picturing Mr. Hurley-Boss with a rifle poised against Pepper's belly. I'd seen the farmer around town from time to time, and was always intimidated by the coal-black points of his eyes. Reaching the barbed-wire fence that separated our property from his, I pried a space for myself to slide between. The barbs snagged my clothes and scraped my skin, yet I forged through it, pain or not.

The sun was hot that day, and my clothes clung to my flesh with the tack of my bloody sweat. I gazed up the hill to where Mr. Hurley-Boss's old gray farmhouse was perched on the horizon. Beyond it, acres of cow-speckled countryside spread itself silently into the distance. I seemed to be running against a current as I pushed forward toward the house, my legs unable to move fast enough, my head so dizzy it felt as though it would unscrew from my body. When at last I reached the front porch, breathless, I bent over and grabbed my knees and tried to regain my composure before approaching the door. Presently, a long cool shadow fell across my body. I glanced up and found myself gazing into Mr. Hurley-Boss's long, drawn face.

"Boy," he said, punctuating the statement with a spit of tobacco.

"My dog," I managed between fast breaths. "Where . . . is . . ." I stopped when his black eyes fell upon me. There was something peculiar in his stare; something hard and knowing.

"Pa?" came a voice, small and barely audible above the thudding of my heart. It was then that I heard the screen door open, followed by a few hesitant footfalls. "This the boy who owns the speckled pup?"

I glanced past the man to where a thin, pale boy stood just outside the doorway. His hair sprouted in small patches on his head, and his skin was wrapped so tightly around his small bones that it pained me to look at him. He seemed to be about my age. I forced a smile.

"Yes, he's my dog. May I take him home now?"

The boy disappeared into the house and quickly returned with my dog, Pepper, on a twine leash. He led him down the stairs to where I stood, and handed me the rope.

"Fine dog," said the boy. His eyes, which seemed like marbles that had been pressed deeply into a ball of clay, moved over me with envy. "Wish I had a fine dog like him."

I seized the leash from his pale fingers, shuddering as my hand brushed against his cold, bony knuckles.

"He'll be dog burgers if I catch him on my land again, hear?" said Mr. Hurley-Boss, gazing at me intently.

I said nothing, merely nodded and clutched the rope tighter in my fist. The boy smiled at me, and I could see that his gums were almost as white as his skin. Trembling, I turned and ran back toward our farm, Pepper following closely at my side.

From then on I kept Pepper tied to a lead in our yard, a few dozen feet from the house. My heart ripped each time he lunged toward a passing bird or rabbit, only to find his quest disrupted by a sharp snap to the neck from the nylon rope. And though I died each time I saw him recoil, frustrated and defeated, I knew it was better than letting him roam free and risking a deadly confrontation with Mr. Hurley-Boss.

Mother grew worse over the following year. Her weight plummeted dramatically and her energy faded from her like flowers left to dry in the sun. By the fall of my eighth year, my mother was completely bedridden, her body a mere presence beneath the pale cotton sheets that swallowed her up. But to say she was my mother is only remotely true. For though she was still the body that had given me life, she was devoid of the spirit that had raised me. Her beautiful smile, full of dimples and teeth, was now replaced with dry, slightly parted lips that never moved and failed to speak. Her blue eyes, which had always followed my own with interest and love, had grown gray and absent and still. By Thanksgiving, the best I could hope for was a weak squeeze of her hand in mine, a sign that my true mother was hiding in some distant corner of her dying flesh. In those last months, my father grew deeply depressed. He moped about the house and hardly slept, and I was lucky if he said a word to me all day.

I didn't see Mr. Hurley-Boss again that summer, nor did I see his waiflike son. Some of the kids in school knew about the boy. They said his name was Kennedy and that he was the only child of Ruppert Hurley-Boss. He attended Brookedale Elementary up until the semester before I enrolled, when the doctors confirmed that he had come out of remission from a five-year battle with leukemia. No one appeared to know whether Kennedy was now dead or alive, nor did they seem to care. I did not fault them for that. Father always said that apathy is more sincere than pity.

It is ten till midnight when Mr. Hurley-Boss finally wanders inside and turns off the front porch light. I can see his hunched silhouette within the downstairs window, his body shuffling across the room before disappearing into the dark cavities of the old house. Confident that he has not seen me, I grope my way around the thick hedge toward the back of the house. As I move, I think about my family—my wife and three children—and how they believe I am in Washington on business. If only they knew, I think to myself as I move blindly across the yard. If only they knew how the images from my youth have haunted me all these years. They'd think I was insane.

But walking across the mineral-scented earth, the cool air chilling my ears, I know I am not insane. There is something special about this place, something more than rolling fields and slow-moving rivers. It is a place where people remember things that the developed world has forgotten. Where the basics of the earth, not technology and progress, control the fates of men. This is where the answers are. This, above any place else in the universe, is Heaven.

Pepper ran away the night my mother died. For years I would associate the two events in my imagination, fantasizing that Pepper had carried my mother's life away with him into the blue twilight, accompanying her soul to its final destination. The fantasy comforted me for a time, then came to disturb me as I grew older and began thinking realistically about the two events. How I, amid the confusion of my mother's failing health, may have been responsible for the coincidence.

My father appeared in my room after he phoned the doctor and Father Kramer. I was sitting on the floor sorting my comics when his silent figure materialized in the doorway. "Your mother is about to leave us, son. Come and say goodbye."

I followed my father down the hall to my mother's bedroom, his arm resting gently on my shoulder. Presently, there was a knock at the door, and he left me to go and answer it. For several moments I stood in the doorway, gazing at my mother across the room. Her breaths were slow and gurgling, her eyelids fluttering above the nonseeing whites of her eyes. I tried to move, tried to force my legs forward to her side, but found myself paralyzed. I could hear my father talking to the doctor downstairs; could hear them quietly uttering words like "pain" and "suffering." As I heard the men approaching the stairs, I turned and ran back to my room, slamming the door behind me. I was not about to let them see me cry.

My mother died in the middle of the night. My father was at her side when she went. He told me that she had slipped away peacefully, though I never have been able to conjure up images of peace when I think back on her illness. The next morning, when I went to tie Pepper to his lead, I could barely hold the thick nylon between my fingers, let alone fashion an adequate knot. My limbs were numb and weak, my body shivering with the chill of cold shock. It is no wonder that a few hours later, without my realizing it, Pepper had broken free. In an instant, gone.

It was freezing that day, the ground a frozen web of grass and weeds. I pushed my body across the hard earth, calling for Pepper. This time, I cared not about the sharp barbs that gouged my skin as I slipped through the fence onto Mr. Hurley-Boss's land. The metal felt good as it pierced my flesh, creating rows of pain in my body to distract me from the agony in my soul.

Mr. Hurley-Boss was perched upon a tractor in the field behind his house. I ran up the hill and stopped beside the grinding machine. He gazed down at me, his body stiff, face grim.

"Where's my dog?" I demanded, my breath meeting the autumn air in a silver mist.

The man turned off the engine and gazed at me expectantly. I gazed back, finding myself lost in the dark pinpoints of his eyes. Drawn in by the hardness of his stare, I let go of the pain in my gut.

"My mother's dead," I blurted. I shuddered at the sound of

my voice speaking the cruel truth for the first time. *My mother's dead.* It sounded so alien to me, like the fading residue of a nightmare. *Dead. My mother's dead.* Before I could stop myself, I fell to the ground and wept. Through a filter of tears, I saw the man climb down off his tractor and step behind me, lifting me to my feet. Silently, he gripped my shoulders and pushed me forward, toward the back of his house. Mr. Hurley-Boss's thick fingers were like steel clamps on my back. I rubbed the tears from my eyes, feeling childish, and let him lead me where he would.

We stopped at the edge of a small patch of tilled earth that had been fenced with the same barbed wire that separated our properties. I scanned my surroundings, looking for Pepper's deep brown eyes and wide, panting grin. He was not there.

Mr. Hurley-Boss dug his fingers into my shoulders, breathed his hot breath onto the back of my head. "Just because people die," he began, his voice low and steady, "don't mean they have to end." At last he let go of my shoulders and pointed a soiled finger toward the small garden.

Maybe I was delirious with grief over my mother's death. Or maybe I was still in bed, dreaming, when I saw what I did. But in my emotion-warped recollection, I remember two unusual plants of various sizes. The one closest to the fence was as tall as a stalk of corn, the other barely a foot from the ground. And although the two plants were in different stages of growth, I could tell that they were of the same strange variety. The mature plant had a velvety red stalk and black, dart-shaped leaves. At the top fruited three almond-colored growths, the size of a man's fist. They resembled coconuts, though their skin was leathery and lighter in color. The stem of the smaller plant was already growing small black leaves with marble-sized buds at the top. And although this sight was so unusual, so absolutely foreign to me, I knew I had seen that little plant before; had encountered it last summer on Mr. Hurley-Boss's front porch, when it told me that I had a very fine dog.

We buried Mother in a small cemetery outside of Richmond, next to her mother. I remember thinking how unnatural the funeral rite seemed. How cruel it was to seal a human being in a box, then bury it deep within the earth's surface where the ground is hard and sterile. And in all the years that have followed, I have not once returned to her grave. I realized long ago that I buried more than my mother that day; I buried my faith in God. And though he never would admit it, I believe my father's faith is buried there too.

I never saw Pepper again, though I didn't stop looking for him until the following spring when my father decided to sell A Fruitful Harvest and move back to the city. And though my life changed and grew more complex over the years, I have never forgotten that morning; the day I lost both my mother and my best friend. Nor have I forgotten the almond-colored fruit that Mr. Hurley-Boss and I plucked from his garden, the one whose peel resembled human flesh in both color and texture, and whose juices ran thick and red like blood.

I do not know whose fruit we picked. He did not say. Perhaps it was his wife, or maybe a sister or mother. All I know is that, sitting with Mr. Hurley-Boss on his front porch, silently taking the sour fruit into our mouths, I felt at peace.

Beyond the hedge, I see them. Two plants towering above the garden, bowing as they struggle to hold their large fruit. Although the garden is overgrown with weeds, neglected, the two plants grow tall and fruitful.

It *is* true, I reassure myself. It is.

I try to contain a laugh, but cannot. It is beyond my wildest fantasies. It is what I have believed in all these years, though I have never felt so sure of until now. Like an atheist opening the front door and finding God, the truth is staring me in the face, and I can deny it no more.

You see, my wife gave birth to our third child last month. A boy, Benjamin. Ten fingers, ten toes, stunning onyx eyes, and no brain. He is still alive, though not expected to live out the week. That is why I had to come. For Benjamin's sake. To give him something more lasting than death.

Benjamin died two months ago. We gave him a service at the funeral home, just a small one with family. Then I came out here and buried him, no coffin, no clothes. Afterward, I went up to the old man's house, knocked on his door and introduced myself as "the boy with the speckled pup." He nodded approvingly when I told him what I'd done with Benjamin, then winked at me with his coal-colored eyes and disappeared into his house.

Each month I return to the old man's land to see. At first I could see nothing beneath the thick weeds that run wild through the soil. Then, in April, I saw a stem. Later in the month, a stalk. Now it is July and there are flowers and the beginnings of small buds in the soft folds of the leaves. I brought my wife here last week. I didn't have to tell her what it was; a mother always recognizes her own. And when my two daughters are old enough, I will bring them out here as well. Together we will harvest the fruit and peel back its leathery skin. And as the meat passes over our gums and into our souls, I will tell them about the things I believe in. About how man was intended to do more than walk the earth; he was meant to put down roots and stay awhile. Yes, that is what I believe.

THE ZIGGURAT

Gene Wolfe

It had begun to snow about one-thirty. Emery Bainbridge stood on the front porch to watch it before going back into the cabin to record it in his journal.

> 13:38 Snowing hard, quiet as owl feathers. Radio says stay off the roads unless you have four-wheel. Probably means no Brook.

He put down the lipstick-red ballpoint and stared at it. With this pen . . . He ought to scratch out *Brook* and write *Jan* over it.

"To hell with that." His harsh voice seemed loud in the silent cabin. "What I wrote, I wrote. *Quod scripsi* whatever it is."

That was what being out here alone did, he told himself. You were supposed to rest up. You were supposed to calm down. Instead you started talking to yourself. "Like some nut," he added aloud.

Jan would come, bringing Brook. And Aileen and Alayna. Aileen and Alayna were as much his children as Brook was, he told himself firmly. "For the time being."

If Jan could not come tomorrow, she would come later when the county had cleared the back roads. And it was more than possible that she would come, or try to, tomorrow as she had planned. There was that kind of a streak in Jan, not exactly stubbornness and not exactly resolution, but a sort of willful determination to believe whatever she wanted; thus she believed he would sign her papers, and thus she would believe that the big Lincoln he had bought her could go anywhere a Jeep could.

Brook would be all for it, of course. At nine, Brook had tried to cross the Atlantic on a Styrofoam dinosaur, paddling out farther and farther until at last a lifeguard had launched her little catamaran and brought him back, letting the dinosaur float out to sea.

That was what was happening everywhere, Emery thought— boys and men were being brought back to shore by women, though for thousands of years their daring had permitted humanity to survive.

He pulled on his red-plaid double mackinaw and his warmest cap, and carried a chair out onto the porch to watch the snow.

Suddenly it wasn't . . . He had forgotten the word that he had used before. It wasn't whatever men had. It was something women had, or they thought it was. Possibly it was something nobody had.

He pictured Jan leaning intently over the wheel, her lips compressed to an ugly slit, easing her Lincoln into the snow, coaxing it up the first hill, stern with triumph as it cleared the crest. Jan about to be stranded in this soft and silent wilderness in high-heeled shoes. Perhaps that streak of hers was courage after all, or something so close that it could be substituted for courage at will. Little pink packets that made you think whatever you wanted to be true would be true, if only you acted as if it were with sufficient tenacity.

He was being watched.

"By God, it's that coyote," he said aloud, and knew from the timbre of his own voice that he lied. These were human eyes. He narrowed his own, peering through the falling snow, took off his glasses, blotted their lenses absently with his handkerchief, and looked again.

A higher, steeper hill rose on the other side of his tiny valley, a hill clothed in pines and crowned with wind-swept ocher rocks. The watcher was up there somewhere, staring down at him through the pine boughs, silent and observant.

"Come on over!" Emery called. "Want some coffee?"

There was no response.

"You lost? You better get out of this weather!"

The silence of the snow seemed to suffocate each word in turn. Although he had shouted, he could not be certain he had been heard. He stood and made a sweeping gesture: *Come here.*

There was a flash of colorless light from the pines, so swift and slight that he could not be absolutely certain he had seen it. Someone signaling with a mirror—except that the sky was the color of lead above the downward-drifting whiteness of the snow, the sun invisible.

"Come on over!" he called again, but the watcher was gone.

Country people, he thought, suspicious of strangers. But there were no country people around here, not within ten miles; a few hunting camps, a few cabins like his own, with nobody in them now that deer season was over.

He stepped off the little porch. The snow was more than ankle-deep already and falling faster than it had been just a minute before, the pine-clad hill across the creek practically invisible.

The woodpile under the overhang of the south eaves (the woodpile that had appeared so impressive when he had arrived) had shrunk drastically. It was time to cut and split more. Past time, really. The chain saw tomorrow, the ax, the maul, and the wedge tomorrow, and perhaps even the Jeep, if he could get it in to snake the logs out.

Mentally, he put them all away. Jan was coming, would be bringing Brook to stay. And the twins to stay, too, with Jan herself, if the road got too bad.

The coyote had gone up on the back porch!

After a second or two he realized he was grinning like a fool, and forced himself to stop and look instead.

There were no tracks. Presumably the coyote had eaten this morning before the snow started, for the bowl was empty, licked clean. The time would come, and soon, when he would touch the rough yellow-gray head, when the coyote would lick his fingers and fall asleep in front of the little fieldstone fireplace in his cabin.

Triumphant, he rattled the rear door, then remembered that he had locked it the night before. Had locked both doors, in fact, moved by an indefinable dread. Bears, he thought—a way of assuring himself that he was not as irrational as Jan.

There were bears around here, that was true enough. Small black bears, for the most part. But not Yogi Bears, not funny but potentially dangerous park bears who had lost all fear of

Man and roamed and rummaged as they pleased. These bears were hunted every year, hunted through the golden days of autumn as they fattened for hibernation. Silver winter had arrived, and these bears slept in caves and hollow logs, in thickets and thick brush, slept like their dead, though slowly and softly breathing like the snow—motionless, dreaming bear-dreams of the last-men years, when the trees would have filled in the old logging roads again and shouldered aside the cracked asphalt of the county road, and all the guns had rusted to dust.

Yet he had been afraid.

He returned to the front of the cabin, picked up the chair he had carried onto the porch, and noticed a black spot on its worn back he could not recall having seen before. It marked his finger, and was scraped away readily by the blade of his pocketknife.

Shrugging, he brought the chair back inside. There was plenty of Irish stew; he would have Irish stew tonight, soak a slice of bread in gravy for the coyote, and leave it in the same spot on the back porch. You could not (as people always said) move the bowl a little every day. That would have been frightening, too fast for any wild thing. You moved the bowl once, perhaps, in a week; and the coyote's bowl had walked by those halting steps from the creek bank where he had glimpsed the coyote in summer to the back porch.

Jan and Brook and the twins might—would be sure to—frighten it. That was unfortunate, but could not be helped; it might be best not to try to feed the coyote at all until Jan and the twins had gone. As inexplicably as he had known that he was being watched, and by no animal, he felt certain that Jan would reach him somehow, bending reality to her desires.

He got out the broom and swept the cabin. When he had expected her, he had not cared how it looked or what she might think of it. Now that her arrival had become problematic, he found that he cared a great deal.

She would have the other lower bunk, the twins could sleep together feet-to-feet in an upper (no doubt with much squealing and giggling and kicking), and Brook in the other upper—in the bunk over his own.

Thus would the family achieve its final and irrevocable separation for the first time; the Sibberlings (who had been and would again be) on one side of the cabin, the Bainbridges on the other: boys here, girls over there. The law would take years, and demand tens of thousands of dollars, to accomplish no more.

Boys here.

Girls over there, farther and farther all the time. When he had rocked and kissed Aileen and Alayna, when he had bought Christmas and birthday presents and sat through solemn, silly conferences with their pleased teachers, he had never felt that he was actually the twins' father. Now he did. Al Sibberling had given them his swarthy good looks and flung them away. He, Emery Bainbridge, had picked them up like discarded dolls after Jan had run the family deep in debt. Had called himself their father, and thought he lied.

There would be no sleeping with Jan, no matter how long she stayed. It was why she was bringing the twins, as he had known from the moment she said they would be with her.

He put clean sheets on the bunk that would be hers, with three thick wool blankets and a quilt.

Bringing her back from plays and country-club dances, he had learned to listen for them; silence had meant he could return and visit Jan's bed when he had driven the sitter home. Now Jan feared that he would want to bargain—his name on her paper for a little more pleasure, a little more love before they parted for good. Much as she wanted him to sign, she did not want him to sign as much as that. Girls here, boys over there. Had he grown so hideous?

Women need a reason, he thought, men just need a place.

For Jan the reason wasn't good enough, so she had seen to it that there would be no place. He told himself it would be great to hug the twins again—and discovered that it would.

He fluffed Jan's pillow anyway, and dressed it in a clean white pillowcase.

She would have found someone by now, somebody in the city to whom she was being faithful, exactly as he himself had been faithful to Jan while he was still married, in the eyes of the law, to Pamela.

The thought of eyes recalled the watcher on the hill.

14:12 Somebody is on the hill across the creek with some kind of signaling device.

That sounded as if he were going crazy, he decided. What if Jan saw it? He added, maybe just a flashlight, although he did not believe it had been a flashlight.

A lion's face smiled up at him from the barrel of the red pen, and he stopped to read the minute print under it, holding the pen up to catch the gray light from the window. "The Red Lion Inn/San Jose." A nice hotel. If—when—he got up the nerve to do it, he would write notes to Jan and Brook first with this pen.

> The coyote ate the food I put out for him, I think soon after breakfast. More food tonight. Tomorrow morning I will leave the back door cracked open awhile.
> 14:15 I am going up on the hill for a look around.

He had not known that until he wrote it.

The hillside seemed steeper than he remembered, slippery with snow. The pines had changed; their limbs drooped like the boughs of hemlocks, springing up like snares when he touched them, and throwing snow in his face. No bird sang.

He had brought his flashlight, impelled by the memory of the colorless signal from the hill. Now he used it to peep beneath the drooping limbs. Most of the tracks that the unseen watcher had left would be covered with new snow by this time; a few might remain, in the shelter of the pines.

He had nearly reached the rocky summit before he found the first, and even it was blurred by snow despite its protection. He knelt and blew the drifted flakes away, clearing it with his breath as he had sometimes cleared the tracks of animals; an oddly cleated shoe, almost like the divided hoof of an elk. He measured it against his spread hand, from the tip of his little finger to the tip of his thumb. A small foot, no bigger than size six, if that.

A boy.

There was another, inferior, print beside it. And not far away a blurred depression that might have been left by a gloved hand or a hundred other things. Here the boy had crouched with his little polished steel mirror, or whatever he had.

Emery knelt, lifting the snow-burdened limbs that blocked his view of the cabin. Two small, dark figures were emerging from the cabin door onto the porch, scarcely visible through the falling snow. The first carried his ax, the second his rifle.

He stood, waving the flashlight. "Hey! You there!"

The one holding his rifle raised it, not putting it to his shoulder properly but acting much too quickly for Emery to duck. The flat crack of the shot sounded clearly, snow or no snow.

He tried to dodge, slipped, and fell to the soft snow.

"Too late," he told himself. And then, "Going to do it for me." And last, "Better stay down in case he shoots again." The cold air was like chilled wine, the snow he lay in lovely beyond imagining. Drawing back his coat sleeve, he consulted his watch, resolving to wait ten minutes—to risk nothing.

They were robbing his cabin, obviously. Had robbed it, in fact, while he had been climbing through the pines. Had fired, in all probability, merely to keep him away long enough for them to leave. Mentally, he inventoried the cabin. Besides the rifle, there had not been a lot worth stealing—his food and a few tools; they might take his Jeep if they could figure out how to hot-wire the ignition, and that was pretty easy on those old Jeeps.

His money was in his wallet, his wallet in the hip pocket of his hunting trousers. His watch—a plastic sports watch hardly worth stealing—was on his wrist. His checkbook had been in the table drawer; they might steal that and forge his checks, possibly. They might even be caught when they tried to cash them.

Retrieving his flashlight, he lifted the limbs as he had before. The intruders were not in sight, the door of the cabin half open, his Jeep still parked next to the north wall, its red paint showing faintly through snow.

He glanced at his watch. One minute had passed, perhaps a minute and a half.

They would have to have a vehicle of some kind, one with four-wheel drive if they didn't want to be stranded with their loot on a back road. Since he had not heard it start up, they had probably left the engine running. Even so, he decided, he should have heard it pull away.

Had they parked some distance off and approached his cabin on foot? Now that he came to think of it, it seemed possible they had no vehicle after all. Two boys camping in the snow, confident that he would be unable to follow them to their tent, or whatever it was. Wasn't there a Boy Scout badge for winter camping? He had never been a Scout, but thought he remembered hearing about one, and found it plausible.

Still no one visible. He let the branches droop again.

The rifle was not really much of a loss, though its theft had better be reported to the sheriff. He had not planned on shooting anyway—had been worried, as a matter of fact, that the twins might get it down and do something foolish, although both had shot at tin cans and steel silhouettes with it before he and Jan had agreed to separate.

Now, with his rifle gone, he could not . . .

Neither had been particularly attracted to it; and their having handled and fired it already should have satisfied the natural curiosity that resulted in so many accidents each year. They had learned to shoot to please him, and stopped as soon as he had stopped urging them to learn.

Four minutes, possibly five. He raised the pine boughs once more, hearing the muted growl of an engine; for a second or two he held his breath. The Jeep or Bronco or whatever it was, was coming closer, not leaving. Was it possible that the thieves were coming back? Returning with a truck to empty his cabin?

Jan's big black Lincoln hove into view, roared down the gentle foothill slope on which his cabin stood, and skidded to a stop. Doors flew open, and all three kids piled out. Jan herself left more sedately, shutting the door on the driver's side behind her almost tenderly, tall and willowy as ever, her hair a golden helmet beneath a blue-mink pillbox hat.

Her left hand held a thick, black attaché case that was probably his.

Brook was already on the porch. Emery stood and shouted a warning, but it was too late; Brook was inside the cabin, with the twins hard on his heels. Jan looked around and waved, and deep inside Emery something writhed in agony.

By the time he had reached the cabin, he had decided not to mention that the intruders had shot at him. Presumably the shooter had chambered a new round, ejecting the brass cartridge case of the round just fired into the snow; but it might easily be overlooked, and if Brook or the twins found it, he could say that he had fired the day before to scare off some animal.

"Hello," Jan said as he entered. "You left your door open. It's cold as Billy-o in here." She was seated in a chair before the fire.

"I didn't." He dropped into the other, striving to look casual. "I was robbed."

"Really? When?"

"A quarter hour ago. Did you see another car coming in?" Jan shook her head.

They had been on foot, then; the road ended at the lake. Aloud he said, "It doesn't matter. They got my rifle and my ax." Remembering his checkbook, he pulled out the drawer of the little table. His checkbook was still there; he took it out and put it into an inner pocket of his mackinaw.

"It was an old rifle anyhow, wasn't it?"

He nodded. "My old thirty-thirty."

"Then you can buy a new one, and you should have locked the door. I—"

"You weren't supposed to get here until tomorrow," he told her brusquely. The mere thought of another gun was terrifying.

"I know. But they said a blizzard was coming on TV, so I decided I'd better move it up a day, or I'd have to wait for a week—that was what it sounded like. I told Doctor Gibbons that Aileen would be in next Thursday, and off we went. This shouldn't take long." She opened his attaché case on her lap. "Now here—"

"Where are the kids?"

"Out back getting more wood. They'll be back in a minute."

As though to confirm her words, he heard the clink of the maul striking the wedge. He ventured, "Do you really want them to hear it?"

"Emery, they *know*. I couldn't have hidden all this from them if I tried. What was I going to say when they asked why you never came home anymore?"

"You could have told them I was deer-hunting."

"That's for a few days, maybe a week. You left in August, remember? Well, anyway, I didn't. I told them the truth." She paused, expectant. "Aren't you going to ask how they took it?"

He shook his head.

"The girls were hurt. I honestly think Brook's happy. Getting to live with you out here for a while and all that."

"I've got him signed up for Culver," Emery told her. "He starts in February."

"That's best, I'm sure. Now listen, because we've got to get back. Here's a letter from your—"

"You're not going to sleep here? Stay overnight?"

"Tonight? Certainly not. We've got to start home before this storm gets serious. You always interrupt me. You always have. I suppose it's too late to say I wish you'd stop."

He nodded. "I made up a bunk for you."

"Brook can have it. Now right—"

The back door opened and Brook himself came in. "I showed

them how you split the wood, and 'Layna split one. Didn't you, 'Layna?"

"Right here." Behind him, Alayna held the pieces up.

"That's not ladylike," Jan told her.

Emery said, "But it's quite something that a girl her age can swing that maul—I wouldn't have believed she could. Did Brook help you lift it?"

Alayna shook her head.

"*I* didn't want to," Aileen declared virtuously.

"Right here," Jan was pushing an envelope into his hands, "is a letter from your attorney. It's sealed, see? I haven't read it, but you'd better take a look at it first."

"You know what's in it, though," Emery said, "or you think you do."

"He told me what he was going to write to you, yes."

"Otherwise you would have saved it." Emery got out his pocketknife and slit the flap. "Want to tell me?"

Jan shook her head, her lips as tight and ugly as he had imagined them earlier.

Brook put down his load of wood. "Can I see?"

"You can read it for me," Emery told him. "I've got snow on my glasses." He found a clean handkerchief and wiped them. "Don't read it out loud. Just tell me what it says."

"Emery, you're doing this to get even!"

He shook his head. "This is Brook's inheritance that our lawyers are arguing about."

Brook stared.

"I've lost my company," Emery told him. "Basically, we're talking about the money and stock I got as a consolation prize. You're the only child I've got, probably the only one I'll ever have. So read it. What does it say?"

Brook unfolded the letter; it seemed quieter to Emery now, with all five of them in the cabin, than it ever had during all the months he had lived there alone.

Jan said, "What they did was perfectly legal, Brook. You should understand that. They bought up a controlling interest and merged our company with theirs. That's all that happened."

The stiff, parchment-like paper rattled in Brook's hands. Unexpectedly Alayna whispered, "I'm sorry, Daddy."

Emery grinned at her. "I'm still here, honey."

Brook glanced from him to Jan, then back to him. "He says—it's Mister Gluckman. You introduced me one time."

Emery nodded.

"He says this is the best arrangement he's been able to work out, and he thinks it would be in your best interest to take it."

Jan said, "You keep this place and your Jeep, and all your personal belongings, naturally. I'll give you back my wedding and engagement rings—"

"You can keep them," Emery told her.

"No, I want to be fair about this. I've always tried to be fair, even when you didn't come to the meetings between our attorneys. I'll give them back, but I get to keep all the rest of the gifts you've given me, including my car."

Emery nodded.

"No alimony at all. Naturally no child support. Brook stays with you, Aileen and Alayna with me. My attorney says we can force Al to pay child support."

Emery nodded again.

"And I get the house. Everything else we divide equally. That's the stock and any other investments, the money in my personal accounts, your account, and our joint account." She had another paper. "I know you'll want to read it over, but that's what it is. You can follow me into Voylestown in your Jeep. There's a notary there who can witness your signature."

"I had the company when we were married."

"But you don't have it anymore. We're not talking about your company. It's not involved at all."

He picked up the telephone, a diversion embraced at random that might serve until the pain ebbed. "Will you excuse me? This is liable to go on awhile, and I should report the break-in." He entered the sheriff's number from the sticker on the telephone.

The distant clamor—it was not the actual ringing of the sheriff's telephone at all, he knew—sounded empty as well as artificial, as if it were not merely far away but high over the earth, a computer-generated instrument that jangled and buzzed for his ears alone upon some airless asteroid beyond the moon.

Brook laid Phil Gluckman's letter on the table where he could see it.

"Are you getting through?" Jan asked. "There's a lot of ice on the wires. Brook was talking about it on the way up."

"I think so. It's ringing."

Brook said, "They've probably got a lot of emergencies, because of the storm." The twins stirred uncomfortably, and Alayna went to a window to look at the falling snow.

"I should warn you," Jan said, "that if you won't sign, it's war. We spent hours and hours—"

A voice squeaked, *"Sheriff Ron Wilber's Office."*

"My name is Emery Bainbridge. I've got a cabin on Route Eighty-five, about five miles from the lake."

The tinny voice spoke unintelligibly.

"Would you repeat that, please?"

"It might be better from the cellular phone in my car," Jan suggested.

"What's the problem, Mister Bainbridge?"

"My cabin was robbed in my absence." There was no way in which he could tell the sheriff's office that he had been shot at without telling Jan and the twins as well; he decided it was not essential. "They took a rifle and my ax. Those are the only things that seem to be missing."

"Could you have mislaid them?"

This was the time to tell the sheriff about the boy on the hill; he found that he could not.

"Can you hear me, Mister Bainbridge?" There was chirping in the background, as if there were crickets on the party line.

He said, "Barely. No, I didn't mislay them. Somebody was in here while I was away—they left the door open, for one thing." He described the rifle and admitted he did not have a record of its serial number, then described the ax and spelled his name.

"We can't send anyone out there now, Mister Bainbridge. I'm sorry."

It was a woman. He had not realized until then that he had been talking to a woman. He said, "I just wanted to let you know, in case you picked somebody up."

"We'll file a report. You can come here and look at the stolen goods whenever you want to, but I don't think there's any guns right now."

"The theft just occurred. About three or a little later." When the woman at the sheriff's office did not speak again, he said, "Thank you," and hung up.

"You think they'll come back tonight, Dad?"

"I doubt very much that they'll come back at all." Emery sat down, unconsciously pushing his chair a little farther from Jan's. "Since you kids went out and split that wood, don't you think you ought to put some of it on the fire?"

"I put mine on," Aileen announced. "Didn't I, Momma?"

Brook picked up several of the large pieces he had carried and laid them on the feeble flames.

"I founded the company years before we got married," Emery told Jan. "I lost control when Brook's mother and I broke up. I had to give her half of my stock, and she sold it."

"It's not—"

"The stock you're talking about dividing now is the stock I got for mine. Most of the money in our joint account, and my personal account, came from the company before we were taken over. You can hang on to everything in your personal accounts. I don't want your money."

"Well, that's kind of you! That's extremely kind of you, Emery!"

"You're worried about the snow, you say, and I think you should be. If you and the twins want to stay here until the weather clears up, you're welcome to. Maybe we can work out something."

Jan shook her head, and for a moment Emery allowed himself to admire her clear skin and the clean lines of her profile. It was so easy to think of all that he wanted to say to her, so hard to say what he had to: "In that case, you'd better go."

"I'm entitled to half our community property!"

Brook put in, "The house's worth ten times more than this place."

Boys here, Emery thought. Girls over there. "You can have the house, Jan. I'm not disputing it—not now. Not yet. But I may, later, if you're stubborn. I'm willing to make a cash settlement . . ." Even as he said it, he realized that he was not.

"This is what we negotiated. Phil Gluckman represented you! He said so, and so did you. It's all settled."

Emery leaned forward in his chair, holding his hands out to the rising flames. "If everything's settled, you don't need my signature. Go back to the city."

"I—Oh, God! I should have known it was no use to come out here."

"I'm willing to give you a cash settlement in the form of a trust fund for the twins. A generous settlement, and you can keep the house, your car, your money, and your personal things. That's as far as I'll go, and it's further than I ought to go. Otherwise, we fight it out in court."

"We negotiated this!"

She shoved her paper at him, and he was tempted to throw

it into the fire. Forcing himself to speak mildly, he said, "I know you did, and I know that you negotiated in good faith. So did we. I wanted to see what Phil Gluckman could come up with. And to tell you the truth, I was pretty sure that it would be something I could accept. I'm disappointed in him."

"It's snowing harder," Alayna told them.

"He didn't—" Emery stiffened. "Did you hear something?"

"I haven't heard a thing! I don't have listen to this!"

It had sounded like a shot, but had probably been no more than the noise of a large branch breaking beneath the weight of the snow. "I've lost my train of thought," he admitted, "but I can make my position clear in three short affirmations. First, I won't sign that paper. Not here, not in Voylestown, and not in the city. Not anywhere. You might as well put it away."

"This is completely unfair!"

"Second, I won't go back and haggle. That's Phil's job."

"Mister high-tech himself, roughing it in the wilderness."

Emery shook his head. "I was never the technical brains of the company, Jan. There were half a dozen people working for me who knew more about the equipment than I did."

"Modest, too. I hope you realize that I'm going to have something to say after you're through."

"Third, I'm willing to try again if you are." He paused, hoping to see her glare soften. "I realize I'm not easy to live with. Neither are you. But I'm willing to try—hard—if you'll let me."

"You really and truly think that you're a great lover, don't you?"

"You married a great lover the first time," he told her.

She seethed. He watched her clench her perfect teeth and take three deep breaths as she forced herself to speak calmly. "Emery, you say that unless I settle for what you're willing to give we'll fight it out in open court. If we do, the public— every acquaintance and business contact you've got—will hear how you molested my girls."

Unwilling to believe what he had heard, he stared at her.

"You didn't think I'd do it, did you? You didn't think I'd expose them to that, and I don't want to. But—"

"It's not true!"

"Your precious Phil Gluckman has questioned them, in my presence and my attorney's. Call him up right now. Ask him what he thinks."

Emery looked at the twins; neither would meet his eyes.

"Do you want to see what a court will give me when the

judge hears that? There are a lot of women judges. Do you want to find out?"

"Yes." He spoke slowly. "Yes, Jan. I do."

"It'll ruin you!"

"I'm ruined already." He stood up. "That's what you're refusing to understand. I think you'd better leave now. You and the twins."

She stood too, jumping to her feet with energy he envied. "You set up one company. You could start another one, but not when this gets around."

He wanted to say that he had seen a unique opportunity and taken it—that he'd had his chance in life and made the best of it, and finished here. All that he could manage was, "I'm terribly sorry it's come to this. I never wanted it to, or . . ." His throat shut, and he felt the sick hopelessness of a fighter whose worst enemies are his own instincts. How would it feel and taste, how would it look, the cold, oiled steel muzzle in his mouth? He could cut a stick in the woods, or even use the red pen to press the trigger.

"Come on, girls, we're going. Goodbye, Brook."

Brook muttered something.

For a brief moment Emery felt Alayna's hand in his; then she was gone. The cabin door slammed behind her.

Brook said, "Don't freak out. She's got it coming."

"I know she does," Emery told him. "So do I, and we're both going to get it. I don't mind for my sake, but I mind terribly for hers. It was my job—my duty—to—"

On the front porch Jan exclaimed, *"Hey!"* Presumably she was speaking to one of the twins.

"I thought you handled yourself really well," Brook said.

Emery managed to smile. "That's another thing. It's my job to teach you how that sort of thing's done, and I didn't. Don't you see that I let her leave—practically made her go—before she'd agreed to what I wanted? I should have moved heaven and earth to keep her here until she did, but I pushed her out the door instead. That's not how you win, that's how you lose."

· "You think the sheriff might get your gun back?"

"I hope not." Emery took off his coat and hung it on the peg nearest the front door. For Brook's sake he added, "I like to shoot, but I've never liked shooting animals."

Outside, the sound diminished by distance and the snow, Jan screamed.

Emery was first out of the door, but was nearly knocked off

the porch by Brook. Beyond the porch's meager shelter, half obscured by blowing snow, the black Lincoln's hood was up. Jan sprawled in the snow, screaming. One of the twins grappled a small, dark figure; the other was not in sight.

Brook charged into the swirling snow, snow so thick that for a moment he vanished completely. Emery floundered through shin-high snow after him, saw a second small stranger appear—as it seemed—from the Lincoln's engine compartment, and a third emerge from the interior with his rifle in its hand, the dome light oddly spectral in the deepening gloom. For a moment he received the fleeting impression of a smooth, almond-shaped brown face.

The rifle came up. The diminutive figure (shorter than Brook, hardly larger than the twins) jerked at its trigger. Brook grabbed it and staggered backward, falling in the snow. The struggling twin cried out, a childish shriek of pain and rage.

Then their attackers fled—fled preposterously slowly through snow that was for them knee high, but fled nonetheless, the three running clumsily together in a dark, packed mass that almost vanished before they had gone twenty feet. One turned, wrestled the rifle's lever, jerked the rifle like an unruly dog, and ran again.

Emery knelt in the snow beside Jan. "Are you all right?"

She shook her head, sobbing like a child.

The twin embraced him, gasping, "She hit me, she hit me." He tried to comfort both, an arm for each.

Later—though it seemed to him not much later—Brook draped his shoulders with his double mackinaw, and he realized how cold he was. He stood, lifting the twin, and pulled Jan to her feet. "We'd better get back inside."

"No!"

He dragged her after him, hearing Brook shut the Lincoln's passenger's-side door behind them.

By the time they reached the cabin, Jan was weeping again. Emery put her back in the chair she had occupied a few minutes before. "Listen! Listen here, even if you can't stop bawling. One of the twins is gone. Do you know where she is?"

Sobbing, Jan shook her head.

"That girl with the hood? She hit Mama, and Aileen ran away." The remaining twin pointed.

Brook gasped, "They didn't hurt her, 'Layna?"

"They hurt me. They hit my arm." She pushed back her sleeve, wincing.

Emery turned to Brook. "What happened to you?"

"Got it in the belly." Brook managed a sick smile. "He had a gun. Was it the one they stole from you?"

"I think so."

"Well—I grabbed the barrel," Brook paused, struggling to draw breath, "and I tried to push it up," he demonstrated, "so he couldn't shoot. I guess he hit me with the other end. Knocked my wind out."

Emery nodded.

"It happened one time when I was a little kid. We were playing kick-ball. I fell down and another kid kicked me."

The image glimpsed through falling snow returned: Brook floundering toward the small hooded figure with the leveled rifle. Emery felt weak, half sick with fright. "You damned fool kid," he blurted, "you could've been killed!" It sounded angry and almost vicious, although he had not thought himself angry.

"Yeah, I guess I could of."

Jan stopped crying long enough to say, "Emery, don't be mean."

"What were you being when you made the girls say I had molested them?"

"Well, you did!"

Brook said, "He tried to shoot me. I saw him. I think the safety was on. I tried to get to him fast before he wised up."

"That rifle doesn't have one, just the half-cock."

Brook was no longer listening. Under his breath, Emery explained, "He was short-stroking it, pulling down the lever a reasonable distance instead of all the way. You can't do that with a lever-action—it will eject, but it won't load the next round. He'll learn to do right pretty soon, I'm afraid."

Jan asked querulously, "What about Aileen? Aren't you going to look for Aileen?"

"Alayna, you pointed toward the lake when I asked which way your sister went. Are you sure?"

Alayna hesitated. "Can I look out the window?"

"Certainly. Go ahead."

She crossed the cabin to the front window and looked out, standing on tiptoe. "I never said you felt us and everything like Mama said. I just said all right, all right, I see, and yes, yes, because she was there listening." Alayna's voice was almost inaudible; her eyes were fixed upon the swirling snow beyond the windowpane.

"Thank you, Alayna." Emery spoke rapidly, keeping his voice

as low as hers. "You're a good girl, a daughter to be proud of, and I am proud of you. Very proud. But listen—are you paying attention?"

"Yes, Daddy."

"What you tell your mama—" he glanced at Jan, but she was taking off her coat and lecturing Brook, "isn't important. If you've got to lie to her about that so she won't punish you, do what you did. Nod and say yes. What you tell the lawyers is more important, but not very important. They lie all the time, so they've got no business complaining when other people lie to them. But when you're in court, and you've sworn to tell the truth, everything will be terribly important. You *have to* tell the truth then. The plain unvarnished truth, and nothing else. Do you understand?"

Alayna nodded solemnly, turning to face him.

"Not to me, because my life's nearly over. Not to God, because we can't really hurt God, only pain him by our spite and ingratitude. But because if you lie then, it's going to hurt you for years, maybe for the rest of your life.

"When God tells us not to lie, and not to cheat or steal, it's not because those things hurt him. You and I can no more harm God than a couple of ants could hurt this mountain. He does it for the same reason that your mama and I tell you not to play with fire—because we know it can hurt you terribly, and we don't want you to get hurt.

"Now, which way did Aileen run?"

"That way." Alayna pointed again. "I know because of the car. There was a lady at the front looking at the motor, and she sort of tried to catch her, but she got away."

"You say—Never mind." Emery stood. "I'd better go after her."

"Comin' with," Brook announced.

"No, you're not. You're going to see about Alayna's arm." Emery put on his coat. His gloves were in the pockets and his warmest cap on a peg. "There's plenty of food here. Fix some for the three of you—maybe Alayna and her mother will help. Make coffee, too. I'll want some when I get back."

Outside, the creek and the hill across it had disappeared in blowing snow. It would have been wise, Emery reflected, for Jan to have turned the car around before she stopped. It was typical of her that she had not.

He squinted at it through the snow. The hood was still up. The intruders—the boys who had robbed his cabin—had no doubt intended to strip it, stealing the battery and so on, or perhaps hot-wire it and drive it someplace where it could be stripped at leisure. There were three, it seemed—three at least, and perhaps more.

Reaching the Lincoln, he peered into the crowded engine compartment. The battery was still there; although he could not be sure, nothing seemed to be missing. Jan, who had told him he should have locked the cabin door, should have locked the doors; but then Jan seldom did, even in the city, and who would expect trouble way out here during a blizzard?

Emery slammed down the hood. Now that he came to think of it, Jan left her keys in the car more often than not. If she had, he could turn it around for her before the snow got any deeper. Briefly he vacillated, imagining Aileen hiding behind a tree, cold and frightened. But Aileen could not be far, and might very well come out of hiding if she heard the Lincoln start.

As he had half expected, the keys were in the ignition. He started the engine and admired the luxurious interior until warm air gushed from the heater, then allowed the big car to creep forward. Alayna felt certain her twin had run toward the lake, and he had to go in that direction anyway to turn around.

He switched on the headlights.

Aileen might come running when she saw her mother's car. Or he might very well meet her walking back toward the cabin, if she had sense enough to stick to the road; if he did, she could get in and warm up at once.

The Lincoln's front-wheel drive, assisted by its powerful engine, seemed to be handling the snow well so far. At about two miles an hour, he topped the gentle rise beyond the cabin and began the descent to the lake.

Aileen had run down this road toward the lake; but in what direction had the boys run? Emery found that though he could picture them vividly as they fled—three small, dark figures bunched together, one carrying his rifle (somehow carrying away his death while fleeing from him)—he could not be certain of the direction in which they had run. Toward town, or this way? Their tracks would be obscured by snow now in either case.

Had they really fled, as he'd assumed? Wasn't it possible that they'd been pursuing Aileen? It was a good thing—

He took his eyes off the snow-blanketed road for a second to stare at Jan's keys. The doors had been unlocked, the keys in the ignition. If the boys had wanted to strip this car, why hadn't they driven it away?

He stopped, switched on the emergency blinkers, and blew the horn three times. Aileen might, perhaps, have run as far as this—call it three-quarters of a mile, although it was probably a little less. It was hard to believe that she would have run farther, though no doubt a healthy eleven-year-old could run farther than he, and faster, too. Not knowing what else to do, he got out, leaving the lights on and the engine running.

"Aileen! Aileen, honey!"

She had told Phil Gluckman that he, Emery Bainbridge, her foster father, had molested her. Had she believed it, too? He had read somewhere that young children could be made to believe that such things had happened when they had not. What about a bright eleven-year-old?

He made a megaphone of his hands. *"Aileen! Aileen!"*

There was no sound but the song of the rising wind and the scarcely audible purr of the engine.

He got back in and puffed fine snow off his glasses before it could melt. When he had left the cabin, he had intended to search on foot—to tramp along this snow-covered road calling Aileen. Perhaps that would have been best after all.

Almost hesitantly, he put the automatic transmission into first, letting the Lincoln idle forward at a speed that seemed no faster than a slow walk. When a minute or more had passed, he blew the horn again.

That had been a shot he had heard as he sat arguing with Jan; he felt sure of it now. The boy had been trying out his new rifle, experimenting with it.

He blew the horn as he had before, three short beeps.

That model held seven cartridges, but he couldn't remember whether it had been fully loaded. Say that it had. One shot fired at him on the hill, another in the woods (where?) to test the rifle. Five left. Enough to kill him, to kill Jan, and to kill Brook and both twins, assuming Aileen wasn't dead already. Quite possibly the boy with the rifle was waiting in the woods now, waiting for Jan's big black Lincoln to crawl just a little bit closer.

All right, let him shoot. Let the boy shoot at him now, while he sat behind the wheel. The boy might miss him as he sat here, alone in the dark behind tinted safety glass. The boy with his rifle could do nothing worse to him than he had imagined himself doing to himself, and if he missed, somebody—Jan or

Brook, Aileen or Alayna—might live. And living, recall him someday with kindness.

The big Lincoln crept past the dark, cold cabin of his nearest neighbor, a cabin whose rather too-flat roof already wore a peaked cap of snow.

He blew the horn, stopped, and got out as before, wishing that he had remembered to bring the flashlight. As far as he could tell, the snow lay undisturbed everywhere, save for the snaking track behind the Lincoln.

He would continue to the lake, he decided; he could go no farther. There was a scenic viewpoint there with parking for ten or twelve cars. It would be as safe to turn around there as to drive on the road as he had been doing—not that the road, eighteen inches deep in snow already, with drifts topping three feet, was all that safe.

Kicking snow from his boots and brushing it from his coat and trousers, he got back into the car, took off his cap, and cleaned his glasses, then eased the front wheels into the next drift.

When Jan and the twins had left the cabin, they must have seen the boys, perhaps at about the time they were raising the hood. Jan had shouted at them—he had heard her—and gone to her car to make them stop, followed by the twins. What had she said, and what had the boys said in reply? He resolved to question her about it when he returned to the cabin. Somebody had knocked her down; he tried to remember whether her face had been bruised, and decided it had not.

The Lincoln had pushed through the drift, and was already approaching another; here, where the road ran within a hundred feet of Haunted Lake, the snow swirled more wildly than ever. Was there still open water at the deepest part of the lake? He peered between the burdened trees, seeing nothing.

When one of the boys had hit their mother, Aileen had run; Alayna had attacked him. Aileen had acted sensibly and Alayna foolishly, yet it was Alayna he admired. The world would be a better place if more people were as foolish as Alayna and fewer as sensible as Aileen.

Alayna had said something peculiar about their attacker. *The boy with the hood. He hit Mama and Aileen ran away.*

That wasn't exactly right, but close enough, perhaps. The boy had worn a hood, perhaps a hooded sweatshirt underneath his coat, the coat and sweatshirt both black or brown; something of that kind.

For a moment it seemed the Lincoln would stall in the next drift. He backed out and tried again. Returning, he could go through the breaks he had already made, of course; and it would probably be a good idea to turn around, if he could, and return now.

Two dark figures stepped out of the trees at the edge of his lights. Between them was a terrified child nearly as tall as they. One waved, pointing to Aileen and to him.

He braked too hard, sending the crawling Lincoln into a minor skid that left it at an angle to the road. The one who had waved gestured again—and he, catching a glimpse of the smooth young face beneath the hood, realized that it was not a boy's at all, but a woman's.

He got out and found his own rifle pointed at him.

Aileen moaned, "Daddy, Daddy . . ."

The smooth-faced young woman who had waved shoved her at him, then patted the Lincoln's fender, speaking in a language he could not identify.

Emery nodded. "You'll give her to me if I'll give you the car."

The women stared at him without comprehension.

He dropped to his knees in the snow and hugged Aileen, and made a gesture of dismissal toward the Lincoln.

Both women nodded.

"We'll have to walk it," he told Aileen. "A little over two miles, I guess. But we can't go wrong if we stay on the road."

She said nothing, sobbing.

He stood, not bothering to clean the snow from his knees and thighs. "The keys are in there."

If they understood, they gave no sign of it.

"The engine's running. You just can't hear it."

The freezing wind whipped Aileen's dark hair. He tried to remember how the twins had been dressed when he had seen them getting out of the Lincoln in front of his cabin. She'd had on a stocking cap, surely—long white stocking caps on both the twins. If so, it was gone now. He indicated his own head, and realized that he had left his cap in the car; he started to get it, stopping abruptly when the woman with his rifle lifted it to her shoulder.

She jabbed the rifle in the direction he had come.

"I just want to get my cap," he explained.

She raised the rifle again, putting it to her shoulder without sighting along the barrel. He backed away, saying, "Come on, Aileen."

The other woman produced something that looked more like a tool than a weapon, a crooked metal bar with what seemed to be a split pin at one end.

"I don't want to fight." He took another step backward. He pointed to Aileen's head. "Just let me get my cap and give it to her."

The shot was so sudden and unexpected that there was no time to be afraid. Something tugged violently at his mackinaw.

He tried to rush the woman with the rifle, slipped in the snow, and fell. She took his rifle from her shoulder, pulled down and pushed up its lever almost as dexterously as he could have himself, and pointed it again.

"No, no!" He raised his hands. "We'll go, I swear." He crawled away from her, backward through the snow on his hands and knees, conscious that Aileen was watching with the blank, horror-stricken expression of a child who has exhausted tears.

When he was ten yards or more behind the Lincoln, he stood up and called, "Come here, Aileen. We're going back."

She stared at the women, immobile until one motioned to her, then waded slowly to him through the snow. His right side felt as though it had been scorched with a soldering iron; he wondered vaguely how badly he had been wounded. Catching her hand, he turned his back on the woman and began to trudge away, trying to brace himself against the bullet that he more than half expected.

"Daddy?"

He scarcely dared to speak, but managed, "What is it?"

"Can you carry me?"

"No." He felt he should explain, but could think only of the rifle pointed at his back. "We've got to walk. You're a big girl now. Come on, honey." It was easier to walk in the curving tracks of the Lincoln's tires, and he did so.

"I want to go home."

"So do I, honey. That's where we're going. Come on, it can't be far." He risked a glance toward the lake, and this time caught sight of ice lit by blue lights far away. More to himself than to the doleful, shivering child beside him, he muttered, "Somebody's out there on a boat." No one—no sane, normal person at least—would have a boat in the lake at this time of year. The boats had been drawn up on shore, where they would stay until spring.

He took off his glasses and dropped them into a pocket of his mackinaw, and looked behind him. Jan's Lincoln would have been invisible if it were not for the blinking red glow of its taillights. They winked out together as he watched. "They're stripping it," he told Aileen. "They just got the alternator or the battery."

She did not reply; and he began to walk again, turning up his collar and pulling it close about his ears. The wind was from his left; the warmth on the other side was blood, soaking his clothes and warming the skin under them, however briefly. Slow bleeding, or so it seemed—in which case he might not be wounded too badly and might live. A soft-nosed hunting bullet, but expansion required a little distance, and it could not have had much, probably had not been much bigger than thirty caliber when it had passed through his side.

Which meant that life would continue, at least for a time. He might be tempted to give his body to the lake—to walk out on its tender ice until it gave way and his life, begun in warm amniotic fluid, should terminate in freezing lake water. He might be tempted to lie down in the snow and bleed or freeze to death. But he could not possibly leave Aileen or any other child out here alone, although he need only tell her to follow the road until she reached his cabin.

"Look," she said, "there's a house."

She released his hand to point, and he realized that he was not wearing his gloves, which were in his pockets. "It's closed up, honey." (He had fallen into the habit of calling both the twins "honey" to conceal his inability to distinguish them.) "Have you got gloves?"

"I don't know."

He forced himself to be patient. "Well, look. If you've got gloves or mittens, put them on." This girl, he reminded himself, was the wonder of her class, writing themes that would have done credit to a college student and mastering arithmetic and the rudiments of algebra with contemptuous ease.

"I guess those ladies didn't give them back."

"Then put on mine." He handed them to her.

"Your hands will get cold."

"I'll put one in my pocket, see? And I'll hold your hand with my other one, so the one glove will keep us both warm."

She gave a glove back to him. "My hand won't go around yours, Daddy, but yours will go around mine."

He nodded, impressed, and put the glove on.

It might be possible to get into his neighbor's lightless cabin, closed or not. "I'm going to try to break in," he told Aileen. "There ought to be firewood and matches in there, and there may even be a phone."

But the doors were solid, and solidly locked; and there were grilles over the small windows, as over his own. "We've had a lot of break-ins," he confided, "ever since they paved the road. People drive out to the lake, and they see these places."

"Is it much farther?"

"Not very far. Maybe another mile." He remembered his earlier speculations. "Did you run this far, honey?"

"I don't think so."

"I didn't think that you would." Somewhat gratified, he returned to her and the road. It was darker than ever now, and the tire tracks, obscured by advancing night as well as new-fallen snow, were impossible to follow. Pushing up his sleeve, he looked at his watch: it was almost six o'clock.

"I don't like them," Aileen said. "Those ladies."

"It would surprise me if you did."

"They took my clothes off. I said I'd do it, but they didn't pay any attention, and they didn't know how to do it. They just pulled and pulled till things came off."

"Out here? In the snow?" He was shocked.

"In the ziggurat, but it was pretty cold in there, too."

He found the point in a drift at which the Lincoln had bulldozed its way through, and led her to it. "What did you say? A ziggurat?"

"Uh-huh. Is it much farther?"

"No," he said.

"I could sit down here. You could come back for me in your Jeep."

"No," he repeated. "Come on. If we walk faster, we'll keep warm."

"I'm really tired. They didn't give me hardly anything to eat, either. Just a piece of bread."

He nodded absently, concentrating on walking faster and pulling her along. He was tired too—nearly exhausted. What would he say when he wrote his journal? To take his mind off his weariness and the burning pain in his right side—off his fear, as he was forced to concede—he attempted to compose the entry in his mind.

"I got in the sleeper thing, but it was so cold. My feet got really cold, and I couldn't pull them up. I guess I slept a little."

He looked down at her, blinking away snow; it was too dark for him to gauge her expression. "Those women took you into a ziggurat—"

"Not really, Daddy. That was a kind of temple they had in Babylon. This one just looks like the picture in the book."

"They caught you," he continued doggedly, "and took you there, and undressed you?"

If she nodded, he failed to see the motion. "Did they or didn't they?"

"Yes, Daddy."

"And they fed you, and you slept a little, or anyway tried to sleep. Then you got dressed again and they brought you back here. Is that what you want me to believe?"

"They showed me some pictures, too, but I didn't know what lots of the things were."

"Aileen, you can't possibly have been gone more than a couple of hours at the outside. I doubt it was that long."

He had thought her beyond tears, but she began to sob, not loudly, but with a concentrated wretchedness that tore at his heart. "Don't cry, honey." He picked her up, ignoring the fresh pain in his side.

The wind, which had been rising all afternoon, was blowing hard enough to whistle, an eerie moan among the spectral trees. "Don't cry," he repeated. He staggered forward, holding her over his left shoulder, desperately afraid that he would slip and fall again. Her plastic snow boots were stiff with ice, the insulated trousers above them stiff too.

He could not have said how far he had walked; it seemed miles before a lonely star gleamed through the darkness ahead. "Look," he said, and halted—then turned around so that his daughter, too, could see the golden light. "That's our cabin. Has to be. We're going to make it."

Then (almost at once, it seemed) Brook was running through the snow with the flashlight, he had set Aileen upon her feet, and they were all three stumbling into the warmth and light of the cabin, where Jan knelt and clasped Aileen to her and cried and laughed and cried again, and Alayna danced and jumped and demanded over and over, "Was she lost, Daddy? Was she lost in the woods?"

Brook put a plate of hot corned-beef hash in his lap and pushed a steaming mug of coffee at him.

"Thank you." Emery sighed. "Thank you very much, son." His face felt frozen; merely breathing the steam from the mug was heavenly.

"The car get stuck?"

He shook his head.

"I fixed stuff like you said. 'Layna helped, and Jan says she'll do the dishes. If she won't, I will." Brook had called her Mother for the length of the marriage; but it was over now, emotionally if not legally. Emery's thoughts turned gratefully from the puzzle of Aileen's captivity to that.

"I could toast you some bread in the fireplace," Brook offered. "You want ketchup? I like ketchup on mine."

"A fork," Emery told him, and sipped his coffee.

"Oh. Yeah."

"Was she lost?" Alayna demanded. "I bet she was!"

"I'm not going to talk about that." Emery had come to a decision. "Aileen can tell you herself, as much or as little as she wants."

Jan looked up at him. "I called the sheriff. The number was on your phone."

Emery nodded.

"They said they couldn't do anything until she'd been gone for twenty-four hours. It's the law, apparently. They—this woman I talked to—suggested we get our friends and neighbors to search. I told her that you were searching already. Maybe you ought to call and tell them you found her."

He shook his head, accepting a fork from Brook.

"You came back on foot? You walked?"

Aileen said, "From way down by the lake." She had taken off her boots, stockings, and snow pants, and was sitting on the floor rubbing her feet.

"Where's my car?"

"I traded it for Aileen."

Alayna stared at Aileen, wide-eyed. Aileen nodded.

"You *traded* it?"

He nodded too, his mouth full of corned-beef hash.

"Who to?"

He swallowed. "To whom, Jan."

"You are the most irritating man in the world!" If Jan had been standing, she would have stamped.

"He did, Mama. He said they could have the car if they'd give me to him, but they shot him anyway, and he fell down."

"That's right," Emery said. "We ought to have a look at that. It's pretty much stopped bleeding, and I think it's just a flesh wound." Setting his plate and mug on the hearth, he unbuttoned his mackinaw. "If it got the intestine, I suppose I'll have hash all over in there, and it will probably kill me. But there would have been food in my gut anyway. I had pork and beans for lunch."

"They *shot* you?" Jan stared at his blood-stiffened shirt.

He nodded, savoring the moment. *It's nothing, sir. I set the bone myself.* Danny Kaye in some old movie. He cleared his throat, careful to keep his face impassive. "I'm going to have to take this off, and my undershirt and pants, too. Probably my shorts. Maybe you could have the girls look the other way."

Both twins giggled.

"Look at the fire," she told them. "He's hurt. You don't want to embarrass him, do you?"

Brook had gotten the first-aid kit. "This is stuck." He pulled gingerly at the waistband of Emery's trousers. "I ought to cut it off."

"Pull it off," Emery told him. "I'm going to wash those pants and wear them again. I need them." He had unbuckled his belt, unbuttoned his trousers, and unzipped his fly.

"Just above the belt," Brook told him. "An inch, inch and a half lower, and it would have hit your belt."

Jan snapped her fingers. "Oil! Oil will soften the dried blood. Wesson Oil. Have you got any?"

Brook pointed at the cabinet above the sink. Emery said, "There's a bottle of olive oil up there, or there should be."

"'Leen's peeking," Brook told Jan, who told Aileen, "Do that again, young lady, and I'll smack your face!"

"Emery, you really ought to make two rooms out of this. This is ridiculous."

"It was designed for four men," he explained, "a hunting party, or a fishing party. You women always insist on being included, then complain about what you find when you are."

She poured olive oil on his caked blood and rubbed it with her fingertips. "I had to get you to sign."

"You could have sent your damned paper to my box in town. I'd have picked it up on Saturday and sent it back to you."

"She couldn't mail me," Brook said. "Are we going to get the car back? My junk was in the trunk."

Emery shrugged. "They're stripping it, I think. We may be able to take back what's left. Maybe they won't look in the trunk."

"They're bound to."

Jan asked, "How are we supposed to get home?"

"I'll drive you to town in the Jeep. There's bus service to the city. If the buses aren't running because of the storm, you can stay in a motel. There are two motels, I think. There could be three." He rubbed his chin. "You'll have to anyway, unless you want to reconsider and stay here. I think the last bus was at five."

Brook was scrutinizing Emery's wound. "That bullet sort of plowed through your skin. It might've got some muscles at your waist, but I don't think it hit any organs."

Emery made himself look down. "Plowed through the fat, you mean. I ought to lose twenty pounds, and if I had, she would have missed."

"A girl?"

Emery nodded.

Jan said, "No wonder you hate us so much," and pulled his bloodstained trousers free.

"I don't hate you. Not even now, when I ought to. Brook, would you give me my coffee? That's good coffee you made, and there's no reason I shouldn't drink it while you bandage that."

Brook handed it to him. "I scrubbed out the pot."

"Good for you. I'd been meaning to."

Alayna interposed, "I make better coffee than Brook does, Daddy, but Mama says I put in too much."

"You should have stitches, Emery. Is there a hospital in town?"

"Just a clinic, and it'll be closed. I've been hurt worse and not had stitches."

Brook filled a pan with water. "Why'd they shoot you, Dad?"

Emery started to speak, thought better of it, and shook his head.

Jan said, "If you're going to drive us into town in the Jeep, you could drive us into the city just as easily."

Setting his water on the stove, Brook hooted.

"You've got money, and you and Brook could stay at a hotel and come back tomorrow."

Emery said, "We're not going to, however."

"Why won't you?"

"I don't have to explain, and I won't."

She glared. "Well, you should!"

"That won't do any good." Privately he wondered which was worse, a woman who had never learned how to get what she wanted or a woman who had.

"You actually proposed that we patch it up. Then you act like this?"

"I'm trying to keep things pleasant."

"Then do it!"

"You mean you want to be courted while you're divorcing me. That's what's usually meant by a friendly divorce, from what I've been able to gather." When she said nothing, Emery added, "Isn't that water hot enough yet, Brook?"

"Not even close."

"I shouldn't explain," Emery continued, "but I will. In the first place, Brook and the twins are going to have about as much elbow room as live bait in the back of the Jeep. It will be miserable for even a short drive. If we so much as try to make it into the city in this weather, they'll be tearing each other to bits before we stop."

Brook put in, "I'll stay here, Dad. I'll be all right."

Emery shook his head. "So would we, Jan. In the second, I think the women who shot me will be back as soon as the storm lets up. If no one's here, they'll break in or burn this place down. It's the only home I've got, and I intend to defend it."

"Sure," Brook said. "Let me stay. I can look after things while you're gone."

"No," Emery told him. "It would be too dangerous."

Emery turned back to Jan. "In the third place, I won't do it because I want to so much. If—"

"You were the one that gave those people my car."

"To get Aileen back. Yes, I did. I'd do it again."

"And you took it without my permission! I trusted you, Emery. I left my keys in the ignition, and you took my car."

He nodded wearily. "To look for Aileen, and I'd do that again too. I suppose you're already planning to bring it up in court."

"You bet I am!"

"I suggest you check the title first."

Aileen herself glanced at him over her shoulder. "I'm really hungry. Can I have the rest of your hash?"

Brook said, "There's more here, 'Leen. You said you weren't, but I saved—"

"I haven't had anything since yesterday except some bread stuff."

Jan began, "Aileen, you know perfectly well—"

Emery interrupted her. "It's only been a couple of hours since they caught you, honey. Remember? We talked about that before we got here."

"I was in there, in the sleep thing—"

Jan snapped, "Aileen, be quiet! I told you not to look around like that."

"It's only Daddy in his underwear. I've seen him like that lots."

"Turn around!"

Trying to weigh each word with significance, Emery said, "Your mama told you to be quiet, honey. That wasn't simply an order. It was good advice."

Brook brought her a plate of corned-beef hash and a fork. "There's bread, too. Want some?"

"Sure. And milk or something."

"There isn't any."

"Water, then." Raising her voice slightly, Aileen added, "I'd get up and get it for myself, but Mama won't let me."

Jan said, "You see what you've started, Emery?"

He nodded solemnly. "I didn't start it, but I'm quite happy about it."

Brook washed his wound and bandaged it, applying a double pad of surgical gauze and so much Curity Wet-Pruf adhesive tape that Emery winced at the mere thought of removing it.

"I might be a doctor," Brook mused, "big money, and this is fun."

"You're a pretty good one already," Emery said gratefully. He kicked off his boots, emptied his pockets onto the table, and stuffed his trousers into a laundry bag, following it with his shirt. "Want to do me a favor, Brook? Scrape my plate into that tin bowl on the drainboard and set it on the back porch."

Jan asked, "Are you well enough to drive, Emery? Forget the fighting. You wouldn't want to see any of us killed. I know you wouldn't."

He nodded, buttoning a fresh shirt.

"So let me drive. I'll drive us into town, and you can drive Brook back here if you feel up to it."

"You'd put us into the ditch," Emery told her. "If I start feeling too weak, I'll pull over and—"

Brook banged the rear door shut behind him and held up a squirrel. "Look at this! It was right up on the porch." The tiny body was stiff, its gray fur powdered with snow.

"Poor little thing!" Jan went over to examine it. "It must have come looking for something to eat, and froze. Have you been feeding them, Emery?"

"It's a present from a friend," he told her. Something clutched his throat, leaving him barely able to speak. "You wouldn't understand."

The Jeep started without difficulty. As he backed it out onto the road, he wondered whether the dark-faced women who had Jan's Lincoln had been unable to solve the simple catches that held the Jeep's hood. Conceivably, they had not seen the Jeep when they had been in his cabin earlier. He wished now that he had asked Aileen how many women she had seen, when the two of them had been alone.

"Drafty in here," Jan remarked. "You should buy yourself a real car, Emery."

The road was visible only as an opening between the trees; he pulled onto it with all four wheels hub-deep in virgin snow, keeping the transmission in second and nudging the accelerator only slightly. Swirling snow filled the headlights. "Honey," he said, "your boots had ice on them. So did your snow pants. Did you wade in the lake?"

From the crowded rear seat, Aileen answered, "They made me, Daddy."

The road was visible only as an open space between trees. To people in a—Emery fumbled mentally for a word and settled on *aircraft*.

To an aircraft, the frozen lake might have looked like a paved helicopter pad or something of that kind, a more or less circular pavement. The black-looking open water at its center might have been taken for asphalt.

Particularly by a pilot not familiar with woods and lakes.

"Emery, you hardly ever answer a direct question. It's one of the things I dislike most about you."

"That's what men say about women," he protested mildly.

"Women are being diplomatic. Men are rude."

"I suppose you're right. What did you ask me?"

"That isn't the point. The point is that you ignore me until I raise my voice."

That seemed to require no reply, so he did not offer one. How high would you have to be and how fast would you have to be coming down before a frozen lake looked like a landing site?

"So do the girls," Jan added bitterly, "they're exactly the same way. So is Brook."

"That ought to tell you something."

"You don't have to be rude!"

One of the twins said, "She wanted to know how long it would take to get to town, Daddy."

It had probably been Alayna, Emery decided. "How long would you like it to take, honey?"

"Real quick!"

That had been the other one, presumably Aileen. "Well," he told her, "we'll be there real quick."

Jan said, "Don't try to be funny."

"I'm being diplomatic. If I wasn't, I'd point out that it's twenty-two miles and we're going about fifteen miles an hour. If we can keep that up all the way, it should take us about an hour and a half."

Jan turned in her seat to face the twins. "Never marry an engineer, girls. Nobody ever told me that, but I'm telling you now. If you do, don't say you were never warned."

One twin began, "You said that about—"

The other interrupted. "Only, it wasn't an engineer that time. It was a tennis player. Did you do it in your head, Daddy? I did too, only it took me longer. One point four and two-thirds, so six six seven. Is that right?"

"I have no idea. Fifteen is smaller than twenty-two, and that's an hour. Seven over, and seven's about half of fifteen. Most real calculations outside school are like that, honey."

"Because it doesn't matter?"

Emery shook his head. "Because the data's not good enough for anything more. It's about twenty-two miles to town on this Jeep's odometer. That could be off by as much as—" Something caught his eye, and he fell silent.

From the rear seat, Brook asked, "What's the matter, Dad?" He sounded half suffocated.

Emery was peering into the rear view mirror, unable to see anything except a blur of snow. "There was a sign back there. What did it say?"

"Don't tell me you're lost, Emery."

"I'm not lost. What did it say, Brook?"

"I couldn't tell, it was all covered with snow."

"I think it was the historical marker sign. I'm going to stop there on the way back."

"Okay, I'll remind you."

"You won't have to. I'll stop."

One of the twins asked, "What happened there?"

Emery did not reply; Brook told her, "There used to be a village there, the first one in this part of the state. Wagon trains would stop there. One time there was nobody there. The log cabins and their stuff was okay, only there wasn't anybody home."

"The Pied Piper," the twin suggested.

"He just took rats and kids. This got everybody."

Jan said, "I don't think that's much of a mystery. An early settlement? The Indians killed them."

The other twin said, "Indians would have scalped them and left the bodies, Mama, and taken things."

"All right, they were stolen by fairies. Emery, this hill looks so steep! Are you sure this is the right road?"

"It's the only road there is. Hills always look steeper covered with snow." When Jan said nothing, he added, "Hell, they *are* steeper."

"They should plow this."

"The plows will be out on the state highway," Emery told her. "Don't worry, only three more mountains."

They let Jan and the twins out in front of the Ramada Inn, and Brook climbed over the back of the front seat. "I'm glad they're gone. I guess I shouldn't say it—she's been pretty nice to me—but I'm glad."

Emery nodded.

"You could've turned around back there." Brook indicated the motel's U-shaped drive. "Are we going into town?"

Emery nodded again.

"Want to tell me what for? I might be able to help."

"To buy two more guns. There's a sporting-goods dealer on Main Street. We'll look there first."

"One for me, huh? What kind?"

"What kind do you want?"

"A three-fifty-seven, I guess."

"No handguns, there's a five-day waiting period. But we can

buy rifles or shotguns and take them with us, and we may need
them when we get back to the cabin."

"One rifle and one shotgun," Brook decided. "Pumps or
semis. You want the rifle or the scattergun, Dad?"

Emery did not reply. Every business that they drove past
seemed to be dark and locked. He left the Jeep to rattle and
pound the door of the sporting-goods store, but no one appeared to unlock it.

Brook switched off the radio as he got back in. "Storm's
going to get worse. They say the main part hasn't even gotten
here yet."

Emery nodded.

"You knew, huh?"

"I'd heard a weather report earlier. We're due for two, possibly three days of this."

The gun shop was closed as well. There would be no gun
with which to kill the woman who had shot him, and none
with which to kill himself. He shrugged half-humorously and
got back into the Jeep. Brook said, "We're going to fight with
what we've got, huh?"

"A hammer and a hunting knife against my thirty-thirty?"
Emery shook his head emphatically. "We're not going to fight
at all. If they come around again, we're to do whatever they
want, no questions and no objections. If they like anything—
this Jeep would be the most likely item, I imagine—we're going
to give it to them."

"Unless I get a chance to grab the gun again."

Emery glanced at him. "The first time you tried that, she
hadn't learned to use it. She was a lot better when she shot
me. Next time she'll be better yet. Am I making myself clear?"

Brook nodded. "I've got to be careful."

"You've got to be more than just careful," Emery told him,
"because if you're not, you're going to die. I was ten feet or
more from her when she shot at me, and backing away. She
fired anyway, and she hit me."

"I got it."

"When you dressed my wound," Emery continued, "you said
that if her shot had been an inch or two lower it would have
hit my belt. If it had been an inch or two to the left, it would
have killed me. Did you think of that?"

"Sure. I just didn't want to say it." Brook pointed to a small
dark building. "There's the last store, Rothschild's Records and

CDs. It's pretty good. I used to have you drop me there sometimes when you were going into town, remember?"

Intent upon his thoughts and the snow-covered road, Emery did not even nod.

"Those girls have got to be either camping or living in somebody's cabin out here. If we can find out where, we could get some guns when the town's open again and go out there and make them give our stuff back."

Emery muttered, "This is the last trip until the county clears the road."

"We're doing okay now."

"This is a state highway. It's been plowed at least once, most likely within the past couple of hours. The road to the cabin won't have been plowed at all, and we barely made it out."

"I'd like to look at the other car and see if they left any of my stuff."

"All right, if we can drive as far as the cabin, we'll do that. But after that, I'm not taking the Jeep out until the road's been plowed."

"They really were girls? I thought you and 'Leen might have been stringing Jan."

"Two of them were." Emery studied the road. "The one who shot me, and another one who was with her. I imagine the third was as well, she seemed to be about the same size."

Brook nodded to himself. "You never can tell what girls are going to do, I guess."

"Obviously it's harder to predict the actions of someone whose psychology differs from your own. Once you've learned what a woman values, though, you ought to be right most of the time—say, seven out of ten." Emery chuckled. "How's that for a man being divorced for the second time? Do I sound like an expert?"

"Sure. What does a woman value?"

"It varies from woman to woman, and sometimes it changes. You have to learn for each, or guess. With a little experience you ought to be able to make pretty good guesses after you've talked with the woman for a few minutes. You've got to listen to what she says, and listen harder for what she doesn't. All this is true for men as well, of course. Fortunately, men are easier—for other men."

"Okay if I throw you a softball, Dad? I'm leading up to something."

"Go ahead."

"What does Jan value?"

"First of all, the appearance of wealth. She doesn't value money itself, but she wants to impress people with her big car, her mink coat, and so on. Have I missed the turn?"

"I don't think so. We've been going pretty slow."

"I don't either—I don't see how I could have—but I keep worrying about it.

"Money has a poetry of its own, Brook. Women are fond of telling us that we don't get it, but the poetry of money is one of the things that they rarely get. One of a dozen or more, I suppose. Are you going to ask why I married Jan? Is that what you're leading up to?"

"Uh-huh. Why did you?"

"Because I was lonely and fell in love with her. Looking back, I can see very clearly that I wanted to prove to myself that I could make a woman happy, too. I felt I could make Jan happy, and I was right. But after a while—after I lost the company, particularly—it no longer seemed worth the effort."

"I'm with you. Did she love you too? Or did you think she did?"

Emery sighed. "Women don't love in the same way that men do, Brook. I said the psychology was different, and that's one of the main differences. Men are dogs. Women are cats— they love conditionally. For example, I love you. If you were to try to kill me—"

"I wouldn't do that!"

"I'm constructing an extreme example," Emery explained patiently. "Say that I was to try to kill you. You'd fight me off if you could. You might even kill me doing it. But you'd love me afterward, just the same; you may not think so, but you would."

Brook nodded, his face thoughtful.

"When you love a woman, you'll love her in the same way; but women love *as long as*—as long as you have a good job, as long as you don't bring home your friends, and so on. You shouldn't blame them for that, because it's as much a part of their natures as the way you love is of yours. For women, love is a spell that can be broken by picking a flower or throwing a ring into the sea. Love is magic, which is why they frequently use the language of fairy tales when they talk about it."

"We're coming up on the turn." Brook aimed his forefinger at the darkness and the blowing snow. "It's right along here someplace."

"About another half mile. Throw your fastball."

"This woman that shot you. Why did she do it?"

"I've been thinking about that."

"I figured you had."

"Why does anyone, robbing someone else, shoot them?"

"No witnesses?"

Emery shook his head. "A thief doesn't merely shoot to silence a witness, he kills. After she had shot me she let me go. I was still conscious, still able to walk and to talk. Perfectly capable of giving the sheriff a description of her. But she let me go. Why?"

"You were there, Dad. What do you think?"

"You're starting to sound like me." Emery slowed the Jeep from ten miles an hour to six, searching the road to his left.

"I know."

"Because she was frightened, I think. Afraid of me, and afraid she couldn't do it, too. When she shot me, she proved to herself that she could, and I was able to show her—by my actions, because she couldn't understand what I was saying— that I wasn't somebody she had to be afraid of."

The road to the cabin was deep in snow, so deep that they inched and churned their way through it foot by foot. Caution, and speeds scarcely faster than a walk, soon became habitual, and Emery's mind turned to other things. First of all, to the smoothly oval face behind the threatening muzzle of his rifle. Large, dark eyes above a tiny mouth narrowed by determination; a small—slightly flattened?—nose.

Small and slender hands; the thirty-thirty had looked big in them, which meant that they had been hardly larger than the twins'. He did not remember seeing hair, but with that face it would be black, surely. Straight or curled? Not Japanese or Chinese, possibly a small, light-complexioned Afro-American. A mixture of Black and White with Oriental? Filipino? Almost anything seemed possible.

The coal-black hair he had imagined merged with the shadow of her hood. "Brownies," he said aloud.

"What?"

"Brownies. Don't they call those little girls who sell cookies Brownies?"

"Sure. Like Girl Scouts, only littler. 'Leen and 'Layna used to be Brownies."

Emery nodded. "That's right. I remember." But brownies were originally English fairies, small and dark—brown-faced, presumably—mischievous and sometimes spiteful, but often willing to trade their work for food and clothing. Fairies sufficiently feminine that giving their name to an organization for young girls was not ridiculous, as it would have been to call the same little girls gnomes, for example.

Stolen by fairies, Jan had said, referring to villagers of the eighteen forties. . . . He tried to remember the precise date, and failed.

Because brownies did not merely trade their labor for the goods they wanted. Often they stole. Milked your cow before you woke up. Snatched your infant from its crib. Lured your children to a place where time ran differently, too fast or too slow. Aileen, who had been gone for no more than two hours at most, had thought she had been gone for a day—had been taken to the ziggurat and shown pictures she had not understood, had slept or at least tried to sleep, had been made to wade into the lake, where blue lights shone.

Where was fairyland?

"Why're you stopping?"

"Because I want to get out and look at something. You stay here."

Flashlight in hand, he shut the Jeep's flimsy vinyl flap. Later—by next morning, perhaps—the snow might be easier to walk on. Now it was still uncompacted, as light as down; he sank above his knees at every step.

The historical marker protruded above the blank whiteness, its size amplified by the snow it wore. He considered brushing off the bronze plaque and reading it, but the precise date and circumstances, as specified by some historian more interested in plausibility than truth, did not matter.

He waded past it, across what would be green and parklike lawn in summer, reminding himself that there was a ditch at its end before the ranch's barbed-wire fence, and wishing he had a stick or staff with which to probe the snow. The body— if he had in fact seen what he had thought he had seen— would be covered by this time, invisible save as a slight mound.

When he stood in the ditch, the snow was above his waist. His gloved hands found the wire, then the almost-buried locust post, which he used to pull himself up, breaching the snow like some fantastic, red-plaid dolphin.

The coyote lay where he had glimpsed it on the drive to town. It had frozen as stiff as the squirrel it had left him, its face twisted in a snarl of pain and surprise. Negotiating the ditch again with so much difficulty that he feared for a few seconds that he would have to call for Brook to rescue him, he stowed the body on the narrow floor behind the Jeep's front seats.

Brook said, "That's a dead coyote."

Emery nodded as he got back behind the wheel and put the Jeep in gear. "Cyanide gun."

"What do you want with that?"

"I don't know. I haven't decided yet."

Brook stared, then shrugged. "I hope you didn't start yourself bleeding again, doing all that."

"I may bury him. Or I might have him stuffed and mounted. That sporting-goods dealer has a taxidermy service. They could do it. Probably wouldn't cost more than a hundred or so."

"You didn't kill it," Brook protested.

"Oh yes, I did," Emery told him.

What they could see of the cabin through the falling snow suggested that it was as they had left it. Emery did not stop, and it would have been difficult to make the Jeep push its way through the banks more slowly than it already was. The world before the windshield was white, framed in black; and upon that blank sheet his mind strove to paint the country from which the small brown women had come, a country that would send forth an aircraft (if the ziggurat in the lake was in fact an aircraft or something like one) crewed by young women more alike than sisters. A country without men, perhaps, or one in which men were hated and feared.

What had they thought of Jan, a woman almost a foot taller than they? Jan with her creamy complexion and yellow hair? Of Aileen and Alayna, girls of their own size, nearly as dark as they, and alike as two peas? The first had run from, the second fought them; and both reactions had quite likely baffled them. From their own perspective, they had crashed in a wilderness of snow and wind and bitter cold—a howling wilderness strangely and dangerously inhabited.

"We could've stopped at the cabin," Brook said. "We can go look for my stuff tomorrow, when there's daylight."

Emery shook his head. "We wouldn't be able to get through tomorrow. The snow will be too deep."

"We could try."

Brook had presumably confirmed their worst fears, as he had himself; and although they'd had his rifle, they had fled at his approach. They had recognized the rifle as a weapon when they had entered and searched his empty, unlocked cabin—empty because he had seen something flash high up on the hill across the creek. . . .

"Is it much farther, Dad?" Brook was peering through the wind-driven snow into the black night again, trying to catch a glimpse of Jan's Lincoln.

"Quite a bit, I believe." Apologetically, Emery added, "We're not going very fast."

The flash from the hill had left a shallow burn on the oak back of his chair. Had it been a laser—a laser weapon? Had they been shooting at him even then? A laser that could do no more than scorch the surface of the chair-back would not kill a man, surely, though it might blind him if it struck his eyes. Not a weapon, perhaps, but a laser tool of some kind that they had tried to employ as a weapon. He recalled the lasers used to engrave steel in the company he had left to found his own.

"Nobody's in that cabin back there now, I guess."

He shook his head. "Been closed since early November. There's nobody out here really, except us and them."

"What do you think they're trying to do out here?"

"Leave." His tone, he hoped, would notify Brook that he was not in the mood for conversation.

"They could've gone in the Lincoln. It wasn't out of gas. I'd been watching the gauge, because she never does."

"They can't drive. If they could, they'd have driven it away from the cabin the first time, when Jan left the keys in it. Besides, the Lincoln couldn't take them where they want to go."

"Dad—"

"That's enough questions for now. I'll tell you more when I've got more of it figured out."

"You must be really tired. I wish we'd stopped at the cabin. There won't be any of my stuff left anyhow."

Was he really as tired as Brook suggested? He considered the matter and decided he was. Wading through the snow past the historical marker had consumed what little strength he had left after losing blood and slogging home with Aileen through snow that no longer seemed particularly deep. He was operating now on whatever it was that remained when the last strength was gone. On stubbornness and desperation.

"Your grandfather used to tell a story," he remarked to

Brook, "about a jackrabbit, a coyote, and a jay. Did I ever tell you that?"

"No." Brook grinned, glad that he was not angry. "What is it?"

"A jay will yell and warn the other animals if there's a coyote around. You know that?"

"Uh-huh."

"Well, this jay was up on a mesquite, with a jackrabbit sleeping in the shade. The jay spotted a coyote stalking the jackrabbit and yelled a warning. The coyote sprang, and the jackrabbit ran, scooting past the mesquite and hooking left, with the coyote after it.

"The jay felt a little guilty about not having spotted the coyote sooner, so he shouted to the jackrabbit, 'You okay? You going to make it?'

"And the jackrabbit called back, 'I'll make it!'

"They went around the mesquite eight or ten times, and it seemed to the jay that the coyote was gaining at every pass. He got seriously worried then, and he shouted down, 'You sure you're going to make it?'

"The jackrabbit called back, 'I'm going to make it!'

"A few more passes, and the coyote was snapping at the jackrabbit's tail. The jay was worried sick by then, and he shouted, 'Rabbit, how do you *know* you're going to make it?' And the jackrabbit called back, 'Hell, I've *got* to make it!'"

Brook said, "You mean you're like that rabbit."

"Right." Emery put the transmission into neutral and set the parking brake. "I've got to make it, and I will."

"Why are we stopping?"

"Because we're here." He opened his flap and got out.

"I don't see the car."

"You will in a minute. Bring the flash."

They had to climb a drift before they found it, nearly buried in snow with its hood still up. Emery reached inside, took Jan's keys out of the ignition lock, and handed them to Brook. "Here, check the trunk. They may not have noticed the keyhole behind the medallion."

A moment later, as he leaned against the snow-covered side of the car, he heard Brook say, "It's here! Everything's still here!"

"I'll help you." He forced himself to walk.

"Just a couple little bags. I can carry them." Brook slammed down the trunk lid so that he would not see whatever is being left behind. A stereo, Emery decided. Possibly a TV. He hated TV, and decided to say nothing.

"You want the keys?"

"You keep them."

"I guess we'll have to call a tow truck when the road's clear. They've taken a lot of stuff out of here." Brook was at the front of the Lincoln, shining the flashlight into its engine compartment.

"Sure," Emery said, and started back to the Jeep.

When he woke the next morning, bacon was frying and coffee perking on the little propane stove. He sat up, discovering that his right side was stiff and painful. "Brook?"

There was no answer.

The cabin was cold, in spite of the blue flames and the friendly odors. He pulled the wool shirt he had put on after Brook had bandaged his wound over the Duofold underwear he had slept in, pushed his legs into the trousers he had dropped on the floor beside his bunk, and stood up. His boots were under the little table, the stockings he had worn beside them. He put the stockings into his laundry bag, got out a clean pair and pulled them on, then tugged on, laced, and tied his boots.

The coffee had perked enough. He turned off the burner and transferred the bacon onto the cracked green plate Brook had apparently planned to use. The bacon still smelled good; he felt that he should eat a piece, but he had no appetite.

Had Brook set off on foot to fetch whatever it was that he had left in the Lincoln's trunk? Not with food on the stove. Brook would have turned down the fire under the coffeepot and drunk a cup before he left, taken up the bacon and eaten half of it, probably with bread, butter, and jam.

There was no toaster, but Brook had offered to toast bread in front of the fire the night before. That fire was nearly out, hardly more than embers. Brook had gotten up, started the coffee and put on the bacon, and gone outside for firewood.

Lord, Emery thought, you don't owe me a thing—I know that. But please.

They had taken Aileen and had, perhaps, been bringing her back when they had encountered him. They might very well have taken Brook as well; if they had, they might bring him back in a day or two.

He found that he was staring at the plate of bacon. He set

it on the table and put on his mackinaw and second-best cap. Had his best one—the one that the women had not let him retrieve—been on the front seat of Jan's Lincoln? He had not even looked.

Snow had reached the sills of the windows, but it was not snowing as hard as it had the day before. The path plowed by Brook's feet and legs showed plainly, crossing the little back porch, turning south for the stacked wood under the eaves, then retraced for a short distance. Brook had seen something; or more probably, had heard a noise from the cabin's north side, where the Jeep was parked. It was difficult, very difficult, for Emery to step off the porch, following the path that Brook had broken through the deep snow.

Brook's body sprawled before the front bumper, a stick of firewood near its right hand. The blood around its head might, Emery told himself, have come from a superficial scalp wound. Brook might be alive, though unconscious. Even as he crouched to look more closely, he knew it was not true.

He closed his eyes and stood up. They had taken his ax as well as his rifle; he had worried about the rifle and had scarcely given a thought to the ax, yet the ax had done this.

The dead coyote still lay in back of the front seat of the plundered Jeep. He carried it to the south side of the cabin; and where firewood had been that autumn, contrived a rough bier from half a dozen sticks. Satisfied with the effect, he built a larger bier of the same kind for his son, arranged the not-yet-frozen body on it, and covered it with a clean sheet that he weighted with a few more sticks. It would be necessary to call the sheriff if the telephone was still working, and the sheriff might very well accuse him of Brook's murder.

Inside, after a momentary hesitation, he bolted the doors. A calendar hung the year before provided the number of the only undertaker in Voylestown.

"You have reached Merton's Funeral Parlor. We are not able to be with you at this time . . ."

He waited for the tone, then spoke quickly. "This's Emery Bainbridge." They could get his address from the directory, as well as his number. "My son's dead. I want you to handle the arrangements. Contact me when you can." A second or two of silence, as if in memory of Brook, and then the dial tone. He pressed in the sheriff's number.

"Sheriff Ron Wilber's office."

"This is Emery Bainbridge again. My son, Brook, has been killed."

"Address?"

"Five zero zero north, twenty-six seventy-seven west—that's on Route E-E, about five miles from Haunted Lake."

"How did it happen, Mister Bainbridge?"

He wanted to say that one of the women had stood against the wall of his cabin, holding his ax, and waited for Brook to come around the corner; it had been apparent from the lines plowed through the deep snow, but mentioning it at this time would merely make the investigating officer suspect him. He said, "He was hit in the head with my ax, I think. They took my ax yesterday."

"Yes, I remember. Don't move the body, we'll get somebody out there as soon as we can."

"I already have. When—"

"Then don't move it any more. Don't touch anything else."

"When will you have someone out here?"

He sensed, rather than heard, her indrawn breath. *"This afternoon, Emery. We'll try to get one of the deputies there this afternoon."*

If she had not been lying, Emery reflected, she would have called him "Mister Bainbridge." He thanked her and hung up, then leaned back in his chair, looking from the telephone to his journal. He should write up his journal, and there was a great deal to write. There had been a cellular phone in Jan's car. Had they taken it? He had not noticed.

He picked up the telephone again but hung it up without pressing in a number. His black sports watch lay under his bunk. He retrieved it, noting the date and time.

09:17 Jan came yesterday, with Brook and the twins. Three small, dark women in hoods tried to strip her car. There was a tussle with Jan and the children.

He stared down at the pen. It was exactly the color of Brook's blood in the snow.

Aileen ran away. I searched for her in Jan's car, which I was able to trade for her. One of the women shot me. They do not understand English

The red pen had stopped.

His computer back home—he corrected the thought: his computer at Jan's had a spell checker; this pen had none, yet it had sounded a warning without one. Was it possible that the women spoke English after all? On overseas trips he had met people whose English he could scarcely understand. He tried to recall what the women had said and what he had said, and failed with both.

Yet something, some neglected corner of his subconscious, suspected that the women had in fact been speaking English, of a peculiar variety.

> *Whan that Aprille with his shoures soote*
> *The droghte of March hath perced to the roote.*

He had memorized the lines in high school—how long had it been? But no, it had been much longer than that, had been more than six hundred years since a great poet had written in a beautiful rhythmic dialect that had at first seemed as alien as German. "When April, with his sweet breath/The drought of March has pierced to the root."

And the language was still changing, still evolving.

He picked up the telephone, fairly sure that he remembered Jan's cellular number, and pressed it in.

A lonely ringing, far away. In Jan's snow-covered black Lincoln? Could a cellular car phone operate without the car's battery? There were bag phones as well, telephones you could carry in a briefcase, so perhaps it could. If the women had taken it to pieces, there would have been a recorded message telling him that the number was no longer in service.

He had lost count of the rings when someone picked up the receiver. "Hello," he said. "Hello?" Even to him, it sounded inane.

No one spoke on the other end. As slowly and distinctly as he could, he said, "I am the man whose son you killed, and I am coming to kill you. If you want to explain before I do, you have to do it now."

No voice spoke.

"Very well. You can call me if you want." He gave his number, speaking more slowly and distinctly than ever. "But I won't be here much longer."

Or at least, they do not speak an English that I can understand. I should have said that I was not hurt badly. Brook bandaged it. I have not seen a doctor. Maybe I should.

He felt the bandage and found it was stiff with blood. Changing it, he decided, would waste a great deal of valuable time, and might actually make things worse.

Brook and I took Jan and the twins into town. Before I woke up this morning, the women killed Brook, outside in the snow.

There was a little stand of black-willow saplings down by the creek. He waded through the snow to them, cut six with his hunting knife, and carried them back to the cabin.

There he cut four sticks, each three times as long as his foot, and tied their ends in pairs with twine. Shorter sticks, notched at both ends, spread them; he tied the short sticks in place with more twine, then bound the crude snowshoes that he had made to his boots, wrapping each boot tightly with a dozen turns.

He was eight or ten yards from the cabin—walking over the snow rather than through it—when his ears caught the faint ringing of his telephone. He returned to the cabin to answer it, leaving the maul he had been carrying on the porch.

"*Mister Bainbridge? I'm Ralph Merton.*" Ralph Merton's voice was sepulchral. "*May I extend my sympathy to you and your loved ones?*"

Emery sighed and sat down, his snowshoed feet necessarily flat on the floor. "Yes, Mister Merton. It was good of you to return my call. I didn't think you'd be in today."

"*I'm afraid I'm not, Mister Bainbridge. I have an—ah—device that lets me call my office at the parlor and get my messages. May I ask if your son was under a doctor's care?*"

"No, Brook was perfectly healthy, as far as I know."

"*A doctor hasn't seen your son?*"

"No one has, except me." After a few seconds' silence, Emery added, "And the woman who killed him. I think there was another woman with her, in which case the second woman would have seen him, too. Not that it matters, I suppose."

Ralph Merton cleared his throat. "*A doctor will have to ex amine your son and issue a death certificate before we can come, Mister Bainbridge."*

"Of course. I'd forgotten."

"If you have a family doctor . . . ?"

"No," Emery said.

"In that case," Ralph Merton sounded slightly more human, *"I could phone Doctor Ormond for you. He's a young man, very active. He'll be there just as soon as he can get through, I'm sure."*

"Thank you," Emery said, "I'd appreciate that very much."

"I'll do it as soon as I hang up. Would you let us know as soon as you have a death certificate, Mister Bainbridge?"

"Certainly."

"Wonderful. Now, as to the—ah—present arrangements? Is your son indoors?"

"Out in the snow. I put a sheet over his body, but I'd think it would be covered with snow by this time."

"Wonderful. I'll call Doctor Ormond the moment I hang up, Mister Bainbridge. When you've got the death certificate, you can rely on Merton's for everything. You have my sympathy. I have two sons myself."

"Thank you," Emery repeated, and returned the receiver to its cradle.

The cabin still smelled faintly of bacon and coffee. It might not be wise to leave with an empty stomach, was certainly unwise to leave with a low flame under the coffeepot, as he had been about to do. He turned the burner off, got a clean mug (somewhat hampered by his home-made snowshoes), poured himself a cup, sipped, and made himself eat two slices of bacon. Three more, between two slices of rye bread, became a crude sandwich; he stuffed it into a pocket of his mackinaw.

The maul waited beside the front door; he locked the door and started off over the snow a second time. When the snow-covered road had led him nearly out of sight of the cabin, he thought he heard the faint and lonely ringing of his telephone again. Presumably that was Doctor Ormond; Emery shrugged and trudged on.

The front door of the dark cabin seemed very substantial; after examining it, Emery circled around to the back. Drifted snow had risen nearly to the level of the hasp and padlock that secured the door. Positioning his feet as firmly as he could in snowshoes, he swung his maul like a golf club at the hasp. At the third blow, the screws tore loose and the door crashed inward.

Clambering through the violated doorway, he reflected that he did not know who owned this cabin now or what he looked like, that he would not recognize the owner he intended to rob if he were to meet him on the street. Robbery would be easier if only he could imagine himself apologizing and explaining, and offering to pay—though no apology or explanation would be feasible if he succeeded. He would be a vigilante then; and the law, which extended every courtesy to murderers, detested and destroyed anyone who killed or even resisted them. He would have to find out this cabin's address, he decided, and send cash by mail.

Of course, it was possible that there were no guns here, in which case Brook's murderers would presumably kill him too, before he could do any such thing. They might kill him, for that matter, even if—

Before he could complete the thought, he saw the gun safe, a steel cabinet painted to look like wood, with a combination lock. Half a dozen blows from the maul knocked off the knob. Two dozen more so battered the three-sixteenths-inch steel door that he could work the claws of the big ripping hammer he found in a toolbox into the opening. The battered mechanism was steel, the hammer-handle fiberglass; for a few seconds that seemed far longer, he felt certain the handle would break.

A rivet somewhere in the gun safe surrendered with a *pop*— the sweetest sound imaginable. A slight repositioning of the hammer and another heave, and the door ground back.

The gun safe held a twelve-gauge over-and-under shotgun, a sixteen-gauge pump, and a sleek scoped Sako carbine; there were shot shells of both sizes and three boxes of cartridges for the carbine in one of the drawers below the guns.

Emery took out the carbine and threw it to his shoulder; the stock felt a trifle small—the cabin's owner was probably an inch or two shorter—but it handled almost as if it had been customized for him. The bolt opened crisply to display an empty chamber.

He loaded five cartridges and dropped more into a pocket of his mackinaw. Reflecting that the women might well arm themselves from this cabin too, once they discovered that the lock on the rear entrance was broken, he threw the shotgun shells outside into the snow.

•   •   •

From a thick stand of pine on the lake shore, he had as good a view of the canted structure that Aileen had called a ziggurat as the gray daylight and blowing snow permitted: an assemblage of cubical modules tapering to a peak in a series of snow-covered terraces.

Certainly not an aircraft; a spacecraft, perhaps. More likely, a space station. Toward the bottom—or rather toward the ice surrounding it, for there had to be an additional forty feet or more of it submerged in the lake—the modules were noticeably crushed and deformed.

Rising, he stepped clumsily out onto the wind-swept ice. A part of this had been open water when the women had brought Aileen from the ziggurat back to the road—water that was open because the ice had been broken when the ziggurat broke through it, presumably. Yet that open water had been shallow enough for Aileen to wade through, although this mountain lake was deep a few feet from shore; such open water made no sense, though things seemed to have happened like that.

There were no windows that he could see, but several of the modules appeared to have rounded doors or hatches. If the women kept a watch, they might shoot him now as he shuffled slowly over the ice; but they would have to open one of those hatches to do it, and he would do his best to shoot first. He rechecked the Sako's safety. It was off, and he knew there was a round in the chamber. He removed the glove from his right hand and stuffed it into his pocket on top of more rounds and his forgotten sandwich.

He had wanted to die; and if they gut-shot him during the minute or two more that he would require to reach the base of the ziggurat, he would die in agony right here upon the ice.

Well, men did. All Men. Every human being died at last, young or old; and he had already lived longer than many of the people he had known and liked in high school and college. Had lived almost three times as long as Brook.

To his right, the tracks of small feet in large-cleated boots left the ziggurat, tracks not yet obscured by snow and thus very recent. He turned toward them to examine them, then traced them back to a circular hatch whose lower edge was no more than an inch above the ice. It was dogged shut with a simple catch large enough that he manipulated it easily with his gloved left hand.

A wave of warmth caressed his face as he pulled the hatch open and stepped into the ziggurat. Heat! They had heat in here, heat from some device that was still functioning, though Aileen had complained of the cold. In that case, heat from a source they had been able to repair since the crash, perhaps with parts from Jan's Lincoln.

Almost absently, he closed the hatch behind him. Before him was a second hatch; beyond it, misty blue light and dark water. Here, then, was the explanation for the ice on Aileen's boots and pants legs; she had waded in the lake, all right, but here inside the ziggurat, where there seemed to be about a foot of water.

Sitting in the hatchway of what he decided must surely be an airlock, he unlaced his boots and tugged them off, crude snowshoes and all, then tied his bootlaces together. It would be convenient, perhaps, to leave boots and snowshoes here in the airlock, but without either he would be confined to the ziggurat; he could not risk it. He took off his stockings and stuffed them into his boots, rolled up his trouser legs, and stepped barefoot into the dark water, the boots and snowshoes in his left hand, the Sako carbine in his right, gripped like a pistol.

The walls and ceiling of the module were thick with dials and unfamiliar devices, and a tilted cabinet whose corner rose above the water promised more; he paused to look at what seemed to be a simple dial, although its pointer shimmered, vanished, and reappeared, apparently a conveniently massless projection. The first number looked like zero, queerly lettered; the last—he squinted—three hundred, perhaps, although he had never seen a 3 quite like that. Pushing a tiny knob at the base to the left increased the height of the numerals until each stood about five thirty-seconds of an inch; the pointer darkened and now seemed quite solid.

There was a slight noise from overhead, as though someone in a higher module had dropped some small object.

He stiffened and looked quickly around. An open hatch in the wall at the opposite side of the half-crushed module gave access to an interior module that should (if the slant of both floors was the same) be somewhat less deeply submerged. He waded across and went in, followed by the dial he had examined, which slid across the metal wall like a hockey puck, dodging other devices in its path, until he caught it and pushed the knob at its base to the right again.

A ladder in the middle of the new module invited him to climb to the one above; he did, although with difficulty, hi

boots and showshoes slung behind his back and half choking
him with his own bootlaces, and the carbine awkwardly grasped
in his right hand. The ladder (of some white metal that did
not quite seem to be aluminum) gave dangerously beneath his
weight, but held.

The higher module into which he emerged was almost intact, and colder than the one from which he had just climbed;
the deep thrumming of the wind beyond its metal walls could
be distinctly heard, though no window or porthole revealed the
snow he knew must be racing down the lake with it.

"Fey," he muttered to himself. And then, somewhat more
loudly, "Eerie." How frightened poor Aileen must have been!

Curious, he put down his boots and snowshoes and the Sako,
drew his knife, and shaved a few bits of metal from the topmost
rung of the ladder. They were bright where the sharp steel had
sheared them, dull on the older surfaces. Tempted to guess,
he suspended judgment. A somewhat bigger piece gouged from
the floor appeared to be of the same material; he unbuttoned
his mackinaw and deposited all his samples in a shirt pocket.

The rectangular furnishing against one wall looked as if it
might be a workbench topped with white plastic. Two objects
of unfamiliar shape lay on it; he crossed the cubicle, stepping
over featureless cabinets and others dotted with strangely
shaped screens.

The larger object that he took from the bench changed its
form at his touch, developing smooth jaws whose curving inner
surfaces suggested parabolas; the smaller object snapped open,
revealing a convoluted diagram too large to have been contained within it. Points of orange and green light wandered
aimlessly over the diagram. After a bit of fumbling, he shut
the object again and put it in the chest pocket of his mackinaw,
following it with several small items of interest that he discovered in the swinging, extensible compartments that seemed to
serve as drawers, though they were not quite drawers.

Without warning, the face of an angry giantess occupied the
benchtop and her shouting voice filled the module. Gongs and
bells sounded behind her, a music grotesquely harmonious amplified to deafening intensity. For a half second that was nearly
too long, he watched and listened, mesmerized.

She was five feet behind him, ax raised, when he turned. He
lunged at her as the blow fell, and the wooden handle struck
his shoulder. Struggling together, they rolled over the canted

floor, she a clawing, biting fury, he with a hand—then both—grabbing at the ax handle.

Wrenching the ax away, he swung it clumsily, hitting her elbow with the flat. She bit his cheek, and seemed about to tear his face off. Releasing the ax, he drove his thumbs into her eyes. She spat him out (such was his confused recollection later), sprang to her feet, dashed away—

And was gone.

Half stunned by the suddenness and violence of the fight as well as the deafening clamor from the workbench, he sat up and looked around him. His stolen ax lay near his left hand; the brownish smear on its bright edge was presumably Brook's blood. His own trickled from his cheek, dotting the uneven metal floor. His boots and snowshoes, and the sleek carbine, lay where he had left them.

Slowly he got to his feet, stooped to reclaim his ax, then stood up without it; he could only carry so much, the carbine was a better weapon, and the ax had killed Brook.

He shook himself. These women had killed Brook. The ax was his ax, and nothing more: a good piece of steel mounted on a length of hickory, a thing he had bought for thirty or forty dollars in the hardware store in town—as foolish to kick the stone you tripped over as to blame the ax.

He picked it up and wiped the blade on one rough sleeve of his mackinaw until most of Brook's blood was gone. The carbine was a better weapon, but if he left the ax where it was the women would almost certainly find it and use it against him. If he carried it outside, he might be able to chop a hole in the ice and drop it in; but dropping it into the dark water at the bottom of the ladder would probably be almost as effective and a hundred times quicker. Soon, perhaps very soon, the one who had just tried to kill him might try again.

The clamor of the bench continued unabated. Childishly, he told it to be quiet, and when it did not respond, chopped at the huge, female, shouting, shrieking face again and again, until silence fell as suddenly as a curtain and the benchtop was white plastic once more. Had it been a teaching device, as well as a repair bench? One that could, perhaps, instruct and entertain the mechanic while she worked?

He laid the ax on it, found a handkerchief, and pressed it to his cheek.

Curious again, he strode to the nearest wall and touched it it was not as cold as he had expected, though it seemed dis tinctly colder than the air around him. "Insulated," he muttered to himself, "but not insulated enough." Did you need a lot of insulation for space? Perhaps not; astronauts stayed outside in their suits for hours. After a little reflection, he concluded that a space station could lose heat to space only by radiation, and a space station at room temperature would not radiate much. The ziggurat was losing heat by convection and conduction now, and convection was almost always the greatest thief of heat.

Retrieving the ax, he carried it to the floor hatch to drop it in, and saw the dead woman's body floating facedown in the shallow water of the cubicle below.

When he left, the marks of his snowshoes coming in were as sharp as if they had just been made, although it was snowing hard. So much snow had accumulated on the ziggurat's terraces already that it seemed almost a rock rising from the ice; if he were to point it out to someone—to Brook, say, although it would be better perhaps to point it out to someone still alive. To Alayna or Jan, say, or even to Pamela, who had been Brook's mother. If he were to point it out to any of those people and say, *That rock over there is hollow, and there are strange and wonderful blue-lit rooms inside, where little brown women will try to kill you,* they would think him not a liar but a madman, or a drunk. For centuries, unheeded men and women in England and Ireland and any number of other countries had reported a diminutive race living in hills where time ran differently, although in Africa, where skins were black, the little people's had been white.

He had made the mistake of turning the dead woman over, and the memory of her livid face and empty, unfocused eyes came back to haunt him. Someone used to jet-black faces would have called that dead face white, almost certainly. He searched his mind for a term he had read a year or two before.

Members of that small, pale African race were *Yumbos,* the people from the hills who crept out to steal cornmeal. Aileen had said the women had given her only bread to eat. Rations were short, perhaps; or rations were being hoarded against an indefinite stay.

If its hood had not been up, Emery would have missed the Lincoln, thinking it just another snowdrift. Both doors were locked (he had locked them out of habit, it seemed, the night before) and the keys were still in Brook's pocket. He broke a window with the butt of the carbine and retrieved his best cap. Brook had left some possession, a TV or home computer, in the trunk; but he would have to shoot out the lock, and he was heavily loaded already with the loot of the ziggurat.

As he passed the lightless cabin he had burglarized, it occurred to him that he ought to find out whether the shotguns had been taken. After a few moments' thought, he rejected the idea. The other two women (if indeed there were only two left) might or might not have the shotguns, and might or might not have shells for them if they did. They were dangerous in any case, which was all he really needed to know.

His own cabin was as dark. He tried to remember whether he had left a light on, then whether he had even turned one on that morning. He had written his journal—had briefly and crassly recorded Brook's death there—so he must certainly have switched on the lamp on the table. He could not remember switching it off.

Would they shoot through the glass, and the Cyclone fence wire with which he had covered his windows? Or would they poke the barrel through first, providing him some warning? There might have been more shells in the other cabin, in some drawer or cupboard, or even in the pockets of the old field coat that had hung from a nail near the front door.

His own front door appeared to be just as he had left it; there were no footprints in the fresh snow banked against it, and its bright Yale lock was unmarred. Could they pick locks? He circled the cabin, careful to go by way of the north side, past his Jeep and the spot where Brook had died, so that he would not have to look at Brook's corpse. Brook was surely buried under snow by this time, as he had told the undertaker; yet he could not help visualizing Brook's contorted, untenanted face. Brook would never go to Purdue now, never utilize his father's contacts at NASA. Brook was dead, and all the dreams (so many dreams) had died with him. Was it Brook or the dreams he mourned?

The rear door looked as sound as the front, and there were no visible footprints in the snow. No doubt he had turned out the table light automatically when he had finished writing his journal. Everyone did such things.

He unlocked the rear door, went inside, stood the Sako in a corner, and emptied his pockets onto the table. Here was the dial that had tracked him, the tool that displayed a diagram larger than itself, the oblong card that might be a book whose pages turned each time the reader's hand approached it, the octopus of light whose center was a ceramic sphere no bigger than a marble. Here, too, were the seven-sided cube; the beads that strung themselves and certainly were not actually beads, whatever they might be; and the dish in which small objects seemed to melt and from which in a few minutes they vanished. With them, cartridges for the carbine, his checkbook, keys, handkerchief, and pocketknife; and the unappetizing sandwich.

Seeing it and feeling his own disappointment, he realized that he was hungry. He lit the gas under the coffeepot and sat down to consider the matter. Should he eat first? Bandage his cheek? Build a new fire? The cabin was cold, though it seemed almost cozy after the winter storm outside.

Or should he write his journal first—set down a factual account of everything he had seen in the ziggurat while it was still fresh in his mind? The sensible thing would be to build a fire; but that would mean going out for wood and trying not to see Brook. His mind recoiled from the thought.

An accurate, detailed account of the ziggurat might be worth millions to him in a few years, and could be written—begun at least—while his food was cooking and the coffee getting hot. He opened a can of Irish stew, dumped it into a clean saucepan, lit the burner under it, then sat down again and pressed the switch of the small lamp on the table.

No light flooded from its shade.

He stared at it, tightened the bulb and pressed the switch twice more, and chuckled. No wonder the cabin had been dark! Either the bulb had burned out in his absence, or the wires were down.

Standing up, he pulled the switch cord of the overhead fixture. Nothing.

How did the old song go? Something about wires down south that wouldn't stand the strain if it snowed. These wires, his wires, the ones that the county had run out to the lake four years ago, had not. He found one of the kerosene lanterns he had used before the wires came, filled it, and lit it.

If the electrical wires were down, it seemed probable that the telephone was out as well—but when he held it to his ear the receiver emitted a reassuring dial tone. The telephone people, Emery reminded himself, always seemed to maintain their equipment a little bit better than the power company.

His cheek next, and he would have to fetch water from the creek as he had in the old days or melt snow. He filled his teakettle with clean snow from behind the cabin. Washing off the dried blood revealed the marks of teeth and a bruise. You could catch all sorts of diseases from human bites—human mouths were as dirty as monkeys'—but there was not much that he could do about that now. Gingerly, he daubed iodine on the marks, sponged that side of his face with hydrogen peroxide, and put on a thin pad of gauze, noting that Brook had depleted his supply in bandaging his wounded side.

Had the woman who had bitten him and tried to kill him with his own ax been the one who had killed Brook? It seemed likely, unless the women were trading off weapons; and if that was the case, Brook was avenged. Let the sheriff take it from here. He debated the advisability of leading the sheriff's investigator to the ziggurat.

He stirred his Irish stew, and decided it was not quite warm enough yet; he'd get it good and hot, and pour it over bread.

He wasn't quite warm enough either, and was in fact still wearing his mackinaw, here inside the cabin. It was time to confront the firewood problem. When he had done it, he could take off his mackinaw and settle in until the storm let up and the snowplows brought a deputy, Doctor What'shisname—Ormond—and the undertaker.

Outside, on the south side of the cabin, he made himself stare at the place where Brook lay. To the eye at least, it was just a little mound of snow, differing from other graves only in being white and smooth; the coyote lay at Brook's head, his mound not noticeably smaller or larger. Emery found that oddly comforting. Brook would have gloried in a tame coyote. They would have to be separated before long, though—in four or five days at most, and probably sooner. It seemed a shame. Emery filled his arms with wood and carried it back into the cabin.

Newspapers first, with a splash of kerosene on them. Then kindling, and wood only when the kindling was burning well. He set the kerosene can on the hearth and knelt to unfold, crumple up, and arrange his newspapers.

There were tracks, footprints, in the powdery gray ashes.

He blinked and stared and blinked again. Stood up and got the flashlight and looked once more.

There could be no doubt, although these were not the clear and detailed prints he would have preferred; they were scuffed, confused, and peppered with some black substance. He rubbed a speck of it between his thumb and forefinger. Soot, of course.

The prints of two pairs of boots with large cleats; small boots in both cases, but one pair was slightly smaller than the other, and the smaller pair showed—yes—a little less wear at the heels.

They had come down his chimney. He stood up again and looked around. Nothing seemed to be missing.

They had climbed onto the roof (his Jeep, parked against the north wall of the cabin, would have made that easy) and climbed down the chimney. He could not have managed it, and neither could Brook, if Brook were still alive; but the twins could have done it, and these women were scarcely larger. He should have seen their footprints, but they had no doubt been obscured by blowing snow, and he had taken them for the ones the women had left that morning when they killed Brook. He had been looking mostly for fresh tracks outside the doors in any case.

There had been none. He felt certain of that; no tracks newer than the ones he himself had made that morning. Why, then, had the women climbed up the chimney when they left? Anybody knowledgeable enough to work with the equipment he had seen in the ziggurat would have no difficulty in opening either of his doors from the inside. Climbing down the chimney might not be terribly hard for women the twins' size, but climbing back up, even with a rope, would be a great deal harder. Why do it when you could just walk out?

He covered the ashes with twice the amount of newspaper he had intended to use, and doused every ball of paper liberally with kerosene. Should he light the fire first or wait until he had the carbine in his hand?

The latter seemed safer. He got the carbine and pushed off its safety, clamped it under one arm, then struck a match and tossed it into the fireplace.

The tiny tongue of yellow flame grew to a conflagration in a second or two. There was a metallic clank before something black crashed down into the fire and sprang at him like a cat.

"Stop!" He swung the butt of the Sako at her. "Stop, or I'll shoot!"

A hand from nowhere gripped his ankle. He kicked free, and a second woman rolled from beneath the bunk Brook had slept

in—the one he had made up for Jan. Awkwardly, he clubbed
the forearm of the woman who had dropped from the chimney
with the carbine barrel, kicked at her knee and missed. "Get
out! Get out, both of you, or I swear to God—"

They rushed at him not quite as one, the taller first, the
smaller brandishing his rifle. Hands snatched at the carbine,
nearly jerking it from his grasp; for a moment, he wrestled the
taller woman for it.

The sound of the shot was deafening in the closed cabin.
The carbine leaped in his hands.

He found that he was staring into her soot-smeared brown
face; it crumpled like his newspapers, her eyes squinting, her
mouth twisted in a grimace of pain.

The woman behind her screamed and turned away, dropping
his rifle and clutching her thigh. Blood seeped from between
her fingers.

The taller woman took a step toward him—an involuntary
step, perhaps, as her reflexes sought to keep her from falling.
She fell forward, the crumpled face smacking the worn boards
of the cabin floor, and lay motionless.

The other woman was kneeling, still trying to hold back her
blood. She looked at Emery, a look of mingled despair and
mute appeal.

"I won't," he said.

He was still holding the carbine that had shot her. It belonged to someone else, and its owner presumably valued it;
but none of that seemed to matter anymore. He threw it aside.
"That's why I quit hunting deer," he told her almost casually.
"I gut-shot a buck and trailed him six miles. When I found
him, he looked at me like that."

The big plastic leaf bags he used to carry his garbage to the
dump were under the sink. He pulled down quilt, blankets,
and sheet, and spread two bags over the rumpled bunk that
had been Brook's, scooped her up, and stretched her on them.
"You shot me, and now I've shot you. I didn't mean to. Maybe
you didn't either—I'd like to think so, anyway."

With his hunting knife, he cut away the sooty cloth around
her wound. The skin at the back of her thigh was unbroken,
but beneath it he could feel the hard outline of the bullet.
"I'm going to cut there and take that out," he told her. "It
should be pretty easy, but we'll have to sterilize the knife and
the needle-nosed pliers first."

He gave her the rest of his surgical gauze to hold against her wound, and tried to fill his largest cooking pot with water from the sink. "I should have remembered the pump was off," he admitted to her ruefully, and went outside to fill the pot with clean snow.

"I'm going to wash your wound and bandage it before I get the bullet out." He spoke slowly and distinctly as he stepped back in and shut the door, hoping that she understood at least a part of what he was saying. "First, I have to get this water hot enough that I'll be cleaning it, not infecting it." He put the pot of snow on the stove and turned down the burner under his stew.

"Let's see what happened here." He knelt beside the dead woman and examined the ragged, blood-soaked tear at the back of her jacket, then wiped his fingers. It took an effort of will to roll her over; but he did it, keeping his eyes off her face. The hole the bullet had left in the front of the jacket was so small and obscure that he had to verify it by poking his pen through it before he was satisfied.

He stood again, reached into his mackinaw to push the pen into his shirt pocket, and found the fragments of white metal he had taken from the ziggurat. For a moment, he looked from them to the newspapers still blazing in the fireplace. "I'm going to lay some kindling on the fire. Getting chilled won't help you. It could even kill you." Belatedly, he drew up her sheet, the blankets, and the quilt.

"You're not going to die. Are you afraid you will?" He had a feeling that if he talked to her enough, she would begin to understand; that was how children learned to speak, surely. "I'm not going to kill you, and neither is that wound in your leg, or at least I don't think so."

She replied, and he saw that she was trying to smile. He pointed to the dead woman and to her, and shook his head, then arranged kindling on the burning newspapers. The water in his biggest pot was scarcely warm, but the Irish stew was hot. He filled a bowl, and gave it to her with a spoon; she sat up to eat, keeping her left hand under the covers to press the pad of gauze to her leg.

The Voylestown telephone directory provided a home number for Doctor Ormond. Emery pressed it in.

"*Hello.*"

"Doctor Ormond? This is Emery Bainbridge."

"*Right. Ralph Merton told me about you. I'll try to get out there just as quick as I can.*"

"This is about another matter, Doctor. I'm afraid we've had a gun go off by accident."

A slight gasp came over the wire as Ormond drew breath. *"Someone was hit. Is it bad?"*

"Both of us were. I hope not too badly, though. We had a loaded rifle—my hunting rifle—standing against the wall. We were nervous, you understand. We still are. Some people—these people—I'm sorry." In the midst of the fabrication, Brook's death had taken Emery by the throat.

"I know your son's dead, Mister Bainbridge. Ralph told me. He was murdered?"

"Yes, with an ax. My ax. You'll see him, of course. I apologize, Doctor. I don't usually lose control."

"Perfectly normal and healthy, Mister Bainbridge. You don't have to tell me about the shooting if you don't want to. I'm a doctor, not a policeman."

"My rifle fell over and discharged," Emery said. "The bullet creased my side—I don't think that's too bad—and hit . . ." Looking at the wounded woman, he ransacked his memory for a suitable name. "Hit Tamar in the leg. I should explain that Tamar's an exchange student who's been staying with us." Tamar had been Solomon's sister, and King Solomon's mines had been somewhere around the Horn of Africa. "She's from Aden. She speaks very little English, I'm afraid. I know first aid, and I'm doing all I can, but I thought I ought to call you."

"She's conscious?"

"Oh, yes. She's sitting up and eating right now. The bullet hit the outer part of her thigh. I think it missed the bone. It's still in her leg. It didn't exit."

"This just happened?"

"Ten minutes ago, perhaps."

"Don't give her any more food, she may vomit. Give her water. There's no intestinal wound? No wound in the abdomen?"

"No, in her thigh as I said. About eight inches above the knee."

"Then let her have water, as much as she wants. Has she lost much blood?"

Emery glanced at the dead woman. It would be necessary to account for the stains of her blood as well as Tamar's. "It's not easy to estimate, but I'd say at least a pint. It could be a little more."

"I see, I see." Ormond sounded relieved. *"I'd give her a transfusion if I had her in the hospital, Mister Bainbridge, but she*

may not really need one. At least, not badly. How much would you say she weighs?"

He tried to remember the effort involved in lifting her. He had been excited, of course—high on adrenaline. "Between ninety and a hundred pounds, at a guess."

Ormond grunted. *"Small. Small bones? Height?"*

"Yes, very small. My wife calls her petite." The lie had come easily, unlooked for. "I'd say she's about five foot one. Delicate."

"What about you, Mister Bainbridge? Have you lost much blood?"

"Less than half as much as she has, I'd say."

"I see. The question is whether your intestine has been perforated—"

"Not unless it's a lot closer to the skin than I think it is, Doctor. It's just a crease, as I say. I was sitting down, she was standing up. The bullet creased my side and went into her leg."

"I'd wait a bit, just the same, before I ate or drank anything, Mister Bainbridge. You haven't eaten or drunk since it happened?"

"No," Emery lied.

"Good. Wait a bit. Can you call me back in two hours?"

"Certainly. Thank you, Doctor."

"I'll be here, unless there's an emergency here in town, someplace I can get to. If I'm not here, my wife will answer the phone. Have you called the police?"

"Not about this. It's an accident, not a police matter."

"I'm required to report any gunshot wounds I treat. You may want to report it yourself first."

"All right, I can tell the officer who investigates my son's death."

"That's up to you, but I'll have to report it. Is there anything else?"

"I don't think so."

"Do you have any antibiotics? A few capsules left from an old prescription?"

"I don't think so."

"Look. If you find anything you think might be helpful, call me back immediately. Otherwise, in two hours."

"Right. Thank you, Doctor." Emery hung up.

The snow water was boiling on the stove. He turned off the burner, noting that the potful of packed snow had become less than a quarter of a pot of water. "As soon as that cools off a little, I'm going to wash your wound and put a proper bandage on it," he said.

She smiled shyly.

"You're from Aden. It's in Yemen, I believe. Your name is Tamar. Can you say *Tamar?*" He spoke slowly, mouthing the sounds. *"Ta-mar.* You say it." He pointed to her.

"Teye-mahr." She smiled again, not quite so frightened.

"Very good! You'd speak Arabic, I suppose, but I've got a few books here, and if I can dig up a more obscure language for you, we'll use it—too many people know Arabic. I wish that you could tell me," he hesitated, "where you really come from. Or when you come from. Because that's what I've been thinking. That's crazy, isn't it?"

She nodded, though it seemed to him she had not understood.

"You were up in space in that thing. In the ziggurat." He laid splits of wood on the blazing kindling. "I've been thinking about that, too, and you just about had to be. How many were there in your crew?"

Sensing her incomprehension, he pointed to the dead woman, then to the living one, and held up three fingers. "This many? Three? Wait a minute."

He found a blank page in his journal and drew the ziggurat with three stick figures beside it. "This many?" He offered her his journal and the pen.

She shook her head and pointed to her leg with her free hand.

"Yes, of course. You'll need both hands."

He cleaned her wound as thoroughly as he could with Q-Tips and the steaming snow-water, and contrived a dressing from a clean undershirt and the remaining tape. "Now we've got to get the bullet out. I think we ought to for your sake anyway—it will have carried cloth into the wound, maybe even tissue from the other woman."

Breaking the plastic of a disposable razor furnished him with a small but extremely sharp blade. "I'd planned to use the pen blade of my jackknife," he explained as he helped her roll over, "but this will be better."

He cut away what remained of her trouser leg. "It's going to hurt. I wish I had something to give you."

Two shallow incisions revealed an edge of the mushroomed carbine bullet. He fished the pliers out of the hot water with a fork, gripped the ragged lead in them, and worked the bullet free. Rather to his surprise, she bit her pillow and did not cry out.

"Here it is." He held the bullet where she could see it. "It went through your friend's breastbone, and I think it must have gotten her heart. Then it was deflected downward, most likely by a rib, and hit you. If it hadn't been deflected, it might have missed you altogether. Or killed you. Lie still, please." He put his hand on her back and felt her shrink from his touch. "I want to mop away the blood and look at that with the flashlight. If this fragmented at all, it didn't fragment much. But if it did, we want to get all of the pieces out, and anything else that doesn't belong." Unable to stop himself, he added, "You're afraid, aren't you? All of you were. Afraid of me, and of Brook too. Probably afraid of all males."

He found fibers in the wound that had probably come from her trousers and extracted them one by one, tore strips from a second undershirt, and tied a folded pad made of what remained of it to the new wound at the back of her thigh. "This is what we had to do before they had tape," he confided as he tightened the last knot. "Wind cloth around the wounded leg or whatever it was. That's why we call them *wounds*. If you were wounded, you got bandages wound around you—all right, you can turn back over now." He helped her.

The flames were leaping high in the fieldstone fireplace. He took the metal fragments out of his shirt pocket and showed them to her, then pointed toward it.

She shook her head emphatically.

"Do you mean they won't burn, or they will?" He grinned. "I think you mean they will. Let's see."

He tossed the smallest sliver from the ladder into the fire. After a second or two, there was a burst of brilliant light and puff of white smoke. "Magnesium. I thought so."

He moved his chair next to the bunk in which she lay and sat down. "Magnesium's strong and very light, but it burns. They use it in flashbulbs. Your ziggurat, your lander or space station or whatever it is, will burn with a flame hot enough to destroy just about anything, and I'm going to burn it tomorrow morning. It's a terrible waste and I hate to do it, but that's what I'm going to do. You don't understand any of this, do you, Tamar?" He got his journal and drew fire and smoke coming from the ziggurat.

She studied the drawing, her face thoughtful, then nodded. "I'm glad you didn't throw a fit about that," he told her. "I was afraid you would, but maybe you were under orders not to disturb things back here any more than you could help."

When she did not react to that, he took another leaf bag from under the sink; to his satisfaction, it was large enough to contain the dead woman. "I had to do that before she got stiff," he explained to the living one. "She'll stiffen up in an hour or so. It's probably better if we don't have to look at her, anyway."

Tamar made a quick gesture he did not comprehend, folded her hands, and shut her eyes.

"Tomorrow, before the storm lets up, I'm going to drag her back to your space station and burn it." He was talking mostly for his own benefit, to clarify his thoughts. "That's probably a crime, but it's what I'm going to do. You do what you've got to." He picked up the Sako carbine. "I'm going to clean this and leave it in the other cabin on the way, and throw away the bullet. As far as the sheriff's concerned, my gun shot us both by accident. If I have to, I'll say you bit my face while I was tending your wound. But I won't be able to shave there anyhow, and by the time they get here my beard may cover it."

She motioned toward his journal and pen, and when he gave them to her produced a creditable sketch of the third woman.

"Gone," he said. "She's dead too. I'd stuck my thumbs in her eyes—she tried to kill me—and she ran. She must have fallen through the hole in the floor. The water down there was pretty shallow, so she would've hit hard. I think she drowned."

Tamar pointed to the leaf bag that held the dead woman, then sketched her with equal facility, finishing by crossing out the sketch.

Emery crossed out the women in the ziggurat as well, and returned the journal and the pen to Tamar. "You'll have to live the rest of your life here, I'm afraid, unless they send somebody for you. I don't expect you to like it—not many of us do—but you'll have to do the best you can, just like the rest of us."

Suddenly excited, she pointed to the tiny face of the lion on his pen and hummed, waving the pen like a conductor's baton. It took him a minute or more to identify the tune.

It was "God Save the Queen."

Later, when she was asleep, he telephoned an experimental physicist. "David," he asked softly, "do you remember your old boss? Emery Bainbridge?"

David did.

"I've got something here I want to tell you about, David. First, though, I've got to say I can't tell you where I got it. That's confidential—top secret. You've got to accept that. I won't *ever* be able to tell you. Okay?"

It was.

"This thing is a little dish. It looks almost like an ashtray." There was a penny in the clutter on the table; he picked it up. "I'm going to drop a penny into it. Listen."

The penny fell with a clink.

"After a while, that penny will disappear, David. Right now it looks just a little misted, like it had been outside in the cold, and there was condensation on it."

Emery moved the dish closer to the kerosene lantern. "Now the penny is starting to look sort of silvery. I think most of the copper's gone, and what I'm seeing is the zinc underneath. You can barely make out Lincoln's face."

David spoke.

"I've tried that. Even if you hold the dish upside down and shake it, the penny—or whatever it is—won't fall out, and I'm not about to reach in and try to pull it out."

The crackling voice in the receiver sounded louder than Emery's own.

"I wish you could, David. It's not much bigger than the end of a pencil now, and shrinking quickly. Hold on—

"There. It's gone. I think the dish must boil off atoms or molecules by some cold process. That's the only explanation I've come up with. I suppose we could check that by analyzing samples of air above it, but I don't have the equipment here.

"David, I'm going to start a new company. I'm going to do it on a shoestring, because I don't want to let any backers in. I'll have to use my own money and whatever I can raise on my signature. I know you've got a good job now. They're probably paying you half what you're worth, which is a hell of a lot. But if you'll come in with me, I'll give you ten percent.

"Of course you can think it over. I expect you to. Let's say a week. How's that?"

David spoke at length.

"Yes, here too. The lights are off, as a matter of fact. It's just by the grace of God that the phone still works. I'll be stuck out here—I'm in the cabin—for another three or four days, probably. Then I'll drive into the city, and we'll talk.

"Certainly you can look at it. You can pick it up and try it out, but not take it back to your lab. You understand, I'm sure."

A last, querulous question.

Emery chuckled. "No, it's not from a magic store, David. I think I might be able to guess where it's actually from, but I'm not going to. Top secret, remember? It's technology way in advance of ours. We're medieval mechanics who've found a paper shredder. We may never be able to make another shredder, but we can learn a hell of a lot from the one we've got."

When he had hung up, he moved his chair back to the side of Tamar's bunk. She was lying on her back, her mouth and eyes closed, the soft sigh of her respiration distinct against the howling of the wind beyond the log walls.

"Jan's going to want to come back," Emery told Tamar, his voice less than a whisper. "She'll try to kiss and make up two weeks to a month after she finds out about the new company, I'd say. I'll have to get our divorce finalized before she hears. They'll back off a little on that property settlement when she gets back to the city, and then I'll sign."

Tamar's left hand lay on the quilt; his found it, stroking the back and fingers with a touch that he hoped was too light to wake her. "Because I don't want Jan anymore. I want you, Tamar, and you're going to need me."

The delicate brown fingers curled about his, though she was still asleep.

"You're learning to trust me, aren't you? Well, you can. I won't hurt you." He fell silent. He had taught the coyote to trust him; and because he had, the coyote had not feared the smell of Man on the cyanide gun. He would have to make certain Tamar understood that all men were not to be trusted—that there were millions of men who would rob and rape and kill her if they could.

"How did you reproduce, up there in our future, Tamar? Asexually? My guess is artificial insemination, with a means of selecting for females. You can tell me whether I'm right, by and by."

He paused, thinking. "Is our future still up there? The one you came from? Or did you change things when you crashed? Or when you killed Brook. Even if it is, maybe you and I can change things with some new technology. Let's try."

Tamar sighed, and seemed to smile in her sleep. He bent over her to kiss her, his lips lightly brushing hers. "Is that why the crash was so bad that you could never get the ziggurat to fly again? Because just by crashing at all, or by killing my son, you destroyed the future you came from?"

In the movies, Emery reflected, people simply stepped into time machines and vanished, to reappear later or earlier at the same spot on Earth's surface, as if Copernicus had never lived. In reality, Earth was moving in the solar system, the solar system in the galaxy, and the galaxy itself in the universe. One would have to travel through space as well as time to jump time in reality.

Somewhere beneath the surface of the lake, the device that permitted such jumps was still functioning, after a fashion. No longer jumping, but influencing the speed with which time passed—the timing of time, as it were. The hours he had spent inside the ziggurat had been but a minute or two outside it; that had to be true, because the prints of his snowshoes coming in had still been sharp when he came out, and Aileen had spent half a day at least there in two hours.

He would burn the ziggurat tomorrow. He would have to, if he were not to lose everything he had taken from it, and be accused of the murder of the dead woman in the leaf bag, too—would have to, if he wished to keep Tamar.

But might not the time device, submerged who could say how deep in the lake, perhaps buried in mud at the bottom as well, survive and continue to function as it did now? Fishermen on Haunted Lake might see the sun stand still, while hours drifted past. Had the device spread itself through time to give the lake its name? He would buy up all the lakeside property, he decided, when the profits of the new company permitted him to.

"We're going to build a new cabin," he told the sleeping Tamar. "A house, really, and a big one, right on the shore there. We'll live in that house, you and me, for a long, long time, and we'll have children."

Very gently, her fingers tightened around his.

ABOUT THE
AUTHORS

WILLIAM BARTON was born in Boston in 1950 and currently resides in Garner, North Carolina, with his wife, Kathleen. For most of his life Barton has been an engineering technician specializing in military and industrial technology. He was at one time employed by the Department of Defense, working on the nation's nuclear submarine fleet, and is currently a freelance writer and computer consultant. Barton's previous books include *Hunting on Kunderer*, *A Plague of All Cowards*, *Dark Sky Legion*, and *When Heaven Fell*, and two collaborations with Michael Capobianco, *Iris* and *Fellow Traveler*. Soon to appear are *The Transmigration of Souls* and a new collaboration with Capobianco, *Alpha Centauri*.

DOUG BEASON's short fiction has appeared in *Analog*, *Amazing Stories*, *Full Spectrum*, *Star Wars: Tales From the Cantina*, and numerous others. With collaborator Kevin J. Anderson, *Assemblers of Infinity* was a Nebula Finalist, and his latest of eight novels is *Ill Wind* (Forge, 1995). Now holding a dual appointment as Director of Faculty Research and Associate Professor of Physics at the United States Air Force Academy, Dr. Beason recently served on the White House staff, working for the President's science advisor under both the Bush and Clinton administrations. He has headed up an Air Force plasma laboratory and served on a Presidential commission headed by astronaut Tom Stafford to provide the President with options for going back to the Moon and Mars.

MICHAEL BISHOP lives in Pine Mountian, Georgia, with his wife, Jeri. His work includes criticism, poetry, short fiction, and novels. Bishop's most recent novel is the Southern Gothic World War II baseball fantasy *Brittle Innings* (Bantam, 1994). He is currently at work on a new novel, *Black Dog Aloft*.

MARK BOURNE's fiction has appeared in *Fantasy & Science Fiction*, *Asimov's Science Fiction*, and assorted anthologies including *Sherlock Holmes in Orbit and Alternate Tyrants*. Mark's M.A. in theater led to his career as a science writer, planetarium scriptwriter, and astronomy educator. Two of his multimedia planetarium productions, *Orion Rendezvous: A "Star Trek" Voyage of Discovery* and *Space Bus*, are among the most popular shows in the international planetarium community. He is currently at work on an illustrated cruise guide to the Universe and his first novel. He lives in Portland, Oregon, with computer artist Elizabeth Griffiths Lawhead.

RICHARD BOWES lives and works in Manhattan. The story, "Fountains in Summer," is part of his novel-in-progress entitled *Minions of the Moon*. Seven other chapters have appeared or will appear in *Fantasy & Science Fiction, Tomorrow, Year's Best Fantasy & Horror #6*, and *Best From F & SF*. His prior genre novels are *Warchild, Feral Cell*, and *Goblin Market*.

EMILY DEVENPORT's first story was published by *Aboriginal SF* in 1987; in 1988 *Aboriginal*'s readers voted her a Boomerang Award for the story "Cat Scratch." Her most recent story has appeared in *Asimov's Science Fiction* magazine. She is the author of three novels: *Shade, Larissa,* and *Scorpianee*; and has two more forthcoming: *Eggheads* (early 1996) and *The Kronos Kid*.

JEAN-CLAUDE DUNYACH, born in 1957, has a Ph.D. in applied mathematics and works in the aircraft division of Aerospatiale, in Toulouse (in the south of France). He has been writing science fiction since the beginning of the eighties, and has already published six novels and two collections of short stories, garnering him the French science fiction award in 1983 and the Rosny Aîné Award in 1992. He writes lyrics for several French singers, which inspired one of his last novels about a rock'n'roll singer touring in Antarctica with a zombie orchestra . . . His short story "In Medicis Gardens" appeared in *Full Spectrum 4*.

LAUREN FITZGERALD made her first professional writing sale to *Seventeen Magazine* when she was sixteen. Since then, she has gone on to sell fiction to publications such as *Pulphouse*, *2AM*, *Eldritch Tales*, *Bizarre Bazaar '93*, *Midnight Zoo*, *Writers of the Future X*, and others. Born in 1966, she spent the three years following high school studying drama and voice in both Washington, D.C., and Los Angeles, but ultimately returned to her passion for writing when she entered the University of Maryland's College of Journalism, where she graduated Magna Cum Laude in 1991. She now lives in Maryland with her husband, Steve, and divides her time among writing, working full-time, and renovating three late nineteenth-century farm houses. It is in one of these houses that she plans to live and write her first novel.

KAREN JOY FOWLER is the author of two collections of short stories: *Artificial Things* (Bantam) and *Peripheral Vision* (Pulphouse). In 1991, she published her first novel, *Sarah Canary* (Henry Holt), which was a *New York Times* notable book and won the Commonwealth Club award for best first novel in California. She has two children and lives with her husband in Davis, California.

JEAN MARK GAWRON is a linguist who has never worked on any Australian languages but perhaps wishes he had, and is the author of four science fiction novels. His last is appropriately entitled *The Last Science Fiction Novel*.

MICHAEL GUST lives in Portland, Oregon, where he scouts locations for commercial film companies in the summer and scripts educational films in the winter. He has sold short fiction to *Pulphouse* and *Deathrealm*.

HOWARD V. HENDRIX holds a B.S. in biology as well as M.A. and Ph.D. degrees in English literature. He has held jobs ranging from hospital phlebotomist to fish hatchery manager to college professor, but now writes full time. His poetry and short fiction have appeared in many magazines—among them *Aboriginal Science Fiction, Amazing Stories, Asimov's Science Fiction, Eotu, Expanse, The Mystic Muse, Starshore,* and *Tales of the Unanticipated*—as well as the anthologies *Full Spectrum 1, 4,* and *5, Syzygy 3,* and *Writers of the Future II.* He is the author of the novel *Lightpaths* (Tor, early 1996). His previous books include *Testing, Testing 1, 2, 3* and *The Ecstasy of Catastrophe.* Currently, he is a book reviewer for the *New York Review of Science Fiction* and *Tangent.* His literary criticism has appeared in *Neuphilologische Mitteilungen, Assays VII,* and many other venues, and he has presented and published several works of science fiction criticism as part of the J. Lloyd Easton conference series. He and his wife make their home in central California. When not writing, he is most often found gardening or hunting edible wild mushrooms in the Sierras.

Of JOHN M. LANDSBERG's story, "Embodied In Its Opposite" (*Full Spectrum 4*), Michael Bishop wrote, "SF evolved for stories like this." The creator and former editor of *Unearth,* his fiction has appeared in *The Magazine of Fantasy & Science Fiction,* and in Silverberg and Haber's *Universe 1* and *2.* A practicing family doctor, he recently directed a feature film, *Confessions of a Marriage Junkie,* now in film festivals. He has photographed rock musicians and child actors for books by Frances Lantz, his wife. Their almost three-year-old son, Preston, keeps him up-to-date on computers.

ANDREW LANE is 32, has a degree in physics, and works for the British Civil Service. He has written three novels based on the long-running SF television series *Doctor Who* (*Lucifer Rising, All-Consuming Fire,* and *Original Sin*) and is currently working on a fourth. His short stories have appeared in *The Ultimate Witch* (Dell,1993) and the British SF magazine *Interzone.*

JONATHAN LETHEM is the author of *Gun, With Occasional Music.* His second novel, *Amnesia Moon: A Road Movie,* will be published by Harcourt Brace in October. He lives in Berkeley, California.

KARAWYNN LONG's first story won the Writers of the Future Grand Prize in 1993. She has sold stories to various anthologies, including *Alternate Tyrants* and *Enchanted Forests.*

She has studied ASL and worked as a substitute teacher at the Texas School for the Deaf. Currently she lives in Seattle, where she is writing more short fiction and researching a novel about the effects of future technology on the Deaf culture.

After getting a B.S. at Cal State Long Beach in marine biology, PAT MacEWEN spent five years bopping around the Channel Islands, digging up worms and other assorted wildlife. She developed a passion for ribbon worms, but later recovered her senses and acquired a substitute addiction to steady paychecks. Thereafter, she explored a variety of occupations, including mainframe computer operator in the aerospace industry, marketing analyst, mystery shopper, inventory crew manager, Kelly girl, trucking dispatcher, book store clerk, proofreader, and, currently, a field evidence technician for the Police Department in Stockton, California. She has published a novelette in *Writers of the Future IV*, short stories in the *Midnight Zoo* and the *Magazine of Fantasy & Science Fiction*.

LISA MASON is the author of *Arachne* (Morrow/Avon), *Cyberweb* (Morrow/Avon), *Summer of Love* (Bantam Spectra), and the forthcoming *The Golden Nineties* (Bantam Spectra). Her short fiction has appeared in numerous publications including *Omni*, *Universe*, *Fantasy & Science Fiction*, *Asimov's Science Fiction*, and *Year's Best Fantasy and Horror*. She lives in northern California.

PATRICIA A. McKILLIP was born in Salem, Oregon, quite some time ago. She received a M.A. in English literature from San Jose State University, also quite some time ago, and has been earning her living writing ever since. She has written fantasy stories and novels for both adults and young adults, as well as some science fiction, and a wayward venture into contemporary fiction. Among her novels are *The Riddle-Master Trilogy*, *Fool's Tun*, and *The Changeling Sea*. Her most recent are an adult fantasy, *The Cygnet and the Firebird*, and *The Book of Atrix Wolfe*. She is currently living in upstate New York.

PAUL PARK is the author of four novels: *Soldiers of Paradise*, *Sugar Rain*, *The Cult of Loving Kindness*, and the upcoming *Coelestis*. He is temporarily living in New Orleans with his wife, Deborah.

ALAN RODGERS is the author of *Bone Music, Pandora, Fire, Night, Blood of the Children,* and *New Life for the Dead. Blood of the Children* was a nominee for the Horror Writers of America Bram Stoker Award; his first story (actually a novelette), "The Boy Who Came Back from the Dead," won a Stoker and lost a World Fantasy Award. During the mid-eighties he edited the fondly remembered horror digest *Night Cry.* He lives in Manhattan with his wife, Amy Stout, and his two daughters, Alexandra and Andrea Rodgers.

NEAL STEPHENSON is the author of *Snow Crash, Zodiac: The Eco-Thriller,* and *The Diamond Age.* He currently resides in Seattle, Washington, with his family.

S. A. STOLNACK has published stories, poems, and book reviews in a handful of professional and literary magazines, and is nearing the end of his second novel. He regularly leads climbs and backcountry ski tours into Washington's Cascade mountains, and lives in Seattle with his wife, daughter, and numerous shrubs, vegetables, and fruit trees.

TRICIA SULLIVAN was born in 1968. She has studied music at Bard College, education at Columbia University, and Goju-ryu karate in Okinawa; currently, she teaches high school. Her first novel, *Lethe,* was published by Bantam Spectra in 1995. *The Question Eaters* is her first short story publication. She lives with her husband, Todd Wiggins, and two cats.

WILLIAM JOHN WATKINS has published over 300 poems, 50 short stories, and fifteen books. His story "Beggar in the Living Room," was a 1993 Nebula Award Finalist and his poetry appears regularly in *Asimov's Science Fiction* magazine. His eighth science fiction novel, *Kosmic Thunder,* will be published by Avon in 1995.

LAWRENCE WATT-EVANS is the author of some two dozen novels, eighty short stories, and innumerable articles and esoterica in the fields of fantasy, science fiction, and horror. He's recently scripted Leonard Nimoy's *Primortals* and Gene Roddenberry's *Lost Universe* for Tekno-Comix; his most recent novel is *In the Empire of Shadow.* He was recently elected president of the Horror Writers Association. He lives in the Maryland suburbs with his wife, two children, two cats, and a parakeet named Robin. His heart is still where it belongs, but he got rid of his gall bladder.

GENE WOLFE was born in New York and grew up in Houston where he attended Edgar Allan Poe Elementary School, an accident that seems to have shaped much of his life. He attended Texas A&M, dropped out, was drafted, and got the Combat Infantry Badge in the Korean War. After becoming the senior editor on *Plant Engineering Magazine,* he resigned in 1984 to write full time. Besides the four novels that make up *The Book of the New Sun,* he is the author of *There Are Doors, Soldiers of Arete, Castleview, Pandora by Holly Hollander,* and other books; currently he is working on the fourth book in his newest series, *Exodus From the Long Sun.* His short stories have been collected in *The Island of Doctor Death and Other Stories and Other Stories* (that is the title, not a typo), *Storeys From the Old Hotel* (ditto), and *Endangered Species.* His work has won the British Fantasy Award, the Prix Apollo, two Nebulas, two World Fantasy Awards, the British Science Fiction Award, and others.

PAT YORK lives near Buffalo, New York, with her husband, research scientist James York, and two children, Ben and Nora. She attended the 1993 Clarion Writer's Workshop, funded in part by a Donald Wollheim Scholarship from the New York Science Fiction Society. "Cool Zone" is her first professional sale. She has also sold to *Tomorrow* and *Realms of Fantasy.*

ABOUT THE EDITORS

Jennifer Hershey is the former Executive Editor of Bantam Spectra. She is now an Executive Editor at Avon Books.

Tom Dupree is a Senior Editor at Bantam Books. He lives in Manhattan with his wife, Linda.

Janna Silverstein is a former Editor for Bantam Books.

Come visit

BANTAM SPECTRA

on the INTERNET

Spectra invites you to join us
in our new on-line forum.

You'll find:

< Interviews with your favorite authors and
  excerpts from their latest books
< Bulletin boards that put you in touch with
  other science fiction fans, with Spectra
  authors, and with the Bantam editors who
  bring them to you
< A guide to the best science fiction re-
  sources on the Internet

Join us as we catch you up with all of Spectra's finest
authors, featuring monthly listings of upcoming titles
and special previews, as well as contests, interviews,
and more! We'll keep you in touch with the field, both
its past and its future—and everything in between.

Look for the Spectra Science Fiction
Forum on the World Wide Web at:

http://www.bdd.com

SF 30 7/96